PRAISE FOR GLYN ILIFFE

'A must read for those who enjoy good old epic battles,
chilling death scenes and the extravagance of ancient Greece'
Lifestyle Magazine

'It has suspense, treachery, and bone-crunching action
. . . It will leave fans of the genre eagerly awaiting
the rest of the series'
Harry Sidebottom, *Times Literary Supplement*

'The reader does not need to be a classicist by any means to
enjoy this epic and stirring tale. It makes a great novel
and would be an even better film'
Historical Novels Review

THE ARMOUR OF ACHILLES

Glyn Iliffe studied English and Classics at Reading University, where he developed a passion for the ancient stories of Greek history and mythology. Well travelled, Glyn has visited nearly forty countries, trekked in the Himalayas, spent six weeks hitchhiking across North America and had his collarbone broken by a bull in Pamplona.

He is married with two daughters and lives in Leicestershire. *King of Ithaca* was his first novel, followed by *The Gates of Troy*.

Also by Glyn Iliffe

King of Ithaca
The Gates of Troy

GLYN ILIFFE

THE ARMOUR OF ACHILLES

PAN BOOKS

First published 2010 by Macmillan

This edition published 2011 by Pan Books
an imprint of Pan Macmillan, a division of Macmillan Publishers Limited
Pan Macmillan, 20 New Wharf Road, London N1 9RR
Basingstoke and Oxford
Associated companies throughout the world
www.panmacmillan.com

ISBN 978-0-330-45253-3

Copyright © Glyn Iliffe 2010

The right of Glyn Iliffe to be identified as the
author of this work has been asserted by him in accordance
with the Copyright, Designs and Patents Act 1988.

1 3 5 7 9 8 6 4 2

A CIP catalogue record for this book is available from
the British Library.

Typeset by SetSystems Ltd, Saffron Walden, Essex
Printed in the UK by CPI Mackays, Chatham ME5 8TD

Visit *www.panmacmillan.com* to read more about all our books
and to buy them. You will also find features, author interviews and
news of any author events, and you can sign up for e-newsletters
so that you're always first to hear about our new releases.

FOR GUY, EMMA,
JEREMY, KATE AND TOM

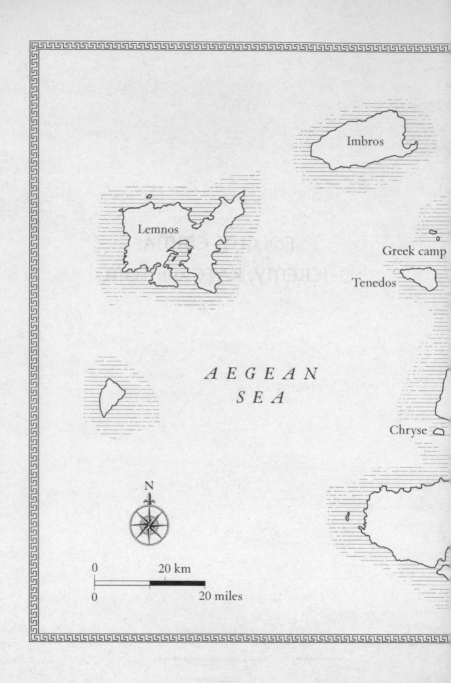

Imbros

Lemnos

Greek camp

Tenedos

A E G E A N
S E A

Chryse

N

0   20 km

0   20 miles

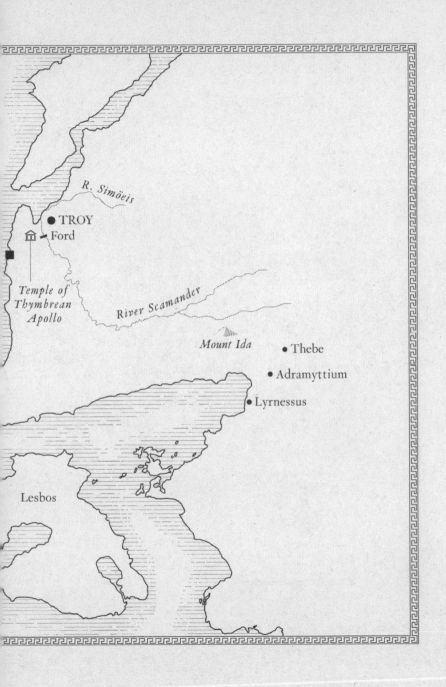

R. Simöeis

● TROY
🏛 Ford

Temple of
Thymbrean
Apollo

River Scamander

Mount Ida

● Thebe

● Adramyttium

● Lyrnessus

Lesbos

GLOSSARY

A

Achilles	— Myrmidon prince
Adramyttium	— city in south-eastern Ilium, allied to Troy
Adrestos	— Trojan soldier
Aeneas	— Dardanian prince, the son of Anchises
Aethiopes	— black-skinned warriors from northern Africa
Agamemnon	— king of Mycenae, leader of the Greeks
Ajax (greater)	— king of Salamis, and Achilles's cousin
Ajax (lesser)	— king of Locris
Alybas	— home city of Eperitus, in northern Greece
Andromache	— wife of Hector and daughter of King Eëtion
Antenor	— Trojan elder
Antícleia	— mother of Odysseus
Antilochus	— Greek warrior, son of Nestor
Antimachus	— Trojan elder
Antinous	— son of Eupeithes
Antiphus	— Ithacan guardsman
Apheidas	— Trojan commander, father of Eperitus
Aphrodite	— goddess of love
Apollo	— archer god, associated with music, song and healing
Arceisius	— Ithacan soldier, formerly squire to Eperitus
Ares	— god of war
Argus	— Odysseus's hunting dog

xi

GLOSSARY

Artemis — moon-goddess associated with childbirth, noted for her virginity and vengefulness
Astyanax — infant son of Hector and Andromache
Astynome — daughter of Chryses, a priest of Apollo
Athena — goddess of wisdom and warfare
Aulis — sheltered bay in the Euboean Straits

B
Balius — famed horse of Achilles, sibling of Xanthus
Briseis — daughter of Briseus the priest, captured by Achilles at Lyrnessus

C
Calchas — priest of Apollo, adviser to Agamemnon
Cassandra — Trojan princess, daughter of Priam
Chryse — small island off the coast of Ilium
Chryses — a priest of Apollo on the island of Chryse
Clymene — Trojan woman, hostage of Apheidas
Clytaemnestra — queen of Mycenae and wife of Agamemnon

D
Dardanus — city to the north of Troy
Deidameia — wife of Achilles
Deiphobus — Trojan prince, younger brother of Hector and Paris
Democoön — Trojan prince
Diocles — Spartan soldier
Diomedes — king of Argos
Dolon — Trojan spy
Dulichium — Ionian island, forming northernmost part of Odysseus's kingdom

E

Eëtion	— king of the Cilicians, allies of Troy, and father of Andromache
Elpenor	— Ithacan soldier
Eperitus	— captain of Odysseus's guard
Eteoneus	— squire to Menelaus
Eupeithes	— member of the Kerosia
Euryalus	— companion of Diomedes
Eurybates	— Odysseus's squire
Eurylochus	— Ithacan soldier, cousin of Odysseus
Eurypylus	— Thessalian king
Eurysaces	— infant son of Great Ajax
Evandre	— cousin of Queen Penthesilea

G

Gyrtias	— warrior from Rhodes

H

Hades	— god of the Underworld
Halitherses	— former captain of Ithacan royal guard, given joint charge of Ithaca in Odysseus's absence
Hecabe	— Trojan queen, wife of King Priam
Hector	— Trojan prince, oldest son of King Priam
Helen	— former queen of Sparta, now wife of Paris
Hephaistos	— god of fire; blacksmith to the Olympians
Heracles	— greatest of all Greek heroes
Hermes	— messenger of the gods; his duties also include shepherding the souls of the dead to the Underworld

I

Ida (Mount)	— principal mountain in Ilium
Idaeus	— herald to King Priam
Idomeneus	— king of Crete
Ilium	— region of which Troy was the capital
Iphigenia	— daughter of Eperitus and Clytaemnestra, sacrificed by Agamemnon
Ithaca	— island in the Ionian Sea

L

Lacedaemon	— Sparta
Laertes	— Odysseus's father
Lemnos	— island in the Aegean Sea
Leothoë	— daughter of King Altes of the Leleges, allies of Troy
Lethos	— Trojan prisoner
Lycaon	— Trojan prince
Lyrnessus	— city in south-eastern Ilium, allied to Troy

M

Machaon	— famed healer, son of Asclepius and brother to Podaleirius
Medon	— Malian commander
Melantho	— Ithacan girl, wife of Arceisius
Memnon	— king of the Aethiopes, allies of Troy
Menelaus	— king of Sparta, brother of Agamemnon and cuckolded husband of Helen
Menestheus	— king of Athens
Menoetius	— father of Patroclus
Mentes	— Taphian chieftain
Mentor	— close friend of Odysseus, given joint charge of Ithaca in Odysseus's absence

Mycenae	— most powerful city in Greece, situated in north-eastern Peloponnese
Myrmidons	— the followers of Achilles

N

Nestor	— king of Pylos
Nisus	— Ithacan elder

O

Odysseus	— king of Ithaca
Oenops	— Ithacan noble
Omeros	— Ithacan soldier and bard

P

Palamedes	— Nauplian prince
Palladium	— sacred image of Athena's companion, Pallas
Pandarus	— prince of the Zeleians, allies of Troy
Pandion	— murdered king of Alybas
Paris	— Trojan prince, second eldest son of King Priam
Patroclus	— cousin of Achilles and captain of the Myrmidons
Pedasus	— horse captured by Achilles at Thebe
Peisandros	— Myrmidon commander
Peleus	— father of Achilles
Penelope	— queen of Ithaca and wife of Odysseus
Penthesilea	— queen of the Amazons
Pergamos	— the citadel of Troy
Philoctetes	— Malian archer, deserted by the Greeks on Lemnos
Phronius	— Ithacan elder
Phthia	— region of northern Greece

Pleisthenes	— youngest son of Menelaus and Helen
Podaleirius	— famed healer, son of Asclepius and brother to Machaon
Podarces	— Thessalian leader
Podes	— Hector's best friend, brother of Andromache
Polites	— Ithacan warrior
Polyctor	— Ithacan noble
Poseidon	— god of the sea
Priam	— king of Troy
Pylos	— city on the western seaboard of the Peloponnese
Pythoness	— high priestess of the Pythian oracle

R
| Rhesus | — king of the Thracians, allies of Troy |

S
Samos	— neighbouring island to Ithaca, also under the rule of Odysseus
Sarpedon	— king of the Lycians, allies of Troy
Scamander	— river on the Trojan plain
Sthenelaus	— companion of Diomedes

T
Talthybius	— squire to Agamemnon
Taphians	— pirate race from Taphos
Tecmessa	— wife of Great Ajax
Telemachus	— son of Odysseus and Penelope
Tenedos	— island off the coast of Ilium
Teucer	— famed archer, half-brother and companion to Great Ajax
Thebe	— city in Ilium

Thebes	– city in central Greece
Thersites	– Aetolian hunchback
Thetis	– chief of the Nereids and mother of Achilles
Tlepolemos	– king of Rhodes
Troy	– chief city of Ilium, on the eastern seaboard of the Aegean

X

Xanthus	– famed horse of Achilles, sibling of Balius
xenia	– the custom of friendship towards strangers

Z

Zeus	– king of the gods

book

ONE

Prologue

ON ITHACA

Penelope, queen of Ithaca, stood tall and stiff, staring at the door to the great hall. The muffled sound of voices came from behind its thick wooden panels, punctuated with frequent bursts of laughter. She knew they were waiting for her – to tell her news of the war that had reached its tenth year, and of her husband, Odysseus, whom she had not seen in all that time – but still she hesitated.

'Should I go now, Mother?' asked the boy at her side, whose auburn hair she was twisting nervously with her slender fingers. 'I know children aren't allowed in the Kerosia.'

'This isn't a gathering of the council, Telemachus,' she replied, looking down at her son and smiling. 'It's a private audience with the men who arrived today. They have news for me, and I have questions for them.'

'Then is it true they're Ithacans, back from Troy?'

Telemachus looked at his mother and she caught a sudden glimpse of Odysseus in his clever green eyes. It made her catch her breath and the only way she could prevent the swell of tears was to avert her gaze to the gloomy, torch-lit corridor that led back into the palace. At ten years old, her son had inherited little or nothing of his father's short-legged, triangular bulk. Instead, he was already showing signs of his mother's height and lean build, as well as her dark, intelligent looks. But his eyes came from his father, and from time to time he would give her a shrewd look or cunning glance that brought memories of Odysseus into painful focus.

After a moment, she looked back at her son and nodded.

'Yes. Eurybates is your father's squire and Arceisius is a member of the royal guard.'

Telemachus's face flushed and his eyebrows puckered angrily.

'Why send a squire? Couldn't he have come himself?'

'No, my dear. His duty is to stay with the army until they defeat the Trojans and win Helen back from the man who took her. Besides, even if he could leave his men I don't think he would.'

'But why?'

Penelope looked at Telemachus and there was a deep sadness in her eyes.

'Because he would never be able to go back. Now, come with me. I want Arceisius and Eurybates to see you with their own eyes, so they can let your father know what a strong and handsome son he has waiting for him at home.'

She pushed the door open and together they walked into the great hall. A fire burned brightly at its centre, casting a vigorous orange glow that fought against the encroaching shadows of night. Its light revealed colourful murals flowing across the white plaster walls, depicting figures of gods and men embroiled in acts of war and violence. Though each wall told a different story, they seemed to move effortlessly into each other, as if the struggles between gods and Titans, and the battles of men against each other, were but one continuous tale. Smoke from the fire coiled up between the four pillars that supported the high ceiling, while around the burning hearth were five chairs, four of which were occupied.

The men stood as Penelope entered.

'Be seated, my friends,' she ordered, circling the hearth towards the fur-draped chair that had been left for her.

They waited for her to sit before lowering themselves into their own chairs. Last of all, Telemachus settled on to a fleece at his mother's feet, his inquisitive eyes roaming the faces of the men as he leaned his cheek against her knee. Penelope laid a hand on his head, drawing comfort from the softness of his hair as she, too, looked at the seated figures.

To her left was Mentor. His handsome face had a natural authority to it and his muscular physique would have marked him as a warrior, were it not for the leather-cased stump of his missing right hand. There was a warm smile on his bearded lips, but Penelope could sense the concern behind it. Mentor was her chief adviser and the closest thing she had to a friend, ever since Odysseus had sailed to Troy. He knew her calm exterior was a façade, hiding the anxieties and uncertainties that were suddenly teeming within her after the arrival of the ships from Ilium. She may have fooled others with her display of regal restraint – bottling herself up in the palace and refusing to follow the crowds down to the harbour to hear the news from Troy – but not Mentor.

Halitherses was to her right, his ageing bulk so tightly packed into the high-backed chair that it seemed the arms would snap off at any moment. He was a veteran soldier and had been a long-standing captain of the royal guard, though his mounting years and the scars of his many battles had prevented him from sailing with Odysseus to Troy. Instead, the king had given him joint stewardship of Ithaca, along with Mentor, to keep the island and its people safe in his absence. And they had not failed him, though the threats to the small kingdom were ever-present and growing. Over the years they had repulsed a handful of raids from the mainland, where groups of armed brigands were filtering down from the north and the rule of law was faltering in the absence of the Greek kings. And then there was the internal menace of Ithaca's own nobles, whose increasingly audacious demands were voiced through the wealthy and treacherous Eupeithes. Odysseus had bought Eupeithes's loyalty many years before with a place on the Kerosia, but neither Halitherses nor Mentor trusted him. Fortunately, the people were loyal to their king and the fear of Odysseus's return kept Eupeithes and his followers in check. For now.

Penelope's gaze turned to the other two men. She had already been informed of their names, of course, but could barely equate the battle-hardened warriors before her with the youths she had once known and had watched sail off to war. Eurybates, seated next to Halitherses, was an exceptional sailor who had been keen to make the voyage to Ilium and exact revenge from the Trojans for stealing Helen, the pride of the Greeks. Now, as he sat before her, his short body looked as hard as if it had been carved from rock, and his curly hair was grown long and had been drawn back into a tail behind his neck. His eyes were tough and uncompromising, though as they rested on his queen for the first time in many years there was a noticeable softness in them.

The other man, Arceisius, she had first known as a young shepherd boy with ruddy cheeks and a roguish grin. His father had been murdered by Taphian pirates, so Eperitus – Odysseus's captain – had taken him under his wing to teach him the profession of war, eventually taking him with him to Troy. Now he was a man, scarred and deeply sunburnt, with eyes that had grown sharp from watching foreign horizons and witnessing horrors that no boy's mind could survive. And yet his cheeks were still red and, unlike Eurybates, there was a light in his eyes that had survived the cruelty of war. It was like the glimmer of gold at the bottom of a pool, that still spoke of happiness and memories of music and dancing, and of young girls in the long grass of Ithaca's meadows. It was then she noticed the garland round his neck and the petals in his hair, from the welcome the ships' crews had received that morning. The sight brought a smile to Penelope's lips.

'Welcome back, Arceisius. Welcome back, Eurybates. I hope your journey wasn't too perilous.'

'Not nearly as perilous as being home again,' Eurybates replied, looking around at the walls. 'I didn't realize how much I'd missed

Ithaca, and the gods only know how we'll bring ourselves to leave again and return to that forsaken country!'

'We'll do it because we're loyal soldiers, sworn to obey Odysseus,' Arceisius answered.

'Aye, we will,' Eurybates conceded with a nod. 'But there's not another man in this world that I'd do it for.'

'Your words reveal more than the depth of your love for my husband,' Penelope said. 'The war, it seems, is not going well.'

'Not going well, my lady?' Eurybates replied. 'That's the problem – it's not going anywhere at all!'

'And you will tell us all about it,' Penelope interrupted. 'Every detail of everything that has happened since the last galleys were sent back five years ago. But I'm being a poor hostess. First we will eat; meat and wine will raise your spirits, and then you can tell us about the war and my husband's part in it.'

She nodded to Mentor, who snapped his fingers behind his ear and brought a servant scurrying out of the shadows. A moment later the steward was running from the hall with his orders, to return a short while afterwards followed by a stream of slaves carrying tables, platters of food and kraters of wine. After washing her hands, Penelope led the libations to the gods by stepping up to the hearth and tipping a slop of wine into the flames. The others followed, muttering thanks to the Olympians as the liquid hissed and sent a puff of steam up into their faces. The rest of the meal was silent as the men helped themselves to strips of roast goat, which they picked up and wrapped in thin saucers of bread before washing it down with mouthfuls of wine, constantly replenished by the waiting slaves. Penelope ate very little, and that only out of politeness, as she watched the faces of her guests. Eurybates quickly lost his surliness as he forgot the war in the taste of Ithacan wine, while Arceisius was enjoying the flirtations of Melantho, the prettiest of the servant girls, who would brush seductively across him every time she refilled his krater and bat her long, dark eyelashes at him. They were men who had seen much hardship, but she could only envy them their trials because at least they had endured them alongside her husband. Indeed, the nearness of the two men – whose arrival had been totally unexpected – gave her a renewed sense of Odysseus, almost as if he were here with them, standing unseen in the shadows. Had they not spent the last ten years with him, listening to his soft voice, witnessing his feats on the battlefield and enjoying the embellishments he would add as they sat around the campfire later? For all the loss of their youth and naïvety, for all their hatred of the thought of returning to Troy, they had still not suffered as much as she had. She reached for Telemachus's head again and was comforted by the touch of his hair beneath her fingertips.

'Enough of this silence,' Halitherses announced, his impatience finally getting the better of him. 'Speak to us about this damned war. What in Ares's name is taking Agamemnon so long? Doesn't he have the greatest of all the Greeks in his army? What about that great oaf, Ajax, and Diomedes, and all those others? Why isn't Menelaus tearing the walls down with his own hands? After all, Helen's his wife and he should be leading the way. And what of Achilles? He's the one they all had their hopes on, isn't he?'

As Halitherses vented his frustration – built up by years of relative inaction at home – Mentor glanced at Penelope, then held his hand up to silence the old warrior.

'What about Odysseus? I'd rather hear about our own king first.'

'Thank you for your concern, Mentor.' Penelope smiled. 'As ever, you know where my heart is. But everything in its right place: first Eurybates can tell us about the war, leaving nothing out; and then, if Melantho can leave him alone, perhaps Arceisius will tell us about my husband.'

There was a pause in which the servants trooped out of the hall or faded back beyond the circle of firelight. Eurybates waited until the last sandals had stopped scuffing across the stone floor, then leaned across the arm of his chair and focused not on Penelope, but on the boy who had remained seated in obedient silence at her feet.

'You must be Telemachus,' he began.

Telemachus nodded.

'Yes, now that I look at you I can see you have your father's eyes,' Eurybates continued. 'I was there when he dedicated you to Athena on Hermes's Mount, when you were just a few days old. He was *so* proud of you, Telemachus.'

'Then why did he go?'

Eurybates's eyes flicked up to meet Penelope's. The queen nodded.

'He left because he had to. He's a king and no man bears more responsibility than a king – to his family, to his people and to his gods, but most of all to his gods. And, as you must already know, Odysseus was bound by a most sacred oath . . .'

Telemachus knew all about his father's oath, of course – to protect Helen, queen of Sparta, which had been taken by all her suitors – and of all the things that happened because of it. But children love stories, especially when those stories involve themselves and the people close to them, and so he listened intently as Eurybates recounted how Helen had been abducted by Paris, a Trojan prince, while he was a guest in Menelaus's palace. Supported by his brother, the powerful and ambitious King Agamemnon, Menelaus had called on the oath-takers to honour their promise. A great fleet was assembled and set sail for Troy, where, with Agamemnon as their elected leader, they laid siege to the city, intent on razing it to the ground and reclaiming Helen for Menelaus.

But the auspices had not been good from the outset. For one thing, Troy was not some poor city that would fall at the first attempt. Its walls were thick, high and strong, constructed by the gods and protected by all manner of prophecies. It was also a rich and powerful city and King Priam, Paris's father, could call on vast, experienced armies of allies from far and wide. Indeed, after the Greeks' first attempt to draw the Trojans out of their walls had failed, Troy's allies had arrived in droves and under the leadership of Prince Hector had forced Agamemnon to make camp on the coast, a safe distance away to the south-west. Since then, countless battles had raged across the hills and plains between the camp and the city, killing and maiming thousands of men for little or no advantage to either side. Every strategy that Agamemnon tried, every ruse that Odysseus had thought up to defeat the Trojans, had been frustrated by Hector's uncanny ability to anticipate their every move. In the end, Eurybates explained with a sigh, the Greeks were too numerous to be pushed back into the sea, while the Trojans always had the safety of their impenetrable walls to fall back on. And so the years had passed, filled with slaughter from spring until autumn, pausing during the cold misery of winter, and then resuming again with the first flowers of spring.

'And now that spring has returned, the sacrifices of previous years need to be replaced,' Penelope said, 'hence your journey back to Ithaca with skeleton crews.'

Arceisius nodded. 'Things have got bad. The longer the war goes on, the more bitter and brutal it gets. We used to be able to exchange our prisoners with the Trojans, but that was when both sides still had a sense of honour. Now most are murdered, unless they're rich enough to fetch a ransom. The toll of war is growing and Odysseus hasn't enough wealth to attract mercenaries to replace our dead – not when the other kings will offer them more. So we need to take as many men back with us as we can fit. The king wants them to be picked in equal proportion from the nobility and the peasantry.'

Penelope sighed. 'There are problems with that.'

'Yes,' Mentor agreed. 'Bandit raids from the mainland are becoming more common, and some of our own nobles are starting to show signs of disloyalty, especially with Odysseus having been away so long. We have to keep a standing force of soldiers.'

'Nonetheless, Odysseus will have his men,' Halitherses countered.

'We can take care of the problems here; just let us know how many the king needs.'

'The problem isn't how many men we can provide,' Penelope said, sitting upright and looking at her two advisers. 'It's with *whom* we send.'

The others looked at her, not understanding.

'What do you mean, my lady?' Eurybates asked.

'I mean there are certain nobles who are not happy about sending their sons and heirs to Troy. They know why you're here, of course, and they want to be allowed to send proxies in place of their own sons – in other words, pay another man to go to war instead.'

Halitherses snorted derisively.

'Well, they can't. In fact, I've a good mind to send the sons of the most troublesome nobles first.'

'Perhaps that's what they fear,' Penelope replied. 'Either way, Eupeithes approached me earlier today pleading their case. He says the nobles are angry and if their sons are chosen we could have a rebellion on our hands, but if we agree to allow paid proxies he might be able to calm things down again.'

'How dare they!' Halitherses exclaimed.

The others exchanged worried glances.

'So I agreed.'

'But my lady—'

'No, Mentor. It's too late. I've asked Eupeithes to tell the nobles I accept their proposal. The war in Troy can't last much longer, and I won't risk a rebellion on Ithaca while Odysseus is away. That has happened before, remember?'

Mentor nodded, followed by Arceisius and Eurybates as each one accepted the wisdom of her decision. At first Halitherses stared at the queen with a blank look on his face. Then a smile broke through his grey beard as he recalled the oracle that had been given to Odysseus before he had married Penelope.

'"Find a daughter of Lacedaemon",' he quoted, laughing to

himself, '"and she will keep the thieves from your house." Now, more than ever, I understand the words of that old prophecy. Odysseus would be proud of you, my lady.'

'He should be,' Penelope replied. 'Just as I am proud of him. And now, Arceisius, you can tell me about my husband, and Telemachus here about his father. Ten years is a long time to be apart, and yet he's never far from my thoughts. He feels like a shadow, something ever present and yet insubstantial, always just beyond my reach.'

She sat back and shook her head, knowing her words had failed to express how she felt. And then she looked directly at Arceisius, silently awaiting his response.

'He made me memorize a few words, my lady,' he said. 'I can't match his voice or speak with his eloquence, but he said to tell you this: that the Walls of Troy will not outlast his love for you. An oracle led him to you, and though all the oceans of the world and Hades itself might lie between, he *will* come back to you.'

Chapter One

LYRNESSUS

Eperitus licked his pale lips, feeling the old lines where they had cracked again and again under a ruthless foreign sun. Ten years of that same sun had given his skin a leathery texture so that when he smiled, which was not often, his teeth were white against his deeply tanned face. With his braided beard and long black hair – combed tightly back and tied behind his neck – he looked more like a savage than the handsome man he had once been. And perhaps he was a savage, for the only trade he had ever known was fighting and there was little humanity in war.

His thoughtful brown eyes, red around the rims and creased at the corners, were fixed on the ridge ahead, waiting patiently for the next battle to begin. The accoutrements of his profession had been strapped and buckled into place long before dawn, each item as familiar and comfortable as if they were parts of his body. On his head was the same bronze cap he had worn since before his exile from Alybas twenty years before. Its battered cheek-guards were tied under his chin by leather cords, which he had tucked into his dirty woollen scarf to prevent them becoming untied in battle. Over his patched thigh-length tunic – once a vivid scarlet but now faded to a watery pink – was a close-fitting, oxhide corslet that bore the scars of countless hand-to-hand combats. Bronze greaves tied about cloth gaiters protected his shins, while hanging from a strap across his shoulder was his grandfather's old shield. This was almost as tall as Eperitus himself and was shaped like two overlapping, convex circles – the broader at the bottom and the smaller on top – with a raised wooden crest running down the centre. Though the shield's four-fold leather had been hacked and pierced innumerable times, and it was of an old and cumbersome style that had long since faded from battlefields, Eperitus refused to replace it, considering it as much a part of himself as his own name.

While his shabby collection of armour had saved him from the spear points and sword blades of countless enemies over the years, it was his weapons that were the tools of his trade. Tucked into his belt was the ornate golden dagger King Odysseus had given him as a token of friendship when they had first met. In a plain leather scabbard under his left arm was his double-edged sword, slung at a height where its silver-studded ivory handle could be found and drawn with ease. Finally, in his right hand was his primary weapon, a tall Trojan spear which he had plundered from its dead owner during a skirmish the previous summer, his own having been launched at a horseman whose mount had then fled, carrying its impaled rider and Eperitus's spear with it. Without these heavy and brutal weapons he was not a warrior, and if he was not a warrior then he was nothing, a mere mortal without reputation or honour who would one day perish and be forgotten.

To Eperitus's right stood Odysseus, king of Ithaca, the man he had followed to this sun-baked, mosquito-infested and scorpion-plagued country. With his short legs, heavily muscled torso and large head – almost devoid of a neck – Odysseus could never be considered a fine-looking man. His long red hair was tied behind his neck and his thick beard, flecked with grey, reached down to his chest. Like Eperitus, there was a tang of fresh sweat about him, mingled with the odour of wood smoke and roast mutton. His breastplate and shield were battered and dusty, while his bronze helmet with its nodding plume of black horsehair had been dented in so many places that its surface rippled in the early morning sunshine. Over his shoulders he wore the thick double-cloak his wife had given him at their parting ten years before. It was threadbare and heavily patched, and the purple wool had faded to a silvery grey at the shoulders, but he would no more replace it than Eperitus would his grandfather's shield. It was all he had left of his beloved Penelope, whose vivid intelligence and bright company he still missed with all his heart, even though her beautiful face was little more than a memory now.

But if Odysseus's appearance was undistinguished and beggarly compared to the other kings who had flocked to Troy, the fact that he was of high birth was unmistakeable. His intelligent green eyes – full of a ready humour – were stiffened by an iron will; his face appeared kind and approachable at most times, but there was an authority lying just beneath the surface that no man would dare cross lightly. More than anything, though, Odysseus's power was in his voice. When he spoke, men listened. He could still a room with a simple sentence and sway even the most adverse opponents with his smooth tones and well-reasoned arguments. There was no other man in the whole Greek army – neither the great Achilles nor the noble Diomedes, the kind-hearted Menelaus nor the fearsome Great Ajax – Eperitus would rather serve.

Standing a little behind the two men was the Ithacan army, arrayed in six ranks of a hundred men each. There was a low murmur of conversation as they waited with bored patience for the order to advance. They had stood there since the first light of dawn, after beaching their ships on the sandy coastline and marching up to the low line of hills that hid the city of Lyrnessus, but they did not complain as their spears and oxhide shields grew heavy in their hands. They had endured much in the past ten years and were no longer the mixture of inexperienced farmers and fishermen who had first answered their king's call to arms. Now they were true warriors, hardened by the long years of fighting that had sifted the weak from the strong. Only those with an instinct for warfare and a fierce anger in battle had survived; the remainder had been killed long ago, their souls conducted to the underworld by Hermes, the shepherd of the dead.

In the front rank were the men of the royal guard. These were the heavily armed elite who had once formed Ithaca's standing army in the days before the war. Well trained and highly motivated, with a fearless devotion to their king, they were the pride of the Ithacan army. Unlike the scavenged weaponry of the levied masses behind them, each guard was equipped with greaves, a plumed bronze helmet with cheek-guards, a breastplate and an oval shield with a flattened bottom edge and a bronze boss. Swords hung from their sides and long daggers were tucked into their belts, while their main weapons were the two spears that each man carried. The guards were the first in every attack and the last in any retreat, a perilous duty that had taken its toll over the years but which they carried out with unquestioning loyalty. Their losses were filled by the bravest men from the rest of the army – those who had proved their courage, skill and thirst for glory during the numerous battles with Troy and her allies.

Odysseus had selected the best warriors from the royal guard to head the assault on Lyrnessus. Each was in charge of ten men with a tall, well-built ladder between them; twenty ladders in total. They would march to the city concealed among the ranks of the other Ithacans, then dash out to the walls, place their ladders and begin climbing. The first up, Odysseus had insisted as he explained the assault to the men of the guard, would be the leader of each group – a dangerous job, especially if the walls were well defended, but one which would bring glory in the eyes of men and gods alike. As he had expected, his words were greeted with a chorus of demands to lead. The loudest were from Polites, who, though normally a quiet man, had a voice to match his giant-like physique when he wanted to be heard, and from Antiphus, the best archer in the army and one of its longest-serving veterans. These two were stood in the centre of the front rank now, the heads of their ladders resting against their calf muscles as they waited with calm indifference for the day's action to begin.

On either side of the Ithacans were the armies of Argos and Phthia: the ranks of the Argives to their left, four thousand men massed behind the tall and handsome King Diomedes, with

Sthenelaus and Euryalus at his side; and the black-clad Myrmidons from Achilles's homeland of Phthia to their right, three thousand of the fiercest and most ruthless warriors in the whole Greek army, formed up behind the stout and hardy figure of Peisandros. Like their Ithacan comrades, both armies were a mixture of irregularly equipped levies fronted by a core of hardened warriors. Large numbers of ladders had been evenly distributed through their ranks, ready for the assault. Standing behind them were the archers of Locris, two thousand men led by the short and angry figure of Little Ajax. These carried no shields and wore only leather caps and jerkins of layered cloth for protection, placing their trust in the wall of infantry before them and the long range of their bows and slings.

In the rearmost ranks of each army stood men carrying tall, bronze-tipped pikes, normally used for ship-to-ship fighting because of their long reach. From the upper third of each pole a canvas banner streamed forward in the breeze from the sea, fluttering and snapping over the heads of the men below. The flags had been Odysseus's idea earlier in the war, to help warriors find their units in the dust and clamour of battle and for other commanders to identify where their allies were amidst the chaos. Each army had its own symbol. For the Ithacans it was a blue dolphin, while the Locrians' banner carried the device of a coiled brown serpent, in honour of the snake that Little Ajax wore around his shoulders at all times. Diomedes's Argives fought beneath a golden fox on a green field, which was now torn and filled with arrow holes from always being at the forefront of battle. In even worse condition was the banner of the Myrmidons, the tattered remains of which featured an eagle with a serpent in its beak.

The four armies had been chosen by Achilles, who had insisted on leading the attacks against Lyrnessus, Adramyttium and Thebe, the cities that guarded Troy's supply route from the lands of Mysia and Lydia in the south. Knowing there was none better who could give him the victory he so desperately needed, Agamemnon had agreed to Achilles's demand. Not that the King of Men expected either city to present a problem. The walls, gates and ditches that protected them were nothing compared to the god-built battlements that had defended Troy for so long. Most significantly, the once powerful garrisons that had deterred earlier attacks had been slowly stripped of their best men to feed the battles around Troy, company after company marching away until all that remained were local militias made up of old greybeards and men wounded in the war – no match for a force of nearly ten thousand Greeks.

'I can hear horses,' Eperitus announced quietly. 'Three of them, approaching fast.'

His senses had been supernaturally sharp ever since he had been brought back from death by Athena nearly twenty years before, and he was easily able to filter out the murmur of the soldiers behind him to focus on the heavy galloping of hooves from the other side of the ridge. Odysseus could hear nothing beyond the hubbub of voices, but he trusted his friend's ears and gave him an assured nod.

'It'll be Achilles, with Patroclus and Antilochus,' he said. 'And about time too.'

A few moments later the thudding beat was heard by every ear, and then with a whinnying neigh and a barked command three horsemen appeared in silhouette at the top of the ridge, surrounded by a billow of dust. The riders paused for a moment to survey the massed ranks below them, then with a shout of 'Hah! Hah!' the first drove his horse straight down the slope towards Odysseus, followed closely by his companions.

'What news, Achilles?' Odysseus called, striding out to meet the riders with his hands raised.

Achilles pulled his horse's head aside with the reins and leapt from the animal's back, landing lightly a few paces in front of the king of Ithaca. He swept his black cloak back over his shoulder to reveal a well-made bronze breastplate and a sword, hanging from a baldric at his side. He carried no shield or spear and his head was helmetless, so that his long blond hair shone in the sunlight as he offered Odysseus his hand.

'Good news, my friend,' he answered, his handsome face breaking into a confident smile as Odysseus gripped his wrist. 'This little fight isn't going to be as dull as I first thought. The gods have given us the chance of some real glory!'

'What do you mean?' Odysseus asked. 'Has the garrison returned since Diomedes and I were here a few days ago?'

'Lyrnessus won't be a problem,' one of the other riders announced, trotting up behind Achilles. Patroclus slid from his mount with an easy motion and stared down his long, pointed nose at Odysseus and Eperitus. 'The battlements are no higher than two tall men and there's only one tower, guarding the southern gateway – just as you reported. As for defenders, I didn't count any more than five men on the walls in total. It'll be a disappointing way to start the year's fighting, I'm afraid, after such a long and tiresome winter.'

'To Hades with Lyrnessus!' Achilles exclaimed. He draped a tightly muscled arm over Patroclus's shoulder and leaned his weight against his companion's tall and sinewy frame. 'We found something much more interesting than that pile of rubble. We found *Aeneas*!'

'Aeneas?' Eperitus asked, surprised to hear the name of one of Troy's finest warriors. 'What's *he* doing this far from Troy?'

'He didn't give me the chance to ask,' Achilles said, slipping his arm from Patroclus and pacing the ground before the two Ithacans. 'We'd almost scouted the full circuit of the walls when we saw half a dozen horsemen coming over the ridge to the north of here. They could hardly have missed ten thousand Greeks waiting on the other side of the hills, so I gave Patroclus and Antilochus here a look and didn't find them wanting.'

He nodded at the third rider, a long-faced youth with cold, grey eyes who was still growing his first beard. Antilochus was the son of Nestor, one of Agamemnon's closest advisers, and had arrived at the Greek camp just a few days before, contrary to his father's wishes. Impressed by the lad's eagerness to fight, Achilles had persuaded Nestor to let him stay, on the promise that he would shepherd the lad through his first battle.

'We weren't going to let them reach the city alive,' Achilles continued. 'And that was when I recognized Aeneas – and *he* recognized *me*. I dug my heels in and set off after him at a gallop, and even with the head start he had he'd never have outrun Xanthus if he hadn't ordered his escort against us. By the time we'd fought our way through them Aeneas was safely inside the city walls. Safe for *now*, at least.'

Odysseus stroked his beard and looked up at the line of hills, in the direction of Lyrnessus.

'I don't like it,' he muttered, as if to himself. 'Eperitus is right – what business would Aeneas have out here?'

'Who cares?' Achilles said dismissively. 'The point is we have one of their best fighters bottled up in that city, and before the day's done I'll send his cowardly soul down to Hades.'

As he was speaking, Diomedes and Little Ajax appeared at Eperitus's left shoulder. The Argive king was a tall, muscular figure, dressed in armour that befitted his wealth. He removed the gleaming bronze helmet from his head to reveal long auburn hair and a stern but handsome face, the only blemish on which was the faint trace of a white scar running down from the tip of his left ear and into his thick beard. Little Ajax, on the other hand, was a short, spiteful-looking man with a flat nose and pockmarked cheeks. A long brown snake was draped over his shoulders, its triangular head raised and its pink tongue slithering out from its lipless mouth, sending a shiver of disgust through Eperitus. Ajax's dark eyes frowned up at Achilles from beneath his single eyebrow.

'What's the delay?' he demanded. 'I've been waiting all winter to kill some Trojan scum and my spear arm's getting restless.'

'The itching of your spear arm is nothing compared to the suffering of Helen,' Diomedes rebuffed him. 'If the fall of this city brings her freedom a step closer, then let's get on with it. Zeus

THE ARMOUR OF ACHILLES

only knows what she's gone through as a prisoner of Troy, kept from her husband and children and forced to endure the lustful attentions of Paris every night.'

'*Forced*?' Ajax scoffed. 'That trollop wanted Paris between her thighs from the first moment she—'

He fell silent as the point of Diomedes's dagger pressed against his throat.

'If you say another word against the queen of Sparta, it'll be your last,' he warned.

Ajax met the cold stare of the Argive king with equal menace, but said nothing.

'We've delayed long enough,' Achilles said, taking Diomedes's wrist and easing the blade away from Ajax's neck. 'The attack will begin immediately – unless Odysseus has any more misgivings?'

Odysseus shook his head.

'Same plan as before?' Diomedes asked, sliding his dagger back into his belt.

Achilles nodded, looking over his shoulder at the ridge. 'The Argives and Ithacans will scale the western walls while my Myrmidons will take the southern gate. Ajax's Locrians can hang back and shoot any Trojan who dares show his head above the battlements. There's still the ditch, but the walls behind it are low and we have the ladders. Even if they're alerted to our presence, nothing can stop Lyrnessus from being ours by midday.'

Without another word he turned and held his hand out to Xanthus. The horse answered his call immediately and soon Achilles, Patroclus and Antilochus were riding to join Peisandros at the head of the Myrmidon line. As Diomedes and Little Ajax returned to their own armies, Odysseus arched his eyebrows and turned to his captain.

'I don't like this, Eperitus. The Trojans have outwitted us too many times over the years, and if Aeneas is here then that spells trouble. He's one of the best commanders they have – Hector wouldn't send him down here without a very good reason.'

'We can hardly turn around and get back in the ships now,'

Eperitus answered. 'We'll just have to climb the walls and see what's inside.'

Odysseus smiled back at him. 'You're right, of course, and we might as well enjoy ourselves while we're at it. Give the order.'

Eperitus turned on his heel and looked at the expectant faces of the Ithacan soldiers.

'Shields ready. Pick up the ladders.'

Similar orders were barked out up and down the Greek lines, followed by a flurry of movement as shields were taken up, ladders lifted and spears readied. Achilles received his spear and shield from two of his men and moved to the head of the Myrmidon army. Raising the spear above his head, he pointed it towards the line of hills. There was a great cheer from the whole Greek assembly and the Myrmidons began to move.

Eperitus instinctively kissed his fingertips and placed them against the image of a white deer on the inside of his shield. He had painted it there to remind him of his daughter, Iphigenia, and though it was grimed and faded where he had repeatedly touched it for luck he felt reassured by its presence. Odysseus discreetly touched the image of Athena painted on the inside of his own shield, then, after a glance at Eperitus, turned to the ranks of Ithacans and waved them forward.

The long lines of warriors advanced with a steady tramp, the Myrmidons, Ithacans and Argives in the lead with the Locrians forming a wide arc behind them. At first the bronze of their helmets and shield bosses shone fiercely in the sunlight, but as they marched slowly up the hillside the dust raised by their thousands of feet shrouded them in a brown cloud that dulled the glimmer of their weaponry. Soon they were topping the crest of the ridge and looking out over a fertile, lightly wooded plain, dominated by a low hill at its centre. On top of the hill was a walled city, its sand-coloured battlements no higher than the scattering of windswept olive trees that surrounded it. A few two-storeyed buildings stood up above the level of the weathered parapets, but the only tower was at the southern end of the fortifications, guarding an arched gateway from which a narrow track wound down to the level of the plain. Here it met the main route from the city of Troy to its southern provinces, but as the ten thousand Greeks filed out across the western edge of the plateau, not a single traveller could be seen up or down the length of the road.

A handful of sentinels stared silently out from behind the walls of Lyrnessus and a low horn call vibrated out across the plain to greet the newcomers, but no reinforcements hastened to join their colleagues on the battlements. Instead, the sombre noise was followed by a silence, which was quickly devoured by the clanking of the Greek army as it spread across the plain like pitch spilled from a bucket, file after file marching relentlessly towards their objective. Soon the soldiers of Argos and Ithaca were in place at the western foot of the hill, a bowshot from the walls, while the Myrmidons straddled the road to the south, facing the gate. The Locrian archers formed a wide crescent behind them, where they began standing their arrows point-down in the grass, ready to be fitted to their bowstrings and fired at any enemy that dared show themselves above the parapets. As the dust cloud the Greek host had raised was carried forward on a gentle breeze to veil the walls of Lyrnessus, Odysseus looked left to where Diomedes stood at the head of his Argives. Diomedes raised his arm and nodded. In response, Odysseus looked right to Achilles and raised his own arm.

'Ladders at the ready,' Eperitus called out behind him, all the time keeping his eyes on the distant, golden-haired figure of Achilles.

Achilles dismounted and gave the reins to one of his men, who in return handed him a bright helmet with a black plume and a visor shaped in the likeness of a grimacing face. Achilles was the only warrior who wore such a helmet, designed not for additional protection but to distinguish him on the battlefield, his reputation being such that the mere sight of the helmet filled his opponents with terror. As the soldier led the prince's horse away, Achilles put the helmet on his head and lowered the hinged visor into place, while Patroclus stood before him and tied the leather thongs beneath his chin. With all eyes watching him, Achilles took up his shield and raised his huge spear above his head. A moment later, the point fell and the Greeks gave a great shout, their voices rebounding from the city walls.

Chapter Two
STORMING THE WALLS

Odysseus did not cheer. Gritting his teeth behind sealed lips, he waved the Ithacan ladder parties forward. The scrambling of leather sandals on hard earth was followed by the sharp smell of sweat and the sound of cursing as the men ran past him, dashing quickly up the long, stony slope towards Lyrnessus. At their head were the groups led by Antiphus and Polites, the former with his bow slung across his back and the latter striding forward as if he would smash down the walls with his bare fists.

'Something's wrong,' Odysseus said in a low voice as he watched the advance on the walls. 'There's not one man on the battlements. Even the soldiers we saw earlier have gone.'

'They've probably thrown away their armour and are cowering in a temple somewhere, hoping their gods will protect them,' Eperitus replied.

Odysseus shook his head. 'If we've learned anything from this war, it's that Trojans aren't cowards. Some of them should be up there at least, trying to save their families from slavery or death. I think they're not on the walls for a reason – either they're expecting help from outside, or they've a better defence than we're guessing. Eperitus, go and warn Ajax to keep a close eye on those hills to the north; I'm going to take the army closer in to the walls before—'

At that moment, as the ladder parties were nearing the ditch, a man climbed up on to the battlements and looked down in haughty defiance at the crawling mass of Greeks before the city. That his dark eyes and large, hooked nose belonged to Trojan nobility – if not royalty – was beyond doubt, and every Greek who looked up at his bearded face sensed that his appearance meant an end to their hopes of an easy victory. The man was tall and strong with enormous shoulders and huge fists that hung at his sides, big enough to kill a man with a single punch. As if to prove the point, though he wore a splendid breastplate of bronze scales and a massive helmet with a green plume, he carried no weapon. Instead, he raised a palm towards the advancing foes and called out in a loud voice:

'Enemies of Troy, go back to your ships. Nothing but death awaits you here. Go back to your ships and sail home to Greece, before the vengeance of Apollo falls upon you. King Sarpedon of the Lycians has spoken.'

'Told you,' Odysseus said, arching his eyebrows knowingly at Eperitus. 'The whole city must be filled with Lycians, just waiting for us to come and throw ourselves on to their spears. Aeneas is in there too, don't forget, and I'll stake my kingdom there's a host of Dardanians with him.'

'Then Hector must have guessed we'd try to take Lyrnessus,' Eperitus said, watching the men with the ladders, who had halted their advance and were looking up at the walls as if death would sweep down on them from the battlements at any moment. 'Either that or the information that the garrison had been stripped was false and we've been lured into a trap.'

'It wouldn't be the first time they've outwitted us,' Odysseus replied. 'And yet our spies told us Aeneas was inside Troy only the day before yesterday. If that's true then he was sent here on purpose – and that means Hector must have known we were coming.'

As he spoke, Sarpedon stepped back down so that only the upper half of his body remained visible behind the stone parapet. A moment of quiet followed in which the ranks of Argives, Ithacans and Myrmidons shifted restlessly, while some of the Locrians fitted arrows and half drew their bowstrings in readiness. Then a slow, mocking laugh broke the silence. Eperitus looked around to see who among the Greeks could draw amusement from the shock of Sarpedon's presence, and saw Achilles leaning on his shield and chuckling as he looked up at the Lycian king.

'Sarpedon, you old fool,' he called, shaking his head and smiling. 'Do you really think we Greeks are going to return to our homes before Troy has fallen? And do you think that by standing on the crumbling walls of this old dung heap you're going to stop *me* from knocking its worm-eaten gates off their hinges and killing every living thing that opposes me? Then let me make *you* an offer: any Lycian inside the walls of Lyrnessus, including yourself, who wants to return to his home now can do so, taking his armaments, his honour and his life with him. All I ask is your word that none will ever come back to the aid of Troy. But any who choose to remain will be slaughtered, without mercy, and his body left as carrion for the birds. Achilles, chief of the Myrmidons, has spoken.'

There was a roar of approval from the Greek ranks, but Sarpedon raised his hand again and they fell silent.

'I am familiar with your reputation, *Prince* Achilles – as a butcher who knows no restraint, a murdering dog whose excesses are shameful even to the Greeks. You strut around the battlefield as if Hades himself cannot claim you, yet all the time the shadow of death is at your heels. Do you think we haven't heard of your own mother's prophecy, that you'll die here in Ilium? Perhaps today your fate will catch up with you.'

Without warning, a spear flew towards the battlements and split the air where, a heartbeat before, Sarpedon's head had been. Slowly, the Lycian's shocked face rose back above the parapet to see Patroclus standing in front of Achilles, his arrogant features twisted with fury.

'Your own fate will strike you down long before a drop of Achilles's blood touches Trojan soil,' he shouted. 'If you ever see your homeland again, Sarpedon, it'll be as a corpse, to be wept over by your wife as she curses the gods for their cruelty.'

Achilles placed a calming hand on Patroclus's shoulder and pulled him back. Stepping forward, he raised his spear above his head then thrust the point towards the walls. Simultaneously, the lines of Greek warriors lifted their shields before them and began to move, closing ranks as they marched up the slope once more. At their head, the assault parties took up their ladders and resumed their advance, while to the rear the Locrians pulled back their bowstrings to their cheeks and waited for the enemy to show themselves.

They did not have to wait long. Sarpedon raised his hand again, but this time it was not to parley. A moment later the city's defences were crowded with armed men – not the weak and badly outnumbered militia the Greeks had originally expected, but a force many hundreds strong, their spearheads blazing like points of fire all along the battlements.

As the Greeks stared up in awe at the defenders, Sarpedon's hand fell. An instant later the air above the city walls was filled with a dark, hissing cloud of arrows that arced high above the heads of the assault parties to fall into the massed ranks of the main army behind. Thousands of men who had lowered their guard at the appearance of Sarpedon were suddenly scrambling to raise their shields above their heads again. Many did not succeed.

Odysseus nodded at Eperitus, who turned sharply to the crouching ranks behind him and barked out the order to advance at the double. More arrows dropped among them and more men fell, but the lull was over and their blood was up, so they came on with a grim determination that showed in every sweat- and dust-caked face. Eperitus felt a touch of pride at the sight of them, but his stern grimace did not falter as he turned and broke into an awkward run.

Odysseus was beside him, with his oval shield raised above his head and his spears clutched in his right hand. The two men had been in more fights together than either could remember and they drew confidence from each other's presence as they ran into battle together, sweating in their armour while dozens of black-shafted arrows fell all around them.

At the top of the slope, the first assault parties had reached the ditch and were raising their ladders against the walls. A deadly rain of spears and rocks were cast down on their heads, felling many as they struggled to plant the feet of the ladders in the base of the ditch. Then, as the first ladders hit the wall, they realized something was horribly wrong.

'They've deepened the ditch,' Eperitus exclaimed, raising his voice above the whistle of arrows and the shouts and cries of men. 'The ladders aren't long enough to reach the tops of the walls.'

Odysseus stared at the tell-tale layer of fresh earth that crowned the top of the slope and watched in dismay as the men of the assault parties poured into the ditch, where only their heads remained visible. He and Diomedes had scouted the walls a few nights before, when the trench that circled the city was silted up by mud brought in by the winter rains. They had built the ladders accordingly, but the defenders had since re-dug the ditch and now the tops of the ladders were falling a spear's length short of the parapet.

'Damn it,' he cursed, suddenly quickening his pace. 'But by all the gods we're not turning back now. We'll take those bloody walls even if we have to climb them on the bodies of our own dead!'

Eperitus followed in the king's wake, staring ahead at the rapidly approaching fortifications. At every point, desperate men were trying to reach the battlements with their outstretched arms, where the defenders speared them with ease or cut off their hands as they seized the parapets. Only one ladder reached the top of the wall, the foot of which was supported firmly in Polites's lap to give it the extra height. Men scrambled on to his back and sprang up the thick wooden rungs, but were easily cut down as they reached the mass of defenders at the top. Antiphus had abandoned his own ladder and was crouching behind the cover of another man's shield, shooting enemy after enemy from the walls.

'It's suicide!' Eperitus protested, seizing Odysseus by his cloak and trying to stop him. 'We need to fall back. We can attack again tomorrow, after we've made the ladders longer.'

'Fall back yourself,' Odysseus grunted, pushing Eperitus's hand away. There was a fierce anger in his eyes, which Eperitus had become more familiar with as the years of the siege had dragged on. 'I'm sick of the Trojans frustrating every attack we make. If we're going to return to Ithaca, then we have to keep fighting until every last one of them is dead.'

'Then join Achilles at the gates, where at least we have a chance of breaking into the city. It's madness to attack walls we can't even reach!'

'To Hades with Achilles!' Odysseus cursed. 'And to Hades with you, too, if you won't come.'

Scowling, he turned and ran the last stretch of the slope, where, with his shield held over his head against the rain of rocks and spears, he dropped down into the ditch beside Polites. A moment later his helmeted head was lost from sight as the ranks of the Ithacan army rushed past the lone figure of their captain, sweeping round him in their eagerness to reach the walls. As the final rank ran by, a sneering voice called out: 'Lost your nerve, Eperitus?'

If the accusation of cowardice was not bad enough, the fact that it had come from Eurylochus was unbearable. The king's cousin had never forgiven Eperitus for being made captain of the guard – a position Eurylochus had always coveted for himself, despite the fact that he was a spineless fool who was only ever to be found skulking at the rear of any battle, where the corpses provided rich pickings. Eperitus caught the man's small black eyes staring at him from over his snout-like nose and multiple chins – maintained along with his ample stomach, despite ten years of camp rations – and felt hot needles of shame driven through his chest. But there were more important things than Eurylochus's mockery to be concerned about.

Uncertain of how they were to scale the walls, his instinct for command took over and he ran up behind the press of Ithacan warriors.

'Stay out of the ditch! Front two ranks kneel and raise your shields; rear ranks, throw your damned spears at those bastards on the wall.'

In response to his orders, the Ithacans began casting spear after spear at the defenders, sending many toppling backwards into their comrades. But more took their places, and among them were the archers who had been massed behind the city walls. With the armies of Ithaca, Argos and Phthia smashing themselves against the battlements, they had been ordered on to the ramparts to shoot directly down into the mass of attackers. But at the same time, Little Ajax had brought his Locrians closer up the slope, where they could pour an equally deadly fire into the crowded Lycians and Dardanians. Many fell screaming into the ditch below, where they were quickly silenced by the hacking swords of the frustrated Greeks.

Then a ladder rose up from the ditch where the Ithacan assault parties were massed. To Eperitus's surprise, as he crouched behind his great shield to avoid the murderous rain of arrows, he saw that the top of the ladder reached just above the parapet. Another ladder of the same length followed it, and then another, and it was only as men began to dash up them with their shields held over their heads and their swords at the ready that Eperitus saw the answer to the riddle: someone was lashing ladders together with leather belts around the middle rungs, giving the extra length needed to reach the ramparts.

'Odysseus,' he said with a grin.

At that moment, he saw Aeneas appear on the walls above the Ithacan army. His rich armour flashed in the sunlight and left no one in doubt of his presence, as his bright sword cleaved the head of one of the attackers from its shoulders and sent the body plunging down into the press of men below. Eperitus's eyes were not on the Dardanian prince, though, but on the warrior who accompanied him. He stood a head taller than the men around him, who moved quickly aside at the sight of his powerful physique, battle-scarred face and dark, merciless eyes. He placed his hands on the stone parapet and, ignoring the Locrian arrows, looked out over the seething mass of soldiers below, sweeping his hard gaze across their upturned faces until it fell on Eperitus. The faintest flicker of a smile touched Apheidas's lips as he met his son's eyes.

Chapter Three

THE TEMPLE OF ARTEMIS

For a moment Eperitus was aware of nothing but the face of his father watching him. The spears, stones and arrows that were sending men to their deaths on both sides of the struggle were no longer a concern. The clash of weapons and the screams of men faded from his hearing, just as the figures moving all around him and on the walls above became colourless blurs, like shadows in a dream. Now all that mattered was the face on the ramparts, the closeness of the man who had haunted his nightmares for two decades, whose death he had wanted for so long that the desire to kill him seemed to have tormented his thoughts for ever. And now, after ten years of searching for his father across the battle-fields of Ilium, he was suddenly and unexpectedly a spear's cast away. All he needed to do was pull back his arm and hurl his weapon and all the hatred and shame would end.

And yet he was unable to move. For the first time in many years he felt afraid. It was not the churning of his stomach before every battle, which soon disappeared after the first arrow was fired or the first spear was thrown; it was the fear of confronting something so integral to his existence for so many years that in destroying it he might destroy himself. Who would *he* be if his father was gone? Apheidas had murdered his own king to usurp the throne, and when Eperitus had refused to join him he had sent his son into exile. The shame of that treachery was the driving force behind Eperitus's desire for honour and glory; his anger at his father's terrible acts gave him his ferocity in battle; and the knowledge that the old traitor had given his service to Troy kept Eperitus's own loyalty to Greece focused and sharp. Indeed, Apheidas made Eperitus what he was.

He looked up at the battlements and into the dark eyes that had controlled him for so long, and despite the fear and the doubt that were tearing at his insides he knew he must kill his father. It was the only way he could be free to discover his own self, to move on from his dark past and become whatever the gods had intended him to be. With heavy limbs he drew back his spear and threw it at the crowd of defenders on the walls above. The black shaft seemed to quiver as it flew straight at its target. For an unbelievable moment Eperitus thought it would strike home, then Apheidas leaned to one side and the bronze head thumped into the chest of a Lycian archer behind him. It tore through the man's tunic of layered cloth, split open his heart and came out through his back, just below the shoulder bone. As he fell, one of his comrades stepped forward and aimed an arrow directly at Eperitus, but before he could release it Apheidas grabbed him by his shoulders and threw him from the walls, to be hacked to death by the attackers below.

With his spear cast, Eperitus felt the heaviness lift from his limbs and the old anger return. He drew his sword and barged through the ranks of soldiers who stood between him and the walls. Leaping into the ditch, he ran to one of the ladders and pulled aside a pale-faced soldier who was about to mount. A large stone thumped into the earth beside him and arrows whistled past his ears, but he raised his grandfather's heavy shield over his head and began to climb.

The rungs were slippery with blood and his progress was awkward without the full use of his hands, but as more stones bounced off his shield and the points of half a dozen arrows nudged through the four-fold leather he felt no fear, only an iron-like determination to reach the top and get among the defenders. On either side of him as he ascended he could see the length of the ditch filled with the dead and the living. Doubled ladders lashed together with belts were being raised at every point now and under the cover of the Locrian archers hundreds of men were renewing the attack on the walls.

'Eperitus!' boomed a voice from a neighbouring ladder.

It was Polites.

'Where's Odysseus?' Eperitus shouted back.

Polites shrugged and pointed to the battlements above, before resuming his ascent in silence. Eperitus looked up from beneath his shield and saw the parapet just ahead of him. As he watched, a pair of hands seized the top of the ladder and tried to push it sideways. The flimsy structure wobbled and Eperitus's body tensed as he struggled to keep his balance, but a moment later he heard a scream and a body fell past him to the ditch below. The ladder straightened again and he quickened his ascent, steadying himself with his sword hand on the rungs before his face. As he reached the top a spear point jabbed through his cloak and scraped across the back of his leather cuirass. Eperitus hooked his shield over the parapet and instinctively lashed out with his sword. The obsessively sharpened edge found flesh and bone and a bitter cry of pain followed; his attacker's spear fell down to the ditch below, a severed hand still gripping the shaft.

Climbing up on to the top of the wall, he found himself looking down at a dozen dark-skinned, bearded faces, eyes wide with fear and exhilaration and the knowledge that death was close. He kicked out at the nearest and sent him sprawling backwards, then jumped down among the others and buried his sword in the chest of a young spearman, killing him instantly. He tugged his weapon free and advanced. An archer tossed his bow aside and drew his short sword against the fearsome Ithacan, only to have his arm lopped off above the elbow. Eperitus barged him aside with his shield and – sensing that more Ithacans were jumping down on to the wall behind him – pushed forward into the mass of Lycians and Dardanians, all the time scanning for signs of his father.

By now the walls were crowded with men from both sides,

jostling against each other in a struggle for mastery. As Eperitus sent another opponent tumbling from the battlements with a heave of his shield, he noticed for the first time the collection of simple, flat-roofed dwellings that both sides were fighting to possess: a homogenous sprawl of dusty houses, brightened here and there by the broader structure of a temple or by an open market square, but otherwise unremarkable and not worth the blood of so many brave men. Then he caught the flash of a bronze-scaled breastplate out of the corner of his eye and turned to see a Lycian noble pushing forward through his men. He carried the tall shield favoured by most high-born Trojans and wielded a huge, double-headed axe, which he swung at Eperitus's head. Eperitus dodged the blow and punched out with his shield, knocking his attacker back into the press of his men.

'Where's Apheidas?' he demanded, speaking in his opponent's language.

'Damn Apheidas! Fight *me*!' the noble responded angrily, the spittle flecking his beard.

He sprang forward, cleaving the air with his axe. Eperitus ducked aside and lunged with his sword, forcing the Lycian to fall back and draw his shield across his body.

'Tell me where Apheidas is and I'll let you live.'

The Lycian laughed and brought his heavy axe down in another attack. The edge sparked against the stone parapet as Eperitus avoided the blow with easy agility. A moment later the point of the Greek's sword found the Lycian's groin and he crumpled to his knees, clutching at the wound in a vain effort to stop his lifeblood pouring out of his body. Eperitus kicked him to the stone floor of the battlements and placed his blade against the man's neck.

'I can kill you now or leave you to a slow death. Where's Apheidas?'

The man looked up at him with pain-filled eyes, his warrior's pride replaced by the humbling certainty that death was near.

'He went back down into the city,' the Lycian whispered

through gritted teeth. 'Now keep your promise and send me to Hades.'

Eperitus pushed his sword point into the man's throat then glared at the remaining Lycians, who looked on in shock at the defeat of their champion. From every part of the wall now there came the sound of bronze beating against bronze, the calls and cries of men and the strange shuffling of leather sandals on stone as crowds of warriors fought desperately to kill each other. Then, as Eperitus raised his shield and readied his sword to attack, an arrow split the air past his right ear and stuck in the throat of a Lycian spearman, who gasped horribly as he struggled to gain control of his dying body.

'Even you can't take them all alone,' said a familiar voice.

Eperitus turned to see the scruffy figure of Antiphus at his shoulder, with the bulk of Polites looming up behind him. A moment later Odysseus joined them, his face spattered with blood and his sword running with gore.

'I knew you couldn't stay out of things for long,' the king said, his earlier rebuke seemingly forgotten. 'It's not in your nature.'

Then he raised his shield before him and ran at the Lycians, shouting his defiance. Eperitus and the others followed, sweeping all resistance before them until the will of the defenders cracked and many began to drop their weapons in surrender. The remainder fled back down the steps that led to the city streets, closely followed by streams of Greeks. As Eperitus joined the pursuit he caught sight of a fresh body of enemy spearmen and archers, standing in ordered ranks at the far end of a broad, heavily rutted street that led to the heart of the city. At the head of this unbloodied reserve were Sarpedon and Aeneas, their armour bright in the sunshine as they ordered the stragglers from the walls to join the solid lines of their comrades. Then, just as Eperitus was thinking that the battle for Lyrnessus was far from over, a great crash from the southernmost point of the city signalled the fall of the gates to Achilles and his Myrmidons. Soon the whole of

Lyrnessus would be filled with Greeks. Realizing there was no hope of defending the city, Sarpedon and Aeneas suddenly began ordering their soldiers to fall back to the northern gate.

Eperitus jumped down on to the dusty, body-strewn street, closely followed by Odysseus.

'They've given up,' the king said, watching the hasty but well-ordered retreat. 'Form the men into lines, quickly – I want to catch them while they're still inside the city. If they get out on to the open plain most of them will escape back to Troy.'

Eperitus looked at Odysseus, whose stern eyes were determined to kill as many of the enemy as possible, and shook his head.

'I can't.'

Odysseus shot him a questioning look. 'Can't?'

'I saw my father on the walls. He's here, somewhere in the city. I have to find him.'

'Apheidas is here! Are you sure?'

Eperitus nodded and Odysseus raised his eyebrows.

'Then I'll come with you. Diomedes and Achilles can lead the pursuit, and Antiphus can command the Ithacans . . .'

'No, Odysseus,' Eperitus replied. 'Sarpedon and Aeneas will fight a hard rearguard and the men will need you to lead them. Besides, I have to face Apheidas by myself. You understand that.'

'Of course,' Odysseus answered. He gripped Eperitus's shoulder and looked him in the eye. 'Go and do what you have to, and may Athena protect you.'

With that, he turned and looked up at the walls, where Diomedes was giving orders for the captives to be properly treated.

'Come on, you old war dog! Leave the prisoners to the guards; there's still plenty of fighting to be had down here.'

'And I'll be in the thick of it before you are, you red-headed laggard,' Diomedes shouted back.

Eperitus left them and ran after the fleeing Lycians and Dardanians, hoping for a glimpse of his father. The force under Sarpedon and Aeneas had already disappeared from sight, but here and there lone soldiers were still running from the walls, desperate to escape death or capture at the hands of the victorious Greeks. Ahead of him was a stumbling figure, covered in blood and clutching at the stump of his arm. Eperitus caught up with him and grabbed his shoulder.

'Where's Apheidas?' he demanded.

The man stared at him blankly, his brown face pale from shock and loss of blood. Eperitus shoved him aside and ran on to where a young soldier, barely more than a boy, was cowering in a doorway. He shrieked as Eperitus sprinted up to him, sword still in hand, and could only shake his head in terror as the same question was pressed on him.

Cursing, Eperitus left him and ran on down the street, his heart beating fast with the fear that his father would escape. He had waited too long to face him and despite his earlier doubt he was now filled with an urgent need to confront Apheidas. He reached a turn in the street and saw a small market square ahead of him. The tail of the enemy rearguard was marching across it, heading towards the gate in the northern wall of the city. An archer recognized his old-fashioned but unmistakeably Greek shield and called to his comrades, who loosed a dozen hasty arrows towards him. They were hopelessly out of range, though, and the nearest bounced harmlessly off the wall beside his head.

Unfazed, Eperitus scanned the retreating army for sight of his father, but knew in his heart that he was not among them. Seeing a narrow side road, he dashed down it as more arrows sailed down to stick into the earth around his running feet.

Soon he was losing himself among the dark, deserted alleyways of Lyrnessus, hoping beyond hope that he would stumble across Apheidas among the shadows. But every door was closed and the windows he passed revealed only empty rooms, devoid of all removable possessions. The city's population had abandoned their homes in a hurry, fearful of the slaughter, rape and enslavement that a triumphant Greek army would bring. Even the dogs had gone, leaving the streets and marketplaces temporarily bereft of the signs of civilized life.

But the void they had left was already being filled. Here and there Eperitus saw the stooping, misshapen figures of wounded men, fleeing the destruction at the gates and on the battlements and desperately seeking a place to hide from the wrath of the victors. Eperitus ignored them, knowing they would be too confused or frightened to be of any use in his hunt for his father. His sharp senses picked up the harsh shouts of warriors drawing in on every side, closely followed by the crackle of flames and the smell of burning. He emerged on to another broad avenue – which he guessed must run from the southern gate – and saw a dozen black-clad men to his right.

'There's one,' a voice shouted.

A spear flew fast and accurate towards Eperitus's head. He leaned to his left and flung up his shield, knocking the missile aside with the flat of the layered oxhide.

'Hold, damn you,' he shouted, as the battle-crazed Myrmidons readied their weapons to attack. 'I'm Eperitus, captain of the Ithacan royal guard.'

'Impossible! Achilles was first in the city, and we were right beside him as the gates fell. The Ithacans are still trying to take the walls.'

Eperitus gave a derisive laugh. 'Odysseus and I were inside the city while you were still knocking on the doors. And if you still doubt who I am, then I know two of you at least are from Peisandros's command. What Trojan would know that? Now get about your business and leave me to mine.'

He ran on, leaving the confused Myrmidons staring after him. He passed more groups of Achilles's men and several bodies as he went. As the sky began to fill with dark palls of smoke he heard the heavy clash of weapons ringing in the distance. The fight with the enemy's rearguard had begun, but whether Odysseus and Diomedes were leading the attack, or whether Achilles had caught up with them first, Eperitus could not guess. Then, as he reached an open space before a squat temple of yellow stone, a man stepped out from a doorway and lunged at him with a sword. Eperitus turned aside at the last moment, just as the blade passed beneath his arm and scraped against his cuirass. The sharpened upper edge slid along the soft skin beneath his bicep, burning like hot iron as it opened his flesh. Wincing with pain, he stepped away and threw his shield across his body as his assailant drew his arm back for a second thrust. The point jabbed at the oxhide, but was too weak to penetrate. Eperitus responded with a foot to the man's groin, doubling him over. Before he could bring his sword down into the man's skull, a second appeared from the same doorway and took the blow on the boss of his oval shield. A third man followed and suddenly Eperitus found himself facing three fully armed Lycians, with no inclination to retreat until they had taken their revenge on at least one Greek.

'Out of my way,' he warned them. 'I've no quarrel with you.'

'But we have with you, you Greek scum,' the third man answered.

They fanned out around him. Eperitus saw the man to his right crouch, ready to spring, and immediately lashed out with his sword. The man lifted his shield, but too late to prevent the point of the blade slicing across his eyeballs and the bridge of his nose. He screamed in agony and fell to his knees, clutching at his face. An instant later his comrades attacked, screaming defiance as their swords beat down simultaneously against Eperitus's raised shield. Using his great strength to throw both men back, he brought his sword around in a low sweep at the legs of the nearest. His opponent saw the attack too late and could only watch in horror as the blade hacked into his left leg below the knee. He collapsed on to his shield, thrashing about with pain and spraying blood across the dry earth of the street.

The remaining Lycian looked at his two colleagues, the first now unconscious and the second oblivious to everything but the pain of his wound, and decided he had seen enough. Throwing down his weapons, he turned and fled. Without hesitation, Eperitus placed his foot on the chest of his second victim.

'Have you seen Apheidas?'

The man gave a great sob of pain and tried to twist free, but Eperitus leaned his weight upon him and slapped the flat of his sword against his cheek.

'I *said*, have you seen Apheidas!'

The man reached out a shaky hand towards Eperitus, begging for mercy. Eperitus placed the point of his sword against the man's throat and drove it through into the earth beneath. The Lycian's lifeless head lolled to one side and he was silent.

'I'm here, Son.'

Eperitus whirled round to see a figure standing in the shadowed portico of the temple. The dull gleam of a drawn blade shone at his side.

'You fought well,' he said. 'If your grandfather was alive he'd have been mighty proud of such a display.'

'Not as proud as he'd have been to see me run you through, traitor.'

Apheidas chuckled. 'Still so angry, Eperitus? Come now, such excessive rage goes against nature and the will of the gods. You must leave it behind.'

Laying his blade casually over his shoulder, he turned and disappeared between the tall wooden doors of the temple. Eperitus felt a bead of sweat trickle down across his cheek. Swatting it away, he gripped his sword so tightly that his knuckles turned white, then he walked up to the pillared threshold. The familiar temple smell of perfumed incense and woodsmoke drifted out from the darkened doorway. In the blackness beyond he could see an avenue of painted wooden columns, fading to grey as the shadows swallowed them, and a floor flagged with stone slabs, worn to a black-edged smoothness by generations of worshippers. He stepped inside and instantly felt the warmth of the sun sucked from his flesh by the chill, stagnant atmosphere of the temple.

He paused and scanned the heavy shadows, waiting patiently for his eyes to adjust, relying instead on the acuteness of his hearing and the supernatural ability of his skin to sense the slightest movement in the air. It reminded him of the ruined temple at Messene, where he and Odysseus had once fought an ancient serpent placed there by Hera. As he recalled the terrifying battle with the giant snake he noticed two points of light at the far end of the temple. They gleamed like eyes in the darkness, and indeed that was what they were – not living eyes, but the glass eyes of an idol. Half his own size, the painted wooden effigy stood in an alcove behind the white-washed stone altar. It had been carved with an ankle-length chiton, large breasts and a golden bow in its left hand. Eperitus shuddered: he was in the temple of Artemis.

There was a movement in the shadows beside the altar. Apheidas stepped from behind one of the painted columns and laid his sword irreverently on the plinth where sacrifices were offered to the goddess.

'How long's it been, Son? Eighteen years?'

'Twenty, and my hatred of you hasn't faded, Father. When you killed Pandion and took his throne for yourself, you brought a shame on our family that can never be removed – except by your death. I intend to claim that honour for myself, now.'

He raised the point of his sword, lifted his grandfather's shield higher and took a cautious step forward.

'Don't be hasty, Eperitus. You've waited this long; at least listen to what I have to say before you do something we might both regret.'

Eperitus took another slow step and saw his father's hand edge towards the handle of his sword.

'There's nothing you can say to me, Father. Your shadow's lain over my life for too long and now I'm going to set myself free of it.'

'A man can change, Eperitus. Twenty years ago I was only a little older than you are now – I was young and impetuous, thinking with my heart and not giving my head a say. I made a mistake.'

'And now you're making another.'

Eperitus lunged, aiming above the leather breastplate at his father's unprotected throat. With astounding speed, Apheidas seized his sword from the altar and brought it up to meet his son's blade. Bronze scraped across bronze until the two hilts locked against each other. Eperitus stared into his father's dark eyes for a moment, but instead of seeing a reflection of his own hatred he saw something infinitely more disarming. For the briefest moment, he saw the father he had known as a boy – a man fiercely proud of his son; a man whom he had looked up to and admired. Then he remembered that his childish admiration had been destroyed by an act of unforgivable evil, and with a snarl of fury on his lips he pushed his father back against the altar and brought his sword down upon him. Again Apheidas's reactions were quicker than Eperitus had expected, meeting the blow with the edge of his blade and at the same time kicking out with his foot, catching Eperitus in the stomach and sending him sprawling across the stone flags. He landed with his back against one of the columns and a cloud of dust fell down over his head.

Springing back to his feet, he moved out to meet the inevitable follow-up attack. But Apheidas did not take the advantage he had created, and instead moved behind the protection of the altar.

'Don't be a fool, Son. Can't you see I regret what I did in Alybas? Your older brothers were killed fighting at my side, but . . .' Apheidas paused, as if struggling with the memory. 'But worse even than that, I lost *you*. Don't you realize you were always my favourite, Eperitus?'

'That's a lie!'

'It's true. Your brothers were fine lads, but you've a greatness in you they could never have matched. Your grandfather knew that.'

'And he would have known I'd never betray King Pandion or tolerate his murderer to live.'

Slipping the shield from his arm, Eperitus leapt across the altar and swung at his father's head. Apheidas twisted out of the way and the blow decapitated the idol in the alcove behind him, leaving the headless torso rocking on its plinth. A sudden fury lit

Apheidas's eyes and he lashed out with his sword, striking sparks from the stone wall as Eperitus ducked beneath the slicing blade. Without pausing to think that his father was now trying to kill him, Eperitus ran beneath his raised sword arm and rammed his shoulder into his chest. Apheidas's spine jarred against the overlapping edge of the altar, causing him to cry out in pain, but he quickly recovered and deflected another swipe of Eperitus's sword. A moment later the temple was filled with the ringing of bronze as the two men struck blow after blow against each other. Then the tip of Apheidas's blade, deflected upward by the edge of Eperitus's weapon, slashed the forehead of the younger man. At the sight of his son's blood, Apheidas's anger left him and he stood back.

'Forgive me,' he said through heavy breaths. 'Forgive me for everything. As the gods are my witnesses, Eperitus, I beg you to let the past go!'

Eperitus felt the sting of the cut and dabbed at it with the palm of his hand. The blood was dark in the gloomy temple as he inspected it.

'Why? You killed a good man because of your selfish ambition. If it wasn't for you, Pandion might still rule Alybas today and I'd never have been ashamed of naming you as my father. What's more, you've betrayed Greece to serve Troy. There's no reason why I shouldn't fight you to the death, right here in this temple.'

'Yes there is. I'm your father, Eperitus, and you're my son. As soon as I knew you'd be attacking Lyrnessus, I insisted on coming here with Aeneas and Sarpedon . . .'

'You *knew* I'd be here? You knew about the attack?'

Apheidas smiled, realizing his mistake. 'Yes, I knew, but don't bother asking me how – unless you intend to come back to Troy with me.'

Eperitus grimaced. '*Troy?*'

'Of course. That's why I came to Lyrnessus – to speak with you, if I could, and convince you of my regret about the past. You're a man of honour, no one can question that, so come and fight alongside me for a worthy cause, in defence of a noble people.'

Eperitus's eyes narrowed. 'Just because you betrayed your king and your country, Father, doesn't mean I'll betray mine.'

'There would be no treachery, Eperitus. Do you think I fight for Troy because I was thrown out of Alybas, or because I'm a mercenary who'll sell my services to the highest bidder?'

'You fight for Troy because you're a man without shame, who cares nothing for his own honour or the honour of his family! Your own father would have killed you for what you've done.'

Apheidas threw back his head and laughed.

'You poor fool,' he said. 'It's because of your grandfather that I'm here in the first place.'

'Speak plainly,' Eperitus replied, angered by his father's mockery.

'Even you know your grandfather wasn't from Alybas,' Apheidas answered, calmly, 'that he killed the man who raped and murdered his wife – my mother – and was forced into exile, taking me with him when I was only an infant. You remember me telling you this when you were a lad? And yet you never wondered where he came from?'

'He would only ever say he came from the east. From Euboea or Attica, I'd always assumed—'

'Your grandfather was a Trojan, Eperitus. *I* am a Trojan, and but for your mother's blood, you are too.'

Eperitus glanced at the square of intense light beyond the door, where he was vaguely aware of voices in the street. His mind was reeling from his father's revelation, wanting to reject it and yet instinctively knowing it to be true. At the same time, part of him understood that it did not matter. Not now, at least. He was born and raised a Greek and had spent the past ten years killing Trojans. Apheidas's news was not going to change that, and somehow he knew his grandfather would not have wanted it to.

He flexed his fingers around the handle of his sword and focused his gaze on his father.

'You're wrong. I'm a Greek. My grandfather was a Greek, too. When he arrived in Alybas, Greece became his new home – that's why he let me believe I was a Greek through and through. What good does it do a man to split his identity? After all, look at *you*.'

Eperitus spat on the floor at his father's feet, then, feeling the old hatred surge into his veins, he lunged forward. Apheidas parried the blow with ease, as if he had expected it all along, and swung his own blade across his son's torso, forcing him to leap backwards. Eperitus attacked again, furious now, but Apheidas smashed his sword aside and brought the hilt of his own weapon sharply up into his jaw, throwing his head back. Eperitus caught his heel, staggered and fell. As if in a nightmare he heard the sound of his sword clattering across the flagstones, and a moment later his armoured body was crashing down on the hard floor. The back of his head smacked against a slab, dazing him, and the next thing he knew his father's foot was on his chest, the point of his blade resting against his throat.

Chapter Four
THE GIFT OF THE GODS

'Kill me, then,' Eperitus said savagely, loathing the dark eyes that were staring down at him. 'Kill me and put an end to it.'

The sword was heavy and sharp against his flesh, but the face above it was bereft of menace. Instead, there was a sadness in it – regret, perhaps, for what could have been.

'Put an end to *your* anger and shame, maybe,' Apheidas said. 'But not mine. Though you hate me, Eperitus, you're my son. You're all I have left. I used to think a man found immortality in a glorious name, covered in brave deeds and built on the bodies of dead enemies. Like Hector, or your Achilles. Do you remember how I used to tell you such things when your grandfather and I trained you to be a warrior? Well, they were the words of a fool. A man is remembered through his children. His glory can fade, but not his offspring.'

Eperitus closed his eyes and thought of his own daughter, Iphigenia, the child of his illicit union with Clytaemnestra, the wife of Agamemnon. Had not Clytaemnestra said the same thing as she begged Eperitus to take her and their daughter to safety – that he should forget glory and let Iphigenia be his legacy? But this was not the same. He had failed to protect Iphigenia. Agamemnon had murdered her to appease the vengeful Artemis, and had lived with that regret for over ten years. But he had *not* brought shame upon her or sent her into exile.

'Don't look to me for your own immortality,' he said, whispering as the point of the sword continued to press against the base of his throat. 'I am no longer your son, Apheidas. You lost me when you killed King Pandion and brought dishonour on your family. So kill me now, for if you don't you have my word I will hunt you down and slaughter you like a sick dog.'

Apheidas's brow darkened for a moment, and then the sound of voices – growing louder in the street outside – distracted him. He looked through the doorway at the blinding sunshine, then stared back down at his son.

'I'll not kill you, Eperitus,' he said, raising his sword and slipping it into its plain leather scabbard. 'And you can forget thoughts of killing me, too. You've neither the skill nor quite as much hatred as a man needs to murder his own father. Look to your heart and you'll know it's true. And when the time is right, you'll know where to find me – inside the walls of Troy.'

He took his foot from Eperitus's chest and knelt beside him. Eperitus looked up at his father and saw his own features reflected back at him: the same oval face, the same straight nose and thin, almost lipless mouth, and the same dark hair. Only their ages and the lighter skin and thoughtful eyes he had inherited from his Greek mother separated them, and for the sake of his Greek blood he would never forget that difference.

Apheidas pulled his fist back and hit him.

When Eperitus awoke it was to the sound of a woman screaming.

He opened his eyes and looked up at the ceiling, on which he could see stars painted in gold against a sable firmament. They were smoke-stained and half lost in the gloom, but at their centre he could see a crescent moon, the symbol of the goddess whose temple this was. Raising himself on to his elbows, he dabbed his fingers gingerly against the bruised cheekbone where Apheidas's fist had connected, then lifted them to the new scar on his forehead. It was deep, but the blood had already caked inside the gash and stopped the flow of blood. With the inside of his skull pounding, he looked around between the wooden columns and noticed for the first time the faded patterns of blue, yellow and red flowers that twined around them. His sword and his grand-father's shield lay close together, halfway between himself and the door of the temple, but of Apheidas there was no sign.

Then another scream broke the stillness and he realized he had not been dreaming. Ignoring the pain in his head, he leapt to his feet and ran over to retrieve his weapons. The scream had come from the street outside, and as he squinted into the fierce daylight beyond the doorway he heard harsh laughter followed by another scream. He dashed out of the temple, blinking against the bright-ness, and saw a black-haired woman clad in a knee-length white chiton, surrounded by a circle of five men. None of the men was Apheidas, but Eperitus recognized them all the same.

'Come on, my sweet, stop playing with us,' said one of the men. 'We only want a little fun.'

'Leave me alone!' she spat. 'I'm a priestess of the temple of Artemis!'

'A virgin, then,' leered the man, wiping spittle from his beard with the back of his hand. 'I haven't had a virgin since I was a young shepherd.'

'And *she* was one of his flock!' said another, raising a laugh from his companions.

'Have you no respect for the gods?' she retorted, scowling at them. 'Have you no *fear* of the gods?'

One of the others snorted, a fat man whose face was red and shining with sweat. 'What are you talking about, girl? Don't you know you're a gift of the gods to us? You're our reward for con-quering Lyrnessus.'

He lunged at her and caught her wrist.

'Let the girl alone, Eurylochus,' Eperitus said from the shadows of the portico, his voice calm and even. 'Let her go, now!'

Eurylochus's surprise at the sudden appearance of the captain of the guard was short lived. Keeping his hold on the priestess, who had stopped struggling and was looking intently at the newcomer, he spat in the dirt and frowned at Eperitus.

'So, the absent hero has returned,' he sneered. 'Though it looks like someone has given you a beating in the meantime. But if you think I'm going to let this little beauty go just so you can have your way with her, then you'll be disappointed.'

Eperitus propped his shield against one of the columns and, sheathing his sword, walked out into the sunshine. Skeins of dark smoke were drifting up into the otherwise perfect blue skies and the smell of burning was thick in the air. He looked at the priestess, whose chiton he now saw was stained with dirt and had been torn open to expose a long, dark-skinned thigh; there were bloody scrapes on both elbows and forearms, and her lips were wet with fresh blood. As he glanced at her, she swept the tangled hair from her face to reveal dark, frightened eyes framed by long lashes. Her beauty took him by surprise and he had to forcefully shift his stare to Eurylochus.

'I told you to let the girl go,' he warned. 'I won't tell you again.'

Eurylochus's face twitched with hatred. There was a moment's indecision, then he shoved the girl into the arms of one of his cronies and pulled out his sword.

'There're five of us, Eperitus, and no witnesses. I tell you now, that girl's a rare beauty in this godforsaken country and you're not going to take her from me.'

Eperitus looked at the other four Ithacans who, except for the man whose arms were struggling to contain the priestess, had also drawn their swords and were fanning out in a crescent around him. He knew them all and none of them was any good as a warrior or as a man, but he left his sword untouched in its scabbard and instead fixed his eyes on each of them in turn. Finally his gaze rested on a skinny, rotten-toothed soldier whose red-rimmed eyes were quick to blink and look away.

'I know you men,' Eperitus told them in a slow, steady voice. 'I know you for the weak-minded, back-stabbing scum that you are. Not one of you is worthy to call himself an Ithacan, and the only reason any of you are still alive is because you skulk at the back of every battle, furthest away from the fighting. How do I know that? Because I'm always in the thick of it, and I've never seen any of your faces at my side. So if you think you can take me – even five of you together – then come on. But if you do, then it's to the death, and any man who pleads for mercy will be taken back to camp and executed. But if you put your swords back in their scabbards and walk away, I'll forget I ever saw you here. Make your choice.'

There was a pause during which the nearby sounds of shouting, laughter and the crackle of flames were carried to them on the breeze. Then the skinny man with the red-rimmed eyes slid his sword back into its scabbard and turned away.

'The girl's all yours, Eurylochus,' he grunted as he shouldered past him.

'Yeah, enjoy her,' said the man holding the priestess, pushing her towards Eurylochus and turning to follow the first man.

Eurylochus grabbed the girl by the elbow and pulled her to his side.

'Where are you going?' he asked, as the other two sheathed their swords and backed away. 'What are you afraid of? He's one man against five. Didn't you seeing him holding back from the battle?'

'There's a difference between cowardice and refusing to march into a trap, Eurylochus,' Eperitus said. All four of Eurylochus's cronies had departed now, leaving him alone with the girl – no longer struggling – at his side. 'And I'm sure you know a real coward when you see one. So what's *your* choice? Shall I draw my sword?'

Eurylochus glowered at Eperitus, then slammed his sword into its scabbard and marched off in the wake of the others. The priestess watched him go, then turned to Eperitus.

'And what do you intend to do with me?' she asked in heavily accented Greek. 'Rape me and cast me aside, as your countrymen would have done? Or take me as your captive, to be raped whenever you wish?'

'Neither,' Eperitus replied, meeting her hostile but enthralling gaze. 'I'm not interested in captives or playthings. You're free to go as you wish.'

Afraid to keep his eyes on her lest he should have a change of heart, he turned and walked back to the temple portico. As he picked up his shield and hoisted it on to his shoulder, he heard her naked feet padding along in his wake.

'Go?' she said. 'Go where? To be found by more Greek soldiers and raped? No, my lord, I'd rather take my chances with you. At least you seem to be a man of honour, which is rare among the enemies of Troy.'

He turned to find her standing directly behind him.

'A man of honour?' he said, raising an eyebrow. 'Can such a thing still exist in this war, on either side? But whether I am what you think or not, I can't take you with me. I have to find my king.'

'You *must* take me with you,' she insisted, reaching out and seizing his hand. 'My lord Eperitus – that's what the fat one called you, isn't it? – forgive me if I failed to thank you for saving me, but you can't just turn your back on me now and leave me to the next group of common soldiers who come along. Take me as your slave. I promise to serve you well, even if you are a Greek.'

As if to emphasize the point, she knelt before him and threw her arms around his legs, resting her head against his thighs. Eperitus reached down and, taking her by the elbow, raised her to her feet. Though the features of her face were still edged with anger, the hostility had left them and as he looked into her eyes he realized she was as beautiful as any woman he had seen in many years. At that moment, shouts erupted from a side street and two men came rushing into the open space before the temple. One was old with snow-white hair and short, spindly legs that seemed too exhausted to carry him any further; the other was a youth of little more than sixteen, whose thin brown arms were desperately trying to help the older man. Neither wore armour nor carried any weapons, and at the sight of Eperitus in the portico of the temple towards which they were heading they stopped and seemed to quail with fear.

Then a group of a dozen warriors came rushing out of the side street after them, brandishing swords and spears. One carried a bow, to which an arrow was already fitted. As he saw the two men he drew the string back to his right ear and released the arrow, sending the younger of the two spinning to the ground. While the older man turned to his dead companion, Eperitus pulled the girl back into the cool darkness of the temple.

'What are you doing?' she protested. '*Save* him!'

'Shut up and come with me,' Eperitus commanded, taking her by the arm and dragging her deeper into the gloom. 'Is there a back way out of this cursed place?'

'But those are Greek soldiers. Can't you intervene to save the old man's life?'

'They're Myrmidons and they're already drunk with killing. One sight of you and they won't care whether I'm a Trojan or a Greek – they'll kill me just so they can have their way with you. Now, if you really want me to help you, then tell me how to get out of here.'

'There'll be a side door somewhere. Behind a curtain, I think.'

'You *think*? But you're the priestess here – shouldn't you *know*?'

A sudden scream announced the demise of the old man. Eperitus looked to the doorway, where he could hear the voices of the Myrmidons in the street beyond.

'They're going to come in here looking for something to steal,' the girl said, her voice rising with panic. 'Come on. There's the curtain over there.'

'And where does it lead?' Eperitus asked, tightening his grip on her arm and eyeing her suspiciously as she tried to pull away.

'To an antechamber. There'll be another door leading out on to the side street that runs beside the temple. We must be quick.'

'No,' Eperitus replied, looking at the girl. Her eyes were pale and wide in the darkness where they stood by the altar stone, but as he heard the voices of the Myrmidons approaching he refused to move towards the curtain the girl was gesturing at or loosen his grip on her arm. 'We're going nowhere until you tell me who you are.'

'I'm the priestess of—'

'The priestess of this temple would have known immediately where the side door was. Who are you?'

The girl struggled against the strength of his fingers for a moment, then heard the metallic slither of a sword being drawn from its scabbard and saw the squat silhouette of a man in the doorway of the temple.

'All right, I'm not the priestess here,' she hissed. 'I don't even come from Lyrnessus. Now, can we leave before his eyes adjust to the darkness?'

But Eperitus was already pulling her across to the corner of the temple, whisking aside the heavy curtain and fumbling with the door. Fortunately, the room beyond was also in darkness and no sudden splash of light betrayed their presence to the soldiers who were cautiously advancing into the temple behind them. They crushed through the narrow doorway together, Eperitus awkwardly conscious of her soft, warm body pressed close to his, then he turned and closed the door silently behind him. Quickly scanning the tiny antechamber, which was lit only by a thin line of daylight coming from beneath a door on the opposite side of the room, he could see it was empty but for a straw mattress and some dishevelled blankets.

The girl looked around the room in disgust. 'To be honest, I'm glad I'm not the priestess of this hovel.'

Eperitus dropped his hand to her wrist and led her to the opposite door. Already there were sounds of destruction coming from the temple behind them and it would not be long before the concealed antechamber was discovered. He threw open the door and together they stepped quickly out into the comparative brightness of the shady side street.

'What's the quickest, least conspicuous way to the north gate?' he asked. 'Assuming you know that much.'

She pulled her wrist free of his grip and took his hand in hers. 'This way.'

Chapter Five

IN THE RUINS OF LYRNESSUS

'So who are you?' Eperitus asked the girl again as they walked through the shadowy alleys and rutted thoroughfares of Lyrnessus.

All around them were the sounds of pillage and burning, disrupted from time to time by the dying shouts of murdered men or the terrified screams of women in peril. The roar of flames was everywhere and a thick plume of smoke shrouded the city, filling their nostrils with its savoury reek. More and more bodies lay scattered around the streets – some still in armour, others stripped naked or left in their woollen tunics – and every now and then they would be forced to sink into the shelter of a doorway or slip down passageways between the ramshackle houses as they saw gangs of rampaging Greeks ahead of them.

'My name is Astynome. I am the only child of Chryses, priest of Apollo on the island of Chryse.'

'Why did you say you were a priestess?'

Astynome gave a bitter laugh. 'Because I thought your countrymen might show some respect for the gods and leave me alone. I should have realized the Greeks have no reverence for the immortals.'

'Then you're not a priestess at all?

'No,' she answered, and with a backward glance added: 'Or a virgin.'

Eperitus looked away, though he did not know why her

admission had embarrassed him. He was not surprised: there was something worldly about Astynome that had seen suffering and knew how to fight – the grazes on her limbs and the blood on her lips showed that. He wondered whether she had a husband, but guessed that a married woman would not be alone in a besieged city.

'I came to Lyrnessus to celebrate the annual festival of Artemis,' she continued, as if reading his thoughts. 'Then Aeneas and Sarpedon arrived with their brave Dardanians and Lycians behind them, saying Greek ships were sailing towards the shore and bringing an army to lay siege to the city. Those who were able took what they could and fled to Adramyttium or Thebe.'

'But you stayed.'

'I trusted in the men who had come to defend the city,' Astynome retorted, a touch of angry pride igniting her pupils. 'At home they say a single Trojan is worth ten Greeks and I believe them. A man who fights for a just cause – defending his homeland – is more than a match for any invader, especially one from such a backward country as Greece.'

Eperitus smiled at her zeal.

'Then your trust was misplaced,' he said. 'Did many others remain behind?'

'A few – the city's militia, the old, the sick and the foolhardy. The two your countrymen killed before the temple were a wine merchant and his son. He stayed on to make some money from the Dardanians and Lycians after their victory, and now he's dead and the Greeks will be drinking his wine for free.'

Before long they reached a small square with a large, two-storeyed house to one side. A dozen bodies were scattered around, all of whom had been disturbed by looters. Though the square was now empty, they could hear the hubbub of many voices coming from nearby. As they crossed, stepping over the debris of corpses, discarded weapons and broken armour, Eperitus asked Astynome how it was she spoke Greek.

'I learned it on Chryse,' she explained, almost stumbling as she looked around in horror at the bodies, some of which were hideously dismembered. 'From the merchants who used to call there.'

'So you were happy to buy Greek goods, and yet you clearly hate Greeks.'

'I did not hate them then. The hate came later.'

'And will you hate me, Astynome, even though you've begged to be my captive? Will you slit my throat late some night as I lie in my tent, before you steal back to Troy?'

Astynome turned to face her new master. 'You have my word I won't try to kill you, my lord. You're not like other Greeks. You remind me more of a Trojan than a Greek.'

He lifted his hand to cup her chin, feeling the distinct cleft with his thumb before raising his fingers to touch her bottom lip. She looked at him intently and for a moment he was tempted by her nearness. Then he let his hand fall to his side and turned away again.

'That's not a mistake you should make again, Astynome. I am a Greek, in heart and mind. But there's one more thing I want to know if I'm to take you under my protection – can you cook? All my men bring me is grilled mackerel and tunny, or goat's meat that's too tough to chew.'

She smiled broadly, the first real smile he had seen on her pretty mouth. 'Yes, I can cook. Even if you have no other use for me, you'll value me for my food.'

They left the square and followed a line of crude dwellings to the city walls. The sound of voices increased and soon they were at the edge of a large space filled with Greek soldiers. At the far end was a low gateway. Unlike the gates that Achilles and his Myrmidons had stormed, there was no squat tower defending the northern entrance to Lyrnessus; instead, the eastern wall doubled back on itself and ran parallel with the western wall for a dozen paces, so that the gateway was positioned between the overlap in the battlements. Though not as well defended as the southern entrance, it did mean an assaulting force was exposed to attack on both sides. The gates were fully open now, and from where they stood in the shadows of a narrow alleyway Eperitus and Astynome could see the gentle plains and wooded hills beyond.

Unlike the bands of men roving the city, the soldiers by the northern gate were still disciplined and acting under orders, giving Eperitus the confidence to lead Astynome out from their hiding place. There had been a battle here but it had long since finished. Some of the victorious Greeks were on the walls, keeping watch, while others were standing fully armed and ready for the possibility of an unexpected counter-attack. The majority, though, had stripped off their armour and weapons and were busily removing the bodies of the dead and stacking them in long rows on either side of the open space before the gates. When Astynome saw the scores of Lycians and Dardanians who had died holding the gates – while their countrymen escaped the pursuing Greeks – she fell to her knees and covered her face as she sobbed quietly. Eperitus looked at the lines of young men who had fallen, many with missing limbs or mutilated faces. It was a sight he had become familiar with since the start of the war, so he was surprised to feel a sudden pang of guilt. Was that Astynome's presence, or the realization these men were not so different from himself, and could even have been his own countrymen but for the exile of his grandfather?

Eperitus lifted Astynome to her feet and allowed her to rest her head against his shoulder, where her tears fell on to his breastplate and mingled with the spatters of dried blood. As her arms wound round him and he stroked her sea of dark hair – watched by the envious eyes of the men in the burial parties – he noticed a young woman leaning over the body of a man, laid out among his dead comrades beneath the shadow of the walls. Her shoulders shook with a slow, mournful sobbing, and despite her red eyes and tear-stained cheeks it was clear she had a powerful beauty. Other than Astynome, she was the only woman present.

'Who's she?' he asked.

Astynome lifted her head and gazed across at the stricken

woman. More tears came to her eyes and she shook her head pityingly.

'It's Briseis,' she answered. 'Daughter of Briseus the priest. And that's her husband, Mynes, she's weeping over, with his brother Epistrophus beside him. They were princes of Lyrnessus and proud men in life.'

'And brave men in their deaths,' added a soldier, stooping beside them and lifting a corpse on to his shoulders. The dead man's arms hung limply down the soldier's back as he turned to look at Eperitus and Astynome. 'Those two were at the heart of the rearguard, refusing to surrender or admit defeat. But Achilles slew them both and now Briseis is his captive.'

'Was it a hard fight?' Eperitus asked.

The man nodded. 'It was worse here than at the walls, a real bloodbath. That Sarpedon commanded the rearguard while Aeneas got the majority of the Dardanians and Lycians out through the gate. And they fought like Furies! If it hadn't been for Achilles they might've held us to a stalemate. But we beat them in the end,' he added, patting the corpse over his shoulder as he saw Astynome's chin raise a little. 'Sarpedon only escaped at the last moment, and Achilles, Patroclus and Diomedes have gone out in pursuit of him and the remainder of his men. He'll be a rich prize if—'

'What about Odysseus?' Eperitus interrupted.

'He was in the thick of it too, as usual, but Achilles asked him and Little Ajax to stay here and put down the last pockets of resistance. They were surrounding a group of militia not far from here, last I heard.'

The soldier pointed in the direction of a column of smoke billowing up from behind a line of ramshackle dwellings to the west, then, with a final glance at the Trojan girl, turned and carried his burden towards the lines of dead.

'Come on,' Eperitus said, taking Astynome's hand and heading towards the smoke.

The battle must indeed have been a brutal one, Eperitus

thought as they weaved a path between the bodies of the fallen. The sun-baked, dusty earth was dark with innumerable bloodstains and here and there he could see small fragments of human remains: several hands; arms severed at the elbow; a sandalled foot; even a cleanly lopped ear lying in a wheel rut. As they passed the gates a wagon laden with bundles of wood squealed its way through the gates.

'For the funeral pyre,' Eperitus explained, seeing Astynome's look of confusion. 'We stopped burying the dead years ago – it took too much time and effort, and by the time we'd dug the pits the carrion birds had already taken the eyes and the softer parts.'

Astynome squeezed his hand tightly and he shut up. Before long they heard the crackle of fire and turned a corner to see a large, two-storeyed house surrounded by at least three score of warriors. Long orange flames flickered up from the windows and sent spirals of dark, ember-filled smoke up into the air. More smoke wafted out into the street, but Eperitus recognized Odysseus's squat, triangular form through the fine haze, with the colossal figure of Polites beside him. As he watched, two men appeared on the flat roof of the building. They were unarmed, but their scaled breastplates and plumed helmets marked them out as warriors. Both were waving their hands before their faces and choking on the smoke. They stumbled to the edge of the low wall that surrounded the roof and looked down at the Ithacans below. Odysseus shouted a command and a moment later there was a loud twang. One of the men staggered against the wall, clutching at the black shaft protruding from his groin, before slowly curling forward and plunging to the floor below. He landed with a dull thud and lay still. His comrade shook his fist blindly at the surrounding Greeks, then retreated into the consuming smoke.

Suddenly there was a hoarse shout and several men ran out from the doorway of the house. They were half-blinded by the smoke, but the dull gleam of their weapons showed they had no intention of surrendering. Odysseus, who had been awaiting their appearance with calm patience, now sprang into action, dashing forward and knocking a man's head from his shoulders with a swift slice of his sword. Polites followed, a captured two-headed battle-axe in his right hand, and within a moment the rest of the Ithacans were behind them. The battle was brief, bloody and uneven, and with Astynome at his side Eperitus felt almost ashamed as he watched the massacre. Then, when the ringing of weapons and the shouts of men were over, he saw Odysseus come striding out with his bloodied sword hanging at his side. He looked strangely savage in the sunlight: his face grimed with ash and spattered with gore; his normally bright and thoughtful eyes red-rimmed from the smoke and filled with a forbidding anger. In his left hand he held a cloak which he had torn from the shoulders of one of his victims, and with which he was slowly wiping the mess from his blade.

'Odysseus,' Eperitus called.

The king looked at him in confusion for a moment, as if startled from a dream, then dropped his sword back into its scabbard and walked towards his captain, forcing a smile.

'Eperitus!' he answered, almost sighing as a great tiredness seemed to press down on his shoulders. 'Thank the gods you're all right. I was concerned for you.'

'Since when have you needed to worry about me?'

'It's a king's prerogative to worry about his subjects,' Odysseus replied, wiping the sweat from his brow and leaving a streak of clean skin through the accumulated dirt. He looked at Astynome. 'I see you've gained a captive during your absence.'

Astynome drew closer to Eperitus, eyeing the king of Ithaca with distrust.

'She captured me, I think. I saved her from being raped and now she's placed herself under my protection.'

'Well, girl, the gods must favour you,' Odysseus said, speaking to Astynome in her own tongue and looking at her with kindness. 'Of all the thousands of men in the Greek army, you were found by the one warrior who still retains a scrap of decency and honour. Anybody else would have left you to your fate – or added to your misery.'

Astynome frowned but said nothing.

'And what of Apheidas?' Odysseus continued in Greek, addressing Eperitus. 'Did you find him?'

Eperitus nodded and lowered his eyes a little. 'We fought in the temple of Artemis, where he gave me this.'

He pointed to the cut across his forehead. Odysseus reached up and pushed aside a lock of Eperitus's hair with his thumb. He stared at the wound and winced, but a moment later his face was transformed by a smile.

'Then you defeated him. He's dead.'

Eperitus shook his head. 'No. He mastered me easily. In fact, I've never met a swordsman like him. We fought when I was a lad, of course, but that was in the training yard, not for real. Perhaps that's why I've always assumed I'd be able to beat him, because I've never *really* seen him fight. But today I did, and he could have killed me any time he wanted to.'

'So why didn't he?'

'Because he wants me to join him in Troy! I thought I was hunting him, but it appears he came to Lyrnessus to find *me*. He knew about the assault, Odysseus. He *knew* I'd be here.'

Odysseus frowned, suddenly serious. He glanced at Astynome, who looked away.

'How?' he asked. 'How could he have known you'd be here, unless . . . ?'

'Unless someone told him,' Eperitus finished. 'Until two days ago only the commanders of the army knew about the attack on Lyrnessus and who would be taking part in it. That means there's only one way the Trojans could have sent an army here in time to meet us. There's a traitor among us, Odysseus. A traitor in the heart of the Greek command!'

Chapter Six

ANDROMACHE'S WOE

Helen, formerly the queen of Sparta, now a princess of Troy, looked out from the lofty battlements of her adopted city. The sun had long since sunk beneath the far horizon of the Aegean Sea, leaving the broad plain before the walls and the hoof-shaped bay beyond it in darkness. The stars were abroad in the moonless sky and for a while Helen gazed up at them, taking simple pleasure from naming the constellations in her mind — both the Trojan names that she was first taught by Paris on the island of Tenedos before their marriage, and the Greek equivalents that she still recalled with a slight pang of homesickness. Out on the black waters of the bay a single light shone. It was most likely a lamp on a small fishing boat, the only vessels that dared to exist in the once crowded harbour. From time to time a merchant would risk the journey, bringing much needed luxuries to Troy at greatly inflated prices, but since the Greeks had taken to sending a galley or two to capture these ships they were now very few in number. And there were no longer any warships in the bay. The whole Trojan fleet had been burned at anchor ten years ago, and the handful that had been constructed since — either in the harbour or at one of the allied cities further up the coast — had all suffered the same fate. In effect, the Greeks had destroyed Troy's power at sea and forced her to rely on supplies brought overland, via the long and arduous routes from the south and east.

Helen turned her eyes to the south-west, where by day she

would have been able to see the humped shape of Tenedos, its wooded slopes blue in the distance. The island had been consumed by the night, though a handful of lights still flickered in the darkness. A little closer, in a wide bay further up the mainland coast, a hazy orange glow marked the fires of the Greek camp. They had been ensconced there since shortly after the start of the war, out of sight and far enough away to be safe from sudden attack or harassments from Troy, and yet close enough to bring battle to the city's walls when they had a mind for violence. Mostly, though, they remained hidden away in their vast, makeshift camp with their hundreds of ships drawn up along the golden sand behind them. Whole weeks might pass without sight of the enemy, other than the occasional cavalry patrol along the banks of the Scamander, or neutral encounters at the temple of Thymbrean Apollo on the hills to the south, where both Trojans and Greeks would go to offer sacrifices and prayers. Sometimes, Helen would walk along the battlements of Pergamos, the high citadel of Troy, and look out at the sea shimmering in the morning light, watching the fishermen casting their nets, or the herds of wild horses running on the plains below, and she could almost forget that Menelaus and Agamemnon – her first husband and his power-hungry brother – were camped with an army of eighty thousand men a short chariot ride away. But they were there. They were always there.

She turned and leaned her back against the parapet, feeling the cold roughness of the stone through the wool of her long dress. Her husband was beside her, resting his elbows on the crenellated walls and looking out at the darkness. She reached across and stroked the backs of her fingers over his left bicep and down to the thick black hair of his forearm. He caught her hand and held it, then turned and smiled at her. Paris could never be described as a handsome man: he had pockmarked cheeks and an old scar that ran from his right temple, across the bridge of his flat nose and into his beard; his features were stern and battle-hardened, and carried an unquestionable authority. By contrast, Helen had beauty beyond the measure of mortal words. Her white skin was carefully preserved from the effects of the sun, and her long black hair framed a face that commanded adoration. Her striking blue eyes, so different from the common brown of all Trojan women, hid a fire that had the power to consume a man's heart, and her body was the desire of men and the envy of women. Rumoured to be a daughter of Zeus, father of the gods, she had once been the queen of Sparta but had chosen to abscond with a Trojan prince – a man who could never hope to be king so long as his brother, Hector, lived and commanded the hearts of the people. But she did not care. Power was not her fancy; it was freedom she longed for, which for a while Paris had given to her. And though the armies of Greece had quickly imprisoned her again, she still loved him with all her soul and prayed for the day when Menelaus and Agamemnon would leave the shores of Ilium in peace.

'What's wrong?' he asked.

'Other than the fact young Trojan men will soon be dying in their hundreds again for my sake? Or that I'm the most hated woman in Ilium because of the misery I've brought to its shores? Or even that I ran away from Sparta seeking freedom and love, only to find myself locked up inside the walls of Troy for ten years, unable even to leave the gates for fear I'll be snatched up by a Greek patrol?'

Paris reached across and took her other hand.

'But you have love,' he said, squeezing her soft palms with his rough fingers. 'And soon the war will come to a head. My father is seeking new alliances with distant countries and, before long, strange and fearsome armies will come to our aid. The Greeks will be thrown back into the sea and we'll be free again. As for being the most hated woman in Ilium, how can you say such a thing? The people worship you like a living goddess! Why do you think, in ten full years of war, they haven't sent you back to Menelaus?'

'Because your father won't let them,' Helen snapped, wilfully. 'It's Priam they worship, not me. All I've brought them is war and devastation.'

'Nonsense. If anyone is to blame for this war, it's me – and I don't give a damn whether the people love me or hate me, just so long as they love you. Which they do.'

Paris pulled her gently to his side, where she could feel the warmth of his body contrasting the chill of the evening breeze blowing in from the sea.

'Look at these men,' he said in a low voice, pointing to the dozen guards stationed at intervals along the western ramparts. Each one was gazing out at the plain below, while straining to hear the conversation between Paris and Helen. 'Do you know that each night the citadel guards throw dice over who will get the early watch on this part of the wall? Just so they can be here when you appear every evening after your meal, to be able to glance at your beauty. Did you also know that—'

A shout rang through the night air, cutting him short. He turned and looked at the tower guarding the entrance to the citadel, where an armed guard was pointing beyond the lower city to the plains in the south-east. Another soldier was leaning over the battlements and calling down to the guard hut just inside the gateway. Moments later dozens of soldiers were spilling out of its doors, hurriedly pulling on shields and helmets or looping scabbards over their shoulders.

'What is it?' Helen asked.

Paris held up his hand for silence as he strained to hear the shouts of the guard on the tower.

'Someone's coming,' he said. 'Horsemen, at speed, though I didn't hear how many.'

'Is it an attack?'

'No, not at night and on horseback. Which can only mean—'

He set off at a run along the broad battlements. Helen followed, walking as quickly as her long, restrictive dress would allow. She joined her husband beside the tower, where he was leaning over the walls and peering down at the darkened streets below. A dozen horsemen were winding their weary way up from the east-facing Dardanian Gate, through the lower city to the entrance to Pergamos.

'Isn't that Aeneas?' Helen enquired, leaning alongside her husband and straining to identify the faces of the men as they were met by the light of the torches fixed on the front of the tower. 'And Apheidas, too.'

'And Sarpedon,' Paris added. 'But why have they abandoned the southern cities?'

'Abandoned?' Helen asked in consternation. 'What do you mean?'

Paris turned to her, his face pale and concerned in the darkness. 'They were sent to defend Lyrnessus, Adramyttium and Thebe. We'd heard the Greeks planned to attack after we'd whittled down the garrisons, but—'

'You mean the fighting has already restarted?' Helen interrupted anxiously.

'Yes,' Paris replied. The sound of horses' hooves on stone echoed from the gateway below. 'And I must go and find out why they've returned so soon.'

He took Helen by the hand and led her down from the walls to where the horsemen were dismounting amidst a crowd of guards. As the horses were led away to be watered and fed – the sweat on their flanks showed they had been ridden hard to reach Troy – Helen could see that the newcomers were exhausted and filthy. To her alarm several of the men appeared to have lost weapons or parts of their armour, and three or four carried light wounds to their heads or limbs. As she appeared among them, white and excruciatingly beautiful in the darkness, every eye fell on her. She sensed the accusation in their tired gazes, the same silent condemnation that she had seen after so many battles in the past. Then Paris stepped forward and gripped Sarpedon by the shoulders.

'What's happened, man? Why have you come back?'

Sarpedon looked around at the faces of the citadel guards and shook his head. 'Not here, Paris. Where's Hector?'

'In his palace, with Andromache,' Helen announced, defying the looks on the faces of the men.

'Then we must go there now,' Sarpedon said. 'We have news that concerns them both. If you'll excuse us, my lady?'

The Lycian king bowed low, then with Paris at his side started up the sloping road to the royal palace, on the third level of the citadel. Aeneas, his youthful face almost unrecognizable beneath the dust and dried blood, gave Helen the glimmer of a smile before joining them. Apheidas gave her a curt nod before turning on his heel and following the others. His usual confident smile was strangely absent and of all the horsemen who had ridden in through the gate he looked the most preoccupied.

Helen began to follow, but her husband held up his hand and shook his head.

'No, Helen. We must discuss this matter with Hector alone.'

'And Andromache?' Helen protested, feeling like a disobedient child.

'Do not envy your friend, Helen,' Sarpedon returned, his words thickly accented but clearly enunciated. 'The news we have for her is not good. But I would be indebted to you if you could see that our escort are fed and rested.'

Helen watched the four men disappear up the cobbled street that ran between the magnificent buildings of Pergamos and felt a pang of dread tear through her insides. Thebe had been Andromache's home before her marriage to Hector. Helen had never been there, but she almost felt she knew the city from Andromache's homesick descriptions: a walled town in a green valley, beneath the wooded slopes of Mount Placus. Her father, King Eëtion, still lived there with seven of Andromache's eight brothers; the eighth – Podes – was Hector's closest friend and fought in the Trojan army. Of all the women in Troy, none had treated Helen with as much love and kindness as Andromache had, so if anything had happened to her family then Helen had to know. After all, the murderous Greeks were only in Ilium because of her own foolish iniquity. Every foul deed they committed was her fault, whatever Paris might say.

She turned to the captain of the guard and gave orders for the remaining horsemen to be fed and given beds. After the lines of soldiers had trudged off to the guard hut, she threw her hood over her head and disappeared into a passage between two high-sided buildings. The stars were bright in the narrow channel of sky overhead, forcing her to seek the shadowy obscurity of a nearby doorway. She listened intently for a moment, then clutched her hands together and bowed her head.

'Mistress Aphrodite, *why* did you curse me with such beauty?' she whispered bitterly. 'What has it ever earned me but trouble? And what's the use of fine looks if men still ignore me and exclude me from their councils?'

'A woman's body is a cage, sister,' said a voice, 'from which there can only ever be one escape.'

A figure emerged from the doorway opposite, draped in a black cloak that gave it the quality of deep shadow. A pointed white chin and pale lips were visible under the hood and for a shocked moment Helen thought it was Clytaemnestra. But her sister was back in Mycenae, of course, where Agamemnon had left her to brood over the murder of her daughter. Then white hands rose up to tip the hood back and reveal a beautiful but melancholy face, framed with thick black hair. Dark, unhappy eyes stared briefly at Helen, then glanced away to the street beyond the narrow passageway.

Helen sighed with a mixture of relief and irritation. It was Cassandra, her sister-in-law – a tiresome and gloomy girl who flitted about at the edges of palace life. She had a fondness for black clothing, just like Clytaemnestra, but there the comparison ended. For Cassandra had never been a widow, and where Clytaem-nestra was stern and hard, Cassandra was detached and miserable. Helen was not aware that she had any friends at all in the palace, despite her alluring beauty and the fact she was a daughter of King Priam. Indeed, even her own father seemed to stiffen and go cold whenever she was near.

'What are you doing here, Cassandra? I thought you were with Pleisthenes.'

'Your son and his friends hate me.' She shrugged. 'So I came here to watch the men come back from Thebe.'

'How could you know about—?'

'I had a vision of them. I saw Mount Placus and Thebe below it, burning. There were soldiers everywhere, killing and putting houses to the torch. I saw Andromache's father, too.'

'King Eëtion!' Helen exclaimed.

Cassandra nodded. 'He was fighting a man wearing a strange helmet. It had a black plume and a metal mask, shaped like a scowling face. The king's sons were lying all around him, killed by the man in the helmet.'

'What happened to Eëtion, to Andromache's father?' Helen demanded, softly.

'The man killed him, too.'

Helen's eyebrows arched upward in momentary horror, before settling quickly into an annoyed frown. Some years ago, before she reached puberty, Cassandra had told Helen that she could see the future. It was a gift from Apollo, she claimed, and only an intermittent one, but when she had refused the god's sexual advances he cursed her so that no one would ever believe a word she said. It was then that Helen realized she was party to a young girl's fantasy, a clumsy attempt to gain a little credence among her betters. After failing to convince Helen, Cassandra had gone on to tell others, even resorting to offering them prophetic words as proof. But no one else fell for her story either and she quickly learned to keep her visions and dreams to herself, speaking only when compelled by the sheer force of some of her revelations. By then, though, she had lost all credibility and her rantings were generally ignored and usually forgotten altogether. Perhaps her vision of a burning Thebe was just another cry for attention.

'Where are you going?' Cassandra asked as Helen stepped out from the shadows and started up the road to the palace.

'To find out the truth,' Helen called back over her shoulder.

Her sandalled feet made small scuffing sounds on the flat

cobblestones as she moved, but there was no one else on the broad streets of Pergamos to see or hear her. As she climbed the steep ramps from one tier of the citadel to the next, she passed between magnificent stone buildings that exceeded anything she had ever seen in Greece, though they barely caught her attention any more after all these years. On the second tier she passed between the temples of Athena and Zeus, monolithic structures that were almost as tall as the lines of poplars that grew either side of the road. Both were fronted by towering, brightly painted statues of the gods, but in the portico of the temple to Athena – most of them sleeping beneath their woollen cloaks – were a dozen soldiers. They were there to ensure the safety of the Palladium housed within, a small wooden effigy, crudely carved, that was supposed to have fallen from heaven when the temple was being built. It was said that as long as the image remained in Troy then the city would never be destroyed.

There were more guards at the foot of the second ramp, leading up to the compound before Priam's palace. They moved aside as the princess approached, bowing, but not so fully that their upturned eyes could not feast on the greatest beauty Troy had ever seen. She passed between them like a ghost, silent and white, and drifted out into the broad courtyard where the fine earth had been trampled and scored by countless feet, hooves and wheels. Ignoring the grand portico of the main entrance, from which more guards were eyeing her, she crossed to a plain, single door in the right-hand wall of the compound and entered. Torches lined the long corridor beyond, their sputtering light throwing strange shadows across the walls and floor as Helen continued between them, not stopping until she reached a narrow passage to her left. She followed this to a low door, where she paused to listen.

After a moment, she opened the door and entered a small, square garden. It lay in darkness except for in the far corner, where a wide, open doorway spilled orange light on to a stone veranda. Voices were coming from within, speaking quickly and in competition with each other. Helen threw her hood back from her head to hear them better, then moved quietly across the lawn to a clump of bushes at the foot of the veranda.

'And after they'd driven you from Lyrnessus and Adramyttium?' said a hard, gravelly voice.

Helen peered between the waxy leaves to see Hector standing by the open doorway. He was an imposing figure whose black tunic and cloak reflected the mood written on his bearded face.

'We retreated from Adramyttium in good order,' answered a voice Helen recognized as Sarpedon's, though she could not see the Lycian king from where she knelt in the damp grass. 'Apheidas here fought a magnificent rearguard and we were able to reach Thebe with most of the army intact.'

Andromache appeared suddenly at Hector's side and slipped her arms round her husband's waist. She was a tall, handsome woman with an air of calm confidence about her, but as she clung to Hector and stared back into the hidden half of the room, Helen could see the fear written on her friend's face.

'Thebe, did you say?' she asked.

'Yes, my lady,' Sarpedon confirmed. 'Your father's city has strong walls in good repair, and the Cilician militia are well trained and numerous. We had much more chance of defending Thebe than the other towns. Besides, most of the refugees from Lyrnessus and Adramyttium had already fled there.'

Hector placed a comforting arm around his wife's shoulders. 'What happened after you'd reached the city?'

'I had hoped the Greeks would be delayed by their plundering, but I was wrong. The next day we looked out from the walls to see them marching across the plain with their banners trailing out in the wind; our own men were still exhausted from the previous battles, but theirs seemed fresh and keen to renew the fight.'

'But you were behind defended walls,' Hector countered. 'There were two thousand of you.'

'And there were ten thousand of *them*!'

'They overran us with ease,' added the voice of Aeneas, sounding bitter and angry. 'We needed more men—'

'We don't *have* any more men!' Hector snapped, silencing the Dardanian prince.

'Then Thebe has fallen,' Andromache said slowly, unwinding her arms from round Hector's waist and falling to her knees. 'What about my father, Sarpedon? And my brothers?'

There was a silence in which Helen could imagine Sarpedon's face hardening to the news it was his misfortune to bring.

'King Eëtion was a brave man,' he began at last. 'As were his sons. Their ferocity in defending their city would have put Ares himself to shame. For a while, even though the Greeks had scaled the walls and broken down the gates, I thought we would be able to drive them back out again. And then Achilles came.'

'Achilles?'

'Yes, my lady,' said Apheidas from further inside the room. 'He killed your father and your brothers, and the heart of the city's resistance died with them. After they fell, defeat was swift.'

Helen buried her face in her hands, unable to watch any more. For a moment there was silence, an oppressed, threatening silence like the flatness in the air before a storm. Then she heard the flap of naked feet on stone and looked up to see Andromache standing on the top step of the veranda, her tear-filled eyes staring down at Helen with a mixture of grief and surprise. A moment later a great shout of fury erupted from the room behind her.

'ACHILLES!' Hector bellowed, his voice rolling out into the night air. 'Achilles, you godless butcher! As the immortals are my witnesses, I swear upon my son's life I'll kill you *with my own hands* before this year is out!'

The door slammed shut, muffling Hector's rage. Andromache burst into more tears and ran across the lawn. Helen ran after her, catching her as she slipped on the damp grass and pulling her into her arms.

'Andromache! Andromache, I'm sorry! All this is my fault –

your father, your brothers – none of them would have died if it hadn't have been for me!'

She pressed her face against Andromache's warm neck and felt the wetness of her own tears crushed against her hot cheeks. Then Andromache's hands were on her arms, pushing her gently away as she looked into her eyes.

'Don't be foolish, Helen,' she sobbed. 'I don't blame you! You didn't ask for this war. No one did; it was the will of the gods.'

'But your father and your brothers . . .'

'My father was an old man,' Andromache insisted. 'I'm surprised he still had the strength to lift a sword, let alone use one – the gods would have claimed him soon anyway. And as for my brothers, I haven't seen them in years. And there's still Podes . . .'

Helen shook her head and turned away, unable to face her friend's excuses for her.

'Helen, you have to stop blaming yourself for this war,' Andromache insisted. 'If it helps, my tears aren't for my father and brothers, but for Hector and our son.'

Helen looked at her friend in surprise.

'You heard his anger,' Andromache continued. 'He hates sitting behind these walls while the Greeks destroy Ilium and all that he loves. But Priam and the elders have always advised this policy of waiting – waiting for the Greeks to give up and go home, or for the gods to deliver Troy from their grip. What else can we do? We don't have enough men to drive the Greeks back into the sea. But that doesn't make it any easier for Hector.'

'You think he'll do something rash?' Helen asked.

Andromache nodded. 'I'm afraid he'll seek Achilles out in combat. And when he does—'

'But Achilles is doomed to die,' Helen cut her short. 'His own mother predicted he'd be killed before the walls of Troy. And who in the whole of Ilium would stand a better chance than Hector?'

Andromache rose to her feet and pulled Helen up with her. 'No one, of course. But if Hector faces Achilles, I fear it will mean his death. And then who will Troy have to protect her?'

Chapter Seven

REPLACEMENTS

'Are you sure — *absolutely* sure?' Odysseus asked, gripping the side of the galley and leaning as far forward as he could, as if to do so would help him see the distant ships more clearly.

Eperitus shielded his eyes against the noon sun, his body rolling naturally with the movement of the sea. The sail flapped noisily overhead and gulls were gliding beside the ship, their feathers brilliant white as they rode the undulating air currents. Astynome, looking pale and uncomfortable, sat curled up beside him with her back against the hull.

'Yes, I'm certain they're ours,' he said. 'And it looks like they've only just arrived — the prows have been driven into the sand and there are lines of men unloading sacks and clay jars.'

'Did you say jars?' asked Antiphus, who was manning the twin rudders. His left hand was against his forehead, blocking the sun as he strained to see the shore. 'That can only mean one thing: they've brought *wine* with them! The gods be praised — I haven't had Ithacan wine in years.'

'It could just be oil,' Eperitus suggested with a playful grin.

'And if it's Ithacan wine, then it's the property of the king, for his use only,' Odysseus added.

'Not unless you want a mutiny on your hands,' Antiphus replied.

Adramyttium and Thebe had been razed to the ground and Achilles was busy organizing a garrison to hold Lyrnessus — a task

that would take a week or more to complete – so the ten ships of
the Ithacan fleet had been sent back to carry news of their victories
to Agamemnon and the Council of Kings. It was a fine spring day
with hardly a cloud in the sky and they had just slipped around
the seaward flank of Tenedos, catching their first sight of the Greek
camp in a crescent bay further up the mainland coast. The vast
sprawl of patched and weather-stained canvas, interspersed with
ramshackle huts of wood or stone, spread thickly upwards from the
edge of the ranging beach on to the deforested slopes above. Twisting grey columns rose from the countless fires that burned day and
night, carrying the smell of woodsmoke, roast meat and freshly
baked bread across the sea to the hungry Ithacan crews as they
drew closer. The long, arcing beach that years ago had been scattered with small fishing vessels – used for catching the shellfish
and oysters found in the bay – was now crammed with double
rows of warships, their black hulls dragged up on to the white sand
to lie bow-cheek to bow-cheek. These were the thousand galleys
that had brought the Greek armies to Ilium ten years before in the
hope of a swift victory, but which had lain there like stranded
whales ever since. Only four gaps existed in the wall of ships:
where the Locrians and Argives were camped on the northern
sweep of the beach; at the southernmost point where the Myrmidons had their camp; and in the centre where the Ithacan ships
were normally found. It was here that Eperitus had spotted the
other two galleys of Odysseus's fleet, back already from their
recruiting mission to Ithaca.

By now, the Ithacan fleet had been spotted from the camp and
men were abandoning their chores and gathering along the beach,
anxious to hear news from the expedition. They looked like wild
savages with their long hair and bearded, sun-tanned faces, contrasting markedly with the groups of men who had formed in two
separate knots around the newly arrived ships. These were the
recruits Odysseus had sent for from Ithaca, to replace those who
had fallen in the past few years of the war. Many were clean-
shaven and short-haired, with their new armour and bright cloaks

marking them out from the veteran warriors who lined the rest of the beach.

'Whom do you see?' Odysseus asked, moving to Eperitus's side.

'Arceisius and Eurybates that I can recognize,' Eperitus answered, squinting against the morning sun and scanning the faces of the newcomers. 'The two score men who went with them. And a whole load of new faces, most of them pale with fear and homesickness.'

'Then I pity them. It might be a long time before they see Ithaca again.'

Odysseus felt his oversized hands trembling at the thought of home and quickly grabbed the bow rail as soon as he noticed Eperitus's eyes upon him.

'You're concerned about the news they might have brought with them?'

Odysseus nodded. 'We've heard nothing since we sent Antiphus and Polites back for reinforcements five years ago. It's my kingdom, Eperitus, and while I'm stuck here there are thousands of people at home who should be relying on *me* to protect them. Anything could be happening there in my absence.'

'Everything'll be fine,' Eperitus reassured him. 'Mentor and Halitherses will keep the kingdom in order, and you can rely on Penelope to pick up whatever they miss. Remember what the oracle said: a daughter of Lacedaemon will keep the thieves from your house.'

'I haven't forgotten,' Odysseus said. 'But I wouldn't be much of a king, would I, if I didn't worry? I'd be even less of a husband and father. And that's what haunts me most of all. I miss my family every day, but I can barely remember Penelope's face any more; and I can't even begin to guess what Telemachus looks like. Ten years old and he's never known his own father.'

'Penelope will tell him all about you,' Eperitus said. 'Didn't Clytaemnestra make sure Iphigenia knew everything I'd ever done, even though she didn't meet me until she was nine years old? You can count on Penelope to do the same with Telemachus.'

Odysseus stared out across the white-capped waves. 'But it's not good enough, Eperitus. This war has me caught between two choices: be an absent husband and father, or dishonour my loved ones by breaking my oath to Menelaus. The first keeps me from the family and home I love, but the second would bring down a curse from the gods, on me and untold generations of my family.'

The identity of the two ships on the beach had become clear to the rest of the crew by now and their chatter was growing louder and more animated as they approached the shore.

'Silence!' the king ordered. 'Keep your minds on your work.'

Astynome stirred at the sound of his barked command and looked groggily up at Eperitus. Odysseus had noticed a bond growing between the two of them in the week since the capture of Lyrnessus, something that was closer than the normal relationship between slave and master. She worked as hard as any of the other captives, but not out of a sense of subservience; in return, he treated her like an equal, giving her the freedom to come and go as she pleased, despite the fact that she could have run away at any time. And for the first time since the death of Iphigenia Odysseus had noticed a lightness in Eperitus's spirit, the sort of lightness Odysseus had not felt himself since he had last seen Penelope – and one he would not feel again until she was back in his arms.

He slammed his fist down on the wooden rail.

'Damn this war, Eperitus, and damn my own stupidity. For all my supposedly clever schemes for capturing Troy I was too blind to see why the Trojans have defeated every one of them. Why didn't I realize there was a traitor?' He lowered his voice as he looked into Eperitus's eyes. 'And it can only be someone in the Council of Kings. Someone at the very top has been selling our plans to Hector, and until your father's slip at Lyrnessus, the Trojans have been far too clever to make it obvious.'

'What do you intend to do?' Eperitus asked.

'Catch him, of course, and catch him soon. The quicker we

stop the Trojans finding out all our plans, the quicker we can bring an end to the war.'

Eperitus glanced down at Astynome, who had closed her eyes again and lay back against the wall of the ship, then across at the benches where the crew were now quietly anticipating the approach of the shoreline and the imminent news from home.

'But you don't know who this traitor is,' he hissed.

Odysseus smiled darkly. 'Yes, I do. I've thought about it and there's only one man I can think of. It's Palamedes.'

Eperitus's eyes widened briefly before contracting back into an unconvinced frown.

'*Palamedes?*' he whispered. 'A week ago you weren't even aware there *was* a traitor; now you're convinced it's Palamedes. How?'

'I have an instinct it's him.'

'An *instinct*, Odysseus? But he's one of Agamemnon's inner circle, one of his closest advisers. This isn't just because he humiliated you last winter, is it, bringing in a ship-load of grain when you hadn't been able to find more than a few bags of mildewed corn in Thrace?'

Odysseus shook his head, slightly irritated at the accusation. Or was it that Eperitus's guess was closer to the mark than he wanted to admit? After all, he had never forgiven Palamedes for exposing his attempt to feign madness when Agamemnon and Menelaus had called on him to honour his oath. Nor had he forgotten how Palamedes had frustrated his efforts at negotiating a peace before the war began. If it had not been for the weasel-faced Nauplian, he would have spent the last decade of his life at home on Ithaca with his family, ruling a peaceful and prosperous kingdom. But if his suspicions proved correct – as he was sure they would – and Palamedes had treacherously deprived the Greeks of victory, then his past anger would be as nothing compared to how he would feel then.

Eperitus crossed his arms and looked at Odysseus disapprovingly.

'You can't accuse an innocent man.'

'I tell you he's not innocent,' Odysseus insisted. 'I admit I don't know why he's doing it, but I have a strong suspicion how and I intend to prove I'm right. But if it makes you feel better I give you my word I won't even *accuse* Palamedes until we can show the council he's a traitor. Does that satisfy you?'

'All right, then,' Eperitus agreed. 'I'll help you get your proof, if you're so certain.'

'I am,' Odysseus replied.

He stood up straight and signalled to Antiphus.

'A little more to the left. As close in as you can get – there're another nine ships to come after us. The rest of you,' he added with a booming shout, 'I want you in the water the moment we hit. Drag her up to the top of the beach so one of the others can get in behind us.'

'Astynome,' Eperitus said, offering the girl his hand. 'Hold on to me. Quickly.'

She took his hand and he pulled her into his arms. A moment later the ship's shallow bottom hit the soft sand beneath the waterline, sending a heavy judder through the thick timbers of the galley. Eperitus stood firm, his feet planted apart on the deck, while Astynome's arms tightened around him. The next instant there was a shout of enthusiasm as, all around, men began leaping overboard into the knee-high water.

'Leave the girl with Polites,' Odysseus ordered, clapping Eperitus on the shoulder. 'You and I are going to speak to Eurybates and Arceisius.'

Eperitus reluctantly gave Astynome to the giant warrior, before following Odysseus over the side and into the shallow water. The galley was surrounded by men who strained and grunted as they hauled her further up on to the sand. Then Odysseus and Eperitus heard a shout and saw Eurybates and Arceisius walking down the sloping beach towards them.

'Greetings from Ithaca!' Arceisius called.

'We've brought gifts,' added Eurybates. 'Ithacan wine and

cheese. New clothes for our noble king, made by Queen Penelope herself. And men – over eighty replacements!'

Odysseus greeted his herald with an embrace.

'It's good to have you back,' he said, slapping him on the back. 'You've already missed three good battles and I've got a feeling the gods are planning a lot more before the year's out. I hope you've brought some decent fighters back with you.'

Eurybates looked uncertain. 'They're good fighters, all right, for the most part, but they won't be what you or Eperitus were expecting.'

'What do you mean?' Eperitus frowned.

'You'll see,' Arceisius said.

He greeted his captain with a tight embrace. Eperitus had taught him to be a warrior, and though he was no longer his squire, Arceisius was pleased to see his former master again after the weeks spent sailing to Ithaca and back. Then he turned to Odysseus and offered the king his hand.

'I'm pleased the gods have brought you back safely, Arceisius,' Odysseus said, pulling him into a hug. His smile stiffened slightly and the light in his eyes grew a shade dimmer. 'But what news of home? Is Ithaca still as beautiful as I remember her? Am I still king?'

'Mentor and Halitherses continue to rule in your name, my lord,' he answered, though without conviction. Odysseus's eyes narrowed slightly, but he said nothing so Arceisius continued. 'And Ithaca is as lovely as it ever was. More so. It seemed to me as if hardly a stone had been moved from its place since we left her all those years ago, and yet . . .'

'And yet?'

'And yet I'd never really understood the beauty of my home until I went back. When I saw her outline on the horizon, with giant Samos beside her, I suddenly realized that my heart had never left Ithaca. All this time I've spent in Ilium I've been like a wraith, Odysseus, a soulless shade of my real self.' He paused and then shrugged, as if his words were of no value. 'I think it would have broken your heart to have returned, knowing you must come back here.'

There was a moment's silence, broken eventually by Eurybates.

'It was a lot colder than I remember,' he said. 'The wind coming off the Ionian Sea just seems to cut through anything. And it rained a lot, even for the tail end of winter. But cold winds and grey skies can't dim the wonder of your own home. Arceisius is right – everything looks the same. It smells the same, too: the dung heap by the palace gates, the livestock in the marketplace, the scent of the pine trees wafting down from Mount Neriton; even the woodsmoke smells Ithacan. It made my heart ache just to hear the birds sing and see the first flowers of spring among the rocks and on the hillsides. The girls were wearing them in their hair as they waved us off.

'And *there*'s another thing about Ithaca that has grown more lovely since we left. I don't know whether it's this gods-forsaken country and the lack of women around these past ten or so years, or whether the immortals have simply blessed Ithaca while we've been gone, but I've never seen so many beautiful girls. And they couldn't get enough of a couple of battle-hardened old sweats like us. Arceisius here even got married.'

'Married!' exclaimed Eperitus and Odysseus simultaneously.

The usually pert and confident Arceisius was suddenly bashful, his naturally red cheeks turning almost crimson.

'Is it true?' Eperitus asked, the corner of his mouth rising in an amused smile. 'The greatest womanizer in the Ithacan camp tamed at last? She must be a real beauty, this wife of yours.'

'She is,' said Eurybates. 'And at least she's Greek. There are too many men in the army taking Trojan captives as wives or concubines.'

Eperitus ignored the comment and offered his congratulations to his former squire. Odysseus took Arceisius's hand again and gripped it firmly.

'You have your king's blessing,' he said. 'Marriage is good for a man – it gives him something to fight for. But who is this girl and where are you hiding her?'

'It's Melantho, my lord, Dolius's daughter,' Arceisius replied. 'I insisted she stay on Ithaca. At least she'll be safe there.'

'I hope she will,' Odysseus said. 'But if Melantho's the same little firebrand I used to know – though she was only a little girl back then – well, I'm sure she can look after herself until you return. But what of *my* wife? Tell me, Arceisius, is she safe? Are Telemachus and my parents safe? There's something about you two that tells me all's not well at home.'

'Have no fear for your wife or family, my lord,' Arceisius replied. 'At least not for now. But if you want to know about affairs at home, don't ask us; we weren't back long enough. You should ask the replacements.'

He indicated the men who had been standing at the top of the beach as Odysseus's galley had run aground. A few were now helping to haul the ships on to the sand, while others were sharing news of Ithaca with the eager crowds of men who had not seen their homes for over ten years. A sizeable group, though, had remained where they stood, aloof from or ignored by the rest. These were generally older than the other replacements and had the bearing of men who had seen battle and for whom war was a way of life. They were perhaps a score in number and at least half of them were tall and armed with long spears. Eperitus eyed the latter with alarm.

'Some of those men are Taphians.'

'I told you they wouldn't be what you were expecting,' Arceisius reminded him.

'Did Mentes send them?' Odysseus asked, referring to the Taphian chieftain. Though the Taphians had been enemies of Ithaca for many years, Odysseus had forged a friendship with Mentes that – though it had not brought friendship or alliance – had at least put an end to the hostility.

'I only wish that had been the case,' Eurybates answered.

'Unfortunately, this isn't a popular war with the nobility back home. The law has been changed, allowing those who can afford it to send a proxy in their place. Of the eighty-four men we brought back with us, twenty-two are mercenaries and twelve of *them* are Taphians.'

'Then we should send them back again at once,' Eperitus said, clenching his fists. 'And when we get home to Ithaca we can settle matters with those nobles who've bought their way out of joining the army.'

Odysseus shook his head. He was concerned and angry that so many of the Ithacan nobility would dare snub his authority so openly, but sending the mercenaries back to Ithaca would only risk more trouble for Penelope and those ruling in his stead. His revenge would wait.

'Let the mercenaries stay,' he said. 'The gods know we need experienced fighting men, and a quarter of the Greek army is made up of mercenaries anyway. Right now, I need to speak to one of these replacements, someone with a good head on his shoulders. Agamemnon, Menelaus and Nestor will be waiting to hear my news, but first I need to learn exactly how things stand at home.'

'Then you'll want to speak to Omeros,' Arceisius suggested.

He pointed to a well-fed youth sitting in the tall grass at the top of the beach. His arms were crossed over his knees and his shaven chin was resting on his wrist as he watched the ships landing one after another and being dragged up on to the sand. His quick eyes were following the activity around the beaked galleys and remained unaware of the four men who were staring at him from among the crowds.

'By all the gods on Olympus, it *is* Omeros,' Eperitus said, shielding his eyes against the high sun. 'I never imagined I'd see him here.'

'Still a dreamer, by the looks of him,' Odysseus said, smiling. 'But if he's as clever and observant as he used to be then he'll know what's *really* happening at home. Eurybates, Arceisius, get those replacements working on the ships – including the mercenaries – and have them ready for my inspection by sunset; Eperitus, come with me.'

As the others bowed and turned to the crowds milling around the galleys, Odysseus and Eperitus walked up the beach towards Omeros, kicking up small fountains of white sand behind them. Omeros only seemed to notice their approach at the last moment, when he stood in confusion and – recognizing his king – dipped into an awkward bow.

'M . . . my lord,' he stuttered. 'My lord Odysseus!'

'Welcome to Troy, Omeros,' the king said, pulling him upright. 'You've grown well since I last saw you.'

'Outwards more than upwards, though,' Eperitus added, grinning.

Omeros placed a hand on his large stomach and looked down at himself in concern, then back at the captain of the guard.

'It's nothing I can't run off, my lord Eperitus,' he answered. 'And may I say that *you*'ve barely changed at all in ten years.'

Odysseus and Eperitus swapped a knowing glance. Since Athena had brought Eperitus back from death he had hardly developed a wrinkle or grey hair, and Omeros had not been the first to remark on this strange longevity.

'But can you fight, lad?' Odysseus asked, looking Omeros up and down and noting his slightly pampered appearance, compared to the lean, hardened figures that populated the rest of the Ithacan army.

'I'll fight with as much heart as any of those others,' Omeros answered, nodding at the mercenaries and Taphians. 'And what some of them have in training and experience, I'll match in enthusiasm and loyalty.'

This broadened the smile on Odysseus's face.

'I'm glad to hear it, very glad,' he said, placing his arm across Omeros's shoulders and steering him in the direction of the sprawling camp, with Eperitus following on Omeros's other side. 'Without loyalty every other fighting quality is useless, especially to a king. And that's what I want to talk to you about. I've been told some of the nobles on Ithaca have hired mercenaries to take their places. Is it true?'

The line of tall grass where Omeros had been sitting marked the furthest extent of the sea's reach, and just behind it were the first tents of the huge Greek army. Most of the Ithacan part of the camp was now empty, though here and there groups of men were preparing food or carrying out other tasks that excused them from the work on the beach.

'It's true, my lord,' Omeros said, ruefully. 'Some of the nobles threatened rebellion if their sons were called to war. Eupeithes told Penelope he could calm their tempers, but only if the Kerosia allowed men of a fighting age to send substitutes in their place. Which meant that while the poor went to serve their king, the wealthy could stay at home and hire mercenaries instead.'

'This doesn't bode well,' Odysseus mused. 'Eupeithes is still a snake, even if a reformed one, and it'll take all of Penelope's skill to keep him in his place. The sooner we can finish this war and return home, the better.'

'Forgive me, lord,' Omeros began, 'but if an army this size hasn't defeated the Trojans in ten years, what chance is there of *ever* defeating them?'

'He's beginning to sound like a veteran already,' Eperitus said with an ironic laugh.

'It seems to me the men don't have any appetite for victory,' Omeros added, hesitantly. 'And I think I know why.'

Odysseus cocked an eyebrow.

'Really, Omeros? So what's the secret of our persistent failure?'

Omeros's chin dropped a little at the king's chiding, but he did not back down.

'Lord, I've been watching the army since I arrived and they look more like barbarians than Greeks: their hair and beards are long, their clothing is foreign, and half of them are equipped with Trojan armour and weapons. All the women in the camp are Trojan and the men speak to them in their own language. Shouldn't it be the other way round? It's as if this camp, this makeshift colony of tents and huts, has become their new home. And as long as they've forgotten who they really are and why they came here in the first place – to rescue Helen and return to Greece – then I don't think they'll ever take Troy.'

Odysseus looked at him with narrowed eyes and pursed lips. Then he shrugged his shoulders and looked away along the curved line of the beach.

'You're right,' he conceded. 'The Trojans have checked our every move for ten years and no army can fail to lose heart after so long. But perhaps you're being a little too hard on us. Some may have given up the hope of victory and a return home, but the rest have just . . . *forgotten*, as you say. But it's forgotten, not *forsaken*. We've forgotten what it's like to stand on our own soil, or to have a solid roof over our heads and be surrounded by our families. All we need is to be reminded of those things and we'd return tomorrow, given the chance.'

'Ithaca hasn't changed much, my lord,' Omeros said.

'So I hear,' Odysseus nodded, placing an arm around his shoulder and leading him into the armada of tents. 'And I wouldn't want it to. But how are my family, Omeros? Are my parents well? What about Telemachus? Does he look like me or Penelope? And how *is* my wife?'

Eperitus dropped back and let them walk on alone.

He watched them head in the direction of Odysseus's hut, then returned to the beach to find Astynome.

Chapter Eight
HOME

Despite his youth, Omeros bore the burden of Odysseus's desire for news admirably. As he described Anticleia's sickening for Odysseus and the way she mourned her son's absence as if he had died, quiet tears fell from the king's eyes; and when he spoke of how Laertes would climb Mount Neriton every evening to look for the homecoming sails of his son's ships, Odysseus just nodded his head and smiled.

'And Telemachus? Is he like me? I mean, can you see anything of me in him?'

'He'll be taller than his father,' Omeros answered, 'and not so broad.'

'Like his mother, then.'

'Yes. Handsome like her, too, but with your eyes. Penelope says she can look at Telemachus and see you looking right back out at her.'

Odysseus laughed with unexpected delight.

'He has your cunning too, my lord, but it's kept in place by his mother's principles. I'd think he could be a very naughty boy if he wasn't so good.'

'As long as he can still be naughty when he has to,' Odysseus said as they reached the entrance to his hut. 'A future king has to know when to lay aside his morals.'

They stooped as they entered the gloom of Odysseus's quarters. A small fire burned in the hearth, filling the enclosed space with warmth and the smell of woodsmoke. Odysseus swept off his cloak and unbuckled his armour, before settling down on his haunches before the flames and indicating for Omeros to do the same.

'What about Penelope?'

Omeros nodded to himself. This was the question that was at the heart of the king's yearning, the question that would prove whether Penelope's faith in him had been justified. He glanced at the king, whose eyes were fixed rigidly on the small tongues of orange and yellow flame while he chewed unconsciously at a thumbnail.

'The queen is well.'

'Well?'

'As well as any queen can be without her king.'

Odysseus's face twitched. A flicker of guilt, Omeros thought.

'And how does she look now? Has she changed much since I last saw her? It's been almost ten years, Omeros, and I can barely remember her face – as if she were nothing more than a dream. I sometimes wonder whether she existed at all.'

'She exists, lord, and she's hardly changed since you departed.'

'Describe her, for me. Just as she looked when you last saw her.'

Omeros sucked in his bottom lip and swept his hand through his hair as he recalled the scene.

'It was night time. No moon, just the starlight. It made her brown hair look black and her skin pale. She stood a little taller than me, dressed in a dark cloak with the hood down.'

'And her face?'

Omeros, who had been staring at the king as he described Penelope, blinked and looked down at the fire.

'She's still beautiful. Not youthful beauty, like Melantho's, or the powerful beauty I imagine Helen has, but something calm and reassuring instead. The sort of beauty you don't think would laugh or sneer at you.'

Odysseus nodded as if recognizing the description, but said nothing.

'My lord,' Omeros continued, the tone of his voice more tentative now. 'She asked me to give you a message.'

Odysseus looked up, expectation and anxiety flickering across his features in the shifting light from the flames.

'What is it?'

Omeros closed his eyes and thought back to the starlit night on Ithaca when he had last spoken to Penelope. It was the night of Arceisius's and Melantho's wedding.

The great hall had been given over to the celebrations. Every table and chair in the palace – and more from the town – had been brought in and were now overflowing with food, wine and guests. The hearth blazed, bathing the hall and its occupants in golden light, supplemented by the numerous torches sputtering on the mural-covered walls. To one side of the central fire a square of the dirt floor had been kept free, bordered by tables on its flanks and the table and chairs of the bride and groom at its head: in this large space, dozens of cheerful – and drunk – young Ithacans were dancing to the music of lyre, pipes and tambourines, while on every side scores of onlookers cheered and sang. Leading the dance were Arceisius and Melantho: he in his battle-scarred armour that spoke of heroic deeds and the glory of war, and she with her white chiton and the first flowers of spring in her black hair. They smiled broadly at each other as they moved in time to the music, delighting in being the centre of attention. Omeros, watching from one side, was pleased for them. Though Melantho had been an immature girl when Arceisius had sailed to war, she was now a woman with all the beauty and allure of youth about her. Arceisius had fallen in love with her almost the instant he had set eyes upon her, and while it was well known on the island that her favours had been given freely to others before, Arceisius was blissfully unaware of the fact. As a soldier who had lived in the shadow of Hermes's cloak, and who had known more than enough slaves and prostitutes in his time, Omeros thought it unlikely Arceisius would have cared anyway.

As he watched them, his poet's ears offended by the loud, clamorous music, Melantho caught his eye and skipped over to him, dragging Arceisius behind her.

'Come dance with me, Omeros,' she pleaded, outrageously flirtatious with her pouting lips and large brown eyes. 'Come on now.'

'You know I hate dancing . . .'

'Nonsense. You're just jealous I didn't marry you instead!'

'No one hates dancing!' Arceisius exclaimed. His eyes were bright with alcohol and love, and with an irresistible laugh he pulled Omeros from his chair and almost threw him into Melantho's arms. 'Now dance!'

Omeros really did not like dancing, but Arceisius's happiness was infectious and the seductive beauty and heady intimacy of Melantho could not be denied. Eventually he was rescued by Eurybates, who took his place and sent the young bard to join Arceisius, who was beckoning to him from one of the crowded tables. As Omeros joined him, Arceisius pushed a krater of wine into his hand.

'Are you concerned?' he asked. 'About the war, I mean.'

Omeros looked at him, surprised by the frankness of the question, and could tell Arceisius was not drunk. His red face was full of light-hearted cheer, and yet in the middle of his own wedding he could still spare a moment to discuss the anxieties of a lad he had not seen for ten years. Omeros was not sure how to reply.

'Well, you needn't be. You have a level head, Omeros, and it's men like you who make the best soldiers. You'll do well in Ilium, believe me, and, anyway, those of us who've seen a few battles will watch over you to start with. But if you want some advice, don't spend the whole of your last evening on Ithaca in here. Go for a walk and say goodbye to the island you love. She'll haunt your dreams while you're gone and no amount of glory in battle can replace the joy of being on your own soil. Besides, you don't know you'll see the place again.'

Omeros nodded. 'I will.'

He drained his wine and stood up, returning Arceisius's smile. Then a thought struck him and he looked down at the seasoned warrior in his leather cuirass with his ever-present sword hanging at his side.

'And what about you? Are you concerned?'

Arceisius's eyes narrowed uncertainly.

'I mean,' Omeros continued, glancing over at Melantho who was draping herself about Eurybates and laughing merrily, 'I mean you're married now. You have more to lose on the battlefield.'

Arceisius gave a small laugh and shook his head.

'Don't worry about me. I can take care of myself.'

The large double doors were wide open as Omeros left the great hall. A slab of orange light lay at an angle across the wooden portico, reaching out far enough to illuminate the trampled soil of the courtyard where the wedding ceremony had taken place earlier. Omeros crossed to the gate in the outer wall, followed by the mingled noise of music, laughter and drunken voices. Arceisius had been right: while others could forget their fears and doubts in the company of wine and friends, it was better to leave the celebrations behind and spend the remainder of his last evening on Ithaca with his own thoughts. Tomorrow he would sail for war, but tonight he wanted to walk beneath the familiar stars, listening to the wind in the trees as he stared up at the dark, humped shapes of Mount Neriton and Mount Hermes. Omeros sighed; though he had volunteered to go to Troy, seeking adventure and glory on the battlefield, now the time was almost upon him to leave he found the place he most wanted to be in all the world was right here in Ithaca.

He stepped through the unguarded gates, intending to walk down to the harbour and look out at the straits between Ithaca and the neighbouring island of Samos. The broad terrace in front of the palace walls was covered with the tents of the men who had left their homes on Samos, Zacynthos and Dulichium to join the expedition. They were empty now, flapping in the wind that came over the ridge from the sea below, and their canvas was a ghostly grey in the light of the countless stars that circled above. Omeros filled his lungs with the briny air, then crossed to the houses on the other side of the terrace.

'There you are,' said a voice behind him.

He turned and saw the black shape of a dog running towards him from the gateway he had just vacated. He flinched instinctively as the animal reached his ankles, but it did no more than bark and sniff a circle around his feet, before pressing its wet nose against his thighs and beating the air with its tail. Omeros recognized Argus, Odysseus's old hunting dog, and ran his fingers over his domed head. Then a tall figure stepped out from the shadow of the palace gates.

'Had your fill of feasting and dancing already?' Penelope asked, walking up to him and slipping her arm through the crook of his elbow.

'I wanted to clear my mind, my lady.'

'Thinking of Troy?'

'I suppose I should be, but the truth is I was thinking of Ithaca. I'll miss the smell of the pine trees and the sound of the gulls following the fishing boats back into the harbour. It's all I've ever known, of course, and now that I'm leaving it behind I feel . . . suddenly uncertain. I don't even know if the stars will be the same on the other side of the world.'

'They will,' Penelope assured him with a smile as they walked between the dark, silent houses of the town, Argus sniffing the ground in their wake. 'And there are trees and gulls in Ilium too, just as there are here.'

'But they won't be the same. It's just that I might not see Ithaca again. After all, I'm not a soldier. I'm just a storyteller.'

'You're stronger than you realize, Omeros, and you're not a coward – although you think too deeply to be a natural warrior,' she added, tapping her forehead. 'Stay close to Arceisius, Odysseus and Eperitus: they'll keep you safe.'

Omeros nodded, smiling at the thought of so many people seeming concerned for his safety. They walked on, following the broad path out beyond the edge of the town and down towards the harbour. For a while they said nothing, then, as they passed the town spring and the poplar trees that surrounded it, Penelope's grip tightened about Omeros's arm.

'I want you to do something for me, Omeros.'

'Yes, of course.'

'I want you to give a message to Odysseus. I want you to give it to him in person, when he's alone.'

'Me? But Eurybates is Odysseus's squire. Wouldn't he . . . ?'

'No, I want you to give it to him. Eurybates has spent the past ten years in Ilium; what can he tell Odysseus about Ithaca? But you've seen everything that's happened here these past ten years. You can let him know everything that's happened while he's been away, in all the detail he could want. More importantly, you can tell him about Telemachus: how tall he's getting, how strong he is, and how he's always talking about his father. Tell him that . . .'

She paused. They could see the harbour below them now, where the two galleys had their sails furled, ready for the morning departure. Penelope stood watching them as they rolled gently on the black, starlit waves that swept in from the straits. Across the water was the vast bulk of Samos.

'Tell him that sometimes I look at Telemachus and see Odysseus staring back out at me. And sometimes I can't bear it. I want him back, Omeros.'

She turned to face him, and though her face was in darkness he could see the tears glistening in her eyes. He took her cold hand and pressed the palm, trying to offer reassurance and yet not knowing how to comfort a queen.

'The gods will bring him back.'

'The gods are fickle,' she replied. 'And yet I still pray and hope. When I saw those galleys a moment ago, I imagined they were his and that he had come home at last. I could almost see him climbing the road from the harbour, as if the past ten years had been an awful nightmare and that he had returned. But this isn't a nightmare; it's reality, and Odysseus is in a darkness that's beyond my reach.'

Omeros lowered his eyes.

'I'll tell him for you,' he promised. 'I'll tell him all about Telemachus and how much he needs his father. And I'll tell him about you, how much you love him and need him.'

'Thank you, Omeros,' Penelope said, laying her hand on his arm. 'But there's something else you must make clear to him, something I will entrust to you alone. Tell Odysseus his kingdom is under threat again.'

Omeros's eyes widened briefly, before settling into a frown.

'If that's true, then the ships should remain here. While you or Ithaca are in danger, our first duty is to defend you. It's what Odysseus would have us do.'

'No. If Eurybates and Arceisius don't return he'll fear the worst and do something rash. Tell him we're safe for now, but the threat will grow the longer he is away. It's Eupeithes again.'

'Eupeithes!'

'Yes. His influence has increased in Odysseus's absence, but never such that he could be a threat. The Kerosia has always been too heavily weighted against him. He bought Polyctor's support long ago, but he'll never win over the rest of the council.'

'Then what has changed?' Omeros asked.

'The arrival of the galleys was the catalyst,' Penelope replied. 'Before then, the people thought the war could not last much longer, but the call for replacements has crushed their hope. Now they are wondering if Odysseus will ever return, and with some of the nobles refusing to send their sons to Troy, Eupeithes's confidence has grown. He's pushing for his son – Antinous – to be added to the Kerosia, as a *favour* for persuading the nobles not to rebel. He won't be allowed – not yet – but if he can gain support among some of the richest families we'll find it hard to resist for ever.'

'Will he try force again?'

Penelope shook her head.

'Not outright: he lost his taste for that the last time. He'll stick to what he's best at – politics of the worst kind – and though I will defend my husband's kingdom in every way I can, I'm not sure how long I can outwit a resurgent Eupeithes for. If he can somehow take control of the Kerosia, with me as titular head of Ithaca, he will be ruler of Ithaca in all but name. Omeros, you must tell Odysseus that if the war isn't over soon he could lose his kingdom altogether.'

Omeros nodded and looked out at the wooded slopes of Samos across the water. If he ever saw his homeland again, he had a feeling it would not be the same place it was now.

Chapter Nine

CALCHAS

The sun was low in the west before Odysseus and Eperitus dismissed the replacements. The inspection had been delayed by Odysseus's report to Agamemnon, where his news of victory had been questioned at great length by the King of Men, aided by Menelaus and Nestor. Now, as the men began to stream back from the beach and into the camp where the rest of the army were preparing their evening meals, the king of Ithaca and the captain of his guard stood looking at the Aegean Sea beyond the black hulks of the Greek fleet, contemplating the merits of the newcomers.

'There's not a man among them who's fit enough yet,' Odysseus said, his face sober with concern. 'Those mercenaries will flag in a prolonged battle, but the lads from home wouldn't even make it through a skirmish.'

'They've been crammed on to those galleys for days,' Eperitus replied. 'It's bound to have left them a bit weak and groggy. But I'll make sure they're put through their paces over the next few days.'

'They need more weapons training, too,' Odysseus added, looking up at the pink skies scored with lines of purple cloud as if great claws had been drawn across the heavens. 'The hired men will be able to stand their ground, but from what we saw of the others the Trojans would cut them to pieces without breaking into a sweat.'

ything else?' Eperitus asked, raising an
g at his friend as they turned and walked back
the camp. 'But don't worry – I'll see they know
too, before we inflict them on the enemy. Besides,
ur own countrymen more than I would those mercen-
t least they have a sense of loyalty and honour.'

What good's honour in this place?' Odysseus said. 'Omeros
was right: remembering who we were and what we've left behind
is the only thing that's going to win this war – that and ruthless
determination.'

'Honour is the lifeblood of a fighting man,' Eperitus protested.
'Without it we're nothing more than murdering brigands. You're
a king, Odysseus, you should know that.'

'I'm a king of nothing unless this war finishes soon. And the
longer we fight the Trojans the more our sense of honour and
humanity is dying out anyway. You saw how the men were by the
time we sacked Thebe – brutal and merciless, like wild animals.
I've watched it growing in them as the years have passed, and the
Trojans are no better. It's despicable, but perhaps we have to
abandon our notions of honour and become the worst kind of
savages if we're ever to see our homes again.'

'If that's what's needed, then perhaps it's best we never return
to Ithaca at all,' Eperitus said.

They walked between the weathered tents where the men were
seated around small fires, eating smoked mackerel and bread
washed down with wine from home. Eperitus looked at the new
arrivals, sitting in twos and threes among the men for whom Ithaca
was nothing more than a faded memory dressed up in nostalgia.
For a short while they would listen to news from their homeland,
of their loved ones and of the places they had once known as
intimately as they knew their own bodies. Then the wine that had
been fermented on Samos would help them forget and instead they
would tell the newcomers stories of the war against Troy and of
the kings and heroes whose names were already becoming legend.
How long, Eperitus wondered, before the newcomers would also

lose their identities as Greeks? How long before they became long-haired barbarians, carrying captured weapons and married to foreign wives who spoke a different tongue? How long before their honour faded and was stained with acts of black cruelty?

'Well, I have no intention of dying here, with or without my honour,' Odysseus said, looking determined. 'You and I are going to prove Palamedes has been passing our plans to the Trojans, and once we've stopped him I'll think up a new way to defeat Hector once and for all.'

'That's assuming Palamedes *is* the traitor, Odysseus. And I can't see how you're going to prove that.'

'I'll find a way,' Odysseus replied confidently. 'The gods will reveal it to me. But now I'm going to my hut; Agamemnon, Menelaus and Nestor tired me out with their questions, and I need time alone to think about this news from home.'

Eperitus watched him pick his way through the campfires to his hut, his shoulders sagging with the burden of what was happening back on Ithaca. It was hard for any man to be away from his family for so long, and whatever Omeros had told him had concentrated that sense of separation. But Odysseus was also a king, and the threat of rebellious nobles when he was trapped in a war on the other side of the world was not an easy load to bear. Unfortunately, it was not a load Eperitus could share, though he wished he could.

'Eperitus?'

He turned to see Astynome standing behind him. She was barefoot, as usual, and her white chiton was covered by the green cloak he had found for her a week ago in Lyrnessus. In her outstretched hands was a krater of wine.

'I brought this for you,' she said, smiling. 'It's Ithacan. Perhaps it will remind you of your home.'

He took it and raised the dark liquid to his lips. After a long day with nothing but water the wine was cool and refreshing.

'Thank you. Try some.'

He passed the krater back to her, but instead of taking it from him she placed her warm hands beneath his and lifted the cup to her mouth, watching him with her dark eyes as she drank.

'It's good,' she said, removing her hands from his. 'Polites gave me a whole skin of it for you. It's at your hut, with the food I've prepared. Come.'

She led the way between the various campfires, walking with her head high and her long black hair cascading down her back. The Ithacan soldiers looked up as she passed them by, staring desirously at the fine, proud features of her face but looking away as soon as they saw their captain a few paces behind her. It was obvious they assumed she was more than just his slave, an assumption he was happy for them to make; after saving her from Eurylochus and his cronies at Lyrnessus, he did not intend to allow the rest of his men to force themselves upon her.

A large fire was burning close to his hut as they approached. Arceisius was stirring the contents of a large pot that hung over the flames, while Polites, Eurybates, Antiphus and Omeros sat around the hearth drinking wine and talking with animated gestures. Sparks and smoke rose into the air and the delicious aroma of stewed meat filled Eperitus's nostrils, making him suddenly aware of how hungry he was. His comrades greeted him enthusiastically as he sat down beside them, while Astynome took the ladle from Arceisius's hands and insisted that she be allowed to serve the meal she had cooked. She poured some of the stew into a wooden bowl and passed it to Eperitus, watching closely for his reaction. As the rich sauce touched his lips he thanked the gods he had been fortunate enough to find such an excellent cook and nodded his approval.

'It's good. Very good.'

Astynome smiled with satisfaction.

'Of course it is,' said Antiphus, holding up his bowl. 'We've eaten better in the past week with Astynome's cooking than we have during the whole of this war. Haven't we, Polites?'

Polites nodded and watched as his own bowl was filled. Silence followed as the men ate, while Astynome passed them baskets of bread and busied herself mixing the wine. She filled Eperitus's krater first and hardly took her eyes off him as she served the others. When she had finished, Arceisius insisted that she fill her own bowl and join them about the fire. She tried to refuse, claiming it was not right for a slave to eat with free men, but the rest would not accept her excuses and eventually she agreed, though awkwardly at first.

It pleased Eperitus to see how well his friends had taken to her, and he knew it was not simply because she was an attractive woman. Despite her display of humility about eating with them, there was a fire in her spirit that defied the fact she was a captive among enemies. She had a natural nobility that came not from birthright, but from her character. Eperitus had quickly come to respect her for it in their short time together, and it seemed the others recognized it too.

As darkness descended the men turned naturally to conversation. While Astynome slipped away to fetch bread and mix more wine, Antiphus made Arceisius tell them all about Melantho and how he had managed to fool the poor girl into marrying him. Next came the tale of the capture of Lyrnessus, Adramyttium and Thebe, which Arceisius and Eurybates wanted in every detail. Antiphus indulged them, while Polites and Eperitus contributed very little – Polites due to his natural quietness and Eperitus because he did not want to offend Astynome. Then it was the turn of Omeros, who fetched his tortoiseshell lyre and began to sing to them of Ithaca and the homes and people they had left behind. Astynome sat down at Eperitus's shoulder, enchanted by the poet's skill even though he sang about a place she had never seen and knew nothing about. Eventually, with the stars filling the sky and the conversations of other campfires slowly dying out around them, Omeros finished singing and declared it was time for him to sleep. The others nodded and unrolled their furs, while Astynome stood and walked to where her blanket lay beside the wall of Eperitus's hut.

Eperitus watched her remove her cloak and roll it up to act as a pillow. Every night since the sack of Lyrnessus he had watched her do the same, making her bed little more than an arm's length away from him as they prepared to sleep beneath the stars. Tonight, he decided, should be no exception.

He stood and walked over to her.

'Sleep in my hut,' he said, a little awkwardly. 'If you wish.'

She looked at him mutely.

'You can make your bed close to the hearth,' he continued. 'I have plenty of furs, and it'll be warmer than out here. Astynome, I'm not asking you to—'

'No, of course not,' she finished, embarrassed by his attempt to explain himself. 'I'd be glad to have a roof over my head again. You're kind, my lord.'

He gave her a half-smile, but felt even more awkward than before and quickly looked away. Astynome laid a hand on his forearm, then picked up her blanket and cloak and entered the hut.

The return to the Greek camp was followed by two weeks of training the Ithacan recruits for war. Replacements were of no use unless they could fight, and Odysseus was determined the new-comers would be as ready as they could be to face the battle-hardened Trojans. The task would not be an easy one: their fighting ability, stamina and physical strength differed greatly, but were generally poor and far below the standard of the rest of the army. Before they could be risked in battle they would have to learn how to use their weapons in attack and defence, manoeuvre as a body of men, and understand orders. Equally important, they would need to attain a level of fitness that would allow them to fight in full armour, all day long if necessary, with the vicious Trojan sun beating down on their shoulders.

Early each morning, Odysseus and Eperitus would march the replacements out on to the plain above the camp, where they were put through their paces until the sun sank into the Aegean and the light began to drain from the world. The pampered Ithacans, who had never known anything other than the sheltered lives of islanders, were driven to the limits of their endurance and beyond. Long marches were followed by weapons training and drill. Exhaustion ensued, making the recruits sloppy and careless, but the slightest inattention invariably led to a blow from the staff Eperitus had armed himself with. Each night they would stumble back to their tents, drained of all energy, bruised, ravenous, and always desperate for sleep. And before the first inkling of dawn was in the sky again, Odysseus, Eperitus and a handful of the other veterans would kick them awake and march them back on to the plain for a new day of drills and exercises.

Eperitus was enjoying the period of training. The mercenaries were developing quickly, and even the ordinary Ithacans – who for the most part had been farmers and fishermen before the call to war – were starting to show promise. But most of all he looked forward to the evenings, when he would sit with his comrades around the campfire, discussing the progress of individual recruits while eating the food that Astynome's skilful hands had prepared. Sometimes, when he was not too exhausted by the day's training, Omeros would join them and sing songs about gods, monsters and long-dead heroes, strumming gently on his battered lyre until he could keep his eyes open no longer. And at the end of the night Eperitus would lie awake in his bed, listening to the sound of Astynome's gentle breathing from the other side of the hut, wondering what would become of the girl he refused to think of as his slave. Whenever he raised the subject of sending her home to her family – reminding her that he had only ever agreed to take her under his protection – she seemed strangely reluctant to discuss the matter. Equally strange was the pleasure he took from her reluctance. For a man who had always been content to look after his own needs, having another person in his life brought benefits he had never guessed at. Astynome could cook, of course, but she could also wash, darn, clean, oil, polish and a host of other things he had never before given much mind to. Suddenly, the many holes in his tunics and cloaks had all been repaired and his armaments gleamed with an almost embarrassing lustre. She was also strong enough to chop wood or carry clay pithoi filled with water, and yet gentle enough to knead the tension from his back and shoulders after a long day's weapon training. But despite all these talents, he valued her most for her company. She did not have the cowed dullness of many slaves. Instead, she was opinionated, lively, fiercely patriotic, often rude, and yet never malicious. She would interrupt the men's conversations with astute comments as she served their wine, or hold long discussions with Omeros about the history and legends of Troy, sometimes teaching him snatches of songs in her own language, made more beautiful by the softness of her voice. She was a gift of the gods, and yet Eperitus knew such gifts were the envy of others and rarely belonged to one man for long.

Odysseus would sometimes join the others around the campfire, though he rarely stayed for long. Since the return of the ships from Ithaca, he had been unusually sombre and withdrawn. But the question of Palamedes remained, and almost two weeks after the king had made his suspicions known, Eperitus took him aside one evening and asked him how he intended to prove the Nauplian was a traitor. Odysseus replied the answer lay with the gods, and that he had the beginnings of a plan.

The next evening, after the day's training was over and Eperitus was about to start on the meal Astynome had prepared, Odysseus appeared with a wineskin hanging from his shoulder.

'Come with me,' he said in a low voice.

He set off without waiting and Eperitus was forced to ignore the wooden dish in Astynome's hand and set off after the king. Odysseus was weaving a meandering path between the sprawl of tents and huts as Eperitus caught up with him. The camp was a small city, temporary in its nature and yet almost permanent in the length of time it had existed within the crescent of hills that overlooked the bay. Tens of thousands of soldiers from every Greek nation lived there with the wives, concubines, children and slaves that they had accumulated during the long years of the siege. Though their commanders had huts of wood or even stone, the tents of the soldiers were no less homely – like intricate beehives where whole communities worked, ate and slept in close company with each other. And just like the cities they had left behind, the camp was filled with smithies, armourers' shops, bakeries, covered stalls from which merchants traded their wares, stables, livestock pens, communal latrines and even the altars and crude temples that were vital to any metropolis. Odysseus did not pause in his course, and in the failing light of day managed to dodge skilfully between guy ropes and washing lines and through the constant traffic of soldiers and the numerous dogs, sheep and goats that wandered freely through the camp. At first Eperitus thought he was planning to visit one of the other kings, but as they passed the well-built huts of Menelaus, Nestor, Tlepolemos, Idomeneus, Menestheus and several others, eventually climbing the surrounding hills to the earthwork and ditch that defended the camp, he began to understand who it was Odysseus was seeking, and why. At the top of the ridge, from which they could see the myriad fires of the Greek camp behind them, and the darkening plains towards Troy ahead, they could hear him among the trees on the other side of the ditch. After Odysseus had spoken briefly with the guards, they crossed one of the causeways and followed the mournful sound of drunken singing.

They found him crouched against the crooked bole of a wind-blasted plane tree. His black robe was pulled tightly about his thin body and his hood was pulled over his face. As they approached, he threw back his hood to reveal pale, skull-like features and a head that was bald but for a week's growth of stubbly black hair.

'Odysseus?' he hissed, leaning forward inquisitively. 'And Eperitus with him. What urgent need brings *them* to my little kingdom, I wonder? Has Agamemnon sent for me? But no, he only ever sends his slaves. Then they must have come for reasons of their own. I wonder what they might want.'

'I was hoping you might already have known, Calchas,' Odysseus answered him, sitting on a rock and laying the wineskin between his feet.

The seer's dark eyes fixed greedily on the leather bag. He staggered to his feet and took a couple of faltering steps towards the king, his black cloak falling open to reveal the grubby white priest's robes beneath. As he came closer both warriors could detect the mingled scent of wine, stale sweat and urine. Eperitus's nose twitched in disgust, but it was nothing compared to the revulsion he always felt in the presence of the renegade Trojan priest, who at the command of Apollo had forsaken his homeland to join the Greeks. It was Calchas who, ten years before, had prophesied that Eperitus's daughter, Iphigenia, must be sacrificed before the Greek fleet could sail to Troy, and who had led her to the altar to be murdered by Agamemnon.

'Might already have known what, my lord?' the priest asked, fixing his bloodshot eyes on a spot just above Odysseus's head. His left arm was hanging limply at his side, while his right dangled before his chest, the fingers constantly clutching at something that was not there. 'Might have known some dark secret of the future? Some omen of Troy's doom, or maybe even . . . *your own?*'

He laughed and then belched, before dropping heavily on to his backside and crossing his legs with clumsy awkwardness.

'Sit down!' he snapped, frowning at Eperitus. The Ithacan captain remained standing and a moment later the priest's sudden anger drained away to leave him sullen and depressed. 'Oh, do what you like – nobody else respects me any more so why should you? A seer whose gift of prophecy has abandoned him and left him with a taste for wine. I should have stayed in Troy, serving my god. You'd have listened to me then, a priest of Apollo! Damn your stubborn, warrior's pride.'

'But the gift hasn't left you, Calchas,' Odysseus said, his voice slow and calming. 'Or so I hear. Agamemnon still sends for you, even if the rest of the Greeks shun you. It's said the King of Men asks you to interpret his dreams and that he confides all his plans in you, and that sometimes – *sometimes* – Apollo lets you see things. Have I heard wrong?'

Calchas gave a small, almost imperceptible shake of his head.

'I thought not,' Odysseus continued, picking up the wine and nonchalantly sniffing at the neck of the skin.

'But the gift's weak and fitful at best,' Calchas protested. 'I see so little now, and then nothing but glimpses of shadows. Apollo has turned away from me . . .'

'Apollo has ordered you to serve the Greeks,' Odysseus countered sternly. 'It was at your own insistence that Eperitus and I took you from Troy to the gathering of the fleet at Aulis. And if you've renewed your old liking for wine since then, we aren't to blame for that. Now, tell me truthfully, do you know the identity of the traitor in the council?'

Calchas opened his mouth to speak, but the words fell away and he frowned in confusion. 'Traitor?'

'Yes, a traitor,' Eperitus replied. 'Has Apollo told you who he is? Is it—'

'Enough, Eperitus,' Odysseus ordered, holding up his hand. Then he picked up the wineskin and stood. 'Answer me, Calchas. Do you know anything about a traitor?'

The priest looked longingly at the skin dangling from Odysseus's fingertips, then shook his head and turned away.

'Then forget we ever came here,' Odysseus said, and with a nod to Eperitus began to walk in the direction of the camp.

'Wait!' Calchas called, leaping to his feet. 'Wait. I think—'

He gave a cry as he stumbled over the rock on which Odysseus had been sitting. The two warriors turned to see him sprawled on his stomach, clawing pathetically at the dust and sobbing with sudden despair.

'We shouldn't have wasted our time on him, Odysseus,' Eperitus said, looking with disdain at the fallen priest. 'I understand why you came here – the proof you seek – but any powers he once had left him long ago, destroyed by wine and too much self-pity.'

'Wait,' Odysseus said, holding up a hand.

He took a step towards the priest, who had stopped crying and was now arching his back with his arms pinned to his sides, as if straining to get up but without using his hands. His whole body began to shudder, quivering from head to foot as if shaken by an invisible attacker. Then he turned his face towards them and they saw his pupils had rolled up into the top of his head to leave only the pink orbs of his eyeballs. A white spume had formed about his lips and was rolling down his chin in long gobbets.

'What's happening to him?' Eperitus asked, shocked.

'I've heard about this,' Odysseus replied. 'It's a prophetic trance.'

'He's faking it. You shouldn't have brought the wine – he's putting on a show to—'

Eperitus fell silent. Though Calchas's body remained arched and quivering, something was happening to his eyes. They were changing, filling with an intense light that came from within. Suddenly beams of silver shot out from each eye, feeling through the darkness like antennae, pulsing, growing in strength until the eyeballs glowed like heated bronze. Eperitus and Odysseus instinctively clutched at the swords in their belts, horrified at the seer's face as he looked up at them, mocking their fear with a broad grin.

'Your swords will not protect you,' he said in a deep, powerful voice that seemed to emanate from the plane trees above their heads.

An instant later the handles of their weapons were searing hot, forcing them to pull their hands away. The voice merely laughed.

'What do you want of me?'

'We want to know who's betraying our plans to the Trojans,' Odysseus replied, flexing his hand and rubbing the unharmed flesh of his palm.

The amusement on Calchas's face changed to a frown as the glowing pupils flicked towards the king.

'Your instincts are correct, Odysseus, son of Laertes,' the voice hissed. 'The traitor is Palamedes. But the proof will be less easy to come by. Nauplius's son is as devious as you are and your cunning must exceed his if you are to catch him out.'

Odysseus shot a victorious glance at Eperitus, but the captain's expression remained sceptical.

'Hear this also,' the voice continued. 'Great Ajax blasphemes the gods with impunity, but the day is coming when we will seek to punish his arrogance. When Ajax sets his jealous heart on the armour of Achilles, the Olympians will look to you, Odysseus, to prevent him from taking it.'

Odysseus's look of triumph was replaced by confusion. Eperitus turned to Calchas and saw the demonic eyes now staring directly at him.

'As for you, Eperitus, son of Apheidas, know this: you were unable to defeat your father in my sister's temple because a part of you still loves him. To kill him now will be even harder, after what has passed between you. But if that is still your wish then you must give up all restraint and turn your energy to savage hatred. If you do not, or cannot, then your only choice is to die at his hand. Or to join him.'

Then the light faded from the priest's eyes and his body went limp. Darkness descended on the three men once again.

Chapter Ten

TO CATCH A TRAITOR

Odysseus and Eperitus returned to the camp with barely a word said between them. Then, as they crossed the causeway over the ditch and passed the guards, the king stopped and turned to his friend.

'What did Apheidas say to you in Lyrnessus?' he asked.

'Nothing.'

'I know you better than that, Eperitus – you've been struggling with something ever since you faced him. I saw it in the way you fought at Adramyttium and Thebe, as if you'd lost your killing edge. At first I thought it was because Apheidas had beaten you, or you'd missed the chance you've been wanting for so long. But it's more than that, isn't it? When Calchas said something had passed between you—'

'Calchas is a drunkard,' Eperitus replied, a little more sharply than he had intended. 'His visions are guided by wine more than they are by the gods.'

Odysseus raised a hand.

'We both know that wasn't Calchas speaking. You saw the eyes, heard the voice. If there's something you need to tell me . . .'

Eperitus shook his head. He knew he could not share Apheidas's revelation about his Trojan ancestry, not even with Odysseus. It was a secret he would have to bear alone.

'Apheidas told me something about my family's past. Something I'm trying to forget.'

'Keep it to yourself, then,' Odysseus said, patting Eperitus on the shoulder. 'But now my suspicions about Palamedes have been confirmed, you *will* help me get the proof I need.'

They returned to their huts without another word. Eperitus's thoughts were so full that he was almost surprised to find the tall, slender form of Astynome waiting for him. She had made a good fire in the hearth at the centre of the hut, over which she had suspended the large pot of thick stew she had cooked earlier, keeping it warm for his return. The rich aroma of meat and herbs filled the tent.

'You must be hungry, my lord,' she said in her heavy accent, lifting the ladle from the bubbling liquid and touching it to her lips.

'Ravenous,' he answered.

He unfastened his cloak and folded it roughly over his arm before tossing it on to his bed. His sword and scabbard followed, but as he stooped to remove his sandals his eyes were drawn to the girl who it had been his good fortune to rescue. She wore a white, knee-length chiton and had washed the day's dirt from her limbs and bare feet; with the firelight playing on her brown skin she looked more beautiful than ever.

'I kept some of the stew I had made earlier, before Odysseus called you away,' she said, pouring some of the soup into a wooden bowl and handing it to him with a spoon. 'It was a fight to keep the others from eating it all.'

He took the bowl and sat at the rudimentary table where he sometimes ate his meals. A basin of clean water was already waiting for him, and after he had washed his hands Astynome replaced it with a basket of fresh bread and a krater of wine. He ate in silence while she moved around the hut with a familiar, busy ease, lending it a sense of homeliness it did not deserve. How different, he thought, to when she had first entered two weeks ago. Then her eyes had fallen at once on the captured armour that hung from the walls, glinting in the darkness. She had walked over to the breastplates and helmets and studied them in reproving silence, running her hands over each piece and placing her finger-tips against the holes where spear or sword had punctured the bronze and brought death to her countrymen. Eperitus had taken them from the Trojan nobles he had defeated in battle – men worthy of having their armour stripped from their corpses – but as she touched each piece of crafted leather and bronze he had felt suddenly and for the first time ashamed of these testaments to his skill and courage in battle, these glorious trophies of his own savagery. Then, in answer to her unspoken accusations, he began naming the former owners of each set of armour she touched, describing how they had looked in life, recalling how well they had fought, and declaring that he would not forget their bravery. Even though their souls had gone down to the Chambers of Decay, he was telling her that they were remembered, that they had not died in vain. And he felt that she forgave him for taking their lives.

He dismissed the memory and sat back in his chair, as Astynome removed the stew from the fire and replaced it with a pot of fresh water.

'That was wonderful,' he declared, washing down the last of the meal with a mouthful of wine. 'I haven't tasted anything as good as your cooking in a very long time.'

'That's because I'm not a clumsy Greek soldier, but a woman who knows about food,' she replied, wrapping a cloth around her hand and removing the pot from the fire. 'And a woman who is grateful to her rescuer.'

She poured the water into a large basin, threw the cloth over her shoulder and knelt before his chair. Taking his feet in her hands, she lifted them into the warm water and began to wash them, gently massaging the tired flesh with her fingers. Her hair was tied back to reveal her long brown neck and smooth shoulders, and as she looked up at him he could see that the anger that had marked her face when they first met was now completely gone. Instead, she looked content and at ease.

'I should get a bigger table so you can eat with me in the evenings,' he said.

'In the day, too, I hope,' she said, removing his feet one at a time and resting them on the cloth in her lap as she dried them. 'Surely you won't be training these replacements for ever?'

'That still wouldn't be long enough for some of them. But Achilles is expected back any time, and when he's around things are never quiet for long.'

'You mean you will have a war to fight.'

'Yes.'

Astynome dried his feet in silence and withdrew to the pile of fleeces around the hearth, where she pulled her legs beneath her and turned to look at the fire.

'Why are the Greeks such a murderous people?' she asked, the flames reflecting in her eyes. 'Why do they stubbornly cling to this small patch of Ilium, spreading misery and death?'

'If we are murderous, then it's the gods and the length of this war that have made us so,' he answered. 'But it isn't in our nature. At heart we're an honourable people. Perhaps you'll find that out for yourself, one day.'

'Then you intend to take me back to Greece with you?'

'I didn't say that,' he said, forcing a smile. 'Though you *are* a useful person to have around.'

'I am,' she agreed. 'But it is not my desire to go to Greece. Do you . . . do you have a wife there?'

Eperitus shook his head.

'But you need a woman to look after you. Perhaps you could remain here with me, when the war's over?'

'In Troy?' he echoed with a small laugh, pushing aside the empty bowl and taking a swallow of wine. Astynome had only added a little water, leaving it strong and potent. 'Whatever the outcome of the war, Troy's no place for a Greek. Besides, what of your own husband? You said . . . you said you weren't a virgin.'

'My husband is dead, my lord.'

'Because of the war?'

Astynome shifted around to sit cross-legged, facing the fire. The hem of her dress rode back over her knees to reveal the smooth flesh of her thighs.

'I was sixteen when we married, just after the Greeks arrived. He wasn't a soldier then, but it wasn't long before all young men were given a shield and spear and sent to fight. He died in the first year of the war, before I could bear him children . . .'

Eperitus left his chair and knelt before her. Her eyes were wet, but no tears had escaped to glue together her long eyelashes or stain her beautiful cheeks.

'Did you love him?' he asked.

'Very much,' she whispered. Then she looked into his eyes. 'You have also lost someone close, haven't you? My instincts tell me you have.'

He nodded. 'My daughter. A storm was bottling up the fleet at Aulis, so King Agamemnon sacrificed her to appease the gods.'

Astynome's eyes narrowed in disbelief. 'That's *barbaric*! And yet you still fight for such men?'

'I fight for Odysseus,' he said. 'And for my own honour.'

He touched her on the shoulder and she turned to face him, as if obeying an unspoken command. As she looked into his eyes he felt almost overwhelmed by the power of her beauty, and yet as he placed his other hand on her arm he could feel her trembling. Her eyes fell to his mouth as inevitably their faces moved closer. There was a moment of hesitation in which he could feel her nervous breath on his lips, and then they were kissing.

Eperitus woke to the sound of voices beyond the walls of his hut, but they were only the low murmurings of men greeting each other as they moved around the camp. It was the light of early morning seeping in beneath the entrance that had woken him — that and the unfamiliar warmth of Astynome's naked body close against his own. They had fallen asleep facing the wall of the hut, with his arm beneath her neck, and her back and buttocks tucked into the curve of his body. Long strands of her dark hair were spread across his face and her feet were laid flat across his, the soles and toes soft and comforting. His other arm was across her abdomen as they lay beneath the furs, his fingers curled up in a fist beneath the smooth mound of a breast, which rose and fell gently as she breathed.

For a while he thought of their lovemaking, how awkward it had been at first and then how quickly they had learned to respond to each other. For him the experience had been rich and unexpectedly moving; Astynome had not reacted with the emotional detachment of a slave, but with passion and tenderness. Perhaps she had been thinking of her husband (she told him there had been no other since his death, a confession by which she had unwittingly revealed the depth of her love for the man), or, perhaps, to be touched intimately after so long had released a deep-seated need in her, expressing itself in an ardour that was both fiery and gentle. But his instincts told him otherwise. The desire she had shown was so much more than the rekindling of a distant memory or a longing for physical contact. She had wanted *him*, not the ghost of a dead husband, but him – his lips upon hers, his body against and within hers. The thought pleased him and for a while, as she lay in his arms, he did not think of Apheidas or the grim warning of Calchas's words from the night before.

The voices outside grew a little louder as more men woke and rose. Eperitus cursed them silently, hoping they would not wake the girl, but something seemed to be happening and the noise increased until Astynome's eyes flickered open. She rolled on to her front and raised herself on her elbows.

'It isn't always this noisy,' she said in a hoarse, croaky voice.

'I wouldn't know,' he replied. 'I don't normally sleep this long.'

He looked at her face, half lost behind thick lengths of mutinous hair and with her eyes squinting against the growing light. She was sleepy and vague, her skin flushed and hot to the touch, and yet he thought her as beautiful now as she had been last night, when the firelight had played on her sweat-damp skin and a fierce passion had burned in her eyes.

She looked at him beside her and broke into a tired smile.

'And I should have been up long ago,' she said, leaning over and kissing his bearded cheek. 'As your slave I should have had your breakfast ready before first light.'

Eperitus returned her smile and moved his hand down to rest on the raised mound of her buttocks. The experience of waking each morning to a breakfast made by Astynome was about to be superseded by the happiness of waking to Astynome herself. It struck him then that his life was about to change for the better. Up to that point, the only pleasures of his hard existence had been the company of his comrades and the prospect of battle – to achieve glory and slowly erase the dishonour his father had brought upon him years before. But now he had Astynome to return to at the end of each day and the thought of her presence thrilled him. Men without women were too prone to savagery – the evidence of that had been around him for years – and now, suddenly, he realized why Odysseus had desperately wanted to return to Penelope for so long.

'You're not my slave, Astynome,' he reminded her. 'I agreed to take you under my protection, that's all.'

'Then I'm free to go whenever I wish?'

Eperitus felt a sinking sensation in his stomach. 'Yes. You can do as you please.'

'Then it pleases me to stay,' she answered, stroking his hair. 'I would only want to go back if you came with me, so until I can persuade you to do that I must masquerade as your slave. And now, perhaps, my lord would like some water?'

'The wine last night *has* left my throat dry.'

Astynome threw back the fur and stepped over him. He watched her cross the fur-covered floor to the other side of the hut, where a skin of water hung from the wall. At that moment, the flax curtain that covered the entrance was swept aside and Odysseus walked in. He looked at the shocked girl as she tried to cover her nakedness, then picked up the cloak from her unslept-in bed and tossed it to her.

'It's been too long since I've seen a naked woman,' he said as Astynome caught the cloak and threw it around herself. Then he frowned and turned to his captain with a purposeful air. 'Achilles is back. I'll wait outside while you get dressed.'

He gave a curt bow to Astynome and left. Eperitus rose at once and pulled on his tunic. Astynome came over to him and slipped her arms around his shoulders, placing a kiss on his lips.

'Does that mean Briseis will be here?' she asked.

'Yes. Plunder and slaves are presented to Agamemnon for even distribution, which usually means he gets to pick the best for himself, regardless of who fought for it. That's why I kept your presence quiet. But if the King of Men has got any sense he'll leave Briseis to Achilles. She's won his heart, from all accounts, and there'll be trouble if he's forced to part with her.'

'Poor Briseis,' Astynome sighed.

The sun was just peeping over the ridge to the east as Eperitus pushed aside the curtain and stepped out. The smell of woodsmoke was already in the air as a few men belatedly warmed water and prepared breakfast. Most of their comrades had already washed and eaten, though, and were streaming down to the beach to see the plunder that had been brought back from Lyrnessus. Odysseus, standing with his arms crossed as he stared in the direction of the sea – hidden behind the forest of tents – turned and greeted his captain with a smile.

'She's a beautiful girl,' he said, nodding towards the hut. 'The gods still hold you in their favour, Eperitus.'

'She hates the Greeks,' Eperitus replied.

'Ah, but I think she has a strong affection for you.'

Eperitus snorted derisively to disguise his sudden interest, then placed his hand on Odysseus's shoulder and led him away from the hut.

'And why would you think that?'

'Because of the look she gave you when I entered. Before she even thought to cover her nakedness she glanced at you, and that's when I saw something in her eyes. I can't say *what*, but I know that look. Now, let's get to the beach.'

They joined the flow of hundreds of men, heading towards the southern end of the bay. This was where Achilles's ships were beached, and it was here that the plunder from Lyrnessus, Adramyttium and Thebe was being gathered. The conversation on every side was focused solely on the amount of gold the expedition had looted, and the rapidly spread rumour that there would be a share for every man in the camp. Eperitus gave the matter no thought; he cared little for wealth and his mind was occupied with thoughts of Astynome and what Odysseus had said about her. And then he saw the gargantuan figure of Great Ajax striding head and shoulders above the crowd before them and his mind returned to the words of Calchas the night before. He saw that Odysseus's eyes were also fixed on the king of Salamis.

'What do you think Calchas meant last night?' he asked. 'About Ajax, I mean.'

Odysseus shrugged. 'Everyone knows Ajax has little respect for the gods, though why he would want Achilles's armour is beyond me. I was more interested in Palamedes.'

'He could have been lying.'

'Why would he lie?' Odysseus frowned. 'He's a drunken fool, but he's not a liar.'

'But what if *Calchas* is the traitor? Have you considered that? He's a Trojan, after all, and he's in Agamemnon's confidence. Didn't he say last night that he regretted leaving Troy? Perhaps he told you it was Palamedes to throw you off his own trail.'

'That could be true,' Odysseus replied, still watching the towering form of Ajax ahead of them. 'And you forgot to say that

Calchas can enter or leave the camp whenever he pleases. The only other man who can do that is Palamedes.'

'Any commander can leave the camp,' Eperitus countered. 'You could, if you wished, and at any time you felt like it.'

'Not without the fact being reported to Agamemnon, Menelaus and Nestor. They keep a tight watch on this camp, whether you know it or not, Eperitus. Any commander crossing the ditch at night without good reason would be reported to them. But Palamedes was the one who thought up the system of sentries and patrols that defend the camp from Trojan raiders. And he regularly goes out to check on the patrols at night – a perfect cover for meeting Trojans and passing on our plans. That's one of the reasons why I suspected him in the first place.'

'And Calchas?' Eperitus asked.

But Odysseus simply smiled and shook his head. 'Palamedes is the one, and I'll prove it to you before the night is out.'

They had come to the beach, and though they could see the masts of the newly landed ships above the heads of the multitude of onlookers (all the other galleys had had theirs removed and stowed), they could see nothing of Achilles or the treasures that had been plundered during the expedition.

'Make way,' Eperitus ordered.

He pushed at the backs of the men in front, who turned – some angrily – but were quick to step aside at the sight of the Ithacan commanders. Beyond them were a line of Myrmidon warriors, fully armoured and cloaked in black, facing the crowds with their spears across their bodies.

'Let them through,' said a deep voice as two of the guards moved towards Eperitus and Odysseus with their weapons raised.

Not waiting for his command to be obeyed, a large, broad-chested man with a wild black beard thrust the two soldiers aside and stepped forward to embrace the Ithacans.

'The plunder has arrived safely, my friends,' he announced after releasing them from his bear-like hug, 'and that means wine and whores aplenty by sundown, if you care to join us.'

'I'll take the wine,' Odysseus replied, 'but you can keep the whores, Peisandros.'

'Still holding out for Penelope, I see,' Peisandros said with a shake of his head. 'Ah well, more for the rest of us, eh, Eperitus?'

'I have my own arrangements,' Eperitus replied. 'But tell me, how much did we take in the end? It looks like a lot.'

He pointed towards the wide beach where at least three score heavy wooden caskets had been unloaded so far, with still more being lowered from the sides of the black-hulled galleys.

'Oh, there's enough to go around,' Peisandros grinned, 'and there are prisoners to be ransomed, too, not to mention a haul of slaves that would be worth a lot back home.'

He jabbed a thumb over his shoulder, indicating a large crowd of frightened-looking women and children, standing at the water's edge and staring wide-eyed at the thousands of men gathering along the top of the beach. Eperitus saw the tall and attractive figure of Briseis among them, her chin held high despite the broken look on her face. Achilles was nearby, talking animatedly to Great Ajax, who had already crossed the sand to greet his cousin. Antilochus watched the two men with undisguised admiration, while Patroclus, as aloof as ever, stood to one side with his arms crossed and a scowl on his face.

'The question is,' Peisandros continued, 'whether our illustrious King of Men will share the spoils equally.'

'Where is Agamemnon?' Eperitus asked.

'He won't be here yet,' Odysseus answered. 'He doesn't think it fitting to his rank that he should come to the victors first; they have to go to him and invite him to inspect the spoils. And here comes his messenger now.'

Palamedes had elbowed his way to the front of the crowd, several of whom cursed him and pushed him angrily out towards the line of Myrmidon guards, laughing as he fell on his stomach in the sand. Two of the Myrmidons approached and hauled him to his feet.

'Get your hands off me!' he snapped in a shrill, whining voice, waving them away as if they were mosquitoes.

Palamedes was a short, black-haired man with a wispy beard and a pointed face. His eyes were narrow and clever, always darting about watchfully, and his thin nose and lipless mouth gave him a hateful look that won him no friends. Though he always wore armour, as if to remind others that he was a warrior, he had neither the physique nor the bearing of a fighting man. His value was in the power of his shrewd brain.

'Ah, Palamedes,' Odysseus greeted him, standing in front of the Nauplian prince and planting his fists on his hips. He did not bother to hide the contempt in his face. 'Come to admire the spoils of our victories?'

'I shouldn't get too fat-headed about it, Odysseus,' Palamedes retorted. 'For a man who failed to bring even a few bags of grain back from Thrace, I doubt very much you were able to plunder more than a handful of wooden bowls from your little play-battles at Lyrnessus and beyond.'

Odysseus's eyes narrowed slightly.

'Play-battles, you say? You should be careful: my friends here and I could have taken offence. But as you wouldn't know what a *real* battle was anyway, Palamedes, we'll forget you opened your sneering mouth.'

'Good. Now, why don't you run off and sulk about your wife and son and let *me* go about the king's business. Oh, I hear you've had news from Ithaca – how *is* little Telemachus?'

Odysseus snatched hold of Palamedes's cloak and drew back his fist, but before he could drive it into the Nauplian's face, Eperitus caught hold of his arm and pulled him away. Palamedes fell back on to the sand in terror.

'Odysseus!' Eperitus hissed. 'If it's come to this, at least find a place where there aren't hundreds of witnesses.'

'You'll apologize for that!' Odysseus spat, glaring at Palamedes.

'You'll have no apology from me!' Palamedes returned, staring back. 'And unless you let me take my message to Achilles, then you'll have the King of Men to answer to.'

'Don't overestimate your influence with Agamemnon,' Odysseus returned. 'Your days as his messenger boy are numbered. Calchas has seen to that.'

'Calchas? What are you talking about?'

Odysseus slipped free of Eperitus's grip and dropped to one knee beside Palamedes, who shrank back into the soft sand.

'You haven't heard his latest vision?' he whispered, his voice too low for anyone other than Palamedes and Eperitus to hear. 'Calchas told Agamemnon *you* aren't to be trusted, that you'll bring doom to the Greeks. I don't know what he means, but you can be sure Agamemnon won't be taking you into his confidence any more.'

Palamedes's eyes narrowed with suspicion. 'That's nonsense. Agamemnon trusts me completely.'

'Oh really? Then you'll know Great Ajax and Menestheus are to launch a surprise attack against the city of Dardanus, three days from now. I thought not. Well, Agamemnon still trusts me,' Odysseus added, lowering his face to Palamedes's and taking a fistful of his tunic, 'so keep *that* bit of information to yourself, or it'll mean trouble for the both of us.'

He stood and took Palamedes by the hand, pulling him to his feet. The Nauplian, his brow furrowed in thought, stared hard at him for a moment, then turned and marched across the beach in the direction of Achilles. Many of the men who had witnessed the argument jeered him as he left, while others cheered Odysseus and shouted his name.

'What was all that about?' Eperitus asked in a low voice. 'You've not mentioned any attack on Dardanus before.'

Odysseus raised his eyebrows and smiled brightly.

'That's because there isn't one. And now the bait's been set, we'll have to see if our little fish takes it.'

Six men sat cloaked and hooded around a small campfire. There was little conversation between them as they stared at the mean flames, sputtering and hissing beneath the fine drizzle that fell from the ceiling of cloud above. Beyond the deep ditch that defended the Greek camp, two more guards stood with their shields slung across their backs and their spears sloped over their shoulders, staring out into the darkness of the plain for signs of life. There were none, of course – the Trojans hardly ever ventured beyond the safety of their walls at night – and thankfully the drunken priest, Calchas, had kept his peace, subdued by the light rain that had rolled in from the Aegean during the early evening. The clouds that had transported it now blocked out the light of the early moon and left the landscape black and featureless, while in the camp behind them the same rain had dampened the drinking and whoring of the army.

A dislodged rock and a quiet curse announced the approach of someone from the camp. Some of the men around the fire turned and raised their hoods a little to stare at the newcomer, while the two guards on the other side of the ditch crossed the narrow causeway that they were guarding and held their spears at the ready.

'Who's that?' demanded one of the men, knowing full well who the cloaked figure that walked towards them was.

'It's me,' said Palamedes, tipping his hood back just enough to reveal his face. 'Have the patrols gone out for the night?'

'Yes, sir. They'll be following the routes you set for them. You're checking them a little earlier than usual, though, if I might say so.'

'No, you may not,' Palamedes replied haughtily, clearly annoyed at the guard's familiar tone. 'It's my prerogative to inspect the patrols whenever I feel like it, or how else will they remain watchful and alert?'

He turned his eyes on the men around the fire, who looked down into the flames. Then he threw his hood forward again and marched across the causeway. The two guards followed him to the other side and watched his black cloak into the distance. When it could no longer be distinguished among the rocks and trees of the plain, one of them gave a low whistle and beckoned to the others around the fire. At once, two men rose and ran to join them.

'He went that way,' said the guard, a tall, sinewy soldier with steely eyes and a Spartan accent. 'You'll have to be quick not to lose him in this darkness.'

'I see him,' said Eperitus, narrowing his eyes slightly. 'He's in a hurry, but we'll soon catch up with him.'

The Spartan guard raised his eyebrows a little, but knew enough about Eperitus's senses not to question how he could see a man in a black cloak in the dead of night. He turned to Eperitus's companion.

'What's this all about, Odysseus?' he asked.

'You'll find out soon enough, Diocles,' Odysseus replied, his voice smooth and reassuring. 'And as a favour to an old friend, I'd be grateful if you didn't tell Menelaus or Agamemnon we left the camp tonight.'

'A few swallows of that Ithacan wine you brought us will help me forget,' Diocles said with a wink, and a moment later Odysseus and Eperitus had slipped into the darkness.

Eperitus led the way, his excellent eyesight picking out the easiest path as they followed the skulking form of Palamedes across the plain. Every now and then Palamedes would stop and throw a glance over his shoulder, waiting a while as his eyes and ears probed the gloom before proceeding again. Each time Eperitus would raise his hand and he and Odysseus would remain still until it was safe to carry on. As they progressed in this silent, halting manner – the rain-sodden wool of their cloaks sticking to their skin and restricting their movements – Eperitus thought about Astynome. He had not seen her since that morning and she would be wondering where he was. Even the other soldiers would not be able to tell her his whereabouts, as none knew, and so eventually she would go to her own, cold bed to fall asleep, wondering about his absence while he was chasing phantoms across the plains of Ilium.

Eventually, they saw the ridge that marked the end of the undulating land between the Greek camp and Troy. Its flanks rose up as a black mass against the cloud-filled sky, while out of sight beyond it a slope led down to the fords of the Scamander and the familiar battle plain before the walls of Priam's city. Many thousands of men had died there over the years of the siege and no Greek could approach the ridge without feeling a pang of terror at what lay beyond. But on top of it was a grove of laurel trees dedicated to Thymbrean Apollo, a neutral place where both Greeks and Trojans went to make sacrifices and offer prayers. It was a sanctuary where men of either side could attend to the god in the knowledge his enemies would not harm him. And it was towards the sacred circle of trees that Palamedes was now climbing. Odysseus and Eperitus followed, clambering up the slope as quickly as they could.

'He's going to leave a message for the Trojans,' Odysseus hissed in Eperitus's ear as they watched Palamedes enter the grove just ahead of them. 'He must have been doing this for years.'

'You know it means nothing unless we can find evidence,' Eperitus responded.

'Perhaps I should have brought Diomedes as a witness,' Odysseus mused. 'Or even Agamemnon himself . . .'

Eperitus grabbed his elbow and pulled him behind the cover of an outcrop of rock. Odysseus opened his mouth to speak, but Eperitus raised a finger to his lips and, a moment later, the sound of horses' hooves broke the silence of the night. They came from the gentler slope on the Trojan side of the ridge, the footfalls of the animals loud on the wet rock and accompanied by snorts and the hushed voices of men. Slowly, the two Ithacans peered above the edge of the rock, just as a group of ten mounted men climbed into view a spear's cast away. At their head was the tall and fearsome figure of Apheidas.

Eperitus grabbed at the sword hanging beneath his arm, but Odysseus seized his wrist and gave him a warning glare.

'Are you mad? We'll never defeat ten of them!'

'I only want to defeat one,' Eperitus replied, trying to pull his arm free of Odysseus's iron grip.

'Now's not the time, Eperitus. But a time will come; trust in the gods for that.'

Apheidas gave orders to his escort, who began to spread out around the sacred grove. Two horsemen passed close to the outcrop of rock where Odysseus and Eperitus were hiding, but the Ithacans drew their hooded cloaks around themselves and were all but invisible in the stygian darkness. Then the Trojans moved further along the ridge, turning their eyes southwards in the direction of the Greek camp, and Eperitus dared to raise his head above the rocks once more. He saw his father dismount and hand the reins to one of his men, then stride to the entrance of the temple and disappear from sight. Odysseus had been right all along: Palamedes, for whatever reason, was passing information to the Trojans, and had probably been doing so for years. How he and Odysseus would convince the council of the fact, especially in view of the known animosity between Palamedes and Odysseus, was another matter. But that was of little concern to him now. He was thinking instead of Calchas's sobering words, that part of him still loved Apheidas and that only with savage hatred would he be able to defeat him. And in spite of his instinct to fight his father, Eperitus knew the hatred that had created that instinct no longer burned in his veins.

They returned to the camp long after Palamedes, who had slipped away while Odysseus and Eperitus waited behind the outcrop of rock for the Trojan horsemen to leave. But where Eperitus had expected Odysseus to be glad that his suspicions had been proven beyond doubt, he found the king unnaturally angry. As they walked back through the darkness – the bank of cloud having rolled away and taken the drizzle with it – it seemed to Eperitus that the futility of the past ten years had snapped something inside his friend. Frustration at the length of the siege had given way to a hot rage, knowing that Palamedes's treachery had delayed the defeat of Troy for so long, and with it his return home. One way or another, Odysseus promised, he would find the evidence to convict the traitor before the Council of Kings.

Quietly, Eperitus pulled aside the curtained entrance to his hut and peered inside. There was a dull red glow from the slumbering hearth and as he looked at Astynome's bed he was pleased to see it unoccupied. But as he gazed across at his own bed, expecting to see her there waiting for his return, he noticed that the furs were empty and had not been slept in. He stepped inside and looked around, but there were no signs of the girl other than the black remains of a stew in the pot over the fire.

He dashed out of the hut to find Arceisius standing before him, rubbing the sleep from his eyes.

'I tried to stay awake until you returned,' he began. 'But you were gone so long—'

'Where is she?' Eperitus demanded. 'Where's Astynome?'

'They took her, sir,' Arceisius replied, reverting instinctively to the formal in the face of his captain's anger. 'Agamemnon found out there was a slave who hadn't been counted among the plunder and properly allotted . . .'

Eperitus ran his fingers through his hair. 'Where is she now?'

'You can't get her back, sir.'

'*Where is she now?*'

'She's in Agamemnon's tent. As soon as he saw her beauty he claimed her for himself.'

Eperitus slumped back against the wall of the hut and stared up at the smattering of stars above. 'That bastard!' he cursed. 'Why *him*? And how did Agamemnon find out about Astynome?'

'I wasn't here when his guards came for her,' Arceisius said. 'But Polites was. And he says Eurylochus was with them.'

Chapter Eleven

THE PHRYGIAN

The following morning, Antiphus and Eurybates, whom Odysseus had sent to keep a watch on the eastern gate of Troy, rode into camp and reported that a large force of chariots, cavalry and spearmen had left the city and headed north in the direction of Dardanus. This final proof of Palamedes's treachery stirred Odysseus to anger once more, though he was careful not to allow anyone other than Eperitus to know of his fury. Eperitus warned him not to be rash, reminding him that Palamedes was a trusted member of the council and if they were to expose him they must have evidence. With a dark face, Odysseus promised his friend he would have all the evidence he needed within two days, before Palamedes could realize there was no planned attack on Dardanus and that he had been tricked into revealing his treachery.

Eperitus did not see the king for the rest of the day. With the help of Arceisius, Polites and Antiphus he took the new recruits down to the beach and continued their preparation for war. The intense training was a convenient distraction from the dark thoughts that had kept him awake all night. His rage towards Eurylochus was ready to spill over into violence – and would have done, if Odysseus's envious cousin had dared show his pig-like face in the Ithacan camp. But Eperitus's loathing of Eurylochus was as nothing compared to his hatred for Agamemnon, the man who had plunged a dagger into his daughter's heart, and had now taken his lover from him. In the three short weeks they had spent together

130

Astynome's powerful beauty and proud spirit had found a weakness in Eperitus's callused, battle-hardened emotions. But now she was the slave of the most powerful man in Greece, a man whose life he had taken a solemn and binding oath to protect, though there was no one in the whole of Ilium he would rather send down to Hades. He had promised to protect Astynome, but she had been moved beyond any help he could give her.

After the setting of the sun had ended the day's training, Eperitus joined Arceisius, Polites and Antiphus around a small fire, where they ate a meal of skewered fish and barley cakes. It was woeful fare compared to the food Astynome had cooked for them over the past two weeks, but there was the wine from Ithaca and soon Omeros joined them, his round, happy face immediately bringing cheer to their hearts. As the stars began to emerge overhead he sat his tortoiseshell lyre in his lap and sang them more of the songs he had learned at home. His fingers stroked the strings with skill and his soft, clear voice seemed to mingle with the fiercely bright embers that spiralled up from the flames, stilling the minds of his audience and unlocking memories of places far away and long ago. Eperitus thought again of Astynome, then of Iphigenia, her face suddenly clearer than he had remembered it in years. Inexplicably, his thoughts turned to Palamedes and the one mystery that remained to be explained. Why was he betraying his countrymen?

A hand fell on his shoulder, startling him. He turned to see Odysseus with his finger across his lips, gesturing for him to follow. Though it was mostly covered by the king's double-cloak, Eperitus saw he held a large box under his arm.

'Where've you been?' he asked, leaving the circle of light, warmth and memory. 'No one's seen you all day.'

'I've been in my hut, thinking,' Odysseus answered.

'And have you come up with anything?'

Odysseus could not prevent a self-satisfied smile. 'We're going to Palamedes's tent. No, not to confront him – he's the last man I'd expect to confess anything. At least not freely.'

'Then what?'

'You'll see.'

They walked between the haphazard rows of tents until they reached the place where the Nauplians were concentrated. As with every other part of the camp, the soldiers here were gathered around blazing fires that chugged great columns of spark-filled smoke into the night sky. The different conversations combined into a low buzz as they swapped stories and washed their evening meals down with wine, no one seeming to notice the cloaked figures walking among them. Eventually, the two Ithacans came to Palamedes's tent. Odysseus drew his hood over his head and sat cross-legged at the back of the nearest fire, where two dozen men were talking animatedly in strongly accented Greek.

'What are we doing?' Eperitus whispered, sitting next to Odysseus and looking around himself uncertainly.

'Waiting for Palamedes, of course,' Odysseus answered, giving a small flick of his head in the direction of the large tent close by. A light was shining within and the blurred outline of a man could be seen against the sailcloth walls as he moved around the interior.

'We're going to follow him again?'

Odysseus placed his fingers against his lips, then turned his face towards the fire and laughed quietly at some comment he had heard. Eperitus, not for the first time annoyed by his friend's ability to keep his own counsel, crossed his arms and stared at the flames, wondering what was in the box in Odysseus's lap. After what felt like a very long time, during which the gods seemed to have drawn a convenient veil over the presence of the two Ithacans, the entrance to Palamedes's tent was pulled aside and the traitor stepped out. Odysseus's face remained fixed on the fire, but Eperitus could not resist turning slightly to watch Palamedes slip quietly into the night.

He tugged at Odysseus's cloak. 'Come on. He's heading up to the edge of the camp.'

'Good. Let him go,' Odysseus replied.

He waited a while longer, increasing Eperitus's sense of consternation, then turned his head discreetly and eyed the large tent. The lights within had been extinguished, leaving only the dull glow of the hearth, the grey smoke from which was trailing up out of a vent in the top of the canvas. Odysseus took the box in his hands, glanced briefly at the Nauplians around the campfire, then stood and moved to the entrance of the tent. Eperitus followed.

'You can't go in,' he hissed. 'What if there are slaves?'

'Palamedes has never owned slaves,' Odysseus replied, pulling aside the entrance flap and peering into the half-light within. 'He doesn't think it right. Now, stay here and warn me if anyone comes.'

Eperitus grabbed the king's shoulder. 'What are you looking for, Odysseus? Surely you don't expect to find anything in there.'

'Everything depends on evidence, Eperitus,' he said with a smile. 'Everything.'

He ducked into the tent and was gone. Eperitus crouched down before the entrance and lowered his hood over his face, watching the nearest campfires intently. The men continued to chatter and laugh, becoming steadily drunker as they pulled at the necks of the wineskins they were sharing. Behind him, Eperitus could hear the small sounds of items being moved about, followed by what seemed like a scratching noise. But as Odysseus showed no signs of finishing his search and time dragged on, he grew more and more tense. Then the thing that he was dreading happened. A man rose from the nearest campfire, swayed slightly, then trudged in a direct line towards Palamedes's tent. Eperitus snatched up the flap and prepared to whisper an urgent warning, just as the man came to a halt and hoisted up his tunic. He staggered a few more steps to the corner of the tent and began to urinate. The arc of water spattered noisily over the canvas and on to the hard earth, changing direction several times as the man leaned unsteadily from left to right. Eventually, the last drops fell on his sandals and – without a single glance at the crouching figure of Eperitus – he swung round and returned to his comrades.

A moment later Odysseus emerged.

'I thought he'd never finish,' he whispered.

'Did you find anything?' Eperitus asked as they skulked away from the tent.

'Not a thing,' Odysseus replied, sounding quite pleased about the fact.

It was then that Eperitus noticed the box had gone.

'Odysseus!' he exclaimed. 'The box – you've left it behind.'

'Box?' Odysseus said. 'What box?'

'The box you brought with you.'

'I don't know what you're talking about,' Odysseus said, shrugging his shoulders.

And it was then that Eperitus noticed the dirt under Odysseus's fingernails.

The next day's training was long and arduous with little to show for the effort Eperitus and the other veterans had invested in the replacements. For all the shouting and bullying of their instructors – kindness had no place in the training of warriors – the same men made the same mistakes again and again and many a beating was doled out to the worst handful. These were the ones who would be killed very early on or, if they were fortunate, might discover a latent fighting instinct that could just make warriors of them. Even Odysseus's presence as he observed them from the top of a sand bank did little to encourage their performance. But as the westering sun turned the sky indigo and edged the thin clouds with gold, the king could tell there were some who were showing promise and many more for whom there was hope. These men would benefit from the days of training they had received, and would stand a good chance of surviving their first battle.

Later that night, he left his hut and walked to the place where the Trojan prisoners were kept. Their numbers had dwindled over the winter as the wealthier ones had been ransomed back to their families and many more had been sold to foreign slave traders. The few who remained were poor and either too weak or too rebellious to become slaves. Odysseus picked a dark-skinned man with black curly hair and a hooked nose whom he knew as a trouble causer and had him released into his custody. They walked to Eperitus's hut and, flinging aside the flap, walked in.

'Odysseus?' Eperitus said, jumping from his bed in surprise. 'Is something wrong? Who's this?'

'A Phrygian we captured last year,' Odysseus answered. 'All he's ever done is eat our rations, so I've found another use for him.'

'What do you want with me?' the Trojan asked in good Greek, shrinking away from the Ithacan king, whose sword was pressed against his kidneys. 'I am a prisoner and should be respected as such.'

'You will be, my friend,' Odysseus reassured him, patting his shoulder. 'In fact, I've decided to let you go. Eperitus and I are going to take you beyond the fringe of the camp and set you free.'

'Free?' said Eperitus. 'Why in the names of the gods would we want to do that?'

'Yes, what reason could you have for releasing me?' the prisoner asked.

'I need you to take a message to King Priam.'

Eperitus narrowed his eyes. '*Priam?* That would be treason, Odysseus, and you know it. And what could you possibly have to say to Priam?'

'You know I'm no traitor, Eperitus,' he answered. 'But I need your help, so you'll just have to trust me.'

He gave the prisoner a clay tablet and told him to tuck it into the folds of his tunic. Then, once Eperitus had dressed and slung his sword and scabbard under his arm, the three men left the hut and made their way up the slope to the top of the ridge. The Trojan led the way, his face suddenly bright with hope, followed by Odysseus and Eperitus. Before they reached the edge of the camp, Odysseus stopped them and ordered Eperitus and the prisoner to change cloaks.

'Eperitus, I want you to cross the ditch further up and wait for me among the trees where we spoke to Calchas. Diocles still has the evening watch, so I'll keep him distracted while you make your way over. And you,' he added, placing a large hand on the Phrygian's shoulder, 'pull your hood down over your face and stay behind me. Don't speak, even if spoken to. Do you understand?'

The Phrygian nodded uncertainly and glanced at Eperitus. Eperitus ignored him and set off up the slope towards the earthen ramparts that edged the ditch. Odysseus watched his friend pull himself up the rampart and cross its broad parapet on his stomach, finally disappearing into the ditch beyond. Then, aware that he could be executed if he was caught escorting a prisoner from the camp carrying a message to Priam, Odysseus gave the Phrygian a warning look and approached the guards on the causeway. There were three of them, cloaked against the cold night air and carrying shields and spears.

'Diocles,' he called. 'Still on watch?'

'Someone has to do it,' the Spartan grumbled. 'Not planning to follow Palamedes again, are you? He passed through a while ago, if you are.'

Odysseus shook his head and indicated the Phrygian with his thumb.

'Not tonight. One of my lads has been having dreams about his father. Worried he's dead, so I said I'd take him to Calchas to see if he could interpret the dreams. He used to be good at that.'

'Used to be, maybe,' Diocles said. 'Not any more, though, if you ask me. Not with his wine-addled brain. No harm in trying, I suppose.'

He waved the other guards aside and Odysseus crossed, followed closely by the Phrygian. They moved to the cover of the trees and moments later were met by Eperitus.

'Lead us to the ravine,' Odysseus ordered. 'To the place where the patrols usually cross on their way back. And keep quiet – Calchas will be asleep near here and Diocles says Palamedes is around again. The last thing I want is for either of them to notice us.'

The ravine was a short march to the south-east of the camp, where rainwater from the eastern mountains had cut a path down to the sea. They found it with ease in the faint moonlight. It opened up as a rocky shelf before their feet, with a steep drop into a dried-up river bed. A little to their right, the shelf fell away and was replaced by a rubble-strewn slope that led down to a bulge in the gully below. In the winter when the river was full this was one of the few places where it could be forded with ease, but all that could be heard now as they stood in the semi-darkness was a slow trickle of water in the shadows below.

Odysseus looked down at the slope and felt a heaviness in his heart. He did not like what he was about to do. Even for a man who was renowned for his sly cunning, it was an act without honour that left him cold. But the alternative was to allow Palamedes to continue his treachery and prolong the war, something that was even more unpalatable with the nobility testing his authority at home and the threat that might bring to his family. With his heart pounding against his ribcage, he turned to the Phrygian.

'You still have the letter?'

The Phrygian patted his tunic. 'Is this where I leave you, my lords?'

Odysseus nodded and pointed to the nearby slope. 'Cross the ravine there and head north-east to avoid the patrols. After a while you'll find another ford by an abandoned farmhouse. Cross back over there and make your way north to Troy. I assume Trojans know how to read the stars?'

The prisoner dismissed the question with a smile. 'Your letter will be delivered before the rising of the sun. Whatever you want with King Priam, I pray the gods will honour you for releasing me.'

With that, he turned his back and took two steps towards the break in the rock shelf. Then with a speed that belied his physique, Odysseus stepped after him, threw his arm around the man's neck and twisted sharply. There was a small snap and the man's body went limp, held up only by Odysseus's muscular arm.

'Gods!' Eperitus exclaimed, stepping back in shock. 'You've killed him.'

'Of course I have,' Odysseus replied sternly, slipping his arms under the dead man's armpits. 'Now, take his feet.'

Eperitus hesitated, still stunned by the unexpected murder of the Trojan prisoner, but a glance at the fierce look in Odysseus's eyes forced him to obey.

'I don't understand,' he grunted as they carried the body to the ravine and threw it over the edge. 'What's this all about? Why did you have to kill him?'

'I didn't. He fell and broke his neck. And by morning the whole Greek army is going to be baying for Palamedes's blood.'

Chapter Twelve

TRAITOR'S GOLD

Palamedes awoke to the sound of barked commands and the stamp of approaching feet. He swung his legs out of bed and pulled on his tunic. As he found his sandals and pulled them on he heard the sound of voices raised in challenge followed by a scuffle. A man cried out. Then the flap of the tent was jerked aside and Agamemnon walked in, followed by Menelaus, Nestor and Odysseus. Eperitus was the last to enter and dropped the flap shut behind him.

'My lords,' Palamedes said uncertainly, bowing low before them.

Agamemnon said nothing. He was a tall, imposing figure dressed in a pure white tunic and a blood-red cloak, fastened at the left shoulder by a golden brooch of wonderful craftsmanship. He threw the cloak back to reveal an ornately decorated breastplate, the gift of King Cinyras of Cyprus, which he wore at all times for fear of an assassin's knife. Its different bands of gold, tin and blue enamel shone in the filtered sunlight, and the finely worked snakes that crawled upward on either side glittered as if they were moving.

Despite his rich garb, Agamemnon's long brown hair and auburn beard were shot through with grey and his fine features had lost their youthful arrogance and self-confidence. The eyes were dark-rimmed, as if sleep was a luxury that his great wealth and power could no longer command. He stood with his hands locked behind the small of his back, staring at Palamedes in forbidding silence, his cold blue eyes revealing nothing of what he was thinking.

Menelaus stood beside him, his forehead and thick eyebrows puckered together in an angry frown. With his bear-like physique, thinning hair and careworn face he bore little resemblance to his older brother, and it was clear from the way he was clenching and unclenching his fists that he did not share Agamemnon's capacity for calm detachment.

'The letter, Nestor,' he said after a few more moments of silence. 'Show him the damned letter.'

Nestor was the oldest of the four kings, a greybeard whose battered face spoke of a lifetime of hardship and battle. He stepped forward and pulled something from inside his purple cloak and tossed it on to the furs at Palamedes's feet. Palamedes frowned in confusion, then stooped to pick up the tablet.

'Read it,' Agamemnon commanded.

Palamedes glanced at the King of Men, then lowered his eyes to scan the marked clay.

'What is this?' he asked, looking back up at Agamemnon with an incredulous frown.

'Read it aloud,' Agamemnon ordered.

'But it's ridiculous.'

'*Read it!*'

Palamedes blinked in surprise and fear. He glanced at Odysseus, whose face was passive and unreadable, then looked back down at the letter.

'To Priam, son of Laomedon, king of Troy. Greetings! Your generous offer of gold is gratefully received. The sacking of Lyrnessus, Adramyttium and Thebe was regrettable, but as ever, I remain in Agamemnon's closest confidence and will send you details of his battle plans for the rest of the year as soon as I can. Your faithful servant, Palamedes.'

He read the letter haltingly, almost unable to say aloud the words that bore his name, then shook his head and looked at Agamemnon.

'But this is a nonsense, my lord,' he protested. 'By all the gods of Olympus, I swear to you I did not write this.'

'The letter was found on the body of a Trojan spy,' Nestor informed him. 'Not far from the boundary of our camp, where he had fallen in the dark and broken his neck. It bears *your* name, Palamedes. What do you say in your defence?'

'It's obviously a forgery.'

'How long have you been in Priam's pay?' Menelaus demanded, suddenly stepping forward and grabbing Palamedes's tunic. 'How long have you been betraying our strategies to him? *Tell me!*'

'Let go of him, Menelaus!' Agamemnon commanded. 'If he's a traitor, I want him to confess freely, not have it beaten out of him. Now tell me the truth, Palamedes: have you been betraying us to the Trojans?'

Palamedes ran forward and fell at Agamemnon's feet, throwing his arms around his knees.

'I swear the letter has nothing to do with me. I would *never* betray you for gold, my lord. If you don't believe me, search my tent. This is an elaborate trick thought up by Odysseus to destroy me, I know it.'

Agamemnon looked at the other kings and nodded. Immediately they began pulling apart the contents of the tent, turning over tables and chairs, tearing open Palamedes's mattress and throwing his clothing into the air. Water skins were slashed open with daggers and boxes were opened and their contents poured on to the ground and searched. Eperitus, still standing guard at the entrance, had by now worked out Odysseus's plan to convict Palamedes and watched with mixed feelings as the traitor's belongings were ripped apart. Then the inevitable happened, as Eperitus knew it would. Odysseus kicked aside the remains of the fire and began to pull up the furs and fleeces that lined the floor of the tent. It was then that Menelaus gave a shout of triumph and pointed to the place where Odysseus had just thrown aside a large oxhide. Every eye in the room fell on the patch of ground where the soil had recently been dug up and replaced. Although smoothed again by the hide that had been placed above it, the surface had gained a slight bulge and was darker than the earth around it. Menelaus grabbed Palamedes's sword from where it hung on the wall of the tent and began to scrape away at the soil. It was not long before he was able to reach down and pull up a heavy leather bag, which he upended to release a cascade of golden ingots.

Nestor knelt down beside the gleaming pile and examined it closely. 'These weren't cast in any Greek smithy, my lord,' he told Agamemnon. 'They're Trojan. I think we have all the proof we need.'

'But they're not mine, I tell you,' Palamedes insisted, looking in wide-eyed shock at the blocks of gold spread across the floor of his tent. 'Someone else put them there . . .'

'Silence!' Agamemnon snapped, glaring at the Nauplian prince. 'I've seen enough. You will remain under guard here, Palamedes, while the council decides your fate. I shall send for you shortly.'

The sun was midway in its passage to the Aegean by the time the council sent Eperitus, Arceisius and Polites to fetch Palamedes. The Mycenaean guards who ringed his tent stepped aside at their approach and inside they found Palamedes kneeling before a crude altar, his head bowed before the clay figures of his household gods. Two were missing heads, irreverently broken off during the ransacking of his possessions earlier.

'What's to happen to me?' he asked as the men entered, his eyes still fixed on the painted figurines.

'You're to be stoned to death,' Eperitus answered.

Palamedes looked at him in horror.

'Stoning! Was that Odysseus's influence?'

'No. The manner of your death does not concern him, just so long as you *are* dead.'

'But it was Odysseus who buried the gold in my tent, wasn't it? And Odysseus who planted the letter on the body. Did he have to kill the man in cold blood too?'

'Odysseus did what he had to,' Eperitus replied. 'And what is the death of one man if it exposes a traitor and shortens the war, saving the lives of thousands?'

'But you don't approve of his methods, do you? I know you better than that, Eperitus.'

Eperitus took a deep breath. '*My* opinion counts for nothing; I'm just a soldier, whereas Odysseus is a king. And what about you? Do you deny you're a traitor, Palamedes?'

Palamedes turned away.

'Odysseus thought it was you the moment we realized someone had told the Trojans of our plans to attack Lyrnessus,' Eperitus said. 'Then he fed you false information about the raid on Dardanus, and that night he and I followed you to the temple of Thymbrean Apollo. We saw you meet with Apheidas.'

Palamedes looked at him in surprise, then his shoulders slumped as if a great weight had been placed upon them.

'Then what's the point of denying it any longer? For years I've lived a dual existence, and now I'm glad it's over. My betrayal has stretched this war to an unnatural length and perhaps I deserve death, but in the end I'm just a puppet of the gods, a plaything that no longer amuses them. But is anyone else any better? Do any of us command our own destinies? Does Achilles? Or Hector? Or Odysseus? Or even you, Eperitus?'

'What I don't understand,' Eperitus said, 'is *why* you did it. You're a Greek; why would you betray your country to foreigners?'

Palamedes stood and picked his robe up from a chair, throwing it across his shoulders.

'You remember the first time we came to Troy, on the peace embassy? You were surprised to learn I could speak the language of the Trojans and I told you it was because my nursemaid was a Trojan. I lied. It was my *mother* who taught me. She was a Trojan slave captured in a raid by my father and taken as a concubine, but when I was eight she escaped and gained passage back to Troy on a merchant ship. I came here more with the intention of finding her again than any notion of honouring my oath to protect Helen. Then, in the first year of the war, I received a message from Apheidas saying Clymene, my mother, was a servant in his household and demanding I meet him in the temple of Thymbrean Apollo. How he discovered her or found out she was my mother he has never said, but he told me that unless I gave him regular information about Agamemnon's plans and strategies then Clymene would die.'

'So you betrayed your country for the sake of your mother?' Arceisius sneered. 'You'd have done better to have let her die and kept your honour.'

Palamedes laughed derisively. 'Why should I have allowed my own mother to die for the sake of a meaningless oath, taken under circumstances that should never have led to a ten-year war in a distant land? And as for betraying my country, I think you're missing the point. If my mother was Trojan, then what does that make me? I'm as Trojan as I am Greek, and I can pick my loyalties as I please.'

Eperitus looked at him in silence for a moment, his disapproval of Palamedes's treachery undercut by the revelation that he, too, bore the burden of a divided heritage. But Palamedes had chosen Troy, whether rightly or wrongly, and now he had to pay the price for that decision.

'We're wasting time,' he announced, pointing to the entrance.

'Promise me something, Eperitus,' Palamedes said, his eyes wide and his face suddenly pale as he realized death had taken a step closer. 'Promise me that you will save my mother's life when Troy falls.'

'And why should I promise you anything?' Eperitus returned.

Palamedes drew nearer and lowered his voice to a whisper. 'Because, for all our differences, you and I have something in common. Apheidas told me you're his son, and that you're half Trojan like me.'

'No, Palamedes, I'm not like you. The difference is that you love Clymene, whereas I hate Apheidas. Do you think I could want to be like the monster who has kept your mother under threat of death for so long? I'm Greek, Palamedes, and as far as I'm concerned, my father's blood counts for nothing. But if it makes your death easier for you, then I promise to do all I can to save Clymene when Troy falls.'

'Thank you, Eperitus,' Palamedes said. 'You're a rare thing in these times: a man of honour. But don't deceive yourself that Greeks are more honourable than Trojans, or Trojans more honourable than Greeks. You'll understand what I mean as this war draws to an end.'

They did not follow the slope down to the beach, where debates and trials were normally held. Instead, with Polites and Arceisius standing on either side of Palamedes and the Mycenaean guards following, they climbed to the top of the ridge and crossed the ditch to the rocky ground beyond the border of the camp. Here, every king, prince and commander of the Greek army was assembled in a great crescent around a tall wooden post. At their centre was Agamemnon, seated on a heavy wooden chair plated with beaten gold and beset with jewels; his blue eyes were as dispassionate as ever as he watched Eperitus escort the traitor to the wooden post. Menelaus and Nestor stood either side of the King of Men, while flanking them were the very greatest men in the army: Achilles, young, handsome and proud; Patroclus, cold and disapproving; Great Ajax, so confident of his own strength that he snubbed the aid of the gods; Teucer, twitching constantly as he skulked in his half-brother's shadow; Little Ajax, driven by spite and the joy of violence; Idomeneus, second only to Agamemnon in wealth and power; Menestheus, the handsome and powerful king of Athens; and Diomedes, his hurt at Palamedes's betrayal clear in his eyes. Other faces were ranked behind them, men of high birth and great honour, their bearded jaws set with hostility, but it was Odysseus who caught Palamedes's eye. The king of Ithaca stood between Diomedes and Tlepolemos of Rhodes, his clever green eyes regarding the Nauplian impassively.

'Odysseus!' Palamedes sneered. 'You rank coward. I know you planted that gold in my tent. But if you think you're the victor in our rivalry, think again. The gods see everything, Odysseus, and they remember. Your base tricks won't go unpunished.'

Eperitus pulled him back against the post. A short cross-spar had been nailed just below shoulder height to the back of the post and Eperitus tucked Palamedes's elbows behind this before binding his hands together with a piece of thick leather rope, which he then looped several times around Palamedes's waist until he was held upright and secure.

'May the gods give you a swift death, Palamedes,' he said in a low voice before turning and walking to where Arceisius and Polites awaited him.

The crowd had not spoken a word since the arrival of the prisoner. As the sun soared high above them, the only sounds were the beating of the waves on the shore below and the sound of birds singing in the trees. Even the vast camp beyond the ditch was silent, still but for the gentle flapping of the tents in the warm breeze from the sea. Then Agamemnon rose from his golden throne and took two paces towards his former friend and adviser. In the king's hand was a golden sceptre as tall as himself, covered from base to tip with many rich jewels and topped by a silver bird, its wings spread in flight. This was the symbol of his power, made by the smith-god Hephaistos for Zeus himself, before being passed down to Hermes, then Pelops, then Atreus and finally to Agamemnon. Its mere presence in his hand increased the king's authority many times over, as if the majesty of the father of the gods had lent itself momentarily to the King of Men, raising him to god-like status.

'Palamedes, son of Nauplius, for your treachery the council has sentenced you to death by stoning,' he announced. Then he turned to the rest of the grim-faced assembly. 'May the manner of this traitor's death serve as a warning to any man who seeks to assist the enemies of Greece.'

Though Eperitus despised traitors, who had no honour and

deserved death, the look of disdain in his eyes was not for Palamedes but for Agamemnon as he handed his sceptre to Nestor and bent to pick up the first stone. For ten years he had barely been able to look at the King of Men without a bitter pang of hatred, recalling in vivid detail how he had sacrificed Iphigenia to the gods – even though he believed the child to be his own daughter – all to gain a fair wind for the Greek fleet to sail to Troy. Now those memories were given a fresh acidity by the knowledge he had taken Astynome for himself. Yet again he cursed the oath Clytaemnestra had tricked him into taking, not only not to kill her husband but to protect him from death at the hands of others, all so that she could take her revenge for Iphigenia when Agamemnon returned to Mycenae.

The King of Men weighed the stone in the palm of his hand and the rest of the council moved closer. Some bent to pick fist-sized rocks from the ground; others had already chosen the instruments of their judgment and raised them above their shoulders, waiting for Agamemnon to start the execution. At that moment, Arceisius turned around and looked away in the direction of the sea, but Eperitus placed a hand on his shoulder and turned him back.

'Watch, Arceisius,' he said, firmly, 'so that you know never to do such a thing yourself.'

'Odysseus!' Palamedes shouted suddenly as the circle tightened around him. 'Odysseus! You think yourself a great warrior, but you're just a thief, a quick-tongued impostor masquerading among his superiors. When this war's over you'll go back to Ithaca and be forgotten, a poor king in a poor country once more. After all, what glory will attach to a man like you, Odysseus? Do you think *you*'ll ever have the fame of Agamemnon, or Ajax, or Achilles? What token or outward show of greatness will you bear? *Nothing!* May the gods curse you.'

Eperitus glanced across at Odysseus, whose face was pallid and hard. Then Agamemnon stepped forward, bounced the rock once in his hand and hurled it with all his strength at Palamedes. It caught him just above the elbow and a sharp cry of pain followed. Then Little Ajax cast his own stone, a small boulder that required both hands to throw; it thumped into Palamedes's breastbone and the whole post shook with the impact. Achilles's rock caught him on the left ear, whipping his head violently to the right and sending up a spray of blood. Another missile hit his right temple, just above the eye, producing a cry of pain that was half strangled by the blood welling up in his throat. More stones followed, pelting the traitor's torso and head, breaking skin and snapping bone until his head dropped forward in unconsciousness. Then Great Ajax stepped forward with a rock the size of a lamb. He hurled it with his immense strength, sending its uneven shape spinning through the air to land on Palamedes's lower thigh and snap his leg inwards, forcing even Eperitus to flinch. Palamedes woke and screamed violently until another rock broke his jaw and silenced him again. It was then that Eperitus saw Odysseus let his own stone fall from his fingers to land in the dust, before turning and melting into the crowd. Eperitus also turned his back on the execution and with a feeling of nausea in his stomach returned to his hut, where he stayed until nightfall, thinking of Astynome and wishing she were with him.

book
TWO

Chapter Thirteen

CHRYSES

Eperitus was woken by a gnawing hunger. Palamedes's execution the day before had robbed him of his appetite and he had retired without any dinner, but as he dressed and exited his tent to be greeted by the smell of cooking fires he felt as if he could eat a whole goat by himself. He ordered Omeros, who was passing, to fetch him something to eat, then returned to his tent to be alone for as long as possible. But when the flap was pulled aside again, it was not Omeros who entered.

'Come on,' said Odysseus, staring at him with tired eyes that looked as if they had not slept all night. 'The council is about to meet. We have a visitor – one who might interest you.'

'Who is it?'

'You'll see. Now, come on.'

Eperitus looped his baldric over his shoulder, fastened his cloak around his neck and followed the king back out into the daylight. They nearly collided with Omeros, who was carrying a bowl of porridge.

'Your breakfast, sir,' he said, hurriedly passing Eperitus the bowl.

Eperitus lifted a spoonful to his mouth then pushed the bowl back towards the young Ithacan.

'You have the rest,' he mumbled, following in the wake of Odysseus.

'But where are you going?'

'To the Council of Kings.'

'Come with us, Omeros,' Odysseus added, pausing. 'Only kings and princes are permitted to speak, but there's always a sizeable crowd from among the ordinary soldiers.'

Omeros nodded eagerly and followed the two veteran warriors, still clutching the bowl to his chest. They joined a great stream of men, leaving their tents and campfires to see what the cause of the impromptu meeting was. Soon they were crossing the soft sand to where the Mycenaean ships lay ashore in double rows, the weathered props beneath their hulls testament to the length of time since they had last been at sea. Gathering before their high black prows was a great crowd of men, all talking at the same time and sounding like a throng of seagulls. Odysseus shouldered his way through, and as men turned and spoke his name the press of bodies began to open up before him, allowing him and his companions access to the heart of the assembly. Soon they were met by a circle of guards, dressed ceremonially in the now defunct armour of an earlier era: banded cuirasses of burnished bronze with high neck-guards that covered the chin and arched plates to protect the shoulders; domed helmets covered with a layer of boars' tusks, with black plumes that streamed down from sockets at the top; tall leather shields covered in a gleaming layer of bronze; and a fearsome array of deadly weapons that were nothing to do with ceremony and everything to do with keeping the horde of onlookers at bay. These were Agamemnon's personal bodyguard, hand-picked warriors who were ruthlessly loyal to their king. At the sight of Odysseus and Eperitus they raised their spears and stepped aside, moving quickly back again to bar Omeros's progress.

'No commoners,' ordered one of the guards. 'You'll wait here.'

Without a backward glance, Odysseus and Eperitus joined the kings, princes and high-ranking captains who were already seated on benches around an unblemished circle of silver sand. They sat at their usual places next to Achilles, Patroclus and Peisandros. Although there was no defined order of seating other than the gold-covered throne of Agamemnon – which always faced inland with its back to the sea – the council members had decided their own order over the years, any contravention of which had become unthinkable. As Eperitus sat beside Peisandros, he could see that all the great men who had taken part in the stoning of Palamedes were present, even Agamemnon, Menelaus and Nestor, who usually arrived last. Only Palamedes's place was empty.

Standing alone at the centre of the gathering was an old man. He was cloaked and hooded in black and leaned upon a tall staff, decked with woollen bands that marked him both as a priest of Apollo and a suppliant. Though his back was bent with age, his eyes were fixed firmly on the King of Men. Agamemnon paid him no attention, preferring to lean back into his throne and pull his red cloak around him to keep out the early morning breeze. He was chatting with Menelaus and only looked up briefly as Odysseus arrived, as if to mark his lateness, before resuming his discussion. After a while the chatter among the hundreds of onlookers and the circle of leaders began to ebb, until only the voices and laughter of the Atreides brothers – Agamemnon and Menelaus could still be heard. Eventually, Agamemnon turned his gaze from Menelaus to the bent figure waiting patiently at the centre of the circular arena formed by the benches. He eyed the old man for a few moments, then stood and held out his hand towards a slave, who hurried to bring him his golden sceptre.

'It is not often we receive Trojans in this camp, unless they are our captives or our slaves,' he began. 'But you come to us as a suppliant and bearing the signs of a priest of Apollo, so we will suffer you here. Speak: tell us your name and put your request before us.'

The old man tipped his hood back to reveal a bald head, suntanned and deeply creased with age to the texture of worn leather, then swept his cloak back over his left shoulder to show the white priest's robes beneath.

'My name is Chryses, priest of Apollo on the island of Chryse,' he announced in a voice cracked with age. 'I have received a message that my daughter was taken captive at the sack of Lyrnessus and that she is held here in the Greek camp.'

Eperitus gripped the edge of the bench as he realized the old man standing before them was Astynome's father.

'What of it?' Agamemnon asked, hiding a yawn behind his fingertips.

'What of it, my lord?' Chryses repeated. 'Astynome is my daughter, an innocent girl caught up in a savage war, and I love her. I want her back and have brought a generous ransom for her release.'

The old man raised his arms and turned to the circle of kings and the hundreds of soldiers on the sloping beach behind them. More men were still arriving, clambering on to the decks of the ships or lining the grassy bank that divided the beach from the mass of tents beyond. To these commoners, as well as the kings, he looked, and in a loud voice that belied his age implored their support: 'Great lords, mighty warriors of the Greek army, show your respect to Apollo and accept the ransom I bring. Give an old man back his daughter and in return I will pray to all the gods of Olympus that the gates of Priam's city fall to you this very year!'

A great shout of agreement rose from the ranks of kings and commoners alike as Chryses slowly turned full circle to face the King of Men once more. Eperitus added his own voice to the cheers all around him. As a mere captain he was powerless to argue for Astynome's return, and his oath to Clytaemnestra, not to kill Agamemnon, prevented the other options that his instincts preferred; but with the appearance of Chryses and his offer of a ransom there was hope that she might yet be saved from the clutches of the man he hated. Standing with the rest of the assembly, he caught the eye of Odysseus and knew in an instant that it was his friend who had somehow sent the message to the old priest. Odysseus nodded and Eperitus smiled back.

As the roar of applause rang from the hillsides, Agamemnon's impassive expression turned cold and stern.

'So Astynome is your daughter, is she?' he said stiffly. 'Then know this: she pleases me greatly, too much for me to let her go in exchange for the trinkets of an old man.'

'I have brought all the wealth I possess as a ransom for my daughter, and it is not a paltry sum – gold and copper ingots, tripods of—'

Agamemnon held up his hand.

'Your wealth means nothing to me, Chryses. I intend for your daughter to return with me to Mycenae as my slave, where she will serve me in whatever function I choose, including as my lover. As for you, you will leave immediately and take your beggar's ransom with you.'

Chryses's lined face became suddenly stern and he pointed an accusing finger at the Mycenaean king. 'Dismiss me now and it will be to the loss of you and your men. I cannot be blamed for what happens if—'

'*Silence!*' Agamemnon commanded. 'Leave the camp now, before I decide you are one of Priam's spies and have you executed.'

'So be it!' Chryses replied, and without a further glance at the King of Men he turned and marched from the now silent arena.

Agamemnon's treatment of the old man received widespread disapproval among the ordinary ranks of the army as well as many of their leaders. Whatever increase the King of Men's standing had gained from the recent victories at Lyrnessus, Adramyttium and Thebe was reversed, and as the Greeks streamed away from the gathering they were already muttering solemnly about the consequences of offending a priest of Apollo. And their superstitions were soon fulfilled.

By nightfall of that day, scores of men throughout the camp were suffering with different combinations of fever, shaking, vomiting and diarrhoea. By noon of the next the number was in its hundreds and a feeling of concern bordering on panic began to creep through the army. By the fourth day the healers Machaon and Podaleirius, the sons of Asclepius, were still unable to identify the strange new plague or find effective ways to treat it. Soon great pyres of the dead – a dozen or more bodies at a time – were sending thick palls of black smoke up into the cloudless sky from every point in the Greek camp. Cries of mourning mingled with chanted prayers and the screams of slaughtered animals, as kings and leaders led appeasing sacrifices to the gods. Most prayers were offered to Apollo, whom many suspected of taking his revenge for the snub to Chryses, but by the tenth day the mysterious plague that was ravaging the army showed no signs of abating. It was then that Achilles called for an urgent meeting of the council.

Once the leaders were seated in a circle on the wide beach, surrounded by a great sea of worried soldiers from every nation in Greece, Achilles rose to his feet and silence fell. He walked over to Agamemnon and received the golden staff from the king's hand. Then, striding out into the centre of the arena, he looked around at the thousands of hushed, attentive faces.

'My lord Agamemnon,' he said, though his back was turned to the Mycenaean king, 'perhaps the cries of the dying have not penetrated the walls of your tent, or the acrid stench of the funeral pyres has failed to reach your royal nostrils, but let me inform you that your great army is being decimated by plague while you sit idly on your throne and do nothing. Would you do the same if Hector and all his Trojans were attacking our camp?' There was a dissentious murmur from the onlookers as Achilles turned his dark gaze on the King of Men. 'I have lost more Myrmidons in the past nine days than I did in the attacks on Lyrnessus, Adramyttium and Thebe combined. They were all good men who deserved to die fighting their enemies, not convulsing in their own vomit!'

Agamemnon regarded Achilles in silence, his blue eyes devoid of emotion as he stroked his beard.

'Then what do *you* propose we do, son of Peleus?' asked Menelaus, compelled to speak by his brother's silence.

'To me the solution is clear,' Achilles replied. 'We've angered one of the gods and yet our prayers and sacrifices are going unheard. We have to discover the nature of our offence before this plague destroys us altogether. Fortunately, there is one among us who claims to have the answer.'

The mumblings of the crowd grew louder, forcing Menelaus to raise his hands for silence while Agamemnon continued to stare icily at Achilles.

'Very well,' Menelaus said. 'I, too, have lost many good men and want to see an end to this murderous plague. Who is it that claims to know why the gods are angered?'

Achilles crossed to the benches and hooked his hand beneath the arm of a man hooded and cloaked in black. He lifted him up and placed the tall staff in his hand, then pushed him into the arena and sat down again. The man shuffled uncertainly to the centre of the circle of kings, his back stooped and his face hung low, and many thought Chryses had returned. But when he lifted his hood over his bald head it was the starkly white face of Calchas that blinked round at the ring of shocked onlookers.

'My . . . my lords,' he began, his voice weak and slightly slurred as his dark eyes were drawn inevitably towards Agamemnon. 'My lord, the gods . . . I have seen . . . terrible things.'

'What have you seen?' Agamemnon demanded, sharply.

'I have seen Phoebus Apollo, seated on the high ridge above the camp.' Swaying slightly, Calchas pointed to the surrounding hills and many followed the direction indicated by his long finger. 'I have seen him, the archer-god, seated on the earthen ramparts with a great quiver of golden arrows at his side, drawing the string of his bow back to his cheekbone and launching missile after missile down into the camp. I have watched him from behind stumps of trees and tussocks of grass, firing arrows from dawn until dusk, each one finding its target in a warrior of Greece and bringing him down to a slow and painful death. He is up there now; I can hear the singing of his bow again and again – a dozen times, at least, since this council began. The plague comes from him as a punishment . . . a punishment for—'

He raised a trembling hand towards the king, then turned his face imploringly to Achilles.

'My lord Achilles, I fear to speak. What am I but a priest without a temple, an outcast whose devotion to the gods has earned him nothing more than scorn and resentment from the Greeks? Will you protect me against the wrath of men greater than myself, if my words stir their anger?'

'Speak freely, Calchas,' Achilles commanded. 'Tell us what the gods have revealed to you, and while I am alive you need not fear any man here.'

'Then let it be known that Apollo's anger is directed towards Agamemnon,' Calchas announced, thrusting an accusing finger at the King of Men. 'It was you, my lord, who refused the ransom brought by Chryses, and because of you the plague will not be cleansed from the camp until Astynome is returned to her father without compensation. Only when she has been sent back to the island of Chryse will Apollo listen to our prayers and accept our sacrifices.'

Eperitus, seated between Odysseus and Peisandros, whispered a prayer to Athena, offering the sacrifice of an unblemished lamb if Agamemnon agreed to return Astynome safely back to her father. But when Agamemnon rose to his feet, it was with a terrible anger in his eyes.

'You cursed harbinger of doom! You drunken preacher of woe! In all the years since you fled Troy and came to haunt the Greeks, have you ever spoken words of comfort or joy? It was *you* who condemned us to ten years of war – and still Troy has not fallen – and *you* who damned me to sacrifice my own daughter at Aulis. But in this latest prophecy of gloom I do *not* hold you responsible, for you are but the mouthpiece of another who hides his own vindictiveness behind the shadow of your cloak.' Agamemnon turned to face Achilles. 'And don't accuse me of being ignorant of the suffering of the Greeks, son of Peleus. More Mycenaeans have been tossed on to the funeral pyres in the past nine days than warriors of any other nation. And now that the cause of this plague has been exposed I will not sit by and allow it to continue. Apollo must be appeased: I will send Astynome back to her father, asking only that the army awards me an equal prize as compensation.'

He moved back to his throne, just as Achilles stepped forward and seized the staff from Calchas.

'And what is this compensation that you expect, my lord? The plunder we took has all been shared out. Nothing remains, unless you intend to take an even greater share when Troy falls.'

'Perhaps I will take *your* share, Achilles,' Agamemnon rounded on him, 'seeing as the prophecies say you will not be there to claim it for yourself! But no, you won't trick me out of my due. Doubtless you are a great warrior and a man without equal in honour or glory, but I am a king, the elected leader of this expedition, and I will not be robbed of my portion until this council agrees to compensate me with an equal prize of my own choosing. Come, let us put it to the vote now – why delay further and send more men to their deaths, when we could be preparing a ship to take Astynome back to her father?'

'Don't get ahead of yourself, Agamemnon,' Achilles warned. 'I know you too well to let you pick your own compensation! How often have you remained in camp dressed in Cinyras's breastplate – for all the world a warrior to look at – while letting the rest of us do the fighting? And how often have we returned with captured slaves and weapons or the plunder from a sacked city, only for you to take the lion's share of what our blood and toil have gained? And now I can see you're scheming for an even greater cut of our hard-won spoils, playing on our loyalty to serve your own greed. Well, you seem to forget that the Trojans never stole anything from us – the only reason we're here is out of pity for poor Menelaus. And if you continue to take us for granted then, sooner or later, we'll be taking our armies back with us to Greece, leaving you to fight the Trojans alone. Then where will you be, *King of Men*?'

Agamemnon, who had stood as if rooted before his throne, now turned and walked back into the arena. Calchas, mistaking his intent, stumbled back to the bench from which he had come, pulling his hood back over his head and leaving Agamemnon and Achilles to face each other, anger and disdain filling their eyes.

'Scuttle back to Phthia, then, if you haven't the stomach to stay here,' Agamemnon said quietly, a tremor of anger in his voice. 'I don't need your kind. Every other man here honours my authority – whether they respect me or not – but *you* have always been obstinate and pig-headed. Even Great Ajax will obey me without question, though he is contemptuous of the gods themselves; but it seems to me *you* will not be content until you have command of the Greeks for yourself! Well, I won't stand for it. As for Astynome, I'll make sure she is returned to her father this very day, though of all the women in Troy I have seen none so fair as her – unless it is the woman you claimed for yourself, Achilles. And just to show you that I am the king and a more powerful man than you, if I must surrender Astynome to Apollo, then you must give Briseis to me. And if you will not give her willingly, then I will come to your hut and take her!'

Achilles's lips curled back into a snarl and his hand moved instinctively to the pommel of his sword, half drawing it from its ornate scabbard. On the benches behind him, Eperitus placed a hand on his own sword, ready to honour his hateful oath to Clytaemnestra and defend Agamemnon if needed. But, after a moment, Achilles let his sword slide back into its sheath.

'You may hold more power than I do, Agamemnon,' he said, his voice filled with dangerous intent. 'But you are not the better man. You have stayed in camp, siphoning off the pick of the plunder when you should have been at the forefront of battle. Your inept command has dragged this war into its tenth year, while men like Nestor, Odysseus and myself have kept your alliance together for you. If it wasn't for us your army would have given up the fight long ago and gone home. And if you intend to take Briseis, who was awarded to me for my part in the storming of Lyrnessus, Adramyttium and Thebe, then I will not stand in your way. But from this moment on I am done with you. The others may be too feeble to stand against your tyranny, Agamemnon, but I swear by this staff that my Myrmidons and I will fight for you no more, even if the hordes of Troy are running amok in the camp and setting fire to your black-beaked ships!'

And with that he flung the staff down into the sand and marched from the arena. Patroclus and Peisandros went with him and were followed by the wordless exodus of every Myrmidon present.

Chapter Fourteen
REUNION AND PARTING

Eperitus had not seen Astynome in the two weeks since she had been taken from his tent, and though they had only spent three weeks together before that, he missed her sorely. He also worried for her safety at the hands of Agamemnon and amid the ravages of the plague. But when Odysseus announced he was to captain the ship returning her to Chryse, and that Eperitus would be coming with him, he was relieved and overjoyed at the thought of seeing her again.

'How did you ever persuade Agamemnon to let you take her back?' he asked Odysseus as they stood on the beach by the galleys. 'I never thought he'd send Astynome back on an Ithacan ship after she'd been found in my hut.'

'I don't think he knew she'd been taken from you,' Odysseus replied. 'As far as he was aware, she was simply an undeclared captive from the recent expedition who had to be "fairly" distributed. Agamemnon was jealous and angry that Achilles had already claimed the best of the pick in Briseis, so when he saw Astynome's beauty he took her for his own.'

'And now he has Briseis anyway.'

'Yes,' Odysseus said with a concerned look. 'But as for getting him to let me take Astynome back, I simply pointed out that our ships had recently been at sea and needed little preparation, unlike most of the fleet.'

'And it was you who sent the message to Astynome's father, I presume?'

'Of course, via a merchant who was heading south to Chryse.'

'Then I'm grateful to you,' Eperitus said, watching the crew lay a gangplank between the beach and the side of the hull and trying to coax half a dozen sacrificial cattle up it and on to the galley. 'The thought of her as Agamemnon's slave has been unbearable. At least she'll be safe with her father again.'

'And here she is,' Odysseus said.

They looked to see Talthybius, Agamemnon's squire and herald, approaching with Astynome at his side. Her dark hair was tied above her head and her beautiful eyes were fixed downward at the sand, refusing to look up and meet Eperitus's.

'Is this the girl who's caused all the trouble?' Odysseus enquired.

'This is her; one look at her face and you can see why,' Talthybius laughed.

'Take her to the crew. They can load her on board with the cattle. And then you'd better return to Agamemnon – I hear he's making a sacrifice of bulls and goats to Apollo.'

'He is,' Talthybius replied sullenly, 'but I've other work to do. He wants me to fetch Briseis from Achilles.'

'Don't be concerned. Achilles has said he will give her up freely and he'll keep his word,' Odysseus assured him. 'I only hope for the rest of us he'll take back his other promise and not refrain from the fighting when it starts again.'

Eperitus watched Astynome as she made her way up the gangplank, but she did not return his gaze. Even as the galley was pushed down into the water and the crew settled at their oars, she stood at the prow and refused to turn her eyes to the stern, where he stood with Odysseus at the twin rudder. Before long the faint swishing of the oars took them past the broadest part of the great crescent of sand, where the Mycenaean ships lay rotting on their props and Agamemnon was beginning the sacrifice to Apollo. Dressed in his gleaming breastplate and a lion's pelt, surrounded by a crowd of kings, priests and attendants, he raised his hands in a prayer that did not carry across the waves to the departing galley, but as he spoke Eperitus saw Astynome's eyes upon him and felt despair and jealousy seize his heart. Had he lost her? In the short time she had been with Agamemnon, had she given her heart to the King of Men, as unbelievable as that seemed to Eperitus? As Odysseus ordered the sails to be unfurled and the galley slipped past Tenedos on the journey south, he resolved to speak to her and moved between the benches towards the prow. At the same moment she turned and looked at him and there was a smile on her lips. Then she ran to him and threw her arms around his neck, kissing him on the mouth with a passion that surprised and delighted him as, all around them, the crew cheered.

'I'm sorry I didn't look at you or speak to you before,' she said as he led her by the hand to the prow. 'But I didn't dare with Talthybius looking on, or with Agamemnon in sight on the beach.'

'Gods, but I've missed you,' he said, dismissing her apology. 'After you were taken I wondered whether I would see you again.'

'But here I am. The gods are merciful.'

'Not to the hundreds who were killed by the plague.'

'All the better for Troy,' Astynome replied. 'Though I prayed that you would survive, my lord.'

'And I prayed for you, too. The thought of you with Agamemnon . . .'

Astynome touched his cheek, seemingly oblivious to the eyes of the crew who had stowed their oars and were busy keeping the cattle quiet or simply sitting idle on the benches. 'Don't worry, my love. He came to me the first night as eager as a bull, but when I told him it was the time of my monthly flux and I was unclean, he didn't touch me. Then, after the plague struck, he was afraid. Despite his rebuttal of my father, I think he knew he had offended Apollo and didn't dare touch me.'

Eperitus smiled and held her close.

By late afternoon they had reached Chryse, a small, wooded island that was low in the sea off Cape Lectum to the south. The sail was furled and the mast stowed as they rowed into the deep waters of the island's only anchorage, a small basin surrounded by white sand, trees and a few stone huts. None of the islanders were visible as the anchor stones were tossed into the shallow water and the gangplank was run out.

'They're afraid to see a Greek galley,' Astynome explained as she, Eperitus and Odysseus walked down to the beach, followed by the crew with the sacrificial cattle. 'It's understandable. But I know where my father will be.'

She led them through the treeline to the foot of a small hillock, where sycamores grew and where they could hear the gurgle of a brook or natural spring nearby. A neatly dressed altar of white stone was visible through the boles of a grove of trees at the top of the slope, where worshippers had left garlands of flowers and items of food. On the opposite side of the slope was a simple wooden hut. Astynome led them towards it, but before they could reach the darkened entrance – whether drawn by instinct or the distant sound of cattle – her father stepped out and, with tears in his old eyes, ran to embrace his daughter.

'Greetings Chryses, priest of Apollo,' Odysseus said with a bow of his head. 'I am King Odysseus, son of Laertes, and by the order of Agamemnon I return Astynome into your care. I also bring ceremonial offerings to the archer-god, who has struck our army countless deadly blows since your ransom was refused. In return for your daughter I ask only that you make sacrifices to Apollo and appease his wrath.'

Though reluctant to release Astynome, Chryses reached across and took Odysseus by the hand.

'Welcome, Lord Odysseus, and thank you for returning my daughter to me, even though she can only be with me a short while. Bring the animals here and I will sacrifice them without delay. As for you, my dear Astynome, go to the town and send my attendants to me with grain, bundles of wood, water and wine. Wait for me there and later we will make our own sacrifices together, in thanks for your safe return.'

'Yes, Father,' she said obediently, and with a final, wistful glance at Eperitus, she walked down the slope and into the trees.

The attendants arrived shortly afterwards – half a dozen lads, too young yet to fight in Troy's army. While two stacked the wood and made a fire, the others poured the water into large wooden bowls and washed their hands before scattering the sacrificial grain around the altar. Chryses washed his own hands, then, turning to the west where the sun was setting through the foliage of the trees, held up his arms in prayer.

'Gracious Apollo Smintheus, Lord of the Silver Bow, when the stiff-necked Greeks refused to return my daughter to me I asked you to punish them. You answered my petitions and sent many to the halls of Hades, forcing Agamemnon to relent. Now I ask you to end their suffering and save your arrows, and in return we offer you these animals in sacrifice.'

One by one the six cattle were brought to the altar, where two of the attendants pulled back their heads by the horns while Chryses slit their throats. Still twitching out their life, they were pulled away by the other lads to be skinned and carved up while the next animal was led to its death. As the thigh bones of each victim were brought to Chryses, covered by a layer of fat with raw meat on top, he placed them on to the burning faggots and sprinkled wine over them, muttering constant prayers as he did so. The attendants waited for the thighs and fat to burn, then removed the half-cooked meat and gave them to the Ithacans, who carried them down to the beach to be cut into small pieces and roasted on spits.

When the last animal had been slain, Odysseus, Eperitus and Chryses joined the ship's crew on the beach to feast on the sacrificial meat. Here, finally, they were joined by the male islanders. Most men of fighting age had long since been called to Troy, and ever since Achilles had sacked Chryse early in the war the surviving occupants had treated the Greeks with caution and fear. But tonight they joined the Ithacans at Chryses's behest and ate and drank until the stars came out and the moon rose above the hills of the mainland. Then Chryses bid Odysseus and Eperitus farewell in his slow but clear Greek and went to be reunited with his daughter.

Eventually the food ran out, the islanders returned to their homes and the singing trailed away. The crew laid their blankets in the sand around the fires they had made and went to sleep, their snores filling the night air as moths gathered around the light of the dying embers and bats swooped out from the trees to devour them. Eperitus placed his head on his rolled-up cloak and looked out to where the galley floated at anchor, a black mass edged with silver from the thin moon. He thought of Astynome, as he had not stopped doing since he had watched her disappear into the trees, and his heart felt heavy with longing. Then, as his eyelids began to droop with the inevitable approach of sleep, his sharp senses were suddenly alert to a presence.

Taking his sword in his hand, he sat up and scanned the treeline at the top of the beach. In the shadows was a deeper blackness, and though even his eyes could not define the detail of her face, he knew Astynome had come to bid him farewell. Letting his sword fall on to his blanket and picking up his cloak, he walked silently across the sand to where she stood.

'Astynome,' he whispered.

She smiled, her face pale in the moonlight that filtered through the canopy of leaves. Taking his hand, she led him through the trees to the foot of the hillock. They sat on the grass, slightly damp with the night dew, and kissed, holding each other tightly.

'I had to see you again,' she whispered.

'I'm glad you came. We've spent so little time together . . .'

She touched his cheek and looked into his eyes, as if wanting to say something but not knowing how.

'Your father,' he said. 'When we arrived he said something I didn't understand. He said you could only be with him for a short while. What did he mean?'

Astynome pursed her lips and lowered her eyes. 'He means I'm going to Troy.'

'*Troy?* But why?'

'Look around you, Eperitus. Chryse is a poor island. The wealth my father found to ransom me was everything this island has left, everything they had stored up for the hardest times. Thankfully, Agamemnon did not take it, but even so, if I remain here it will be in poverty. That's why he is sending me back to Troy.'

Eperitus thought about all he had seen since arriving at Chryse – the ramshackle houses around the bay, the meagre priest's hut at the top of the hill, the peasants who had shared the Ithacans' food on the beach, many of whom had hidden meat under their threadbare clothing to take back to their families.

'What do you mean, "back" to Troy?' he asked.

'When you found me at Lyrnessus, I hadn't gone there from Chryse but from Troy. I am a maid there, in the service of my husband's former commander. My husband was mortally wounded defending him from Greek cavalry, and in return he promised to take me as a servant in his household to save me from the poverty that has befallen so many widows in Troy. I have been his maid ever since.'

'And you are *just* a maid?'

'Nothing more.' Astynome smiled, lying back in the grass and staring at her lover. 'He even sends provisions to my father, and for that reason – and the insistence of my father, who believes I will be safer and better kept in Troy – I have agreed to go back in a few days from now. Besides, Chryse is so far away from everything. At least in Troy I can be of some use to the war.'

'But on Chryse I will be able to see you again. That'll be impossible if you return to Troy.'

'Then come with me. There are Greek prisoners from the early years who have decided to fight for Troy, and I'll vouch for you with my master, he'll—'

'You don't understand, Astynome,' Eperitus said, lying beside her and stroking the long strands of her hair. 'I'm sworn to serve Odysseus and, more than that, he's my friend. But even if I could turn my back on him, there are other, much darker things that will keep me out of Troy, even for your sake.'

She slid her leg over his and sat astride him. Though the night air was cool, she unclasped the brooch on her shoulder and her chiton fell away to reveal her breasts, pale in the moonlight. He placed his hands on her waist, enjoying the touch of her skin beneath the press of his thumbs as he slid them up to her ribs.

'Come with me, Eperitus. It's not right that you should fight for the man who murdered your daughter. Odysseus would understand that. And what does any of it matter if you love me and I love you?'

Her admission filled him with joy, and at the same time made the thought of leaving her even more unbearable. He moved his hands round to her buttocks, feeling the gooseflesh beneath his fingertips. The sight and touch of her body called to him, and yet his desire for her was tempered by the thought that he might not see her again. There were other Greeks who had chosen to fight for Troy, a quiet voice reminded him. And wasn't he half Trojan himself? But it was a weak voice, and even his love for Astynome could not make him fight on the same side as his father, or break his loyalty to Odysseus.

He shook his head.

'I can't. It would be impossible for me.'

'Then I will find a way back to you,' she said, leaning across him and planting her lips on his. 'I promise.'

Chapter Fifteen

HELEN AND PARIS

Andromache and Helen sat side by side on a stone bench, their hands on their knees and their eyes fixed on the pillared antechamber to Priam's throne room. They were seated on the shady side of the courtyard, silently waiting for the meeting between the king and the leaders of his army to end. Hector and Paris were both inside, along with Apheidas, Aeneas, Sarpedon and many other high-ranking nobles. But since the start of the gathering, shortly after sunrise, the great portals of the throne room had only opened once, to admit an exhausted and dust-covered soldier who had ridden in from one of the outposts.

Helen cast a sidelong glance at the beautiful but solemn features of her friend. Though she had said nothing, Helen knew Andromache was concerned at the change in Hector. For ten long years her husband had carried the expectations and hopes of Ilium on his shoulders. Troy and its allies did not have the strength to throw the Greeks back into the sea, so Hector had patiently waited for the invaders to expend their superior numbers against the impenetrable walls of the city. But the tenacity of Agamemnon's army was greater than he had anticipated, and with the slaughter of Andromache's father and brothers he was no longer prepared to wait for them to leave. Suddenly he was determined that the Greeks should be defeated once and for all. Most worryingly for Andromache, he had also sworn to face Achilles in battle and avenge the death of King Eëtion.

Helen's concerns were no less than her friend's. It was enough that every widow in Troy blamed her for their woes, but if Hector were to challenge Achilles and be killed then all would hate her without reserve. Even Andromache and Priam, who loved her like a sister and a father, would demand that Paris return her to Menelaus. Worse still, Paris himself could be killed. He had fought in every battle of the war, earning himself a reputation for courage and skill that was second only to his brother's. But as the war dragged on, so his sense of guilt at causing it increased and his recklessness in battle along with it. If it were not for his love of Helen – as fresh and consuming now as it had been that first time their eyes had met in the great hall at Sparta – she felt sure he would have thrown his life away, unable to cope any more with the slaughter he had brought on his people. Her only comfort was that Pleisthenes, now of fighting age, had not been called into the army because of the withered hand he had had since childhood. Even then, her son had an indomitable desire to fight the Greeks and had contrived to blame his mother that he was not allowed to take his part in the war, treating her with scorn when she so needed his love.

As if sensing her doubt and concern, Andromache placed a hand on Helen's and smiled at her. Just then the doors of the throne room opened and Apheidas stepped into the shadowy antechamber. Andromache and Helen rose simultaneously and crossed the courtyard towards him as he swept out into the bright daylight.

'What news, Apheidas?' Andromache asked.

Apheidas paused, noticing the women for the first time. He was clearly in a hurry, but after a moment's consideration he turned and bowed.

'My ladies,' he greeted them. 'The news is good, for those of us who are tired of being penned behind these walls like sheep in a fold. Hector's anger can no longer be contained: he has persuaded his father that Troy and her allies must now wage all-out war if an end is ever to be reached.'

He bowed again and turned to go, but Helen placed a hand on his arm.

'Paris spoke to me of new allies coming to help us. Will we not even wait for them?'

'Paris should not have mentioned such things, even to you, Helen,' Apheidas continued, reluctantly. 'But it's true. Priam has negotiated for the Amazons and Aethiopes to come to our aid, but they will not arrive before the summer and Hector is impatient. Even then I think Priam would have resisted, had Hector not benefited from the support of the fighting men in the assembly. Antenor, Antimachus, Idaeus and the other elders were on the king's side, but Paris, Aeneas, Sarpedon, Pandarus and many more want war now.'

'Yourself among them, no doubt,' Andromache commented, wryly.

'Yes, my lady,' Apheidas replied. 'But now I must go. Word's arrived that the Greeks are leaving their camp and forming on the plain. Hector wants to march out at once and meet them beyond the fords of the Scamander and he's sent me to get the army ready.'

Apheidas bowed again and set off across the courtyard.

'Apheidas!' Andromache called after him, her face pale and her voice tremulous. 'Stay close to Hector. Promise me you'll keep him away from Achilles.'

'I shall stay as close as I can,' he answered. 'But your husband is his own master and will do as he pleases.'

'Hector doesn't need looking after,' Helen said, watching Apheidas disappear down the ramp towards the city. 'No warrior in the whole of Ilium can match him in battle.'

A lone tear rolled down Andromache's cheek. 'Achilles will kill him, Helen. I can feel it in my blood. The end is close for all of us.'

The doors opened again behind them, followed by a gust of conversation as the various leaders began to leave the throne room in twos or threes, hurrying back to their different commands.

Their languages were mingled, reflecting the diverse nature of Priam's alliance of cities and nations. Andromache looked for Hector among the sober faces and when she could not see him, she ran between them into the throne room.

'Deiphobus,' Helen called, spotting her brother-in-law among the stream of warriors.

He was walking between Sarpedon and Pandarus, an archer prince from Zeleia, but at the sight of Helen he left his companions and strolled across to her.

'Sister,' he greeted her, placing his hands on her arms and smiling into her blue eyes. 'What are you doing here? I thought you'd be—'

'Deiphobus, where's my husband?'

The prince moved his hands to her shoulders, fighting the impulse to lift his fingertips to her cheeks or run them through her soft black hair. But he mastered his instincts and stepped back again, dropping his arms to his sides.

'He's gone to put on his armour,' he answered. 'We're going to war again, Helen. You shouldn't distract him . . .'

But Helen was already running across the courtyard to one of the side doors. Entering the cool, gloomy corridor within, she ran as fast as her long dress would allow her, ignoring the greetings or curious glances of the palace slaves until she had found the annex that Paris had built after their marriage. Breathing hard, she pushed open the door of their bedroom to find Paris and his armour bearer, who was fitting the prince's bronze-scaled cuirass around his chest.

'You would go to war without saying goodbye to me?' she demanded.

'Leave us,' Paris commanded his armour bearer, tightening the final buckle himself. As soon as the man had left, he turned to his wife and sighed. 'You speak as if you don't expect me to return.'

'That's the risk I live with every time you don that breastplate, Paris.'

'A man lives for glory, not for love,' Paris retorted, though without conviction. 'He risks his mortal existence to win honour and renown on the battlefield and a name that will last for eternity.'

'A man of honour keeps his word, even when it's to a woman, and you promised me you would not fight.'

'Don't bring that up again, Helen. It was a long time ago and I've been in many battles since then.'

'Yes,' she admitted, turning aside. 'But won't you at least hold yourself back from the fighting? You fought too hard last year, harder than ever, and you've earned the respect of the people – you don't have to keep on with this recklessness. Even if you hold yourself responsible for this war, throwing your life away won't absolve you.'

'Then what else can I do?' Paris snapped. 'Thousands of Trojans have died because I brought you back from Sparta. Every time I march out to war I can feel the eyes of the army upon me, watching for the slightest hesitation so that they can accuse me of weakness or cowardice. The only way I can keep their respect is to show them I'm prepared to fight as hard as they are – and harder! I can't afford to relent until Menelaus and his Greeks have been driven from our shores.'

Helen turned her blue eyes upon him. 'This is a sickness of the mind, Paris. Some malign god is trying to drive you to your death, don't you see that? And if you do die out there, throwing your life away in some reckless deed, what will become of me? The people will turn on me like a pack of dogs.'

'Never!' Paris protested, seizing her white arms. 'That will never happen! My father loves you as if you were his own flesh and blood. Whatever happens to me, he will protect you.'

'He's old, Paris, and growing weaker by the month. If you were killed, the people would send me straight back to Menelaus. Everything you've fought for would be lost; all Troy's suffering would have been in vain. But what would it matter? I'd rather they throw me alive from the towers of Ilium than go on living without you! You're everything I've ever existed for. Before you came, my whole life had been lived in anticipation of you; if you were to die, my grief would never end.'

'Don't say that,' Paris sighed, lifting her chin gently. 'I've survived this long, haven't I? Pray to your immortal father, Helen; ask for his protection on me.'

'I have prayed and sacrificed to all the gods for your sake, my love,' Helen replied. 'And I will continue to plead with them on your behalf. But will you not help the gods and withdraw from the fighting? Will you at least promise me that you won't tempt Hades so often and so determinedly – hang back a little and let the other men of renown be your equals?'

She wrapped her arms around him and kissed him on the lips, pressing her body against the cold bronze scales of his cuirass. Her perfumed skin and hair dizzied his senses, just as the softness of her mouth on his drew his thoughts away from the impending battle. But as her fingers slipped through his black hair and she drew her nails lightly across his scalp, he pulled back and shook his head.

'You know I can't, Helen. If this war is ever to end, then I must fight with *more* determination, not less. And not because I don't care for you, but because I love you more than my own life. What sort of an existence is this, living under Menelaus's shadow year upon year, unable to leave the walls of the city without fear? If we're to be fully free to love one another, then I have no choice but to fight.'

Helen drew back.

'Abandon me, then! But there's a much quicker and surer way of ending this interminable conflict. If you insist on risking your life so wantonly, then I will find a way out of the city and go back to Menelaus. I would rather return to Sparta with him and know you are alive, than live a widow in Troy with nothing but my grief and the memory of you. Don't underestimate my love for you, Paris!'

She turned on her heel and ran out of the bedroom, leaving

Paris confused and speechless behind her. The tears streamed down her face as she fled through the dark corridors, cursing the return of the fighting and the inevitable procession of death that would accompany it.

Chapter Sixteen
THE ARMIES MEET

Twelve days had passed since the quarrel between Agamemnon and Achilles. The Phthian prince had not left the Myrmidon camp in all that time, nursing his anger against the King of Men and refusing to be appeased by the noble Greeks who visited him. When even Great Ajax – Achilles's cousin and closest friend, after Patroclus – could not persuade him to put aside his dispute, a deep concern began to spread through the army. Some feared that without their greatest bulwark against the Trojans, Hector's fighting prowess would defeat the Greeks and drive them back into the sea. But Agamemnon was determined to show them they did not need Achilles and had determined that he himself would lead them to victory.

As the sun climbed towards noon and Hector was mustering the Trojans and their allies for war, the armies of the Greek nations poured over the causeways that crossed the ditch around their camp and formed up on the plains beyond. The grassy plateau where large flocks of sheep and goats still grazed was already beginning to dry in the heat of spring and the movement of countless sandalled feet, hooves and chariot wheels raised a dust cloud that was visible from the high towers of Troy. At their head was a screen of archers, whose role in the coming battle would be to drive away their Trojan counterparts and then break up the ranks of enemy spearmen with their deadly fire. Following them was a long line of two-horsed chariots, each carrying an armoured nobleman and his driver. These were the elite warriors of the vast Greek army who would leap down from their chariots and lead their countrymen into the heart of battle, remaining there until the day was won or death claimed them.

Behind the chariots were file upon file of spearmen, the bronze of their armour and weapons glinting in the sunlight as they marched. The banners of the different kings fluttered and snapped over their heads: the lion of Mycenae tearing out the throat of a stricken deer; the white maiden of the Spartans, which Menelaus had chosen to represent Helen; the Cretan galley in full sail; the golden fox of Argos; the blue dolphin of Ithaca; the serpent of Locris; the goddess Athena for Athens; and many more. Only the eagle and serpent of the Myrmidons was missing.

In the foremost ranks of each nation were the professional soldiers, the men whose experience, courage and loyalty could be relied upon by their leaders. Every man was equipped with a bronze or leather cuirass, a plumed helmet and greaves tied around woollen gaiters. On the left arm he carried a broad, oxhide shield shaped like the moon a few days from its zenith, while in his right hand were two long spears with socketed bronze points. Should these break or be lost, each warrior also carried a sword at his side and a dagger in his belt, weapons which came into their own during the close and bloody work of hand-to-hand combat.

The professional soldiers were supplemented by equal numbers of well-armed mercenaries, but the bulk of the army was provided by the peasantry of Greece with their scavenged armour and weapons. Among them were the most recently arrived drafts, who remained inexperienced and poorly equipped. These were pushed out front with the skirmishers or herded into the rearmost ranks of the battle order, to live or die as the Fates dictated.

Though the nobles would claim the glory, it was the ferocity and nerve of these thousands of spearmen that would decide the outcome of the day's battle – that and the will of the gods. But the heavy infantry were slow and unwieldy, and if their flanks could be turned the fight would be lost. For this reason, hundreds of spear-wielding cavalry swarmed at each end of the battle line, ready to drive off attacks from the enemy or, if the opportunity arose, exploit gaps in their opponents' defences. Mounted on horses that had been captured and trained from the wild herds that roamed the plains, the riders carried no shields and relied on the speed of their animals for protection. They were of little use attacking solid lines of spearmen, but against an undefended flank where shields and spears could not easily be turned to face them they were deadly.

As the army filed out on to the plain, the men looked north-east and saw the distant wisps of woodsmoke that marked the great city of Priam. There, in front of the walls of Troy, many of them would die before the sun sank below the far edge of the Aegean. Like thousands of their comrades before them, their souls would be ushered down to the Chambers of Decay to spend an eternity mourning the sweet joys of the life they had lost. It was a terrible fate and many shook with fear at the thought of it, but there were just as many who faced it with grim anticipation. These knew that death was the one certainty in life, and yet to die fighting was to reach out towards immortality. For glory and fame could only be found in the thick of battle, and glory and fame were the only way a man's name could live beyond his mortal existence.

Odysseus stood in his chariot and stared through the heat haze towards the edge of the plateau, beyond which were the fords of the Scamander and the wide plain where battle would soon be joined.

'Keep them steady,' he snapped as Eurybates struggled to control the team that pulled their chariot.

The beasts snorted with excitement, shaking their heads defi-antly while Eurybates leaned back on the leather reins and cursed at them. Odysseus looked around at the other drivers manoeuvring their chariots into place at the head of each army, some shouting at their charges and laying their whips across their backs, while others encouraged their animals with calming words and loud clicks of their tongues. To his left was Eperitus, squinting in his chariot against the fierce north wind that haunted the plains of Ilium. Like Odysseus, he wore his shield across his back to leave both hands free for his spears, while relying on his helmet and breastplate to ward off enemy weapons. His driver, Arceisius, wore only a light corslet over his woollen tunic and a bronze cap to protect his head. As he had but one role in the battle – to steer the chariot into and out of danger – he carried no weapons other than the sword that hung from a baldric beneath his left arm.

A little further on were King Menestheus and his Athenians, proud and numerous in their bright armour. Beyond them the hordes of Mycenae were led by Agamemnon, standing in his golden chariot with Talthybius at the reins. After sacrificing a five-year-old ox to Zeus, he had taken his place with much fanfare at the head of his troops. He wore the breastplate Cinyras had sent him and a helmet with twin crests of bronze and a horsehair plume that fell down to the middle of his back; his round shield was covered with concentric rings of bronze, boasting the shaped image of a gorgon's head at its centre. On either side of the king were two dozen chariots carrying the nobles of his personal bodyguard, who had swapped their heavy, ceremonial armour for light cuirasses and the smaller shields favoured by the rest of the army. Next to the Mycenaeans were the Spartans, with Menelaus at their head. His bearded jaw was set firm and his eyes were narrowed on the smoke trails of Troy, eager to rejoin battle and fight for the return of his queen. Barely visible through the dusty haze beyond him were the chariots of Diomedes and a dozen other lesser kings.

Odysseus turned his head to the right, where the chariots of Nestor of Pylos, Idomeneus of Crete, Tlepolemos of Rhodes and the rest of the Greek leaders were arrayed, each one surrounded by their noble retainers and backed by vast armies of spearmen, their different standards streaming out in the wind. Nestled between the hordes of Pylos and Crete was the small force from Salamis, headed by the Ajaxes and Teucer. Little Ajax, whose Locrian archers were among the advance screen of skirmishers, had positioned his chariot next to his larger namesake and was looking around himself with an evil glare, eager to join battle and spread misery among the unfortunate Trojans. In contrast, Teucer twitched nervously behind the curved panel of his own chariot, hating to be even just a few paces away from the protection of Great Ajax's towering shield, which he would shelter behind in battle while picking targets for his bow.

His half-brother, meanwhile, stood motionless in his chariot, glowering impatiently towards the north-east as he awaited the order to advance. The handrail of the chariot, which was just below hip height for most men, barely reached the middle of Great Ajax's thigh, while the spoked wheels and the oak axle seemed to sag beneath his weight. Only the largest and strongest horses in the whole army could pull him for any distance, and as he stood in the car behind them he looked like the oversized effigy of a god being paraded for a religious festival. His great shield was slung over his back by a leather strap, and of all the nobles in the Greek army only Eperitus had a shield of the same cumbersome, anti-quated style. But whereas Eperitus's shield had belonged to his grandfather and was retained out of a sense of respect and nostalgia, Ajax preferred the older design because nothing else was capable of covering his massive body.

With Achilles's withdrawal from the fighting, the hopes of the Greeks now rested on Ajax. No man could claim a greater sense of pride or thirst for glory after Achilles himself, and the army looked on him with soldierly adoration, envying his brute strength and the terrible fury with which he would destroy every enemy in his path. The only Trojan who had ever defeated him was Tecmessa, daughter of King Teuthras. After sacking Mysia in the early years of the war and slaying Teuthras, Ajax had fallen in love with Tecmessa and she had borne him a son, whom Ajax had named Eurysaces after his own shield.

Of all other Trojans, it was said that only Hector would be able to withstand Ajax in battle. Ten years before, the Greeks had expected to sweep to victory, crushing their enemies with ease and taking their city within months, despite the prophecies of Calchas. But so far Calchas had been right, and the reason for their frustration – other than the great walls of Troy – was Hector. His reputation among the Greeks as a tactician, a commander and a fighter had grown with each year of the war, and though Ajax had often boasted that he would seek Priam's eldest son on the battlefield and send his ghost to Hades, few shared his confidence.

The army was now assembled and with a great shout Agamemnon raised his sword in the air and thrust the blade in the direction of Troy. Thousands of voices cheered in response and, within moments, the multitude of archers, chariots, spearmen and cavalry were moving. At Odysseus's command, Eurybates gave a flick of the reins and the chariot lurched forward. Odysseus glanced at the line of Ithacans behind him, then across at Eperitus, who met his gaze and nodded. A grim resolve was in his eyes, a determination and severity that Odysseus understood and shared, though for different reasons. Whereas Eperitus was preoccupied with finding his father and ending the disgrace that had haunted him for so much of his life – and which had been made all the more acute since they had faced each other at Lyrnessus – Odysseus's thoughts were on hastening the end of the war and returning home to his family. The news from Ithaca had refocused his mind, though his instincts told him there would be much suffering and death before he saw Penelope again.

The army moved and the ground trembled beneath its collective weight, sending more dust into the warm, windswept air. Few could see beyond the thick haze, but from his raised position Odysseus watched the green pastureland roll away beneath the wheels of his chariot and the smoke trails of Troy growing ever nearer. It was a long march from the safety of the Greek camp to the raised mound on which Priam's city had been built, but eventually, as the sun passed its noon position and started to roll westwards, Troy's gleaming white towers and sloping battlements came into view, larger and grander than anything Odysseus had ever seen in his native Greece. At its highest point was the citadel of Pergamos, a fortress within a fortress, its palaces and temples protected by an inner ring of thick walls where armed guards kept an unfailing watch. Further down, sweeping southwards from the citadel like a half-formed teardrop, was the lower city. Here rich, two-storey houses slowly gave way to a mass of closely packed slums, where many hundreds of people had once lived in discomfort and squalor. Now, though, they were forced to share their meagre homes with thousands of soldiers drawn from across the vassal towns and allied states of Priam's empire.

As the Greeks topped the ridge that marked the edge of the plateau, the ground fell away towards the plain of the Scamander, where the winter floods had receded to leave a rich carpet of clover, parsley and galingale. It was a beautiful sight in the spring, but they took little notice of the white-and-yellow-flowered water meadows or the twisting river, with its high banks lined with elms, weeping willows and tamarisk bushes. For the armies of Troy and her allies had crossed the fords and were now arrayed in their thousands across the marshy pastureland at the bottom of the slope. It was as if the Greeks had been met by a great mirror, in which throngs of archers preceded hundreds of chariots, followed, in their turn, by deep ranks of spearman and flanked on both sides by dark, threatening masses of cavalry. Even Odysseus, who had fought in every battle since the start of the war, had never seen such a force of Trojan men and horses before. It seemed to him that every fighting man in Ilium had been disgorged from the gates of Troy, intent on meeting the invaders and throwing them back into the sea.

Agamemnon raised his hand and, up and down the line, kings and their officers shouted for their men to halt. The relentless tramping of thousands of feet and hooves suddenly stopped, to be followed by an unnatural hush that seemed to roll down the long slope and silence everything before it. Though seagulls screeched overhead and horses whinnied nervously, not a man spoke. Even the women and children watching from the parapets of the city did not dare to break the silence as the two armies faced each other. Then a single chariot sprang forward from the Trojan lines, cutting a channel through the screen of archers and slingers and dashing up the slope towards the Greeks. Before it had covered half the distance separating the opposing skirmishers, who were barely within bowshot of each other, the driver steered aside and brought the chariot to a halt. In the car behind him was a tall warrior with broad shoulders and great, knotted muscles on his arms and legs. Beneath the folds of his black cloak he wore a coat of scaled armour that reached to his thighs, while on his head was a tall helmet that flashed in the sunlight. A black plume flowed down from a socket at its peak and the leather cheek-guards framed a face that was stern, fearless and menacing, promising only suffering and death as he stared disdainfully at the ranks of invaders.

As Hector stepped down and planted his large fists on his hips, he was greeted by a shower of arrows from some of the Greek archers. He did not flinch as the nervous, poorly aimed volley thudded into the ground around him, and only a sharp command from Agamemnon prevented further arrows being released. Then Hector raised his arms and looked from one army to the other.

'Brave warriors of Greece,' he began in his gravelly voice, speaking in the tongue of his enemies, 'we are about to fight a battle in which no quarter will be given; in which many thousands of good men will die. Before the sun sinks in the west and brings a natural end to the day, the soil of Ilium will be dark with our spilled blood and the carrion birds will have more flesh for their beaks than even *they* can stomach. And for what? So you Greeks can regain Helen, or we Trojans can keep our homeland safe? Or to fulfil the whims of the uncaring gods, whose sport is to set men against each other like dogs in a pit? Then listen to me and we can end this destructive war once and for all – you Greeks can sail back to your homes in Sparta, Mycenae, Pylos and beyond, while we Trojans can return to our families in Troy, Dardanus, Mysia and the many other cities of Ilium.'

As he spoke, a second chariot passed through the lines of Trojan archers and drove up the slope towards him. Paris stood behind the driver, dressed in a coat of scaled armour with a panther's skin thrown around his shoulders. In his right hand were two tall spears, while across his back was the feared horn bow with which he had caused so much damage to the Greeks during the years of war. Gripping the rail with his free hand, he stared up at the long, silent lines of the enemy army spread across the ridge above him.

'To this end,' Hector continued, offering Paris his hand and helping him down from the chariot, 'my brother has suggested that the armies lay down their weapons under truce while he and Menelaus fight in single combat for Helen. If Paris wins, the Greeks under Agamemnon will leave Ilium and never return, while if Menelaus is victorious, we Trojans will return Helen to him without further argument. What do you say?'

For a moment there was silence as the shocked Greeks contemplated the sudden end of the conflict that had bound them to Ilium for so long. But before Agamemnon could reply, Menelaus urged his chariot through the line of Greek skirmishers and down the slope towards Hector and Paris.

'I accept the challenge,' he announced as his driver, Eteoneus, stopped the chariot a spear's cast from Priam's sons. The king of Sparta's face was dark with anger as he glowered at Paris. 'This war should have ended long ago, but I will not deem any of the past years wasted if I can bring you down in the dust now, Paris, and hold Helen in my arms again. But first I demand a solemn oath before the Sun, the Earth and Zeus, the father of the gods. Let Priam himself be brought from Troy to make sacrifices with my brother, promising that the truce will not be broken and that both sides will hold to their part of the bargain. Unless he does there will be no duel, for I don't trust the word of his sons. Who can forget how Paris broke the pledge of friendship he took to me in my own home, dishonouring himself and all Trojans when he stole my wife from me?'

'Stole her?' Paris responded, scornfully. 'Is that what you believe, you old fool? Didn't your slaves tell you how she came willingly, only too eager to have a *real* man in her bed?'

'You lying, Trojan scum!' Menelaus snarled, leaning across the handrail and shaking his fist at Paris. 'You murdered her guards and seized her against her will, taking my youngest son as a guarantee that she would come with you to Troy!'

'Enough!' Hector commanded, placing a hand on his brother's chest before he could respond and forcing him back towards his chariot. 'King Priam will be fetched from the city, as you request, Menelaus. I will also send for sacrificial sheep, while the armies lay down their weapons and await the outcome of the duel. Will that satisfy you?'

Menelaus nodded and Hector shouted for a messenger to be sent to Priam. As the horseman splashed across the ford, Menelaus gave Paris a last, baleful look then ordered Eteoneus to drive back to the safety of the lines.

'Did you hear what he said?' he asked, stepping down from his chariot and walking towards Agamemnon. 'Does he really expect me to believe Helen left me for *his* sake?'

'It's what the Trojans have always claimed,' said Odysseus, joining them with Eperitus at his side. 'As a salve to their consciences, of course.'

'They can claim whatever they like,' Menelaus said dismissively. 'It won't matter one way or the other when I lay Paris's corpse out in the dust and—'

'You'll do no such thing,' Agamemnon announced, his cold blue eyes focused on his brother.

'Oh no? Believe me, brother, I'm going to kill that wife-stealing oath-breaker in front of the whole Trojan army, with my bare hands if necessary.'

Agamemnon lowered his voice, no longer able to restrain his anger. 'You stupid oaf! Surely you don't think the only reason I've brought the armies of Greece halfway across the world is for your sake? I've come here to wipe Troy out of existence! I want the city sacked, the men killed, the women enslaved and those accursed walls reduced to rubble so that Troy will never, *ever* be a thorn in our side again! Don't you understand? Have you *never* understood? With Troy gone, Greece will be the greatest power on both sides of the Aegean, but if you kill Paris, then all we'll have to show for ten years of war is the return of your strumpet wife.'

'Then what do you suggest I do?' Menelaus replied, his voice trembling with anger. '*Lose?*'

'At least that would rid me of your interfering stupidity!' Agamemnon snapped. 'You're the cunning one, Odysseus – think of something to get us out of this.'

'There's no honourable way around a solemn oath,' Odysseus replied with a shrug. 'Your best hope is to start the battle before Priam arrives – a misfired arrow could find its way into the Trojan ranks, or—'

'Too late for that now,' Eperitus said, pointing to the pair of chariots that had just exited the Scaean Gate and were now dashing towards the fords of the Scamander. 'Priam's already on his way.'

'Then all you can do is drag the fight out, Menelaus,' Odysseus continued. 'Wound him and feign exhaustion so you can't deliver the fatal blow, then let him escape.'

'I'll be a laughing stock,' Menelaus protested. 'And what about my wife? Do you think I'm going to leave Helen with these savages for a day longer than I have to?'

'You'll do as Odysseus suggests – wound him and let him go,' Agamemnon insisted. 'Until then, I want the army to sit down while Priam and I carry out the sacrifices. It'll be interesting to meet my enemy face to face at last.'

He turned and looked towards the Trojan lines, beyond which the two chariots were cutting the spume in the shallow waters of the ford, then placed a hand on Talthybius's arm and spoke in a low voice. As the herald leapt down from the chariot and began shouting commands for the army to lay down its weapons and sit, the King of Men beckoned to Odysseus and set off through the ranks of archers to where Hector was waiting. Odysseus signalled for Eperitus to follow – knowing his captain would be eager to scan the Trojan battle line for sight of his father – and noticed the look of rebellion on Menelaus's ruddy face.

Chapter Seventeen

THE DUEL

The two armies laid their weapons on the ground and sat down in lines. Agamemnon, Odysseus and Eperitus strode down the slope to where Hector was waiting for them, while Paris returned to the lines to ready himself for the coming duel. As Odysseus looked in awe and admiration at the might of the Trojan army, the ranks opened and the two chariots from Troy dashed through. The first was driven by Antenor, whose hunched back and blind left eye Odysseus remembered from his first visit to Troy ten years before, when he had come with Eperitus and Menelaus to request the peaceful return of Helen. Gripping the handrail beside him was Priam, king of Troy. He was strikingly tall and erect in his flowing purple robes and at first sight appeared to be a man in his middle years. Then, as he came closer they could see his hair had been dyed a glossy black and his skin thickly powdered to disguise his age; and his eyes were unmistakeably those of an old man, filled with care and great loss. As Antenor brought the chariot to a halt beside Hector, Priam stepped down and looked across at the proud form of Agamemnon before him, dressed for war.

'So you are the man whom all this multitude of warriors serve,' he said in his stiff Greek, indicating the massed ranks at the top of the slope. 'You are the one by whose commands my people have been murdered and my land ravaged.'

Agamemnon swept his red cloak back over his shoulder,

revealing the intricately crafted breastplate beneath. As he eyed his enemy, tall in form and yet stooped in spirit, the King of Men began to feel a sense of his own superiority. In all the long years of war, he had never seen Priam except as a distant figure watching the battles from the walls of Pergamos; and now he understood why the king of Troy had not dared to step outside the gates of his own city. He was weak. He was the defeated king of a beaten people, and the sight of him made Agamemnon smile.

'Your losses have been brought about by your own actions, Priam. You shouldn't have let your sons goad a more powerful nation into war. For Greece is greater than Troy and we will defeat you.'

'Paris was foolish,' Priam admitted, 'but he has offered to fight Menelaus to the death and spare the rest of us further bloodshed. And though I love him dearly – with more love than a man like yourself could ever feel or understand, Agamemnon – I am willing to see him die and the lovely Helen returned to Menelaus if it will rid Ilium of your foul hordes.'

'We shall see what happens,' Agamemnon replied. 'Have you brought the sacrifices?'

Priam raised his hand and Idaeus, his ageing herald, stepped down from the second chariot. He hauled a black ewe and a white ram from the floor of the car and cut the bonds around their ankles. Next he took a goatskin and poured water on both kings' hands, while the driver brought a skin of wine and a bowl for mixing. As soon as Agamemnon had washed his hands and shaken off the excess water, he took the dagger from his belt and cut a handful of wool from the heads of the dazed animals.

'Great and glorious Zeus, father of the gods,' he began, raising his face and arms to the clear blue firmament above, 'all-seeing Sun and great Mother Earth; solemn and terrible Hades below, witness the vows we take in your presence. If Paris kills Menelaus, the Greeks shall call an end to this bitter war and sail home, recognizing without dispute that Helen is his wife. But if Menelaus slays Paris, then the Trojans must return Helen to him without hesitation, or face ceaseless war until their city lies destroyed and their people scattered.'

Without further delay, he closed his large hand around the jaws of the ewe, pulled its head back and slit its throat. Next, he slaughtered the ram, and after cleaning his blade on its fleece and returning it to its scabbard, he left the animals in pools of their own blood and took the krater of wine that Idaeus handed to him. The two kings poured libations on the ground and drank, then Priam lifted his own hands to the heavens and prayed, calling on the immortals to preside over the truce between the two armies, and bring death to any who should dare break it, as well as death to their children and the enslavement of their wives. His petition to the gods over, he stepped back into his chariot.

'I hope for my people's sake and yours that this duel will bring an end to the fighting for ever,' Priam said. 'And yet, now that I have met you face to face, I do not trust you to keep to your word. You are a monster, Agamemnon. You came here to build an empire at any cost, even sacrificing your own daughter, and whatever the outcome of this duel I fear you will not leave Ilium until you have what you want.'

He gave a brief nod to Odysseus and Eperitus, then ordered Antenor to return to Troy.

'The old man's not stupid,' Odysseus said in a low voice as they watched the chariots depart.

'No,' Eperitus agreed. 'Fortunately for the rest of us, I don't think Menelaus has any intention of following Agamemnon's orders. He won't just wing Paris then let him crawl away.'

'Of course he won't, though if he thinks Paris will be easy to kill then he's going to be shocked — or dead! Either way, as long as one of them dies we'll soon be on our way home, and it couldn't have come at a better time. They must have sent every man in Ilium against us.'

'The slaughter would have been terrible,' Eperitus mused. 'And yet, if this is the end of the war, then I can't leave for Ithaca with you. Not yet.'

'Your father?'

Eperitus nodded. 'Until he's dead I'll always live in the shadow of his dishonour. But there's Astynome, too. I want to take her back to Greece and have children. You have Penelope and Telemachus to return to, Odysseus, but since Iphigenia was killed, I have no one.'

'Every man should have a family.'

They turned to see Hector standing behind them, his helmet removed and sitting upturned in his hands.

'Except, perhaps, in times of war,' he continued, 'when the thought of our loved ones tests our courage and weakens our resolve. But now the war is to end as maybe none of us had foreseen, and you and I, Odysseus, must cast lots for who will throw the first spear.'

Odysseus nodded and picked up two stones from the ground, one sharp-edged and black, the other smooth and grey.

'The black for Menelaus,' he announced, dropping the stones into Hector's helmet. 'So, even the great Hector thinks of his wife and son before he goes into battle.'

Hector shook the helmet. 'Always. But there are other things that compel a man to battle. Love of his country. Duty to his king. Vengeance. Tell me, Odysseus, where is that bane of Troy, Achilles?'

He tipped the helmet and the grey stone sprang out first. Paris would have the opening cast.

'What do Achilles's whereabouts matter now?' Odysseus replied as Hector tipped out the other stone and pressed his helmet back down on his head. 'The war will soon be over.'

'I'll tell you where Peleus's son is, Hector,' Eperitus announced, 'if you tell me where to find Apheidas.'

Odysseus gave him a silencing stare.

'You will find him with Prince Pandarus among the Zeleians,' Hector answered. 'Over there.'

Eperitus looked in the direction in which Hector was pointing and saw Apheidas at once – tall and fearsome with his leather cuirass catching the sunlight and the hem of his black cloak blown around his calves by the strong north wind. As if sensing his son's gaze, Apheidas turned his head and stared back at him with a dark intensity that cut through the din and movement of the battle lines.

'If you bear him a grudge, you would be wise to forget it,' Hector continued, noticing the dark look in Eperitus's eyes. 'Unless your heart is set on death, put Apheidas out of your mind and sail back to Greece with your life.'

'I could give the same advice to you, Hector,' Eperitus replied. 'But if your desire to face Achilles is greater than your need to see your family again, you will find him back among the Greek ships, where his feud with Agamemnon is keeping him out of the fighting.'

Aeneas pulled the cheek-guards of Paris's helmet under the prince's chin and knotted the leather laces together.

'May the gods be with you, Paris,' he said, clapping a hand on his shoulder. 'Don't let your anger and hatred cloud your judgement: kill Menelaus when the opportunity reveals itself and tonight we will offer sacrifices in the remains of the Greek camp.'

Paris nodded, his mouth too dry and his mind too distracted to give any other answer. As he looked up the slope to where Menelaus was standing, resplendent in his bronze cuirass, plumed helmet and flowing green cloak, he felt the nausea he always suffered before battle, the nervous stirring in the pit of his stomach that long experience told him would fade as soon as the first spear was cast. *His* spear. He held out his hand and Aeneas placed the two ash shafts in his palm, then, with a deep breath, he moved through the ranks of seated archers to the empty ground between the two armies.

If only he had never vowed to Helen not to face Menelaus in battle, the war could have been decided by single combat years ago. But Helen's beauty was hard to resist, and she had always known how to twist him to her will. He could still picture her standing before him on their wedding night, with flowers woven into her hair and wearing the dress Andromache and Leothoë – one of Priam's many wives – had made for her: seven layers of gossamer, which she had removed one by one while the room was filled with the heady scent of her perfume. How could he have refused her when she asked him to take a solemn vow not to face her former husband in battle? How could he say no to such beauty, or such love?

But now he was about to break that vow, just as he had broken his promise before the war that his days as a warrior were over. What choice did he have? Helen had threatened to give herself up to Menelaus for his sake and he believed her, so the only way to stop her would be to kill Menelaus first. Perhaps news had reached her in Troy and she was even now watching from the city walls, fearing that the man she loved would be killed. But it was too late to prevent the duel now. Hector had resisted the idea for a while, reluctant to see his younger brother's life risked against the indomitable fury of Menelaus, and still burning with his own desire for vengeance on Achilles. But Paris had quickly persuaded him that it would save many Trojan lives and was for the best.

And so he looked again up the hill towards the man who had tormented his happiness for too long. The sun was now in the west, blinding Paris and the whole of the Trojan army behind him; the Greeks never attacked before midday if they could avoid it, preferring the sun to be in the eyes of their enemies rather than their own. The slope also gave Menelaus the advantage of height but, ultimately, these factors were of no consequence. The winner of the duel would not be decided by the sun or the slope, but by the gods.

'Having second thoughts, Paris?' Menelaus scoffed loudly, for all to hear as he closed some of the distance between them. 'I thought you said you were a real man!'

There was a ripple of tense laughter from the Greek ranks.

'I was man enough to take your woman, Menelaus,' Paris replied, moving up to meet him. 'And I'm man enough to take your life, too.'

Menelaus's face darkened and he spat on the ground.

'Prove it, Trojan!'

With a silent prayer to Ares and all the gods of Mount Ida, Paris thrust one of his spears into the ground and raised the other so that the black shaft almost touched his right cheek. As he closed one eye and stared down the length of the spear towards Menelaus, who spread his feet a little wider and wiped a trickle of sweat from his brow, he felt his nervousness leave him. Then, with a sudden lunge, he hurled the weapon towards its mark. Menelaus leaned to his right just in time, angling his shield so that the spearhead skipped across its surface and plunged into the earth behind him. The Greeks gasped loudly, then cheered as they realized their champion had survived.

Menelaus now seized one of his own spears and launched it with all the strength of his hatred at the Trojan prince. It flew with deadly accuracy towards Paris, who raised his shield at the last moment. The bronze spearhead punched through the layers of oxhide and wicker, causing him to cry out as he felt the point graze his body armour and tear through the folds of his cloak. There was a shout of dismay from the Trojan ranks behind, followed by a cheer as he turned to show them he was unharmed. Then, with a roar of fury, Menelaus pulled his sword from its scabbard and charged towards him.

Paris took his own sword and ran to meet him. Menelaus was the first to strike, bringing his blade down with tremendous force against Paris's shield and knocking him backwards. Paris stumbled on the slope but quickly regained his footing. Ducking low, he thrust the point of his sword towards the gap beneath Menelaus's round shield. Menelaus anticipated the move and smashed the rim of his shield down on Paris's blade, while sweeping his own weapon in a wide arc towards his opponent's neck. Thrown off balance by the blow on his sword, Paris parried the strike with his shield and withdrew, circling to his right and bringing himself level with his enemy.

Menelaus attacked again, the snarl on his bearded lips visible above the top of his shield as he rained blow upon blow against Paris's defences. The Trojan retreated before his anger, skilfully turning back the relentless assault with his sword so that the air rang with the din of bronze.

'You're wearing yourself out, old man,' he taunted. 'Your fear is undoing you.'

Menelaus growled in reply and with terrifying speed dashed Paris's sword arm aside and brought his weapon down on to the crown of his bronze helmet. It hit the socket from which his white horsehair plume streamed, snapping the blade in two. Paris fell to his knees, his head pounding with the blow that should have killed him. A trickle of blood seeped out from beneath the rim of the helmet and ran down his left temple. Then, realizing the gods had saved him, he looked up at Menelaus's shocked face and laughed out loud with a mixture of relief and joy. Menelaus stared incredulously at the broken blade in his hand, then with a howl of frustration tossed it aside and launched himself on his enemy. The two men threw their arms around each other, rolling down the slope as they fought. One moment, Menelaus was on top, trying to close his large fingers round Paris's throat, then Paris gained the advantage, throwing the Spartan bodily aside and raining punches down upon him. Above and below them the armies of Greece and Troy were now on their feet, shouting at the tops of their voices for one champion or the other, filling the valley with their urgent voices. Then Menelaus, realizing Paris was his match in strength and sensing the younger man's stamina might outlast his own, thrust his knee into Paris's groin, forcing him to roll aside in pain. With a roar of triumph, the Spartan leapt to his feet and seized the Trojan's helmet by its plume, dragging him back up the slope towards his equally jubilant comrades. Paris, his face purpling as the knotted lace beneath his chin cut into his neck, wrapped his hands around Menelaus's wrists in a desperate attempt to prise his fingers from the plume. Suddenly, the lace snapped and the helmet came away in Menelaus's hands.

Paris rolled aside, choking for air and rubbing the scored flesh of his throat. Menelaus tossed the helmet towards the Locrian archers and ran at his enemy. Forgetting his pain, Paris leapt forward and drove his head into Menelaus's abdomen, punching the air from his body and knocking him back to the ground. But as Paris was about to leap on the Spartan once more, he saw Menelaus's second spear from the corner of his right eye, buried point-down in the earth. He ran to it and plucked it from the ground, turning with an exultant grin towards Menelaus.

'It's over,' he said. 'Helen is mine and your brother's army will have to leave these shores for ever. But you're a better man than I thought, Menelaus, and so I'll send your spirit down to Hades with honour.'

Menelaus backed away slowly, looking for the sword that Paris had dropped when they had wrestled on the slope earlier. It was nowhere to be seen but, as he glanced behind himself he saw Paris's second spear standing upright in the earth halfway towards the Trojan lines. Paris saw it at the same moment and, realizing Menelaus's intention, raced his enemy down the slope towards it. Menelaus reached the spear first, snatching it up in both hands and spinning round just in time to parry the thrust aimed at his stomach. As Menelaus turned the point aside, Paris swung the shaft of the spear with both hands into his forehead, stunning him and knocking him to the ground. But if the gods had shattered Menelaus's sword and broken the strap of Paris's helmet, now they turned their favour on the Spartan. As Paris steadied a foot on a boulder and made ready to plunge his spear into Menelaus's gut, an agonizing burst of pain seared through his brain. The spear dropped from his grip and he clutched both hands to the wound on his head, stumbling beneath the intense agony. Menelaus immediately kicked Paris's legs from under him and jumped to his feet, holding the point of his weapon against the Trojan's throat.

'Now whose victory is it?' he crowed, triumphantly. 'You've fought well, Paris, though you're an oath-breaker and a wife-stealer, but the gods have finally decided between us. Helen is – and always *was* – mine.'

Apheidas had been watching the battle from among the ranks of Zeleian spearmen. Ever since Paris had decided to face Menelaus in single combat he had positioned himself next to Pandarus – the most renowned archer in all the armies of Troy after Paris himself – and persuaded him to ready his gold-tipped bow. He knew that if Paris won, Agamemnon would find a way to break his oath, but that if Menelaus gained the victory, and Helen was returned to him the King of Men would be unable to persuade the Greeks to continue the war. In which case Eperitus would return to Greece and the plans Apheidas had been nurturing for so long would fail. With this in mind, he had informed Pandarus that Hector had no intention of letting Paris die or of giving Helen back to the Greeks, and that he would reward any Trojan who prevented Menelaus from winning. And so, as Apheidas saw Paris stumble, and watched Menelaus gloating over him, he placed his hand on the Zeleian prince's arm.

'Now, Pandarus!' he hissed. 'Shoot Menelaus and save Paris's life.'

Pandarus drew back the horn bow and with a whispered prayer to Apollo, released the arrow from the string. It flew with terrible speed, piercing Menelaus's belt and cuirass. The Spartan king dropped his spear and clutched his hands to his side as the warm blood gushed out between his fingers, then blackness overcame him and he slumped to the ground.

Chapter Eighteen

THE BATTLE BEGINS

Shocked silence fell across the two armies. Then a voice cried out and Agamemnon's chariot burst through the stunned ranks of Greek archers and sped down the slope towards his brother. As Paris crawled back to the safety of the Trojan lines, to be placed in his chariot and rushed back to Troy, the King of Men jumped down and lifted Menelaus's inert body from the ground. A moment later Talthybius was whipping the horses back up the slope, driving them as quickly as they could go with the weight of the wooden chariot and its three passengers behind them. Trojan arrows peppered the ground around them as they fled, to be answered by the singing bows of the Greeks and the hiss of their missiles as they arced down into the thick mass of enemy archers, sending many crashing down to their deaths.

'What have I done?' Agamemnon said, clutching his brother's great bulk to his chest. 'Why did I listen to Hector's false assurances and allow you to fight Paris? Without you this whole expedition will have been for nothing. Now the kings will take their ships back to Greece, leaving Helen to the victorious Trojans while your tomb will stand as a monument to *my* folly. May Zeus open the earth beneath my feet, I am going to become a laughing stock on both sides of the Aegean!'

'Courage, brother,' Menelaus said groggily, opening an eye and looking up at Agamemnon. 'Death won't find me such an easy victim. My belt and cuirass stopped the force of the arrow, though

. . . though it succeeded in piercing my flesh. It was the effort of the fight and . . . and the shock of the wound that overcame me, nothing more.'

'Zeus's beard!' Agamemnon exclaimed, staring at his brother's pale face as the chariot rolled into the safety of the lines. Then, seized by a sudden urgency, he grabbed Talthybius by the arm. 'Take him to Machaon at once. Have him apply all his skill to the wound and tell him that if anything happens to my brother I will make his own life forfeit.'

Talthybius gave a shake of the reins and drove the chariot through a channel in the dense ranks of the army, where other chariots were also being driven to the rear as their passengers leapt down and prepared to face the Trojans. Agamemnon turned on his heel as a Locrian screamed and fell heavily beside him, an arrow protruding from his chest. More feathered shafts whistled down among the skirmishers, spilling several to the ground while their comrades returned fire, seemingly ignorant of their own safety.

'They're coming!'

Agamemnon looked down the slope to where the companies of Troy and her allies were massing. Though the enemy archers were aided by the north wind, the Greeks enjoyed the advantage of the slope and were causing far greater casualties among their counterparts. Soon the Trojan skirmishers would be swept aside, exposing the densely packed spearmen behind to the deadly arrows. Accepting this inevitability, Hector was ordering his heavy infantry up the hill towards the waiting Greeks, and the sight of them as they marched towards him, yelling at the tops of their voices as they were struck by wave after wave of arrows from the Greek archers, filled Agamemnon's heart with panic. He looked around himself and saw Odysseus and Eperitus nearest, with Menestheus at their side, all three calmly watching the approach of the heavily armoured Trojans.

'You!' he bellowed. 'What do you think you're doing, standing around like fishwives at a market? Order your men down that hill before I charge you with cowardice in front of the rest of the army!'

Odysseus's sun-tanned skin flushed red and his brow furrowed as he turned to face the Mycenaean king.

'There isn't a man in the whole army more keen to end this war than I am, Agamemnon. I haven't seen my wife or son in almost ten years, thanks to your ambitions, and my spear is as ready as yours to lay out Trojans in the dust. The only thing keeping us at the top of this slope is good military sense!'

Eperitus saw the confusion, impatience and panic vying together on Agamemnon's face.

'By the time they've struggled to the top of this slope they'll have been decimated by our archers, my lord,' he said, indicating the wall of advancing Trojans with a contemptuous flick of his thumb. 'And those who are left will have to fight uphill against fresh troops.'

Agamemnon cast another glance down at the approaching enemy, their dense ranks twitching as the clouds of Locrian arrows rained death upon them. And yet his pride told him he was right.

'Stay here, then,' he sneered, 'and we'll see whose military sense is best.'

He ran on, past the steady ranks of Mycenaeans and Spartans to where Diomedes and Sthenelaus waited at the head of the massed Argives.

'In the name of all the gods, Diomedes, what are you waiting for? It's no surprise to see Odysseus hanging back, but *you* claim to be a son of the great Tydeus! If your father were here I wouldn't need to goad *him* to attack the enemy.'

'If Tydeus was great, then his son is greater,' Sthenelaus responded, angrily. 'You forget, my lord Agamemnon, that Tydeus and my own father, Capaneus, died attacking Thebes. But when Diomedes and I laid siege to the city to avenge their deaths *we* left it in ruins.'

'Well spoken, Sthenelaus,' Agamemnon replied. 'But words count for very little on the battlefield. If you don't have the stomach to face Hector and his Trojans, then I will lead the attack myself.'

'I'll not quarrel with you, Agamemnon, but neither will I be accused of cowardice,' said Diomedes. 'If you want me to attack, then give the command, or else stay your tongue and go back to your Mycenaeans.'

'Of course I want you to attack. And, for all our sakes, do it before they reach the top of the slope and cut us to pieces!'

Turning to the men behind him with a furious look in his eyes, Diomedes raised his spears above his head.

'Argives! *Advance!*'

The great shout rolled along the top of the ridge and, a moment later, the first ranks of the Argives began to move. There was a pause, as if the whole Greek army was drawing breath, and then a series of commands were barked out. From left to right, the long lines of spearmen closed up and locked their shields together, ready to move down the slope and meet the Trojans head on.

Eperitus slipped his own shield from his back and took its weight on to his left arm. He kissed the tips of his fingers and placed them against the faded image of the deer on the inside, silently praying to the gods and the spirit of Iphigenia. Then he plucked his spears from the ground and looked across at Odysseus. The king nodded sternly before turning to the ranks of spearmen behind.

'Ithacans!' he cried. 'For ten years the Trojans have sat behind the safety of their walls, rarely daring to meet us in battle. But now they've emptied the city against us! The moment we've been praying for is here, so call on all your courage, ruthlessness and hatred and *fight*! Show no mercy; do not stop killing until every one of them is dead, or you yourselves have been ushered down to Hades. Think of your homes and families and *kill*!'

'*Kill!*' the Ithacans echoed with one voice.

The king thrust his spear forward and the line of shields began to advance. All along the ridge the armies of Greece were moving through the screen of archers and down the hill towards the

Trojans, who by now were reaching the upper climbs of the slope. Even Eperitus, who had seen many battles, felt awed by the sight of tens of thousands of men marching towards each other, their helmets, shields and breastplates gleaming in the sun, the deadly points of their spears now lowering towards each other. The tramp of their feet beating together was like the heartbeat of the earth itself, while the clatter of hooves behind and on either side of them was like the rushing of waves across a pebble beach. On they marched, relentless, inexorable, and yet not unstoppable; for behind those magnificent walls of leather and bronze were bodies of flesh and blood that in the space of a moment could be torn and broken.

As the gap between the two armies narrowed, orders were shouted in a dozen different languages and dialects as thousands of men drew back their spears and took aim. The Greeks launched the first volley, darkening their air with missiles that arced over the first rank of Trojan shields and into the densely packed ranks behind. Screams followed as socketed bronze tips found exposed necks and faces, or tore through shields and scaled armour to penetrate the soft flesh beneath. Then the Trojans cast their own weapons and a similar chorus of screams followed from the Greek ranks as men were thrown violently back into the dust.

With a furious roar, the two sides lowered their remaining spears and charged. Eperitus held his grandfather's shield before him and crashed into the hedge of Trojan spears, feeling the sharpened points scrape across the oxhide surface. One missed his exposed right flank by a hand's breadth. Suddenly walls of flesh and hardened leather closed in from every side and he was locked in a dark, struggling press of men. In desperation, he pushed his spear beneath the circular shield of a Trojan and felt the bronze bite into the unarmoured flesh of the man's groin, knocking him screaming to the ground. Eperitus did not pause but thrust the raised wooden boss of his shield into the bearded face of an enemy soldier, splitting his nose and toppling him back into the ranks behind. Two more men leapt forward, one on either side, and jabbed at him simultaneously with their spears. He turned the first aside with his shield, while shrinking to his left to let the other plunge past his right hip. With an instinctive thrust, he sank the point of his spear into the neck of one of his attackers and killed him instantly. Then Arceisius appeared – his spear already lost and his sword drawn – and with a backhanded swing he slashed its sharpened edge across the other man's forehead, sending him spinning out of the battle.

'Thought you needed some help,' he said, grinning.

'You just watch out for yourself,' Eperitus replied as more Trojans moved to take the places of the men they had killed.

The chaos of battle was raging all around them now. To Eperitus's right the gigantic form of Polites – his helmet lost and his face spattered with gore – was cutting a swathe through the ranks of Trojans, supported by Antiphus and Eurybates on either side. Even Omeros had worked his way to the front ranks and was duelling with a Trojan spearman, his eyes wide with terror and his young face pale as his opponent thrust at him again and again. Then Arceisius seized Eperitus's arm and pointed to their left, where a short, heavily built warrior had cut down three Ithacans in easy succession and was now making for Odysseus. The Ithacan king had already struck dead several opponents and was exhorting the Ithacans to greater destruction when he sensed the man's approach and turned to face him. All around them the fighting broke off as the two sides edged backwards.

'I am Democoön, son of Priam,' the Trojan grunted, speaking in his own language. 'Name yourself, Greek, so I can know whose ghost I'm sending to the Underworld. I want to boast of my victory when I've stripped the armour from your corpse.'

'I am Odysseus, king of Ithaca and son of Laertes, but to you and all other Trojans who stand in my way, my name is Death!'

A moment later his spear was flying through the air towards Democoön, who flung his shield up instinctively and had it torn from his grip by the force of the cast. He replied immediately, but his weapon missed Odysseus and buried itself in the groin of the man behind him, a lad called Leucus who had arrived with the most recent shipment of recruits from Ithaca. He fell forward, groaning in agony as his lifeblood poured out on to the soil of Ilium.

Odysseus plucked the spear from his dead body and, with a shout of fury, ran straight at Democoön. The Trojan only had time to wrap his fingers around the ivory handle of his sword before Odysseus sent the point of his own spear through his temple and out the back of his head, dropping him lifeless to the ground. A moment later, he had seized the corpse by the arm and was dragging him back to the safety of the Ithacan lines, there to strip it of its armour.

With a cheer and renewed fury, the Ithacans charged once more into the Trojan ranks. Undeterred by the loss of their chieftain or the casualties that had already been inflicted on them, the Trojans kept their discipline, filled the gaps that had been made and held their ground stubbornly. Though none could stand for long against the anger of Odysseus, the skill of Eperitus or the brute strength of Polites, they were tenacious men who fought for their homeland and their families, and soon the corpses of both sides were clogging the hotly contested slope. The fighting became so close that Eperitus was forced to abandon his spear and draw his sword from its scabbard, using it to parry the thrusts of enemy weapons or stab down across his opponents' shield rims and into their exposed throats. The air was now filled with a brown haze of dust, kicked up by countless sandalled feet as they struggled for a grip on the dry earth; it stung eyes and parched throats so that men longed for water and the cries of their struggles were dry and muted. The senses were further stifled by the reek of sweat from thousands of toiling bodies, clogging a man's nostrils so that only the stench of warm blood could compete against it. Even the ever-present north wind seemed to die away and leave the armies to suffer amidst the stink of their own folly. Worse still was the din of the fighting, a sound that would have drowned even the smithies of Hephaistos, manned day and night by the Cyclopes as they beat out Zeus's thunderbolts in the fires of Olympus. Its ceaseless clanging deafened men as they fought, so that the survivors were left with the echo of its ringing in their heads for days.

All across the plain the sounds and smells, the pain and exertion, the tragedy and triumph were the same. Men on both sides called on the gods to help them, exhorting the aim of Apollo, the brute strength of Ares or the skill of Athena, and in response Zeus sent terror, strife and panic to increase their suffering. He filled some with bravery, exhorting them to acts beyond their standing, while others he robbed of their courage and sent fleeing from the battle line, to be shot or stabbed from behind. But the Greeks had the advantage of the slope and their archers had already thinned and disrupted the ranks of their opponents, and so it was that the Trojans began to fall back before them. Great Ajax increased their misery, slaying scores of warriors in his thirst for glory and stripping the armour from the best of them. Teucer's bow – a gift from Apollo – and Little Ajax's spear brought down many others as they fought alongside him. Agamemnon did not shrink from the battle, either, and felled several opponents of high rank or otherwise, not discriminating in his hatred of the men of Ilium. Even Menelaus had joined the fray, ignoring all advice to return to the ships and returning to lead his own men. But nowhere was the slaughter greater than before the ranks of the Argives and their king, Diomedes. They drove all before them, leaving a trail of dead on the slopes as they pushed the Trojans perilously close to the fast-flowing Scamander. Even when Pandarus – whose arrow had felled Menelaus and broken the truce – drove out against them and shot Diomedes in the left shoulder, it did not stop the king's fury. Instead, he ordered Sthenelaus to pluck out the arrow then killed Pandarus with a spear throw which passed through his cheekbone and out the back of his neck. And thus the Zeleian archer's treachery against the gods was repaid.

But Hector saw the salient the Argives had cut into the Trojan ranks. It stretched out from the Greek lines like the blade of a sword, long, narrow and exposed, with the banner of the golden fox at its tip where Diomedes was leading. Urging the rest of the Trojans to hold their ground and assuring them that Achilles – the man they feared above all others – was refusing to fight, Hector sent his chariots against the extended flanks. The men of Argos heard the thunder of hooves and heavy wooden wheels through the clouds of dust that obscured the battlefield. Moments later the rancorous Trojans were bursting through on three sides, bringing swift terror to their enemies. Now it was the turn of the Argives to litter the ground with their bodies. The chariots punched holes in the once solid lines of spearmen, spreading fear and alarm through the men behind. Trojan infantry followed, exploiting the gaps that had been created and cutting Diomedes's army to shreds. Their king, suffering from the wound to his shoulder, ordered a fighting retreat and suddenly the battle was turning in Hector's favour.

As the Argives fled back up the slope, panic spread through the rest of the Greek army and they gave ground before the resurgent Trojans. The Ithacans moved back with them, fearful of leaving their flanks exposed as their neighbours retreated on either side. They passed the bodies of the men who had died in the earlier fighting, many of whom Eperitus knew, as well as many others who were unrecognizable beneath the layers of gore and dust that covered them. But this was the glory he had longed for all his life, he reminded himself. Only amidst the litter of the battlefield could a warrior find immortality, winning renown with his spear at the risk of a painful and bloody death. That was the warrior's creed.

But it was a creed he knew he was losing faith in. Each time he scanned the sweating, resolute faces of his opponents, he was reminded of the Trojan blood that flowed in his own veins. When his father had exiled him from Alybas, he thought he had turned his back on the last surviving member of his family. But now he realized that the men he was fighting could be his distant cousins, men with whom he shared a common ancestry. What was more, the dark skin and black hair that he had always considered the mark of an enemy race now reminded him of the woman he loved. Every time he brought down a Trojan in the fury of battle, he thought of Astynome and how she despised the Greeks for killing her countrymen and destroying her homeland. And as he surveyed the destruction around him and listened to the terrible clamour of battle, he understood her hatred. The Greeks had brought nothing but suffering and death to the people of Ilium, and all for the lust of one man and the greed of another.

The lines parted as the exhausted Greeks drew further back up the slope and the Trojans were temporarily too tired to pursue. The pause had not lasted more than a few short moments, though, when a chariot rode out from the enemy ranks with Sarpedon standing proud and upright in the car. He shouted a challenge in his own tongue and Tlepolemos, the king of Rhodes, ran out to meet him. As Eperitus watched he was reminded of the young, baby-faced suitor whom he had first seen twenty years ago in the great hall at Sparta. He had only been a prince then, with a fledgling beard and a full head of curly hair, vainly hoping to win the hand of the most beautiful woman in Greece. Now his beard was full and he had proved himself again and again on the battlefield, but Eperitus sensed that Tlepolemos had as much chance against Sarpedon as he had had of marrying Helen.

The two kings cast their spears simultaneously. An instant later, a cheer erupted from the Greek ranks as Sarpedon's thigh was gashed open and he fell from the car to roll in the dust. Then the cheer died in their throats as they realized the point of Sarpedon's own spear had passed through Tlepolemos's neck, killing the king of Rhodes instantly.

The small force of Tlepolemos's followers gave a shout of anger and rushed forward, to be met head on by Sarpedon's army of Lycians as they ran to defend their wounded king. Through the cloud of dust that obscured the battlefield, Eperitus saw the men of Rhodes overwhelmed and cut down. Though they fought gallantly, the disciplined spears and shields of their enemies were too numerous for them. Gyrtias, their captain, who had accompanied

Tlepolemos to Sparta and befriended Odysseus's small escort of Ithacans there, slew a tall Lycian spearman before being impaled on the spear points of three or four others and sent to accompany his king to the halls of Hades.

With a shout of rage, Odysseus threw his spear into the swarm of Lycians and ran towards them, brandishing his sword. Eperitus and the rest of the Ithacans followed, casting what spears they had left and bringing down several men, but too slow to catch up with their king. Caring little for his own safety, Odysseus tore into the tired enemy soldiers with a blazing fury, hacking wildly to left and right. A man crumpled to his knees, dropping his weapons as he cupped his hands over the gash in his stomach; another fled back through the Trojan lines, holding the stump of his wrist towards the heavens as if imploring the uncaring gods to restore his severed hand; a third crashed into the dust, a corpse with no sign of wound or blood on him. As the Lycians fell back, Odysseus tossed his shield aside, angered by the encumbrance, and began swinging his sword with both hands, knocking shields from men's grips, dashing the weapons from their hands and cutting into flesh so that he became spattered with their gore.

Eperitus and Arceisius joined the fight at their king's side, just as the redoubtable Lycians began to edge around him. Though his limbs were heavy with the long afternoon's toil, Eperitus punched the boss of his shield into an opponent's face and sank his sword into the man's liver. Arceisius severed another's arm from above the elbow and, as the man staggered back in surprise, ran the point of his sword through his throat. The Lycians' discipline crumbled without their king to bolster them and they began to fall back. Led by Odysseus, the Ithacans and the remaining Rhodians fell on them with a new fury. Then a horn blast ripped through the noise of the battle and Hector came racing up in his chariot behind the collapsing Lycians, bellowing at them to hold their ground. He leapt down from the car with two spears in his hand and a fearsome look on his face that struck terror in friend and foe alike. Striding through the ranks of Troy's allies, his mere

GLYN ILIFFE

presence was enough to halt their flight and turn them back up the slope to meet the Greeks. He hurled one of his spears through the shield and breastplate of an Ithacan guardsman, then took the other in both hands and threw himself into the fray, driving all before him.

At the same moment, Eperitus saw Odysseus retrieve his shield and move towards the towering form of the Trojan prince.

'Odysseus!' he shouted, running to the king's side. 'Odysseus, what are you doing? Challenge Hector and he'll kill you for certain. Even Achilles would think twice . . .'

'Do you see Achilles on the battlefield?' Odysseus snapped. 'And even if he was here, do you think I would shirk my duty as a king, to face my enemies whoever and wherever they are? Hector is my enemy, Eperitus, and he is not immortal.'

He turned to go but Eperitus seized his arm.

'But the gods are with him, Odysseus.'

Odysseus threw his hand off with an angry sneer. 'Is he a god himself?'

'Then if Hector is to be challenged, let *me* do it.'

'And what about *me*, Eperitus? Do you think I haven't forgotten that Palamedes accused me of being a coward in front of the whole council? He called me a thief and an impostor, a poor king without fame. And perhaps he was right. Perhaps I've wasted too much time trying to end this war by cunning, when I should have been winning renown on the battlefield like Achilles or Ajax.'

'So that's what this is about,' Eperitus said. 'A sudden desire for glory, just because of the accusations of a traitor? Well, Palamedes was a fool, and what's more he's a *dead* fool – and if you face Hector, you will be, too. In the name of Athena, remember why you've fought so hard all these years, Odysseus – for your family's sake, so you can see them again!'

'Didn't the Pythoness say I'd survive the war and return to Ithaca?' Odysseus countered. 'And what better chance to end this war now than to face Hector and bring him down in the dust? And when I've killed him, no one will ever brand me a coward again.

210

Even Achilles's glory will fade next to mine. So may Athena be with me.'

'Athena is with you,' said a voice.

They turned to see a tall warrior standing behind them. He carried the shield and long spear of a Taphian mercenary, though his skin was oddly white and his hair was not black or brown, but a bright blond that seemed to catch the sunlight wherever it fell from the rim of his helmet. Neither Odysseus or Eperitus could remember seeing his face before, but there was nevertheless a strange familiarity about the large eyes, the thin lips and the straight nose that did not dip at the bridge. The Taphian bent his stern gaze on the Ithacan king, then poked him on the breastplate with his forefinger.

'I am with you, Odysseus – as I have always been – but even *I* can't save your worthless hide if you choose to throw yourself on Hector's spear.'

Odysseus fell to his knees and bowed his head, Hector's presence forgotten.

'Mistress Athena!' he exclaimed.

The goddess quickly pulled him to his feet, making light of his heavy bulk.

'Not in the middle of a battlefield,' she scolded him. 'Can you imagine what others will say if they see the mighty king of Ithaca bobbing and scraping before one of his own mercenaries? A subtle bow would have sufficed. And that goes for you, too, Eperitus.'

Shamed by his omission, Eperitus gave an uncertain nod of his head. Athena rolled her eyes and clicked her tongue.

'I haven't seen you for ten years, my lady,' Odysseus said, looking at the goddess with subdued wonder. 'Not since—'

'I appeared to you on Samos, I know. But it does not mean I've been apart from you all that time. On the contrary, I have kept a very keen eye on you – on *both* of you, in fact. And now a time is coming that will test you, each in your different ways; a test of the strength of your characters and your worthiness to conquer Troy. But your test is not to face Hector, Odysseus, and

I forbid you to pick a fight with him. Leave that trial for those the gods have already chosen.'

'Then am I to be a coward king as Palamedes declared, my name forgotten and without glory?'

Athena shook her head and smiled, reaching out to brush her fingers down the side of Odysseus's beard.

'It's rare that Eperitus speaks with any intelligence, but he was right when he told you Palamedes is a fool and a dead one at that. You will find your glory, son of Laertes, though I know few men more heedless of the warrior's creed. Just use your cunning, the greatest asset the gods awarded to you, and your fame will be established for ever.

'As for you, Eperitus,' she added, turning her grey eyes on him. 'I know the challenges in your heart. And yet your heart is much clearer than your mind, so follow it as you have always done and it will not let you down.'

At that moment another horn call rose above the battle and they turned to see Hector mounting his chariot and riding to another part of the field, where Ajax was driving a company of Trojans back down the slope and leaving chaos and destruction in his wake. Odysseus watched him disappear with a wistful look in his eyes, but when he and Eperitus looked about again Athena was gone.

Chapter Nineteen
HECTOR AND AJAX

The battle raged back and forth and fortunes changed from one side to another as the afternoon wore on. As their men tired, still their captains rallied them to new endeavours, desperately trying to break the deadlock that was slowly beginning to impose itself on the exhausted armies. But for all the efforts of Agamemnon, Menelaus, Diomedes and the other Greek leaders, wherever the fighting was at its hardest and most dangerous, Hector would appear, giving the men of Ilium new courage and determination, while filling their enemies with dismay as he charged into their ranks and brought down their best warriors.

Eventually, the sun began to dip towards the rim of the western ocean, promising twilight and an end to the fighting. Even the hardiest warriors – their limbs aching from the struggle, now barely able to lift their heavy swords or raise their shields for protection – wanted night to come and bring respite so that they could quench their thirsts, rest their weary muscles and count their losses. And so the two armies parted, taking up the positions they had held before Menelaus and Paris had started the day's struggle. Now, though, the opposing battle lines that had filled the slope for as far as the eye could see, their armour gleaming in the sun, were but a phantom of their former glory. The ranks had been thinned hideously and those who remained standing were caked with dust and blood, their shields and helmets dinted and dull. Meanwhile the bodies of their comrades carpeted the plain, banked up in lines where the tides of battle had raged most furiously. Here and there broken forms twitched or called out for help. But none came, for their countrymen were too fatigued to leave the battered mass of the living.

And yet the day's fighting was not over, for into the field of human debris stepped Hector. Though his armour was scarred and dusty, his limbs damp with sweat and gore, he looked unwearied as he raised his spears above his head and faced the Greek lines.

'Trojans! Men of Greece!' he began, speaking first in his own language and then in Greek. 'Whether by treachery or the desire of the gods, the truce we agreed to earlier has been broken. Zeus means the war to go on, and many strong and courageous men have died today to please his will. But the sun is only now entering the waters of the Aegean; there is light still to fight by, if Greece can produce a champion who is worthy of me. Send out the best man you have, and if he can kill me, he can strip me of my armour and boast a greater victory than any other Greek has ever claimed before. Equally, if I kill him, then I will take his armour and dedicate it to the undying gods. Only, let the loser's body be taken back to his own lines for burial and the raising of a tomb that will stand as a monument to himself and his conqueror.'

With that, he pushed his spears into the ground and stood with his arms crossed, surveying the depleted ranks of his enemies. For a long time there was silence as the weary Greeks searched their courage, knowing that Hector's challenge could not go unmet, but each hoping that another would step forward to answer it. Only Odysseus had the desire to face him, still desperate to disprove Palamedes's accusation, but a quick look from Eperitus reminded him of Athena's words and kept him from stepping out. Then, when their silence began to hang over the Greeks like a cloak of shame, Menelaus slipped the shield from his back and took up his spears.

'Not you, brother,' said Agamemnon in a low voice, stepping in front of Menelaus. 'You've fought one duel today, and whether you admit it or not the wound you received has weakened you. I'll not have you throw away your life – and this whole war – for nothing.'

'Have you no shame?' Menelaus hissed. 'Hector is mocking us, while we quake in our armour like children.'

Agamemnon scowled at the suggestion.

'There's no shame in refusing to fight! Even the *great* Achilles is afraid of Hector. Why else has he avoided him on the battlefield for so long?'

'My cousin has never avoided a fight and you know it,' Ajax said beside them in his deep, rumbling voice. 'Achilles is a better man than any here, myself and Hector included. But if no other Greek wants the honour of confronting Hector, then I'll take up the challenge myself.'

'Then we will pray to Zeus for your victory, my friend,' Menelaus said, as Ajax raised his tall shield to his shoulder and picked up his spears.

'Save your prayers for yourselves,' Ajax sneered. 'Any man can claim victory if the gods are with him, but when I've sent Hector's ghost down to the Underworld I want the glory to be given to me alone.'

He walked out from the Greek lines towards Hector, cupping a spear in his right hand as he picked his way across the dead and dying. The sounds of battle had been replaced by the hum of flies and the cawing of carrion birds. To his left the bloated orb of the sun had almost disappeared into the sea, leaving a blood-red smear across the horizon and casting long shadows over the battlefield. The north wind fanned Ajax's face and found its way into the joins of his armour, cooling the hot skin beneath his sweat-sodden tunic. Hector raised his own spear above his shoulder and began to circle, trying to turn his opponent so that he was facing what remained of the sun. Ajax responded by moving closer, keeping the advantage of the slope and forcing Hector back. Then the Trojan gave a shout and hurled his spear. It twisted through the air towards Ajax, too quick to avoid, and punched into the many-layered oxhide, almost ripping the broad shield from his powerful grip.

But it failed to pierce the thick leather and fell into the dirt, the bronze point bent.

Now Ajax advanced, a confident smile breaking his dust-caked beard and face. He pulled his spear back, took aim and launched it with a loud cry that rolled across the battlefield. Hector ducked aside as it sailed past his shoulder, then, with a shout of terrifying rage, charged up the slope with his remaining spear held before him. Ajax lifted his shield and took the point of Hector's weapon full on the boss, turning it aside and catching his opponent off-balance. With terrifying speed, he stabbed upwards with his spear and the force of the thrust cut through the layers of Hector's shield, biting into the side of the Trojan's neck. Hector cried out in pain and flung his shield arm wide, tearing the spear from Ajax's grip.

The two men fell back, Hector clasping his hand over the gash on his neck while Ajax looked around for another spear. Spotting a large rock close to, Hector lifted it above his head and heaved it towards Ajax with a grunt. It struck the rim of the Greek's shield and knocked him back into a heap of corpses, where a momentary darkness covered his eyes and he struggled to draw breath. A jubilant cheer rose up from the Trojan armies at the bottom of the slope as Hector drew his sword and strode confidently towards the fallen giant. Before he could reach him, Ajax staggered to his feet and seized the same boulder that had struck him down. He lifted it above his head as if it weighed no more than a child and sent it whirling towards Hector.

It caught the Trojan on the front of his shield, crumpling the wooden frame and smashing him to the ground. With a shout of triumph, Ajax drew his sword and lumbered towards his prey. At the last moment, Hector sensed Ajax's shadow fall across him and rolled aside, just as the king of Salamis plunged his blade into the ground where Hector's body had been. Hector's dazed senses snapped back into focus and he aimed a kick at the huge warrior as he stood over him, catching him just above the groin and sending him reeling backwards, howling in pain. Then he found his sword and, prising another shield from its dead owner's fingers, leapt to his feet just in time to stop Ajax's blade from splitting his head down the middle.

They threw themselves at each other now with a terrifying fury that silenced the armies above and below them and had men looking on at the duel in awe. Their blades made hollow thuds against the leather of their shields as they forgot their tiredness and tried to beat each other into submission. But the sun had sunk below the horizon and a dusky light had settled over the battle-field, choked by the haze of dust that still hung there. And then two horns sounded above the noise of battle.

Ajax and Hector both turned to see Agamemnon, Talthybius and Idaeus. The Greek and Trojan heralds held horns in their hands, while Agamemnon signalled for the two combatants to part.

'Friends, the sun has gone and the light is following fast. Hold your arms now and call the fight a draw. Be satisfied that you both live and have earned more honour for yourselves.'

'If our fight is to end honourably, then let Ajax and I part as friends, if only until tomorrow,' Hector said, his breathing heavy and his voice more hoarse than ever. Returning his sword to its scabbard and unslinging it from his shoulder, he presented the silver-studded handle towards his opponent. 'Ajax, I have never before fought a man like you. Truly, unless another of your comrades can find the skill to beat me in battle, you are the greatest of the Greeks and I give you honour and friendship.'

He bowed and Ajax took the weapon from his hand, admiring the craftsmanship on the handle and the ornate sheath, before withdrawing the blade and feeling its weight in his hand. Then he draped the baldric over his shoulder and unslipped the purple belt from about his own waist, offering it to the Trojan prince.

'Any man who can still get up and fight after I've flattened him with a boulder is worthy of my friendship. Take this belt as a reminder of our fight and wear it with honour, knowing that today you faced a man who has no equal in battle – mortal or immortal.'

'A dangerous boast, even for a warrior of your quality,' Hector

217

replied, fastening the belt around his waist. 'The time may come when the gods will make you regret your words. But now we must thank them we are still alive and call the day's fighting over.'

Paris lay on the wide, fur-covered bed, his eyes firmly closed in sleep. He was dressed in a white, knee-length tunic – his armour long since removed – and Helen was curled up beside him, resting his head in her lap while she dabbed at his wounded scalp with a damp cloth. The bedroom smelled of her perfume, and though the sun had gone down, the stuccoed walls, white drapes and large windows kept the room bright and airy. The only sound was the swish of the cloth as Helen dipped it into a bowl of warm, slightly scented water; although from time to time, when the north wind dropped a little, the sound of wailing women could also be heard rising up from the lower city.

Helen looked down at her husband and smiled. With Menelaus dead, she thought, the Greeks would soon give up the fight and return home, and then she and Paris would at last be free to enjoy their marriage. There would be no more slaughter for her sake, no more worry that her husband was throwing himself recklessly into battle because of a misguided sense of guilt. And if there remained widows and orphans who could not forgive her presence in their city, that was something she could live with. Had she not left Pergamos at night on countless occasions, veiled and cloaked, to leave gifts of food, even silver and gold, for those who had lost husbands and fathers? She would have to live with the blame for Troy's dead for the rest of her life, but after so long trapped behind the city's walls she did not intend to remain imprisoned for their sake. Besides, there were many who loved her, including Priam and Hector, Hecabe and Andromache, and as long as they were happy for her to live with them then she would be content.

She dampened the cloth again and continued gently dabbing it against the wound, careful not to press too hard where Menelaus's sword had crushed Paris's helmet into the flesh of his head. Then she heard raised voices in the corridor beyond their bedroom and as she looked up the door burst open and a man in dust-covered, bloodstained armour came crashing into the room. He carried a tall spear in his right hand and a Greek shield over his left shoulder, while strapped round his waist was a belt of bright purple. Helen gasped in shock, momentarily fearing the Greeks had somehow entered the citadel. Then, through the dust and gore, she recognized her brother-in-law.

'Hector!'

'Get up!' Hector ordered, ignoring Helen and pointing a finger at Paris. *'Get up this instant!'*

'He's sleeping,' Helen protested, bending over her husband protectively as Hector strode across the room towards them. 'He collapsed the moment he was brought into the city and hasn't woken since.'

Hector seemed unable to hear her. Seizing the bowl from beside Helen's feet, he poured the contents over his brother's face before throwing it into a corner, where it smashed into smithereens. Paris shook his head and sat up, wiping the water from his eyes.

'Where am I?'

'In the comfort of your own house, damn it, while every other man in Troy has been toiling and dying for your sake! The plains are black with bodies and all the time you've been lying here in your wife's arms. You disgust me!'

'But it's—' Paris began, then looked through one of the windows to see the first stars pricking the evening sky. 'Gods! Have I slept all this time? Why wasn't I woken?'

'You needed to rest,' Helen replied as his eyes fell on her. 'So what if others have had to fight without you for a while? Don't you already do more than your share in this war?'

Hector grabbed his brother by the arm and pulled him from the sodden bed.

'As long as Paris is responsible for Agamemnon's presence on our shores, sister, he can never be seen to do more than his share. The men of Ilium have suffered grievously today, as have the

Greeks – thousands dead and nearly as many badly wounded. At this very moment the elders are debating whether to return you to Menelaus and end the war, and if Paris wants to keep you here he had better get down to the palace gates and defend himself before it's too late.'

Paris and Helen looked at each other.

'But Menelaus is dead,' Helen declared.

'I saw him shot,' Paris added. 'He fell before my very eyes and his body was carried away by Agamemnon.'

'You fool,' Hector chided him. 'It was a flesh wound only and, unlike you, Menelaus rejoined the fighting as soon as he could. Now, get your cloak and sandals and get down to the palace gates before they send your wife back to Menelaus in your absence.'

Paris gave his brother a black look, but knew that his anger was justified. While he had been allowed to sleep through the day, Hector had performed Zeus only knew what feats on the battlefield on his behalf.

'I'm sorry, Hector,' Paris said, pulling on his sandals and throwing a cloak around his shoulders. Then, with a final glance at his wife, he swept from the room.

'Aren't you going?' Helen asked Hector as Paris's footsteps finally receded out of earshot.

'I've already argued your case,' he replied, a little calmer now, 'but it'll help if Paris is there to defend himself. Apheidas and Aeneas are also standing up for you, but there are some among the council whose sons won't return from the battlefield. They're stirring up a storm of anger against you.'

'Then will I be sent back to Greece?'

For the first time since entering, Hector smiled. 'You forget the final decision always lies with Priam, and he loves you above all his sons' wives. And now I must return to Andromache, if only until dawn calls me out to the plain again. Goodnight, Helen.'

'You were too hard on him, you know,' she said, taking hold of Hector's hand. 'Paris would have gone out on to the battlefield again. It was my fault for not waking him. The whole war is my fault.'

'The blame for this war lies with no man or woman, sister,' Hector assured her. 'It's the will of the gods and nothing more. As for my anger against your husband, I ask you to forgive me. I love Paris, and I'm only worried that voices will be raised against him for his absence today. *I* know he would have been there.'

With that he took his spear from the doorjamb where he had leaned it and, giving a final bow, left the room. Helen flopped back down on to the bed, confused and concerned. Though Hector had sought to reassure her about the outcome of the debate – and she did not want to leave Troy and be forced to return to Sparta – it also meant the war would continue and Paris would again take unnecessary risks in battle. When she had threatened to return to her former husband if Paris continued to pointlessly endanger himself, she had not expected him to respond by challenging Menelaus in single combat; and now she was worried he would do the same again. Was that what Hector really wanted, for his brother to sacrifice his life needlessly? Did he want the war to end in such a way and all the Trojan lives that had been lost to count for nothing? And did he not love Helen and want her to remain in Troy? Then surely he would listen to reason and order Paris to stay out of the fighting.

Suddenly she knew what she had to do. She pulled a cloak around her shoulders, drew the hood over her head and ran out into the corridor, her sandals making faint scuffing sounds on the stone floor. Hector lived in an annex of the palace close to the city's northern watchtower, and it was but a matter of moments before she was at the pillared threshold of his house. The slaves were busily lighting torches in the small courtyard beyond, where the scent of flowers mingled with the smell of the flames. They bowed as she swept past them and up the stairs to the second level, where Hector and Andromache had their bedroom. She rehearsed what she would say as she walked the corridors, wondering whether to rely on her feminine charm or appeal to Hector's pity to get him to order Paris out of the fighting. But as she approached the bedroom door she heard low voices, one of them tearful, and felt suddenly awkward at the thought of intruding. Instead, she moved quietly to the door and peered through the gap where it had been left ajar.

Hector was still in his grimed and battered armour. Andromache was holding his giant hands in hers, her fine white dress smeared with dust and blood where she had embraced her husband. Her cheeks were stained with tears as her dark eyes looked up into his.

'I couldn't bring myself to watch the battle,' she said, sniffing. 'But my maids were on the walls. They said you were always where the fighting was hardest, like a man stamping out fires, always leaping into your chariot and riding from one point of the battle to another.'

'Then they've reported truthfully,' he said with a smile, raising a curled forefinger to her cheek and brushing away a tear. 'But now I'm back in your arms, my love.'

Andromache choked back a sob, then lowered her head and let the tears flow freely.

'Then where were Paris and Aeneas, and Sarpedon and Apheidas, and all those other kings and princes and captains of Ilium? Are you to run all the risks yourself?'

Hector wrapped his arms around her and folded her into his armoured chest.

'The fighting was the hardest I've ever known it, and those of us whom the gods made leaders bore the worst of it. Paris was struck down by Menelaus and should have died, if the sword hadn't broken. Aeneas was almost killed by Diomedes with a rock; Sarpedon was wounded in the leg; Pandarus was killed, and many other men of high renown besides. And that left Apheidas holding the centre and myself dashing around like a Fury.'

'But this bravery will be the end of you,' Andromache protested. She pointed to a wooden cot at the foot of their bed. 'Don't

Chapter Twenty
THE VALLEY OF THE DEAD

That evening the Greeks moved back to the top of the ridge, away from the mangled corpses of the fallen. The ordinary soldiers gathered in sullen groups around large fires, to mourn their dead comrades and rue the absence of Achilles, who most believed would have turned the battle in their favour. While his army grumbled against him, Agamemnon declared a great victory and celebrated it with the sacrifice of a five-year-old bull. Ajax was awarded the choicest cut of meat for his duel against Hector, and even Diomedes, who had also fought with god-like valour, did not dispute that the king of Salamis deserved the honour. But the mood among the other leaders was as melancholy as their men's, tired as they were by their exertions and disheartened by their failure to rout the Trojans. Despite the King of Men's triumphant claims, few could deny their enemies had proved they were a match for the Greeks; many were already beginning to believe the tenth year of the war would prove as inconclusive as every other before it.

After the meal, Nestor called the leaders to council. Few spoke as a thick bank of cloud rolled out of the east and extinguished the heavenly lights above them. Odysseus was particularly quiet, his eyes dark and brooding as he sat beside Eperitus and held his palms out to the hastily made fire. Eperitus looked at the handful of gaps left by the captains who had fallen, Tlepolemos chief among them, and understood his friend's mood. A chance to finish the war had come and gone, and Odysseus must have been wondering if he would ever see his home and family again. He must also have been pondering the words of Athena, as Eperitus was himself.

Agamemnon prayed to Zeus for victory and, after they had poured libations into the dust at their feet, Nestor took the staff from the king of Mycenae's hand and turned to face the circle of men. He began by suggesting they call for a two-day truce to gather and burn the dead, and after receiving the firm agreement of the council added that they should also use the time to finish the camp's defences – building the wall that had been suggested long ago but never started, fitting gates and deepening the ditch. The King of Men objected immediately, calling the proposal defeatist and holding his hand out for the staff. Nestor ignored him and, turning back to the council, began extolling the courage of the Trojans and Hector in particular. The Greeks needed a last line of defence if the gods continued to favour the Trojans, he argued, for they could no longer count on Achilles to help them. This angered Agamemnon, but the rest of the council supported Nestor and agreed that the wall should be built.

Eperitus was woken the next morning by the feel of rain on his face. His limbs were stiff and heavy and he was tempted to throw the blanket over his head and fall back into sleep, but instead he raised himself on one elbow and looked to the east, where a faint greyness was creeping over the distant mountains. All around him were the humped shapes of his comrades, some fully covered by their blankets, others continuing to snore despite the light drizzle that was falling from the stony heavens. Odysseus was close by, silent and still, only the faint movement of his shoulders indicating he was still breathing.

Quietly and stiffly, Eperitus stood and rolled up his blanket. Then, shaking out his balled-up cloak, which had acted as his pillow, he threw it around his shoulders and went over to the nearest picket fire. Polites and Omeros were there, staring down the slope at the thousands of dark, formless shapes that were just becoming visible in the pre-dawn light. Both men looked up at him as he joined them, their faces pale and their eyes starkly white in the gloom.

'The rain woke me,' he explained as he sat down, but Polites raised his fingers to his lips and nodded down the hill.

Eperitus could see anxiety in his face, something he had never known in the giant warrior before, and realized it was more than the stress that followed a hard day's fighting. He peered down the slope, his keen eyesight struggling against the darkness and the shroud of thin, clinging rain. For a while all he could see were the shapes of the dead, blurred and indistinct and devoid of the individuality that life had once given them. And then he saw it, another shape moving over the heaped corpses, its cloak catching in the light wind that blew out of the north. For a moment Eperitus thought someone was despoiling the dead – a common feature of battlefields in darkness – but then he noticed that the tall figure seemed to be gliding slowly, not pausing or stooping to rob the broken bodies at its feet. Suddenly Eperitus understood who the figure was and a chill of recognition shuddered through him.

'He's been there most of the night,' Omeros commented, his eyes fixed on the slope below. 'He was there when Polites and I came on watch, and the men we replaced said they had first noticed him at dusk. No one has dared go down to challenge him. We think he's a god – or a ghost.'

'It's Hermes, collecting the souls of the dead,' Eperitus said, recalling his own experience of the god many years before.

Omeros simply nodded and pulled his knees to his chest, resting his chin on them and looking with dejection at the figure in the semi-darkness. Somehow he had survived his first battle, but the young singer of songs also knew one small twist of fate could have meant his own ghost being caught up beneath Hermes's cloak and ushered down to the Underworld. The thought of it put fear in his eyes as he watched the god moving over the bodies of the slain, but Eperitus could see that it was a controlled fear. His own long experience of war had shown him more than enough men who had lost all discipline in the face of terror and succumbed to dumb panic. Omeros, he was pleased to note, was not one of them.

As they watched, the darkness slowly became suffused by a grey half-light. Scattered voices began to break the silence of the sleeping army behind them, causing the figure on the slopes to turn and stare at the picket fires on the ridge, as if noticing them for the first time. Then it began to laugh, a deep, mocking sound that seemed to rise up from the ground beneath their feet, filling their heads with despair and loathing as if a finger of doom had been laid upon the whole army. Eperitus pressed his hands over his ears and squeezed his eyes shut, only opening them again when he felt the heaviness suddenly lift from his heart. Hermes had gone, like smoke in a breeze, but in the nascent light of the new day he saw that another shape was picking its way towards them over the bodies of the dead. But this was no god: it was Idaeus, the ageing Trojan herald, who raised a ram's horn to his lips and sent a long, clear note into the air above the battlefield.

He was taken to Agamemnon, where a two-day halt to hostilities was arranged so that both sides could retrieve their dead. After he had gone, Nestor advised that each king or leader should divide his men in half, sending the less hardy back to the camp to build the walls with as much speed as possible, while the more resilient were to remain on the ridge and begin the painful process of gathering the fallen. After the sun had cleared the eastern mountains, though unseen behind the belly of grey clouds that filled the sky from horizon to horizon, the men ate a cold breakfast and then the army was split into two. As half marched back to build the walls, carts and chariots passed them in the opposite direction, sent to collect the bodies and take them back for burning.

The different contingents of the Greek army moved to the parts of the slope where they had fought the day before, looking for their comrades among heaped corpses. The rain fell more heavily now, rattling on helmets and breastplates and soaking into woollen clothing so that every man was soon cold to the bone. It turned the powdery dust of the battlefield to mud, making men slip and struggle as they lifted armoured bodies on to their shoulders and carried them to the waiting carts. Ironically, the rain was not heavy enough to wash away the dust and blood that made many of the dead unrecognizable, so men were detailed to carry pails of water and wash the filth of battle from their faces. Others had lost heads or were too disfigured to identify, and only their armour or clothing distinguished them as Greek or Trojan. Occasionally there would be a shout of despair or a stifled cry as men came across their friends, but Agamemnon had forbidden displays of grief before the Trojans and so the warriors shed their tears in silence.

Similar orders must have been given to the Trojans, so that the only sound that persisted through that long day was the hiss of the rain and the trickle of the small brown rivulets that had formed on the hillside and ran down to join the Scamander. The men of both sides – murderous enemies only a day before – now mingled cautiously as they searched the same heaps of bodies for their comrades. Occasionally a Greek might give a surly nod to a Trojan, or vice versa, and sometimes one side would separate their enemy's dead from their own and then call across to indicate the pile. Otherwise there was little communication between them: they were still rivals in a deadly contest, and the previous day's fighting had left feelings of hatred and revenge on both sides.

Eperitus spent as much time scanning the faces of the Trojans as he did the pale, lifeless faces of the dead. After years of loathing the men of Troy, he found it hard to believe their blood ran in his own veins or that he could have anything at all in common with them; and yet, as he watched them gather their dead, he could not help but admire the strength they had shown in battle. Before yesterday, they had only ventured beyond their own walls to fight limited skirmishes – small clashes to foil Greek plans and in which they had been aided by information from the traitor Palamedes. But now they had attempted to break the deadlock – perhaps because they had been blinded by the loss of Palamedes and could no longer anticipate the next Greek attack – and had proved themselves a formidable enemy, worthy of respect. As he looked at them he found himself thinking of Astynome and how she had asked him to go with her to Troy, even to become a Trojan. Had he made the right choice? he wondered, and the moment the thought entered his head he was appalled that he should think such a thing. Had not the Pythoness warned him against betraying his friends for the sake of love, all those years ago? Was this the challenge in his heart Athena had spoken of? He stared around at the faces of the dead, gazing up into the rain with soulless eyes; too many of them were Greeks, killed in a war that the Trojans had caused. Picking up the body of one of the most recent batch of Ithacan reinforcements, a lad whose name he had heard but could not remember, he threw it across his shoulder and trudged angrily up the slope towards a half-filled cart.

'Eperitus!' called a voice.

He dropped the body into the cart and turned to see the barrel-like figure of Peisandros jumping down from the back of a newly arrived wagon.

'Eperitus,' he repeated, seizing the Ithacan's hand and pulling him into a hug. 'I'm glad to see you survived the fighting. They say it was a hard day.'

'See for yourself,' Eperitus replied, sweeping an arm towards the corpse-strewn battlefield, where more than half the bodies still remained where they had fallen. 'We could have done with the help of the Myrmidons. Is that why you're here? Has Achilles decided to rejoin the fighting?'

Peisandros shook his head despondently. 'You know how proud he is, Eperitus; it'll take a lot of grovelling from Agamemnon before he takes up his spear and shield and fights for the Greeks again. No, I came here to see if things are as bad as they're saying back at the camp – and from the corpses I passed on the way and those that are left, I'd say it was worse. What about Odysseus and the others?'

'I'm well,' said the king, appearing beside the cart with a body over his shoulder. He laid it down on top of the others and paused to brush a tumble of hair from its face, then embraced the Myrmidon spearman warmly. 'And the others, too – Eurylochus, Polites, Arceisius and Antiphus all came through safely. But why's Achilles still hanging back, Peisandros? Can't he see he's missing all the glory, and that we *need* him?'

Peisandros rubbed his chin and looked down the slope.

'He knows you need him. In fact, it's *his* fault the Greeks are being slaughtered in the first place.'

'How can it be Achilles's fault?' asked Eperitus.

'You forget his mother is chief of the Nereids. He asked her to speak to Zeus for him, so the father of the gods would give the upper hand to the Trojans. He wants Agamemnon to be humiliated and the Greeks made to see they're helpless without him.'

'But that's ludicrous,' Odysseus protested. 'He's fought at our sides the whole campaign; why would he turn against us for the sake of Agamemnon's arrogance?'

'Do you think we haven't asked ourselves the same question?' Peisandros retorted. 'It has to be this war. We've had ten years of fighting and the savagery gets to us all in the end, even Achilles. Perhaps him most of all. After all, he's lived every day here knowing he will never leave Ilium alive, and that can't be easy for any man. That and his rigid pride; I'm only surprised something like this hasn't happened before. Anyway, now I'm here I'll help you with the bodies. We've a lot of work to do if we're to clear the field by sundown.'

They moved back down the slope, Peisandros looking with sad eyes at the terrible slaughter all around him, and resumed the work of retrieving their dead countrymen. Above them, cart after cart squealed away with their bloody burdens, the teams of oxen plodding slowly through the thick mud and sheet rain. That the heavens could contain so much water seemed impossible to those that toiled beneath it – especially in the middle of a Trojan spring – but as Peisandros commented, at least it kept the flies off the bodies. Then Odysseus spotted Omeros, sitting among the dead with his head in his hands. Beside him was Elpenor, another of the recent arrivals from Ithaca, whose young face had gained years in a single day; a skin of wine was clutched between his knees and his glassy eyes were staring emptily across the Scamander towards Troy. Together they had carried the bodies one by one to the carts, but now it seemed the task had defeated their will to carry on. Odysseus took pity on them.

'Omeros,' he called, 'give us a song, lad.'

Omeros lifted his head and stared vaguely at his king.

'A song, my lord? Here?'

'Yes, here. If men can sing *about* battlefields, why can't they sing *on* battlefields? Give us something to take our minds off . . . off our work.'

'Yes, sir.'

Omeros dragged himself to his feet and looked down into the valley of the dead. His cheeks were flushed with tears and for a moment Eperitus thought he might just sit back down and bury his face in his hands once more. But he remained standing and, after accepting a swallow of wine from the skin Elpenor held up to him, he cleared his throat and raised his chin a touch.

At first, his voice was a soft, quiet sound, almost drowned by the patter of the rain. A few of the men looked up and saw a small, pale-faced lad standing on the slopes above them, before ignoring him and returning to their grim work. Eperitus looked at Odysseus and was about to speak, but the king placed a finger to his lips. As he did so Omeros's voice rose a little and the words became more distinguishable. But where Eperitus had expected a dirge, he was surprised to recognize a popular song about the seven heroes who had fought to conquer Thebes during the dark days of the Greek civil wars. It told of their deaths before the walls of the city, of their heroism, courage and sacrifice for one another, and as the young bard's voice found itself and began to rise above the sound of the rain, Eperitus felt his throat thicken and tears come to his eyes. The men on the slopes stopped working and looked up, standing and listening as the song's words spread their net about them, pulling them in deeper and deeper as the young bard grew in confidence, forgetting the rain and the oppressive darkness and singing as if he would never have the chance to sing again.

Then another voice added itself to Omeros's, low and resonant but equally engaging. Eperitus looked at Odysseus in mute surprise, then began to sing himself, quietly at first but with growing conviction as the combined voices rang out across the battlefield. Even the Trojans were stopping and listening.

Before long the song was being picked up and repeated along the whole line of the ridge, by Ithacans, Argives, Spartans, Mycenaeans and men of every nation, honouring the glorious dead with their voices as they carried their bodies to the waiting carts.

Chapter Twenty-One

THE STORM

The rain hissed in the courtyard outside the great hall on Ithaca. It drummed against the doors and the roof of the portico, and came in through the vent in the centre of the ceiling. Penelope stroked her fingertips lightly over Argus's head as he lay beside her chair, thumping his tail against the floor. Phronius sat opposite the queen on a high-backed chair, his white hair and beard still matted with the rain. His cloak was hanging from the back of another chair, turned about so that it faced the flames of the hearth. A faint steam was rising out of the thick wool.

'He offered you *gold* to resign from the Kerosia?' Mentor asked, the disbelief clear in his tone.

'You heard me right,' Phronius croaked toothlessly. 'Enough gold and other wealth to see me through to my dying day. Very generous, I'd have called him, too, if he wasn't such a devious old serpent. Not that he ever fooled Laertes or me with his supposed *change of heart*.'

'I wonder if he ever really fooled Odysseus,' said Penelope.

'I didn't mean any criticism of the king . . .' Phronius protested.

'Of course you didn't, and your loyalty to him has put Odysseus in your debt. The fact that Eupeithes was prepared to offer you a bribe proves my suspicions were true – he wants to take control of the Kerosia, and perhaps he's not that bothered who knows it.'

'He should be,' Halitherses snarled. 'I'll collect a dozen guards-men in the morning and arrest him.'

Mentor shook his head.

'He wasn't so careless as to make the offer in person. It was only suggested through an acquaintance and, despite Phronius's convictions, Eupeithes wasn't mentioned by name. We have no proof.'

'Give me tomorrow morning with him in a quiet storeroom and I'll get you all the proof you need,' Halitherses replied, gripping the edge of his chair.

'We aren't tyrants, old friend,' Penelope said, her calm voice belying the look of concern in her eyes. 'We have no choice but to wait for him to make a mistake and reveal his crooked inten-tions more openly. Until then, we will have to simply watch our backs.'

'You must look out for the boy, too,' Phronius added, leaning forward on to his staff as he slowly levered himself from his chair. He signalled for one of the servants to fetch his cloak. 'If Eupeithes is gambling Odysseus won't return and thinks he can take power through the Kerosia, at some point he will have to deal with Telemachus. Even if Odysseus doesn't come back from Troy – forgive me, my lady – Telemachus will inherit the throne at twenty-one. Eupeithes knows that.'

He emphasized his point by staring at each of the others in turn, Penelope last and longest. Not that he needed to make her understand: she had long known the dangers that surrounded her son, and more so with the reawakening of Eupeithes's treacherous nature. Her fears had not been helped by an instinctive knowledge that the fighting in Ilium had started again, and that her husband was in greater danger than he had ever been before.

The servant draped the cloak over Phronius's frame and the old man, too bent already to make a meaningful bow, satisfied himself with a nod to the queen.

'And now I will beg your leave. It may be a short walk to my hut for some, but at my age it's still quite a trek.'

'Let me walk with you, Phronius,' Halitherses offered, rising from his chair. 'It's growing dark and—'

Phronius gave a dismissive wave of his stick and stumped off to the doors of the great hall, which were opened for him by two armed soldiers. Outside, the rain had slowed to a steady drizzle, but the uneven courtyard was a patchwork of puddles, the largest forming a small lake at the bottom step of the portico. Phronius made a resigned huffing sound and stepped into it. The water was above his ankles in an instant, and by the time he had reached the gates and the terrace beyond, both feet and the hem of his cloak were soaked and filthy with the mud of the courtyard.

Phronius's hut lay a little beyond the eastern edge of the town, on a grassy shelf of rock that overlooked the sea. It was distant enough for him to keep his own company – which he preferred to the pestering interference of town life – and the views at sunrise were enough to make a man happy just to be alive. The seagulls cawed and screeched from dawn until dusk and the crashing of the waves on the rocks below the grassy shelf never ceased, but he had grown used to the din of it many years ago and now he doubted he would get to sleep without it.

Before long, even at his creeping pace, he had passed the outskirts of the town and could see the grey wisp of smoke rising up from the roof of his own hut. It was barely visible in the growing darkness, through the haze of fine rain, but he greeted the phantom-like column with a satisfied grunt, knowing he would soon be tucked up in his bed until the first glimmer of dawn woke him. Indeed, his body was so heavy with tiredness, he felt as if he would sleep for ever.

Then he saw a figure rise up from the rocks at the side of the path. The man stepped out in front of him and planted his legs shoulder-width apart.

'Who's there?' Phronius asked, slipping his hand down to grasp the neck of his staff. In younger hands it would make an effective club; in his feeble, arthritic fingers it did not even amount to a threat.

'Friends,' came another voice, this time behind him.

Phronius twisted around to see a second man blocking the route back to the town – as if he would have been able to escape anyway. His voice was young and faintly familiar, despite being muffled by the cloth that hid the lower half of his face.

'Friends to whom?' Phronius challenged.

'That depends. Have you thought about the offer that was made to you?'

'Hmph!' Phronius replied.

He carried on along the path towards the first man, who had also masked his lower face. To Phronius's surprise he stepped aside and let him pass, but both men followed him at a short distance.

'That's not an answer,' the second man called, raising his voice over the crash and boom of the waves as they neared Phronius's hut.

'It's all the answer you'll get.'

Phronius reached the grassy shelf of rock and drew confidence from the sight of his hut, built under the shelter of an inward-leaning cliff face. He could smell the woodsmoke much more strongly now, as well as the pot of stew he had left warming over the embers of the hearth. If he could get inside, the old spear he kept behind the door would even matters. But he never reached the hut. In a few easy strides, the first man placed himself between Phronius and his home, and this time his cloak was thrown back to reveal the gleam of a dagger in his belt.

Then a hand fell heavily on Phronius's shoulder and he was dragged forcefully to the lip of the rock shelf. He caught a glimpse of the black waves far below and the foaming lines of jagged boulders that awaited his frail body.

'Think carefully, old man,' hissed the second assailant, clutching at his robe and dangling him backwards over the cliff edge. His eyes were fearful and uncertain, but with a dangerous edginess about them. 'You've proved your loyalty to Odysseus time and time again, nobody can deny that. But the king won't be coming back from Troy, so it's time for you to stand down from the Kerosia and let a younger voice take your place.'

With a speed that surprised even himself, Phronius hooked his fingers into the cloth that covered the man's mouth and tore it away from his face.

'Antinous!' he exclaimed, recognizing the haughty features of Eupeithes's only son. 'I should have realized it was you. And will the voice that replaces mine on the Kerosia be yours?'

'Yes, and why not? The Kerosia needs some younger heads to replace the old fools Odysseus left behind.'

'Go to Hades, Antinous. You'll be nothing more than a mouthpiece for your treacherous father, and I'd rather die than allow that to happen.'

'So be it,' Antinous sneered.

He splayed his fingers, releasing the folds of Phronius's cloak. The old man's heels scuffed pathetically against the cliff edge for an instant, kicking off one of his sandals, and then he was falling into nothingness. He felt a momentary lightness and freedom from the cramped and twisted prison of his body, then his ankle caught an outcrop of rock, spinning him around so that his head was mangled by the cliff face. Phronius was dead before his body could be impaled on the black teeth below, or the powerful waves could snatch him away and fill his lungs with salt water.

On the slopes above the Scamander, the passing of the sun was marked only by a deeper greyness; with the onset of night came distant rumbles of thunder and an increase in the wind. Lightning lit the clouds above the eastern mountains, and by its intermittent flashes the last of the bodies were hauled from the battlefield and carried away.

While the rest of the army struggled to make fires in the wind and rain, Odysseus offered to take Peisandros back to the ships in his chariot. After a difficult journey in the darkness, they passed between the great mounds of the dead – fifty of them at least – and so came to the edge of the camp. By this time the storm had rolled westward towards the sea, and as a bolt of lightning parted the clouds the newly built walls sprang up from the other side of the ditch. They had already been raised to the height of a man and the rain-washed bricks gleamed wetly as the stark light bounced off them, before disappearing again and leaving only an impression of a deeper darkness where the walls had been. They reached a causeway marked by torches and guarded by bronze-clad soldiers, where Peisandros leapt down. He accepted Odysseus's hand in farewell, as the blustering wind made words useless, and then the king turned his chariot around and sent the frightened horses back as fast as they would go to the ridge above the Scamander valley.

As the next day arrived, overcast but without rain, Agamemnon changed his mind about the wall and decided that every effort should now be thrown into making it higher and thicker, while the ditch before it should be dug deeper and filled with sharpened poles. Perhaps unnerved by the sight of the dead piled up on the plain beyond the camp, he ordered the army back from their positions overlooking the Scamander and set them to work on the defences. This caused resentment from the men who had fought to defend the ridge and strongly worded protests from their leaders, who knew the strategic value of such a position in the face of a Trojan army that was suddenly intent on facing them in the open. But Agamemnon refused to listen, insisting the men were needed to help build the wall and cut down hundreds of trees, to supply wood for the gates and the stakes, as well as provide fuel for the funeral pyres.

These were lit at midday and quickly filled the air with the stench of burning flesh. Great columns of black smoke twisted upwards to mingle with the low clouds, and shortly afterwards were followed by similar columns from Troy. The different Greek armies stood around the pyres where their comrades' bodies were stacked and as the flames fed greedily the men raised their spears and shouted three times to the heavens. It was a shout of grief and despair, pride and defiance, and glorification of the dead. Once they had saluted the fallen they returned to their tasks, their already stiff limbs labouring hard in the sunless warmth. Eventually, as the sun went down on the second and final day of the truce, the wall was complete, its gates fitted and its ditch made almost uncrossable by man or horse. The Greeks set a line of pickets on the plain and more guards on the wall, then returned to their tents. Here they feasted and drank, easing their grief and tiredness with a newly arrived shipment of wine from Lemnos. As they lay down to sleep the sky rumbled with distant thunder, but no storm came and the rain held.

At dawn, the gates in the new wall were thrown open and the chariots of the Greek leaders dashed out, followed by endless columns of infantry and cavalry. They trudged over the causeways that bridged the ditch and formed up in dense blocks on the plain beyond with their standards trailing above them. Overhead, the skies were like an ocean of pale grey marble, streaked with skeins of darker cloud that twisted and curled across the face of the monotonous mass. The distant thunder of the previous evening still rumbled over the tortured surface of the Aegean, and as the army began its slow, all-consuming march towards Troy, the rain began to fall.

Eperitus heard the approach of the Trojan army long before any of the others and knew that they must have spent the night camped on the ridge where the previous battle had taken place. Now they were advancing across the pastureland towards them, and this time the Greeks would not have the advantage of the higher ground. Then, through the curtains of grey that swept west to east across the plain, he saw them: row upon row of shields, helmets and spears, shining dully in the pallid light that filtered from above. He called to Odysseus who, trusting to his captain's eyesight, drove his chariot across the line towards Agamemnon. Soon, orders were being shouted and the whole army tensed like a muscle, the lines of warriors drawing closer together and their lumbering movement becoming suddenly tighter as their step found a unified rhythm. In contrast, the units of skirmishers moved forward at a run, losing any sense of formation as they spread out and pulled the bows from their backs.

Now every man in the army could see their foe in the near distance. The terrible fighting of three days before seemed to have had no effect on their numbers, as the wall of their shields spread in a long line across the plain, the threatening packs of cavalry only just visible on each flank. The skirmishers of both sides rushed into range and released deadly swarms of arrows at each other. Men fell thickly, their death cries strangely dampened by the hissing rain. But the main armies did not wait for the archery duel to be decided: kings and princes sent their chariots to the rear and led their men into battle on foot, quickening their pace as they passed through the archers and came within spear-shot of their hated enemies.

Odysseus tossed his spear up so that it sat in the palm of his right hand, then, pulling it back over his shoulder, dashed forward and hurled it with a great shout at the Trojan lines. No order had been given, but on both sides men instinctively knew the range at which their weapons would be effective and the two armies surged forward simultaneously to fill the air with missiles. A moment later the bronze points bit home, piercing shield, cuirass and helmet as if they were little more than wool. Screams rang out and men crumpled all around, driven into the ground by the unstoppable force of the spears that took their lives. Brief holes appeared in the densely packed ranks of men, only to be filled in an instant as the two armies lowered their weapons and surged towards each other.

Odysseus sensed Eperitus's familiar presence at his side, and though they were running headlong at a line of viciously sharpened spear points he felt no fear knowing that his friend was there. Then, letting out a shout of defiance at his enemies, he plunged between their long lances and pushed the head of his weapon into the shoulder of a man whose face was but a momentary blur as the bronze tore through his flesh and sent him crashing to the thick mud at his feet. Eperitus downed the man next to him and together he and Odysseus began to drive a wedge into the enemy line, not allowing their foes time to close up the gaps left by their headlong charge. A man pushed his spear at Odysseus's stomach, only for the king to knock it aside with his shield and bury his own spear into his attacker's chest. It pierced the overlapping bronze scales and ruptured his heart, felling him in a moment. Eperitus was less precise. He punched his shield into a Trojan warrior, knocking him to the ground and stepping across him to sink his deadly bronze into the throat of the soldier behind, a youth whose ill-fitting helmet had slipped forward over his eyes and blinded him.

On either side of them the Ithacans were fighting with equal fury, many striking down their opponents and as many more falling to the ill-fortune of war. The air was filled with the clamour of battle: the metallic clang of weapons that rang in a man's skull for days afterwards; the familiar grunts and cries of men fighting and dying; the hiss of rain and the sound of it drumming on leather and bronze; and over everything the rumble of the storm as it drew inland. Light flickered in the belly of the cloud, followed short moments later by a loud crash. Odysseus glanced to the side and saw Eperitus hacking left and right with his sword, his face an unrecognizable mask of wrath as he spread havoc and death among his enemies. Then he sensed a figure rushing towards him and twisted aside as the head of a spear skipped across his body armour. It was quickly withdrawn again and Odysseus turned to see the young face of a Trojan noble, this time aiming his weapon higher at the king's chest. Odysseus swung his shield before him, stopping the point of his assailant's spear and thrusting it back. Raising his own spear over his shoulder, he stabbed down at the dark, handsome face of his opponent. The Trojan ducked aside and rushed forward, punching his shield into Odysseus's and trying to force him back. The man was strong, but Odysseus was stronger. As they stared hard at each other across the rims of their shields, Odysseus dropped his spear and tugged his sword free of its scabbard. His enemy did the same. Their blades clashed, but as they withdrew in an effort to give themselves space to fight, a trickle of rain ran into Odysseus's eye, momentarily blurring his vision. The Trojan saw his chance and leapt forward with his sword at arm's length. Half-blinded, Odysseus sensed the move and pulled, while striking downwards on to his attacker's sword hand. The blow severed his thumb at the knuckle and, dropping the weapon, the Trojan fell to his knees and clutched the injured hand under the armpit of his other arm.

'Mercy!' he shouted in Greek, as Odysseus raised his sword for the killing blow. 'Have mercy, my lord, I beg you. My father is rich and will pay any ransom you demand of him for my return. Spare me and I will honour your name among my fellow Trojans, so that not only wealth but also glory will be yours.'

Odysseus looked at the man kneeling before him and hesitated. There were tears of pain and despair in the Trojan's eyes as he held his maimed hand into his body, but he had fought well and perhaps deserved life more than many who would survive that day.

'What's your name, lad?' he asked.

'Adrestos, my lord. My father is a merchant who traded goods with Greeks from Mycenae and Crete; that's how I learned your language. I hold no grudge against the Greeks. If Paris hadn't taken Helen, this war would never have happened.'

'It would have happened all right, one way or another,' Odysseus replied. 'And now it's up to us to finish it. But if I ransom you, you will rejoin the fight. Perhaps you will kill Greeks who would otherwise have lived – you're no mean warrior, Adrestos – and perhaps you will make this war last a little longer. I cannot allow that to happen, not for all the gold and glory in Ilium if it means even one more day apart from my wife and son. I'm sorry.'

He raised his sword again, but was stopped by a shout.

'Odysseus!'

The two men turned to see Eperitus running towards them. His eyes were burning with the ferocity of battle and the rain that ran from his armour and sword was pink with the gore of his victims.

'What are you doing? You can't kill an unarmed man, especially one who's thrown himself at your mercy. It's nothing less than murder!'

An angry flicker crossed Odysseus's features. He had never been the most principled of men, but he did not need to be reminded of the ruthlessness of his intentions – least of all by a man who did not have a family and a kingdom to influence his high-minded notions.

'He's *my* prisoner, Eperitus,' Odysseus warned his captain. 'And if you think we're ever going to win this war by sparing our enemies to fight another day—'

'You're letting your desire to go home cloud your judgement,' Eperitus interrupted, his sodden clothes clinging to him as more rain beat against his armour. 'First the prisoner at the ravine, then Palamedes, and now this. Cruel logic isn't the way to defeat Troy. There's no honour in it.'

'Honour means different things to different men,' Odysseus informed him coldly, sheathing a sword and plucking a spear from the body of a dead Ithacan. 'And your old-fashioned notion of it has no place in this war.'

As he spoke, Adrestos sprang up and made to run. A moment later he was face down in the thick mud, Odysseus's spear protruding from his back.

'Let that be an end to the matter,' the king growled, retrieving the weapon. 'Come on. This fight is far from over yet.'

All around them were dead and dying men and yet the battle lines had hardly shifted from where the two sides had first clashed. Though the Greeks were gaining ground in some places, in others it was being taken from them by the resolute Trojans. Odysseus and Eperitus rejoined the battle side by side, angry with one another and yet not so angry that they did not seek the safety and comfort that the other man's presence offered. Again they fought until their muscles ached, with arrows flying over and around them and the heavens above rumbling and flashing with a sound like a thousand drums beating together at once. Strangely, the storm did not move on, and those that were not in the forefront of the fighting began to say that it was sent by the gods to increase their torment and fill men with fear. And then, as the morning wore on towards another deadlock, men sensed a change in the air. The clouds rose higher, but instead of breaking up or moving south, driven away by the north wind, they grew darker and seemed to churn with an inner anguish. Then a loud crack sundered the sky and a bolt of lightning flashed downwards into the terrified ranks of the Greek army. A man was struck dead, while those around him clapped their hands to their eyes and staggered away from the blast. Then a second strike followed, overturning a Greek chariot and sending its crew spilling to the ground. After that, no man was in doubt that the favour of Zeus had been given to the Trojans.

Suddenly the stalemate was broken. The Greeks began to fall back, some even tossing their weapons aside and fleeing headlong in the direction of the camp, which was still a long march across the plains to the rear. Odysseus and Eperitus looked around at the chaos of running men and speeding chariots then, realizing that widespread panic could mean the destruction of the entire army, began ordering the Ithacans to re-form the line. Further along Idomeneus was doing the same with his Cretans, but the two armies were only small islands of discipline among a sea of anarchy. What was happening beyond the sheet rain even Eperitus's eyes could not see.

For a moment the Trojans seemed too shocked to press home the attack and allowed their enemies to retreat before them. Then shouts and horn calls filled the air and, with a roar of triumph, the long ranks of warriors surged forward, hurling their spears at the tattered Greek line. Many fell beneath the deadly hail, while many more simply broke and fled in the face of the charging Trojans. A handful of Ithacans ran, Eurylochus and his cronies foremost among them, but the remainder stood firm beneath the dolphin banner of their king.

The Trojan spearmen fell on their retreating enemies with the ferocity of men who had been kept too long behind the walls of their city. They wanted revenge for years of siege and bloodshed, and though the Greeks fought hard they were pushed inevitably back in the direction of their camp. Then, as Odysseus fought with Eperitus and Arceisius at his side, horn calls sounded behind them and a dozen chariots came driving out of the rain and crashed into the enemy ranks. At their head were Diomedes and Nestor. The younger man was leaning over the chariot rail and beheading terrified warriors with his long sword, while the older cut down several more with thrusts of his spear as the Trojans were thrown into disarray.

'Form a rearguard,' Nestor shouted to Odysseus, spotting him in the thick of the fighting. 'That fool Agamemnon's ordered the army back to the wall, but it's a long way back and someone has to keep the retreat from becoming a rout.'

As he spoke, an arrow hit one of his horses in the forehead. It fell heavily, pulling the other horse and the chariot over with it and throwing Nestor and his driver to the ground. Diomedes ordered his chariot around and went to the old king's aid, just as Hector came dashing out from the thick curtains of rain on the Trojan side. He saw the overturned chariot and with a howl of triumph steered his horses towards it.

'Help us, Odysseus!' Diomedes cried, leaping down from his chariot and running to Nestor's side.

The king of Pylos lay on all fours, his helmet lost and blood in his grey hair. As he heard Diomedes's shout for help, he threw out his hand and shook his head.

'No, Odysseus. Form the rearguard or the army is doomed. Everything depends on you.'

Odysseus stared wild-eyed at the scene before him, the indecision contorting his face. Men and chariots were in full flight before the Trojan onslaught, but there were still whole companies of warriors who had not lost their nerve and were making a fighting withdrawal. If there was a leader who could pull them together, they could keep their pursuers at bay while the rest of the army sought the safety of the Greek walls. And yet if he abandoned Diomedes and the stricken Nestor then Hector and his victorious Trojans would quickly overwhelm them. He was also mindful of Athena's order not to face Hector.

'Eperitus; Arceisius,' he said, 'give all the help you can to Diomedes and Nestor – and don't be drawn into a fight with Hector, if you can avoid it. I'll take charge of whoever is left and form a rearguard.'

He clapped a hand on Eperitus's shoulder, then with a brief smile and a nod he moved into the lines of Ithacans, shouting for them to fall back. Whether he would be able to knit together a body of men who could hold off the Trojans – and most especially their cavalry – Eperitus did not know, but if any man in the army could do it, that man was Odysseus. Then he turned and saw Diomedes helping Nestor towards his own chariot, where Sthenelaus waited at the reins. Nestor's driver had regained his feet and, though dazed, had seen Hector approaching rapidly across the battle lines, a spear balanced in the palm of his right hand. He scrambled to pick up a discarded shield and spear from the many dead that lay all around.

'Come on,' Eperitus said.

He sprang forward, closely followed by Arceisius, knowing at a single glance that they would never cover the ground to Diomedes and Nestor before Hector reached them. Then Nestor's driver dashed forward and threw his spear with reckless aim. It crossed the path of the Trojan chariot, narrowly missing the horses and causing them to turn aside. A smack of the reins and a harsh shout from their driver pulled them back on course. Then Hector hurled his own weapon and Nestor's charioteer fell back into the mud. An instant later, Hector's second spear was in his hand as his chariot now charged headlong at the kings of Argos and Pylos.

Eperitus knew there was but one chance to save them. He stopped and pulled back his spear, taking aim along its black shaft. Then a shout to his right announced the approach of a group of enemy soldiers, who had spotted the lone Ithacans and were running at them with murderous intent.

'Arceisius!' Eperitus barked.

The young warrior nodded and ran to meet the new threat, somehow slipping between the hedge of spear points and bringing his sword to bear on the disadvantaged enemy. Eperitus watched him cut down his first opponent, then turned his attention back to Hector's speeding chariot. The Trojan was almost upon the stricken forms of Diomedes and Nestor, the former trying desperately to drag his wounded comrade towards his waiting chariot. Eperitus took aim again, lining up the point of his spear with the galloping horses, just as Hector pulled back his own weapon. Drawing on all his experience and instinct to judge the throw, Eperitus uttered a prayer to Athena and launched his heavy spear. It caught Hector's unarmoured driver in the chest and sent him crashing backwards from the car. Panicked by the loss of control, the horses saw the wreck of Nestor's chariot before them and veered aside, almost spilling Hector into the mud. Then the chariot disappeared into the thick rain, Hector desperately hanging on to the rail with one hand and reaching for the reins with the other.

Eperitus did not spare himself a moment to exult over the small victory. He pulled his sword from its scabbard and ran to where Arceisius was struggling to fight off his attackers. Already two lay dead, but four still lived and were trying to form a circle around the reckless but skilful Greek, whose wildly swinging blade kept them at arm's length. Then Eperitus was upon them, burying his sword into the liver of the left-most Trojan and killing him instantly. The others, already dismayed by Arceisius's ferocity and seeing Diomedes's chariot approaching, quickly turned and fled.

'I'm taking Nestor back to the camp,' Diomedes announced as Sthenelaus reined the pair of horses in beside the Ithacans. 'Join

Odysseus with the rearguard and tell him I won't abandon him. He just needs to hold on until I can organize a counter-attack.'

Sthenelaus gave a tug on the reins and the horses kicked forward. As they broke into a gallop, Diomedes turned back to Eperitus and cupped his hands around his mouth.

'And thank you for saving our lives,' he shouted before vanishing into the sheet rain.

Chapter Twenty-Two
THE REARGUARD

The Greek camp was in turmoil. Beneath the wind and rain, the bellowing thunder and staccato flashes of lightning, thousands of exhausted men stood or sat, many wounded and many more leaderless and confused. Some were without their weapons, which they had discarded on the battlefield, while others had run down to the ships in blind panic, expecting the walls to tumble and fifty thousand Trojans to come rushing in on them at any moment. But in the thick of the chaos order was being restored. Kings, princes and captains shouted orders and marshalled what was left of their armies, sending some to man the walls and others to defend the gates, through which a constant stream of stragglers was pouring into the relative safety of the camp. The fact that they were able to do so was down to the fighting rearguard that had been organized from the broken units of a dozen Greek states and were at that moment repelling wave after wave of Trojan infantry. It was only a matter of time, though, before their resolve collapsed and they, too, were driven back to the walls.

Agamemnon stood in his chariot and looked around in anger and despair. He did not blame himself for what had happened – it was clearly the work of the gods – and yet he burned with shame that, not so far away, Achilles would be sitting in his hut laughing at his misfortune. He would no doubt be boasting to his Myrmidons that the Greeks were nothing without him, and that the great King of Men himself was unable to stop Hector and his allies.

He surveyed the chaos with as much restraint as he could muster, his eyes offended by the sight of soaked and bedraggled soldiers and his ears assailed by the groans of the wounded. How could his splendid army have been reduced to this? Then he saw the once-proud kings who had sworn to help him raze Troy to the ground: Menelaus, brooding and sulky at the defeat; Diomedes, tending to Nestor's wounds as if he were the old man's nursemaid; Idomeneus, busy organizing the defenders on the walls in an effort to cover his disgrace on the plains; and the two Ajaxes, who dared to look at Agamemnon with disdain, though they were clearly incapable of stemming the Trojan victory themselves.

'Shame on you!' Agamemnon shouted, succumbing to his wrath at last. 'Shame on you all! Call yourselves Greeks? Greek women, perhaps! I remember your boasts at Aulis, when you feasted night by night in my tent and said that each of you was worth a hundred Trojans. It seems to me the whole crowd of you couldn't stand up to Hector alone.'

'I can and *have*!' Great Ajax shouted, drawing the sword Hector had given him after their duel and holding it aloft as evidence.

'It wasn't any of *us* who ordered a retreat,' Diomedes added, furiously. 'But I promised Odysseus I would go back for him, and now I've brought Nestor to safety I intend to keep my word. My Argives will ride out to help the rearguard, but who will come with us?'

'We will,' Great Ajax answered, indicating Little Ajax and Teucer.

'And I will,' said Menelaus, leaping up into his chariot and turning to the soldiers around him. 'Spartans! Now is not the time to sulk over a setback or mourn the day's dead. If any of you still call yourselves men, then take up your spears and follow me.'

And with a roar of anger the Greeks followed their kings back to the causeways.

By the time Diomedes had left Eperitus and Arceisius, the tide of battle had already washed over them and left them behind the main force of Trojans. But the gods had not abandoned them and somehow – perhaps mistaken for Trojans by the companies of enemy spearmen and cavalry they passed through – they found their way across the field of bodies to the last wall of Greek shields. There were but two or three thousand of them, flanked by troops of horsemen on either side who struggled to master their mounts in the intense storm. But even here the two Ithacans were almost killed by a volley of their countrymen's spears as they approached, only saving themselves by waving their arms and calling out in Greek.

They joined a group of Euboeans as a shower of arrows and spears fell among the rearguard, felling several and announcing a new attack. Moments later a horde of Trojans came screaming at them. The Greeks stood their ground and drove their assailants back again after a short but ferocious fight that left many dead on both sides. Then Eperitus heard the familiar voice of Odysseus over to their right, ordering the ever-dwindling force of men to resume the steady march back to the camp. As the rearguard lifted their shields and shouldered their spears, many casting anxious glances over their backs, Eperitus gestured to Arceisius and ran to the centre of the line where he had heard Odysseus. The king saw them approach and greeted them both with an embrace, giving Eperitus a look that told him their earlier argument was forgotten. Then the recently constructed ramparts around the Greek camp came into view through the squalls of rain and the men gave a cheer. This was immediately followed by another hail of arrows falling out of the rain-filled skies and tumbling more men into the thick mud. A new attack followed and was repulsed again, but before long as they recommenced the march towards the walls – which were now tantalizingly close – they heard the snorting of a large number of horses, followed by the shouts of men and the tramping of hoof beats behind them.

'This is it,' Odysseus announced. 'They're sending the cavalry to break us.'

The Greeks had faced the Trojan cavalry on many occasions over the years of the war and had learned to fear them. But they had also learned how to fight them. Odysseus shouted orders for the front rank to kneel and the second and third ranks to create a wall of spears – an obstacle that only the most disciplined animal would attack. The order was relayed along the line and Odysseus shouldered his way into the front rank, with Eperitus and Arceisius flanking him. Kneeling and planting the butts of their spears into the soft ground, they looked into the pelting rain and saw the long lines of horsemen approaching at a disciplined canter. Eperitus's keen eyes could see the fear on the animals' faces as the thunder ripped open the sky above and bolts of lightning tore down into the sea away to their right. Any moment now the riders would stab their heels into the horses' flanks and goad them into a charge; the thunder above would then be matched by a thunder in the earth itself as thousands of hooves tore up the ground in a frenzied sprint towards the lines of bronze spear points. Whether they would carry it through depended on their training, the command of the rider, the storm-induced panic and the discipline of the tired spearmen, for if any of the Greeks broke and fled, the horses would herd into the gaps and bring a terrible destruction upon them.

But as Eperitus clutched at the wet spear and prepared himself for the assault, the sound of horns came blowing out of the storm behind him. He looked over his shoulder and saw streams of chariots and horsemen leaving the walls of the Greek camp and dashing over the causeways. Diomedes was honouring his promise to save the rearguard.

Chapter Twenty-Three

DISHONOURABLE PRIDE

The whole Greek camp seemed to be groaning with pain and misery. Wounded men lay everywhere among the tents and huts while their comrades tended to their injuries, or tried to shut out their cries and find much-needed sleep. Though the storm had passed on to leave a cloudless, star-filled sky, the earth was still sodden from the heavy rain and the soldiers were chilled to the bone as they tried to dry their clothing around the countless campfires. The unexpected catastrophe and loss of life on the battlefield had left their mood sullen and despairing, while beyond the walls the fires of the victorious Trojan army were as innumerable as the stars above, threatening another day of intense fighting and death. And if the walls did not hold, then nothing would prevent Hector from torching the ships and bringing about the utter annihilation of the Greek army.

Eperitus was pondering these things as he followed Odysseus through the camp towards Agamemnon's tent. Though the force of chariots and cavalry led by Diomedes had caused great slaughter among the Trojans and enabled the rearguard to slip back behind the protection of the walls, it had only been a small success in a day of resounding defeat for the Greeks. With the Trojan army now besieging the camp, no man could draw any kind of solace from the day's struggle. Some tried to encourage their comrades or subordinates by recalling Calchas's prophecy of victory in the tenth year, but such remarks were met with scorn or bitter sneers. There was hardly a man who did not know in his heart that the next morning would bring only more loss, humiliation and death.

Chief among the doubters, it seemed, was Agamemnon himself. Rumours had swept through the camp that the once proud King of Men was declaring the war as good as lost and blaming everyone but himself for the defeat. Odysseus had tried to scotch the rumours among his own men, telling them Agamemnon had summoned the Council of Kings to his tent and together they would devise a way of beating Hector. But as he and Eperitus entered the vaulted pavilion, with its canvas walls billowing pregnantly in the wind, they found the tales of Agamemnon's mood were not exaggerated.

As the last of the council took their seats, the Mycenaean king faced the grimed and bloodied circle of leaders with a look of angry despondency in his eyes.

'Greeks,' he announced, clutching at his golden sceptre, 'comrades in suffering, can any of you deny that Zeus has finally decided between myself and Priam? Is there a man among you foolish enough to say the Son of Cronos hasn't given victory to the Trojans? We sailed here in the greatest fleet the world has ever seen, expecting to conquer swiftly and share the rich spoils of Troy. But who now can look out from the ramparts we built in our foolish pride and not know the doom of our army is camped on the plain?

'Let us take to our ships, then, while we still can, and leave this place of sorrow to its true masters. If the choice is retreat with ignominy or death with honour, then let us unfurl our sails at dawn and go home.'

If Eperitus hated the cold, emotionless king who had murdered his daughter to wage war against Troy, he had felt no less contempt then for the defeated fool who stood before the men who had elected him their leader, lamenting his treatment at the hands of the gods and declaring defeat because of a single day's fighting. But as the kings and princes looked at each other in silence,

Diomedes stepped out from among them and snatched the sceptre from Agamemnon's undeserving hand.

'Is it just three days since you called me a coward in front of the whole army, my lord?' he sneered. 'Three short days, in which you've managed to throw away a tenth of your men and let the Trojans push us back inside the boundaries of our own camp. Then I congratulate you: you've gained a triumph very few of *us* could have achieved! But now you've excelled yourself with this talk of sailing home. Zeus may have given you a splendid sceptre and the command of all the Greeks with it, but one thing he did not give you was *courage*. Go, then! No one will stop you – you're the King of Men, after all. And if there are any who want to go with you, then let them. In fact, let every Greek leave Ilium, for all I care; Sthenelaus and I will fight on alone with our Argives, until Troy falls or the last of us is sent down to Hades. For we are men of honour, warriors who will not return home in shame. We choose to stay and fight.'

Diomedes's speech was met with a chorus of approval, many of the kings leaping to their feet and beckoning for the sceptre, keen to add their own words of rebuke for Agamemnon. But Diomedes had already given the staff to Nestor, who held up his hands and refused to speak until the last man had returned to his seat.

'My lord Agamemnon, Diomedes is right to rebuke you. For one thing, the fleet is in no condition to sail: timbers have rotted, sails are moth-eaten, and ropes are frayed to snapping point. But even if our ships were seaworthy, why would any of us want to leave now? Have we fought for ten long years to leave empty-handed, when victory can still be claimed even at this dark time?'

'Victory!' Agamemnon snorted. 'So the years have finally caught up with your brains, Nestor, as well as your body. Why do you try to placate me with false hopes when you know the gods are against us?'

'You *conveniently* forget my wife is still a prisoner of the Trojans!' Menelaus snapped, glowering at his brother. 'If Nestor says we can still win then *I* want to know what he's got in mind.'

'Haven't you already guessed?' Nestor replied. 'Victory lies with one man – Achilles. If Agamemnon will forget his pride and offer to return Briseis, the greatest warrior we have may yet come to our aid. Even Hector won't stand against *him*, and with his battle-hardened Myrmidons still fresh they'll sweep the Trojans from the field. What do you say, Agamemnon?'

Nestor had voiced the hope of every man present, who now turned as one to the King of Men. But Agamemnon stared down at his feet as if his aged adviser had not spoken.

'What do you say, my lord?' Great Ajax insisted, rising to his feet. 'Will we approach my cousin for his help, or turn tail and flee like an army of washerwomen?'

Agamemnon lifted his face and fixed his cold blue eyes on the king of Salamis.

'Do I have a choice in the matter? It seems to me now that the gods aren't so much with Priam and the Trojans as with *Achilles*. Ever since I argued with that man nothing has gone right for me: not only has my army been decimated, but my enemies are ensconced before the gates and unless I humble myself at the feet of that stubborn young goat even my most trusted advisers and allies will turn upon me. Then so be it!'

He stood and crossed the floor of his tent, seizing the sceptre from Nestor and rounding angrily on the others.

'Go to Achilles! Offer him whatever you see fit from my wealth – gold, slaves, as many tripods and cauldrons as his vanity requires; even my best horses if he demands them. And if that won't appease his cursed pride, then offer him part of my kingdom and Menelaus's too – after all, it's your damned wife we're here for,' he added, staring down his brother's unspoken protest. 'And tell him Briseis is his, untouched by me. I give him my word on that.'

There were tears of anger on his face as he shook the sceptre at the commanders of his army.

'Just make sure he submits himself to my authority again. If *I* can debase myself for his sake, then the least he can do is accept my peace offering and save us from the Trojans. After all, even the will of the gods can be turned by a show of humility. And if you're determined on this course – which is *not* what I would do, if you gave me a choice – then, for the sake of all the gods, send someone he's going to listen to. You, Odysseus; you can win any man's heart with your words, whether honest or deceitful. And you, Ajax; you're Achilles's cousin and there's no man closer to his heart, other than Patroclus. Go at once. We'll await your return here, though you go with a fool's hope.'

And so Ajax and Odysseus – accompanied by Eperitus – left the assembly and walked along the sand towards Achilles's hut. The low groaning of the wounded was all around them, like the strained breathing of an injured animal, and yet as they approached the tents of the Myrmidons they were met by the sounds of laughter and feasting. It irked Eperitus to hear the skilled strumming of a lyre drifting out across the beach, while a voice sang softly of long-dead heroes and their feats. Were Achilles and his soldiers somehow unaware of the suffering of the rest of the army, he wondered, or was this their way of mocking them for daring to face the Trojans without their help? He looked out at the black ocean to his right and prayed to Athena that he would contain his growing anger.

The Myrmidons' tents were pitched a short distance away from the rest of the camp, at the southernmost point of the bay. It was a psychological detachment as well as a physical one, and the difference between the two camps had never been more noticeable to Eperitus than it was to him then. The numerous fires that sent columns of orange sparks twisting into the night sky were a world away from the misery he had temporarily left behind, while the groups of warriors who sat drinking wine and chattering noisily among themselves seemed like figures from a forgotten past, where pain and suffering were just words in a story. They fell silent, though, as the three men appeared among them, and watched with muted fascination as they made their way towards

Achilles's hut at the upper edge of the beach. It was from here that the song that seemed to mock the suffering of the rest of the army was emanating. Smoke rose from a hole in the apex of the hut's roof, while four armed men guarded its entrance. They quickly moved back at the sight of Odysseus, Ajax and Eperitus and waved them inside.

The interior was dimly lit by the low flames of the hearth, but by the orange light the newcomers could see a dozen Myrmidon nobles lying on fleeces and picking at the remains of a meal. Many had half-naked slaves in their arms and in the darkened corners of the hut Eperitus could see the dim outlines of figures coupled together, making no effort to quieten their exertions. On the opposite side of the fire, seated on the floor with his back propped against a stool, was Achilles. A lyre was in his hands, his fingers stroking the strings with greater skill than any bard Eperitus had ever heard. He sung of Meleager and the Calydonian boar, and his voice threw a web of enchantment over his audience that even the sounds from the corners of the hut could not disrupt. Patroclus was at his side, leaning against the same stool and stroking his fingers through the back of Achilles's long blond hair.

As he recognized Ajax, Odysseus and Eperitus, Achilles stopped his song and gave the lyre to Patroclus. He stood and clapped his hands twice.

'Out, all of you!'

At once the nobles jumped to their feet, spilling the slaves from their laps or hauling them up by their wrists and dragging them towards the door. The noises from the corners of the hut stopped abruptly as six or seven naked figures left the shadows, the women clutching their clothing to their chests as the men herded them unsympathetically outside. When only Achilles and Patroclus remained, the prince leaned forward with a smile and took each of the visitors' hands in greeting.

'Welcome, friends,' he said with warm enthusiasm. 'I was expecting Agamemnon to send someone, but you don't know how pleased I am he chose you. Be seated.'

He nodded to Patroclus, who fetched three heavy chairs draped in purple cloth from the shadows.

'Fetch wine, too,' Achilles added. 'Not too much water, though. And bring more meat, Patroclus. No one's visited my hut in nearly a week and I want to show these men a real welcome.'

'Some of us have been *fighting*,' Ajax growled, squeezing himself into his chair.

Achilles glanced at him out of the corner of his eye, smiling as he cleaned bits of meat from his teeth with his tongue.

'Let's not be bitter, cousin. You know how much I love a scrap, but you also know the offence that forced me to withdraw from this war. Which, I imagine, is what you've come to talk about. But first let us share wine and meat together, as friendship demands.'

Patroclus entered with a large bowl of mixed wine, which he placed on a bench before drawing cups for Achilles and his visitors, frowning at the menial task he had been relegated to. As the four men poured their libations to the gods and drank, a soldier brought in the sides of a sheep and a goat and laid them out next to the bowl of wine. Achilles began jointing and carving up the meat at once, while Patroclus tended to the fire and prepared the spits. While the Myrmidons busied themselves with the meal and Odysseus and Ajax leaned in towards each other to speak in low voices, Eperitus looked around at the large hut with its deep shadows. The wide floor was covered in the soft fleeces of sacrificed sheep, many of which had been misplaced and rucked up by the exodus of noblemen and their slaves. The walls were hung with a collection of weapons and armour that Achilles had stripped from his more illustrious victims as tokens of his victories, while in the gloom against the far side of the hut was a rack from which hung Achilles's own armaments: his long sword and dagger in their ornately worked sheaths; his bronze greaves with silver clips at the ankles; his round, leather shield with its scooped bottom edge, giving it the shape of a waning moon; his sculpted bronze corslet with the dents and scars of many battles upon it; and his black-plumed helmet with its grimacing visor. As Eperitus stared into its empty eyeholes, he was reminded of the many times he had seen Achilles wear it into battle and the terror that the mere sight of it had instilled in his enemies. How different would the outcome of the day's fighting have been if the helmet had been seen among the ranks of the Greek army?

After the meat had been cooked, the ritual pieces burned for the gods and the meal eaten, they refilled their cups and sat down to face each other.

'We thank you for your hospitality, Achilles,' Odysseus began. 'But as you've already guessed, we're not here to pass the evening drinking wine and telling you of our deeds on the battlefield. We were sent here by the Council of Kings.'

'You mean Agamemnon sent you.'

'It was the will of the council we come here,' Ajax growled.

Odysseus held up a hand for silence.

'Ajax is right, Achilles, but as you know the council does nothing without Agamemnon's say-so. It's by his authority we're here and every word we speak is uttered on his behalf. You don't need me to tell you that the Trojans have mastered us in battle and at this very moment their campfires are lapping against the walls of our camp like a great ocean. Zeus's favour is with them now, not us, and unless that changes there's little chance we'll ever force them back to Troy, let alone sack the city and rescue Helen as we promised ourselves we would do. What's more, one determined attack by Hector and those mud brick walls we threw up so hastily will be sent crashing back down again. I'm afraid tomorrow will see the Trojans torch our ships and kill us to a man.'

'Afraid, Odysseus? Achilles interrupted with a half-smile. 'Then do you fear death?'

'Death, no. But I fear not seeing my wife and child again. Telemachus turned ten this year, you know. If my own son were to walk into this hut I wouldn't even recognize him. What's worse, I can barely remember what Penelope looks like any more. That's what I fear most of all, Achilles – going down to Hades without a last look at my family.'

Achilles leaned back in his chair, running the tips of his fingers back and forth across his lips. 'Yes, I understand,' he said, nodding. 'I understand the desire to go home.'

'Then come and fight with us again! If not for the sake of your friends, who look to your help, then for your own sake. Heap glory upon yourself in the eyes of the army; give them victory so they can go back to Greece and tell your deeds to everyone, honouring you like a god! You know no man can withstand you in battle, even the great Hector, though he roams the battlefield with impunity in your absence. Rouse your Myrmidons, Achilles, and save the Greeks before it's too late!' Odysseus paused and leaned forward, spreading his hands with an imploring gesture. 'Agamemnon acknowledges he was wrong to treat you as he did – *you*, the greatest warrior in his army! You should have seen the tears rolling down his cheeks as he begged us to speak with you on his behalf.'

'Then why didn't he come himself?'

Odysseus laughed and shook his head. 'He knows you wouldn't listen to him, even if he came in sackcloth and covering his head with ashes, as a man might humble himself before the gods. But he *does* know you'll listen to your friends, whose own suffering is close to your heart, and that you'll listen to them even more keenly if they bring promises of gifts. For anybody else an apology from the King of Men would be more than sufficient, but *you*'re not anybody. He knows your renown is only equalled by your pride, and so he offers gifts as an open symbol of his apology, for all to see.'

'What gifts?' Patroclus asked.

'*Ten* talents of gold; *twenty* copper cauldrons and seven tripods, none of them yet touched by fire; his twelve *best* racehorses; *seven* of his most skilled slaves – your choice – and if that isn't enough, he offers your pick of the wealthiest towns from his own kingdom, to rule over as you wish. But he also realizes that these gifts on their own aren't enough to right the wrong that was done to you;

so Agamemnon will return Briseis to you at once, with his solemn oath that she has not been touched by him or any man since she left your side.'

Odysseus sank back in his chair and looked at the prince, whose eyes had been fixed on the flames as the gifts had been enumerated. Ajax, Eperitus and even Patroclus also stared at him, but Achilles did not lift his gaze or make any effort to respond.

'What do you say, my lord?' Odysseus urged. 'The offer is a generous one and would bring you great glory. If the stubborn gods will listen to prayer and change their minds, then it would be profane to let your own pride keep you from accepting.'

'Nevertheless, I will not accept it,' Achilles answered. 'Ten long years I've fought for Agamemnon. I've sacked no fewer than twenty-three towns and cities in Priam's kingdom and the kingdoms of his allies, and for what reward? Every time I've brought back the spoils and laid them before him, not withholding anything, only to see this *King of Men* take the greater share and divide the rest equally, regardless of who stormed the walls or who stayed with him by the ships. Even then, I was content to serve under his command until he took Briseis from me. I won her with my own spear and she won my heart, but he dared to take her from me in front of the whole army. Did he rob you, Odysseus, or you, Ajax? No, just *me*, and for that I will never forgive him!'

There was a rage now in Achilles, growing as he spoke so that his knuckles were white about the arms of his chair.

'And as for his gifts, I care nothing for them. I have towns of my own back in Phthia and wealth enough not to miss these meagre offerings he insults me with. Does he think I don't know this is but a tiny portion of the wealth and slaves he has gleaned? After all, *I* captured it for him in the first place! No, Odysseus, if Agamemnon wants to save his precious ships from Hector then he must rely on you and the other kings to do it for him. At first light tomorrow, my ships will unfurl their sails and return home, and if you have any sense you will come with me.'

A long silence followed Achilles's refusal, but as the others stared at the glowing embers of the hearth – unable to look each other in the eye – Eperitus fought a losing battle to contain his own sense of outrage. Eventually, he slammed his fist down on the arm of his chair and spoke.

'I've seen you fight, Achilles, and there's not a man like you anywhere in Greece or Ilium. Even Ajax, here, couldn't match you, and yet I look upon him with the greater honour. I look upon the least of the soldiers lying dead on that plain out there with more honour than I do you. Damn it if even *Agamemnon* hasn't more honour than you do!'

Achilles leaned forward in his chair and Eperitus felt as if Hades himself were staring at him, but his own anger was too great to feel any fear.

'Men speak of you and they talk of honour and a name that will live until the end of time,' he continued, 'and yet *I* see a man whose renown has been overmastered by his pride. If the gods will bend their will in the face of humility, then who are you to remain so obstinate? I've more reason to hate Agamemnon than you do, but even I can see he knows when to acknowledge he's in the wrong. Not only has he offered you gifts that will give you glory – even if you don't need the wealth – but he's also prepared to give you back the woman you claim to love. Isn't that enough? He took my woman, too, you know, though you revel in the thought that you're the only man to have been robbed by Agamemnon. I'd have given anything to have taken her in my arms again, so why don't you accept this offer and return to the army? Or are you more interested in nursing this grievance of yours than having Briseis back?'

Achilles continued to stare at him, his nostrils flaring slightly as he fought to contain his temper, but Eperitus did not flinch. And then the prince took a deep breath and sat back in his chair, though his eyes did not for a moment leave Eperitus's.

'You are my guest, Eperitus. We have shared wine and meat and therefore you are at liberty to speak your mind, and no doubt you also speak with the passion of your heart. But do not claim to hate Agamemnon more than I do, when every time I argue with him *you* come to his rescue. Do you think I've forgotten that time on Tenedos, when I would have killed him but for your intervention? But none of this matters any more, for no words – appeasing or offensive – will change *my* mind.'

He pointed at Odysseus. 'Are you the only man who can wish for home, Odysseus? Am I doomed to stay in Ilium, my bones turning to dust beneath some mound that future generations will call the "Tomb of Achilles", discussing my deeds in awe as their sheep graze on top of me? But it doesn't have to be so, for my mother foresaw two paths for me, did she not? To live a short and violent life here, earning a name that will echo down the ages; or to enjoy a long and peaceful existence back home, forsaking eternal renown for the love of a family in Phthia. You would have chosen that path, wouldn't you Odysseus? Then so have I!'

'What?' Ajax exclaimed, rising from his chair. 'Have the gods robbed you of your mind, Achilles? You're the greatest warrior of our age; how can you talk of giving up your renown? No one hungers for glory more than you do – not even myself – and that's why I've come to love and revere you above all other men. Do you think I don't worship Tecmessa and dote on Eurysaces? Yet I would rather give up my wife and son than give up my honour, as you are proposing to do. Listen to what you're saying, cousin, and admit your place is on the battlefield with us, not on some farm in Phthia. Accept the gifts Agamemnon is offering and put aside this stubborn pride, before it's too late for all of us.'

'My lord Ajax, there isn't a man amongst the Greeks I love and respect more than I do you,' Achilles replied. 'We are cousins by blood, but we are brothers by our prowess in battle and our desire to win fame. By the same token, you more than anyone should appreciate the humiliation I had to suffer when Agamemnon took Briseis from me, and because of that I will not relent. And mark this, too: if you continue to favour Agamemnon over me and speak on his behalf, then it will not matter that we are cousins or friends, for my love for you can be turned to hatred. I forgive

Odysseus and Eperitus, who have always curried favour with Agamemnon, but you I would have expected to support my cause, not his. Now, all of you, leave my hut and take my reply back to the King of Men. Make sure he realizes the depth of the affront he has caused me.'

'Let's go,' Ajax said gruffly as Odysseus and Eperitus rose from their chairs. 'That an argument over a girl should bring about such an impasse is beyond my understanding. But even though you're abandoning us by this ruthless arrogance of yours, Achilles, I hope that you will still think of us as your friends.'

'I have none greater,' Achilles assured him, taking each of the men by the hand as they followed Patroclus to the doorway.

'Come with us a moment,' Odysseus said in a low voice as Patroclus pulled aside the canvas for them.

Patroclus frowned, but after a quick glance at Achilles – who had picked up his lyre once more and was plucking angrily and discordantly at its strings – he followed the Ithacan king outside. A thin moon was casting weak shadows among the tents, and the air was filled with the smell of brine and woodsmoke. Waves crashed against the nearby shore and the sound of voices came from the Myrmidon campfires, while here and there the distant cries of wounded men rose up to offend the peacefulness of the night.

'What is it?' Patroclus asked.

'You need to do something,' Odysseus replied in a low voice, looking furtively around at the scattered guards. Ajax was waiting just out of earshot, while Eperitus was at Odysseus's shoulder, curious to know why the king had asked Patroclus to follow them.

'What do you mean?'

'Don't feign indifference, Patroclus,' Odysseus said. 'Do you think I wasn't watching your face in there as Achilles refused every argument we put to him? He's letting his pride get the better of him and you're as concerned about it as we are.'

'Of course I am, but what do you expect me to do? You can see for yourselves how difficult he is to talk to once his mind is set.'

'I don't know what you should do, but unless you can convince him to lead the Myrmidons back into battle, then I fear everything we've fought for will be lost. *We* can do nothing to influence him – indeed, our efforts only seem to make him worse – but *you*'re his closest friend, Patroclus. He'll listen to you.'

Patroclus gave a derisive snort and cast a jealous glance over at Ajax. Odysseus caught the look and knew what was in the Myrmidon's mind.

'Achilles and Ajax share the same passion for glory and they admire each other for it, but even Ajax couldn't persuade Achilles to give up this feud with Agamemnon. You, on the other hand, have known Achilles longer than anyone else; you share his meals by day and it's said his bed by night; he loves you more than any other, including Ajax, and because of that you are the only one who can bring him back to the fight. You must do what you can, Patroclus. I have a feeling the fate of the whole army rests with you.'

Chapter Twenty-Four

THE NIGHT RAID

Odysseus delivered the news to the assembled leaders with uncharacteristic bluntness: Achilles had not only flatly refused Agamemnon's gifts and his offer of reconciliation, but he had also promised to set sail for Greece the next day and had advised all others to do the same. The council fell into a stunned silence, with Agamemnon sinking into his fur-draped throne and glowering at the flames of the hearth. When he finally looked up again, his blue eyes were filled with hopeless despair.

'Now what do we do?' he asked, looking around at the expectant faces of the kings and princes who had followed him to Troy. 'The only thing that stands between Hector and total victory is a ditch and that pile of mud bricks Nestor persuaded us to build only a few days ago.'

'If it hadn't been for the wall, our ships would be charred wrecks by now and we would all be dead,' Diomedes countered, standing and pacing the floor of the tent with his hands locked behind his back. 'But who knows what tomorrow will bring? I for one don't believe the gods have abandoned our cause – not yet, at least – and you seem to overlook another fact, my lord Agamemnon: we still have a great and powerful army, and men of renown to lead it. The storm seems to have passed and the sight of the sun tomorrow will give the men heart again.'

'It will lift Trojan spirits, too!' Agamemnon exclaimed. 'I tell you, Hector will brush aside our defences in the morning and put us all to the sword.'

Nestor slapped his hand on his thigh in anger.

'No!' he said firmly. 'You set too much store by Hector, my lord. Have you forgotten that Ajax there fought him to a standstill only three days ago? And Diomedes is right, we still have an army that is more than a match for the Trojans, even if Zeus has tipped the balance in their favour for a short time. All we need is to take the initiative – find out the Trojan dispositions and how they plan to attack us, then focus on their weak points and take the battle to them.'

Menelaus stepped forward. 'And how do we do that, old friend? Walk into the Trojan camp and ask Hector to tell us all his plans?'

There was a hollow laugh from some of the men on the benches, but Nestor ignored them. He spoke quietly to Antilochus, who sat next to him, then stood and raised his hand for silence.

'You mock, Menelaus, but that is almost exactly what I suggest we do. All it needs is two or three brave men to slip across the ditch and into the Trojan camp: it's a dark night and there are plenty of Trojan helmets and shields around to provide them with a disguise. Once they're among the campfires, it'll be nothing to snatch a prisoner – some nobleman of rank – and bring him back here for questioning . . .'

'I'll do it,' Diomedes said, standing purposefully and adjusting his scabbard as it hung over his shoulder. 'And Odysseus and Eperitus will come with me.'

'I'll come, too,' Great Ajax added, rising to his full height so that his head almost touched the canvas roof.

Diomedes shook his head. 'Three is enough, my friend, and your size will attract too much attention. What do you say, Odysseus? Is a second mission in one evening too much?'

Odysseus and Eperitus rose from the benches, both men pulling their cloaks about themselves in readiness to meet the chill night air outside.

'You'll need someone with intelligence if you're to come back alive,' Odysseus said. 'I just hope we don't meet as much opposition in the Trojan camp as we did in Achilles's tent.'

§

The shallow moon had sunk below the horizon, leaving the stars to shine brightly above them as they made their way up to the gates. It was now the third watch of the night, but there was still plenty of time to carry out their mission before the first glow of dawn infused the eastern skies. Before leaving Agamemnon's tent they had equipped themselves with Trojan armour and weaponry, earning curious looks from the strong guard who watched the gates. More men were on the walls above and several companies of soldiers slept nearby, ready to arm in an instant if the Trojans showed any sign of attacking. But as the gates were opened and the three crossed the narrow causeway to the plain beyond, everything remained still and quiet. Many hundreds of fires still burned, where the Trojans had camped well out of bowshot from the walls, but the only signs of life were the occasional figures of sentinels silhouetted by the bright flames.

They looked about themselves at the dark, indistinct shapes of the dead who lay everywhere. The ditches on either side of the causeway were filled with bodies, some still impaled on the sharpened poles. Here most of the fallen were Trojans, where Hector had flung his spearmen against the defences in a last, desperate effort to win the day as the Greeks retreated behind their walls; but out on the plain most of the fallen were Greek, shot down by Trojan archers or speared by Trojan horsemen as they turned and ran back to the gates. The chaos of those last moments had been something none of them would forget easily: the lashing rain and the thunder erupting from the clouds above; the clawing sense of panic as men retreated back to the open gates; the glittering blasts of lightning illuminating the terrified faces of men fighting for their lives. Now, though, all was tranquil as they stood on the shadowy stretch of land that separated the two armies.

'There's a gap in the watch fires over on the right,' Diomedes said in a low voice. 'Let's follow the ditch until we're opposite, then cut across.'

He set off at a quick jog and the others followed, instinctively running at a slight crouch as their eyes searched the darkness ahead and to their left, where the Trojan campfires flickered on the plain. But before they had gone very far, Eperitus's keen ears heard soft footsteps and a quick glance revealed the figure of a man coming towards them from across the battlefield.

'Hide yourselves, quickly!' he hissed.

He scrambled into the ditch, followed by Diomedes and Odysseus, who threw themselves down on either side of him.

'What is it?' Diomedes whispered, raising his head just above the lip of the trench and squinting into the darkness.

Eperitus replied by pointing ahead of them where, after a few moments, all three were able to see a skulking figure emerging from the gloom.

'Who do you think he is?' Odysseus asked. 'A straggler?'

'He's a Trojan, whoever he is,' Eperitus answered. 'He's not wearing any armour, but he's dressed like a Trojan and he's got a Trojan cap on his head.'

Diomedes smiled grimly. 'Then he must be a spy, hoping to find a way into our camp. It won't be the first time, after all, though he must think the gods are with him if he expects to slip over this wall unnoticed.'

'He's coming our way,' Odysseus added. 'I say we capture him and see what he knows. It might save us having to slip into the Trojan camp and find a prisoner.'

They drew their swords slowly and silently then lay as if dead. As the man came closer they could see his pale eyes in the darkness, wide and fearful. He wore a wolf's pelt around his shoulders and carried a short spear and a bow. He was stepping carefully, but most of his attention was on the walls and the positions of the sentries.

'Drop your weapons!' Diomedes ordered, leaping up and holding

271

the point of his sword beneath the man's double chin. He spoke in the Trojan tongue, though his accent revealed him as a Greek. Odysseus and Eperitus stood either side of him with their own weapons held ready.

'Oh, mercy!' the Trojan squeaked, releasing his spear and bow and raising his trembling hands in the air. 'Mercy, my lord, mercy!'

'Tell me what you're about or I'll cut your throat,' Diomedes threatened, pressing the blade a little closer.

The man seemed to melt before them, sinking as low as Diomedes's sword would allow and covering his head with his hands, while large tears began cascading down his cheeks. Despite their stolen armour, there was no mistaking the three men for Trojans.

'Oh, no, no, no, don't be hasty now. Don't be hasty! My father will pay a good ransom for me, for sure – I'm worth much more to you alive than dead.'

'Indeed you are,' said Odysseus, looking the man up and down as he circled. 'Now, tell us your name and your mission.'

'Dolon, sir. I, oh gods . . . I got a little lost and . . .' Dolon's voice rose sharply as Diomedes lifted his chin with the point of his sword. 'I mean, I've been sent to scale the walls and spy on the Greek camp. Hector forced me into it. He threatened to kill me if I—'

'Stop lying,' said Eperitus irritatedly.

'Excuse my friends,' Odysseus continued, raising a hand. 'They're a little impatient and easily angered. I wouldn't provoke them, if I were you.'

He signalled to Diomedes, who reluctantly lowered his sword and stepped back. Dolon edged away, rubbing his neck and swallowing.

'Of course not, my lord,' he said, eyeing Diomedes nervously. 'All I want is my life. I'll tell you anything I know.'

'That's good,' Odysseus said, smiling and clapping a friendly hand on his shoulder.

To their surprise, the terrified Trojan knew more than the three men had ever expected to learn from any prisoner they might take. Despite his feeble appearance he was a nobleman and a lesser captain in the Trojan army, and had therefore been present at the meeting between Hector and the other leaders that evening. Not only did he reveal the watchword for passing the sentries and give them all the dispositions of the army as they lay camped in their different factions before the Greek walls, but he also gave them a summary of Hector's plans for the next day's attack, all the time wringing his hands with a mixture of guilt at betraying his countrymen and shame at his own cowardice.

'How do we know we can trust him?' Diomedes asked, sceptically. 'Look at him: he doesn't strike me as the sort of man Hector would send out to spy on our camp. I say we should kill him and take another prisoner.'

Dolon thrust out his hands imploringly. 'No, don't kill me. Test what I've told you: go to the far edge of the lines, where I said King Rhesus and his Thracians are camped. The watchword I gave you will get you past the sentries and then you'll find the Thracians sleeping like babies – they're newly arrived to the war and haven't learned to fear you Greeks yet. If you've a mind to take them, Rhesus has a team of splendid horses that are as white as snow and as fast as the wind. It was prophesied that if they drink from the Scamander then Troy will never fall; Rhesus intends to drive them to the fords at dawn tomorrow, but if you capture the horses tonight, you can make sure the prophecy is never fulfilled. You must believe me! Tie me up and leave me here until you return, and when you know I haven't lied to you perhaps you'll ransom me back to my family, like you promised.'

'We'll test the truth of what you're saying,' Diomedes said, 'but I don't remember promising to ransom you. And if you think I'm going to leave you here to wriggle out of your bonds and raise the alarm, then think again.'

Dolon's eyes widened and he opened his mouth, but before he could speak Diomedes's sword had cut his head from his shoulders and sent it rolling into the ditch. Eperitus frowned in disapproval and glanced down at Dolon's upturned face. The fear had left his dead eyes, though they remained in a look of permanent surprise.

To their relief, the watchword Dolon had given them got them past the four sentries who stood warming their hands by the furthest fire in the Trojan outer line. There were more fires further in as they walked slowly into the midst of the enemy camp, but every one was surrounded by snoring soldiers, curled up beneath their blankets and with their armaments lying close to hand.

'Sleeping like babies,' Diomedes whispered. 'Just as he said they'd be.'

'And those must be the horses he spoke of,' Odysseus added, spying four tall white mounts with blankets thrown across their backs to keep them warm. They tossed their heads and snorted as the strangers approached.

'By the gods, they *are* beautiful,' Eperitus said. 'But we'd never get them past all these men.' He indicated the dark shapes that littered the floor all around the beasts. 'It's more important that we get back and report what we've heard to the council.'

'We're not going back without the horses,' Odysseus countered. 'You heard what Dolon said: if they drink from the Scamander, then Troy will never fall. We can't risk that happening.'

'And think of the glory we'll add to our names if we can ride these beauties back,' Diomedes added, his eyes wide as he admired the Thracian horses. 'Not to mention the dismay we'll bring to the Trojans. Draw your sword, Odysseus: there's work to be done.'

He fell to one knee by one of the sleeping Thracians and clapped a hand tightly over his mouth. The man's eyes opened briefly, just as Diomedes's blade sliced through his windpipe and released his soul from his body. Odysseus hesitated, then knelt and cut the throat of another sleeping soldier. Eperitus watched as, within moments, another two of Troy's allies were dead, and then two more. Then Odysseus hissed at him and pointed to the bodies, indicating he should move them from the path of the horses.

As he took each one by the ankles and dragged them to one side, a couple of the horses began to stamp and tug against their pickets. Suddenly, one of the Thracians sat up, blinked, and looked at the three stooping figures nearby. Odysseus was on him in an instant, pushing the point of his sword into the man's heart and thrusting his hand against his mouth to stifle his last cry. Eperitus and Diomedes look around, their swords ready in their hands, but nobody else stirred.

It did not take long before a route had been cleared between the horses and the edge of the circle of Thracians. All that was needed now was to lead the horses out, mount them and ride to the edge of the camp. But as Odysseus and Eperitus took the animals, stroking their oiled manes and calming them with hushed voices, Diomedes held up his hand for them to wait.

'What is it?' Odysseus asked in an urgent whisper. 'Come on, Diomedes. We've pushed our good fortune far enough as it is. Let's go.'

'Not yet – that must be King Rhesus,' Diomedes replied, pointing his sword at a tall man sleeping on a mattress under a canvas awning. His armour lay nearby, draped in cloth through which only a glimmer of metal could be seen. 'I'm going to teach the Thracians not to sleep too soundly when there are Greeks nearby. And I'm going to take that armour.'

'No,' Eperitus whispered, but Diomedes was already standing over Rhesus with his sword at his throat.

At that moment, Rhesus opened his eyes and let out a cry of alarm. It was the last sound he ever made as Diomedes's sword hacked halfway through his neck, but in an instant his men were waking on every side and sitting up. Diomedes made a grab for the king's armour, pulling the cloth away to reveal a breastplate of ornately worked gold.

'Come on!' Odysseus shouted as he and Eperitus mounted two of the horses.

'But . . .'

'Leave the armour and come *now*!'

Shouts of dismay were echoing around the camp as the Thracians saw the piled corpses of their comrades and the Greeks in their midst. A man leapt to his feet and ran at Eperitus, who kicked him in the face and sent him sprawling backwards.

Diomedes gave the armour a last look, then tossed it aside and leapt on the back of one of the animals Odysseus was holding. Suddenly all three of them were kicking their heels into their horses' flanks and driving them through the dozens of unarmed Thracians who were running at them with their arms held wide. Eperitus cut one man down with a sword stroke across the face and severed the hand of another. The rest fell back, searching desperately for any weapons that were to hand.

But Dolon had not lied when he had said the king's horses were fast. As arrows whistled past them, the Greeks galloped their captured animals through the midst of the startled sentries at the edge of the camp and into the obscuring blackness of the night.

Chapter Twenty-Five
TO SAVE A KING

Agamemnon stood in his golden chariot, his breastplate gleaming in the bright morning sunshine. The red plume of his helmet and his red cloak fluttered in the north wind as he stared across the plain at the thick ranks of Trojan soldiery, positioned just beyond the range of the Greek archers. The king's round shield hung on his back and in his hand he carried two tall spears, for today he intended to lead the army into battle himself. Despite the defeat of the day before, today the Greeks would have the upper hand: the spy Odysseus and Diomedes had captured had revealed the weaknesses in Hector's battle plans, and Agamemnon planned to exploit them to the full.

Eperitus watched the King of Men with more than his usual contempt. His failings as a leader, both on and off the battlefield, had made themselves disastrously obvious in recent days, and the thought that he would be leading the attack did not fill the Ithacan captain with confidence. Fortunately, there were many much more capable men in the Greek army and as long as they still fought there was a hope the Greeks could save their ships and drive the Trojans back inside the walls of Troy. But it was only a hope: any victory against Hector and his allies would be hard won without Achilles; and as company after company of Greek spearmen marched out on to the plain, the Myrmidons and their prince were already raising the masts and cross-spars in their galleys and stowing their goods and provisions for the long journey home.

The Ithacans stood at the centre of the line, with the Mycenae-ans to their left and the Argives under Diomedes to their right, their individual banners trailing in the wind above them. Odysseus was shielding his eyes against the sun as he observed the motion-less files of enemy spearmen, waiting patiently for the Greeks to advance. His presence gave the battered Ithacans a sense of reassurance, but Eperitus could tell the king was not happy.

'What is it?' he asked, quietly.

'Dolon said the regiments at the centre had taken the most casualties and were the weakest in the whole Trojan army,' Odysseus said. 'Your eyes are better than anybody's, Eperitus: how do they look to you?'

'Quiet. That's as bad a sign as any in fighting men.'

'Then maybe Dolon was right: one determined attack and the centre of the Trojan line will break. And yet . . .' Odysseus added as the last of the Greeks crossed the causeways and the gates closed behind them with a thud, 'and yet Hector's always proved a good commander. Surely he wouldn't put his weakest units at the centre of the line?'

'He has to make a mistake some time, my lord,' said Arceisius, who was standing behind Eperitus. 'And now he doesn't have Palamedes to feed him our plans, perhaps we're going to see he's human after all.'

'Don't underestimate him,' Eperitus replied, glancing over his shoulder at his former squire. 'We're the ones fighting to survive now, don't forget.'

To his surprise, he saw Omeros standing next to Arceisius, with Polites on the other side of him. The young bard's eyes were wide, but whatever fear he felt he was able to master it as Agamemnon raised his arm above his head and gave the signal to advance. The skirmishers were the first to move. Lightly armoured, some almost naked, they dashed forward across the freshly dampened earth and fitted arrows to their bows or placed stones in the woollen pouches of their slings. The spearmen followed, their heavy equipment rattling about them as they marched. Meanwhile, Agamemnon jumped down from his chariot and led his Mycenaeans on foot. The other kings and princes followed his lead.

On the opposite side of the battlefield, the Trojans also began to move. The spring sunshine had already dried up most of the surface rain from the storm of the day before, leaving the earth dark but firm beneath the feet of the two armies. The bodies of their comrades who had died in the previous day's fighting still littered the ground in great numbers. Though some had been stripped naked by scavengers in the night – their bodies pasty, disfigured lumps among the thick grass – there were so many dead that most had retained their armour and were shrouded by their cloaks. But the living soon forgot the dead as the sound of bowstrings hummed in the warm air, accompanied by the undulating swish of slings. Thousands of eyes looked up in momentary fear as the skies were crossed by throngs of arrows that quickly fell amongst the skirmishers, killing or wounding scores on both sides. More volleys followed and, as the two armies came closer, the sound of slingshot rattling against bronze and leather joined the growing cacophony of battle. Then it was the turn of the spearmen: the first to cast their missiles were the Greeks, their heavy spears ripping great holes in the densely packed Trojan ranks. The Trojan reply was even more murderous, the Greeks less able to judge the fall of the weapons as they fell out of the sun. And as spears were retrieved and thrown back again and again, piles of fresh corpses were added to the pale and distended victims of the earlier battle, until eventually Agamemnon realized there was no advantage to be gained from continuing the exchange. He raised his spear above his head and with a great shout of anger signalled his army to attack.

The Greeks lowered their spear points and advanced in silence, grimly determined to avenge themselves for the destruction the Trojans had caused the day before. They passed through the depleted skirmishers, who re-formed behind them and continued firing into the enemy mass. The Trojan skirmishers did the same as their own infantry moved forward to present a wall of shields barbed with spears. Then Agamemnon shouted an order and the whole army emptied their lungs in a collective howl of rage as they charged at the enemy ranks.

The two sides met with a heavy thud as thousands of shields clashed against each other, followed instantly by the sudden and terrifying din of ringing bronze and men crying out in anger and agony. The sound was heard as far away as the walls of Troy, where Helen and Andromache were among the silent, ashen-faced women on the wide battlements, each one of them hoping the gods would accept their prayers and sacrifices for their husbands. Many had hoped in vain, for the gods were more intent on death than mercy.

The Ithacans drove into their opponents with ferocity and skill, felling several and pushing the remainder back with ease. Eperitus stepped over his first victim and lunged with a combination of spear and shield at the next man, who retreated meekly before him. To his left, Odysseus was engaging a Trojan captain who was much taller than him and had the look of a veteran warrior, but who seemed to have no stomach for a fight as he shrank away from the king's attacks. Even the inexperienced Omeros was beating back his opponent, while beyond him Polites and Arceisius were driving a wedge into the enemy line.

'What's up with them today?' Eperitus asked, shouting to Odysseus across the clamour.

'They don't want to fight,' Odysseus called back as the Trojan chieftain ducked away from another thrust of his spear. 'Dolon wasn't exaggerating when he said the centre was weak. But they're not running, either; I think it's time we threw caution aside, Eperitus.'

With that, he pulled back his spear and hurled it at his opponent with enough force to punch through the bronze scales of his armour and pierce his chest. The man fell heavily, dead in an instant, and in the same moment Odysseus drew his sword and threw himself at the Trojan line. Eperitus also dashed forward, battering aside the thrust of his enemy's weapon and lunging at his stomach with his own spear. By skill or good fortune the Trojan managed to deflect the attack with his shield, but Eperitus was in no mood for further delay. With the old lust for blood and glory coursing through his veins again, he kicked the man's shield aside, drew back his spear and plunged it into his groin.

'Come on!' he shouted angrily, turning to the rest of the Ithacans. 'This isn't a drill, damn you. Kill or be killed!'

With a shout, the Ithacans surged forward. It was all that was needed for the rest of the Trojans to break and run. Suddenly Eperitus was witnessing something he had never expected to see after the heavy fighting of the previous battles. The Trojan line was melting away before them. Men who had fought like lions days before were now turning their backs and fleeing for their lives. And a brief glance across the battlefield revealed it was not just the company that faced the Ithacans who were breaking: though the flanks of the Trojan army still held fast, the whole of its centre was collapsing before the onslaught of Mycenaeans, Ithacans and Argives.

Eperitus ran after Odysseus, whose short legs belied the speed he was capable of as he outstripped the rest of the Greeks in his pursuit of the fleeing Trojans, cutting them down as he caught them. Only Agamemnon and a handful of his bodyguard were further ahead in the hunt. Eperitus spotted the Mycenaean king through the crowds of men who were streaming across the plain, and it was as if a god had descended on to the battlefield to wreak terrible havoc among mortal flesh, killing with divine fury while seemingly immune to injury himself. The banded metal of his breastplate flashed in the golden sunshine as he brought Trojan after Trojan crashing to the earth, exulting with each death and only regretting that he did not have time to strip them of their armour. One turned to fight, but had already tossed his heavy shield aside and soon fell to a thrust of Agamemnon's spear. Another cast his weapon in a desperate attempt to stop the King of Men, but Agamemnon merely ducked aside before chasing the man down and plunging his spear between his shoulder blades. His guards, though never far from their king, joined in the butchery with equal relish.

Eperitus was distracted from the sight by a heavy thump against the top of his shield. Turning, he saw a man a short distance away dressed in nothing more than a short tunic, fitting another stone to the woollen pouch of his sling. Without thinking about it, Eperitus stooped to retrieve a discarded spear and launched it at the Trojan skirmisher, who screamed as it punched through his stomach. Picking up another spear from the grass, Eperitus ran on to where Odysseus had stopped in the middle of the battle and was looking about himself.

'Look,' the king said as Eperitus reached him. He used the point of his sword to indicate both flanks of the battle. 'Trojan chariots and cavalry massing on each side of us. I knew this was too easy.'

Eperitus followed the arc of Odysseus's sword point and saw hundreds upon hundreds of horses and chariots forming into lines to the north and east, while beyond the fleeing crowds ahead of them he could see a new force of infantry marching into view from a deep defile in the plain.

'Then this whole rout was a feint,' he said. 'They're leading us into a trap and it's about to be sprung.'

'Dolon wasn't the coward we thought he was, either,' Odysseus commented. 'He gave his life to feed us false information and we took the bait. Gods, how could I have been so stupid? And yet I respect the man's cunning – anyone who can fool me is worthy of recognition.'

'They're preparing to charge,' Eperitus warned.

Odysseus forgot his admiration of Dolon and looked up. 'You're right. We need to call the men to order at once!'

He turned and shouted for the Ithacans to halt and form line. The Greeks had already pushed far beyond the safety of their flanks, which were held firm by the wings of the Trojan army, and it was in the hands of the gods whether the disordered soldiers of

Ithaca, Argos and Mycenae could be alerted to their danger. Then Eperitus thought of Agamemnon, who dashing ahead of his own men would quickly be cut off and surrounded by any attack.

At that moment, horns sounded on both sides of them, followed quickly by the war cries of hundreds of cavalrymen and charioteers as they spurred their horses into the attack. The ground thundered with the familiar and terrifying sound of approaching hooves, filling everyone who heard it with fear. Eperitus drew instinctively closer to Odysseus, readying his shield and spear to defend the king. Then he remembered his promise to Clytaemnestra, that he would do everything in his power to protect her husband's life. Wavering for the briefest of moments, though it seemed an age amongst his feverish thoughts, he looked from Agamemnon to Odysseus and back again. And as Agamemnon continued to kill Trojan stragglers, oblivious to the fast-approaching horde of chariots and horsemen, he knew what he had to do.

Odysseus was already running towards the lines of Ithacans.

'Eperitus!' he called over his shoulder. 'Eperitus, come on!'

'I have to warn Agamemnon,' Eperitus shouted back. 'He'll be surrounded and killed unless someone helps him.'

Odysseus looked across, saw the danger and nodded. As he watched him join the other Ithacans, Eperitus suffered a pang of doubt. Was he right to abandon his own king to the threat of a cavalry charge, all for the sake of the reviled Agamemnon and an oath that he'd been tricked into taking? Then he saw that Diomedes had also realized what was happening, and he was reassured by the sight of him forming his doughty Argives up next to the Ithacans. Whatever happened now would be the will of the gods, he told himself, before throwing his shield across his back and sprinting towards Agamemnon.

By now, the small band of Mycenaeans had spotted the peril they were in and had formed a circle about their king. The Trojan cavalry swept around them, throwing their heavy spears at the knot of men. Many of the bronze points were turned aside or stopped by the broad leather shields, but some found flesh and spilled men backwards, forcing the survivors to draw closer in on themselves. A few hurled spears back at the lightly armoured horsemen, bringing several down from their mounts to crash into the long grass below.

While the Trojans concentrated on wearing down the Mycenaeans, Eperitus ran up unnoticed and plunged the point of his spear into a passing rider's ribcage, piercing his heart and killing him instantly. As he fell, Eperitus seized the reins and hauled himself on to the horse's back. He slid his sword from its scabbard, kicked his heels into the animal's flanks and sent it dashing towards the Mycenaeans. As he did so, another Trojan cavalryman turned his mount skilfully and aimed a spear at Eperitus's head. It flew over his shoulder, only a hand's breadth from piercing his eye. A moment later Eperitus charged down on his assailant and swung his blade into the man's neck, tumbling his dead body to the ground.

He raced on, seeing the last of the Mycenaeans now surrounded by cavalrymen, their swords rising and falling as they hacked the Greeks to death. For a moment he forgot whose life he was trying to save and felt a pang of fear that he was too late, and then Agamemnon stumbled out from the knot of horsemen, followed by Talthybius, his herald. Both men were armed with sword and shield and each felled a Trojan before running as fast as they could in the direction of the distant walls. Three horsemen broke free from the melee in which the last of Agamemnon's bodyguard were giving their lives so their king could escape, but did not see Eperitus as they chased after the fleeing Mycenaeans. He charged in from their left and sank his sword into one man's spine, before hacking the blade with a backward blow across a second's face. The third dropped his spear – useless at such a close range – and pulled out his sword, only to have his arm severed below the elbow by another swing of Eperitus's blade.

As the man fell to the ground, shrieking with pain, Eperitus saw a chariot cut across the path of Agamemnon and Talthybius and draw to a halt. Whether they knew they were facing the leader of the Greek army, or whether they had simply seen his armour and decided to take it for themselves, the two Trojans jumped down from the car and ran at Agamemnon. Both were tall and heavily built, alike enough to be brothers. The first rammed his shield into Talthybius's face, swatting him aside like one of the many mosquitoes that haunted the plains of Ilium. The second leapt at Agamemnon with his spear, but the king twisted aside with surprising agility and punched the point of his own weapon into his attacker's throat. The man dropped with nothing more than a grunt, but as Agamemnon turned, the second Trojan was already upon him, piercing his forearm with the tip of his spear. The king fell back with a shout of pain and surprise, letting his sword fall from his fingertips. Taking his spear in both hands, the Trojan raised it high above the plume of his helmet to deliver the killing blow. In the same instant, Eperitus's blade swept his head from his shoulders. The torso fell forward and gushed blood over the King of Men, who kicked it aside and got to his feet, still clutching at his wounded arm.

'Eperitus!' he exclaimed, wide-eyed. 'Where did you come from?'

Eperitus ignored the question and dismounted. He found Talthybius, dazed and with a bloody nose, and helped him back to his feet; then he tore a strip of cloth from a dead man's cloak and bound it around Agamemnon's wounded forearm. Leading the two men to the abandoned chariot, he handed Talthybius the reins and put a hand on his shoulder.

'Take Agamemnon back to the camp as quickly as you can. Machaon or Podaleirius can tend to his arm there. I must go and find Odysseus.'

'Wait!' Agamemnon ordered. He stood in the chariot and looked around at the chaos of battle: bodies lay everywhere, their nationalities indistinguishable; knots of Greeks struggled to return to their comrades, where, by a miracle, the gap left in the line had been plugged and the Trojan cavalry were still being held at bay. But it was only a matter of time before the Trojan reserve – which

Eperitus had seen marching up out of the defile where they had lain hidden – arrived and threw their weight into the fighting. 'I don't understand, Eperitus. We had them running before us . . .'

'It was a trap, my lord,' Eperitus explained, trying to hide the sneer from his voice. 'Hector sent Dolon to feed us false information.'

'But why?' Talthybius asked.

'To draw us out from the safety of the walls and massacre us on the plain,' Eperitus answered. 'And they may yet succeed. Now, go.'

He slapped the hindquarters of the nearest horse and, with a snap of the reins and a shout from Talthybius, the chariot set off at a dash towards the Greek lines. Eperitus ran back to his captured mount and leapt lightly on to its back. The added height enabled him to take in the battlefield at a glance, and to his horror he saw the Ithacans and Argives being attacked by a mass of Trojan cavalry. He tried to spot Odysseus amongst the struggling men but could not, and with a sudden chill sensed that the king was in mortal danger.

'EPERITUS!' boomed a familiar voice. '*EPERITUS!*'

He pulled on the reins and turned the horse to face Ajax, who was running towards him with great strides. Menelaus was at his heels and both men looked concerned.

'Why aren't you with Odysseus?' Menelaus demanded, his voice accusing.

'I left him to save your brother's life,' Eperitus retorted. 'And now I'm going back to find him. You should get back to the safety of the lines too, my lords. The Trojan reserve will be upon us at any moment.'

He indicated the mass of men marching towards them across the plain. The two kings looked and their eyes widened briefly.

'We've just seen Diomedes being driven back to the ships by Sthenelaus,' Ajax said, tearing his eyes away from the force that would certainly spell doom for the Greeks. 'He told us Odysseus needed help.'

'He'd been shot in the foot by Paris,' Menelaus added, seeing the look on Eperitus's face at the news Diomedes had abandoned his friend. 'That's why we're here.'

'Come on, then,' Eperitus said, sliding back down from the horse and pulling his shield on to his arm.

The three men ran to where the Trojan cavalry were almost overwhelming the beleaguered armies of Ithaca and Argos, falling on the horsemen from behind and cutting a swathe through the tightly packed mass. Ajax felled several riders with his spear, and when the weapon stuck fast in the body of one of his victims he used his height and strength to punch men from the backs of their mounts instead, even knocking horses to the ground in his battle rage. Menelaus, too, was lost in a frenzy of killing, desperate to find the elusive Paris and finish their duel of four days before. But Eperitus was a match for both men. The strong sense that Odysseus was in danger filled him with urgency. As the horsemen struggled to turn about in the dense throng and face their attackers their light armour was no match for the sharp bronze of Eperitus's spear. One man after another dropped to the ground before the terrible onslaught of the three Greeks. Panic spread through the Trojan ranks and soon they were scattering before them like sheep before wolves. Then Eperitus saw Odysseus, standing before a line of Ithacan spearmen, his shield stuck with arrows and his bloody sword in his hand. Omeros was on the ground behind him, struggling to pull himself to safety across a carpet of dead men as his king defended him from a mounted Trojan.

The rider's scaled armour was expensive and marked him as a chieftain. Oblivious to the terror that was forcing his countrymen to flee, he reared his horse so that its hooves flailed in the air above Odysseus's head. Odysseus threw his shield up and in the same moment his opponent pushed down with his long spear, piercing Odysseus's side and toppling him backwards across the struggling form of Omeros. Eperitus gave a shout and sprang forward, followed by Ajax and Menelaus. The Trojan turned, the look of triumph dropping from his face as Eperitus's spear pushed up into his armpit, almost severing the limb at the shoulder. He let out a cry of pain, but somehow managed to turn his horse with one arm and ride away. The Trojan cavalry followed, streaming back across the plain in the wake of their captain.

Chapter Twenty-Six

IN AGAMEMNON'S TENT

Eperitus knelt beside Odysseus and cupped his hand beneath the back of his head. Antiphus and Eurybates appeared and pulled Omeros free, while casting anxious glances at their king's pale face and the blood seeping out from his right side.

'Odysseus!' Eperitus urged. Odysseus's familiar green eyes stared back at him blankly. 'Say something, Odysseus.'

Odysseus blinked with pain and gave a groan. 'As long as you don't want me to sing.'

Eperitus's face broke into a grin. He helped Odysseus to sit up, while Ajax tore strips from a woollen cloak and pressed them against the wound.

'It's not fatal,' he said, though his stern tone failed to completely hide his relief. 'Nothing vital's been hit; just a flesh wound with a lot of blood loss. You'll live to fight another day, my old friend, though not *this* day. I'll take you back to the ships in my chariot.'

Odysseus shook his head. 'Let Eperitus take me; you and Menelaus are needed here. The Trojans will be on us any moment and it's up to you to organize a fighting retreat. Get the army back to the walls.'

'And concede defeat again?' Menelaus spat. 'Not while Paris is on the battlefield.'

'Odysseus is right,' Ajax countered, rising to his feet and looking to where the Trojan reserves had come within spear range.

289

Hector was at their head with Paris at his side, both men encouraging the ranks of fresh warriors with loud war cries. 'We have to salvage the army or face ruin.'

As he spoke, Antiphus arrived with a chariot. Eurybates lifted the unconscious Omeros into the car, while Eperitus followed with Odysseus leaning heavily on his shoulder. Despite his weakness, the king stood and clutched the rail for support, so that as many of his men as possible could see he was able to stand. Then Eperitus took the reins and, with a shout, sent the horses racing back towards the walls, the wheels bouncing over the countless bodies that littered the ground. Odysseus threw a glance over his shoulder as the hordes of Trojans threw their spears and charged.

'They'll make it back,' Eperitus reassured him. 'It's a long time since the Ithacans were simple fishermen and farmers.'

'I have confidence in them,' Odysseus answered, weakly. 'And Hector and Paris will find their match in Ajax and Menelaus. But you must return as soon as you can and take charge of the Ithacans, at least until my wound has been tended to.'

Eperitus nodded. He slapped the reins across the horses' backs and fixed his gaze grimly on the tall gates that were looming up ahead of them.

Achilles stood in the prow of his beached ship, looking beyond the sea of tents to the walls at the top of the slope. All around him the Myrmidons were busy preparing their galleys to leave, some walking up and down springy gangplanks with loads on their shoulders while others raised masts or readied sails and rigging for the long journey home. Patroclus and Peisandros directed their movements reluctantly and without haste, hoping that the prince would yet change his mind. And as they watched him – his gaze focused intently on the walls as if his eyes could pierce the bricks and wood to see the battle raging beyond – it seemed as if at any moment he would call for his armour and summon the men to arms. But still he remained there as if he were carved from stone, listening motionless to the distant sounds of battle and watching the streams of wounded come limping through the gates to choke the tents with their broken bodies and fill the whole camp with their cries.

'Patroclus!' he shouted, suddenly. 'Patroclus!'

Patroclus threw a glance at Peisandros, then dashed up the nearest gangplank, knocking one of the Myrmidons and his load on to the sand below.

'My lord?' he asked.

'Another chariot has just come through the gates. Run and find out who it is, and ask them what's happening on the plain. I'm tired of not knowing what's going on.'

Patroclus hesitated, hoping that Achilles might also send for his armour, but when the prince returned to his impassive stance he gave a short bow and ran back down to the beach.

'Are we fighting?' Peisandros asked urgently as he passed.

Patroclus shook his head, then sprinted across the sand towards the centre of the camp, where Agamemnon's tent stood like a white Olympus among the smaller peaks of its neighbours. As he passed the wounded from the battle they called out to him, stretching out their hands for help; but when they saw he was a Myrmidon their cries of anguish became insults and shouts of anger. Even the dying looked up at him with disdain or turned away, preferring to suffer than implore the aid of one of Achilles's men. But Patroclus did not begrudge them their bitterness. He was used to being treated with scorn – hated as he was for his arrogant nature – and he would have felt the same in their place. There was not a man in the whole Greek army – not on the whole face of the earth – that Patroclus did not admire or love as much as he did Achilles, but even he knew that the prince's pride had gone too far this time. Pride was the prerogative of great men, but when it came at the expense of honour it was a perversion. He averted his eyes from the wounded and ran on.

A line of chariots waited outside the great tent of Agamemnon, where the first man Patroclus saw was Eperitus. He had always looked down on Odysseus's captain, a low-born noble like himself, but things had changed in the past few days and he found his old conceit waning rapidly.

'Have you come to tell us your master has decided to fight?' the Ithacan asked, unlooping two skins of water from the rail of a chariot.

Patroclus shook his head. 'He remains the prisoner of his stubborn honour.'

'Honour?' Eperitus snorted, turning and walking to the mouth of the tent. 'That's not honour.'

Patroclus followed him. 'I agree with you, Eperitus. And I think *he* does too. It's destroying him to wait by his ship and do nothing while his comrades fight and die on the plain.'

'Then why has he sent you here, assuming he has?'

'He wants to know who are the wounded men he's watched being brought back from the battle.'

'Then come inside and see for yourself,' Eperitus replied, indicating the tent with his open hand.

Patroclus led the way into Agamemnon's headquarters. The sun still streamed in through the heavy canvas, but the familiar sense of order and majesty that had once marked the King of Men's seat of power was gone. The benches where the council sat had been dragged aside without ceremony to make way for a dozen wounded men, who lay on mattresses or were sitting in fur-draped chairs in the centre of the tent. They were waited on by slaves with bowls of steaming water and lengths of bloodstained cloth, which they used to stem the bleeding and clean the wounds. The air was close and smelled strongly of blood and pungent herbs. Though the groans were more muted than out among the rest of the sprawling camp, the shock for Patroclus lay not in the condition of the wounded men but in their identities. At the far end of the tent was Agamemnon himself, seated gloomily in his golden throne as fresh bandages were wrapped around his forearm by a female slave. On a mattress at the centre of the tent was the great Diomedes, who still wore his armour but for the greave on his left leg, which had been removed to allow Sthenelaus to bathe the arrow hole in his foot; the shaft and the broken head of the missile lay beside him. Then there was Machaon, the healer, who sat on a chair while Nestor dabbed gingerly at the wound in his shoulder. Every now and then he would bark out instructions to the dozens of slaves tending to the injured, before slumping back into his chair, exhausted.

'Paris shot him,' Eperitus said, watching Patroclus's gaze. 'He shot Diomedes, too, and Eurypylus over there.'

He pointed to one of the kings from Thessaly, a sandy-haired man who lay on a mattress, biting on to a folded leather belt as a soldier pulled an arrow from his thigh.

'He's been making a nuisance of himself with that bow and arrow,' Odysseus commented, rising to his feet from a corner of the tent and taking Patroclus by the hand. His armour had been removed and his midriff swathed in bandages; a pink stain on his left side, below the ribs, showed where he had been stabbed. 'After his scrap with Menelaus, I think Helen must have persuaded him to stay out of the real fighting and rely on his archery instead.'

'I can hardly believe it,' Patroclus stuttered. 'So many of you wounded.'

'There are more still on the battlefield, fighting to save what's left of the army,' Eperitus said. 'Both the Ajaxes, Menelaus, Idomeneus, Teucer, Antilochus . . .'

'To name only the best, but even they won't last indefinitely against Hector,' Odysseus added. 'He's like a lion out there, and he has the support of Paris, Sarpedon, Aeneas and Apheidas. There's only one hope left now for the Greeks.'

'And he remains implacable,' said Patroclus.

'But have you spoken with him, as I asked you to?'

'He won't listen. Even now, while the Greeks are streaming from the field and crying out in their suffering, he's done nothing more than send me here to take a tally of the wounded. I've appealed to him in every way I can, Odysseus, but now I'm starting to believe *nothing* will ever move him to fight again. All he wants to do is go back to Scyros for his wife and son, then return to Phthia. Nobody else matters to him any more, not even the men he has fought alongside all these years.'

Odysseus turned away and Eperitus caught a glimmer of something in his eye – that familiar look that came across him when he was struck by an idea.

'*Nobody*, you say?' he mused. 'Then you underestimate how much he cares about *you*, Patroclus. But enough of that. If Achilles won't be drawn into battle, it's up to you to act on the advice your father gave you before you left Phthia. Have you forgotten that Menoetius told you to be an example to Achilles, whose pride he knew would cause him trouble?'

Patroclus snorted his derision, but Odysseus placed his great hands on the Myrmidon's arms.

'Why don't *you* lead the Myrmidons into battle? If you can convince Achilles to lend you his armour and visored helmet then the Trojans will think he's returned to the fight. It'd strike terror into their hearts; you'd send them fleeing back to the city and be responsible for saving the army! Better still, a man like you could face Hector and win – who would dare to call you a lesser noble then?'

Patroclus stared at Odysseus for a long moment, then shrugged off his hands and turned to Eurypylus, who was grunting with pain as the arrow was torn from his thigh and his blood began to pump out over the rich furs.

'He'll never agree to it, Odysseus,' Patroclus insisted, before snatching some bandages from a slave and going to help the struggling Thessalian.

Odysseus turned to Eperitus with a knowing smile on his lips.

'I'll talk to him again,' he said quietly, taking the skins of water Eperitus had brought. 'You should go back to the plain and take charge of the Ithacans. The sound of battle's much closer now and you'll do more good up there than you can here.'

'Let me go too, my lord.' Omeros emerged from the shadows

at the side of the tent, the wound on his forehead freshly bandaged. 'I'm no use here and I want to go and fight.'

Eperitus looked at Odysseus, who nodded; then with Omeros following at his heels he left the tent and walked out into the bright sunshine. As they climbed the slope to the walls, Eperitus looked back and saw the calm waters of the bay with the sun gleaming on the wave caps as they rolled in towards the beach. All along the sandy curve of the great cove the Greek ships were drawn up out of the water, like a vast and peaceful colony of seals basking in the midday warmth. Most had barely touched the water for the whole decade of the war and their silent, empty timbers were as dry as tinder. One lick of flame to each would see them burn. Eperitus imagined the beach awash with Trojans, tossing torches into the hulls so that they blazed like a line of funeral pyres, the wind fanning the flames and spreading them from ship to ship.

'May the gods forbid they ever get that far,' he muttered to himself.

'Sir?'

'Nothing, Omeros,' he replied, then, looking up to the walls, he saw that the last of the Greeks had escaped the battlefield and were thronging the top of the slope. 'Come on – let's see who's left of the Ithacans.'

They set off at a run, following the well-trodden paths to the top and kicking up sprays of dust from the ground. Soon they had joined the host of weary soldiers on the ridge, whose tired, dispirited eyes stared out from grime- and blood-encrusted faces as their commanders tried to shepherd them into some sort of order. Streams of wounded were being helped down to the ships and many more must have lain dead on the plain. But the gods had been merciful: thousands upon thousands had escaped the battle-field and now packed the narrow crescent of ground that topped the ridge above the camp. Hundreds more manned the walls above them and were hurling rocks or firing arrows into the invisible

attackers beyond, whose mingled cries of pain, rage and determination could be heard roaring like a storm-wracked sea. Some of
the men on the walls fell back as black-feathered Trojan arrows
found their mark, but Eperitus could see the mighty figure of
Great Ajax exhorting the defenders to hold and fight, while his
half-brother, Teucer, picked out targets with his bow from behind
the cover of Ajax's tall shield. On the other side of him was
Menestheus, the Athenian king, hurling spear after spear into the
seething mass of men below.

Suddenly there was a loud yelling and Eperitus saw the tops of
ladders – clearly brought up from Troy during the night – lodging
against the battlements. Moments later the walls were beset with
Lycian spearmen, clambering over the parapets with Sarpedon at
their head and bringing havoc to the defenders. As the Greeks on
the ridge behind looked up in horror, Eperitus balanced a spear in
his right hand, took aim, and sent a Lycian chieftain spinning from
the battlements into the spike-filled ditch beyond. Then an enormous boom shook the air and every eye turned to the gates, where
trails of dust were still falling from the timbers as they quivered
beneath the blow that had hit them. Another boom followed,
smashing the gates from their hinges and sending them whirling to
the ground. Through the haze that followed their destruction a
figure emerged. Hector tossed aside the large boulder he had used
to break down the gates, then, with a metallic scrape, drew his
long sword from its sheath and with a loud cry led the Trojans
into the Greek camp.

Chapter Twenty-Seven

PEACE OFFERINGS

The Trojans poured through the broken gates with Hector at their head. He crashed into the shocked Greeks and cut a swathe through their packed ranks, wielding his sword to left and right with murderous effect. On either side, men were leaping from the walls and fleeing from Sarpedon and his victorious Lycians, many abandoning their weapons in panic as they ran. The hideous discord of bronze upon bronze broke out once more, deafening men as they struggled face-to-face with their enemies, driven by anger, hatred or fear as they stabbed and hacked at one another. Clouds of dust rose up from beneath their feet to dry throats and sting eyes, and very soon every man was locked in a personal battle for survival.

'Stay close to me,' Eperitus instructed, glancing briefly at Omeros before dashing across to join the battle for the gates.

Here the fighting was hardest as the Greek line bent back before Hector's onslaught. No quarter was given by either side as men already exhausted by their efforts fell upon each other with renewed vigour, killing and being killed in droves. While the spearmen struggled to contain the swarming enemy, the lightly armed skirmishers had fallen back and were firing at short range into the mass of Trojans. But their efforts were to no avail: the Trojans had tasted victory and were fighting with a drunken recklessness, slaughtering the Greeks and pushing them inexorably back down the slope before them. Only the hard-won experience of the veteran warriors and the dogged determination of each man not to betray his comrades kept the Greeks from full flight. Eperitus and Omeros fell back with them and soon the thousands of struggling men were trampling the outermost tents and expended fires of the once-unassailable Greek camp, the battle now stretching diagonally from the farthest point of the bay in the north to the top of the ridge in the east.

Eperitus ducked instinctively as a spear passed over his head and buried itself in the chest of the man behind him. Startled, he saw Hector away to his right, taking another spear from one of his soldiers. This time he did not cast the weapon, but charged into the attack. Eperitus spared a moment to push Omeros back, then raised his defences to meet the full force of Hector's assault. Their shields clashed with an arm-numbing impact that sent Eperitus stumbling backwards. He steadied himself just in time to avoid the ensuing thrust of Hector's spear, then brought his sword down against the Trojan's shield. Hector swatted the blow aside with contempt and lunged forward again. This time the point penetrated the thick leather of Eperitus's shield, just missing his shoulder. Eperitus twisted the heavy shield aside and snapped the socketed head away from the shaft, then rushed forward and swung his blade at Hector's scowling face. The Trojan leapt back with the agility of a man half his size, throwing the shaft of the broken spear aside and drawing his sword with a menacing, metallic scrape.

Eperitus braced himself, but the expected attack did not come. Instead, Hector paused and narrowed his eyes against the dust their battle had raised.

'Odysseus's squire,' he said at last, recognizing the blood- and dirt-stained figure before him. He stepped back and lowered his weapon slightly.

'His friend,' Eperitus corrected.

'Then Odysseus is blessed in his friendships – you're a good fighter. I would have been honoured to strip your armour from your corpse and add it to my growing collection.'

'*Would* have? Then you concede I am the better warrior?'

Hector smiled. 'No, but I won't fight you. You're still looking for Apheidas, I take it?'

'Yes,' Eperitus answered.

'Then perhaps you'll be glad to know he's looking for you, too – and I have no intention of spoiling his fun.' Hector backed away and sheathed his sword as one of his soldiers passed him another spear. 'If you've got any sense you'll beg that loathsome coward, Achilles, to let you sail back to Greece with him: if Apheidas finds you on the battlefield, even the gods won't be able to help you.'

He said something in his own tongue to the men around him and pointed at Eperitus, then bowed briefly to the Ithacan before slipping back into their ranks. Within a moment the Trojans were attacking again. It was as if Hector had never appeared, except for the noticeable fact that none of the enemy would come near to Eperitus. Whenever he attacked them, they would close their shields like a wall against him, refusing to cross their weapons with his. In return, Eperitus's sense of honour forbade him to kill men who would not fight.

'Just think, sir,' Omeros said, crouching beside him as the maelstrom of battle whirled around them, 'if all men simply refused to fight, there would be no wars and we could all live happy and peaceful lives.'

'Then warriors and poets like us would starve,' Eperitus replied. 'But I'll be damned if I'm going to be kept out of the battle; we'll find another place, where the struggle's just as desperate and the Trojans haven't been ordered not to fight me.'

'Idomeneus and his Cretans are hard pressed on the right flank,' Omeros said, craning his neck to look eastward, before turning his gaze to the north, 'and things are even worse on the left. They're nearly at the ships!'

Eperitus followed his stare, using his keen eyesight to distinguish between the mass of figures at the far end of the bay, even though there were many thousands of them and all were shrouded in dust.

'Both the Ajaxes are there,' he announced, 'and Teucer with them. They're holding the Trojans back, for now at least. But wait! Hector's making his way there, and Paris is with him. That's where we're needed, Omeros, before they get among the ships and start putting them to the torch. Zeus's beard, if Achilles doesn't forget his foolish pride soon we're going to be destroyed!'

They pulled back from the fighting and set off at a run, through the scattered ranks of skirmishers and the disorderly tents – some of which had been set ablaze by flaming arrows and were sending columns of black smoke into the air – and on to where the struggle was at its fiercest. Arrows and spears fell all around them as they ran, while the ground was choked with countless wounded, groaning with the pain of severed limbs and other ghastly wounds. Then they felt the soft sand beneath their feet and to their left the tall beaks of the galleys were rising up like a leafless forest, the symbolic goal of the Trojan horde as they wrought havoc across the camp.

Suddenly the two Ithacans were in the thick of the battle again. They joined the rear of the throng, where the cowards hung back from the fighting, and quickly pushed their way through to the front, where the mounds of the dead had made a low wall over which the two armies were trying to bring their arms to bear. Here they saw the towering form of Great Ajax, a bastion of destructive fury amongst the fading strength of the Greeks. Teucer was lurking at his side, an almost comical parody of manhood were it not for the arrows that sped with deadly efficiency from his bow, bringing one Trojan down after another. Then there was Little Ajax, standing on the piled corpses with his pet snake about his shoulders and holding the severed head of a man by his black hair, which he tossed into the crowded enemy with a yell of triumph. It landed at the feet of Hector, who kicked it aside contemptuously and, with a shout that rose above the din of war, ordered his army to renew the attack. The air filled with heavy spears and hummed to the sound of hundreds of arrows speeding towards their targets, tearing the life from the flesh of scores of men and dropping their corpses into the dust. Then the Trojans gave a cheer and fell upon the faltering Greeks. It was enough. Even the fearful presence of the Ajaxes could not stop the cracks that now raced through the Greek ranks. First the men at the back scattered, then the rest fell away before the force and fury of the Trojan assault.

Eperitus ran back across the sand towards the beached galleys, where amazingly men were trying to heave the heavy vessels back into the sea, so desperate were they to escape the vengeful Trojans. Others were clambering up the black hulls, hoping to avoid death on the decks above, while a few simply threw away their weapons and crashed into the waves, thinking they could swim to safety with their armour weighing about them. And yet there were many more who turned again and fought, encouraged by the presence of Great Ajax as he bellowed commands over the ringing of weapons and the crashing of the waves. Eperitus watched him run up a gangplank to the deck of a galley – closely followed by Teucer – where he seized one of the long spears used for ship-to-ship fighting and began stabbing at the Trojans swarming below. The last Eperitus saw of him was as he pushed the weapon into the chest of a young man running towards the ships with a lighted torch in his hand, ready to toss it on to the bone-dry decks. The lad fell back into the sand with a scream, still clutching the torch as his legs quivered in the last throes of life.

Eperitus turned to Omeros, but found he was no longer with him. He looked around, desperately searching the many figures running this way and that across the beach, but could see no sign of the young bard. A pang of regret coursed through him, then he saw a man from the corner of his eye, running towards him with his sword raised.

Eperitus threw up his shield and took the blow on the thick leather hide, forcing his attacker's arm wide. Before the man could bring his shield across, Eperitus had plunged his weapon into the gap and found his abdomen, punching a hole through the leather armour and on into his soft stomach. Dark blood gushed out on to the sand as he withdrew his sword from the wound, and the Trojan fell quivering and whimpering to his knees, his eyes wide with the shock of the pain. Eperitus spared him the long and agonizing death of a stomach wound with a swift jab to his throat, but as the body collapsed at his feet he saw another figure approaching. This man, however, was in no hurry. He swept aside his black cloak to reveal scaled bronze armour that gleamed in the bright sunshine. Tugging at the cords beneath his chin, he seized the plume of his helmet and pulled it from his head.

'We meet again, Son,' Apheidas said.

Patroclus stood at the mouth of Agamemnon's tent and looked north, where the fighting was at its fiercest. The distant roar and clatter of battle was unbearable to his warrior's ears, powerless as he was to follow his instinct and go to the aid of the Greeks. There had been no sign of action from the Myrmidon camp beyond the continuous loading of the galleys, and no recall from Achilles, ordering him to don his armour and prepare for battle. As far as anyone knew, the greatest fighter in the Greek army was still standing on the prow of his ship, tending to his grudge and gloating over Agamemnon's discomfort while his countrymen perished at the hands of the Trojans. Patroclus gave a frustrated snort and kicked the sand at his feet.

'Here you are.'

Patroclus turned to see Odysseus, leaning on his spear with his body armour hanging from his other hand. His bandages were dark with sweat from the warm, humid air, and the bloodstain on his left side had spread in a wide circle beneath his ribs.

'Is it still going against us?' he continued. 'Agamemnon refuses to come out and see for himself. Nestor and I had to persuade him against giving the order to launch the galleys back into the sea and head for home.'

'There wouldn't be time anyway.' Patroclus dismissed the notion. 'The Trojans would be on you before you could remove the props and push the hulls back down into the water. Only the Myrmidons will come away from these beaches alive today.'

'Ah, the Myrmidons,' Odysseus said, glancing south to where the Phthian camp lay hidden beyond the sea of tents.

Patroclus drew a deep breath through his teeth, then, exhaling through his pinched nostrils, he turned to Odysseus. 'You don't have to die with the rest of them, you know. Achilles will be more than happy to take you with us. And Diomedes and Nestor, too, if they're willing.'

Odysseus shook his head. 'Nestor won't leave without Antilochus, and Diomedes has too much pride. As for me, I've no wish to abandon my countrymen and my honour on the shores of Ilium, though I thank you for the offer, Patroclus. If this is the end, then I will die fighting where I stand, and cursing the gods with my last breath for their false promises. Here, give me a hand with this, will you?' He raised the body armour and pointed to his large, triangular abdomen.

'Surely you don't expect to fight in your condition?'

'Diomedes and I can make a stand together. At least we'll have a few of them to accompany us to Hades; and it's far more preferable than lying on our sick beds, waiting for a cold dagger across our throats. Unless you can convince Achilles to let you lead the Myrmidons into battle, of course.'

Patroclus shook his head and looked westward to the calm ocean.

'It's impossible.'

'It's *not* impossible. Go to him, Patroclus. Tell him how we're suffering. Plead with him, if you have to, but in the name of Athena make him let you fight! He *will* listen to you, I know it. Why do you think he sent you here if it wasn't because his heart is out there with the rest of the Greeks? Whatever he may think of Agamemnon, he won't want to see his old friends destroyed by the Trojans. All you have to do is convince him that it has reached that point — the destruction of the whole expedition — and he'll relent.'

'*All right.*' Patroclus shouted. Then, looking at the battle raging only a bowshot away, he realized that Odysseus was right: the Greek army was on a precipice, being edged towards annihilation, and only the return of Achilles – or someone the Trojans believed was Achilles – would save them now. 'All right. I'll speak with him again. I'll convince him to let me lead the Myrmidons into battle. And when he says yes, I'll drive the Trojans from the battlefield in his name.'

He reached out and took Odysseus's hand in farewell. There was a look of relief in his eyes, now that he had finally made his mind up to do what had been in his heart ever since Odysseus had spoken to him the night before. Then, with a last determined glance at the lines of battle as they drew ever tighter around the camp, he turned and sprinted southward.

❧

As Eperitus looked at his father, the anarchy of the battle that raged around them faded away, so that the only thing he was conscious of was the dark figure before him. He reached up instinctively and touched the scar across his forehead, which Apheidas had given him in the temple of Artemis.

'You've thought about what I said?' Apheidas asked, tossing aside his spear and slipping his sword from its scabbard. 'In the temple.'

'I gave you my answer then,' Eperitus replied. 'I promised that if you let me live I would hunt you down and kill you. And I intend to keep my word.'

He sprang forward, knocking his father's defences aside with his heavy shield and swinging his sword down at his helmetless head. But the blow was too slow and Apheidas slipped aside with ease.

'Where's your enthusiasm, Eperitus? A man with half your skill could have done better than that.'

Eperitus narrowed his eyes and curled back his lip, desperate to muster the familiar hatred he had lived with for so long and angry with himself that it would not come. He lunged again, thrusting towards his father's chest with the point of his sword. Apheidas forced the blade upwards, but Eperitus punched his shield into his side and sent him staggering backwards. He leapt after him, but Apheidas raised his shield against the repeated strikes of his son's sword.

'That's better, lad,' he said. 'But still you don't possess the hatred to kill me, do you? Even the bit of fight you showed at Lyrnessus has gone out of you. In fact, I believe you *have* been thinking about my proposition, haven't you?'

Eperitus felt his anger and loathing rising at last, but knew his feelings were directed at himself for his sudden weakness. For twenty years he had wanted to kill his father; he had dreamed of nothing other than to avenge his family's honour in the traitor's blood. But now the opportunity had come he found his hatred suddenly impotent, just as Calchas had warned. He swung wildly at Apheidas's shield, but it was as if his muscles had turned to water or the bronze blade was suddenly too heavy to lift; the blow reverberated against the layered leather with no more threat than if he had been using a wooden training sword.

He looked at his father, but instead of the mockery he had expected he saw sympathy.

'You know I'm right, don't you, Eperitus? You can no more hate me than I can hate you. You're divided inside: between your loathing of what I did and your love of who I once was – and could be again; between your loyalty to the Greeks, and your realization that *you* are half Trojan, fighting against a people who deserve more than to be wiped out by Agamemnon's lust for power.'

Eperitus thought of how Astynome had asked him to live with her in Troy. He remembered her face and felt his longing for her again. Then he thought of Agamemnon, the man who had sacrificed Iphigenia just so that he could sail to Ilium and bring the towers of Troy down in ruin. He glanced down at the white hart painted on the inside of his shield in memory of his daughter, and as he looked he was reminded that the shield itself was his grandfather's, a man who would have put honour ahead of family, and oaths of fealty before blood. And so, Eperitus resolved, would he.

'You've misjudged me, Father,' he said. 'My loyalty is to Odysseus and no blood-ties will break that. As for you, even if you're right and I can no longer find the hatred in me that I used to have for you, my honour still demands your death.'

He stepped forward, protecting his left side with his grandfather's shield and driving the point of his sword at his father's face. Apheidas used his own shield to block the jab and send it skidding upwards, while at the same time swinging his blade at Eperitus's shin. Eperitus skipped back two paces, avoiding the blow and taking a second on his shield before pushing forward again, using the heavy leather to batter Apheidas's own defences aside. He thrust the point of his sword forward with deadly speed, only for his father to twist aside with equal swiftness and the blade to skid across his body armour without finding his flesh. As he jumped back, Apheidas hacked downwards, knocking the weapon from Eperitus's hand. Eperitus turned and brought up his shield just in time to stop a second blow that would have taken his head from his shoulders.

'You're forgetting yourself, Father,' he mocked as he fell back, stooping to retrieve a discarded spear from the sand. 'Perhaps you've misjudged your own feelings, too.'

'I'm not the one who's confused,' Apheidas replied, the fury of battle sharpening his features.

He lunged again. Eperitus twisted away from the blow and arced the point of his spear at his father's face. Apheidas ducked and swung at Eperitus's legs, only to be checked by his tall shield. The two men fell back and stared at each other, breathing hard.

'I told you before, you don't have the skill or the hatred to defeat me, Eperitus,' Apheidas hissed. 'But at least listen to what I have to say.'

'Save your breath, Father.'

'I understand your anger with me, Eperitus, but if you won't forgive my past mistakes, maybe you'll have more compassion for your comrades. Look at them – they're dying in their hundreds. How much longer will they hold out? How long before Hector sends the last Greek to Hades? But *I* can save them.'

'What do you mean?'

'I command a quarter of the army. If I pull my companies out of the battle – I can find excuses later – it'll spread confusion and panic among the Trojans and give the Greeks time to reorganize, then use their greater numbers to drive Hector back out of the camp. All I ask is that you come with me to Troy. I have a plan that will bring a peaceful end to this war, but I can't do it without your help.'

Eperitus looked around at the battle. He heard the crackle of fire and turned to see the first galley going up in flames; columns of black smoke were billowing upwards as Hector laughed drunkenly on the beach below. Chariots and horsemen were galloping in every direction, pursuing fleeing Greeks or launching their ash spears into the ranks of those who still resisted. He saw Paris with his deadly bow, Sarpedon at the head of his Lycians, Aeneas leading his Dardanians, and for as far as he could see in every direction, men killing and being killed. And suddenly it was in his power to stop it. All he needed to do was say yes and the battle would be over; his friends would live and the army would be saved from destruction. What was more, if Apheidas's words were true, he could end the conflict that had claimed so many lives on both sides; he could be reunited with Astynome, and Odysseus could at last return to his beloved Ithaca.

But he would also lose his honour. In saving his comrades – above all, Odysseus – he would betray the oaths he had taken and be cursed by his former friends and the gods alike. Could anything be worth such a price?

He thought not.

'No, Father, not even for the sake of my friends. I would rather die here with them than betray the oaths I've taken and return with you to Troy.'

Apheidas's lips tightened. His hand shook visibly as he raised his sword to renew the battle. Then he shook his head and let the blade fall.

'It's said Agamemnon murdered his own child to appease the gods and sail to Troy,' he sighed. 'But whatever you may think of me, Eperitus, I won't commit the same crime. I won't fight you any more.'

As he finished, a horn call rang out across the battlefield. It was long and clear and for a moment men on both sides forgot their struggles and looked to the south. Then it sounded again and a murmur began to sweep through the scattered knots of men, a murmur that soon became a shout. Trojans raised their voices in dismay and Greeks called out in hope, all saying the same thing.

'Achilles! Achilles is coming!'

Chapter Twenty-Eight

ACHILLES RELENTS

Patroclus ran across the sand towards the Myrmidon galleys, watched by his countrymen as they carried heavy loads to the ships or took down the tents they had slept under for ten years. They looked on him with concern as he sprinted past them, but the only eyes Patroclus was aware of were observing him coolly from the prow of the foremost galley.

'What kept you so long?' Achilles asked sternly as his cousin ran up the gangplank, but when he saw the tears in Patroclus's eyes, his look of disapproval was replaced by one of surprise and concern. 'You're – you're *weeping*? What is it? What disaster could bring tears to your proud face, my friend? If you'd had news that either of our fathers had died, *that* might be worth your grief; but then surely I'd have heard of it too.'

'By the sword of Ares, Achilles, has your damned pride made you into that much of a fool?' Patroclus snapped. 'Force your gaze to the north, where the armies of Greece and Troy are fighting the most desperate battle of the war. See the trails of smoke from the burning tents and listen to the clash of weapons and the screams of the dying! Turn your eyes *that* way and witness the destruction of your friends and all their hopes – all for the sake of your cursed pride.'

Stunned by his cousin's rebuke, Achilles turned his head towards the great clash of nations, which he had been observing with anxious concern ever since he had sent Patroclus in search of news. The battle lines were closer now, trampling the tents and campfires to the east and stretching in a long curve of furious activity to the north, where the fighting had reached the furthest ships. Here the Greek flank seemed to be breaking up: men were streaming back across the beach, hotly pursued by cavalry while knots of their more resilient comrades fought on against overwhelming numbers of Trojan infantry. Spirals of grey smoke twisted up into the bright blue sky, where not a single cloud impeded the light and heat of the sun. Even on the high prow of his galley, the sound of the fighting pounded the inside of Achilles's head as if every battle he had ever contested had been rolled into one. And somewhere among the shouts of victors and vanquished he knew his friends were suffering.

Patroclus placed a hand on his shoulder.

'Diomedes and Odysseus are lying wounded in Agamemnon's tent, as are Machaon, Eurypylus and Agamemnon himself. Some say Great Ajax is dead. But even if Menelaus, Idomeneus and a few others remain, what chance do they stand against Hector, Paris and Sarpedon? Do you still refuse to cast off your pride, Achilles, even when your comrades are suffering so terribly?'

Achilles did not reply, but the tightening of his lips and the narrowing of his eyes were answer enough.

'Then let *me* lead the Myrmidons out in your name. Lend me your armour, too, so that when the Trojans see your visored helmet on my head they'll think you've returned. It'll strike the fear of Hades into them. Besides, they're so exhausted from days of fighting that a fresh force of spearmen now will sweep them away from the ships and back on to the plains.'

'I will not help Agamemnon,' Achilles said angrily, still staring out at the dreadful slaughter consuming the camp. 'When he took Briseis from my hut he created a greater enemy for himself than Hector or any number of Trojans. But . . . but you're right. With so many already fallen, the Greeks need our help now. Go then, Patroclus. Take my armour and lead the Myrmidons into battle if your heart is moved to save them.'

'It is, my lord,' Patroclus replied. 'Thank you.'

Achilles turned and stared at his cousin. There was a strange look in his eyes.

'Don't thank me, Patroclus. You're simply doing what I should have done some time ago, and perhaps you're a better man for it.' He frowned at the notion, but continued quickly. 'Take the Myrmidons and drive the Trojans back beyond the walls, but *don't* go any further! I don't know why, but I fear for you, my friend. You've lived a long time in my shadow and your skill as a fighter has been less appreciated than it should have been, though I believe you're a greater warrior than Menelaus, Diomedes or even Ajax himself. Nevertheless, I forbid you to pass the walls of the camp.'

He stepped forward and gently cupped his friend's chin in his fingertips, looking him in the eye. The other men on the ship's deck glanced away or busied themselves with their work.

'I'll take care,' Patroclus assured him, folding his fingers around Achilles's wrist.

Achilles smiled, then pulled away and looked back at the battle raging about the camp like a stormy sea.

'Besides,' he added, 'it wouldn't be right for your deeds to outshine my own. You're a lesser noble whereas I'm the son of a goddess; even if you feel Zeus himself is with you, don't pursue glory but remain at the walls. Go now. My armour is sitting idle in my hut; put it on while I call the Myrmidons to arms.'

Patroclus stroked his chin where Achilles's fingers had touched him. For a moment, he stared at the back of the prince's blond head and felt both love and hatred in equal measure. Then, without another word, he turned on his heel and marched down to the sand below. As he ran into the hut, Achilles climbed up on to the prow of his ship.

'Myrmidons!' he called out in a loud voice, pausing while his men left their tasks and came running to stand before him. 'For days now you've sat around your campfires cursing me for a bull-headed and heartless monster, nursing my ruthless anger while the

Greeks are dying on the battlefield. And don't shake your heads as if I'm a liar, too – do you think I don't know *you*, my own men? Well, I'm not the pitiless fool your whisperings have made me out to be. I am sending you to fight in my place, with Patroclus at your head. And if any man has looked on me with spite these past few days, then let him fight twice as hard now that *I* have relented. Put on your armour and collect your weapons, and remember that when you face the Trojans, you fight not only for your own glory but also for mine!'

The gathered soldiers shook the air with their cheers, before scattering in every direction as their captains barked order after order at them. And as the Myrmidons prepared for war, Achilles saw the first of the Greek ships go up in flames to the north.

Chapter Twenty-Nine
THE MYRMIDONS RETURN

Penelope looked at the lines of fish on the market stall. Expressionless eyes stared back from silver-grey bodies that twisted and arched in helpless agony, longing for the sea. The fisherman – suntanned with heavy muscles and a thick grey beard – poured a pail of seawater over his catch, causing the fish to thrash about with renewed vigour until the last of the briny liquid had cascaded off the sides and on to the grass. Looking up, he recognized the queen and gave a curt bow.

'My lady!' He smiled, showing good white teeth. 'Take a good look. These are the fattest fish in the whole market. Ain't no little wrigglers ever come off my boat, 'cause I always goes out the furthest to where the best shoals are – all the strongest fish with the tastiest flesh.'

Penelope closed her eyes briefly and nodded. All fishermen claimed their boats went furthest out and caught the best fish, but in this case there was no denying the man's catch were fine-looking creatures. She turned to Actoris, her body slave, and pointed down at the table.

'Pick the eight biggest, Actoris, and have him deliver them to the palace kitchens. He can settle with the cook.'

Leaving Actoris with the fisherman, who shouted cheerful thanks after her, Penelope wandered off alone through the crowded market place. The mid-morning sun was already hot and the warm air was thick with the smells of freshly slaughtered meat, different spices, just-baked bread and a multitude of pungent vegetables and fruit. The market was a good place to lose oneself, she thought; where people were too wrapt in choosing and haggling for their wares to pay much attention to the wife of their absent king. As she pushed between different bodies, avoiding bony elbows and plump backsides, she looked across to the walls of the palace where Telemachus and a collection of other boys were being taught military manoeuvres by Halitherses. The old man sat on an upturned bucket waving instructions with his stick at the double line of children, who were armed with staves or poles and wore wicker baskets for helmets. Penelope paused to watch her son, his solemn but shambolic attempts at spear drill earning him sharp reprimands from his instructor. Halitherses was particularly keen for the future king to learn the art of war, but Penelope knew her son was not an instinctive fighter. He had too much of his mother's sensitivity about him.

And yet, she thought, if his father did not return from Troy soon, little Telemachus would have to learn to fight to defend his kingdom. Ithaca's wolves had woken from their slumber and were regarding his inheritance with hungry eyes, while the forces that stood in their way were growing weaker in comparison. A silent, undeclared war had begun and Phronius, it seemed, was its first victim. The old man had fallen to his death in the sea below his isolated house, leaving a single sandal at the cliff's edge to show he had not disappeared completely. In public people said he must have stumbled in the darkness and fallen on the rocks, from whence the waves had taken his body out to sea. But in private there were many who believed his death had been no accident.

He had also left a vacancy on the Kerosia, and it had taken less than two days for the chief wolf to call upon Penelope and demand a replacement be chosen. Someone young, Eupeithes had suggested, to counterbalance the grey heads of Laertes, Halitherses, Polyctor and himself, not to mention that the other two members of the Kerosia – Nisus and Mentor – were both in their forties. His proposition, as he had sat with Penelope in the great hall the night before, was that his own son, Antinous, should take Phronius's place.

Penelope had laughed off the suggestion, but Eupeithes was not one to be easily dissuaded. She recalled his pale, mole-covered face, orange in the firelight as his fat body sat wedged into the chair opposite her. His long, feminine hands were folded together beneath his chin and his dark, intelligent eyes stared at her without wavering, though the friendly, understanding expression did not fool her for a moment. He wanted to know why she did not want his son on the Kerosia, and before she could reply he gave a long exposition of Antinous's qualities. Penelope countered with a list of reasons why he was unsuitable, but Eupeithes dismissed each objection with kind and respectful ease until, finally, her arguments for rejecting Antinous had been stripped bare, leaving only her *insistence* that he should not be allowed on the Kerosia. At that point, Eupeithes had leaned back in his chair with a defeated sigh, nodding his acquiescence to her decision. But if Penelope had thought she was the victor in their contest, she was soon to realize otherwise. Eupeithes had simply been manoeuvring her into a corner. Now, with her resistance worn thin, he took every one of her arguments against Antinous and turned them into reasons *for* electing Oenops, one of the nobles most aggressively opposed to the conscription of replacements to go to Troy. And indeed, Oenops would have made an excellent member of the council were it not for the fact he was every bit Eupeithes's man. But Penelope's arguments against Antinous could not now be turned on their head to reject Oenops, and when Eupeithes reminded her of how she was in his debt for preventing a rebellion of Ithaca's nobles, she gave in.

She looked again at Telemachus and felt she had betrayed him. She had called a meeting of the Kerosia for that evening and was not looking forward to telling Laertes, Mentor and Halitherses that Oenops was its newest member. Now only Nisus – the seventh member, and every bit loyal to Odysseus – continued to ensure that Eupeithes, with Polyctor and Oenops, did not control Ithaca's governing council.

Suddenly, more than at any time since those first few months after Odysseus had sailed for Troy, Penelope wanted her husband back. There was a strength about Odysseus that was like a wall, keeping all the dangers of the world at bay so that to those he sheltered the world seemed a safe and happy place. She would have given anything to see him on his throne again, bringing stability back to his island; but her deepest longing was to have him back in the intimacy of their bed, to be able to love him with all her mind and body again and know the long years of loneliness were over.

But Odysseus was gone and his return seemed more distant now than it had ten years ago, when he had left her to defend his kingdom in his absence. What was more, Penelope knew it was up to her to protect Telemachus. For if the wolves wanted Ithaca, they could not have it while Odysseus's son lived.

'Achilles! Achilles is coming!'

Eperitus and Apheidas looked to the south, where dozens of Trojan horsemen were galloping back across the sand and between the broken tents. They were shouting the name of Achilles and the fear in their eyes was clear enough. As they passed, the Trojan infantry pulled back from the beleaguered bands of Greeks they had been attacking and looked in the direction of the panic; their opponents did the same. Everyone sensed a wind of change was now blowing across the battlefield, crushing the victorious ardour of the Trojans and raising the spirits of the Greeks.

'Achilles,' Apheidas repeated cautiously, before turning his eyes on Eperitus. 'If it's true, then perhaps the war won't end today. But if Hector is denied his victory, don't think that Agamemnon will find his. The war will go on, Eperitus, and only you and I can end it. Remember my offer of peace, Son: peace between us for the sake of peace between nations and the salvation of many.'

He gave him a last, lingering look, then turned and ran towards a throng of Trojan spearmen. As Eperitus stooped to retrieve his sword, watching his father disappear amongst the shields of the retreating enemy, he heard a deep voice call out to him. He turned to see Ajax staggering across the body-strewn beach, the blazing galley pouring sparks and smoke into the sky behind him.

'Eperitus!' he gasped, exhausted. Eperitus went to support him but his help was dismissed with a wave of the king's giant hand. 'No, I'm not hurt – though Hector came closer than any man has ever done to killing me. But is it true what they're saying, that Achilles has returned? The mere sound of his name has sent the Trojans running from the ships and saved the fleet from being torched.'

'I don't know,' Eperitus answered, looking over his shoulder to where the sound of battle had gained a renewed fury. 'Where's Hector?'

'He went to stem the retreat, and if he hadn't I might not be here now.'

For the first time Eperitus saw the shadow of defeat in Ajax's eyes. How different from the day when he had first seen him, twenty years ago in the palace at Sparta. Then he was young, powerful and arrogant as he laid his claim on Helen. But today his confidence in his own supremacy had finally been broken.

'You forget you nearly beat him on the slopes above the Scamander,' Eperitus comforted him. 'If he mastered you today it's because you've taken on the greater burden of the fighting, that's all.'

'And Hector hasn't?' Ajax laughed, ironically. 'No, Eperitus, the difference today was that Hector could smell victory in the smoke from the galley. He was like one of the gods, assured of his own immortality. But it seems the Olympians aren't going to destroy us today, after all. Let's find Achilles and throw the Trojans back on to the plain.'

As he spoke a great cheer erupted from the Greek soldiers, who raised their spears in the air and cried out in delight. At the same time, the scattered Trojans fell back from the beach altogether and reformed in a dense line amidst the remains of the camp. Then Achilles rode up in his chariot drawn by a pair of pure white horses, the immortal Xanthus and the mortal, but equally splendid, Pedasus. Achilles's gore-spattered spear was raised high above his head and his black-plumed helmet shone like a mirror in the sunlight, the grimacing mask that formed the visor both wonderful and terrible to look on. The bronze breastplate was shaped and patterned with equal skill – though it was criss-crossed with the scars of war – and the shield on his arm was stuck with arrows that had failed to pierce the many-layered leather. The sight of the famous armour alone had sapped the courage from the veins of the Trojans and sent them reeling back in fear of its owner; and as the chariot rode up to the burning galley – with the Myrmidons behind him in five, solidly packed companies – Eperitus and Ajax felt their own fighting spirit revived in equal measure.

'Achilles!' Ajax shouted exuberantly, his near defeat by Hector forgotten as he ran up to the chariot. 'Thank the gods you're back, and not a moment too soon. I *knew* you couldn't resist a rich fight like this!'

But the man did not remove his helmet or take Ajax enthusiastically by the hand, as Achilles had always done whenever they had met on previous battlefields. Instead, he looked down on him with cold indifference, his eyes gleaming behind the narrow eyeholes; then he ordered the chariot about and, signalling for a group of Myrmidons to douse the fire in the galley, moved slowly towards the waiting Trojans, leaving Ajax silent and confused on the sand.

'Hey, there! Eperitus!' boomed a voice.

Eperitus turned to see Peisandros standing at the head of a company of Myrmidons. His well-fed torso was encased in armour and he held a tall spear in his large fist, which he let fall into the crook of his elbow as Eperitus ran across and took his hand.

'What made Achilles change his mind?' Eperitus asked.

'There'll be time for questions once we've pushed the Trojans out of the camp,' Peisandros growled. 'Until then, why don't you join my company? We can avenge the blood of our comrades together.'

Eperitus nodded and slipped into the ranks of the Myrmidons. Just then a hail of arrows arced up from behind the Trojan lines and fell amongst the Greeks; the Greek archers replied, followed by the infantry, who hurled their spears with angry shouts at the enemy shield-wall. Then the order to advance was given and the Myrmidons sprang forward, eager to come to grips with the Trojans after idling by their campfires for so long. The rest of the Greeks charged too, while ahead of them all ran the chariot of Achilles, its heavy wheels bouncing across the shattered remains of the dead and dying. Patroclus pulled back his arm and cast his spear into the massed enemy. The bronze point struck a Trojan noble in the shoulder, severing the ligaments at the base of the arm and wrenching the bone from its socket. As the man tumbled backwards with a scream, Patroclus leapt down from the chariot and dashed in amongst the Trojan spearmen, felling more men and tearing a hole in the line as the rest broke and scattered.

An instant later, the rejuvenated Greek army crashed against the wall of shields that Hector and his captains had been busy organizing. But their efforts were to no avail. On every side, Achilles's Myrmidons used the strength of their fresh limbs to beat down the exhausted enemy, slaughtering the Trojans like sheep until the front line had been shattered and those behind were sent streaming back to the gates. In a few short, frenzied moments the battle for the ships had been lost, and along with it the Trojans' best hope of ever ridding their country of the hated invaders.

The Greeks chased them out of the gates and on to the plain where the carnage continued with a vengeful lust, transforming men into monsters. They killed without mercy, thinking only of the friends and kinsmen they had lost. But as the retreat turned into a rout, Patroclus halted his chariot at one of the causeways that crossed the ditch and looked out at the fleeing army before him. It was a sight that would warm any warrior's heart: a broken enemy with no strength to fight and no hope of refuge on the open flatlands. To massacre them as they ran would leave the walls of Troy defenceless; the Greeks could plunder Priam's city and put it to the torch that very day. And yet, as the daylight grew strangely dim for the early afternoon, Patroclus recalled Achilles's warning not to go beyond the gates. Then he looked out and saw the Trojans were re-forming again, led by Sarpedon and his Lycians. The tipping point had come: should he recall the Myrmidons and leave the exhausted Greeks to fight on alone, surely giving the Trojans the chance to save most of their army and fight another day? Or should he order the pursuit and destroy them utterly, bringing total victory and earning himself the glory that Achilles had never allowed him? And then a quieter, darker voice spoke from the back of his mind: did he always want to live on the crumbs of glory that fell from Achilles's table? Was he not a great fighter in his own right, capable of killing Hector himself and breaking open the gates of Troy? Did not the name of Patroclus, son of Menoetius, deserve to be immortalized? His face was transformed with an angry scowl as he let the words take hold of him, and a moment later his chariot was dashing towards the wall of Trojan and Lycian shields.

Eperitus watched him speeding across the dry grass where the bodies from two days of fighting still lay. Once more, the open ground before the walls was the scene of battle, though this time it was the turn of the Trojans to be harried to their deaths. Everywhere, the men of Troy and her allies were falling to their knees and begging to be taken prisoner, physically and mentally too exhausted to continue the fight. Many others did not dare risk their lives to the mercy of the Greeks and either ran headlong in the direction of Troy or turned and fought. Of the latter, some stood alone and were quickly overwhelmed, while others formed small, desperate bands of warriors and fought on for as long as they could. Still more had seen the stand the Lycians and Trojans were making under Sarpedon and ran to join them. All around the terrible din of battle rose into the air once again, like the clatter of hundreds of woodsmen felling trees on a hillside: sword against sword, spear against shield, axe against helmet. And as the Greeks cried out with the joy of battle, cutting down their enemies with ruthless energy, Eperitus's heart sank. There was little glory in the slaughter of men who were throwing away their arms and begging for clemency, and as the sun's light faded in a cloudless sky he knew he had to do something. The warrior's creed called for a man to slay his enemies and bring glory to his own name, but it was not an excuse for murder.

He began to run from one man to another, calling on them to spare the Trojans who had thrown themselves at their knees, reminding them that there was more to be gained from ransoming prisoners or selling them into slavery than opening their throats like sacrificial animals. Some cursed his efforts and carried on the butchery with frenzied eyes, while others stayed their weapons and felt the grip of sanity return to them. Then, amid the horror of ringing weapons and screaming men, Eperitus felt his heart go cold and his senses reel in confusion. The light was being slowly sucked out of the day, turning the very air heavy and brown. Others sensed it, too, and many cowered down as their primeval instincts told them something was wrong. Looking up, Eperitus cried out in fear as he saw that the brilliant face of the sun was slowly turning to black. Many others shouted in dismay also, some even dropping their weapons and throwing their arms over their heads in terror as the bright sunshine was turned to a stifled gloaming.

And then a voice cried out over the battlefield: 'A sign! A sign from Zeus. Troy's doom is at hand.'

Eperitus turned and saw Achilles in his chariot, raising his spear over his head and exhorting the Greeks to press their attacks harder. And yet he knew the voice did not belong to Achilles.

The Myrmidons were the first to throw off their stupor and launch back into the fray. They bore down on the shield-wall

Sarpedon had marshalled against them, felling several of their enemy as they remained in awe of the partially eclipsed sun. But the Trojans were quick to recover and soon checked the attack with a furious effort, inspired by the figure of Sarpedon at their backs. The dust that rose from the battle was as grey as ash in the dusky half-light, choking both sides as they struggled against each other, pushing this way and that like treetops caught in a gale as yet more men were brought down into the long grass, spilling their blood over the dry earth and sending their souls to the Underworld.

Peisandros ordered his company to join the fray and Eperitus ran with them, all the time throwing glances at the man in Achilles's chariot. Something more than the sound of his voice told him that the man was not Achilles, and he had resolved to get a closer look when a shout of defiance rang out across the lines of battle. Sarpedon rode up in his chariot and hurled a spear at the commander of the Myrmidons. It missed its target and thumped into the mortal Pedasus, toppling the chariot on to its side as the animal fell and throwing its occupants to the ground. Patroclus was on his feet in an instant and, snatching up his spear, threw it with deadly accuracy at the Lycian king. Sarpedon twisted aside at the last moment and the weapon took his driver in the chest, sending him flailing backwards from the car.

Crying out with fury, Sarpedon took hold of his second spear and jumped to the ground. The lines of men between him and Patroclus herded aside as the king drew back his weapon and took aim; but the throw was hasty and the long shaft passed harmlessly over Patroclus's shoulder. Determined to kill the man he believed was Achilles, Sarpedon slipped his sword from its scabbard and ran at his opponent, while behind him his men filled the air with their cheers. But before he could cover half the distance between them, Patroclus snatched a spear from one of his soldiers and launched it at the Lycian. It caught him just below the heart, stopping his great bulk dead as the bronze tip punched through his armour and bored a channel into his flesh and bone beneath. Sarpedon's eyes widened with shock as blood gushed from his mouth to darken his beard and chest. He seized the heavy spear with both hands and pulled it slowly from his body, before falling to his knees and dropping face-forward into the grass.

Tasting the glory that had been denied him for so long, Patroclus gave a triumphant shout and leapt on the huge form of Sarpedon. Cutting the chin strap with his dagger, he pulled the crested helmet from his head and tossed it into the jubilant ranks of his Myrmidons. Next he sliced through the leather buckles that held Sarpedon's scaled cuirass in place and tore it from his muscular torso, hurling it with a grunt in the wake of the helmet. Then, as he tugged the greaves from his victim's shins, a groan escaped Sarpedon's lips and his arm reached out towards the Lycian lines.

'Avenge me,' he called out as his countrymen stood rooted to the ground with shock and grief. 'Do not let the Greeks drag my body away, to be devoured by their dogs. Avenge me!'

And with that he fell back into the grass and his last breath exited his lips. Patroclus, still kneeling at the dead king's side, sensed movement among the wall of enemy spearmen and looked up. By now the darkness had grown to a thick haze that weighed heavily in the air and sapped the hope from men's hearts. And through the veil of ash-like dust that swirled with mesmerizing slowness over the bodies of the fallen, he saw Hector standing at the front of the Lycians, his sword in his hand with the tip resting in the dirt. His dark eyes were fixed on the corpse of Sarpedon and he barely seemed to be breathing, though his nostrils were wide and his free hand was trembling.

'When I left Troy,' he said, his gravelly voice shaking with suppressed anger as he turned his gaze on Sarpedon's killer, 'I swore I would avenge the deaths of King Eëtion and his sons. You killed them, Achilles, in your god-forsaken wrath. You killed the father and brothers of my wife, just as you have killed countless other Trojans and our allies. And now you have brought even the magnificent Sarpedon down into the dust, sending his ghost to

Hades to whisper your glory amongst the halls of the dead. He was a great friend of Troy and he was *my* friend too; but I will not send him on his final journey alone. *You* are going with him, and I swear before Zeus and Apollo before this day is over I will strip the armour from your dead body and take it for my own.'

Patroclus stood slowly, his eyes fixed on the terrible figure of Hector as he slid his sword from its scabbard.

'This armour was given to Peleus by the gods themselves, and now I wear it. But it is too great for you, Hector, just as *I* am too great for you. Already I have claimed the life of Sarpedon and soon I will claim yours also. The bards will be lifting my name in song before the vultures have finished picking the flesh from your bones, and when I sail back to Phthia your wife will come with me, to spend the rest of her days as my plaything—'

'NO!'

Hector ran forward, striking Patroclus's shield with such force that it was torn from his arm. The fighting around them had stopped and the watching Greeks gave a cry of alarm as Patroclus was sent stumbling backwards, almost falling as he raised his blade instinctively against a second powerful blow. Peisandros gripped his spear in both hands and stepped forward as Hector pressed his ferocious attack upon Patroclus, but Eperitus seized the Myrmidon's wrist and pulled him back. Then Patroclus slipped beneath another blow and turned, thrusting his sword with terrifying speed at Hector's exposed right flank. This time the Trojans and Lycians shouted in fear as they expected their champion's heavy bulk to crash into the long grass. But Hector twisted aside with impossible agility and the edge of the blade skidded across the scaled plates of his armour. Turning, he punched out with the point of his sword, high and to the left, catching Patroclus on the shoulder and causing him to cry out as the bronze bit through his armour and into the flesh. He fell back, grimacing and shocked by the sudden pain as Hector rounded on him.

'So the great Achilles can bleed!' he crowed, his eyes wide with vengeful triumph.

Still gripping his sword, Patroclus raised his fingers to his throat and unslipped the laces from beneath his chin.

'Achilles remains by the ships,' he announced, pulling the visored helmet from his head and dropping it in the grass. There were shouts of surprise from the onlookers. 'And though I love him and honour him above all men, he has forsaken his chance of glory and given it to me. And in killing you, Hector, I will become his equal.'

He lunged with his sword, the speed and power of his attack almost burying the point in Hector's chest. But the Trojan had been waiting for the attack and caught the blade in the toughened leather of his shield, before burying his own sword in Patroclus's stomach, driving it clean through. A stream of dark blood flowed down the blade as Patroclus slid back and fell into the grass.

'You were never your master's equal,' Hector mocked, though there was disappointment in his eyes that he had been robbed of the destruction of Achilles. 'Although you boasted you would leave me to the vultures and take Andromache back with you to Greece, I have taught you the hollowness of your words. Instead, you can tell the shades in the Underworld that you were beaten by Hector, the greatest warrior in all Ilium.'

He knelt beside the dying Patroclus and stripped the breast-plate from his chest. Then he tore away his tunic to expose his flesh for the vultures, leaving him naked and pale in the brown half-light.

'You are right in one thing, Hector,' Patroclus croaked as the greaves were torn from his shins. 'I never was the equal of Achilles, and for my arrogance I will not see his beauty with my living eyes again. But you are not the greatest warrior in Ilium. He is, and when he learns of my death he will hunt you down without mercy. You will not escape him, Hector.'

'I don't intend to,' Hector said, standing and placing the point of his sword against Patroclus's throat.

Patroclus stared up at silhouette of the Trojan prince. The half-eclipsed sun shimmered over his right shoulder, a sign not of the end of Troy as Patroclus had hoped, but of his own end. And then Hector leaned his weight on the hilt of his sword, cutting through Patroclus's windpipe and releasing his spirit from his body.

The Lycians and Trojans thumped their spears rapidly against their shields as Hector rejoined their ranks, the armour of Achilles piled in his arms. Then, their fear dispelled, they gave a hoarse shout of triumph and charged. The Myrmidons ran to meet them with Eperitus and Peisandros at their head.

book
THREE

book THREE

Chapter Thirty
THE VOICE OF THETIS

Achilles sat at the southernmost point of the beach, where large black rocks rose out of the sea and the long sickle of sand was bare of ships. At last, Zeus's anger seemed to have been appeased and the darkness that had covered the face of the sun was slowly receding. But the return of the soft light of late afternoon did not diminish the darkness that had taken hold of Achilles's heart. It was clear Patroclus had disobeyed his orders and taken the Myrmidons out on to the plain, and as he sat in the sand and watched the gentle waves roll back and forth along the shoreline he sensed something terrible had happened. The foreboding he had felt when Patroclus had begged to lead the Myrmidons into battle was stronger now, filling him with an inescapable dread for his friend's life.

Then he heard horses and the rattle of an approaching chariot. One set of braying he knew intimately and with a rush of joy turned to see Xanthus at the top of the beach, standing tall and magnificent with Achilles's own chariot behind him. But the sense of relief that Patroclus had returned quickly drained away and was replaced by apprehension as he saw that the horse next to Xanthus was not Pedasus – the horse he had captured at Thebe and had been putting through its paces – but another animal, an unfamiliar brown mare that looked frightened and blown. And the man who leapt down from the chariot was not his cousin but Eperitus, caked with blood and dust from the battle and his armour slashed and dinted with many fresh scars.

The Ithacan trudged across the white beach towards him, lifting small clouds of sand behind his heels. The look on his face was sombre and anxious and Achilles knew in an instant the news he had brought with him. Suddenly the heart in his great chest seemed to stop beating and he reached out for something to support himself against, but there was nothing to hold him and he fell back in the sand, tears already welling up in his eyes.

'My lord Achilles,' Eperitus began, his words hurried as if he knew he must impart his news now or lose the courage to speak. 'My lord, your cousin is dead!'

Achilles dropped forward on to his knees like a beggar.

'You mean Ajax! Ajax is dead.'

Eperitus blinked with surprise. 'No, my lord, I mean Patroclus. Patroclus is dead.'

Achilles lowered his head, his face lost behind the long curtains of his blond hair. Suddenly his whole body felt heavy, heavier than he had ever known it, hanging between his limbs like a sack of grain that he no longer had the strength to lift. Then he felt Eperitus's hand around his wrist, hauling him to his feet, and as he stumbled under the leaden weight of his body Eperitus caught him and held him firm. Achilles looked into his brown eyes and saw the depth of his concern.

'He died a warrior, Achilles, covered in glory. It was he who drove the Trojans from the camp and saved the ships, and I watched him kill Sarpedon with my own eyes and strip the armour from his dying body – such a feat of arms that men will sing about for generations to come. And yet, in the end, the gods were against him . . .'

'Hector!' Achilles spat. 'It was Hector, wasn't it? Oh, foolish Patroclus! Why did you dare to face the best man in all Troy?'

He looked up at the empty skies and let out a despairing wail, then seized his tunic at the neck and tore it down to his belt. He ran across to the remains of an old campfire, knocking aside the tripod and pot that straddled it and tearing up handfuls of cold ash that he poured over his hair, all the time shouting Patroclus's name as the tears flowed down his handsome cheeks. At the top of the beach a maidservant ran out from a tent and, guessing what had happened, began to beat her breast with her fist and call out in grief. Others joined her from the surrounding tents, and though all of them were Trojan slaves they also took up the mournful cry. It was a scene Eperitus had witnessed many times about the walls of Troy, as the womenfolk came to claim their dead after a battle, but as he watched the captive maidservants grieving for one of their country's enemies he felt himself deeply moved.

He turned to Achilles, now lying face down in the remains of the campfire, and knelt beside him, placing a hand on his shoulder.

'You should know that he died with your name on his lips, Achilles, declaring that he loved and honoured you above all other men.'

'Where is he now? Where's his body?'

'Still on the battlefield. Ajax and Menelaus sent me back to you with the news while they fight to save Patroclus's corpse from the Trojans. Ajax has killed many, but still they fight on, eager to take the body back to Troy as a prize. But your armour could not be saved; Hector has that.'

'What do I care for armour when Patroclus is dead?' Achilles declared, dragging himself to his feet and facing the west, where the sun was now dipping towards the rim of the ocean. It was a sight he had seen thousands of times in his ten years at Troy, but today it felt as if the sun was going down and would never rise again. 'I sent him to his death by my own arrogant pride, Eperitus. It's as if I killed him, not Hector.'

He walked back down to the shore and waded out into waves until they reached his waist. For a moment Eperitus feared that his grief had driven him from his senses and he was about to drown himself, but as he splashed down into the water behind him Achilles threw his arms wide and closed his eyes.

'Mother!' Eperitus heard him whisper. 'Oh Mother, hear me in my grief. Menoetius's son has been killed by Hector and now I wish my anger had never been provoked by Agamemnon, or that I had never been given reason to plead for your help. How the gods mock us mortals. Even you, my own mother, must have known that my prayers would lead to the death of Patroclus. Why didn't you tell me? If I'd put aside my fury at Agamemnon's arrogance things would never have come to this. But it seems this whole war has become nothing more than an exchange of savage fury between friend and foe alike. It's no longer the thing of honour and glory that I left Greece in search of. And what do I even care for such trifles as *honour* and *glory* any more? Patroclus has fallen and now I have nothing but the darkness of grief – and this heaviness I feel is but the beginning. Unless I can find solace beneath these waves?'

He beat the water with the flats of his hands and a sudden desperation filled his eyes, but Eperitus reached out and took him by the arm before he could throw himself under.

'There was one other thing Patroclus said – his last words before his soul left him. As Hector took the armour from his dying body, Patroclus said that you would avenge him.'

'Hector?' Achilles echoed, as if the name were new to him. Then his eyes narrowed and a shadow fell over his handsome features. 'Yes, Hector. Patroclus must be avenged.'

'Then you will die, my son.'

Eperitus looked around in surprise for the source of the voice, which did not come from the air but the very waters in which he and Achilles were standing. It sounded gentle and sad, but as ageless and vibrant as a waterfall that calls to the thirsty man with the promise of refreshment and new life. Achilles instantly raised his head.

'Mother!'

'Listen to me, Achilles,' the voice continued, though there was no sign of its owner. 'If you choose the path of vengeance you will not live long; for it is your doom that once Hector's soul has departed this world, yours will surely follow. But I would not have

332

it this way. Even now you might escape the fate that has long been assigned to you.'

'Then I choose death!' Achilles insisted bitterly. 'My pride condemned Patroclus to his fate, so why should I go on living without him? All I want is to grant him his dying wish and bring Hector down into the dust. After that, nothing matters. After that, I will gladly give up this pathetic existence and join Patroclus in the Underworld.'

'And I will spend eternity weeping for you, my dearest child!' Thetis replied. 'But even you cannot return to the fight without armour. Restrain your lust for vengeance until tomorrow and meet me here before the sun rises. I will ask Hephaistos to make you a set of arms that will be the envy and desire of all men, though even Hephaistos's craftsmanship cannot save you from your death.'

A gust of wind tore at Eperitus's hair, waking him from the dreamlike trance the voice of Thetis had cast over him. Only then, as a white-tipped wave came rolling towards them, did he realize the waters about him and Achilles had been still and flat while the goddess spoke.

Achilles's grief – like the pride that had come before it – was excessive. He returned to the beach to pour more ash over his head and wallow in the depths of his despair, surrounded all the time by the Trojan maidservants he and Patroclus had taken from the cities they had sacked. The sound of battle raging on the plain drifted over the camp and filled the wounded with fear for their comrades, but the great warrior did not hear it in his anguish as he beat the sand with his fists and tore his clothes and hair. Eventually the sun dropped below the horizon, draining the colour and light from the world and bringing a natural end to the fighting. The remnant of the Greeks fell back behind the relative safety of their walls – the shattered gates having been repaired during the afternoon's fighting – and the Trojans set up their tents on the plain once more. Everything was the same as the evening before, except that the plain and now the camp itself were filled with thousands more corpses of all nationalities, while the groaning of the wounded had become even louder.

There was one other exception. The following day would see Achilles return to the fight. But as the evening darkened into night he lay prostrate across the dead body of his friend, his face hidden in the crook of his arm and his whole body shaking with harsh, relentless tears. By the efforts of Menelaus, Little Ajax and, above all, Great Ajax, the body had been dragged step by step back to the walls, while all the time the Trojans had fought like Furies for possession of it, as if that single corpse represented the winning of the whole war. Then, as Achilles had led the general mourning – washing the blood and dust from the battered body of Patroclus before covering it with a white sheet and a cloak – Eperitus had slipped away to look for Odysseus and the other Ithacans.

He found them by their ships, battered and exhausted by the prolonged fighting and with a hundred of their number left behind on the battlefield, carrion for the vultures and wolves. As he approached their silent campfires he could see the despondency on their faces, but then a deep voice called his name and he saw Polites limping towards him, his leg bandaged and his bulging limbs and torso crossed here and there with new scars. Eperitus embraced him, ignoring his sharp intake of breath, and to his delight saw Antiphus and Omeros sharing a campfire and signalling for him to join their meal. But he was most pleased to see Arceisius grinning at him from behind the flames, alive and well.

'I'd given you up for dead,' he said, gratefully accepting a warm bowl of porridge from his old squire. 'In fact, I'd given you *all* up for dead.'

'You should know we're not that easy to get rid of,' Arceisius said, his voice heavy with tiredness.

'You least of all, I suppose,' Eperitus said and smiled back, laying a hand on Arceisius's shoulder. 'Especially after all the years I spent training you.'

'You can claim some of the credit, old friend, but not all of it. A glorious death isn't as appealing as it used to be, not since I married Melantho. I've a good reason to survive now, and as soon as we get back to Ithaca the first thing I'm going to do is set about having lots of sons.'

'Then Zeus save the girls of Ithaca if they're anything like you,' Eperitus responded. 'And perhaps we'll be returning to Ithaca sooner than we thought: Achilles is going to return to the fighting.'

The others exchanged looks of surprise and elation, glad that their greatest warrior would be returning to their ranks.

'What of our casualties?' he continued.

'Too many,' Antiphus answered. 'Half of the new recruits, but a lot of our best fighters too — and some of the old guard with them.'

Eperitus was silent for a while.

'I'll go round the survivors soon, but first I have to see Odysseus.'

'He's waiting for you in his tent,' Polites informed him, 'with Eurybates and Eurylochus.'

Eperitus did not voice his disappointment that Eurylochus was still alive, though the news did not surprise him. Taking a mouthful of wine from a skin offered by Arceisius, he took his leave of his friends and went to find the king. Fortunately, the small Ithacan camp had avoided the worst of the destruction and he found Odysseus's hut much as it had always been. His friend was inside discussing the formation for the next day's fighting, but when he saw Eperitus he gave him a broad grin and came to embrace him. Eurylochus scowled and excused himself while the others sat and discussed the battle, as slaves brought tables of roast meat and bread with kraters of wine to wash it down. Odysseus listened intently to everything that Eperitus and Eurybates had to say about the battle — both men having experienced different viewpoints while their king's wound had forced him to remain in the camp — but his interest increased even further when

Eperitus mentioned hearing the voice of Thetis as he stood with Achilles in the sea.

'And she will return to him before sunrise tomorrow?' he repeated.

'Yes, down by the rocks at the northern end of the bay.'

Odysseus raised an eyebrow. 'That should be something to behold. But for now I need to rest this wound and get some sleep. I suggest you two do the same: even if Achilles settles his differences with Agamemnon tomorrow and rejoins the fight as you say he will, Eperitus, it's going to be another hard day for us all. Goodnight.'

His companions stood and left, welcoming the thought of sleep and a rest after the toils of the day. But, though Eurybates went straight to his own tent, Eperitus stayed awake a little longer, visiting the Ithacan campfires and testing the morale of the men – which was good, despite their losses – before encouraging them to grab some hard-earned rest. A little while later, he curled up under his blanket and was instantly taken by a deep and dreamless sleep.

Chapter Thirty-One

THE ARMOUR OF ACHILLES

Odysseus placed his hands on Eperitus's shoulders and shook him gently.

'Come on,' he whispered. 'It's not long until dawn.'

'What of it?' Eperitus replied, rubbing the sleep from his eyes. 'Where are we going?'

But Odysseus was already at the door of his hut, beckoning for him to follow. Eperitus kicked off his blanket and dressed quickly, throwing his cloak about his shoulders and grabbing his sword. The brightest stars were still shining overhead as they stepped out, but a faint light was infusing the skies to the east and turning them a deep blue. With Odysseus leading the way, the two men jogged between the tents and campfires where the hunched forms of sleeping men were snoring heavily, ignorant of the groans of the wounded that still undulated from different parts of the camp like the wailing of lost souls. Soon they reached the beach where the Myrmidon ships were drawn up and found the wooden bier on which Patroclus's body had been laid. It was empty.

Odysseus gave Eperitus an inquisitive glance as they paused to look at the discarded shroud and the white cloak that had covered the body. Then he set off again, kicking up gouts of sand as he sprinted past the tall, black prows of the galleys.

It was not until they passed the last Myrmidon ship and saw the jagged rocks that marked the southernmost edge of the bay, that they spotted Achilles, a dark shape lying close to the water's edge. Patroclus's pale, naked body was with him and the prince lay prostrate across his friend's chest, shaking with tears as the waves washed repeatedly over his outstretched legs. Odysseus ducked down behind a low boulder and signalled for Eperitus to join him.

As the rock was only a short distance from the shore they could see Achilles clearly, and for a while they crouched in silence listening to his heavy sobs amid the consolatory hushing of the waves. The sky grew gradually lighter and objects that before had been black and indistinct now became colourless shapes in the greyness. A gentle mist had formed over the surface of the sea and was threatening to wash inland when Eperitus seized Odysseus by the shoulder and pointed at a spot close to the shore, where two black rocks jutted upwards like the broken pillars of an ancient gateway.

'Do you see it?' he whispered.

Odysseus nodded. There was a movement in the water, a frantic splashing as if someone were drowning. It grew quickly, rising up in a column like an inverted whirlpool that swirled round and round, fast at first but getting steadily slower as it began to take shape. Then, as the first hint of dawn crept into the sky and brought small dashes of colour back to the world, the two men were amazed to see the figure of a young woman forming from the water, her translucent arms reaching up to clutch at the air. And as she caught the light in her fingertips the liquid became flesh, transforming the hands and arms first, followed by the head, breasts and stomach until they were staring at a girl of little more than twenty years old, standing waist-high in the waves.

Slowly, she lowered her arms and stared at Achilles, who remained oblivious to her presence. Her hair was blond like his and flowed over her shoulders and down her back to run in rivulets over her buttocks; her skin was as white as ivory and her face had all the beauty of unblemished youth, but in her sea-green eyes sat all the knowledge and wisdom of an immortal. She walked ashore, unhindered by the waves because she was part of them, her lower body taking shape from the water as she moved and changing into flesh until she stood naked on the sand, looking down at her son.

'This is not the time for mourning, Achilles,' she said.

Achilles snatched up the sword that lay in the sand beside Patroclus's body and spun round. Seeing his mother, he dropped the weapon and leapt to his feet, throwing his cloak about her nakedness before taking her into his arms. Eperitus almost expected her to dissolve into a shower of spray as the prince embraced her and laid his head on her shoulders, but her flesh was as real as his own and she kissed his head and ran her long fingers through his hair.

'Restrain your grief until you have avenged Patroclus,' she whispered. 'When Ajax brought him to you, you swore before all the gods that you would not let his death go unpunished; that you would make Hector pay for it with his own life. Now there can be no turning back, my son. You have chosen the path of doom and so you must make amends with Agamemnon and take up your spear once more. But even though I dipped you into the River Styx as a baby in the vain hope of making you an immortal like myself, you can still suffer the pain of wounds. What is more, the heel by which I held you remains mortal, the one place where the bite of a weapon can end your life. And so I have fulfilled my promise and brought you new armour – made by Hephaistos himself.'

She swept her arm across the waves that were lapping the beach and suddenly they retreated before her, rolling back to reveal a pile of metal in the damp sand that gleamed and glittered as the sea water drained from its ornately carved surfaces. At the same moment the first molten glimmer of the sun topped the distant mountains to the east and its light touched on the heap of gold, silver and bronze, making it blaze as if consumed by tongues of red fire. Wide-eyed with awe, Odysseus and Eperitus clutched at the rough edges of the boulder and pulled themselves up to get a better view, not noticing as the sharp stone cut at their tightly grasping fingers. Achilles, too, was stunned at the sight. He released his mother and took a step towards the collection of armour. Then he staggered forward – the wet sand sucking at his bare feet – and lifted the golden helmet in both hands, raising it above his head so that the shaggy red mane of its plume dripped salt water on to his chest. His mouth was open and his jaw quivered as if he wanted to speak but, instead, he fell to his knees, laid the helmet down reverently in the sand and lifted up the tin greaves, admiring the life-like curves and the crested waves that had been engraved over every surface.

After a moment he set them down beside the helmet and took hold of the heavy cuirass, which had been perfectly shaped to mimic his own muscle-bound torso, even down to the circles of his nipples and the chute of his navel. The bronze was so highly burnished that he could see his face reflected clearly in the chest muscles, framed by lightening skies that were traced with pink cloud. The red-rimmed eyes that looked back at him had forgotten their grief and become consumed with desire, and the sight of them forced him to release the breastplate and look away.

But he did not look far, for his eyes fell upon the large round shield that stood behind the other pieces of armour, its lower lip buried in the sand but otherwise without any visible support. If the helmet, greaves and breastplate were works beyond Achilles's wildest imaginings, the shield was beyond his comprehension. He stared at it dumbfounded, letting his eyes feast on the intricate designs that adorned it, designs that moved with a life of their own. At its centre, forming the boss, was the disc of the Earth, covered with mountains, forests and rivers depicted in silver; encircling this was the Sea, dotted with islands and populated with giant marine creatures that constantly plunged into the waves before rising up again, spewing water. Bounding Earth and Sea were the heavenly bodies of the Sun, Moon and Stars. As the golden Sun set into the Sea the silver Moon would rise and the constellations that Zeus had set in the sky would twinkle and gleam, fading only when the Sun rose again.

The central circle was ringed by four more circles, each one filled with designs that moved in cyclical patterns. The second circle was divided into two halves, on which were depicted two cities: one filled with celebrations and banqueting as a wedding procession moved through its golden streets; the other in turmoil as besieging and defending armies wrought bloody havoc among each other's ranks. In the first, young women in bridal robes of ivory danced to the music of reed pipe and tortoiseshell lyre; in the second, larger-than-life figures of Athena and Ares fought amid the two armies, slaying with impunity while all around them mortal warriors struggled over the armour of their dead and dying victims.

The third circle showed, on one side, a large meadow being ploughed by teams of oxen, where the golden soil was being turned black by the plough blades, and on the other a rich estate filled with vineyards and fields full of tall wheat. In the latter, golden vines grew on silver frames and brought forth grapes made from gleaming jet; the whole was surrounded by a fence made of tin and an irrigation ditch that flowed with blue enamel. The fruit was being carried away by teams of young men and girls as they danced to the music of a lyre, while in the fields men were harvesting the wheat with sickles and others were tying them into sheaves, all under the close supervision of a majestic king.

In one half of the fourth circle was a herd of ten cattle, depicted in gold with horns of tin. They were accompanied by four drovers, also in gold, and nine dogs that barked as the cows were driven down to a river to drink. But as Achilles watched, a pair of lions leapt out from the rushes and brought down the first animal, tearing out its throat and then feasting on its entrails as the drovers and their dogs tried in vain to scare them off. In the other half were great flocks of sheep with ivory fleeces, grazing in a wide valley where a farm and several sheep pens were depicted in silver.

The fifth circle of the shield showed a vast dance. Young men held the hands of pretty girls as they circled each other in time to the music of a lyre. The maidens wore beautiful silver chitons and flowers in their hair, which Hephaistos had fashioned with minute threads of gold and tin. As for the men, their skin gleamed as if oiled and they wore silver belts with golden daggers. Large crowds of older men and women watched in delight, as if filled with memories of their own youth. Finally, the concentric circles of the shield were bound by the Ocean Stream, which marks the end of all things.

Achilles plucked it from the sand and looped his arm through its leather straps, finding its weight surprisingly light. As he turned, the shield caught the rising sun and its ever-moving designs were displayed in their full glory to Odysseus and Eperitus.

'In the name of Athena!' Odysseus gasped, his eyes widening as they took in the impossible detail of the shield's design.

Not caring that Achilles and Thetis would know he had been spying on them, he stood and crossed the beach towards the Phthian prince. Achilles was momentarily surprised to see him, but instead of admonishing the Ithacan he ran towards him with the shield on his arm.

'Look at it, Odysseus!' he declared, turning it this way and that in the sunlight. 'Can you *believe* such a thing? Hephaistos made it, and as Zeus is my witness, I swear its equal has never been seen on earth or Olympus.'

Odysseus nodded his head in agreement but said nothing, too absorbed by the continuous movement of the figures on the shield. And the more he looked the more he sensed that the scenes depicted his own life, as if the shield had been meant not for Achilles at all, but *himself*. Among the islands that populated the depiction of the Sea, he could clearly make out the shapes of Ithaca and its larger cousin, Samos. And what were the wedding scene and the besieged city meant to represent but his own marriage to Penelope, followed by the attack on Ithaca and the defeat of the Taphian invaders? The king in the third circle could only be himself, presiding over the ten plentiful years that Ithaca had enjoyed under his rule. And as for the cattle in the fourth circle, there was one animal for each year of the war and the tenth – which was being seized by the two lions as he watched –

represented the final victory of the Greeks over Troy. The dancers in the fifth circle surely represented the celebrations on his return to Ithaca. And yes, there amongst the crowd was a woman and her son – Penelope and Telemachus – both depicted in gold to pick them out from the other onlookers who were shown in silver.

But as he looked at the great shield and the pride with which Achilles was displaying it, he realized his fantasies were but foolish imaginings. Surely the armour was beautiful – as beautiful an object of metal as Helen was of flesh – and his heart was filled with desire for it, telling him that here was the outward show of greatness Palamedes had predicted he would never possess. And there was no doubt in his mind that the mere sight of it would spark a similar lust in all fighting men, whether enemies of Achilles or friends, such was the lure of all things that came from the gods, and Odysseus had almost been drawn in by its promise of glory. But he also remembered how he had once tried to make Helen his wife; and as foolish as that thought had been twenty years ago, so he knew it was a foolish desire to want Achilles's shield now. For though the shield was magnificent, the mere possession of it did not bring a man glory or honour. Such lustre could only come from great deeds, and unless a man could first kill Achilles and take the shield from his dead body it was nothing more than a splendid token.

He turned to look at Thetis, wondering whether her eyes would reveal that she, too, knew the shield would be a snare to the Greeks. But the sand where she had stood was empty except for the ashen corpse of Patroclus, its waxy flesh disfigured by the marks of combat.

Chapter Thirty-Two
THE FEUD ENDED

O dysseus and Eperitus helped Achilles on with his new armour then followed him along the beach as he called out at the top of his voice, summoning the Greeks to assemble. The last of the night had been chased away and powder-blue skies now formed an endless ceiling over the world, but the calm of the heavens was not mirrored for long in the sprawling camp below. From every point, soldiers left their cold breakfasts and herded down to the meeting place on the shore opposite Agamemnon's tent, where the clamour of their excited voices grew until it drowned out the cawing of the many seagulls and the gentle crashing of the waves upon the sand. Though they were exhausted by their exertions and many of them bore wounds from the battles of the previous days, the Greeks were suddenly filled with confidence at the appearance of Achilles. The fact that he had left Patroclus's bier could only mean he was ready to put aside his grief and go to war, and the multitude of warriors shared his eagerness for vengeance in Trojan blood. But if the prospect of following the prince into battle had loosened their tongues, the magnificence of his armour set them racing.

'It's the work of a god,' Ajax said as he joined Odysseus and Eperitus on one of the benches being set out hastily by Agamemnon's personal guards. He was accompanied by Teucer and Little Ajax, whose pet snake hung about his shoulders and hissed at the

Ithacans. 'The breastplate and helmet alone are beyond the skill of any man, but that shield!' He gave a whistle and shook his head disbelievingly.

'Magnificent, isn't it?' Odysseus agreed without removing his eyes from the object as it hung on Achilles's arm. 'And yet—'

'In the name of Ares!' Ajax exclaimed, placing his hands on his knees with his elbows out and leaning forward. 'The designs on the shield – they're . . . they're *moving*! From the top of the beach I thought it was the sunlight playing on the silver and gold, but they're actually *moving*. How is that possible?'

Little Ajax squinted doubtfully at the shield, and then, for the first time since Eperitus had known him, a look of wonder transformed his mean features. He turned to Teucer, who was huddled in close by Great Ajax's enormous frame, but the archer's gaze was transfixed by the shield and he paid no attention to the Locrian king.

'Teucer, I forgive you for waking me while I was with Tecmessa,' Ajax said, placing a thick arm about the scrawny shoulders of his half-brother. 'Just to see such a thing was worthwhile, and the more I look at it . . .'

He paused and frowned, staring hard at the shield with a mixture of surprise and growing recognition. At the same moment the crowds of soldiers standing around the benches where the kings, princes and other leaders were sitting parted. Agamemnon entered through the gap, sceptre in hand and followed by Menelaus and Nestor. The King of Men threw a quick glance towards Achilles – who remained with his back to the assembly, staring out at the rollers as they folded in on the shore – then leaned in towards his companions and spoke in a low voice.

Eperitus gave Agamemnon a contemptuous sneer and turned to Ajax.

'You were going to say something about Achilles's shield,' he prompted.

Ajax blinked as if waking from a dream. 'Your eyes are the best in the army, Eperitus,' he said, taking the Ithacan by the arm and pointing at the shield. 'Tell me – does one of those islands look like Salamis to you?'

'I wouldn't know. Salamis is your kingdom, not mine, and I've only seen it from the western side.'

'Never mind,' Ajax said dismissively. 'But look at that city under siege – it's Teuthrania, the city I sacked where I took Tecmessa as my captive. And the next scene is of my marriage to Tecmessa – and that's our son, Eurysaces! Look, all of you: it's as if the shield was made for *me* and not Achilles at all!'

He stood up as if he intended to claim the object there and then, but Odysseus seized his wrist and pulled him back down again.

'Don't be a fool, Ajax,' he hissed, staring at the giant warrior with a strange look in his eye. 'Eperitus and I saw Thetis bring the armour to Achilles. Besides, the shield could just as well be showing Achilles's marriage to Deidameia, whom he wedded back on Scyros. Why should it be you and Tecmessa when it could easily be Menelaus and Helen, or even myself and Penelope? And which of us hasn't laid siege to one city or another?'

Ajax shook Odysseus's hand off and stared at him.

'You're wrong, Odysseus. This armour was meant for me, I can feel it in here.'

He tapped his fist against his chest.

'Ajax, listen to me. The armour has some sort of enchantment about it – I felt its pull myself, only a short while ago. But it was made for Achilles, at the command of his immortal mother. Since when have the gods lavished gifts like this on ordinary warriors like you or me?'

'I'm no ordinary warrior, Odysseus. I'm the equal of any god in battle – even Zeus himself!'

The others drew back, Little Ajax frowning and hissing through his teeth at his namesake's blasphemy. But Great Ajax just glared at them contemptuously.

'Fools! Superstitious old women have less fear of the gods than you do. But I tell you the truth, I've never needed an Olympian's help in any battle I've ever fought. Even the great Achilles calls on their help before each fight, but not *me*! And if any of them dared face me in mortal form then I would master them by my own strength alone.'

Eperitus shook his head. 'I remember a short while ago you thought you'd met your match in Hector. Now you're saying you could beat the father of the gods himself?'

'A comment made in a moment of exhaustion and weakness,' Ajax replied, scowling. 'I have the skill to beat anyone, Hector included, and the fact the gods have sent this armour to me proves it.'

'But the armour belongs to Achilles,' Odysseus reminded him. 'Unless you think you can take it from him.'

Ajax looked at him thoughtfully, then shook his head.

'There's no treachery in my heart, if that's what you're implying, Odysseus. But one way or another, I tell you the armour is meant for me.'

At that moment Agamemnon stepped forward and raised his arms for silence.

'Achilles,' he called out in a stern voice, 'you have called us to assembly. State your reasons and be quick about it; the rest of us have a war to fight.'

Achilles did not answer immediately. He took a deep breath, enjoying the smell of the sea and the feel of the breeze against his face. Then he turned to look at Agamemnon and for the first time the King of Men saw the shield in all its glory. His eyes widened and his sceptre – which had also been made by Hephaistos – almost fell from his fingers.

'Agamemnon, son of Atreus, king of Mycenae,' Achilles began, the red plume of his helmet flickering lightly in the breeze. 'It was your decision to take Briseis from me that caused this feud between us. And yet I would rather the girl had died first and my anger had never been provoked, for it has brought calamity on the Greeks and death to Patroclus, my beloved friend. But these things have happened and I have taken a solemn oath that I will not bury

Patroclus until I have avenged his death with Hector's blood, so for my part I declare this feud over. If you will accept it, my spear is at your service once more, King of Men.'

His words were greeted by a ringing cheer from the watching soldiers. Those who were fully armed clashed the shafts of their spears against their shields, while even their leaders – Ajax, Odysseus and Eperitus among them – rose from the benches and shouted their joy at Achilles's announcement. Only one man remained seemingly unmoved, though there was a glimmer of a smile on his thin lips.

'You aren't the only one, Achilles, to place the blame for our feud squarely on my shoulders,' Agamemnon declared, staring round at the gathered men, many of whom looked down at the sand as his eyes passed over them. 'Every man here was angry at me for driving you into your hut and away from the fighting, though none dared voice it. And yet I tell you the fault for our rift was not mine. It belongs with the gods, who blinded me with folly in order to heap more misery and suffering upon mankind. But as there can be little doubt that the immortals have betrayed me, or that they have shown you their favour' – he pointed at the shield and his eyes lingered a moment on the constantly moving designs – 'I will honour the gifts Odysseus promised you on my behalf. Let them be brought to you now – Briseis first – so that the whole army can witness my offer of reparation and the end of our feud.'

The assembly raised their voices in agreement, but Achilles stepped forward and drew his sword, holding it up like a sceptre.

'Let the gifts wait until after we have driven the Trojans back to their city and Hector's blood is soaking the soil of Ilium.'

The voices were louder in response, Ajax's chief among them, but when Odysseus stepped forward and took the staff from Agamemnon, they soon fell away again.

'Stem your anger, Achilles. We don't all have your strength and our limbs aren't as fresh as yours. The men must eat before they go out to battle and the gods have to be honoured with sacrifice for ending your quarrel. Agamemnon has acknowledged that the immortals overruled his own judgement and has offered reparation; you should have the grace to accept it. The Trojans will still be there once the right customs have been observed, and then we can all make them pay for the suffering they've inflicted on us.'

Reluctantly, Achilles conceded and the army set about preparing their breakfast, though the prince stubbornly refused to eat until the day's fighting was over. Even when Briseis was brought before him, along with the slaves and the other wealth that had been promised him, Achilles hardly seemed to notice the woman over whose ownership his costly feud with Agamemnon had taken place. Instead, he sat on one of the benches as his Myrmidons took Briseis to his hut, watching impatiently as Talthybius brought a boar to Agamemnon and the King of Men invoked Zeus's blessing on their restored friendship. Then, as soon as Agamemnon had slit the creature's throat and Talthybius had hurled its carcass into the sea, Achilles stood and returned to the Myrmidon camp to prepare his chariot for war.

Chapter Thirty-Three
HECTOR'S DILEMMA

Hector stood looking at his shadow as it lay across the crushed grass, pointing like a long, black finger towards the shining sea. He wore the armour he had stripped from Patroclus's body, the magnificent breastplate, shield and helmet that for many years he had longed to pull from the corpse of Achilles himself. About his waist was the purple belt Ajax had given to him after their inconclusive duel. They were symbols of honour, won in combat against men whose spears had brought many a good warrior down into the dust, and yet they gave him no pleasure as he awaited the slaughter of another day's fighting.

Aeneas and Apheidas stood to his left, Paris and Deiphobus to his right, their own shadows thin and black before the bright sunshine. On the plain between them and the walls of the Greek camp were strewn the bodies of the men who had been slain in the previous days' battles. They lay singly or heaped one upon another, hardly recognizable as the living, breathing, articulate beings they had been only a little while before. Now, scattered groups of vultures picked at their dead eyes or probed open wounds with their hooked beaks, occasionally flapping their large wings to give themselves leverage as they tore off strips of flesh. Elsewhere, packs of wild dogs buried their sharp teeth into exposed limbs and torsos, ripping open stomachs and pulling out long, purple entrails that the other dogs would then pounce on in a frenzy. Hector watched them impassively. He could send groups of soldiers to chase the vile creatures away, but what good would it do? The animals would soon come back and he would only be tiring his already exhausted men further.

He sighed audibly and Aeneas, who had been fidgeting impatiently, took this as a sign that the debate could begin.

'Any moment now, those gates are going to open and the entire Greek army will come pouring out again,' he said. 'And if they find us still here, they're going to massacre us. It's a long way back, Hector; we need to return to Troy with the army intact, while we still can.'

'Aeneas is right,' Paris added, tracing his finger along the scar that crossed his face from forehead to beard. 'The men are exhausted, but worse than that, they're *afraid*. With Patroclus dead, Achilles is going to want revenge. *He*'ll be leading the Greeks this time, not Agamemnon, and if he was difficult enough to fight before he'll be like a lion among lambs now. Face it, Brother, for all our efforts we've fallen short of victory. I say let's return to the safety of the city and save our forces for another day.'

Hector folded his hands behind his back and watched one of the broken forms on the battlefield wave a weak arm at a vulture, which hopped out of reach and waited for the arm to flop back down before closing in again. Aeneas and Paris were right, of course. Morale was low with the certainty that Achilles was going to return to battle, so one fiercely pressed attack could break the army's will to fight and force them into open retreat across the plain. Better perhaps to turn back now and find shelter behind the city walls, where they would be safe and could rebuild their strength. With new allies getting nearer by the day – the Amazons led by Queen Penthesilea from the east and the Aethiopes under their king, Memnon, from the sun-parched south – it would not be long before they could sally out again and trap the Greeks in the middle, there to be annihilated.

But allies would demand a high price for bringing victory. And Hector still had his pride: marriage to Andromache may have softened his youthful ambitions, but it had not taken away his warrior's lust for glory. He wanted to defeat the Greeks himself, and, most of all, he wanted to face Achilles and take vengeance for the murder of Andromache's father and brothers.

'The walls will keep us safe, no doubt about that,' said Apheidas, staring out at the carnage on the plain. 'But they won't send the Greeks from our shores or give us victory. Our only chance of that is to stand our ground here and defeat them, or to die in the attempt. If we go back now, Troy may hold out for another couple of years – but the Greeks will triumph in the end. Hector knows that.'

Like the other commanders, Apheidas was ignorant of the new allies Priam had won over, so Hector was able to ignore the provocation in his tone. But the young and impetuous Deiphobus could not.

'Apheidas is right. The only way we can save Helen is to destroy the Greeks now, while we have a chance. We've fought hard and lost many men, but so have they. All it needs is for one of us to kill Achilles and the rest of them will fold.'

'I couldn't agree more,' Hector answered, turning to his comrades. 'Get rid of Achilles and the rest is a matter of time. But who is going to kill him? Will you, little brother?'

Deiphobus blinked in surprise. He had fully expected Hector, the bulwark of Troy and its greatest hope, to see the sense of his argument and announce he was going to face Achilles at last. The notion that he would accept the advice of Paris and Aeneas and *retreat* had never occurred to him. It was almost as bad as the thought of his beautiful sister-in-law, whom he had loved since the first moment he had seen her, being trapped inside the city walls for more long years or being taken back to Sparta by Menelaus.

'I will kill him!'

The five men turned to see a short, stocky warrior strolling towards them. His shield was slung across his back and he clutched two spears in his right hand, while his helmet dangled by its chin strap from the fingers of his left.

'Podes!' Hector exclaimed, rushing to embrace his friend. But the next moment he pulled away and stared hard into the man's dark eyes. 'What's wrong? Why have you left Troy when I gave strict orders for you to stay there with the militia? And who's protecting my wife and son?'

'Andromache's my sister, don't forget, and Astyanax is my nephew – do you think I'd leave them if they weren't safe? The fact is they never needed my protection in the first place and that's why I'm here. I'm sick of waiting on the walls with frail old men and boys too young to fight, listening to rumours and watching the wounded and captured streaming back through the Scaean Gate. I've come to avenge the evil the Greeks have done to our beloved homeland – and to fight at *your* side, Hector, as I have done in every battle up until now.'

'That all changed when Achilles killed King Eëtion and your brothers,' Hector declared, his gravelly voice strained. 'You're the last of Andromache's family. If you die, it'll destroy her, so think of your sister rather than yourself and return to the city at once.'

'No! *You*'re the one who should go back to Troy and let the rest of *us* do the fighting for a change. You never give yourself any respite in this war, my friend, no doubt because you don't trust us to hold off the Greeks without you. But if you fall, then Troy will fall with you, and Andromache and Astyanax's fate will be sealed! Go back to them now and let me face Achilles – it's my duty and my heart-felt desire to avenge the deaths of my father and brothers, whom he slew in his vile and ungodly anger at Thebe.'

As the last word left Podes's lips, the different gates along the Greek wall flew open with a crash and streams of men began pouring across the causeways. First came the cavalry, the horsemen quickly assembling on each flank and the chariots forming a long line opposite the waiting Trojans. Hordes of archers and slingers followed, running on to the plain to create a thick, disorderly screen of skirmishers. Then came the dense ranks of heavily armoured spearmen, their bronze and leather equipment clanking as they drew themselves up into well-disciplined oblongs before the ditch. The sun sparkled on the breastplates and helmets of the assembled army, but from the armour of one man in particular it blazed like a great beacon, too fierce to look at. The red plume of his helmet fluttered in the ever-present wind like a jet of fresh blood, while on his arm was a shield as brilliant as the face of the sun.

The Trojans looked on their foes with dismay. Their numbers seemed hardly diminished by the days of hard and terrible fighting that had taken such a toll among their own ranks, and though none could see his face, every man knew that the warrior with the bright armour in the leading chariot really was Achilles this time, fresh to the battle and seething with the desire for revenge. Hector looked from the resurgent Greeks to the faces of his own men, standing in their companies behind the small group of their commanders, and he knew what he had to do.

'We cannot fight them,' he announced, though his heart was heavy and he had to force the words from his lips. 'The army's exhausted and doesn't share your enthusiasm for this fight, Podes, despite its skill and courage. I will speak to Agamemnon and call a day's truce to gather the dead again, and then we'll withdraw to the city during the night.'

Podes spat in the dust and glowered his disapproval at his brother-in-law.

'Back down now and all is lost,' he warned. 'You're a greater man than that, Hector, and Troy is tired of surviving to fight another day. You must lead us to victory – or say farewell to everything you love.'

'He's right,' Apheidas agreed, clutching at the hilt of his sword and looking at the prince sternly. 'You'll not get another chance like this.'

Hector thought of the Amazons and the Aethiopes who were drawing closer to the city with each passing day and shook his head as he turned to face his men.

'I've made my decision. I'm going to parley with Agamemnon and—'

'Podes!' Aeneas shouted.

They turned to see Podes leap on to Hector's chariot and shove the surprised driver back into the dirt. He seized the reins and with a shout sent the horses leaping across the plain.

'Stop him!' Hector ordered.

At once Aeneas took up his spears and dashed forward, calling to the driver of his own chariot. The man was quick to react and a moment later Aeneas had jumped on to the car and was pursuing Andromache's brother towards the Greek lines. As he watched the chariots speed across the battlefield, Hector knew there was no chance now of a truce and little hope of an unmolested return to the safety of Troy.

'Apheidas,' he said through gritted teeth, 'prepare your cavalry to cover the army's retreat, if need be. Paris, Deiphobus – pray to the gods and call on all your courage. We're going to attack.'

Raising his spear above his head, he turned to the ranks of skirmishers and spearmen whose tired faces looked at him with grim expectation. Then he thrust the weapon towards the Greek lines and, with a great shout that sent the vultures flying slowly and awkwardly up from the bodies of the dead, the army advanced.

Out on the plain, Aeneas quickly overhauled Podes – whose horses were struggling to obey his unfamiliar voice – and shouted for to him to turn back. Podes ignored him, but as Aeneas prepared to cut across and force him away from the Greeks, Achilles spurred his own chariot forward and came rushing towards the two men at a fearful pace. Knowing there was no escape, Aeneas hurled his spear at the approaching warrior, only to watch Achilles raise his shield and swat it aside as if it were nothing more than a toy arrow fired by a child. The Greek's reply was rapid and accurate, the point of his heavy spear punching through the oxhide layers of Aeneas's shield and tearing it from his arm. A storm of arrows from the Locrian archers followed and as Aeneas ducked behind the low screen of his chariot his driver steered the horses away and drove them back towards the Trojan lines.

'Achilles!' Podes shouted, bringing Hector's chariot to a halt and jumping down to the ground. 'Achilles, you murderous dog! I am Podes, son of King Eëtion and brother to his seven sons, all of whom you murdered when you sacked my home city of Thebe. I have come to face you and take revenge for their deaths.'

'Brave but foolish,' Achilles replied, stepping down from his chariot and retrieving his spear from the shattered remains of Aeneas's shield. On either side of him the Greek and Trojan armies were advancing at a run, the heavy tramp of their feet shaking the foundations of the earth as the sky above was darkened by the exchange of their arrows and spears. 'Your father and brothers fought well, but what makes you think you are any better than they were? You'd have honoured their memory more by preserving your life at home, not seeking death from the same man who sent them to Hades.'

'Damn you!'

Podes hurled his spear with a grunt at the Phthian prince. Achilles fell to one knee and raised his shield over his head, letting the point of the weapon glance across its surface. Then, as Podes's eyes fell on the shield and were mesmerized with awe by its ceaselessly shifting designs, Achilles rushed forward and thrust his ash spear into his chest. The Trojan cried out as the sharp bronze pierced his scaled armour and punctured his heart, then fell in a heap as his soul rushed down to join his father and brothers in the Underworld.

'No!' Hector cried out.

He had sprinted far ahead of the army, his speed unchecked by his heavy armour as he rushed to save his friend from his folly. But despite his great strength he had not been fast enough. As he watched Achilles pull his spear from Podes's chest and Podes fall dead to the ground, he knew he had failed not only his closest companion but also his wife, whose entire family had now been murdered by one man. In an instant he recalled that long night only a short time ago when Andromache had been unable to sleep for grief at the death of her father and brothers; and as she loved

Podes above them all, how much deeper would her suffering be now?

Hector's despair turned to hatred. He charged at the Greek monster who had caused his people so much misery and saw the same hatred reflected back at him in Achilles's face. There was no time for words, no time for the courtesies or insults great warriors loved to exchange as they sized each other up – there was only the briefest instant in which each man could judge the approach of his enemy, take aim and cast his deadly missile.

They threw their spears at the same moment. Hector's passed over Achilles's shoulder and disappeared into the mass of soldiers running up behind him, while Achilles's skimmed past Hector's shield and thumped into the ground, where the heavy shaft stood vibrating with the force of the impact. Shouting with rage, both men drew their swords and dashed at each other, followed closely by the long walls of Greek and Trojan spearmen.

Hector swung his blade down with a crash against Achilles's shield and was amazed to see that not only did the myriad figures of men and animals leap aside from the blow, but also the long, thin dint that it left quickly closed up and filled out again. His moment's wonder nearly cost him his life, for Achilles's own blade swept swiftly down beneath the edge of Hector's shield towards his knee. Hector leapt back before it could slice through the skin, muscle and bone and bring him crashing down into the grass, but Achilles was quick to follow, thrusting his shield against Hector's and stabbing with the point of his sword above the rim. It scraped across the scowling bronze visor of the helmet Hector had stripped from Patroclus's body – the same helmet Achilles had worn into battle ever since he had first killed a man – but as the Trojan fell back, he lashed out and caught Achilles on the upper arm. The obsessively sharpened edge cut into the flesh and was only stopped at the shoulder by the god-made cuirass.

Achilles pushed Hector away with his shield and glared hatefully at him, paying no attention to the wound on his arm. But before he could attack again, Hector lunged with the point of his sword at his stomach. The attack came quickly and skilfully and with all the weight of Hector's bulk and strength behind it, but Achilles's instincts had pre-warned him and he parried with ease. His counter-thrust should have found Hector wrong-footed, but the Trojan was too clever a warrior for that and his own shield turned the blade away. And yet, for all his ability and experience, Hector had no answer for the depth of the Greek's hatred. With an energy and speed that knew no bounds, Achilles now launched himself furiously at his sworn enemy, driving him backwards with blow after blow, just as the Greeks on either side of him were besting the Trojans and pushing them back with great slaughter. And as each angry strike of Achilles's blade came closer to finding a gap in Hector's defences, so the Trojan prince began to think that he would not be able to defeat Achilles. In all the years of the war, the two men had exchanged spears but never engaged in hand-to-hand fighting, and with a sudden dismay that doused the fires of his own anger, Hector realized he might never see Andromache or Astyanax again. Though he had fought countless battles and always been at risk of falling to sword, spear or arrow, he had never before sensed the nearness of his own death as sharply as he did now.

He thought of his chariot, standing where Podes had left it, and recalled his friend's words to him – that if he fell, then Troy would fall with him, and Andromache and Astyanax's fate would be sealed. In that moment he knew that his duty was not to fall needlessly to Achilles's wrath, but to swallow his fatalistic pride and take the army back to Troy. He could fight Achilles another day.

The Phthian prince came at him again. Hector met the blow with his sword and pushed his shield into his enemy's chest, sending him reeling backwards and buying himself enough time to turn and sprint to the waiting chariot. Leaping into the car he glanced back at Achilles, whose face was now a mask of wrath. Ares himself would fear to confront such a man, Hector thought, and though he was not one of the immortals, he seemed barely human, either – a demonic creature, physically perfect and yet twisted by equal and opposing forces of pride, grief and unquenchable anger. For a moment he felt pity, then he whipped the reins across his horses' backs and sent them surging through the ranks of his army, shouting for them to retreat.

Chapter Thirty-Four

DEUS EX MACHINA

As Hector rode away and the Trojans fell back in disorder, Odysseus drove his chariot through the chaos to where Achilles stood. Eperitus was in the car beside him, his spears expended and his sword wet with gore from tip to hilt.

'You're hurt,' Odysseus said, forced to shout over the sound of ringing metal and the yells of struggling men.

'It's nothing,' Achilles grunted irritably, not even looking at the deep gash on his upper arm.

He watched Hector disappear behind the shattered ranks of his army, then ran back to his chariot and seized the yoke that hung between the shoulders of the horses. Pedasus's place had been taken by the immortal Balius, brother of Xanthus. The siblings were magnificent beasts and proud, but the prince looked at them sternly.

'My friends, carry me into battle so that I can take my vengeance on these miserable Trojans. And when the day's fighting is over, bring me out alive again; don't leave me dead on the field, as was Patroclus's fate.'

Xanthus stamped his foot and lowered his head, whinnying pitifully as his mane stroked across the high grass. Achilles's eyes widened with surprise, then he cupped his hand beneath the animal's chin and raised his head up again.

'Don't prophesy to me, Xanthus,' he said. 'My mother has already told me I won't live long after Hector dies, but she didn't deter me and neither will you. If a man cannot face his fate, he is not worthy to call himself a man. Now, take me after Hector or I will cut your throats and find other, less wilful horses.'

Odysseus and Eperitus exchanged glances as Achilles stepped into his chariot and lashed the reins. Xanthus and Balius shook their manes and neighed loudly, then shot forward. Odysseus watched Achilles disappear behind the clouds of dust that had enveloped the fighting, then turned to Eperitus.

'Did you hear what he said?'

'He thought the horse was prophesying,' Eperitus answered.

'And did you hear the horse say anything? I mean, you've got sharper ears than I have . . .'

'Horses don't talk, Odysseus. If Xanthus spoke, it was in Achilles's head. His grief has turned his mind.'

Odysseus nodded and dropped a hand on his captain's shoulder. 'Maybe it has. And maybe a man of his quality was never quite sane in the first place. Either way, the beast inside him has been unleashed at last and I doubt either Hector or the walls of Troy will be able to stop him any more. Come on, let's get after him.'

The Trojans were in open flight across the plain now. All semblance of order had gone and though a few fought a rolling rearguard under the direction of Paris, Aeneas and others, many lesser men simply tossed their weapons aside and fled in terror, hoping to reach the safety of Troy before they could be cut down. Achilles, though, was relentless in his pursuit. Odysseus and Eperitus followed in his wake, watching with a mixture of awe and horror as he cut down one man after another, riding down the living or driving over the slain so that clouds of red gore sprayed up from the heavy wheels of his chariot. The pitiless efficiency with which he slaughtered the Trojans seemed to inspire the whole of the Greek army, who chased their hated enemies back across the battlefields of the preceding days until, eventually, they reached the slopes overlooking Troy, with the broad, gleaming ribbon of the Scamander below.

Until this point, only a series of quick, skilfully directed attacks by Apheidas's horsemen had saved the Trojans from utter destruction. By forcing the Greeks to keep their order, they prevented the pursuit from becoming a rout and enabled many Trojans to escape the worst of the butchery. But the Greek archers and cavalry had taken their toll of Apheidas's men, and as the Trojan foot soldiers fled down the slope towards the fords and the city beyond, the cavalry turned tail and went with them.

Achilles drove through the middle of the human stampede, followed by Odysseus, Eperitus and a dozen other chariots. They split the Trojans in two, letting the greater part flee across the fords but driving many into a bend of the river, where the banks were high and the waters between them deep. Without stopping to strip off their armour, the panicked soldiers leapt into the fast-flowing waters and tried to get to the safety of the far bank. Those who could not swim drowned quickly, while many who could, drowned anyway beneath the weight of breastplates and greaves, or the sheer mass of men who were struggling to escape certain death on the grassy slopes above.

Heedless of his own heavy armour, Achilles halted his chariot, threw his shield across his back and jumped into the river after the Trojans. The water by the banks was shallow enough to stand in and was thick with rushes. He waded through them and began laying about himself with his sword, ruthlessly killing any man who could not escape beyond the circle of his reach. Odysseus and Eperitus left their own chariot and ran down to the lip of the slope, where they looked on in horror at the scene before them. Though both men had witnessed much slaughter in their lives, they were appalled to see the water turn pink with the blood of Achilles's victims and the banks become choked with their corpses. Equally horrifying was the sight of hundreds of Trojans drowning in their panic as they fled, or being shot by the arrows of the Locrian archers who had reached the riverbanks and were pouring missiles into the press of bodies, regardless of whether they were alive or dead. The air was filled with screams of pain and anguish, and it took Odysseus a moment to realize that Achilles was calling to him as he pushed a young noble through the rushes.

'Bind his hands with his belt and send him back to the camp,' he shouted.

Odysseus took the shocked youth by the wrist and hauled him up the muddy embankment, but no sooner had he secured his hands behind his back than Achilles sent another nobleman after him. Another followed and then another so that, even with Eperitus's help, Odysseus had to call some of the archers from their sport and get them to assist with the prisoners. Why Achilles had stopped killing he could not guess, as up to that point he had cut down any Trojan he could find without pity or remorse; but soon twelve young men stood cascading water on to the grass, their hands tied and their heads hung low, though doubtless thankful to be alive.

Odysseus and Eperitus returned to the lip of the bank, expecting more prisoners as Achilles waded further into the congested water. But as the Trojans held out their hands in gestures of submission, he began to kill them again without mercy, lopping off heads and limbs or opening stomachs so that men fell into the water surrounded by their own entrails. As the killing resumed, one Trojan ducked under the sweep of Achilles's blade and fell to his knees before him, throwing his arms about the prince's legs so that only his head remained above the water.

'My lord Achilles,' he pleaded, speaking in Greek. 'Do you not recognize me?'

His words pierced the killing trance that had fallen on the Phthian prince and Achilles looked down at him.

'Who are you?'

'Lycaon, one of Priam's sons. You captured me in battle last year and we shared a meal together before you sold me into slavery on the island of Lemnos. I escaped and came back to my father only a few days back, but you fetched a good price for me then and you'll surely get the same or more now.'

'My days of showing mercy to Trojans ended with the death of Patroclus.'

'But the men on the bank—'

Achilles took Lycaon by the hair and forced his head back.

'I have something else in mind for them,' he said as he raised his sword.

'But you can't kill a suppliant,' Lycaon protested, flinching and shaking with fear, but unable to escape Achilles's iron grip. 'You'll bring the wrath of the gods upon yourself!'

Achilles smiled sardonically and brought the blade down through Lycaon's neck and collar bone.

'What more can the gods do to me, Lycaon?' he mocked, still holding the dead youth by his black hair. 'Nothing! Go and feed the fishes, son of Priam; as for the rest of you, I will bleed Troy white for the death of Patroclus, and neither this river nor those walls will save you from my wrath.'

He launched himself once more upon the Trojans, whose bodies clogged the river now and sullied its once clear waters with their blood. A few had made it to the other side – those who were strongest and who had fought their own comrades to reach the embankment – but those who remained alive in the water had either thrown away their weapons or did not have the will to resist the terrible figure of Achilles. They fell before him like sacrificial goats, kicking and clawing at each other in their efforts to escape, but were shown neither compassion nor clemency as Achilles continued his butcher's work.

Then the river level dropped suddenly and began to draw back against the natural direction of its flow, revealing the jumbled mass of armoured corpses that had been dragged to its stony bed. As Achilles stood knee-high in the water, dumbfounded by the sudden draining of the waters, there was a sound like a strong wind approaching from the east.

'What is it?' Odysseus asked, as all eyes were turned upriver.

Then he saw a wall of water like a giant ocean wave come rolling down the course of the Scamander at an incredible pace,

bringing rocks and chunks of bank with it as it came. He shouted
a warning to Achilles, who saw the danger and waded as quickly
as the shallow waters would allow him to an elm tree on the far
bank.

'Run!' Odysseus shouted, grabbing Eperitus by the arm and
dragging him towards the slope.

'Wait,' Eperitus protested, pulling back. 'Achilles'll be washed
into the bay and drowned. We have to help him!'

Odysseus paused and looked down at their stricken comrade,
frowning in consternation at what to do. While the archers on the
bank turned and fled, the men trapped in the river could only
throw their arms up in terror as the water carried them away.
Many were killed outright by the rocks, or were drowned quickly
by the volume and pressure of the water as it overwhelmed them.
The elm that Achilles had thrown his powerful arms about
collapsed and fell into the river, damming its flow for a moment
before the pressure swept it away, and Achilles with it.

Odysseus and Eperitus sprinted after him, following the river's
edge in the hope of intercepting the prince at the ford. As they
ran, the Scamander broke its banks behind them and spread across
the marshes, rolling the corpses of the drowned and murdered
Trojans before it. Chariots were tossed on to their sides and
smashed to pieces, releasing their teams to gallop up the slope in
panic, while many of the escaping archers they passed were caught
by the waters and bowled over. The Greek cavalry, which was
crossing the ford in pursuit of the Trojans, turned and galloped
back up the slope to safety, while Odysseus and Eperitus had their
legs knocked away as the deluge passed beneath them.

'There he is!' Eperitus cried out, pointing downriver.

Achilles was using all his strength to hold on to a large rock
that had once marked the centre of the ford. He still wore the
helmet and breastplate his mother had brought for him from
Hephaistos's smithy, but the magnificent shield was nowhere to
be seen.

'We'll never reach him there,' Odysseus shouted over the roar of the water that was now up to their shins and threatening to take their legs away from beneath them. 'The river's too deep. And even if we did . . .'

But Eperitus was not listening. He ran to the edge of what had once been the riverbank and dived in, instantly disappearing beneath the fast-flowing water. He bobbed up again a few moments later and began to swim with the current to where Achilles was being pounded by the relentless Scamander.

'And even if we *do*,' Odysseus shouted after him, 'how are we going to get back to dry ground?'

Shaking his head, he leapt in after his friend. The cold water shocked the breath from his lungs as he plunged below its surface. For a moment everything was a turmoil of darkness and bubbles, mixed with the pounding of his heart in his eardrums as the angry river sucked him down towards its bed, aided by the weight of his treacherous armour. He kicked against it with all his strength and shot upwards, gulping in a lungful of air as he broke free of the raging waters. Then the violent force of the current seized hold of him and swept him inexorably towards the finger-like rock, where he caught a glimpse of Eperitus and Achilles holding on to each other as their strength began to fade.

Odysseus turned and began swimming against the current to slow his approach to the rock, all the time looking over his shoulder so that he would not be driven directly against it. Then, at the last moment, he turned again and was swept into the waiting arms of Eperitus and Achilles.

'The flood can't last for ever,' Eperitus shouted over the roar of the Scamander as they stood chest-high in the water. 'We just have to hold on to the rock and each other.'

'And pray!' Achilles added.

Odysseus nodded, squinting against the spray. He turned his back to the rock and linked arms with Eperitus, the pressure of the water thrusting them back against the rock.

'Mistress Athena,' he yelled. 'If ever you've been pleased with the sacrifices we three have offered to you, help us now! If ever—'

He stopped and looked down into the tumultuous waters. There, but a little way to the right of the rock, was Achilles's shield, its gold, silver and bronze gleaming beguilingly at him from beneath the surface of the river. All he needed to do was wade out a little into the waters and reach down, but as soon as the temptation had formed in his head he knew that the force of the Scamander would sweep him away. It was as if the shield were trying to lure him to his death.

Then a large shadow passed over them and all three men looked up to see a long-winged bird sweeping down out of the sun. They ducked instinctively and heard a loud splash. When they raised their heads again they saw a woman standing in the water before them, impossibly tall and with brilliant white skin and golden hair. She wore a long white chiton filled with a light that seemed to emanate from her body. On her head was a bronze helmet, from beneath which her stern grey eyes were staring at them intently. The river passed around her, releasing the men from the grip of its power; and it was a good thing, for they would have been swept away in their surprise. Achilles's jaw dropped as he looked up at her, but Odysseus and Eperitus recognized the goddess at once and were quick to bow their heads.

'Mistress,' Odysseus acknowledged her.

'It seems you and Eperitus are still incapable of surviving without my help,' Athena replied, her haughty tone betrayed by the twinkle in her eye. 'And as for you, Achilles, you went too far when you massacred the Trojans in the river. You made the Scamander angry enough to rise against you himself.' She spat into the river and stretched out her arm so that the tasselled aegis hung down like a curtain. 'But this is not your time to die, so I've been sent to save you from his wrath. And Hephaistos has come with me – look.'

The men turned to see a giant figure standing at the flooded delta where the Scamander fed into the wide bay before Troy. His muscular chest and arms were out of all proportion to his spindly legs, one of which was crooked and bent inwards; but if this gave his listing body a comical appearance there was little else to laugh at about the smith-god. His eyes were black coals rimmed with orange fire, staring out from a face that – like his whole body – was covered in a mass of dark, curly hair. In his upturned hands were columns of flame, and as he thrust his arms out – first to the left, then to the right – streams of fire leapt out, igniting the elms and willows that lined the submerged banks of the river. Soon every tree was ablaze, sending waves of intense heat over the surface of the Scamander and turning its waters back in hissing gouts of steam. Achilles, Odysseus and Eperitus threw their arms across their faces and Athena swept her aegis over them to protect them from the scalding inferno. Then Hephaistos limped forward and moved his arm in an arc over the flooded river and plain. The hundreds of bodies of men and horses that floated there burst into flames at once, spewing tongues of fire like white petals and forcing the water back even further.

'Listen to me,' Athena said, her voice louder than the roar of fire and the hiss of water raging all around. 'Amazons are coming to Troy from the distant land of Scythia in the east. They are female warriors, fighting priestesses of Ares who have come to Priam's aid, but your male arrogance should not underestimate them. They are slower and weaker than men, but their fighting spirit is a match for any of yours. Their strengths are their command of horses and their skill with the bow: they can shoot a man down from horseback – at long range and on the move – and wheel out of range before their enemies can fire back. It's a tactic they use to great success in their own lands. I want you to destroy them, and most especially their queen, Penthesilea. These viragos are an affront to the gods – though Ares and Artemis both favour them – and if you do away with them I will consider that ample payment for saving your hides now.'

'Then they will die, Mistress,' Achilles said.

'Be wary of Penthesilea, my prince,' Athena warned him. 'She has the ability to master even you. Be advised by the guile of Odysseus, and don't rely on your own strength.'

'As for you, Odysseus,' she continued, looking directly into the king's eyes, 'the gods have appointed a special task to you. Something you must keep to yourself.'

Odysseus looked left and right at Achilles and Eperitus, but neither man seemed to be listening.

'Only you can hear me,' Athena said. 'And only you can carry out this command. Eperitus cannot help you this time, and you must not tell him until the task has been carried out. It will not be an easy thing for you to do.'

Odysseus looked at the goddess who had watched over him since his childhood, protecting him and occasionally guiding his footsteps. He saw the look of affection and sadness in her divine features, knowing that somewhere in her immortal heart she loved him for his cunning mind and quick wits, qualities for which she herself was famed.

'What do the gods require of me?' he asked, though the question was heard by Athena alone.

'Great Ajax has blasphemed the gods too often. We want our vengeance upon him, as a lesson to all others who defy us in their pride and arrogance. The day will come when he will lay claim to Achilles's armour — Hephaistos placed an enchantment on the shield to fool the weak-minded, though it was aimed at Ajax in particular. When he does, you must stop him, Odysseus. Make the armour your own by any means at your disposal, fair or foul.'

Odysseus looked down at the glimmering circle of gold beneath the surface of the river, recalling Calchas's prophetic words spoken that night on the fringes of the Greek camp. As his sharp mind mulled over what they meant, the boiling waters retreated to leave a vast cloud of steam that hovered over everything like an ethereal sea. When, finally, the thick fog began to dissipate, they saw that Athena and Hephaistos had gone and the Scamander was once more contained within its own high embankments. On the other side of the fords, the plain was silent and empty but for the howling of the north wind. The Trojan army had escaped into the city and the battle was over.

And yet, as the mist thinned and was blown away from the walls and towers of Troy, they saw a lone figure standing before the Scaean Gate, the bronze of his helmet and breastplate shining in the sunlight. It was Hector.

Chapter Thirty-Five

HECTOR AND ACHILLES

The streets of lower Troy were crowded with exhausted soldiers. Many had collapsed against walls and in doorways, where they were given water and helped out of their heavy armour by the womenfolk and old men of the city. Those who still had enough strength to stand were staring vacantly, too shocked to answer the questions thrown at them by people searching for husbands, sons or brothers among the survivors. A few gave quiet thanks to the gods for their deliverance, while others tended to their wounded comrades – of whom very few had reached the city – and tried to comfort them in their pain. The most stout-hearted assembled in their companies, in case the Greeks followed up their victory on the plain with an assault against the walls.

Amid the cacophony of groaning and weeping, a tall, hooded figure dressed all in white pushed her way through the mass of people and horses, her terrified and yet beautiful face turning this way and that. She looked stunningly pure among the dust and bloodstained soldiery and there were many who forgot their suffering as they saw her, their eyes keen to drink of her loveliness; but there were many more who scowled as she passed them by, cursing her under their breath for the perfect looks that had brought unthinkable disaster and misery to Troy.

'Helen!'

She turned to see a young man in expensive armour – now

371

much abused and covered in dried gore – waving to her from a group of wounded soldiers. He left the man he had been tending and shouldered his way through the crowd towards her.

'Deiphobus,' she gasped. 'Oh Deiphobus, you don't know how glad I am to see you alive.'

The prince smiled with pleasure at her words, then, seeing the anguish written in her wonderful face, stepped forward and caught her up in his arms. For a moment he said nothing, content to hold her against his chest and feel her soft, scented hair against his cheek, his only regret being the armour that prevented him from enjoying the warmth of her body next to his.

'What is it, Sister? What's wrong?'

'Is your brother alive, Deiphobus? Have you seen Paris?'

Her eyes were filled with desperate urgency, which turned to relief and joy when Deiphobus nodded his head.

'Yes, he's alive and well. I'll take you to him . . .'

'No, Deiphobus. You have work to do here – your men need you. Just tell me where he is and I'll find him.'

Deiphobus gave her a weak, disappointed smile and nodded towards the battlements. 'He was by the gates when I last saw him. I don't think he will have moved.'

Helen kissed him on the cheek, picking up a smear of dirt on her nose and chin as she did so, then pushed her way back into the crowd. Most moved aside at the sight of her, though some of the women spat on the road before her feet and others stared at her with undisguised malice. Then a soldier took it upon himself to go ahead of her, clearing the way with his shield until the tower of the Scaean Gate was looming over them.

'This will do,' Helen said, and the man bowed low and disappeared back into the crowd.

She cast her gaze around at the walls, where scores of wounded or exhausted men were sitting in the shadows. Many were leaning against each other and sleeping, or resting their foreheads on their raised knees and silently reliving the horrors of the battlefield. But one had placed his tall shield against his shins so that his face could not be seen, though Helen instantly recognized the bow leaning against the wall next to him.

She ran over and pushed the shield away, then knelt beside him and pulled his head into her chest.

'Oh, Paris, Paris!' she whispered, stroking his matted hair. 'It's your Helen. Everything's all right now. You're safe.'

He said nothing, but after a moment she felt his trembling hand slip gingerly on to her hip. Suddenly a rush of tears poured down Helen's cheeks and she sat beside her husband, throwing her arms about his neck and covering his face with kisses. Cupping his chin in her fingers, she raised his head a little so that his eyes met hers. She choked back a new wave of tears as, with deep shock, she saw the emptiness within.

'What's happened to you, Paris?' she sobbed. 'What is it? Is it Hector? *Where is he?*'

She shook his shoulders gently, but Paris closed his eyes and let his head fall again.

'He's outside the gates,' said a voice, 'waiting for Achilles.'

Helen turned to see Apheidas staring down at her. His armour was not as dusty or bloodstained as most of the rest of the army – the result of having fought the battle from horseback – though there was a gash on his thigh and his skin had an ashen tinge to it.

'He's outside *alone*?' Helen asked, her eyes stern through the redness of her tears. 'You left him there to fight that monster?'

'He ordered everyone else back into the city,' Apheidas replied, turning away from her and walking towards the road that led up to the citadel. 'There was nothing I could do.'

'Don't turn your back on me!' Helen snapped.

When Apheidas continued walking – a slight limp evident in his right leg – Helen kissed Paris hurriedly on the forehead and, promising to come back shortly, ran after him.

'Didn't you try to dissuade him?' she demanded. 'Achilles is a butcher with only one mortal weakness. Hector will die out there if he faces him, and the last hope of Troy will die with him.'

Apheidas rounded on her.

'Hector is not Troy's only hope! And he's no fool, either; he knows where Achilles is vulnerable.'

'By Aphrodite's veil, you just left him there to die on his own, didn't you! You know Achilles will win, but you said nothing to discourage him. Your guilt's written all over your wicked face, Apheidas.'

'Guilt! How can *you* lecture me about guilt? Isn't the plain out there littered with dead men because of *your* iniquity?'

Helen slapped him hard across the cheek. Apheidas's eyes blazed for a moment and his fists clenched at his sides, but he was quick to restrain the flash of his own temper.

'As for *discouraging* Hector,' he sneered, 'I was the one who *persuaded* him to stay and fight! You were there that night, skulking in the gardens when he took an oath on his son's life to kill Achilles before the year was out. *I* reminded him of the fact when he was ushering the army back through the gates, while the river was in flood. I also reminded him that Achilles murdered Podes before his very eyes – what, Helen? Shocked to hear of another victim of your lust? And last of all, I told him that he had to fight Achilles sooner or later; their rivalry is the fulcrum on which the scales of this war are balanced, and until one of them has been dispatched to Hades the suffering and the death will carry on interminably.'

'I can't believe he listened to you. It doesn't have to be like that!'

'Doesn't it?' Apheidas smiled. 'Well, Hector agreed with me. And what's more, he confessed his shame at fleeing before Achilles when they met earlier today, at a time when he could have struck him down and saved the army from devastation.'

'Confessed, Apheidas? Or did you goad him?'

Apheidas's eyes narrowed as he looked away. 'If you'll forgive me, my lady, I have wounds that need tending to and then I must see to what's left of my men and horses.'

He gave a curt nod before turning and forcing his way into the crowd. A moment later Cassandra appeared, short-breathed with panic. Her hair and clothing were dishevelled and her face was even paler than usual.

'Helen!' she gasped. 'Oh, Helen, thank the gods. Have you seen my half-brother, Lycaon? I had a terrible dream about him and warned him not to go out and fight, but he wouldn't listen. Now Leothoë's looking for her son and we can't find him anywhere.'

Leothoë was one of Priam's many wives and had been a good friend to Helen ever since she had first arrived in Troy. Helen took Cassandra's hands in her own and squeezed them reassuringly.

'There are a lot of soldiers here, Cassandra. He must be somewhere. But tell me, where's Andromache? I have to speak to her urgently.'

'She's in the palace, preparing Hector's bath as she always does after a battle.'

'Then fetch her at once. Hector's outside the gates, waiting for Achilles. If anyone can persuade him to come back behind the safety of the walls, it's Andromache. I'll look out for Lycaon and send him up to the palace the moment I find him.'

Cassandra stared at her briefly, shocked at the news, then nodded and ran back the way she had come. Suddenly the sluggish, densely packed crowd on the road stopped its wailing and fell silent. A moment later armed soldiers appeared, pushing aside those who were too slow to move. The fact that their armour was pristine, expensive and brightly polished, and the men themselves were tall, young and strong, told Helen instantly that they were palace guards come down from the citadel. Then she saw Priam's black hair and painted face at their centre – the thick powder on his cheeks stained with tears – with the short, plump figure of Hecabe beside him. They marched past Helen in a hurry and took the broad stone stairs up to the walls. Helen followed, along with a great crowd of the ordinary Trojans who thronged the streets.

'Hector, my boy,' Priam called, his voice cracking as he leaned over the battlements. 'Hector, what is this madness that has possessed you? I've lost too many sons to Achilles already, but I'd gladly lose the rest of them before I saw you murdered at his hands. Come inside at once, my beloved son, I implore you.'

Helen pressed against the ramparts with the rest of the crowd – mostly women – and looked down to see Hector standing just beyond the shadow of the gates. He had removed the helmet he had stripped from Patroclus as he lay dying and thrown it on the ground beside the sacred oak that stood a little further beyond the walls, but his tall shield was on his arm and a single spear was in his hands. He made no response to his father's appeal, focusing his attention instead on the fords of the Scamander, where three Greeks stood knee-high in the babbling waters. One had a blood-red plume and a bright shield that caught the light like a mirror; instinctively, Helen knew she was looking at Achilles.

'Then I will order the army out again,' Priam declared in a high voice. 'Even Achilles cannot defeat the whole might of Troy.'

'Keep the army where it is, my lord,' Hector replied without looking up. 'They have earned their rest. I must face Achilles alone – it's the will of the gods.'

'He's coming!' Hecabe shouted, throwing a hand to her cheek in horror and pointing at the figures in the ford, who were now wading through the water to the near bank. 'My dear son, the very sight of him fills me with dread! If you have any love for the mother who suckled you as a baby, then come inside now. There's no dishonour in it.'

'What does a woman know of honour?' Hector replied, this time looking up at his parents. 'If I turn and flee now I will be no more of a man than you are, dear Mother.'

The usual stern self-confidence was gone from his face, and at the sight of this change Helen suddenly realized that Hector knew he was going to die. Perhaps others sensed it too because a few amongst the crowd began to wail, raising their voices in the monotonous sound of mourning that had been heard too often in Troy in recent days.

'Silence!' Priam ordered, raising his shaking hand high. 'My

376

son is *not* dead yet. He stands as he has always stood, defending the gates of Troy against those who would seek to conquer it.'

The wailing fell away. Then, as Achilles strode across the plain with his shield blazing like the sun, someone tossed a handful of flowers from the ramparts. The stems scattered about Hector's feet and the yellow petals stared up at him, bright and cheerful in the warm glow of the afternoon. He looked at them, transfixed by their simple beauty, and for a moment the darkness that was sweeping towards him was forgotten. Then another clutch of flowers was thrown from a different part of the walls, and another, and another. More followed, until Hector stood amid a carpet of red and white, yellow and blue, green and pink, while the air around him was filled with petals, floating like snow to settle in his hair and on his cloak.

Helen hid her face in her hands, ashamed of her tears before such bravery.

As the mist evaporated in the warm sunlight Odysseus splashed across the clear, slow-running river and lifted Achilles's shield from its shingle bed. Eperitus watched the water stream off it to reveal the gold and silver figures moving beneath. Odysseus balanced it on his arm for a moment, enthralled by its beauty and craftsmanship, then quickly slipped it off again and handed it to Achilles.

'I need a weapon,' Achilles announced, passing the strap of his shield over his shoulder and staring across the plain at Hector, who was still standing defiantly before the Scaean Gate. 'Every breath that man takes is an offence to me and the sooner I kill him the sooner I can return and mourn the one whose life he took.'

So this was it, Eperitus thought as he slid his sword from its scabbard and handed the hilt to Achilles: Hector had decided to stop running and face the inevitable. He must have known it was his destiny to fight Achilles and that the outcome of their combat would ultimately decide the outcome of the war; and yet Eperitus was surprised to see him standing there. For ten years he had led the Trojans in battle, skilfully repulsing one Greek attack after another, and yet always reluctant to face Achilles or challenge him to single combat. Had some part of him – as with every warrior – baulked with fear at the sight of Achilles? Or was it that Hector was more concerned with preserving his city for as long as possible, rather than risking everything in a duel with Achilles? Whatever the answer, he did not flinch now as Priam and Hecabe pleaded with him from the city walls, or show any signs of fear as he leaned on his spear and looked across the plain towards his enemy in the middle of the ford.

Achilles took the proffered sword and, with a snarl of hatred, began wading towards the opposite bank of the Scamander. Odysseus and Eperitus followed, while behind them the massed ranks of the victorious Greeks came streaming down the slopes to the fords, which could once again be crossed in safety. As Achilles stepped out on to the plain before Troy, the stamp of hooves and a loud cry made him look over his shoulder to see Peisandros driving the prince's chariot into the water. A few moments later he called the team to a halt beside Achilles and jumped down.

'Your spear, my lord,' he said.

Achilles took the thick, monstrously long weapon and smiled grimly as he stared up at its broad head.

'Wait here,' he ordered.

Then, balancing its familiar weight in his hand, he ran towards the sun-bleached walls of Troy where Hector waited for him, surrounded by a ring of flowers that the women of the city were still tossing to him from the battlements. Peisandros stayed where he was, stroking the noses of Xanthus and Balius, but Odysseus and Eperitus ran after the prince. They were soon within bowshot of the walls, where Achilles came to a halt and planted his spear in the ground. The early afternoon sun flared up from his armour, blinding the watchers on the walls, but the look on his face as he glared at his enemy was as dark as the deepest pit of Tartarus. Hector moved back and, for a moment, Eperitus thought he would run, but some god must have breathed courage back into his limbs for on his third step he halted. He took his spear in both hands and held it across his body as if to bar Achilles from the city.

'I'm done with avoiding you in battle, Achilles,' he said. 'For ten years we've danced around each other, too fearful to fight and too proud to run, but now the time has come for Zeus to decide between us. I expect you to show me no mercy, for I will show you none, but I will make one request of you before we fight.'

'What is it?'

'If Zeus's favour rests on me and I succeed in killing you, I will not dishonour the father of the gods by mistreating your corpse. I'll take your armour as a trophy of my victory, but your body will be returned to the Greeks for cremation with the proper rites. I ask you to do the same for mine, if you defeat me.'

'No,' Achilles responded, scowling at Hector. 'You and I are enemies, not friends to make cosy bargains with one another. That armour you wear with such pride is already mine, loaned to Patroclus, not you. And for the suffering you have caused me by his death I will drag your body back to the ships and give it to the dogs. No flames to devour *your* dead flesh, Hector, only the teeth of savage beasts!'

He plucked his spear from the ground, pulled it back behind his ear and hurled it with a shout that shook the air. Hector ducked aside at the last moment and the bronze point buried itself in the old oak opposite the Scaean Gate. He turned his shocked eyes upon it, realizing it had only missed him by a finger's breadth; but as he watched its long shaft still quivering with the force of the throw he also understood that the gods had preserved his life and handed him the advantage. He looked back at Achilles, who had drawn his sword and was now charging across the open ground towards him, snarling with anger. But the distance between them was still wide and Hector no longer felt any fear. The lethargy of dread and doom that had given his muscles a leaden heaviness was lifted from him and he felt a rush of nervous energy burst through his whole body. Drawing back his spear, he took careful aim down the shaft and launched it with all his force, bellowing his rage and resentment.

The slender missile rushed with deadly accuracy at Achilles, catching him full on the shield and knocking him on to his back in a cloud of dust. The crowds on the wall shouted out in joy, but their elation was short-lived. Achilles staggered back to his feet and kicked aside the broken halves of Hector's spear, the force of the blow having failed to pierce even the outermost layer of his magical shield. Now it was Achilles's turn to cry out in triumph. His face a mask of hatred, he dashed forward and hewed his sword down against Hector's shield, sending the Trojan reeling back towards the sacred oak. Achilles came on relentlessly, swinging with terrifying speed and force at his opponent's neck. The arcing blade would have taken the head off any ordinary man, but Hector's instincts did not fail him; he ducked the blow and launched himself shield-first at the Phthian, knocking his legs from under him and rolling him over his back to crash in the dust behind him. Hector turned on his heel and drew his sword in the same movement, only to find Achilles back on his feet again and charging at him with the speed and energy of his pent-up hatred. Their blades clashed and scraped against each other, echoing back from the walls of Troy and mingling with the horrified shouts of the onlookers above. But the fury of Achilles's attack forced Hector back, battling with all his skill and experience just to survive. Then the Greek lashed out and the tip of his weapon drew a line of red across Hector's forehead. The Trojan rocked back beneath the blow, clapping his hand to the stinging wound, and Achilles circled swiftly to block his escape route to the Scaean Gate.

As the two men eyed each other from over the rims of their shields, Achilles edged back towards the oak tree – watching Hector closely for any attempt to run towards the gates – and pulled his spear free with a grunt. Hector closed the distance again, not wanting to give Achilles the chance for another cast. Then a voice called his name from the battlements and he looked up to see Andromache. Her beautiful eyes were red and her cheeks stained with tears. Helen was at her side, supporting her, but as she looked at her husband facing the monstrous Achilles, her courage left her and she buried her face in Helen's neck.

By now the Greek army, with the Myrmidons in the van, was crossing the ford and forming a dense barrier of shields and spears just beyond the range of the archers on the city walls. Hector glanced over his shoulder and knew he was trapped, but he no longer cared. He turned to Achilles, renewed hatred burning through his veins. There before him stood the black heart of all Troy's suffering, but if he could strike him down now it would end the war and release Ilium from the stranglehold of the Greeks. The farmers would take up their ploughs again and the fishermen their nets; merchants from the east would no longer bring weapons and armour, but coloured garments and silver ornaments for the women of the city; Andromache would smile again and little Astyanax could play beyond the walls for the first time in his life. There would be peace again and the only fighting would be in the songs of the bards, sanitizing the memory of the war and glorifying the sons of Troy, with Hector foremost among them.

But the songs had not been written yet, and would not be until Peleus's son was dead. Hector mumbled a quick prayer, surrendering himself to the mercy of Apollo, and ran forward. Achilles ran to meet him, his spear held in both hands and the point aimed at Hector's stomach. Hector twisted aside and turned as Achilles rushed past him, striking out with his sword. The blow rang out against Achilles's helmet but failed to pierce the thick metal. Shouts of dismay rose up from the walls, but Hector barely heard them as Achilles rushed at him with renewed vigour. They met head on, their shields clattering loudly against each other and for a moment Achilles's long spear left him at a disadvantage against Hector's sword. In that brief instant of time, drawn out by the quickening of his senses, Hector recalled the one weakness that Achilles was said to possess – his heel. Against all his warrior's instincts to strike at the head or torso, he hacked down at the back of his opponent's foot. But Achilles was quicker. He punched the shaft of his spear into the Trojan's face and knocked him to the ground. With a triumphant shout, he moved to plunge the sharpened bronze into Hector's prostrate body. Hector kicked out in desperation, finding Achilles's stomach and sending him sprawling back against the bole of the sacred oak. Hector leapt to his feet and ran after him, his sword raised over his head.

In an instant Achilles's shield was raised, catching the sun as the figures of men and animals moved rhythmically through the concentric circles that spread out from its centre. It was enough. Hector's eyes followed them for a moment too long, noticing the enchanted designs for the first time, and Achilles's spear found the gap between his breastbone and his throat. The momentum of Hector's attack carried the point through his body and back out by the nape of his neck, stopping him dead. He hung there for a few beats of his heart, then the weapon was pulled free and his heavy body crashed backwards into the long grass.

A sudden, incredulous silence swept across the plain. Even Achilles looked surprised as he stared down at his defeated enemy, his bloodstained chest still rising and falling with its final breaths. Then he stabbed the air with the point of his spear and sent a mighty shout of exultation up to the heavens. His triumph was echoed by the Greeks, while on the battlements of Troy the shocked silence gave way to hysterical cries of disbelief and anguish. As Eperitus ran with Odysseus to join Achilles, he looked up to the walls and saw Helen, her pale face even whiter now as she tried to stop Andromache hurling herself from the parapet.

When they reached Achilles he was already tugging the shield from Hector's limp arm and throwing it behind him, before kneeling at his side and unbuckling the purple belt Ajax had given him after they had fought on the slopes above the Scamander. The Trojan's huge body was motionless but for the faint movement of his chest. His eyes were closed and his chin and neck were stained with fresh blood. Then, as Achilles began to unfasten the ties that held his breastplate in place, Hector seized hold of his wrist.

'Achilles,' he whispered, though the effort brought on a fit of impulsive coughing as more blood flowed into his throat. 'Achilles, don't throw my body to the dogs. Ransom me to my parents so they can give me the proper rites and cremate me with honour.'

Achilles knocked his hand away and spat in his face.

'You'll have no honour from me. Be thankful your corpse'll be left for the dogs and carrion fowl; if I had the appetite, I'd carve your flesh right here and eat it raw before the walls of your own city! Not even if Priam were to offer me your weight in gold would I give your body back to him, not after what you've done to me.'

'Damn you, Achilles!' Eperitus protested, stepping forward. 'Hector has fought well; he deserves to be treated with honour. Leave his body here for his own people to claim him, or be cursed by the gods for your savagery.'

'Savagery?' Achilles snapped, pulling the breastplate from Hector and throwing it at the Ithacan's feet. 'What man can endure a war like this and *not* succumb to savagery? Can you, Eperitus? And you needn't look at me with such disdain either, Odysseus. Do you think I don't know who planted the gold beneath Palamedes's tent?'

Odysseus's eyes narrowed slightly but he said nothing as Achilles stripped Hector of his greaves and his tunic to leave him naked in the long grass. Then, as Peisandros drove up in Achilles's chariot, the prince drew his dagger from his belt and slit the tendons at the back of Hector's feet, from heel to ankle, causing him to cry out pitifully. Next he passed Ajax's purple belt through the slits and, dragging Hector behind him, tied him to the back of his chariot. Peisandros jumped down lightly and joined Eperitus and Odysseus as the prince piled the captured armour in the back of the car. The wailing from the walls of Troy grew in intensity as Achilles stepped into the chariot and, with a shout at the horses, sent it trundling off towards the ford.

Eperitus watched Hector dragged to his death, his head knocking over the stony ground, and was filled with contempt – for Achilles, for the war, and even for himself for standing by and allowing such things to happen. Though he had endured ten long years of fighting with little complaint, and knew that with Hector defeated Troy could not stand for much longer, he was filled with a sudden urge to leave Ilium and never bear weapons again. The nature of the war had changed; or maybe he had changed; or maybe it was both. But his heart for fighting had left him and, like Odysseus, all he wanted now was to go home and find peace.

Chapter Thirty-Six

AFTER THE FUNERAL

O meros drew on the strings of his tortoiseshell lyre and began to tell the tale of Orpheus's journey to find Eurydice, his beloved wife, who had been killed by a snake bite and condemned to eternity in the Underworld. It was a sad story that did little to lift Eperitus's already melancholy mood as he sat next to Odysseus in the king's hut. Eurybates, Antiphus and Eurylochus were also seated around the blazing hearth, while two more chairs sat empty between them, the fleeces that covered them glowing orange in the light of the flames.

'More wine, sir?' asked a slave, peering over his shoulder and seeing the empty cup in his hand.

Eperitus nodded and handed him his cup. As the dark liquid reached the rim and the slave moved off to serve Eurylochus, whose hateful eyes were ever flickering towards Eperitus, Omeros reached the climax of his tale. Having persuaded Hades to release Eurydice, Orpheus broke the one condition imposed by the god of the Underworld – not to look back before he reached the land of the living – and lost his wife for ever. For some reason, whether it was the wine or Omeros's skill as a bard, Eperitus felt his heart sink lower and he let his gaze fall on the flames quivering over the hearth.

While the others listened intently to the conclusion of the song, the words faded into the back of Eperitus's mind and he recalled the horrors and excesses he had witnessed over the previous days. More than anything, as he watched the fire, he was reminded of the funeral pyres on the plain and the countless bodies of Greeks and Trojans burning brightly in the darkness. It had taken the exhausted army the rest of the afternoon after Hector's death and the whole of the next day to gather the slain, while the Trojans had done the same under truce. So many had been killed on both sides that the wood for their pyres had to be collected from as far away as the foothills of Mount Ida, and every wagon and cart, mule and bullock had to be commandeered to bring it back. That was twelve days ago now, but Eperitus could still smell the burnt flesh as clearly as the spices in his wine.

But if the scene on the plain had been horrific, the cremation of Patroclus by the ships was opulent, ghoulish and profane in the extreme, making Eperitus shudder with disgust at the memory of it. The humble mourning of the rest of the army for their lost comrades was made a mockery of by the excessive grief of Achilles for his friend. Refusing to wash the caked gore of battle from his own body, he laid Patroclus on top of the great mound of wood and then fetched Hector's corpse, which he threw face-down in the dust before it. Sheep and cattle were sacrificed by the dozen, but instead of offering the fat and thigh bones to the gods as he should have done, Achilles laid them on top of Patroclus's body and slung the carcasses of the slain beasts upon the piled wood around him – a blasphemy that caused even Great Ajax to turn away in shame. Next he slaughtered four horses and two of Patroclus's hunting hounds to add to the growing heap of death, before placing jars of honey and oil between the cadavers – gifts suitable to a god, but not a mortal man. His final act was to murder the twelve prisoners he had taken during the fight in the river, slitting their throats one by one and throwing their bodies on to the pyre, which welcomed them greedily. This stunned the onlookers and raised murmurs of dissent among the attendant kings and leaders, appalled by the affront to the gods. But Achilles ignored them and none dared challenge him while he was in such a fell mood, for fear of having their own corpse added to the heap; but there were few

now who did not doubt his sanity as he stood before the raging
flames with his arms held up to the night sky, shouting defiance at
the gods. His voice was lost in the howling wind and the roar and
crash of the waves out at sea, but even though Eperitus's sharp
hearing could not hear the words, he knew the immortals did. And
whatever curses may leave a man's mouth, the gods always spoke
last.

The following day Patroclus's bones were sealed with fat in a
large jar and a barrow was raised over the ashes of his pyre.
Funeral games followed, with Achilles providing rich gifts for
winners and runners-up alike. Diomedes won the hotly contested
chariot race, while Odysseus competed against Little Ajax in a foot
race that recalled their competition in Sparta twenty years earlier,
when Odysseus had won the hand of Penelope by using his cunning
against the Locrian's greater speed. Once again Odysseus was
victorious, despite being the slower man, though this time his ploy
was to have Omeros spread fresh dung across the final stretch of
the course, causing Little Ajax to slip and fall face down in the
mess while Odysseus swerved around it and sprinted to victory.
More competitions followed with ever more luxurious prizes and
growing bitterness between the proud and stubborn competitors.

When the wrestling match was announced Odysseus stood up
at once, but when Great Ajax rose to challenge him Eperitus
noticed a strange hesitation in Odysseus's face. After the two men
had stripped naked, they began a series of exercises to form a layer
of sweat over their skin, making it harder for their opponent to
get a grip. But as they knelt to dry the palms of their hands in the
sand Eperitus saw the same doubtful look in Odysseus's eye again,
though it was more a guilty pause than a wavering of fear. Then
they closed with a shout, throwing their arms about each other in
a fierce embrace and trying for the first throw of the three required
for victory. But both men were too seasoned and much too strong
to give away such an easy advantage, and within moments their
arms were locked about each other's backs and their heads were
thrust into their opponent's shoulder, pressing ear to ear so that

their senses must have been filled with the sound of their own grunting and the stink of fresh sweat. Each tried to wrong-foot the other and trip him, using the techniques and tricks they had been taught and had practised since childhood, but with little success. Then, as the cheering died down and the crowds began to lose their enthusiasm for the contest, Ajax's superior strength prevailed and he lifted Odysseus from the ground.

'I have you now,' he groaned.

But in the same instant, Odysseus kicked his heel back against the bend of Ajax's knee and cut his legs from beneath him. The son of Telamon crashed into the sand with Odysseus on top of him, while all around them the crowds exploded back into life, leaping into the air and cheering.

The two men were soon back on their feet with their arms tight about each other's backs. Though their stamina was waning, Odysseus was filled with renewed confidence and tried to lift Ajax from his feet for another victory. He raised him a little, but Ajax's pride had already been hurt and he was determined not to be thrown a second time. He resisted with all his might, and as Odysseus felt his strength give, he abandoned the lift and attempted a hasty knee-hook, bringing both men crashing side by side to the ground.

Sensing the contest could carry on until sunset without conclusion, Achilles stepped forward and declared the match a draw, announcing that the prizes and the honour would be shared equally. The crowd applauded the decision with relief and Ajax offered Odysseus his hand. The Ithacan took it quickly and withdrew, leaving Ajax looking puzzled.

'What is it?' Eperitus had asked, handing Odysseus his tunic and cloak.

'What's what?' Odysseus replied, refusing to meet his captain's eye as he walked past him.

Last of all was the competition for the furthest spear cast, but when Agamemnon offered to compete, Achilles pronounced that the King of Men was clearly the best spearman of all the competitors and awarded him the prize without a missile being thrown. This act of flattery towards Agamemnon, and the Mycenaean's equally sycophantic acceptance of it, disgusted Eperitus almost as much as any of the other shameful events connected with the funeral of Patroclus. It was as if the feud that had cost the lives of thousands of men had never happened, as if their deaths were but an unfortunate chapter in the breaking and mending of the relationship between the greatest of the Greeks.

But if Achilles's animosity towards Agamemnon had been laid to rest, his hatred of Hector had not. The morning after the funeral games, he rose at first light and went out to Patroclus's barrow, where Hector's corpse had been left unburied in the dust for the carrion beasts to have their way with it. When he found the Trojan prince's body untouched and his wounds miraculously closed up, Achilles flew into a fury and hacked at it with his sword, before tying it to the back of his chariot and dragging it three times around the broad mound where Patroclus was entombed. It was a sacrilege that he had repeated every morning since, and every night the gods closed the new wounds and left Hector's body lying as if in a deep sleep.

Omeros's song ended with a flourish on the strings of his lyre. A moment later the flap of canvas over the hut door was pulled aside and Arceisius entered, followed by the vast bulk of Polites, who had to stoop to fit through the low entrance.

'You sent for us, my lord?' Arceisius asked.

'Come in and sit down,' Odysseus said, indicating the two empty chairs.

They lowered themselves into the seats, wondering why they had been summoned to the king's hut and looking uncertain of themselves. Odysseus sensed their discomfort and gave them a reassuring smile.

'Relax, both of you. I don't often ask you here, but that's going to change from now on.'

'I don't understand,' Arceisius said, taking the krater of wine that the slave was holding before him and leaning forward to pour a libation into the flames.

He shot a questioning glance at Eperitus, who looked away and raised his wine to his lips to disguise the smile that had appeared there.

'My commanders often come here to discuss tactics and other matters, so you might as well get used to the place,' Odysseus explained with a grin. Then, seeing the look of confusion on their faces, he opened his hands out wide and shook his head in disbelief. 'I'm *promoting* you both. Since Pelagon and Tychius were killed in the fighting, two of my companies have been without commanders – I want you to take their places. I would have said something before now, but I didn't want you walking around with broad grins while everyone's still supposed to be grieving for the dead. Anyway, the official mourning period ended today, so I'm giving you charge of Pelagon's two ships, Arceisius, and all the men in them; Polites, you'll have Tychius's.'

'Thank you, my lord,' Arceisius said, standing and bowing.

Polites, still looking confused, followed suit.

'To Polites and Arceisius,' Eurybates said, standing and raising his cup. 'May their service be long and glorious.'

The others stood, poured fresh libations to the gods and drank to the new commanders. Eperitus caught Arceisius's eye and nodded, proud that the shepherd boy whom he had made his squire so many years before was now a captain in his own right.

'Time you chose a squire of your own now,' he said, smiling. 'It's a commander's privilege.'

As Arceisius opened his mouth to speak, the canvas flap was pulled aside and a guard ducked inside.

'Sir,' he said, addressing Eperitus. 'There's a man outside who wants to see you.'

'Who is it?'

'A farmer, sir. One of the men who brings fodder for the animals.'

'What would he want with me?' Eperitus frowned. 'Tell him I'm busy.'

'I already did, but he says it's urgent. He said to tell you it's about the girl in the temple of Artemis, whatever that means.'

Astynome! Eperitus thought. He glanced at Odysseus, who looked back with concern but nodded his consent. Eperitus retrieved his cloak from the table by the entrance and threw it about his shoulders, then followed the guard out into the night air. The sky above was cloudless and pricked with stars, though their lustre was dimmed by the light of the moon as it hung low in the east. A skinny man with a wide-brimmed hat was standing close to the entrance, tugging anxiously at his pointed grey beard and muttering to himself.

'What do you want?' Eperitus asked sternly, though his heart was beating rapidly at the thought the man might have brought word from Astynome.

'I have something for you, my lord,' the farmer answered in thickly accented Greek.

'What is it? A message?'

'It's in the back of my cart, sir,' he replied, lowering his voice and looking nervously at the guard. 'You'll have to come with me.'

Eperitus narrowed his eyes suspiciously, but nodded his consent. The man set off at a quick pace between the tents and fires of the Ithacans, until he reached one of the main thoroughfares that ran through the Greek camp. An old cart sat at a camber by the side of the broad path, with a sore-covered and fly-infested mule yoked before it. A small, bored-looking boy sat on the bench dangling a long stick over the animal's back. He sat up as the farmer and Eperitus approached and eyed them in silence.

'In here,' the farmer said, leading Eperitus around to the large heap of hay on the back of the cart.

He looked furtively about himself, then thrust his arms into the hay and began pushing great heaps of it over the side. A blanket appeared with something beneath it, and then the something moved. Eperitus stepped back in alarm, gripping the hilt of his sword. At that moment the blanket was thrown aside and a girl sat up, blinking in the moonlight. Her tousled hair was threaded with hay, but her lovely face and dark eyes were as beautiful as the first time Eperitus had seen her.

'Astynome!'

'Eperitus!' she replied, smiling with joy and an instant later bursting into tears.

He rushed forward and lifted her out of the cart. Her arms slipped round his neck and she kissed him, filling his senses with the feel of her soft lips and the smell of perfume in her hair.

'Praise the gods you're still alive,' she said, kissing him on his bearded cheeks and running her fingers through his long hair. 'With all the fighting I feared the worst might have happened to you.'

'It takes more than an army of your countrymen to kill me,' he said smiling. 'And I've no intention of dying yet, not when I have you to live for. But what are you doing here? If Agamemnon were to find out . . .'

'Never mind Agamemnon, I had to know you were still alive. And there's something else. I need your help.'

'So this is what's keeping you so long.'

They turned to see Odysseus emerging from between two of the tents at the side of the path.

'I saw the lad keeping watch, so decided to come round the back,' he added in explanation for why he had not come along the path.

'My lord Odysseus,' Astynome said, bowing low before him.

'It's a pleasure to see you again, Astynome,' he replied with a smile. 'How did you get past the gates?'

Astynome picked up the blanket and shrugged at the simplicity of the ruse.

'I see,' Odysseus said, peering in to the back of the cart and stroking his beard thoughtfully. 'Very clever indeed. But it's not safe for you out here – if Agamemnon should find out . . . well, you understand. Why don't you come to my hut?'

'I'd rather not trouble you, my lord,' the girl said. 'I just wanted to see that Eperitus was alive.'

'Yes, I overheard. And something else about needing his help.' He leaned back against the cart and gave her a searching look.

'Perhaps Astynome would rather I speak to her alone, Odysseus,' Eperitus suggested.

'It's all right,' she said, laying her hand gently on Eperitus's forearm. 'Odysseus is your friend and king, I trust him.'

'Then come back to my hut and we will both be able to help you,' Odysseus said.

'Not with Eurylochus there,' Eperitus warned.

'Leave him to me,' Odysseus replied. 'Come on.'

Astynome gave quick instructions in her own language to the farmer, who nodded slowly, then she took Eperitus's hand and followed Odysseus back to the Ithacan camp. The occupants stood as they entered Odysseus's hut, staring with surprise at the beautiful Trojan girl. Eurylochus shot her a venomous look, which she returned with defiance.

'Listen to me, Eurylochus,' Odysseus warned, staring at his cousin. 'If Agamemnon – or anyone else for that matter – learns of Astynome's presence then I will hold you personally accountable, and the next battle we fight I will have you at my side in the front line. Do you understand?'

Eurylochus frowned at the king but saw that he meant what he said.

'Yes, my lord.'

'Good. Now, bring a seat for our guest, if you please. Astynome, anything you say will not go beyond the walls of my hut. You have my word on that.'

Astynome sat and looked about at the circle of warriors as Odysseus and Eperitus resumed their places. Then she sighed and placed her hands on her knees.

'My lords, you are the enemies of my people, but you are also warriors and men of honour. What I tell you now could hand you a swift victory over Troy – and though I trust Eperitus and Odysseus implicitly, I must also trust that the rest of you will respect the word of your king and not use my information to your advantage. The father of our city, King Priam, is beside himself with grief for Hector. He has heard of the treatment his son's body is suffering at the hands of that monster, Achilles, and in desperation has decided to set out at midnight tonight with a ransom for Hector's return. His wife has tried to dissuade him, as have Andromache, Helen and his nine remaining sons, but he won't listen – he will come, even though it means he may be captured and forced to order Troy's surrender.'

The Ithacans exchanged surprised glances but said nothing.

'If he can reach Achilles's hut and appeal to him as a suppliant,' she continued, 'Achilles will be obliged by the laws of *xenia* to offer him protection and a safe return to Troy, even if he refuses the ransom. But if he is captured on the plain or at the gates, he will be taken prisoner and there will be no limit to the price Agamemnon will be able to ask for his return. When I heard this I knew there was only one hope – to find you, Eperitus, and ask you to get Priam into the Greek camp. It was always a small hope, as you are only one man, my love; but my hope increases with the knowledge that King Odysseus will also help.'

'Don't worry,' Eperitus said, smiling at her. 'I'll do everything I can, and I'm certain Odysseus will be able to think—'

'By Zeus, are you mad?' Eurylochus exclaimed. 'This is a gift from the gods! If we can take the old man alive, the Trojans will be forced to give Helen back and pay us as much compensation as we want on top. We haven't had an opportunity like this in ten years of fighting. The war could be over in days!'

'Don't be so sure of that, Eurylochus,' Odysseus said coldly. 'For one thing, Agamemnon won't be happy until Troy has become a Mycenaean colony, and the Trojans will never agree to that. For another, I have no intention of taking a heart-broken old man prisoner, even if it means we could sail back to Ithaca tomorrow. I've done shameful things to try and shorten this war, but I won't do that. Besides, Astynome brought this news to us in good faith and we must help her if we can.'

'Even more so, if it means Achilles will accept the ransom and stop his defilement of Hector's corpse,' Eurybates added. 'I can't bear to see him dragging it around Patroclus's barrow any longer.'

There was a muttering of agreement, at which Odysseus stood up and raised his hand for silence.

'Very well, then. This is what we're going to do . . .'

Chapter Thirty-Seven

PRIAM IN THE GREEK CAMP

There were six guards on the southernmost gate and not one of them was able to refuse the wine that Astynome brought to them. After all, it was a gift from Prince Achilles, she told them – his best wine, offered in celebration of the end of the official mourning period. Equally, none of the guards was able to resist the powerful drug that Odysseus had added to it and soon they lay slumped by their posts, snoring loudly.

It took but a moment for Odysseus and the others to take their places and open the gates, allowing Eperitus to slip out on to the moonlit plain. The night was already reaching its zenith and he knew that he had to be quick if he was to intercept the Trojan king and his ransom-laden wagon. Fortunately, the gibbous moon shed its silvery light over the plateau, illuminating the numerous rocks and gullies and the newly raised barrows of the dead, and with his exceptional hearing he was soon able to hear the faint squeaking of a wooden axle under stress. Following the direction of the noise, his sharp eyes quickly picked out a humped shape moving in an arc to the east of the walls, obviously trying to avoid detection by the patrols that the Greeks had once been in the habit of sending out, though the practice had waned after the death of Palamedes.

Eperitus ran to intercept the wagon. As he got closer he could smell the pungent odour of fresh human sweat mixed with the reek of the mule's hide; he could also see that there were two men in the cart, both hooded. After glancing around for any sign of an escort, of which there was none, he hid behind a rock and waited until the cart was but a few paces away.

'Good evening, my lords,' he said, emerging from his cover and raising his hands before the mule.

The animal stopped and one of the men threw back his hood. It was Idaeus, Priam's herald.

'We're simple farmers going about our business. Let us be!'

'It's a little late to be off to market, isn't it? And your Greek's very good for a simple farmer.'

'But farmers we are, nonetheless, and I'll remind you that both armies respect our right to move about the land. Your leaders wouldn't be best disposed towards you if we stopped supplying the Greeks with food now, would they?'

Eperitus laughed. 'And what food do you have in the back of your cart, friend? I'm feeling a little hungry myself. Perhaps if you give me a bite to eat I'll let you pass.'

'You won't find anything you can stomach back there, lad,' said Priam, tipping back his hood. His black wig was gone, revealing thin strands of grey hair that clung to his white scalp. 'And we're no more farmers than you are, as well you know.'

'I know, my lord,' Eperitus answered, dropping to one knee and bowing his head. 'You are King Priam, and this is your herald, Idaeus. You've come with a ransom for the body of your son, and I've been sent to escort you in safety to Achilles's hut.'

The two men looked at each other in surprise.

'Then the noble Lord Achilles knows I'm coming?'

'No,' Eperitus answered, standing and placing a hand on the mule's yoke. 'You have a faithful subject, Astynome, daughter of Chryses, who loves you and doesn't want to see you come to harm. She journeyed ahead of you to seek my help, and I agreed to bring you to Achilles in safety.'

'The daughter of Chryses the priest? Yes, I know her,' Priam said. 'A pretty girl and no doubt you are in love with her. That's good. But I also know your face from somewhere.'

'I am Eperitus, my lord, commander of the army of King Odysseus. We came to Troy ten years before, with Menelaus and Palamedes.'

Priam's eyes narrowed a little and then he smiled.

'Of course. I nearly had you killed, and perhaps I should have done – Menelaus, above all. But there's no point ruing past judgements, not now. Lead on, Eperitus.'

The gates swung open as they approached and Odysseus ushered them through, bowing to King Priam as he joined Eperitus. Together, they led the cart down to the southernmost corner of the bay, where a faint trail of grey smoke was rising up from the roof of Achilles's hut. They passed between the fires of the Myrmidon camp, where the men were asleep beneath their blankets, and halted the wagon a few paces from Achilles's hut. Odysseus helped Priam down while Idaeus remained on the bench, huddled beneath his thick double-cloak. Eperitus disappeared behind the back of the cart.

'What do you want?' the guard asked brusquely, lowering his spear as Odysseus and Priam approached.

'Do you realize who you're talking to, man?' Odysseus snapped. 'Stand aside and let me in.'

The guard straightened up at once. 'Sorry, sir, but I can't do that. Lord Achilles is still grieving for Patroclus and has given orders for no one to enter, not even King Agamemnon himself.'

'He'll let us in,' said Eperitus, coming up behind the guard and striking him over the head with the pommel of his sword.

Odysseus pushed the flax curtain aside and stepped in, followed by Priam and Eperitus. A fire burned brightly in the hearth, painting the walls of the hut orange and casting flickering shadows behind the captured weapons and armour that hung there. The lone figure of Achilles sat in a great wooden chair at the side of the hearth; he was bent over, looking at something white and bulbous held between his hands. He looked up in surprise and quickly hid Patroclus's skull in a fold of his robe.

Before Achilles could do or say anything, Priam threw back his hood and fell to his knees before him, locking his arms about the prince's legs in supplication. Taking one of Achilles's hands in his, he pressed his lips to its knuckles and began to weep.

'King *Priam*?' Achilles said, shocked.

He looked questioningly at Odysseus and Eperitus, who said nothing.

'Have mercy, my lord,' Priam said. 'Pity an old man who has seen so many of his children slain. Pity me! I had fifty sons, the best men in the whole of Ilium, and now but nine are left to me. And those I would gladly see dead if I could bring back the one whose life you took before the Scaean Gate.'

He laid his forehead on Achilles's thighs and sobbed, his once muscular frame shaking as his tears fell on to the Greek's legs. Achilles looked down at him in disbelief, not knowing what to do or say.

'It's for his sake that I've come,' the old king continued. 'Won't you give up your anger at Hector and release his body to me? You cannot harm him any more by denying him a burial, but you are *killing* me. Have mercy, Achilles; accept the ransom I have brought – my own son's weight in gold and many other lordly gifts besides. Show compassion to a father who has forced himself to do something no man should ever do, to kiss the hand of the man who murdered his son.'

He seized Achilles's hand again, gripping it firmly as he pressed his lips to the tanned skin. Achilles looked down at him, his other hand hovering over the old man's head as if ready to push him away. Then the tension seemed to leave his body; his chin dropped slightly and his hand moved to Priam's head, stroking the thin strands of grey hair. And both Odysseus and Eperitus could see the tears rolling down his cheeks.

'You . . . you remind me of my own father, Peleus, on the day I left Phthia for Aulis. He knew he would never see me again and he came to me dressed not in his kingly robes, but in sackcloth, weeping as if already in mourning for me. He begged me not to go and I turned my back on him. *I turned my back on my own father!* But

I will not turn my back on you, Priam. The gods themselves have sent you here, and I will not ignore them. As of this moment my feud with Hector is ended. I will accept your ransom and the honour it brings to my name, and in return you shall have Hector's body.'

And with that he folded Priam's old head in his arms and wept openly.

It was a long journey back to the temple of Thymbrean Apollo, overlooking the moon-silvered trail of the Scamander and the ghostly walls of Troy, where Eperitus left Priam and headed back to the Greek camp. The old king had not spoken a word since Hector's body had been laid in the back of the cart and he had planted a simple kiss on his son's white forehead. Mounting the wagon with Idaeus at the reins, he had drawn his hood down across his face and allowed the mule to be led away again. Odysseus had only accompanied them to the gates, but was still there with the others when Eperitus returned in the pitch blackness, the moon having slipped behind the distant hills.

Odysseus insisted Eperitus return to his hut, where Astynome was waiting for him. He found her asleep in his bed, her dark hair spread across the white fleece and one arm on top of the furs that hid her naked body. Eperitus laid a hand on her shoulder and the coldness of his fingers woke her.

She smiled up at him, sleepily. 'Is he safe?'

Eperitus nodded. 'And Achilles relented. Tomorrow the whole of Troy can mourn her greatest son.'

She sat up and the furs fell away, revealing her white breasts. Eperitus took the cloak from his shoulders and hung it about her.

'You'll get cold.'

'Not if you join me.'

'But you need to leave before dawn. If anyone recognizes you—'

'Don't worry, my love. The farmer who brought me will return after sunset tomorrow and take me back the same way. I'm yours until then.'

Eperitus could not keep the smile from his lips and had to stop himself from leaning forward and kissing her.

'What about your master? If he misses you, you'll be punished.'

Astynome shook her head and removed Eperitus's cloak from her shoulders. Then she unbuckled the belt from around his waist and reached down to untie his sandals.

'He knows I'm here,' she said, lifting his tunic over his head so that he was naked before her. 'Join me.'

She moved aside as he slipped into the bed beside her, then swept the heavy furs back over them both. She ran her fingers through his dark hair and looked into his eyes before kissing him, slowly and gently. Hesitantly, he slipped his arm about her waist and pulled her warm body against his.

'What is it, Eperitus?' she asked, drawing away from another kiss and staring at him with concern. 'You seem . . . I don't know . . . *sadder* than before. Is it . . . do you no longer want me?'

He narrowed his eyes in brief confusion, then smiled. 'Never, Astynome. I wasn't lying when I said I loved you. Every day without you has been . . .' He shook his head, not knowing how to describe the anguish of wanting her and knowing she was in the one place he could not reach her.

Astynome touched his cheek affectionately. 'Then what is it?'

'I hadn't thought about it, but I suppose you're right. Something is wrong with me, and it's this war. There was a time, in the early years, when the fighting was hard but not dishonourable. *Xenia* was still observed, as were truces and parleys; the dead were respected and prisoners sold or exchanged. There was free movement for those who did not bear arms and their neutrality was never violated. But things have changed: small atrocities and acts of vengeance have chipped away at the honour of both sides, leaving us bitter and hateful. I've seen it affect Odysseus and even myself, a little. But Achilles's reaction to Patroclus's death was too much for me.'

'Perhaps the nature of war itself has shifted, Eperitus,' she said. 'Perhaps you are clinging to ideals that have become meaningless. But even so, doesn't Achilles's change of heart absolve him, at least in part?'

'No, not in my eyes. He treated Patroclus like a god, even made human sacrifices to his corpse! And his defilement of Hector was an affront.'

'The rumours have been heard in Troy,' Astynome said, running a finger thoughtfully down Eperitus's chest and to his hard stomach. 'He was a very great man and deserved better, much better. We Trojans loved him and his death has filled us with despair. But there is yet some hope, even of peace.'

She glanced up at him, running her tongue thoughtfully along her bottom lip. Eperitus sensed she had something else to say and waited.

'Eperitus, my love, there was another reason for my coming here.'

'Yes?'

'My master in Troy found out about you from my father. He doesn't approve, of course – being a warrior who has spent years fighting the Greeks   but he mentioned your name to another of the commanders, a powerful man call Apheidas.'

Eperitus felt his muscles tense and his jaw set. He stared hard at Astynome, who looked guilty suddenly.

'I'm sorry I didn't tell you before. It was more urgent that Priam was brought to the camp safely, and then everything happened so quickly. But . . . but I have a message for you from this Apheidas.'

'Do you know who he is?' Eperitus said, gripping her arm more fiercely than he had intended. 'Did he tell your master anything about me?'

Astynome reached up and touched his dark hair, avoiding looking into his brown eyes.

'He says he is your father. I always thought there was more of the Trojan about you than the Greek, my love.'

'He's a dangerous man, Astynome. Don't trust him.'

'He says he wants to meet with you on neutral ground, in the temple of Thymbrean Apollo. Whenever you are ready.'

'Does he?' Eperitus said scornfully. 'Well, *I* don't want to meet him.'

'But he says it's to discuss peace between our two nations, something that only you can help with. Peace, Eperitus – an end to this wretched war that we both hate so much!'

'And what can Apheidas possibly offer that will bring about peace? With Hector dead the Trojans can never hope to win this war, so why should the Greeks agree to terms?'

'You forget our walls. They were made by Poseidon and Apollo and can still hold out for many more years. Besides . . .'

She paused.

'Besides what?'

'There's a rumour that more allies will be arriving soon. Female warriors from the east, they say, and Aethiopes from the distant south, where the sun is so hot it burns their skin black. But whether the rumours are true or not, peace will mean you and I can be together. I love you, Eperitus, and I want you to marry me and live with me here in Ilium.'

She leaned forward and kissed him, pressing her body against his and temporarily exorcizing the savage memory of war that had haunted his thoughts for so long. As she slipped her soft thigh over his hip and looked into his eyes, it was easy to imagine that the long siege was over and that he and Astynome were already married.

'We can have children,' she added in a whisper.

He thought with a painful jolt of Iphigenia, then tried to smooth the memory by picturing what his children with Astynome would look like: they would have their mother's thick black hair and large eyes, but his courage and sense of honour. He smiled briefly as he entertained the fantasy, then the reality of what her proposal entailed quickly snuffed it out again and he frowned.

'But I could never live here,' he said. 'I'm a Greek, for one thing. People would hate me.'

'You're half Trojan,' she retorted. 'And your father is one of the most powerful commanders in the army.'

'My father brought shame on our family when I was young and our only words since then have been over crossed swords,' Eperitus said bitterly. Then, seeing the look in Astynome's face, he smiled and touched her cheek. 'But why do we have to wait for peace when you can come with me to Ithaca? We could marry and have as many children as you want there.'

Astynome shook her head gently. 'You can't leave Ilium until this war is over, my love, and that could be many long, hard years away yet. But if you meet your father and it brings an end to the war, then what else matters? I will even go back with you to Ithaca, though it's on the opposite side of the world.'

'It's still not that simple,' he said. 'Twenty years ago an oracle warned I would one day face a choice between everlasting glory gained in battle and shame brought about by love. Only now do I see what the prophecy meant: if I do as you ask, it will be for love, and to meet with Apheidas would be an act of treachery against my countrymen and my king. But I will not betray my oath to Odysseus, no matter how sick I am of this war; not even for you, Astynome.'

'Don't forget that *Odysseus* is sick of this war, too – you told me so yourself,' she reminded him. 'Perhaps by betraying your king you will also bring him release. But all I ask is that you think about your father's offer and do not reject it out of hand, for all our sakes. This peace may be the will of the gods.'

'It may,' Eperitus agreed, reluctantly. 'I will consider Apheidas's offer. I can say no more than that.'

Astynome smiled and moved on top of him, covering his face with her hair as she lowered her lips to his.

book
FOUR

Chapter Thirty-Eight
WOMEN OF ARES

Helen stood on the roof of the palace, looking east. The sun had gone down behind her and turned the skies crimson, which faded into purple darkness as they stretched towards Mount Ida. In the waning light she could see Hector's barrow on the plain before the Dardanian Gate, its freshly heaped earth dark against the sun-bleached grasslands. They had cremated him that morning amid great cries of grief from the city streets, but for the nine days previous, since Priam had brought him back from the Greek camp, his body had lain on a bier in the Temple of Athena, where the people of Troy had queued day and night to mourn their greatest son. Priam's choice of resting place had been a clever one, of course, for Hector's corpse had been deliberately set before the crudely carved Palladium. Though one of Troy's great bastions had fallen, the king was reminding his subjects that as long as the Palladium still remained within its walls the city would never fall to enemy attack.

And even now, while Hector's ashes were still cooling beneath the earth of his homeland, a new hope was arriving to replace him. News had arrived that an army of Amazons was approaching the city, and as the evening settled about her Helen could see the horses of the lead party dashing across the plain, raising a small dust cloud behind them.

Paris laid his hand against the small of Helen's back. It felt warm in the chill air of dusk.

'Did you know that Amazons only mate to have children, never for pleasure?' he said. 'They take several partners at the same time so that the paternity of the child can never be known.'

Helen turned to give him a doubtful frown.

'No, it's true. Where they come from, beyond the River Thermodon, the women do the governing and fighting while the men are given the household chores. It's said they break one arm and one leg of every infant boy, so that when he grows to manhood he will never be able to fight and he will never be able to run away.'

'But that's ridiculous,' Helen scoffed. 'And if they hate men so much, why are they coming to help Troy – a city ruled by men?'

Paris smiled knowingly. 'Because Queen Penthesilea is indebted to my father. When she was younger she accidentally shot and killed her sister, Hippolyte; Father gave her refuge and purified her of the guilt.'

Helen shook her head. 'I still don't see how an army of women is going to help Troy. The Greeks will make pretty carcasses of them all.'

'Oh, they're not pretty, sister,' said Deiphobus, who was standing on the other side of her and watching the troop of fifty or so horses approach the Dardanian Gate. He turned and smiled at her. 'Not if the rumours are true, anyway. But they're supposed to be fine cavalry and second to none in archery. It's even said they cauterize the right breast of every baby girl so that it won't grow and hinder the pulling of a bow when they reach fighting age.'

'And Troy needs all the allies she can find now,' Paris added. 'With Hector gone, the future of our city could rest in the hands of these women and the army of blacks marching up from the south. If they fail us, then all our hopes may fail with them.'

'Well, they sound perfectly vile to me!' Helen replied. 'But now they're here I suppose we should go and see if all these rumours are true.'

They found King Priam already in the courtyard before the

palace, awaiting the arrival of the Amazons with Apheidas and Antenor. The two older men were dressed in their finest robes – the first time Priam had worn anything other than sackcloth since the mourning for Hector had begun – and Apheidas wore his ceremonial bronze-scaled armour, which reflected the watery pink of the late evening sky. As Helen, Paris and Deiphobus joined them, they heard a series of shouts followed by the clatter of hooves on the cobbled streets of the lower tiers of Pergamos. Moments later, the guards at the top of the ramp that led up to the courtyard were being brushed aside and thirteen horses and riders came galloping on to the open space before the palace, quickly forming a line opposite the small group of Trojans. Helen looked at the riders with disbelief, though she hid this behind a display of haughty indifference. All were dressed like warriors: half-moon shields and bows across their backs; leather caps on their heads, with flaps of fur to cover their napes; and swords and daggers hanging from their belts. Though they wore no greaves, their shins were protected by layers of fur tied around with strips of leather, while in place of tunics and breastplates they wore thick animal skins. The mounds of their left breasts could be seen beneath the fur, but the right sides of their chests were flat, proving the rumours Deiphobus had heard were true.

Two of the riders dismounted and crossed the finely raked soil of the courtyard. The older of the two was around thirty years of age, while the younger was perhaps half that. Both were tall and long limbed, with finely honed muscles, but though their facial features could have been considered beautiful, Helen thought, the effect was spoiled by their severe, hard-bitten expressions. The eldest stopped opposite Priam, planting her legs apart in the soil and thrusting her fists on to her hips.

'I am Queen Penthesilea of the Amazons, daughter of Otrere and Ares,' she announced, fixing the king with her light-brown eyes. 'This is Evandre, my cousin.'

Priam nodded genially to them both.

'It's been a long time, Penthesilea,' he said. 'You were but a young girl when I purified you of your sister's death, and now you are a strong and fierce queen of your people. Welcome to Troy.'

He opened his arms and the queen's aloof stance melted away as she stepped forward and embraced him.

'Priam, my old friend,' she said, pulling him into her and thumping his back with the heel of her hand. 'It's been too long and these are not the circumstances I would have chosen to have returned under. But here I am. Where's that big-headed braggart, Hector? Your son would sire fine daughters and I've a mind to mate with him while I'm here.'

Priam drew away, though he left his wrinkled hands on Penthesilea's shoulders.

'You passed my son's barrow as you rode in. He was killed before the Scaean Gate by a man called Achilles.'

Penthesilea stared at Priam and nodded sagaciously.

'Then I am pleased for you and for Hector – it is a much greater thing to die in battle than in bed. But Hector was my friend once. I will be pleased to avenge his death for you.'

She passed her gaze over the others until it rested on Helen. The princess shifted a little under the scrutiny of Penthesilea's cruel eyes and was quickly forced to look away, albeit with a sneer.

'So this must be the *woman* who started everything,' Penthesilea said scornfully, walking up to Helen and taking her chin between her thumb and forefinger. Helen frowned harshly, but said nothing as the Amazon forced her head first one way then the other. 'Beautiful indeed – to the sentimental eyes of men, who love to dwell on baubles. But such finery would soon find itself at a loss among us Amazons. Any woman who cannot fight is a burden on the rest and must be disposed of quickly.'

This raised a laugh from her companions, in whom there was not the least intimation of femininity. Helen looked at them with hateful derision, angry that the potent charm of her beauty was powerless against them.

'Mock me if you like, my fair queen, but never forget that you

Amazons are simply women masquerading as men. What are you but an abomination? At least I am true to my nature.'

'Your nature?' Penthesilea scoffed. 'You should be ashamed to call yourself a woman!'

'She's more of a woman than you are!' Deiphobus snapped, stepping forward and pulling the queen's hand away from Helen.

Penthesilea immediately reached for her sword, followed by her twelve bodyguards. Deiphobus, Apheidas and Paris did the same, but Priam raised his hands with a gesture for calm before laying an arm across Penthesilea's shoulders.

'Come now, all of you, save your aggression for the Greeks. And on that subject, when will the rest of your army arrive? How many horses and men – forgive me, women – will we need to provide for?'

'Army?' Penthesilea replied. 'Our army is at home in Thermiscyra, fighting our own wars and keeping an eye on the men. *We* and the forty riders waiting outside the gates are all the aid you will receive from the Amazons, my lord.'

Priam's jaw dropped. Antenor and Apheidas looked at each other in silent surprise, while Paris and Deiphobus let their hands slip limply from their sword hilts. Penthesilea smiled reassuringly.

'And we are all the aid you will *need*, old friend. The Greek leaders are all men, yes?'

'The whole army is, of course.'

'Then they will be arrogant and conceited, if you'll forgive me for saying so. Their pride won't allow them to refuse the challenge of a few dozen women, will it? Tomorrow morning we are going to ride to their ships and invite the best of the Greeks to face us, man against woman. And when their leaders come out to fight us we will kill them all. How do you think their army will function when *we* have cut off its head?' She thumped the flat half of her chest with pride and grinned at the old king. 'And now we will stable our horses and eat. I assume our arrival has warranted that much?'

Priam shook his head in dismay at his own lack of hospitality.

'Of course. Apheidas here will show you to the stables, while my son, Deiphobus, will send for the rest of your escort. Antenor and I will await you in the great hall. And, Penthesilea, my thanks to you for coming.'

He hugged her once more, and only those who knew the king would have been able to read the disappointment in his eyes.

Paris wrapped his arm about Helen's waist as they watched the Amazons dismount and lead their horses to the stables, following Apheidas, Penthesilea and Evandre. The army they had expected had not arrived, but the fact the Amazons had only seen the need to send so few warriors was a greater stain on the city's pride than if they had arrived in full force and filled the streets with their obnoxious arrogance. Paris sighed.

'And so the manhood of Troy is finally and truly undone,' he said.

❧

The next day the Greek kings and leaders were gathered around a large table in one of the annexes of Agamemnon's tent. Outside, the wind was sending ripples through the cotton and flax sheets that in turn were casting strange, rolling shadows over the table and the odd assortment of objects that were spread across it.

'This is the valley I mean,' Nestor said.

He pointed to two baskets that had been turned upside down to represent hills. A trail of oats passed between them, running from a small circle at one end of the table that had been formed from a belt, to a larger pair of circles – one within the other and also formed from belts – at the other.

'The road from Lyrnessus in the south to Troy in the north,' he continued, tapping the smaller circle, then the larger pair of circles, 'runs straight through the middle of it. The slopes on the western side are scree-covered with plenty of rocks and trees. You can hide a thousand archers there with ease, and as many spearmen beyond the ridge as you like.'

'And if these Aethiopes want to reach Troy, they have to go directly through this valley?' Menelaus asked.

'Certainly, if they want to follow the main road and don't want to be delayed by the hills on either side.'

Eperitus looked at the crude re-creation of Ilium that had been mapped out on top of the table and tried to picture the different terrains in each part. Though he had informed Odysseus of what Astynome had told him, and Odysseus, in turn, had told Agamemnon that an army was approaching from the south, the King of Men had dismissed the intelligence as worthless (especially as Odysseus had been forced to say he was told by a local farmer, so as not to mention Astynome's visit to the camp). Only when a horseman had found his way to the camp that morning, claiming to be the lone survivor from the garrison at Lyrnessus, did he decide to call the Council of Kings. Here they had heard from the exhausted rider of how a force of warriors, each one as black as night and as tall as an afternoon shadow, had stormed Lyrnessus and put every living thing to the sword, including the few Trojans who had found their way back to their homes. He had also reported the army to be in its thousands upon thousands, but this was dismissed by most of the council as the exaggerations of a frightened man. The garrison itself was only a few hundred strong and could easily have been taken by a thousand attackers; and where, they argued, could Priam find such a powerful ally this late in the war? At most, two or three thousand mercenaries were approaching from the south, and the plan was to ambush them before they reached the Dardanian Gate and swelled the defenders of Troy.

'Then we'll send a force to intercept them,' Menelaus announced. 'A thousand Thessalian spearmen under the command of Podarces, supported by a thousand Locrian archers under Little Ajax. That should be more than enough to deal with these southerners.'

'I agree, Brother,' Agamemnon said, taking a swallow of wine.

'We'll crush these Aethiopes and the last hope of Troy will die with them. Then we can bend all our efforts to taking the city itself!'

'You'll need more soldiers.'

The men around the table looked at Odysseus.

'A lot more,' he continued. 'Eperitus and I have visited the valley and it's a good place for an ambush, but it has its disadvantages too. A determined force could quickly storm the slopes and sweep your thousand Locrians away, and if there are enough of them, they'll push back the reserve force of Thessalians too. It's a long way from there to the safety of the Greek camp, and if the survivor from Lyrnessus was correct about the numbers of these southerners, then we'd be lucky if any of our own men make it back at all. You should send three or four times the number, or none at all.'

'We're severely under strength as it is,' Idomeneus countered. If we send a larger force to ambush the Aethiopes, there's a risk they could be caught by Trojans from the city and wiped out. That would leave the rest of the army too few in number to continue the siege. It would end the war with one blow.'

Odysseus opened his mouth to speak, but raised voices at the mouth of the tent stopped him. The interruption was followed by the appearance of Thersites, the hunchback whose provocations and vulgar taunts at the assemblies of the army had always proved a scourge to the members of the council. Today, though, he was red-faced and short of breath, the usual antagonism absent from his hideous features. He shuffled in on his club-foot, his left shoulder so badly deformed that his arms dangled unevenly at his sides and his cone-shaped, balding head sunk almost down to his chest. One of his eyes was set in a permanent squint, while the other was as wide as an egg, the dark pupil revolving this way and that as he stared at the council.

Agamemnon shot him a stern look.

'Well?'

'My lord,' Thersites replied, 'there's been an attack on the gates.'

'An attack? What do you mean?'

'A small group of cavalry appeared a short while ago and shot half a dozen guards before wheeling out of range. Then they did it again and now no man dare put his head above the parapet, my lord.'

'And why is this important enough to bother me?' Agamemnon said, his icy blue eyes narrowing. 'Isn't it obvious I'm in discussion with the council?'

'But no armed sorties are permitted without your permission, my lords. Are we to give up command of the plains to such a small force?'

'You've always thought yourself a great warrior, Thersites, using the Assemblies to tell *us* how to run the war,' Diomedes mocked. 'So why don't *you* take fifty archers out and deal with this small band of horsemen yourself. We give you our permission.'

'But, my lord, I don't think they're men at all,' Thersites replied, wringing his hands. 'They look like women.'

There was a sudden discord of different voices as the kings and princes reacted in shock. Only Odysseus and Eperitus stayed quiet, recalling Athena's warning in the River Scamander and exchanging glances. Achilles, too, kept his silence as he looked thoughtfully at the messenger.

'That's ridiculous,' Menelaus scoffed. 'Women can barely ride, let alone fight!'

'I've struggled with a few in my time, but most of them succumb in the end,' Agamemnon added, raising a laugh. 'Send fifty men out to deal with them, as Diomedes ordered. And if they think it beneath themselves to fight women, then tell them they can do what they like with any they take alive.'

There was a roar of laughter and Thersites gave another bow and left. Odysseus watched him go, then turned to Eperitus and whispered: 'Follow him and see what happens. I have to stay with the council, but I want you to watch from the battlements and observe how these women fight. Hopefully Thersites will see them off, but that oaf's all scabbard and no sword; he's bound to make a mess of things.'

Eperitus nodded and followed the hunchback out into the bright sunlight. Arceisius and Polites were waiting by the entrance, playing dice with a group of Athenians.

'Arceisius, come with me,' Eperitus ordered.

The two men left Polites looking puzzled and set off in Thersites's wake. Despite his club-foot, he was surprisingly quick on his legs and they were soon at the walls of the camp. Here, a large group of soldiers had gathered to investigate the rumours of female warriors dealing death from horseback. They were staring curiously at the bodies of the dead guards laid out on the ground, all of whom had long, feathered arrows protruding from their bodies. Their collective voices formed an angry drone that only died a little at the approach of Thersites.

'I need fifty men,' Thersites shouted. 'And Agamemnon says we can do whatever we want with the ones we take alive.'

The angry drone became an aggressive cheer as crowds of men surged forward. Though all were armed to some degree, they were not prepared for battle and very few had full armour. Thersites stared at the collection of soldiers from all the Greek nations, muttering indecisively to himself until, finally, he waved away the men at either edge of the central group and ordered the remainder to form up and turn about to face the gates. There was a frenzied borrowing of shields and helmets from those who had not been selected, and then the guards swung the tall wooden portals back on their hinges.

'Thersites,' Eperitus called. 'Diomedes said to take archers. If those women can pick men from the walls while on horseback, think what they can do to your rabble of spearmen.'

Thersites looked doubtfully at the men he had gathered, who had already begun to exit the gates without waiting for his order, then waved a dismissive hand at the Ithacan captain and followed them out, belatedly shouting the order to advance.

'What's this all about?' Arceisius asked.

'You'll see,' Eperitus replied, pointing to the battlements, where a handful of soldiers were crouching behind the parapet to avoid being shot. 'Come on.'

They ran up the steps to the narrow walkway and looked out over the plain. Thersites's company of spearmen had crossed the causeway and were forming into a line three deep – more from experience and training than because of Thersites's powers of command. The grasslands before them were dotted with sheep and goats from the army's livestock that had been taken out to pasture earlier that morning; the bodies of half a dozen herdsmen lay scattered among them, face down in the dust with black arrows jutting up from their backs. Further out were the fifty or so archers who had shot them down, every one dressed in furs and seated on a fast pony. They had formed a line beyond bowshot of the walls and were waiting patiently for the force of Greek infantry to march out to them.

Arceisius leaned over the parapet, shielding his eyes from the sun and squinting.

'Surely . . . surely they're *women*!'

Eperitus nodded. His arms were folded as he studied the faces of the Amazons, his superior eyesight enabling him to see the brutal, disdainful looks on their features. They seemed to scorn any armour beyond their shields and leather helmets, and though each carried a tall bow the swords hanging from their hips also spoke of a readiness to fight hand-to-hand. Their limbs were muscular and sun-tanned, and while they did not possess the bulk of male warriors, their hardy aspects nevertheless belonged to seasoned fighters. At their head were a handsome, dark-haired woman and her younger companion, both tall and proud as they surveyed the force of Greeks gathering before the gates. Eperitus wondered whether the Council of Kings would still laugh if they could look on the faces of these women, battle-hardened and filled with calm self-confidence.

The soldiers who had been hiding beneath the protection of the parapet now stood, shamed by the bold presence of Eperitus and Arceisius. Soon they were being joined by the men who had not been chosen to join Thersites's sortie. As they pressed against the rough, sun-baked battlements, Thersites shouted an order and the small body of spearmen began to move. The Amazons waited until the distance between them had been halved, then the older of the two women at the front gave a signal and the whole company turned and galloped westward towards the shoreline. Thersites's men gave a shout and wheeled about to follow, quickening their pace in their eagerness to come to grips with the women who had shot down their comrades.

'They're putting the sun behind them,' Arceisius said in a matter-of-fact tone, his chin resting on his fist as he leaned on the parapet.

'And drawing them out of range of the walls,' Eperitus added. 'Thersites is going to wish he'd picked more archers.'

Then the battle started. The Amazons reined in their mounts, stretched back their bows, and released a shower of missiles at the closely packed infantry. The north wind carried faint cries to the watchers on the walls, and as their countrymen advanced on the waiting enemy they left half a dozen lifeless forms on the ground behind them. Eperitus saw the Amazon leader signal to her left and right and a moment later two groups of her followers had split off and were galloping around the flanks and to the rear of the Greeks. A smattering of arrows sped after them from the knot of armoured men, but none found a target among the fast-moving horsewomen. The Amazons fired another volley in reply – this time from three sides – and more soldiers fell and lay still. The rest of Thersites's company now stopped moving and turned their shields outwards in a defensive circle, from which a tiny huddle of archers began shooting at the surrounding foes. A single rider was hit and slid from the back of her horse. At another command from their leader, the other

Amazons now poured a hail of arrows into the centre of the Greek ring, killing the few bowmen and half a dozen others. With the reply from the soldiers now muted, the women began to circle about the wall of shields and pick men off with impunity.

The spectators on the battlements had barely raised a single voice as they watched their countrymen slowly massacred. Then, when there was but a handful of Thersites's company left, the survivors suddenly began running as a pack towards the Amazon leader. Their frenzied shouts carried on the wind, exciting a chorus of encouragement from the men on the walls, willing them to close on their tormentors and teach them the true meaning of combat. But they were met with a cloud of arrows, felling all but a handful. Eperitus's sharp eyes saw Thersites fall, too, though he did not rue the loss of such a fool. Then the Amazon leader screamed out a command and the arrows stopped. Spurring her horse forward, she drew her long sword and rode in among the last of the Greeks. Wielding her blade to left and right, the bright sun flashing from the burnished bronze, she brought all five men down in a matter of moments.

'By all the gods, I've never seen anything like it,' Arceisius exclaimed, standing.

The bodies of the fallen men lay scattered in a broad circle. A few twitched or tried to crawl towards the now distant walls, but the riders were quick to dismount and cut their throats so that soon every last soldier who had exited the gates with such enthusiasm now lay lifeless, their souls already making the long journey to the Underworld.

The tall Amazon who had single-handedly killed the last of the Greeks now came galloping towards the gates, her horse's hooves kicking up a trail of dust behind her. Some of the men on the walls called for archers, but Eperitus countermanded their hasty shouts.

'She's not coming to fight,' he announced. 'Look, she's alone. She's come to talk.'

She reined her mount in before the gates and raised her gore-stained blade to the men above.

'I am Queen Penthesilea, daughter of Otrere and Ares,' she announced in Greek. 'My Amazons are not slaves to men as the women are in your lands; we are priestesses of Ares, trained from childhood to fight and kill. Tell King Agamemnon he is a craven coward and I challenge him to come forth and face me in combat: the best men in his army against the best women in mine. We will await him here on the plain.'

And with that she rode away again, her laughter ringing out in mockery of the Greeks.

Chapter Thirty-Nine

QUEEN PENTHESILEA

After agreeing that Nestor and Great Ajax should add their own armies to the force being sent to waylay the Aethiopes, the council settled into a detailed discussion of how the ambush should be carried out. Then, as more wine was brought, another spate of urgent words broke out at the mouth of the tent and Eperitus entered, followed by Arceisius.

'My lords,' Eperitus began, 'your orders have been carried out. A company of men left the gates under the command of Thersites the hunchback.'

'Good! Perhaps now we can continue discussing a *real* battle,' Menelaus said. He turned to Nestor and tapped one of the upturned baskets representing the site of the proposed ambush. 'What about cavalry, Nestor? Is the terrain suitable for—'

'Thersites and his men were massacred,' Eperitus continued. 'Not one of them escaped alive.'

Heads that had been turned to the table now snapped back to stare at Eperitus with shock.

'That's impossible!' Diomedes exclaimed. 'Fifty men killed by . . . by a pack of *women*!'

There were mutterings of agreement, but most were too incredulous to speak.

'It's not impossible, Diomedes,' Achilles announced, turning to the Argive king. 'Athena herself warned me that female warriors – Amazons – were coming to Priam's aid, and that they were skilled horsewomen and archers. Are they still waiting before the walls, Eperitus?'

Eperitus nodded and leaned on the table, looking around at the faces of the council.

'Their leader calls herself Queen Penthesilea and sends a message to King Agamemnon, challenging him and the best men in the army to combat. She says . . . she says the King of Men is a coward and no match for her or her companions, whom she claims are priestesses of Ares.'

Diomedes slammed his fist down on the table.

'Zeus's beard! Since when have women been allowed to attend on the god of war? They're not priestesses at all, they're perversions of nature! I accept the challenge – who's with me?'

A clamour of angry voices followed, all of them keen to fight the Amazons. Agamemnon raised his hands, commanding silence.

'Very well, we'll go out to face these harpies. But first I want to know what it is we're going up against. Clearly these aren't ordinary women – tell us, Eperitus, how did they kill fifty of my seasoned warriors?'

Eperitus explained to them what he had seen, and when he had finished answering their questions, the King of Men looked about at their circle of faces and picked out the leaders who would accompany him on the battlefield.

'I doubt Queen Penthesilea and her priestesses intend to fight us one against one,' Odysseus said as Agamemnon finished speaking. 'Their strengths are with the bow and the horse, not the spear and the shield, and if we let them fight on their terms we will lose. But if you'll listen to me, I have an idea that will rid them of their advantages.'

A little later the thick wooden gates at the centre of the Greek wall swung open and fifty men moved out on to the sun-baked plain. Agamemnon had insisted that they should match the Amazons warrior for warrior, but Odysseus had also advised at least half of the force should be archers, picked from the best of Little Ajax's Locrians. The remainder were made up of spearmen, including the men who had been chosen from among the council: Agamemnon, Menelaus, Achilles, Diomedes, Machaon, Great Ajax, Odysseus and Medon, the leader of the Malians ever since Philoctetes had been stranded on Lemnos in the first year of the war. They marched across the narrow causeway and formed a line on the other side of the ditch.

Odysseus raised a hand to shield his eyes from the sun, which had passed its apex in the cloudless sky and was moving towards the ocean. By its unfettered light he could clearly see the bodies of the failed sortie lying in the long grass of the plateau, the tall black stalks of arrows protruding from their still forms. Beyond the litter of corpses and out of range of the walls were the Amazons, sitting patiently on their small horses as they waited for the Greeks to approach. Even among the most wilful and courageous noblewomen he had known — Helen, Clytaemnestra and Penelope chief among them — there had always been something in their expressions that revealed the acceptance, however grudging, that they were socially and physically inferior to men. But these women had none of that. They looked at the greatest of the Greeks as if they were merely swine to be slaughtered, and about as dangerous.

Agamemnon pushed his hand forward and gave the order to advance. Odysseus lifted his shield and moved in a line with the front rank, while the archers followed close behind, also carrying spears and shields to make it look as if the whole company was made up of spearmen. Eperitus was to Odysseus's left, his grandfather's shield covering almost his whole body, and Arceisius was to his right, both men watching the Amazons closely and waiting for them to draw their bows. But the priestesses remained motionless, showing no signs of being drawn prematurely into action.

While they were still within bowshot of the walls, Agamemnon raised his hand again and ordered the company to halt. At a signal from Penthesilea, a score of Amazons rode forward and peppered them with arrows. The Greeks raised their shields and the volley caused no casualties. The Amazons fired again and this time a man cried out as an arrow pierced his forearm, but there were no more shouts of pain and no bodies fell into the dust.

'Keep your shield up,' Odysseus snapped as one of the Locrians reached for the bow across his back. 'They're testing to see if we have any archers. I'll tell you when you can shoot back.'

As he finished speaking, Penthesilea barked an order and the party of Amazons returned to the main body. Then she signalled left and right and two larger groups rode out to the flanks of the Greek line, ready to force them into a defensive circle as they had done to Thersites. But the men who had come out to meet the Amazons this time were not fools and as the horses galloped to either side and readied their bows to fire, hundreds of archers stood up on the walls of the camp and sent a swarm of arrows towards them. The Amazons turned away just in time and Penthesilea gestured for them to return to the main body.

'So far, so good,' Eperitus muttered, touching his fingers to the image of the white hart inside his shield and raising them to his lips.

'I'm not so sure of that,' Odysseus replied, looking to where the man who had been hit in the forearm had just fallen heavily on to his back, his dead eyes staring up at the skies above. 'It looks like they're using poison arrows.'

'Here they come!' Achilles shouted from the centre of the line.

Shields that had been momentarily lowered were raised again as the whole body of Amazons dashed forward and loosed a hail of missiles at the Greeks. Those men who had noticed the death of their comrade drew back from the poisoned tips wherever they broke through the many-layered oxhide; two more were not so lucky and fell back as arrows slipped through the wall of shield and bit into flesh. The Amazons fired another volley, galloping closer this time as they sought to find clearer targets among the Greek line. Two more men fell, one of them dead in an instant as an arrow pierced his eye. The three wounded dragged themselves back from the front line, already weakened by the poison spreading through their veins.

'Archers!' Odysseus commanded, raising a hand above his head.

The Locrians threw away their shields and spears and slipped the bows from their shoulders. Two of them fell to the third Amazon volley, but they held their discipline and took careful aim as they waited for Odysseus's signal.

'Remember, shoot the horses,' he shouted, and let his hand fall.

Bowstrings hummed and a score of arrows were sent flocking towards their targets. The distance was still long – Odysseus had predicted Penthesilea would not risk her warriors within range of the Greek spears – so the Locrians had been ordered to aim for the mounts. Eleven horses fell to the first volley, causing shouts of dismay and surprise from the Amazons. A second volley followed in the confusion and a dozen more animals plunged into the dust, bringing their riders down with them. At that moment, Agamemnon punched the air with his spear and the front rank of Greeks charged headlong at the Amazons.

Chaos ensued. With almost half of their number horseless, and many of those trapped beneath the weight of their dead ponies, the mounted Amazons had no intention of leaving their stricken comrades to the oncoming foes. They fired another volley, which fell half among the spearmen and half among the archers behind, but the aim was hurried and only felled two of the now unprotected Locrians. Seeing that her plan to draw the Greeks out and shoot them down at long range had failed, Penthesilea now threw away her bow and drew her sword, screaming for her fighting priestesses to do the same. She was answered by the ringing of blades and shouts of grim defiance as the remaining cavalry cantered forward to form a line. Then their queen kicked her heels back and sent her mount into a gallop, lowering the point of her blade towards the line of Greeks. The others followed and two dozen horses drummed the ground with their hooves, sending up clods of earth as they dashed into battle.

There was no time now for the spearmen to form a shield-wall. Achilles, running ahead of the rest, threw his spear and plucked a screaming Amazon from her mount. The others followed, and though their aim was hasty and poor two other riders and a horse were brought down. Far greater damage was done by the archers, who loosed two rapid volleys into the oncoming enemy so that only nine Amazons remained on horseback to charge down on the Greeks. Penthesilea was the first among them, her sword scything the head from a heavily built soldier as he ran at her with his spear. Driving on into the scattered men, she hewed the forearm from one and stabbed the point of her sword into the face of another. Away to her right, Agamemnon was struggling against one of the queen's bodyguard, a tall, muscular girl with red hair who reared up her horse to flail at the air above the king's head, but Menelaus came running up behind and impaled her on his spear. Meanwhile, Evandre drew her bow and sent an arrow into Medon's throat, killing the Malian captain instantly. She leapt down from her horse, eager to strip the armour from her first kill in battle, when a soldier rushed at her with his sword held in both hands above his head. Her own sword was still in its scabbard, and with no time to draw it out, she threw up her shield and took the blow on the wooden boss. Snatching a dagger from her belt with her other hand, she thrust it into her attacker's stomach. He fell on top of her, shouting with rage and pain. Then his large hand found her throat, the fingers contracting quickly to squeeze the air from her windpipe. With her strength fast failing, she stabbed again and again until the man's grip relaxed and he slumped down on top of her, gushing blood from his many wounds.

Achilles, Diomedes and Great Ajax led half the remaining spearmen against the dismounted Amazons, who were now rushing into the fray behind their mounted comrades. The battle was now raging beyond any hope of order or command. Amazon and Greek murdered each other with fanatical hatred, neither side giving any quarter as they threw themselves at each other. A warning shout from Arceisius saved Eperitus's life as a horse came galloping up behind him and a sword swept down in an arc at his head. He rolled to one side as the rider's blade cleaved the air above him. A moment later he heard his attacker call out in agony as Arceisius's spear point caught her in the chest and brought her crashing from her horse. Eperitus had no time to thank him, though; through the dust cloud kicked up by the battling figures, he saw Odysseus struggling to hold back a lone rider whose sword was raining a frenzy of blows down on his raised shield. Eperitus ran to help him, just as an arrow thumped into the woman's chest and toppled her into the long grass. Looking over his shoulder, Eperitus saw the surviving Locrians running to join the fight, some with bows drawn and others armed with swords or spears.

At the centre of the maelstrom was Penthesilea, the only mounted figure remaining on the battlefield. She withdrew her sword from the throat of the spearman she had just killed and looked around at the chaos that surrounded her. Her plan to decapitate the Greek leadership had failed, and instead she and her Amazons had themselves been drawn into a carefully thought-out trap. As she watched her glorious priestesses battling on every side of her, killing and being killed, she knew there was little chance of any of them ever reaching Thermiscyra again. Their horses were dead or scattered, preventing any quick escape across the plain to the safety of Troy, and the Greeks were already gaining the upper hand – thanks in no small part to a man whose magnificent armour could only belong to their leader, Agamemnon. Penthesilea watched him with admiring eyes, almost forgetting that the warriors he was slaying with such murderous efficiency were her own. Turning back to the battle around her, she saw that those who had charged into the enemy line with her were now outnumbered with the arrival of the Greek archers. And yet, had she not told Priam it was more glorious to die in battle than in bed? She grinned at the thought; and if she could take a few more men with her into the Underworld, the greater her glory would be.

She gripped her sword hard. Nearby, a priestess was fending

off the attacks of two Greeks. As Penthesilea watched, she plunged her sword up to the hilt in one of the men's chests. He grunted and fell back, but the other had seen his opportunity and with a backhanded stroke of his blade sliced the Amazon's head from her neck. With a shout of rage, Penthesilea spurred her horse at the victor.

Machaon, the famed healer, heard the shout and turned to see the queen of the Amazons charging towards him. He parried the swinging blow aimed at his head and spun about as Penthesilea turned and came at him again. Taking his sword in both hands – his shield having been lost in the earlier fighting – he swung the blade at the horse's face, intending to bring the animal down and its rider with it. But the queen had guessed his intentions and, reining her pony's head aside at the last moment, lunged with the point of her sword and found Machaon's chest. His leather cuirass was useless against her sharpened bronze, which found his beating heart and stopped it in an instant. He fell dead and Penthesilea turned again, looking for her next victim.

As her queen continued to wreak havoc, Evandre pushed away the body of the man she had killed and staggered to her feet. She looked about and saw the bodies of her fellow priestesses lying among the Greeks they had slaughtered. The fighting that had raged so terribly just a short while before was now dying out as the last combats were resolved. Then she looked and saw a man approaching, his golden armour gleaming in the late afternoon sun. He wore a red plumed helmet and on his arm was a shield of magnificent craftsmanship, which seemed to move as her dazed eyes stared at it. But in his other hand was a long spear, running with blood as bright as his plume. There was a fierce scowl on his handsome face, driven by an inhuman anger that filled her with terror. Quickly, she swept her sword from its scabbard and held it out before her, planting her feet apart in the hard earth to give herself balance.

Achilles laughed, knocking the weapon from her grip with a contemptuous swipe of his spear before plunging the point into her soft, unprotected stomach. The gore-spattered Amazon tried to cry out, but instead just opened her mouth in shocked silence as she slumped to her knees, clutching at the fatal wound. She looked up at her killer but did not say a word as he withdrew his spear and placed the point against her chest, pushing it through her heart.

Now only the queen remained. Too far away to save her cousin, she had watched in horror as the warrior she had mistaken for Agamemnon took her life. She cried out in anguish then, kicking back, rode her horse to where Evandre's body had fallen. The remaining Greeks – no more than a dozen in number – fell back as Penthesilea approached and leapt down from her mount. Kneeling beside the dead girl, she cradled her head in her lap and wiped the hair from her still face.

'Who are you?' she demanded in Greek, glowering hatefully at Achilles.

'I am Achilles, son of Peleus.'

'The same Achilles that killed Hector? Then I will have twice the satisfaction in sending your ghost down to Hades!'

Letting Evandre's body slump to one side, she leapt at the Greek and scythed the air with her sword. Achilles checked the blow with his shield and thrust at her stomach with his spear, only to find she had skipped aside and was now behind him. He turned, grinning with pleasure at her agility and skill, then lunged at her again. Penthesilea met his spear with her shield, which collapsed beneath the force of the attack, compelling her to retreat quickly as she tossed the shattered remains of leather and wicker from her arm. He attacked again, and this time she twisted away from the plunging spearhead and in the same movement aimed the point of her sword at Achilles's chest. It scraped across the rim of his shield and sank through the bronze of his breastplate, penetrating the flesh beneath his right collarbone.

Achilles stumbled backwards in pain and shock, looking down at the blood on Penthesilea's blade as it was withdrawn from the wound. Then, his face contorted with rage, he leapt forward and drove his sword through Penthesilea's breastbone, killing her instantly and sending her lifeless body spinning back to join the other corpses in the long grass.

Achilles slumped to his knees, touching his fingers in disbelief to the blood that was seeping through the gash in his armour. Ajax and Diomedes rushed to help him.

'The blood's already stopped flowing,' Diomedes announced in amazement as he lifted away Achilles's breastplate and touched his fingertips to the gore-drenched tunic beneath.

'Of course it has,' Achilles snapped, knocking his hand away impatiently and standing. 'I can bleed just like any other man, but my wounds heal rapidly – always have.'

'Damned witch!'

They turned to see a hunched figure standing over the body of Penthesilea.

'Thersites!' Eperitus exclaimed. 'We thought you were all dead.'

'*They* are,' the hunchback answered, indicating the soldiers of the first sortie who lay all where the Amazons had shot them. 'But I feigned death among the corpses of my friends while the gods protected me from the arrows of these bitches. They didn't protect *you* though, did they?'

He looked down hatefully at the fallen queen, then lifted his spear and began stabbing at her eyes. His mad laughter rang out, shocking the others until Achilles leapt forward and pulled the weapon from his hands. He snapped it over his knee and threw the two halves into the long grass.

'How *dare* you?' he shouted, seizing Thersites's tunic. 'How dare you defile the body of a warrior who was worth a hundred cowardly scum like you!'

'Don't preach to me about abusing the dead, Achilles! You're the one who refused to bury Hector and dragged his body behind your chariot every day while you were mourning Patroclus, and if any Trojan deserved honour, it was him!'

'Shut your vile mouth!'

'And why are you any less vile than I am?' Thersites continued angrily, heedless of the murderous rage that was building up in Achilles.

'Achilles is a royal prince and his mother is a goddess,' Odysseus warned as Eperitus and Diomedes took hold of Achilles's arms and pulled him away. 'You, Thersites, are a foul-minded commoner who needs to remember his place if he wants to live.'

'Really?' Thersites sneered, emboldened by the fact that Achilles was being restrained. 'Or is it that this Amazon not only pierced the noble prince with her sword, but with her looks also? He fell for her in the same moment he killed her, and now he wants to ravage her corpse while the flesh is still soft and warm. Isn't that so, Achilles?'

With a great bellow of fury, Achilles threw off the arms that were holding him and ran at his accuser. Thersites could only squeak in terror before the prince's fist smashed into his face, killing him instantly.

Chapter Forty

CALCHAS'S DREAM

Mentor wrapped his double cloak more tightly around himself and pressed on up the steep path that led to the top of Mount Neriton. The wind was howling and the sun had already sunk beyond the rim of the western ocean, making it difficult to find his footing in the deepening twilight. Behind and below him he could see the glow of lamps and fires starting to show in the windows of the town, and over to his right similar clusters of lights were winking out at him from the dark-blue flanks of Samos.

Why Halitherses should want to meet with him in such a remote place as the top of Mount Neriton, he could not be certain. But he could guess. Eupeithes had an uncanny ability for finding out bits of information he had no right knowing, and Halitherses had often warned Mentor to be careful of spies. Clearly, his old friend wanted to discuss Eupeithes and he did not want eavesdroppers. And, if Mentor's own concerns were anything to judge by, Halitherses probably wanted to talk with him about the way power was being slowly wrested from their fingers.

Not that either man blamed Penelope for allowing Oenops on to the Kerosia. Mentor knew from years of experience how persuasive Eupeithes could be, and the only men he had ever known who seemed totally immune to his arguments were Laertes and Odysseus – Laertes through sheer hatred of his old nemesis, and Odysseus because no man knew his own mind better than the king. And how Mentor wished his friend were back on Ithaca to put things back in order: having to face the combined forces of Eupeithes, Oenops and Polyctor in the Kerosia was now a regular struggle, but one on which the well-being of Ithaca depended.

By the time he reached the top of Mount Neriton, the first stars were peppering the sable sky and the chill of a cloudless spring evening was biting at his toes and fingertips. The lookout post – a thatched canopy on four stilts that gave protection from the sun but not the wind or rain – was deserted. The lookout had passed Mentor on his way back to the town after sunset, but Mentor had expected to find Halitherses there waiting for him. Something must have delayed him, he told himself as he stamped his feet against the cold and looked out at the dark mass of the Peloponnese in the distance. As he often did whenever he came up to the lonely peak, he wondered what Odysseus and the other Ithacans were doing at that moment, far off in Ilium. Had it not been for a traitor's sword severing his hand twenty years ago, he would have been there with them, winning glory on the battlefield rather than fighting a political war where enemies were undeclared and masqueraded as friends, biding their time for the right moment to strike.

Mentor suddenly stopped stamping his feet and froze. Something at the unconscious extremities of his senses told him another human presence was with him. And maybe more than one.

'Halitherses?' he asked, turning about and looking into the darkness. 'Speak up, man. What sort of time and place do you call this to meet up?'

There was no reply, but by the light of the bloated moon that was rising slowly in the north-east he saw a tall figure rising up from the stones at the edge of the small plateau on which he stood. Sensing more movement, he turned to his right and saw another, equally tall figure rise up. A naked blade gleamed in his hand.

Mentor felt for the sword hanging at his hip and slid it from its scabbard. As he balanced it in his one hand, he saw a third figure standing to his left, ensuring he was now trapped on all sides.

'Who are you? What do you want?'

The only answer was the dull, menacing scrape of swords being drawn. It was answer enough: the men were there to kill him, doubtless sent by Eupeithes to reduce his opposition in the Kerosia. Halitherses's summons was false, of course, and had merely been the bait to draw him into an ambush, delivered by a palace slave who had been deceived into relaying the message. It was a well-laid trap and Mentor's chances of survival were thin: he had no armour and had not used his sword in anger for two decades. As his opponents drew nearer he could see they were Taphians, among the most ruthless enemies a man could face. Mentor instinctively flexed his knees and prepared to meet the first attack.

It came quickly. The man to his left rushed at him, grinning with malicious confidence. Mentor sidestepped the move and retreated so that he was now facing all three assailants. His heart beating fast, he withdrew to the edge of the plateau. Behind him he could hear the sea crashing against the rocks below, but at least now the Taphians could not run a sword through his back.

'Jump and save us the trouble,' one of the assassins suggested, his voice husky and heavily accented.

'Jump yourselves.'

The man spoke to his comrades and advanced, intending to finish the Ithacan himself. He leapt forward and their blades clashed, glinting in the moonlight. Mentor was barely able to react in time to the Taphian's rapid cuts and fell back, feeling the ground fall away sharply behind his heel. The man smiled at him, confident of his superiority, then lunged with the point of his sword at Mentor's chest. Mentor turned aside at the last moment and lashed out blindly with his own blade, finding by grim chance the angle between the Taphian's jaw and neck. If Mentor had not used his sword in a long time, it did not mean he did not keep a keen edge on it; the bronze opened up his enemy's throat and he fell back, choking as he died.

His companions now raised their blades and came at the lone

Ithacan together, but Mentor knocked the first attacker aside and ran through the gap towards the top of the path that led back down to the town. The remaining Taphians ran after him, cursing in their own dialect. Mentor reached the path quickly enough, but his pursuers were close behind and their legs were longer and faster than his. He paused briefly as the land fell away before him to reveal the sharp, boulder-strewn slope and the lights of the town below. Ignoring the meandering path, he gave a shout and jumped, landing in a heap some way down and rolling for a short distance until he was stopped by a large boulder. Bruised and disorientated, he staggered to his feet and reached for his sword where it had fallen in the long grass. A moment later, he heard a thud and a cry as one of the Taphians fell awkwardly only a few paces away.

The man had chosen to take the same risk as Mentor – leaping down the hill instead of following the safer, slower path – but had not enjoyed the Ithacan's good fortune and appeared to have injured himself. Looking up, Mentor saw the man's companion shuffling in a direct line down the slope, avoiding the boulders while trying to prevent his momentum from taking his legs away beneath him. In that split moment Mentor had the choice to continue fleeing in the hope that he would reach the town before his pursuers, or to attack while his enemies were momentarily divided. He gripped his sword and with a shout ran at the nearest man. The Taphian struggled to his feet, weapon still in hand, and turned to see the Ithacan charging at him. He lunged clumsily and died with Mentor's sword in his chest, but not before his own bronze had pierced his assailant's thigh.

Mentor cried out, more in surprise at the sudden, burning sensation in his leg than at the pain of it. But before he could give it another moment's thought the last Taphian was upon him, leaping down from the slope with his blade in both hands above his head. It narrowly missed Mentor, who twisted aside at the last moment, and struck a boulder, sending a flash of sparks into the darkness. Mentor's instinct was to run, but his wounded leg gave way and all he could do was turn as his attacker bore down on him again. The sword passed beneath his arm, where Mentor trapped it with his own in instinctive desperation. Together, the two men fell into the grass and the Taphian cried out as Mentor brought the hilt of his sword down into his face. He was too close to stab and Mentor felt himself weakening from loss of blood, so he brought the hilt down again, and then again, continuing until the man's face became so disfigured that it no longer looked human. Eventually, the muffled groaning of his victim died out and he stared at Mentor with dead eyes. Mentor felt exhaustion overcome him and he let his sword slip from his hand before he passed out.

Eperitus leaned back in his chair and stared across at the wide bay. The hulls of the ships stood black against the sparkling ocean, while in the foreground was the barrow that had been built over the ashes of Patroclus's funeral pyre. Its sun-baked sides were bare but for the prostrate figure of Achilles, who lay there in mourning for his lost friend.

'When will he give up this excessive grief?' Diomedes asked in a strained voice, clearly annoyed. 'Doesn't he care what the rest of us think, or even the effect he's having on his own Myrmidons?'

'You forget we've known him much longer than you have, Diomedes,' said Peisandros, whose broad abdomen was tightly squeezed between the arms of his chair. 'We Myrmidons *expect* Achilles to be excessive, whether it's in war, anger, love or grief. We suffer with him for the loss of Patroclus and our loyalty to him is as strong as ever.'

Odysseus finished his porridge and dropped the wooden bowl on to the ground by his feet.

'Yes, but it wavered during his feud with Agamemnon, when he refused to fight,' he said.

'A few disgruntled comments,' Peisandros countered with a

dismissive flick of his hand. 'Would you expect anything less of warriors being kept back from battle?'

'Soldiers will be loyal to their leaders, for the most part,' said Diomedes. 'But Achilles shouldn't expect to get away with everything. Thersites was a distant cousin of mine; it's not a fact I'm proud of, but what Achilles did to him was nothing short of murder. The gods will hold him to account for it.'

'The gods care more for Achilles than Thersites, my friend,' Odysseus said, leaning across and patting Diomedes's shoulder. 'Besides, the hunchback had it coming. He's crossed us all in his time – you and me included – but he should've known better than to keep goading the likes of Agamemnon and Achilles. After all, even I wouldn't dare accuse Achilles of wanting to commit necrophilia!'

He gave Diomedes a smile, but the Argive king continued to stare across at Achilles stretched over Patroclus's barrow. As silence fell between them again, Eperitus took a mouthful of wine and let his thoughts wander to the night before. With the defeat of the Amazons, he had returned to his hut to find the hearth ablaze and Astynome lying naked in his bed. This was the third time she had smuggled herself into his hut, since Priam had taken Hector's body eleven days before, and Eperitus's joy grew with each unexpected appearance. After they had made love she had rested her head upon his chest and, with her long fingers tracing the lines of his rib muscles, asked him whether he had thought any more of Apheidas's offer.

'I won't betray my oath to Odysseus,' he had replied flatly.

'But the Aethiopes will arrive soon,' she had sighed. 'Some say they'll drive the Greeks back into the sea and bring victory to Troy. Others claim they'll breathe new life into our defences and prolong the siege for a few more years. Either way, isn't it better to have peace now? If your father thinks he can negotiate an end to the war, why don't you put away your anger and speak to him? I can't bear to be apart from you for much longer; I want the fighting to stop so that we can be married.'

Eperitus thumbed a tear from her cheek and stroked her hair. 'So do I, my love. But my hatred for Apheidas is irrelevant now. These Aethiopes that Priam puts his faith in will never set foot in Troy; we've set an ambush for them in the hills about the road to Troy. And so long as Achilles is still fighting and Helen is held prisoner by Paris, there'll never be peace between Greeks and Trojans, whatever my father might say.'

They had talked a little while longer, about the war and whether it would ever end, but Astynome said nothing more about Apheidas's offer. Instead, her tone had become increasingly depressed as she convinced herself that she and Eperitus would never now be together and find the happiness they sought. She had dripped tears on to his chest and wound her limbs tighter about his body, while he had tried to assure her the city was prophesied to fall before the end of the year and that they could then be married. But the prospect of Troy's destruction had only made her more tearful. Eventually they had drifted into sleep, and when Eperitus awoke with the first glimmer of dawn Astynome had already gone.

Peisandros lifted the wineskin from the sand beside his chair and poured a little in his cup before offering it to the others. Diomedes refused, but as Odysseus took the skin a series of horn calls rang out from the gates. Recognizing the alarm, all four men jumped up from their seats and looked to the walls that lined the slopes above them. The rest of the camp had also burst into life and men were already hurrying to and fro, pulling on armour and retrieving weapons as they wondered what new threat could be calling them to arms. Then, through the middle of the chaos, a single horseman came weaving his way between the tents and campfires, cutting a path down towards the beach. Eperitus recognized him as one of Nestor's captains, who should have been with the expedition that had set out that morning to ambush the Aethiopes. He ran to intercept him, closely followed by Odysseus, Diomedes and Peisandros.

'Whoaa!' Eperitus called, holding up his arms. 'Where are you heading and what's your hurry, man?'

The rider heaved back on the reins and looked down at the four men. His face was caked with blood and dust and his eyes were wide with fear and urgency.

'I have a message for the King of Men and for him only. Many lives depend on me getting it to him, so I beg you not to delay me any more than I have been already.'

'Get on your way, then,' said Achilles, striding up behind the others, his grief temporarily put aside. 'We'll follow.'

The horseman kicked back his heels and gave a shout, sending his mount galloping the short distance to Agamemnon's brilliant white tent, where he dismounted and ran to speak to the guards. They seemed reluctant to let him enter, but the arrival of Achilles, Diomedes and Odysseus, accompanied by Eperitus and Peisandros, quickly persuaded them to relent. The senior soldier, one of Agamemnon's personal bodyguard in full ceremonial armour, led them into the tent.

'What's the meaning of this interruption?' Agamemnon snapped, rising from his fur-draped throne as the captain of the guard entered. 'I gave orders not to be— Ah, Achilles! And Diomedes and Odysseus, too. Well, come in, come in.'

The King of Men appeared to be alone but for a few slaves, who hurried to bring chairs for the newcomers. He waited until all were seated – except for the battle-grimed horseman, who insisted on standing with his helmet in the crook of his arm and a look of disciplined impatience on his face – then nodded for the captain of the guard to leave. As kraters of wine were brought by the slaves and libations poured to the gods, Agamemnon's gaze scanned across the seated guests, finally coming to rest on Achilles.

'And to what do I owe the pleasure, Prince Achilles? Something to do with the alarm being called, no doubt.'

Achilles did not answer, nodding instead towards the standing horseman. The messenger took this as permission to speak.

'My lords, I've ridden directly from the battle against the Aethiopes.'

'Then you bring news of victory, I expect,' Agamemnon said, in a tone that seemed to warn the man against telling him otherwise.

Eperitus looked at the horseman. From the moment he had seen him riding through the camp he had sensed that the news he carried was bad; now, as he watched the man's urgent demeanour deflate before the King of Men, he knew the ambush against the Aethiopes had met with disaster.

'No, my lord.'

'*No?*' Diomedes questioned. 'But Nestor assured us the ambush couldn't fail.'

'And the king was right, sir. Or would have been, if it hadn't been for a cruel twist of the fates. We took up our positions long before the enemy came into view on the road below, and when they finally appeared – every one of them as black as deepest night, with blood-red eyes and snarling teeth – they didn't know we were waiting for them. I'm sure of it.'

'So what happened?' Eperitus asked, trying to suppress his eagerness.

'What happened, sir?' the man replied, turning to Eperitus with an incredulous smile on his lips. 'The Trojans arrived! We heard a clamour of fighting and horn calls behind us and a moment later a mass of chariots and cavalry was topping the ridge and charging down towards us. We turned, but what could we do? They were in among us in moments, killing at will and laughing as they did so. Then the black men on the road below saw what was happening and came rushing up to close the trap. By an ill chance, or the malice of the gods, the Trojans had sent a force to meet the Aethiopes just at the place where we had planned to ambush them!'

Odysseus shot Eperitus a sceptical glance, then turned to the messenger.

'Then what happened? How did you escape?'

'I didn't escape, my lord,' the man replied proudly, raising his chin a little despite the tears of anguish in his eyes. 'Little Ajax and Nestor pulled us together, while Great Ajax brought the reserve over the ridge to our aid. Though we were being attacked on three sides and were badly outnumbered, we showed no fear and for a while held our own against them. Then Paris shot one of Nestor's horses, sending his chariot toppling and the king with it. Antilochus saved his father's life and helped him to escape from the black spearmen, but as they were retreating the Aethiope leader cut Antilochus down and stripped him of his armour.' At this, the others in the tent stirred uncomfortably in their seats and looked at each other in silent shock, while Achilles glowered at the messenger in disbelief. 'From that point on we were fighting a lost battle. With Nestor wounded and his son dead, the Ajaxes commanded the rest of us to retreat. I and five others were ordered to ride back to the camp and bring reinforcements. I'm the only one who made it through.'

'You did well,' Diomedes said, rising from his seat and offering the rider his wine. He drank greedily.

Achilles also stood.

'You'll have your reinforcements!' he said, punching the palm of his hand. 'I'll order my Myrmidons to arm at once!'

'You're forgetting yourself, Achilles,' said Agamemnon. 'As the elected leader of this army, that decision is mine to make, not yours.'

A sudden silence fell in the airy tent, disturbed only by the brushing of the wind across the flaxen walls. Eperitus watched as Achilles and Agamemnon locked eyes in a battle of wills.

'How many men do the Ajaxes need?' Agamemnon asked, breaking eye contact and looking at the messenger.

'They did not say, my lord. As many as can be spared. There must be at least five thousand of the combined enemy.'

'We will send five thousand against them, then. But under Diomedes's command.'

'Ten thousand,' Achilles demanded, stepping forward. 'With me at their head.'

'No,' Agamemnon replied, fixing the prince with his icy blue eyes. 'You have fought hard and earned your rest, Achilles. Diomedes can go, and he'll have enough to chase away the Trojans and their new allies, no more.'

Achilles took another step towards Agamemnon and for a brief moment Eperitus thought the prince was going to draw his sword and strike the arrogant and imperious King of Men dead. Remembering his promise to Clytaemnestra, he moved forward in his chair and laid a hand on the pommel of his own weapon.

'Give me ten thousand soldiers,' Achilles insisted, 'and I will give you Troy. Calchas once said the city would fall in the tenth year, and I say that day has come. I can feel it in my blood, Agamemnon – can't you?'

There was such a passion in Achilles's voice that, for a moment, Eperitus believed him. Even Agamemnon's calculating gaze was suddenly eager as the Mycenaean king slowly nodded. Then a movement in the shadows at the back of the tent broke the spell and a stooping figure shuffled forward into the light.

'It's true I said Troy would fall in the tenth year, but it won't fall today. And it will never fall by *your* hand, Achilles.'

Every eye turned to look at Calchas, the seer, as he tipped back the hood from his bald head and peered round at Agamemnon's guests.

'So this was why you didn't want to be disturbed,' Achilles sneered, glancing at Agamemnon. 'And I thought you'd stopped taking your lead from this fool!'

'I came here of my own will,' Calchas responded. 'To tell Agamemnon of the dream Apollo sent me last night.'

'Another wine-soaked fantasy?' Diomedes mocked.

Calchas ignored him and peered up into Achilles's eyes, scrutinizing him closely.

'I dreamed of your death, Achilles. Today. That is why Agamemnon wants Diomedes to command the reinforcements.'

The colour drained from Achilles's face, leaving him pale as he stared back at Calchas.

'Who will kill me?' he asked, slowly. 'The Aethiope king?'

'Have no fear of the blacks, or of any mortal. It is by the hand of Apollo himself that you will perish, in vengeance for his son, King Tenes, whom you slew.'

Achilles turned away and looked down at the fleeces beneath his feet, balling his hands into fists and breathing deeply.

'You're wrong, Calchas,' he said in a low voice. 'You're wrong, I tell you! You; my mother; the endless prophecies about me – they're *all* wrong! Weaklings are slaves to the Fates, but the real test of greatness is to command one's own destiny.'

'Achilles is right,' Odysseus said. He rose from his chair and placed his hand on the prince's shoulder, staring at him with fervent eyes. 'A man does not have to be subject to oracles and the will of the gods. It was once in my power to overturn a prophecy and forge my own future, and it will be so again – as it can be for you, son of Peleus!'

Achilles nodded at the king of Ithaca and smiled as his confidence began to return. Then he drew his sword and pressed the point against Calchas's breastbone.

'Tell me, priest, what does Apollo say about your fate today? Will you live or die? Is that the will of the gods or mine? Either way, you are a fool and a weakling who blunders through life like a blind man, staggering from one circumstance to the next. But I am no plaything of any god – not Apollo or even Zeus himself. Today I will take the Scaean Gate and slaughter every Trojan I come across. I will dash their children's brains out against the walls of their houses and rape their wives in their own beds. And before I sleep in Priam's palace tonight, I will summon you to my side and allow you to choose *your* own fate – to beg my forgiveness for your lies, or to wash my blade with your blood!'

Achilles sheathed his sword again and turned to Agamemnon.

'My lord, I will wait outside the walls with Odysseus here and a thousand of my Myrmidons. I give you leave to choose the other nine thousand men under my command, but respectfully ask that you do not delay in sending them. We have a battle to fight and a city to conquer.'

Chapter Forty-One
MEMNON

O nce more the plain beyond the walls of the Greek camp was filled with rank upon rank of soldiers, their spear points gleaming in the fierce sunlight as they marched towards the call of battle. At their head were the chariots of their commanders: Achilles foremost – splendid in his god-made armour and spoiling for the fight – with Odysseus, Menelaus, Diomedes and Idomeneus each leading their own factions. On either side of the massed infantry were the cavalry, the horses' legs hidden beneath the haze of dust raised by their hooves so that they seemed to be floating to war.

Standing on the woven floor of his chariot, with Arceisius at the reins, Eperitus's eyes flicked constantly between the north-east horizon, where the battle would still be raging, and his king and friend in the next chariot. Odysseus's eyes were fixed firmly ahead, having lost none of their passion since he and Achilles had set out to deny the Fates and take the gates of Troy. Turning his gaze once more to the distance, he thought he could see a cloud of dust through the heat haze. He leaned forward across the chariot rail, squinting slightly, then turned his head to listen. And then he heard it – the thrilling and terrible sound of battle. Still some way off, lost among the folds of grassland, the din of clashing weapons and raised voices had melded into a low hum that sounded like heavy rainfall.

'Achilles,' he shouted, pointing in the direction of the noise. 'That way.'

Achilles spoke to Peisandros, who turned the team of Xanthus and Balius a little more to the east before raising their pace to a canter. The infantry followed, wheeling slightly and then breaking into a heavy jog. A force of cavalry dashed forward from each flank to scout the positions of the enemy and the beleaguered Greeks ahead of them, but even before the first messengers could return the army had topped a low ridge and could see the battle in the near distance.

'Can you make out what's going on?' Arceisius asked Eperitus, his eyes burning with excitement. 'What's happening?'

'The Greeks are surrounded, by the looks of it. Cut off, with enemies on every side.'

Although he could not see in the detail that Eperitus could, Achilles knew the situation was dire and he was not a man to dither when action was needed. He turned to the infantry and barked out a series of commands. Spears were lowered and shields moved from backs to shoulders as the thick lines of Greek warriors closed formation. On either side of them the remainder of the cavalry dashed forward, while Achilles raised his enormous ash spear over his head and gave the signal to advance. At the same time Odysseus lifted a thickly muscled arm in the air and drove it forward, just as Menelaus, Diomedes and Idomeneus did the same. The army gave a cheer in response and began to move down the long, gentle slope that led to the battle.

Arceisius snapped the reins and the chariot bounced forward across the rocky ground. Eperitus took one of his spears from its leather socket on the inside of the cab and balanced it over his right shoulder. As they drew closer to the fighting he could see the force of Greeks standing back-to-back in a circle, where the Trojan cavalry had cut off their retreat and forced them back in on themselves, only to be caught and surrounded by the combined forces of the Trojan and Aethiope spearmen. The southerners reminded Eperitus of giant spiders, with their long, spindly limbs and dark skin; and though he had seen Aethiope slaves before, the sight of thousands of black warriors crawling over the plain filled him with awe.

Fierce hand-to-hand combat was raging at every point. Men tried to skewer each other with their spears, but there was no time to exult or plunder the armour from their fallen foe if they succeeded. Instead, every dead enemy was replaced by another, and another, as Greek or Trojan, black man or white, fought with a raging fury to the death. It was then that Eperitus noticed the gigantic figure of Ajax, faced by an equally tall, though rangy, Aethiope. The two men had drawn their swords and were hacking away at each other with one angry blow after another. Both skilfully parried the attacks of their opponent, but the black warrior landed two strikes for every one of Ajax's and the Greek was faltering. The tall shield of sevenfold leather that he usually wielded with ease now seemed to be made of lead as he swung it this way and that against his enemy's skilful lunges, while his thick legs trembled under his own weight. It seemed the mighty stalwart of Agamemnon's army would not endure for much longer.

Then a series of shouts rang out from among the Trojans and Aethiopes. At last, they had spotted the mass of reinforcements storming down the slope towards them, and with a flurry of panicked activity many broke off from the fighting and hurried to form a line of spears between the newcomers and their struggling countrymen. The Trojan cavalry pulled away from the battle and formed two groups on either side of the spearmen, ready to meet the opposing swarms of Greek horsemen. At that moment Achilles's voice roared out above the cacophony of battle as he spurred his chariot forward into a headlong charge. It was too early, Eperitus thought to himself: any ordinary team of horses would be blown long before they could carry a battle-laden chariot into the lines of Trojans and Aethiopes. But Achilles's horses were not of ordinary stock. They were the immortal offspring of the Zephyrus, the west wind, given as a wedding present at the marriage of Peleus and Thetis. And few who watched them leap forward into battle could have doubted their lineage as they took their mighty master sweeping towards the spear-tipped ranks of the enemy. While the rest of the Greeks were just beginning their charge,

Xanthus and Balius bore down on the Aethiopes with such fury that the spearmen's courage failed long before that of the horses, and throwing down their weapons they turned and ran into the thick files of men behind them. Achilles was upon them in an instant, plunging his spear into their exposed backs and sending many of their ghosts to Hades.

Arceisius lashed the reins with a shout and sent the chariot rushing down the grassy slope towards the enemy. Eperitus shifted the balance of his spear in his cupped hand and eyed the wall of black spearmen that was awaiting him. For a moment, as the wind tugged at his beard and he watched the flowing manes of his two horses ahead of him, he felt as if he and Arceisius were alone and detached from the world around them. The thunder of hooves filled his ears and the whole chariot shook beneath his feet. He looked out at the long grass that covered the ground and thought of the sea, as if he was leaning over the prow of a speeding galley with the surface of the ocean flashing past on either side. And then he glanced to his left and saw Odysseus shouting at the top of his voice – though Eperitus could not hear his words in the cacophony of battle – and pulling back his spear over his shoulder. Eperitus did the same, gripping the chariot rail with one hand and taking aim along the shaft at the mass of scowling Aethiopes ahead of him. Yelling as loud as his lungs and the competing wind would allow him, he launched his spear.

Whether it found its mark he never knew. A few heartbeats later he had swept his long sword from its scabbard and was staring in heady exhilaration at the gleaming spear points ahead of him. Arceisius let out a whoop of joy as he slapped the reins one final time across the backs of the horses and drove them on into the enemy. Suddenly it was as if their spears had been swept aside by the hand of some benevolent god, for both horses and men were unscathed as they broke through the terrified Aethiopes, Eperitus's sword hacking at their uplifted faces and dispatching many to the Underworld. For a long, glorious moment in time he felt almost immortal, as if no weapon could harm him, as if his chariot were surrounded by a pocket of invulnerability that could not be pierced. Though there were enemy spearmen on all sides, yelling and stabbing at him, his shield thwarted every attack while the point of his sword sent one assailant after another to oblivion.

Then they were through the hastily assembled line of defenders and driving across open grassland once more. The main battle was now ahead of them and they could see the backs of their enemies as they were busy attacking the besieged remnants of the Greeks. To one side, cut off and surrounded by Aethiopes, Ajax was still struggling to fend off the attacks of the tall Aethiope, who Eperitus realized could only be the famed Memnon. His handsome face grinned at his fading opponent with the assured confidence of a hunter closing in upon a wounded lion.

Arceisius saw the unequal fight and, without waiting for orders, steered the chariot towards it. Sensing movement to his left, Eperitus turned to see three Trojan horsemen dashing towards him, their spears couched beneath their arms as they leaned into the attack. He swung his shield around to face them, but as the nearest rider approached he gave a sudden lurch and tumbled forward from his mount, a long ash spear protruding from his back. His comrades turned in panic, just as Achilles came racing up in his chariot and sliced the top off the nearest man's head with his sword. The remaining horseman veered aside, straight into the path of a third Greek chariot. Odysseus grinned triumphantly and hurled his spear, catching the Trojan in the throat and spilling him from the back of his horse. Eperitus looked beyond the speeding chariots of Odysseus and Achilles and saw that the mass of newly arrived Greek spearmen had already crushed the thin line of Aethiope infantry and were yelling with bloodlust as they charged to the aid of their encircled countrymen.

'Memnon's mine!' Achilles shouted as his chariot swept past Eperitus and raced to save Ajax.

A scattering of spears split the air above Eperitus and Arceisius's heads, warning them that the other Aethiopes were no longer ignorant of their approach. As Odysseus drew alongside –

Eurybates gripping the reins and driving the horses as fast as they would go – Eperitus looked ahead to see a score of black warriors running towards them and casting their spears. Two found their marks in the breast of one of Eperitus's horses, bringing it down in an instant. The last thing he saw as the chariot skewed to the left and threw him from the car was Achilles driving into a line of Aethiope warriors, who had hurried forward to defend their king from the new opponent. Then he hit the ground with a thump and everything went dark.

He came to lying on his back and staring up into the noon sun. The wreckage of the chariot was a few paces away; the fact that one of the wheels was still spinning, and the surviving horse was struggling to get to its feet, told him that he had only been unconscious for a few moments. Then he saw the bloodied and inert form of Arceisius lying beneath the broken cab. He tried to raise himself, but was forced back down by a surge of pain. Grunting through gritted teeth, he tried again and managed this time to turn on to his side. Then a tall shape blocked out the sun and he looked up to see a black warrior standing over him, his long spear in his hands. Eperitus rolled aside just as the bronze spear point bit into the hard soil where a moment before his stomach had been. Suddenly a wave of energy burst through his body, eliminating the pain of his wounds and giving him fresh strength. Grabbing the neck of the spear for leverage, he swung his right leg into the back of his attacker's left knee and knocked him on to his back. As he fell, Eperitus drew back his leg and kicked with all his force, connecting with the man's head and snapping it sideways.

Three more Aethiopes came running up, their spear points lowered towards him. Eperitus spotted his shield, but it was beyond his reach and he knew he would never get to it in time. Then he saw two figures come charging in from the corner of his vision. Eurybates despatched one of the Aethiopes with a slashing cut of his sword that sheared through flesh and bone, while Odysseus sank the point of his spear into the throat of another, before pulling it out again and ramming the sharpened base of the shaft into the remaining man's groin. As the man staggered backwards, clutching at his wounded neck and coughing blood, Odysseus finished him off with a thrust of his spear.

'No time to lie around,' he said, turning to Eperitus and pulling him to his feet. 'Achilles and Ajax need our help.'

Eperitus retrieved his shield and a discarded spear then – seeing that Eurybates was helping Arceisius to his feet and that the young Ithacan was not badly hurt – followed Odysseus towards where they had last seen Achilles driving into the Aethiope shield-wall. All that remained there now was Achilles's chariot with Peisandros at the reins, surrounded by a circle of black bodies. Peisandros said nothing, but pointed to the east where a little further on they could see Achilles standing in front of an exhausted Ajax, who knelt with his head bowed and blood and sweat shining on his powerful limbs. Achilles's magnificent armour gleamed in the bright midday sun and somehow he had retrieved his gigantic ash spear. Facing him was Memnon, backed by a large force of Aethiopes.

'Stay out of this,' Achilles warned as Odysseus and Eperitus ran to join him.

The Ithacans moved forward and lifted Ajax to his feet, while Achilles kept his eyes firmly on the Aethiope king. Memnon made no move to prevent Ajax being taken away; though he regretted not being able to claim the armour of such a fierce and powerful warrior, the breastplate, helmet and shield of the man who had come to aid him would provide a much more worthwhile trophy.

'There was nothing I could do against him,' Ajax admitted despairingly. 'He was too quick for me.'

'But you survived,' Odysseus consoled him, observing the many new wounds that crossed the giant warrior's body. 'From what I've heard of Memnon, there are no others who can boast such a thing.'

Ajax smiled weakly, but the greatest sign of his tiredness was that he was prepared to forgo his pride and lean his weight against Odysseus. Eperitus glanced over his shoulder at the main battle, where the Greek infantry under Menelaus, Diomedes and Idomeneus had broken the stranglehold on their countrymen and were now forcing the Trojans and Aethiopes backwards with great slaughter. Then he turned back to look at the figure of Memnon, prowling from left to right and back again like a trapped lion. Achilles stepped forward.

'I am Achilles, son of Peleus and the goddess Thetis. I slew Hector, and I will slay you, Memnon, son of Tithonus.'

'You claim a goddess for a mother,' Memnon replied in Greek, 'but you don't mention that my own mother is also a goddess – Eos, the Dawn, who brings the new day to the world. I've heard of you, Achilles, but I don't fear you. Rather, it's *you* who should fear *me*!'

With terrifying speed, he lifted his spear above his shoulder and hurled it at Achilles. Achilles ducked down behind his shield, which took the full force of the attack and snapped the spear at the point where the socket joined the shaft. He replied in kind, a deadly throw that would have passed straight through Memnon's armoured chest and spirited his ghost away to the Chambers of Decay, were it not for the speed with which the spindly warrior twisted aside from the missile's aim. The next moment the two men were drawing their swords and running at each other, their blades clashing in mid-air and their shields meeting with a heavy thud. Achilles pushed his opponent away and lunged again with his sword point, piercing the oiled leather of Memnon's shield but failing to meet the flesh beyond. As he tugged the blade free, Memnon drove at Achilles's flank. Achilles batted the attack aside with ease and smashed the razor-sharp edge of his sword down against the Aethiope's shield. The supple leather shuddered but held, while only Achilles's quick instincts saved him from the low, scything reply that would have taken off his lower leg. A second blow rebounded off Achilles's helmet, leaving nothing more than a long dent and a ringing in the Greek's head. Numbed, he stumbled backwards with his shield raised against the swift blows that followed. But Achilles's battle impulses had not deserted him;

anchoring himself with a backward thrust of his right leg, he parried two more blows before ducking low and pushing the point of his sword beneath the edge of Memnon's crescent shield. Memnon leapt back, but not before the blade opened his inner thigh and released a gush of dark blood that spattered over the ground below. He wobbled a little, as much with surprise as pain, but Achilles allowed him no time to recover. As Memnon raised his shield, he rained a series of savage blows down upon it that crumpled the wicker frame and sent the black warrior staggering backwards. Then the wounded muscle in his leg gave way and he fell to one knee, raising his weapon instinctively over his head to meet the next attack. But Achilles brought his sword down at an angle, severing Memnon's hand just below the wrist and sending his blade – with his hand still clutching the hilt – spinning through the air.

The handsome black face that had earlier been filled with arrogant pride and self-assurance now stared up at Achilles with disbelief. The expression remained etched on his features even as Achilles sliced off his head and sent it rolling towards the feet of his shocked men, who gazed down at it in horror.

Achilles fell to one knee beside the headless torso and, while the warm blood was still jetting from the open neck, began to strip off the silver cuirass and the ornate, leather and gold scabbard that hung from a baldric about the chest. Odysseus and Eperitus instinctively moved forward to protect the Phthian prince as he claimed his trophies, each of them eyeing the Aethiope line with unease, aware that they would be outnumbered ten to one as soon as the enemy spearmen shook off their stupor and chose to attack. But as Eperitus clutched his spear and stared over the rim of his shield, a man left the opposing ranks and placed a foot on the decapitated head, rolling it slightly so that the dead eyes stared back up at him. That the man was an Aethiope chieftain was evident from his silver helmet with its long white plume and the gleam of the decorative bronze breastplate beneath his rich black robe. He held a long sword in his hand, which he slowly sheathed before taking hold of the ram's horn that hung at his hip and raising it to his mouth. He blew a long, clear note that rose into the air like a wailing lament. Even the discordant clash of weapons from the main battle faded beneath it as Aethiope, Trojan and Greek alike heard the call and looked for its source. Then, suddenly, the black spearmen let out a cry of despair and began to pull away, turning their backs on battle as they ran towards the chieftain with the ram's horn.

Chapter Forty-Two
APOLLO'S REVENGE

Achilles dumped Memnon's armour on to the ground and joined the others as they turned to face the swarm of approaching Aethiopes. But the southerners were not interested in fighting any more; their leader was dead and with him their brief allegiance to Troy. They were not Priam's vassals, like the Dardanians, the Zeleians or the Cilicians, but had been persuaded to fight by ancient friendships and promises of Trojan gold. These no longer mattered, and so they swept around the small knot of Greeks like a stampede of wild horses avoiding an outcrop of rock, following in the wake of their countrymen who were already in retreat across the plain.

With their left flank now gone, the Trojans broke off the fighting and began to fall back. Menelaus, Idomeneus and Ajax – his pride getting the better of his exhaustion – led their armies in pursuit, while Diomedes and Odysseus prepared their men to go after the Aethiopes.

'Let the cavalry hunt them down,' Achilles said. 'I came here to take the city. The moment the Scaean Gate opens for the Trojan survivors, we're going to follow them in.'

He turned to the lines of spearmen and raised his sword in the air.

'Listen to me! You men fought hard and suffered while I let my pride keep me in my hut. But since my return I've killed Hector, Penthesilea and now Memnon, and today I will lead you into Troy itself! Every man here who does his duty and fights well can take all the women and gold he can lay his hands on – and if Agamemnon or Menelaus tries to stop you then they'll have *me* to answer to. We've waited many years for this day to come; now's the time to make names for ourselves that will linger on men's lips long after our ghosts have gone down to Hades. To Troy!'

'To Troy!' they echoed, punching the air with their spear points.

Eperitus took the reins of Odysseus's chariot while Eurybates and Arceisius joined the Ithacan ranks. As the many wounded began to trail back to the Greek camp – Nestor among them, still unconscious from his wounds and unaware that his son was dead – the rest of the army chased the Trojans back across the grassland. Their pursuit was slowed by the delaying tactics of the enemy cavalry, who wheeled and charged again and again to prevent the Greeks from coming to grips with the retreating infantry. But as the pursuit passed over the temple of Thymbrean Apollo and down the slopes beyond to the Scamander, the Trojan horsemen had no choice but to join the rest of the army as they forded the river. Suddenly Achilles, who had bided his time for this very moment, gave the order for every man to throw himself into the attack. With a great roar, the Greeks splashed through the shallow water and fell upon the Trojans. The ringing of bronze and the screams of injured men mingled with the gentle babbling of the water and the call of the gulls overhead; all around, men fell by the score and fed long streamers of blood into the fast current. The Trojan resistance was ferocious but short-lived. Dispirited, outnumbered and outfought, their line wavered and broke.

'Follow them!' Odysseus shouted, pointing across the sea of helmeted heads to where Paris and Deiphobus were turning their chariot about and driving back to the Scaean Gate.

Eperitus flicked the reins across the backs of the horses and sent them springing forward. The heavy wheels bounced across rocks and the softer bodies of dead men beneath the water, before biting into the mud of the far bank and driving up on to the sun-baked plain. All around them Trojans were running in headlong panic, no longer concerned with fighting but only with reaching the safety of the city walls. Some fell beneath the speeding chariot, while others were caught by the pursuing Greeks and cut down without mercy. Then Paris turned and saw Eperitus and Odysseus gaining on him. With a quick word to his brother, who gave a shout and drove the tired horses even harder, Paris fitted an arrow to his bow and took aim. Odysseus quickly threw up his shield, catching the bronze-tipped shaft in the upper rim. Paris fitted another arrow and Eperitus wrenched the reins to the left, running down a group of Trojan spearmen as the second shaft flew past his right ear.

'Get after them!' Odysseus hollered, watching in angry dismay as Paris and Deiphobus escaped towards the Scaean Gate.

Eperitus steered the chariot back round to the right, just as a series of shrill horn calls announced the opening of the Scaean Gate. In the same moment he heard Achilles's loud voice booming over the din of battle.

'The gates are opening! To the gates! To the gates!'

He swept past them in his chariot, his immortal horses riding down any man in his way as he dashed headlong towards the yawning gap opening up in the Trojan walls. He drove forward with such speed that, for a moment, Eperitus thought he would reach the gates and take them single-handedly, overturning all the prophecies of doom, and with one act of courage and shining skill eclipse the feats of every warrior who had lived before him, even Heracles himself. Men fled as he bore down on them, or leapt aside and threw their arms over their heads in fear. But as Paris and Deiphobus disappeared through the gate a new series of horn calls sounded from the walls above. They were followed by loud cheering as hundreds of heavily armed men came rushing out to meet the Greeks.

Paris jumped down from the back of the chariot, followed by Deiphobus. All around them the streets were packed with soldiers and civilians, mingling chaotically as the panic of war took hold of the city once more. In one direction, massed companies of fresh troops marched out to meet the encroaching enemy, while in the other the survivors of the battle were trickling in through the gate to slump exhausted against the cyclopean walls, there to have their wounds treated by the flocks of anxious-looking women who were waiting for them. Again, Achilles had helped the Greeks turn defeat into victory and Paris felt his frustration turning to anger.

'Apheidas!' Paris called, seeing the tall captain leading the reserves. 'Apheidas, keep the Greek infantry away from the gates – the archers on the walls will help – but let Achilles push in closer. He'll not wait for the rest and I want him to be separated from them.'

Apheidas frowned down at the prince.

'That's too risky, my lord. If he reaches the gates it could mean the fall of Troy.'

'Apheidas is right, Brother,' Deiphobus agreed. 'Let's just get as many men as we can back inside the walls before—'

'No!' Paris snapped. 'Achilles killed Hector and I'm going to avenge his death with my own hands *now*. If I fail and Troy falls, what of it? She'll succumb sooner or later anyway, if Achilles isn't killed.'

Apheidas's gaze remained on Paris for a short while, then without a word he turned and rejoined the stream of spearmen flooding out of the gates, the hooves of his horse echoing loudly between the high walls. As he went, Paris selected a particular arrow from the leather quiver at his hip and turned its long, black shaft between his fingers. The tip had been smeared with a dark grey paste that had dried to a textured hardness. What was in the paste Paris did not know; but when he had requested the arrow from Penthesilea – having heard of the deadliness of Amazon barbs

– she boasted it would kill any man, woman or beast, however great, if it so much as pierced their flesh. And there was only one man he intended to use the arrow on.

He ran up a flight of steps to the top of the walls, followed closely by Deiphobus. The battlements were filled with archers, pouring a deadly fire into the horde of Greeks beyond the line of the sacred oak tree, where the Trojans were barely managing to keep their onslaught at bay. Paris shouldered his way between them and, fitting the arrow to his bow, peered down into the morass of struggling men below.

The sound of the battle washed over him like a strong wind and for a while he could barely identify any individual among the closely fought press. Then he noticed Apheidas directing more reserves towards the fight with the Greek infantry, while ordering others on his right to move back. And then, following the direction of Apheidas's orders, Paris saw him – the hated figure of Achilles, now dismounted from his chariot and fighting in the shadow of the walls. He was alone in the midst of a crowd of Trojans, who refused to attack or retreat as they formed a circle about the most feared of all the Greeks.

Paris sneered with hatred as he fitted the well-made arrow to his bow.

'Lord Apollo, hear my prayer. If you will make my aim straight – if you will aid me in killing Achilles this day – you shall have the fat and thigh bones of twenty calves before darkness falls.'

As the words left his lips he heard a rushing of wind coming, it seemed, from a great distance. He closed his left eye and took aim down the shaft of the arrow, letting the bronze tip wander this way and that until he found Achilles again, causing murderous havoc with his sword among the Trojan spearmen. His heart quickened in his chest and at the same time the firmness of his grip wavered, letting the point of the arrow drift alarmingly away from its target. He felt the sweat on his fingertips and knew his grip on the base of the arrow was beginning to slip. Unless he regained command of himself the shot would be wasted. And then the wind grew louder and a moment later he felt it fanning his hair and cloak as a great shadow fell over him.

The noise of battle raged about Odysseus and Eperitus. Having seen Achilles leap down from his chariot and plunge into the thick of battle, they had followed the prince's example and rushed in after him on foot, only to be held back by the fleeing Trojans as they turned and fought, heartened by the arrival of reinforcements from the gate and supporting fire from the archers on the battlements. The Greek infantry caught up and charged into the hastily formed Trojan line, but were greeted by a hail of arrows that stopped them as effectively as if they had run into a stone wall. They charged again and the struggle that followed was as frenzied and confused as any battle Eperitus had ever known. The Trojans fought with a fury Eperitus had rarely seen before, and which was only matched by the determination of the Greeks to follow Achilles through the Scaean Gate and into the streets of Troy.

Eperitus pushed the head of his spear into a Trojan's chest, only for another to leap into the gap and swing at him with a double-headed axe. Eperitus met the shivering blow with the boss of his shield, before despatching his attacker with a rapid thrust of his spear as he pulled back his axe for a second time. Stepping over his body, he was met by a young lad armed with nothing more than a crude leather shield and a dagger.

'So this is the level Troy has been lowered to,' he said, staring at his enemy. 'Sending boys on to the battlefield with nothing more than knives.'

There was no fear on the lad's face, only angry determination as he rushed at Eperitus with his blade held before him. Almost without thinking, Eperitus reached across and grabbed the boy's wrist, twisting his arm aside until, with a shout of pain, he dropped the dagger into the trampled grass. Eperitus kicked the weapon away just as Odysseus appeared at his side. Eurybates, Polites and Antiphus were with him.

'Come on,' the king shouted over the din of battle. 'We've got to reach Achilles before the Trojans overpower him and drag his body into the city walls.'

He plunged into the press of Trojans, followed by the others.

'Go home to your mother,' Eperitus said, releasing the lad's wrist.

He shoved him forcefully back towards his comrades, then followed the giant form of Polites into the fray. The Ithacans were cutting their way man by man through the swarming Trojans, and as their enemies were slowly pushed back, Eperitus caught a glimpse of Achilles ahead of them, fighting alone against a press of spearmen. Any other man would have fallen beneath such numbers. And yet no other man possessed Achilles's all-consuming lust for glory, a lust that could only be satisfied by taking the gates of Troy and denying the doom his own mother had laid on his shoulders. But his savage fury was met with equal determination on the part of the Trojans, who were prepared to sacrifice everything in the defence of their homes and families, even to the point of sending boys into battle. Watching them throw themselves at the unstoppable Achilles, Eperitus realized that such men could never be defeated by the Greeks. They had a cause worth dying for, whereas Agamemnon's army had forgotten why it had come to Ilium in the first place. Its leaders cared for nothing more than their own personal quests for glory, and pride alone would never give them victory.

Then Eperitus sensed a shadow fall across the battle. Others felt it too and looked up, only to see clear blue skies overhead. But as Eperitus lifted his gaze to the crowded battlements, he thought he saw a giant presence warping the air above the archers there, distorting the emptiness over their heads so that it seemed to shimmer like the heat haze on a distant horizon. No physical form was visible, but Eperitus knew a god was standing on the walls of Troy and casting its shadow over the fighting below. Then his eyes fell on Paris, who was leaning over the parapet with his bow pulled back, and suddenly Eperitus could see the shadowy outline of a tall figure standing over him, moving back its right hand as the Trojan prince drew the bow, and bending its head just as Paris bent his own head to take aim along the line of the arrow. Then the bowstring sang out and the missile struck its target.

Achilles cried out in pain. It was a sound Eperitus had never heard from Achilles before, nor had he ever expected to: high and clear and filled with extraordinary anguish, then slipping into despair as the great warrior knew his end had finally come, just as his beloved mother had warned him it would. He staggered, clutching at the long black arrow that had buried itself in his right heel, then fell.

As he disappeared among the circle of his enemies the clash of weapons and the shouts of men drained away, every Trojan and Greek sensing that something strange and terrible had happened. Then the shadow departed from the battlefield and the heaviness lifted from men's hearts. Paris leaned over the wall and shook his fist.

'That's for Hector! And just as you mistreated his corpse, so will I mistreat yours. Bring the body to me!'

'No!' Odysseus exclaimed, running towards the place where Achilles had fallen.

The battle erupted back into life. Eperitus dashed after Odysseus, who was cutting down any man who dared stand in his way; they were followed by Polites, Eurybates, Antiphus and a handful of Ithacans. Within moments they had driven back the Trojans surrounding Achilles and, while the others fought to hold them off, Odysseus and Eperitus knelt beside the fallen prince.

Odysseus removed Achilles's helmet and took his head in his lap, brushing the long blond hair from his face. As his fingers stroked across his forehead, Achilles's eyes flickered open and looked up at the Ithacan king.

'Odysseus!' he whispered, trying to smile despite the pain of approaching death. 'Odysseus, my friend, it seems Calchas was right after all. And yet it's better this way, I can see that now. The honour of killing Hector was given to my hand, though in the end it was a victory for hatred and revenge rather than for Achilles the man; but the glory of taking Troy must belong to another. To you, I think. And now I'm going down to Hades, where a man's soul knows only misery.'

'But your name will remain here on earth,' Odysseus said. 'Here among the world of the living.'

Achilles gripped Odysseus's arms with the last of his strength, and suddenly there was doubt in his eyes. Doubt, at the last, that he had achieved immortality.

'Can you be sure of that?' he gasped.

'Yes,' Odysseus reassured him. 'Yes, Achilles, you've earned that much at least.'

'But . . .' Achilles's back arched with a stab of pain, forcing Odysseus to hold him tight until the convulsion ebbed away again. 'But are you the only one who has come to save my body from the Trojans?'

As he spoke, a thunderous shout of anger rose above the cacophony of battle. Odysseus and Eperitus looked over their shoulders to see the titanic form of Ajax striding towards them from the Greek lines. Forgetting his wounds and exhaustion in his fury, he brushed aside Trojans as if they were nothing more than children.

Unaware of Ajax's approach, Achilles reached up and clutched at Odysseus's shoulder, his fingers tightening with pain and his eyes suddenly wide with fear.

'*He*'s coming, Odysseus! Hermes is coming for my soul! Lean closer, quickly; let my final words in life be to you, my friend.'

Odysseus bent down and placed his ear to Achilles's lips, which moved briefly and were still. An instant later Ajax burst in among the encircled Ithacans, his great shield bristling with arrows and his sword running with fresh gore as he stared down at the body of his cousin.

'He's dead,' Odysseus announced, passing his fingers over Achilles's eyelids and closing them for ever.

Ajax, his dirt-stained cheeks wet with tears, bent low and lifted the fallen warrior over his shoulder.

'Come, Odysseus, we must take him back to the ships. I can carry his body, but I can't easily fight Trojans at the same time. You and Eperitus must protect me.'

He turned and ran back towards the Greek line, while Odysseus and Eperitus launched themselves at the wall of Trojans.

Chapter Forty-Three

THETIS

E peritus lay on his side, supporting his head on his fist as he watched the shadows moving across the walls of his hut. Astynome was beside him, her breathing barely audible as she slept. He looked down at her chest as it gently rose and fell; the skin was orange in the firelight and every dimple and line was carefully picked out by the soft, wavering glow. Her face was turned away from him and he spent a few moments admiring her profile – the straight line of her jaw, the small nose and the closed eyes with their long, black lashes. A few strands of dark hair were stuck to the thin film of sweat on her forehead, while the rest of it lay tousled across the rolled-up furs that pillowed her head. He reached out and brushed a lock of hair back behind her ear, half hoping she would wake, but she did not.

It was now seventeen days since Paris had shot Achilles before the Scaean Gate, his hand guided by Apollo. After the battle there were many who claimed to have seen the god standing atop the battlements. None had, of course, but it was beyond doubt that the Olympian archer had finally avenged the death of his son, Tenes, whom Achilles had killed ten years before in the first battle of the war. Tomorrow the period of mourning set by Agamemnon would be over and the great warrior's body burnt. And it was about time, Eperitus thought. Unlike the divine protection that had preserved and restored Hector's body during the days of abuse by Achilles, the Phthian prince's own corpse had been afforded no such blessing. Despite every effort of the Greeks, the process of corruption was well advanced and the white sheet that covered the body could not disguise its foul stench. Only the faithful Myrmidons who guarded their prince could endure the smell, while the rest of the army said the rapid decay had been sent by the gods in revenge for Achilles's impious treatment of Hector.

Eperitus did not agree with them. Neither did Odysseus. Despite his excesses, Achilles was too great a warrior to earn the loathing of the Olympians. Few men could boast an immortal mother or a full set of divinely made armour, and none could claim to have killed as many famed opponents as Achilles had. Nor would the Trojans have fought with such savagery to claim the body of any other man. With Paris urging them on, they had pursued the Greeks back across the fords of the Scamander and up the slopes beyond it to the plain above. Warriors had died in their hundreds on both sides, giving their lives for possession of a single corpse, devoid of its precious spirit. While Ajax had carried Achilles's lifeless body across his massive shoulders – oblivious to the deadly hail of arrows and the shouts of the victorious Trojans – Odysseus and Eperitus had fought like trapped lions to protect his retreat, assisted by the strength and size of Polites, the bow of Antiphus and the spear of Eurybates. Finally, as Paris prepared his troops for another attack, Zeus himself intervened in the shape of a sudden storm, darkening the skies with clouds and calling on the winds to drive sheets of rain into the faces of the Trojans as the Greeks slipped away.

Astynome had come to his tent that same night, desperate to know that he had survived. She had treated his wounds then made love to him – tenderly, so as not to reopen his many cuts, but with a strong passion driven by relief at being in his arms again. The fierceness of the fighting and the inescapable closeness of death had given their relationship an urgency that neither had experienced in love before, making Eperitus hate the times when she had to leave him and return to her master in Troy. But until the war was over he knew this was how they would have to live –

furtive meetings at night, spending their short time together in his bed until dawn, when she would seek out her friends the farmer and his son, who would take her back to the one place Eperitus could not join her. Not, that was, unless he gave in to her pleading and accepted his father's offer of a meeting to discuss peace – an offer she had reminded him of on the evening after Achilles's death and again tonight, as she lay in his arms after making love. And again he had refused.

'But there's no other way to end this war,' she had protested, slapping his chest in frustration and looking even more beautiful in her anger. 'Troy can never be victorious, not with the Amazon queen dead and what's left of the Aethiope army in full retreat back south. But neither can the cursed Greeks, now Paris has killed Achilles. It's a stalemate. Surely if your father can bring about peace then you have a duty to listen to him – a duty to Odysseus, to me, and even to yourself.'

'I don't trust Apheidas, for one thing,' he had replied, 'and I will not allow him to think I've forgiven the things he did, or that my shame at being his son is in any way reduced. The answer's no, Astynome, now and every other time you ask me.'

'Then I will ask you no more,' she had said, brushing the tears from her eyes as she lay down next to him.

But as he listened to her rapid breathing gradually slow down until sleep overtook her, he knew that she was right. There was a growing sense of frustration among the ordinary Greek soldiers, bordering on open rebellion as they began to think that the war would never end and they would not see their homes and families ever again. Achilles's very presence was worth an army in itself, and now that he had gone down to the halls of Hades, the camp seemed empty and subdued. Whatever men may have thought about the ruthless Phthian and his excessive pride, none would deny that he had been the fighting soul of the army. And now that he was dead the army's hope had died with him. Despairing soldiers were daring to defy their captains, while some even deserted, preferring to brave the hostile lands about them in a hope of finding a way home than spend any more time under the doomed command of Agamemnon. On one occasion an angry mob of Cretans caught Calchas sneaking away from Agamemnon's tent and threatened to kill him unless he confessed he had lied about the war ending in the tenth year. The priest had refused and only the arrival of Agamemnon's own bodyguards saved his life. The King of Men had one of the Cretans strung up as an example to the rest of the camp and a resentful peace had followed.

But it was more than the despair of the Greeks that convinced Eperitus the war would not be won by either side. As he lay staring into the twitching shadows cast by the fire, he could not help but think of the boy soldier he had faced in the battle before the Scaean Gate. Any city that was prepared to arm children with daggers and throw them against seasoned warriors would not give in until every man who could hold a weapon was dead. And as Astynome never ceased to remind him, all the Trojans needed to do was wait behind their god-built walls until the Greeks found a way to break them down, or gave up and sailed home.

He thought of the boy again and was consoled by the knowledge that he had not killed him. Achilles would not have thought twice about hewing that young head from its shoulders in his all-consuming rampage towards glory – the same glory that Eperitus had once hankered after with all his heart. But no more. All he wanted now was to take Astynome back with him to Ithaca and let his name be preserved by their children rather than his deeds on the battlefield. He kissed her on the shoulder and lay down to sleep.

Odysseus was dreaming of Ithaca. He was in the bed he had made for Penelope and himself, with its four thick posts that rose from floor to ceiling and which were inlaid with patterns of gold, silver and ivory. One of the posts was the bole of an old olive tree that had been there before he had extended the palace, and which he had played in as a child. Staring up at the smooth ceiling, he could see the stars that had been painted there, the constellations positioned just as they had been in the month when the bedroom had been finished, forever a spring evening. And beside him he could feel the presence of his wife.

He turned to look at her. She was naked beneath the furs and in his dream he could feel the warmth emanating from her body. But her handsome features were sad and regretful.

'What is it?' he asked.

'I tried to keep the thieves from your house, Odysseus, but you were gone too long. Now Eupeithes's son is king in your place.'

'*Antinous?*' Odysseus exclaimed, propping himself up on one elbow.

'Yes, Antinous,' Penelope had replied, rolling over so that her back was turned to him. 'My new husband.'

Odysseus reached out to touch her and woke, his arm half-stretched out from beneath his furs. He pulled it back and took a deep breath, unsettled but relieved to realize it was only a dream. He stroked his beard and closed his eyes, trying to recall Penelope's face. But she was gone.

And then his senses told him he was not alone in his hut.

He flung aside his furs and leapt from his bed, reaching for the sword that hung in its scabbard from the wall above.

'That wouldn't do you any good, if I had a mind to harm you.'

He turned to see Athena, sitting in his own chair by the hearth. She was dressed in her white chiton, her shield, helmet and spear absent, and her large eyes seemed unconscious of his nakedness as they stared at him. Odysseus blinked in surprise for a moment then knelt and bowed his head.

'Am I still dreaming?' he asked, looking up slightly.

'No.'

'Then things must be coming to a climax. This is the third time you've appeared to me in just a few weeks, Mistress.'

'Come closer, Odysseus,' she commanded, rising from the chair and reaching out to take his hand. Her touch was cool and smooth, not at all human, and there was a tender, almost pitying concern in her grey eyes. 'Things are indeed coming to their end and you are likely to see more of me as this war reaches its conclusion. But – strange as it might seem to you – the plans of the gods cannot be fulfilled without human intervention.'

'Is that what brings you here from Olympus?'

She reached out and stroked his red hair. 'You haven't forgotten what I said at the river?'

'No, Mistress.'

'Good, because the time is nigh. Tomorrow, Ajax will lay claim to Achilles's armour. You must challenge him and stop him from winning it.'

Odysseus frowned and let his hand slip from hers.

'When you spoke before, I thought you meant Ajax would seek the armour by treachery. But now Achilles is dead, Ajax has a blood right to his possessions. What right do I have to make a claim?'

'Have you already forgotten Achilles's last words?'

'But Achilles thought I was the only one who had come to save him. And without Ajax's great strength his body and armour would never have been saved from the Trojans at all.'

'And did you not fight off the Trojans while he carried his cousin's corpse?' Athena said, her face growing sterner at Odysseus's protests.

Odysseus looked down at the flames.

'I did, and I don't deny part of me wants the armour, my lady. Ever since I laid eyes on it I felt the pull of its enchantment. And I haven't forgotten how Palamedes called me a poor king of a poor country, with nothing to speak of my greatness.'

'The armour would give you that,' Athena said, softly once more.

'But it's not right. The armour should go to Ajax, not me. His pride won't stand it going to someone else.'

'Do you think we immortals care what *you* think is right or wrong, Odysseus?' Athena warned him, angrily. 'Ajax will be punished for his constant blasphemies and unless you want yourself and your family to face our fury you will do as we command – and you will do it alone, without telling Eperitus or anyone else. Claim the armour and make it your own, by whatever means you can!'

As she spoke, the hearth blazed up, forcing Odysseus to shield himself from the heat. But a moment later the flames died back down, and as Odysseus took his hand from his face the goddess's harsh expression had softened again.

'There's another thing you should know. If Ajax takes the armour he will keep it to himself. But Zeus has decreed it should go to another, one even more worthy of it than Ajax. Unless that man joins the army and takes Achilles's place, Troy won't fall. And unless Troy falls, you will never see Ithaca, or Penelope, or Telemachus again. Human intervention, Odysseus.'

'But who is this man you speak of?'

Athena shook her head, her form becoming insubstantial. Like smoke in a breeze, she drifted into nothing before Odysseus's eyes.

'That will be revealed in its own time,' her fading voice replied. 'But if you want to go home, my dear Odysseus, win the armour.'

The king of Ithaca wetted his finger and held it up in the air. It was all for show, of course: the wind always blew from the north-west and he could tell its direction from the way it fanned the sweat on his naked body, not to mention the fact that the pall of smoke from Achilles's funeral pyre was trailing away towards the south-east. But the funeral games were as much a spectacle in respect of the dead as they were a competition for rich prizes and the honour they carried with them, so Odysseus went through all the required motions before the eyes of the thousands of soldiers who were crowded along the edge of the beach.

He stretched his arms behind his back, interlacing his fingers and locking his elbows so that the muscles of his back and arms tensed. After a few moments he let his arms fall to his sides and began to roll his shoulders in forward circles, loosening the muscles there while at the same time tipping his head back and closing his eyes against the bright midday sun. Finally, he placed his fists on his hips and, keeping his back straight, bent his knees several times in succession as the crowd clapped or jeered, depending on which of the competitors they supported.

His limbering-up exercises complete, he turned and raised his hand to the line of benches where the Greek leaders sat in expectation, backed by crowds of noisy soldiers. In the centre were Menelaus, Agamemnon and Nestor. Menelaus was leaning forward and chewing on a finger, while Nestor seemed distant and tired, his wise head greyer and even more bent with age since the death of Antilochus. Between them, reclining in his bulky, fur-draped throne, the King of Men's blue eyes scrutinized Odysseus with cold detachment. Then he gave a curt nod and Odysseus turned to his left.

A few paces from where he stood was a mound of earth that formed a dark circle on the white sand. The palm prints of the men who had patted it into shape were still visible, though the smooth surface had since been broken by the footmarks of the two previous contestants, Sthenelaus and Podarces. Beyond the mound was a long stretch of clear beach marked off by the mass of onlookers to the right and the line of galleys and the sea to the left. At the far end was the barrow Achilles had erected for Patroclus, with the smoking remains of Achilles's own funeral pyre tumbled and blackened before it. A large altar had been set up a little to the left, where the many animals that had been sacrificed to Achilles's memory had bathed it red with their gore and darkened the sand in a large circle around it.

But Odysseus gave no mind to these remnants of the morning's funeral. He narrowed his eyes in determination and stepped up to the mound. Eperitus, who had been standing a few paces behind, followed and handed him something dull and heavy. Odysseus took the discus in his right hand and looked down at it: a lump of cast iron, about the size of a small plate but heavy enough to strain at the hard muscles of his forearm and bicep. Nodding at Eperitus, who returned to where he had been waiting, Odysseus tipped the discus back against the heel of his thumb and gripped its lower edge with the ends of his fingers, before swinging his body round so that his weight shifted on to his right leg. Leaning forward and placing his left hand on his right knee, he began to swing the discus while using the toes of his free foot for balance. A moment later he fixed his stern gaze on the distant barrow, raised the discus as high as he could over his right shoulder, then, with a great shout, swung his body round and let go. The discus arced high and long through the air, silencing the onlookers as it spun over the stretch of naked beach, its flight seemingly interminable as it continued to rise like a bird on the wing, only reaching its zenith as it passed over the marks of Podarces and Sthenelaus before smacking the sand and bouncing on into the remains of the funeral pyre, where its long course ended in a puff of ash.

The incredulous pause that followed was quickly broken by a long roar of approval from the crowd of spectators. Even the men who had jeered him before now joined in the celebration as Odysseus raised his arms to the crowd, his bearded face broken by his beaming smile. He turned and met Eperitus's exultant embrace, and the two men were soon surrounded by a crowd of Ithacans, cheering and shouting their king's name.

'Stand aside!' ordered a booming voice. 'Or have you forgotten that I also put my name forward for this competition? The prize is not yours yet, Odysseus.'

Silence fell and every eye turned to see Great Ajax standing ankle-deep in the soft sand. He had stripped naked and was holding a large discus in his right hand. It was twice the normal size and must have been four times as heavy, but Ajax carried it with ease in his fingertips. On either side of him were Teucer and Little Ajax. The former twitched nervously as he hid in his half-brother's shadow, while the latter scowled with disdain, the snake about his shoulders hissing and flicking its forked tongue at the Ithacan king.

'Of course,' Odysseus answered, stepping down from the mound.

'That was a good throw for a short man,' Ajax said, squinting as he looked to where Odysseus's discus had landed. 'Perhaps Athena lent you her strength, as usual. But I will beat it, and without the help of any god!'

He spat on the sand and assumed the same position Odysseus had adopted, quickly swinging the discus back and forth until he felt the momentum reach its peak. Then he opened his fingers and let it go, emptying his lungs in a deafening bellow as the heavy weight went spinning high into the air. Odysseus shielded his eyes with the flat of his hand and watched it soar over the marks of the first two casts before dipping in a straight line towards Patroclus's barrow. He knew the instant it had left Ajax's hand that it would surpass his own throw, but it was with dismay that he saw it sail clean over the top of the tall mound to bury itself in the sand beyond.

Ajax ignored the roar that erupted from the ranks of the Greeks, choosing instead to turn and look triumphantly at Odysseus. Agamemnon stood and raised his sceptre in both hands over his head, keeping it there until silence had fallen.

'I announce Ajax the winner,' he called in a clear voice. 'Bring the prize.'

A group of male slaves appeared from a nearby tent, carrying three copper tripods and matching cauldrons between them. Agamemnon pointed at Ajax and the men struggled over the soft sand towards him, only for the giant warrior to give his prize a cursory glance and send the slaves in the direction of his own tents at the far end of the beach.

As if to reinforce Odysseus's humiliation, the King of Men now beckoned him forward to receive the runner-up's prize – a donkey's foal that brayed loudly as it was dragged from the tent. But before the attendant slave could hand him the rope that was tied around its neck, a commotion broke out among the crowd of soldiers. Men were pointing towards the sea and crying out in a mixture of disbelief and terror. The kings and princes, too, rose from their benches and stared in shocked awe at where the breakers of the Aegean were crashing upon the beach.

Odysseus turned and ran back down to where Eperitus and Ajax were looking in silence at the sea.

'What's happening to the water?' Ajax asked, looking confused.

Odysseus ignored him and took the cloak Eperitus was holding out to him. By now a stretch of sea beyond the black hulls of the galleys was bubbling and smoking, as if a great fire had been lit beneath the waves and the waters were boiling in agony. Then shapes began to rise up from the turbulence, liquid in form and translucent at first, but quickly changing into flesh as they caught the sunlight. To the amazement of the thousands of onlookers – and no less so to Odysseus and Eperitus, who had seen it before – the first shape took the form of a young woman as she walked up out of the sea, a golden urn held in her hands. A dozen more sea nymphs followed in her wake, all of them young, beautiful and naked, finally halting on the beach halfway between the edge of the water and the throne of Agamemnon.

'I am Thetis, mother of Achilles,' the first announced. She spoke slowly, the grief in her immortal eyes clear for all to see. 'I have brought this urn for my son's ashes, a gift for him in death from the gods who forsook him in life.'

Overcoming his initial shock, Agamemnon snapped his fingers and waved Talthybius forward. The herald approached slowly and fearfully at first, until – remembering the eyes of the Greek army were upon him and finding his courage – he reached out and took the urn from the goddess's hands. As he retreated in the direction of the funeral pyre, Agamemnon rose from his throne, took a few steps towards Thetis, then fell to his knees before her and bowed his head. With a great rustling like the wind sweeping across the canopy of a forest, the rest of the army followed his example.

'My lady, accept our condolences for the loss of your son, whose like will never be seen on this earth again. May we also offer you our gratitude for his services to the army and invite you to join us in a feast honouring you and the glorious Achilles?'

'Your words are tipped with honey, oh King of Men, but in your heart there is no grief for my son's passing. He has been a thorn in your side ever since the fleet left Aulis: always the most difficult to control, the hardest to please and the most terrible to cross. He was your best fighter, yet you and many others are relieved he is dead. Do you deny this?'

Agamemnon kept his eyes fixed on Thetis's white feet and said nothing.

'I do not condemn you, King Agamemnon, for my son was always headstrong and proud. Much though his father loved him, even Peleus was relieved when he left for this war of yours. Achilles was too much of a man to be content in peacetime and only a little less at ease in war. And yet you are a fool if you think your internal problems ended with his death. He may have passed down to the realms of the dead, but he leaves a legacy of strife behind him. Behold, Greeks, the armour of Achilles!'

Odysseus and Eperitus, along with every other man in the army, raised their heads to see that the armour was now at Thetis's side. The heavy cuirass that was the image of Achilles's muscle-bound torso stood at the centre, with the golden helmet and its flowing, blood-red plume planted in the sand before it; the ornately patterned greaves – with the shaped cup on the right greave that had failed to prevent the designs of another god penetrating Achilles's heel – lay crossed over each other to the right of the helmet; while leaning against the left side of the breastplate was the broad shield with its concentric, intricately carved circles depicting scenes of war and peace.

'The Olympians have sent me here,' Thetis continued, 'to award this armour to the bravest of the Greeks who fought before the Scaean Gate, in the battle where my son was slain. But you must decide between yourselves who was the most courageous. If any man here thinks he showed the greatest valour – or believes he is *worthy* to wear the armour of Achilles – then let him step forward to be judged by his peers under King Agamemnon!'

The challenge rolled out across the wide bay and settled on the hearts of every soldier present. For a moment, all those who had fought in the battle felt the temptation to state his claim. Even Eperitus found himself reflecting on his part in the retreat and the number of Trojans he had killed. Without him, Achilles's body would never have been brought back to the ships; surely, a smooth voice whispered in his head, he had as much right to the prize as any other man. And with a sudden greed his eyes fell on the gleaming armour at Thetis's side.

But his ardour cooled as quickly as it had gripped him. A more sobering voice had stilled his mind, telling him he would be a fool to think his part in the retreat had been greater than that of some others – and of two men in particular: Great Ajax, who had carried the heavy corpse back to the ships without any weapons to defend himself, despising all thoughts of his own danger in his desire to save his cousin's body; and Odysseus, who had fought with a fury Eperitus had never seen in the king before, throwing the Trojans back again and again with no regard for their numbers. Some had been so afraid of him that they had abandoned their arms in fear and pleaded to be spared his wrath.

The same conclusion dawned on Diomedes, Menelaus, Little Ajax and a host of others, and they lowered their eyes so that the sight of the splendid armour would not tempt them to make fools of themselves. Of all the great warriors who had taken part in the fighting, only two now rose to their feet and walked towards Thetis. Odysseus and Ajax had accepted the challenge.

Chapter Forty-Four
THE DEBATE

Thetis left her son's armour on the beach and returned to the sea. Her nymphs followed, singing a mournful dirge as the waves reabsorbed their watery bodics. Their voices were so sweet and ethereal that the Greeks were held in thrall for a long time after they had gone, their hearts torn with renewed sadness for the great Achilles. It was Agamemnon who finally broke the spell, rising from his throne and ordering the benches of the council to be formed into a circle with his own seat at its head. The awarding of the armour would be decided by a debate between the two claimants, but first he insisted that Ajax and Odysseus return to their huts and prepare themselves.

Odysseus sighed, wishing Athena had not given the task to him. After she had departed his hut he had spent the remainder of the night pondering what he had to do, knowing there was no open and honest way to prove himself more worthy of Achilles's armour than Ajax. That, of course, was exactly why the gods had chosen him: since the death of Palamedes, no one else in the army had the same instinct for trickery and cunning that would be needed for the job. But he was also concerned about how Eperitus would react. His captain's clear-cut view on what was right and what was wrong would be sorely tested, and yet Odysseus knew he would have to rely on Eperitus's witness if he was to win the debate – at least, not without resorting to baser methods. But the king had no choice in the matter, a fact that Athena had made very clear: carry out the will of the gods; intervene on their behalf, or suffer the war to continue without end, a punishment for the disobedience of mankind. He only wished she had not forbidden him to tell Eperitus.

'Why in Athena's name do you want Achilles's armour?'

Odysseus turned to see Eperitus at his shoulder, looking angry and confused.

'You heard what Achilles said to me,' Odysseus replied, hating himself for the deceit he was about to carry out. 'Besides, I *earned* it, bringing his body back to the camp. And do you remember how Palamedes called me a coward, saying I'd be a forgotten king without glory? What do you think he'd say if he saw me wearing the *armour of Achilles*, made by Hephaistos himself?'

Eperitus's eyes widened in disbelief as the king spoke, though his growing anger was not without concern at the strange shift in his friend's character.

'Listen to yourself, Odysseus! Can this really be *you* speaking? You know the armour should go to Ajax, and as for what Achilles said—'

Odysseus held up a finger.

'Enough, Eperitus. I'm going to my hut to prepare and I'm taking Omeros and Eurylochus with me. *You* are to stay here and keep a close eye on the armour – I don't trust that oaf Ajax not to come and take it while I'm gone. But listen, old friend,' he added, softening his tone and putting his hands on Eperitus's shoulders. 'I'm serious about winning this debate, and I want you to witness for me. Can I count on you?'

Eperitus's eyes narrowed.

'You know I'll always serve your best interests,' he answered.

When Odysseus returned it was to find Ajax already there, standing Titan-like before the ranks of seated warriors with Teucer and Little Ajax standing at his shoulders. His massive fists were balled up on his hips and he looked for every man on the beach as if the armour were already his. Odysseus entered the circle of benches where the Council of Kings was ready to sit in judgment, wearing a plain tunic and the faded purple cloak Penelope had given him at their parting on Ithaca ten years before. He had always scorned fine clothes and decorative armour in a debate, feeling they were the cheap tricks of lesser men, hoping to awe their audience with a show of wealth and power, rather than winning them over by the skill of their argument.

The two warriors stood almost shoulder to shoulder before the King of Men, who kept them waiting – along with the council and the rest of the army – while he spoke in low tones with Nestor and Menelaus. Ajax crossed his hands over the small of his back and looked at Odysseus from the corner of his eye.

'What are you hoping to gain by this, Odysseus?' he whispered. 'If you wanted something from me, you know all you needed to do was ask. But challenging my claim—'

'I have a right to the armour, too.'

'Is it because I beat you in the discus throw? Or are you just trying to antagonize me? Because if you are, you're succeeding. But if you drop your claim now I'll think none the worse of you.'

Odysseus looked up at the towering form of Ajax, catching his fierce eye.

'I don't have that choice, Ajax. And if I lose your friendship over this, then I'm sorry.'

Ajax glared back at him, then began rocking on his heels, making his impatience obvious to Agamemnon as he fidgeted and blew through his teeth. That he was the greatest fighter in the whole Greek alliance could no longer be disputed since the death of Achilles, and if the King of Men's decision was to be based on fighting prowess alone then the victory would doubtless be his. But Odysseus had two assets that Ajax had not – his shrewd intelligence and his voice. The eventual owner of Achilles's armour would not be decided in battle, but by argument and counter-argument. And as the bloated sun shimmered above the distant edge of the ocean, the contest was wide open.

Finally, the whispered discussion between the three kings ended and Agamemnon turned to Ajax and Odysseus. Sliding his left ankle up on to his right knee, he leaned back and placed a thoughtful finger to his lips.

'Of all the men in this army,' he began, 'there are few I rely on for counsel and strength in battle as much as you two. But only one of you can win this debate and claim the armour of Achilles; the loser, I fear, will regard the other with jealousy and even animosity. For it *is* a glorious prize, the likes of which no man has been tempted with for many generations. So, for the sake of our greater goal – the defeat and sack of Troy – I ask you to relinquish your claims and forsake this divisive contest before it begins.'

'I will not surrender my right to the armour,' Ajax announced, glaring at the King of Men. 'Achilles was my cousin. I was as close a kinsman to him as any here, and that alone would raise my claim above all others.' He glanced sidelong at Odysseus, then, unclasping his hands from behind his back, stepped forward and punched a finger towards Agamemnon. 'But I make no blood claim on his armour. I don't *need* to. Thetis said it should be awarded to the most courageous of the Greeks who fought before the Scaean Gate, and that man is me!'

There was a rumble of approval from the seated ranks of the army, but Odysseus showed no sign of doubt or fear. Agamemnon sighed and leaned back in his gold-plated throne.

'And what evidence do you have to back your statement?' he asked in a calm voice.

'What *evidence*?' Ajax exclaimed. He turned and looked at the faces of the seated kings and leaders. 'What evidence, he asks. Well, perhaps, my lord, you were too far back in the ranks to notice that *I* have been in the front line of every battle we have fought since arriving in this accursed land. I can't even begin to count the Trojans I've killed, and if I listed the names of the noblemen who've fallen to my spear then we would be here until long after the moon has risen.

'But I *know* you were there, my lord Agamemnon, when I

fought Hector to a standstill on the slopes above the Scamander. As was Odysseus, who said nothing when Hector challenged us to offer up a champion. No, it was left to me on that occasion. And where were you when the Trojans breached the walls and attacked the ships, Odysseus? I didn't see you when I was fighting them off from the prows of the galleys, because *you* were skulking in Agamemnon's tent with a mere flesh wound! Am I wrong?'

Odysseus looked briefly down at his feet as he composed himself, then placed his hands carefully on his hips and shook his head.

'You know you're wrong, Ajax. We all do. I was neither skulking, nor was it just a flesh wound that kept me from the struggle. While you were fighting a losing battle, hoping that brawn alone could hold back the victorious Trojans, I was convincing Patroclus to put on Achilles's armour and lead the Myrmidons into the attack. While your muscles were saving a single galley, my brains were saving the whole army.'

He spoke calmly, without anger or mockery, and in a tone that convinced every listener of the truth of what he was saying. There were nods and murmurs among the crowd of onlookers as men accepted his argument, only surprised they had not realized it before.

'I've done my fair share of fighting, too,' Odysseus continued. 'I've been in as many battles as you have, Ajax, and more. Where were you when Achilles and I captured Lyrnessus, Adramyttium and Thebe, for instance?' Ajax opened his mouth to protest, but Odysseus held up a finger to silence him. 'Save your objections; I don't deny you've killed more Trojans than I have and could probably recount each of their names one after another until the cock crows. But there's much more to war than blind savagery, and not least for those of us who have the privilege of command. *We* must be in the forefront of every battle or risk losing the respect of our men, but we must also have an eye on the greater goals. And in that I surpass you, Ajax. What were you doing when the army was close to mutiny during the winter months? Well, while you practised your discus throwing with Achilles, I was suggesting the attacks on Lyrnessus, Adramyttium and Thebe to keep the army busy and to bring in some much-needed loot, not to mention cutting Troy's supplies from the south. And I was the one who thought up a way to defeat the Amazons. Without me, Ajax, the best men in Greece – yourself included – would have been dead on the plains with poisoned arrows peppering their rotting corpses, while the rest of the army sailed back home in defeat.'

Ajax spat on the sand.

'Words and tricks – is that all you have to boast of, Odysseus? When all's said and done, a man's courage and honour is determined by his performance in battle; *courage* is the measure by which Achilles's armour will be awarded, and in that *I* surpass *you*! Was it intelligence and cunning that carried the body of Achilles out of the clutches of the Trojans and all the way back here, in spite of their countless spears and arrows? Of course not – it was the strength and bravery of Ajax, son of Telamon!'

His words were greeted by a rumble of approval from the army crowded about the circle of benches.

'And was it my intelligence and cunning that covered your back as you carried Achilles?' Odysseus replied, turning to look his opponent in the eye. 'No, it was my courage and skill that saved you, Ajax. Without me you wouldn't even have reached the fords of the Scamander. My bravery is a match for yours and you know it!'

'By Ares's sword!' Ajax snapped. 'If you hadn't have been there, Odysseus, I would have fought the Trojans with one hand and dragged Achilles's body back to the ships with the other.'

'The armour should be given to Ajax!' Little Ajax shouted, raising his arms in the air. 'Odysseus is nothing but a clever fraud. Award the armour to Ajax!'

Suddenly knots of men stood and began to cheer and shout Ajax's name. Odysseus recognized them as a mixture of Locrians and Ajax's own men, who had been deliberately spread out among the army. But they were quickly joined by others and soon almost every man was on his feet and roaring approval for Ajax. At last the chanting died away as the heralds persuaded and cajoled the dense ranks to sit back down in the sand.

'You've heard what Odysseus and I have to say, my lord,' Ajax said, turning to Agamemnon with a triumphant smile. 'And you've heard what the army thinks. Now it's time to make your decision—'

'Not quite,' Odysseus interrupted. 'There's one other opinion that should be heard, an opinion more important than either mine, Ajax's, or even that of the whole army.'

Agamemnon narrowed his eyes at Odysseus, then slowly scanned the circle of benches. Complete silence had fallen as the vast audience waited in expectation.

'Whose?' Agamemnon asked after no one else had stepped forward.

'The opinion of Achilles himself.'

'Achilles?' exclaimed Ajax. 'What nonsense is this? Can you conjure up the dead now, Odysseus?'

Odysseus took a step closer to Agamemnon.

'When Achilles fell, Eperitus and I were the first to reach him. I took his head in my lap and tried to comfort him as the fear of death settled upon him. Then he clutched at me and asked that I hear his final words. I bent my ear to his mouth.'

The faces of the council were rapt in awe as Odysseus paused for effect, each of them clearly desperate to know what Achilles's final words had been. Even Ajax was staring wide-eyed and dumbfounded as Odysseus brushed away a dramatic tear. Words and tricks, Ajax had sneered; but words and tricks were going to steal the armour of Achilles from his fingertips. The king of Ithaca looked up and scanned the faces of the waiting audience.

'He pulled me near with the last of his strength and whispered these words: "To you, Odysseus, I bequeath my glorious armour, to be worn honourably as a token of my gratitude." As Athena is my witness, I swear this was his last wish. But don't take my word for it. Ask Eperitus.'

There was uproar. Men of every rank suddenly began talking at the same time, their exclamations of disbelief and shock growing increasingly louder as they shouted to be heard. And as more and more turned to face Eperitus, Odysseus looked at his friend and saw the doubt and internal debate reflected in his eyes.

'Silence!' Agamemnon bellowed, standing and raising his golden staff above his head. The babble of voices fell away. 'This contest is not decided yet. If your claim is true, Odysseus, the armour of Achilles is yours. But first I must have confirmation from Eperitus.'

Ajax, who had been aghast and speechless up to that point, stepped forward.

'No! Eperitus is Odysseus's man. He will say whatever Odysseus wants him to say.'

'Eperitus is a man of honour,' Agamemnon countered, turning his cold blue eyes on the Ithacan. 'I will take him at his word. Tell us truthfully and on your oath, Eperitus: did Achilles promise Odysseus his armour?'

Eperitus looked at Odysseus, then raised himself slowly to his feet.

'It's true, Achilles did confer his armour on Odysseus,' he admitted. 'But those were *not* his last words. "To be worn honourably as a token of my gratitude," he said, "*for of all the Greeks, you alone have come to my aid.*" He uttered this with his final breath, unaware that Ajax was fighting off the Trojans only a few paces away.'

Eperitus dropped back down on the bench and put his head in his hands, just as all around him every other member of the council leapt to their feet and began to shout again. But this time they were not calling out in shock or disbelief. Now they were hurling curses and accusations at the king of Ithaca, while Odysseus stood in the eye of the storm staring at his captain. Had Eperitus told the truth to uphold his own sense of honour, or was he doing what he thought was best for his king? Odysseus knew it was the latter, and he did not blame him.

'Shut *up*, damn you all!' Menelaus yelled.

When the voices showed no sign of abating, he pointed to Talthybius, who raised a horn to his lip and blew. Once again a reluctant silence fell over the debate.

'Then the judgment has yet to be made,' Ajax declared. 'Come, Agamemnon, you've seen the trickery and deceit this man is capable of. Make your decision and make it quickly.'

Agamemnon sat back down and shook his head.

'I've a mind to bury this cursed armour along with Achilles's ashes in that barrow, where it can't cause any more trouble.'

'And have some grave robber steal it when the war has ended and we've all sailed home?' Odysseus replied. 'That would be folly indeed. But I've another suggestion, if you'll hear it. Ajax and I have proved ourselves equal in our valour: but if you want to know who was the most courageous, then ask the Trojans we fought. Let them decide between us.'

'A fair proposal,' Agamemnon said. 'What do you say, Ajax?'

Ajax gave a surly nod and Talthybius was sent with an armed escort to fetch a dozen of the men who had been captured during the retreat from the Scaean Gate. It was not long before Talthybius returned, followed by a procession of bruised and dishevelled-looking Trojans with their wrists bound together by leather cords. Most were tired old men or frightened lads, and without their armour and weapons they looked little better than a band of slaves. Only three had the demeanour of true warriors, their bodies marked with old battle scars and their eyes proud and still belligerent. It was one of these that Agamemnon beckoned forward.

'What's your name?' he asked in the Trojan tongue.

'Lethos, son of Thymoites.'

'You fought in the battle by the Scaean Gate?'

'I fought by the Gate, my lord, where Achilles was killed. And then I joined the pursuit of your army across the plain.'

'Where you surrendered your arms and your honour,' Agamemnon non replied, a hint of stiffness in his voice. 'I want you and

GLYN ILIFFE

your countrymen to answer a simple question. Reply truthfully and you will enjoy meat and wine for a month, instead of bread and water. Do you speak Greek?'

Lethos nodded.

'Then tell us who the Trojans fear most among the Greeks,' Ajax demanded, towering over the man.

Lethos looked up at the giant warrior, then about at the faces of the rest of the council. He walked back to join his comrades and spoke with them in whispers, before returning to stand between Agamemnon and Ajax.

'I know you, my lord. Many times I have seen you in battle, killing without mercy or prejudice. I also saw you carry away the body of the Butcher – Achilles – as strong and tireless as an ox. Yes, the name of King Ajax is well known and greatly feared in Troy.'

Ajax gave a satisfied nod and looked at Agamemnon. 'You hear? I am the one they fear the most. Give the armour to me.'

'Your pardon, my lord,' Lethos interrupted, narrowing his eyes determinedly while taking a step back. 'We were not asked who we feared the most, but who fought with the greatest courage at the Gate. Though you proved your strength, there was another who wrought havoc among our ranks, killing Trojans by the dozen and preventing us in our fury from capturing Achilles's body. He was the man who captured me, and he is standing there.'

The assembly erupted in uproar once more as he pointed at Odysseus, but another blast on Talthybius's horn brought silence.

'Then the matter is decided,' Agamemnon declared. 'Talthybius, take these men back and give them meat and wine. Odysseus, come forward and claim what is yours. But first I insist that you and Ajax take oaths of friendship to each other . . .'

'*Friendship?*' Ajax boomed. 'With a liar and a cheat? No, not I! Take your armour, Odysseus, and wear it with a fool's pride. You may have frightened these Trojan women into choosing you, but I tell you now that armour will never bring you glory. As far as I'm concerned, it will be a mark of shame. May it be your downfall!'

He spat in the sand at Odysseus's feet then stormed past him, shoving aside Idomeneus and Sthenelaus and kicking over one of the benches before forcing a passage through the packed soldiers beyond. On the opposite side of the circle, Eperitus rose heavily and slipped away into the crowd, unable to watch as Odysseus stepped forward to claim the armour of Achilles.

'What will you do now?'

Eperitus turned to see Arceisius following him, an anxious look on his ruddy face.

'I can't stay here, that's for sure. I told the truth before the council, thinking I was saving Odysseus from his own folly, and then Agamemnon awarded him the armour anyway.'

'You only did what you thought was right.'

'I *betrayed* him! Perhaps all that's left to me now is to get a horse and ride south, possibly find a ship back to Greece.'

'And Astynome?'

Eperitus looked at Arceisius. In his shame at his disloyalty he had not thought about the woman he loved. Just then, Omeros appeared.

'What is it?' Eperitus snapped, annoyed by the concern on the young bard's face.

'I just wanted to say you were right to tell the truth back there, sir.'

Eperitus felt a sudden stab of guilt. He looked at Omeros and shrugged his shoulders.

'Was I? Or am I just letting my foolish sense of honour get in the way again? And how have I profited from it? The greatest friendship I've ever had is over and I'm back where I was twenty years ago – an outcast without anywhere to call home. Perhaps it's the judgment of the gods upon me that he was awarded the armour fairly in the end, without resort to lies or trickery.'

'But he wasn't, sir,' Omeros said, shaking his head.

'What do you mean?'

'You remember Eurybates and I accompanied him to his hut? Well, it wasn't the only place we visited. After he'd bathed and dressed we went to those old cattle pens where they keep prisoners before they're sold or exchanged. He told them they might be called upon to say who they thought was the bravest Greek, and promised to release them if they chose him.'

Eperitus looked at him with disbelieving eyes. 'Then the whole debate was a fraud from beginning to end.'

'But *why*?' Arceisius asked. 'Why would Odysseus dishonour himself for the sake of another man's armour? I don't understand.'

'I think do,' Eperitus answered. He paused to collect his thoughts, then looked at his companions. 'Somehow, Odysseus believes the armour of Achilles will give him the glory he lacks. But, more than anything, it's the war itself. It's sucking the humanity out of all of us. Look what it did to Achilles and what it's doing to Ajax. And me, too – I've been so full of my own pride I haven't realized the people I care most about are being destroyed. But it's in my power to change it, and by all the gods on Olympus I'm *going* to!'

'But how?'

'Never mind, Arceisius. I'm leaving the army – I've no choice about that anyway – but I'm not heading south. There's something else I need to do, but you and Omeros have to delay Odysseus while I escape.'

'I'm coming with you.'

Eperitus looked at his friend and smiled. For a moment he recalled the first time he had seen him, twenty years ago on Ithaca: he had been a young shepherd boy then, but now he was a veteran warrior with responsibilities to his king.

'No, Arceisius. When this war's over you have a wife to go back to on Ithaca, and what's more you're no longer my squire. You haven't been for a long time now. Your place is to serve Odysseus, and the best way you can perform your duty is to keep him away from the Ithacan camp until I'm gone.'

He slapped Arceisius on the shoulder, nodded to Omeros, then turned and disappeared among the hundreds of soldiers still lingering on the beach. When he reached his own hut it was to find Astynome busy cooking a delicious-smelling stew for their evening meal. She walked over to embrace him, but he slipped away from her fingertips and ran over to the table where his armaments were laid out.

'What's the matter?' she asked, her beautiful face suddenly anxious as she came over to help him with the buckles of his leather cuirass.

'Never mind me. Put your sandals and cloak on. We're leaving at once.'

She looked at him, momentarily confused, then without further question lifted the stew off the flames and did as she was instructed. Within moments they were ready – Eperitus fully armed with his spear and grandfather's shield, Astynome in her plain travel-cloak with the hood thrown over her black hair. As they left the hut and saw the bands of purple, vermilion and red filling the sunset sky, she turned and placed her hands on Eperitus's shoulders.

'Stop, now. Tell me where we are going or I refuse to take another step.'

'Then I'll carry you!'

She ducked away from him and held up an admonishing finger.

'Tell me, Eperitus. I won't resist or question you, I just want to know.'

Eperitus took a deep breath and looked around himself. The Ithacan soldiers were returning from the debate in twos or threes and had already set about making fires and preparing their evening meal. There was a jovial mood about them, pleased at Odysseus's success. But there was no sign of the king.

'I'm leaving the army for good.'

'Leaving Odysseus?'

'Yes, and you're coming with me – at least to the camp gates.'

Astynome frowned. 'And beyond the gates?'

'We'll take a couple of horses and then I want you to ride back to Troy.'

'Not without you.'

'Only for a short time, then we can be together for good. I want you to find my father and tell him to meet me at the temple of Thymbrean Apollo at midnight. No more questions now. Let's go.'

They turned and headed up the slope towards the walls that protected the camp. As they left, Eurylochus stepped out from behind the corner of the hut, where he had been listening to every hushed word of the conversation. He smiled to himself and slipped off to find Odysseus.

Chapter Forty-Five
THE MADNESS OF AJAX

'Who's the woman, Eperitus?'

Diocles and the other guards swung the gates open as Eperitus and Astynome approached.

'A friend of mine,' he replied, slapping Astynome's backside so that the Spartans understood what he meant. Astynome shot him a glance from beneath her hood but said nothing. 'I'm taking her back to her father's farm. I pay well for his goods and I wouldn't want them to get lost.'

'No, I'm sure you wouldn't,' Diocles said, eyeing the fine figure beneath the cloak. 'Are his goods for sale to anyone else?'

'You'll find my father's "goods" are very picky, Greek!' Astynome snapped.

'She's just as fiery in bed,' Eperitus added, holding up his hand apologetically as Diocles's face suddenly darkened. 'If the Trojan men had her temper they'd have beaten us years ago.'

Diocles's frown receded a little, while behind him the other guards laughed and jeered at him.

'Well, just you make sure you escort her out of the camp every time she visits, because if I catch her I might just have to teach her some manners.'

Eperitus smiled and gave a tug on his horse's reins, leading it over the causeway towards the open plain. Astynome followed, pulling her smaller mount behind her. The sky above them was already a deep blue and marked with a smattering of early stars.

The mountains in the east had darkened to a jagged line of black peaks against the horizon.

'Couldn't you have thought of something better to say?' Astynome berated him as they moved out of earshot. 'I'm no prostitute and I don't like being compared to one.'

Eperitus did not reply. The charade at the gate over, his heart was heavy again and his mind filled with dark thoughts. The only comfort was the presence of Astynome – despite her temporary exasperation – and he tried to distract himself by thinking of the rest of his life spent with her. Then his sharp ears caught footsteps following behind and he turned to see a familiar figure coming towards them in the dusky half-light.

'Arceisius! What are you doing here?'

'Where are you going, Eperitus? I think you should tell me.'

'I can't stay with the army.'

'You're going to Troy with Astynome, aren't you?'

There was a strange look in Arceisius's eye, as if he knew the truth but could not bring himself to believe it. Eperitus hesitated, not knowing how to answer.

'Yes, he is,' Astynome answered, reaching out and placing a calming hand on Arceisius's upper arm.

'I'm going to end the war, Arceisius. I'm going to meet my father in the temple of Thymbrean Apollo—'

'Your *father*!'

'Yes. He says he can bring peace and I'm willing to give him a chance. I don't think he's acting on behalf of Priam, but peace is peace and I'm at the point where I'll take it in any form it's offered.'

Eperitus crouched beside Astynome's horse with his hands cupped together. Astynome stepped on to his crossed fingers and mounted.

'But you hate Apheidas,' Arceisius continued. 'You've hated him for as long as I've known you. And now you're betraying Odysseus for his sake? How can you, after all you and Odysseus have been through together?'

'You can call me a traitor if you wish, Arceisius, but I'm doing this for Odysseus's sake, and for Astynome's. Do you think I'd ever give up my honour for personal gain?' He mounted his horse and took the reins, turning the beast to face Arceisius. 'My honour is everything I've ever had, but if I can stop this war by surrendering it, then it'll be worthwhile. Odysseus needs to get back to Ithaca before he loses all trace of who he really is; and I'll not have Astynome raped or worse if the Greeks ever succeed in taking Troy.'

Suddenly the point of Arceisius's sword was pressed against his stomach, just beneath the line of his cuirass.

'I won't let you go, Eperitus. You're ill – a fever or something – but whatever it is, you're not yourself. You're not thinking clearly.'

'My thoughts are clearer than they've ever been, my friend. For years all I've wanted is glory and honour, and all it's ever brought me has been pain and loss. And I believe my father has changed, too. He regrets the past, I'm certain of it, and I'm going to give him the chance to redeem himself. So if you want to stop me, you're going to have to kill me.'

There was a pause, broken only by the flapping of the north wind in their cloaks. Then Arceisius withdrew his sword and slipped it back into its scabbard.

'Go then, traitor. And may the gods forgive you.'

Ajax sat hunched up on a boulder on the northernmost slopes of the bay. The myriad stars above him seemed to be reflected in the camp below, where thousands of fires guttered and glimmered in the breeze from the sea. The dark, countless shapes of the galleys stood out against the grey of the beach, where their high sterns were lapped by the moon-brushed breakers of the Aegean, charging and retreating again and again across the sand. The roaring of the waves that had hushed the dreams of every Greek for ten years seemed suddenly fresh and soothing to Ajax as he sat with whetstone in hand, repeatedly sweeping it across the blade of the sword Hector had given him after their duel, so many weeks before. All around him were the vast herds of sheep, goats, cattle and oxen that fed the Greek army. They had settled for the night and were lying close to each other for warmth, filling the air with the pungent smell of their bodies. Occasionally a beast would stir, causing a chain reaction of shifting and bleating, but Ajax took no notice of them. Instead, he kept scraping his whetstone over the gleaming blade and staring down at the grey mass of Agamemnon's tent.

A large fire burned on the sand nearby, sending a column of spark-filled smoke into the air. Black outlines could be seen against the flames, busy jointing and carving up a score of carcasses for the feast that was taking place inside. Every king, prince and captain in the army had been invited to celebrate the end of the official mourning period for Achilles; all of the chief Greeks would be inside, cramming food into their mouths as if Achilles had never existed. But for Ajax, the mourning period was not yet over. When the messenger had arrived with Agamemnon's invitation, Ajax had refused even to acknowledge his presence. How dare Agamemnon ask him to attend his banquet after he had denied him Achilles's armour, which was his by blood right *and* by right of the fact that he was the greatest warrior in the whole army? And no doubt Menelaus, Nestor and the others would all be there to gloat over his defeat! They hated him to a man, jealous of his strength and ferocity in battle, and the fact that he had always covered himself in greater glory than the rest of them combined. What was worse, he could not stand the thought of being in the presence of Odysseus, who would doubtless be showing off Achilles's armour and taking every opportunity to remind Ajax of his victory. A victory for injustice and nothing more.

Ajax swiped the whetstone over the blade one final time, then returned it to the small leather pouch that hung from his belt. He held the sword up and watched the faint light of the full moon cascade down its length. It was a good sword and a far greater token of glory than the armour Odysseus had been awarded, for at least Hector had given it to him in honour of his fighting prowess. Now he would use both sword and prowess to show the rest of the Greeks that he was not to be dismissed lightly or made a mockery of. He slid down from the rock and strode determinedly through the long grass, an angry sneer contorting his features.

'If you go down to that tent, Ajax, I promise you it will end in disaster.'

Ajax spun round to see a young shepherd sitting on the boulder he had just vacated. He was as tall as Ajax, but white-skinned and of slender build. His hair shone like silver in the moonlight and he stared at Ajax with large grey eyes that seemed wise and ageless and yet filled with energy and laughter. In his right hand was a tall crook and over his left arm was draped a fleece of silvery wool.

'Who are you?' Ajax demanded. 'Where did you spring from?'

'Come now,' the shepherd replied, 'don't you recognize an immortal when you see one? You may grudge our help in battle, son of Telamon – always reluctant to share your glory – but you still honour us with sacrifices. Only the other day you offered me a bullock . . .'

'Mistress Athena!' Ajax exclaimed, bowing his head and dropping on to one knee. 'Forgive my slowness.'

'And where are you off to on this fine evening, Ajax?'

Ajax stared at the ground, glad the goddess could not see the guilt written on his features. 'To . . . to Agamemnon's tent. There's a feast.'

'A good idea. Best not to let your anger fester – speak with the King of Men and Odysseus, let them know you bear them no ill will. But give me Hector's sword first. I will take it back to your hut for you.'

'I'd rather not, Mistress.'

'I see,' said Athena, though she had seen all along. 'Then you're set on teaching Agamemnon and Odysseus a lesson, and perhaps a few of the others too, in your anger.'

'Yes,' Ajax answered, raising his angry eyes to the goddess.

'Yes! They humiliated me in front of the whole army and I can't stand it. I won't stand it!'

'Don't blame Agamemnon or Odysseus, or even the Trojan prisoners. Blame yourself, Ajax! You have insulted the gods too many times. Do you think we have turned a blind eye to your proud insolence? Well, we haven't. It was Zeus's will that Achilles's armour was given to Odysseus – not for anything Odysseus has done, but to punish you. And if you continue on this course you're planning, then the vengeance of the gods will be complete.'

'Then let Zeus strike me down!'

'No, Ajax. You have lived your life without our help, so let your demise be in the same manner. But I have come to tell you it is not too late. You have your admirers on Olympus, myself among them. Beg our forgiveness and mend your ways and all may yet be well with you. Don't forget your wife and child . . .'

'It's for their sake I have to do this,' Ajax retorted. 'I will not have Eurysaces bullied by other children because his father let himself be mocked by lesser men. And if the gods are against me in this, then *curse* the gods!'

Athena slid down from the rock and faced him.

'Poor fool,' she said, and struck him over the forehead with her crook.

When Ajax came to it was with a pounding headache and blurred vision. He looked up and saw the stars were somehow distorted, as if he were viewing them through a glass. He closed his eyes and rubbed at them with his knuckles, until slowly he felt the thickness in his head pass. When he looked at the stars again he could see them clearly and noticed they had barely moved in their stations, telling him he had only blacked out for a short time. He looked around for Athena, but there was no sign of her and he concluded he must have been dreaming. Then, with a sudden resurgence in his appetite for revenge, he slipped Hector's sword from its scabbard and set off down the slope.

Four guards stood at the entrance to the tent, their ceremonial armour gleaming orange in the light of the nearby fire. A few paces away were a dozen or so slaves, busily preparing food and wine to supply the feast inside the vast pavilion. The noise of it was spilling out through the different entrances, along with the sounds of a lyre, drunken singing and the playful laughter of women.

The guards were chatting idly among themselves and only saw the glimmer of Ajax's sword when it was too late. The first fell to his knees with the point in his throat, before keeling over without a sound. Another had his neck sliced almost clean through so that his helmeted head hung down over his back. The last two ran into each other in their panic and fell across one of the guy ropes. Ajax finished them quickly, then turned to face three slaves who were running towards him with torches and carving knives. Despite their bravery they were no match for Ajax's strength and skill and soon all three of them lay dying in pools of their own blood; the others ran off among the tents, thinking only of saving their own miserable lives.

Ajax saw the blood on his sword and grinned to himself. Behind him, the sound of music and singing seemed to grow louder as the revellers remained ignorant of the threat that was but a moment away from bringing murder and destruction into their midst. He edged closer and for some reason was reminded of the time when he had first entered the great hall at Sparta and staked his claim on Helen. There had been a fight on that occasion, too, though a ban on weapons had saved many men their lives.

Suddenly a man came staggering out of the tent, pulling up his tunic and looking for a place to urinate. Ajax recognized him as Peisandros, one of the Myrmidon captains.

'Ajax,' he said, focusing drunken eyes on the giant figure before him.

Then his gaze fell to the pile of bodies. A moment later Ajax's sword was in his heart and his corpse dropped to the ground. Ajax stepped across him and pushed open the large canvas flap.

The scene inside was one he had witnessed many times before. Slaves carried platters of meat and kraters of wine to tables that were already overflowing with food and drink. High-born warriors from every city across Greece sat arm in arm on long benches, singing loudly and tonelessly. Girls in varying states of undress floated here and there like bees, drifting from one lap to another. Every leader in the army was present, along with their captains and favourites, all of them roaring drunk and only sitting because they were too intoxicated to stand. And there, against the west wall of the tent, were Agamemnon and Odysseus, seated next to each other like gods presiding over an Olympian wedding. As Ajax had expected, Odysseus was wearing Achilles's breastplate and greaves, with the shield and helmet at the side of his heavy wooden chair.

At first no one seemed to notice Ajax, despite his vast size and the sword in his hand dripping gore on the fleece below. Then a half-naked slave girl leapt from the lap of Menelaus and screamed, pointing at the blood-spattered newcomer. With three giant strides, Ajax crossed the floor of the tent and hewed her pretty head from its body. The screaming – along with the music and singing – stopped, only to be followed by a new cacophony of terrified shouts and the crash of overturned chairs and tables as people ran to the door of the tent.

But Ajax was quicker than all of them and, turning, began to lay about himself with Hector's sword. The first to fall were the slaves, herded before their masters like sheep. The unfortunate bard was among them, holding up his lyre for protection; Ajax's sword smashed through it with ease and opened up the man's chest and stomach, spilling his intestines over the luxurious rugs below. Then Sthenelaus, Diomedes's companion, attacked Ajax with a carving knife and was killed by a thrust through the heart. In his rage, Diomedes picked up a table and charged at Ajax, but the giant warrior knocked it away with a swing of his arm and sliced his obsessively sharpened sword down into Diomedes's skull. His death shocked the other kings, who turned to the walls of the tent and began to arm themselves with the trophies Agamemnon had taken from the Trojans he had killed. But Ajax was no longer concerned with fighting battles and winning glory: he wanted to avenge himself in the blood of the men who had forsaken him, and he fell on them with the full might of his wrath. Menestheus's arm was severed as he charged at Ajax with a spear; next Idomeneus fell, his throat opened neatly so that he dropped to the floor and poured a dark mass of blood over the heaped furs and fleeces. Many others followed, and as their bodies piled up, someone slashed open the opposite wall of the tent and sent the remaining slaves to fetch help. Then, from the ranks of the leaders – who were too proud and foolish to flee – Teucer and Little Ajax stepped forward with their hands raised. Ajax was shocked to see them there at first, but as they began to plead with him to come to his senses he realized they had betrayed him and had gone over to Agamemnon. He leapt at them in a fury and plunged his sword into his namesake first, who screamed loudly as his soul was torn from his body. Teucer followed, stabbed through the back as he turned to run. Suddenly, Ajax caught the gleam of a blade as a figure lunged at him from his right. He turned instinctively, recognized the squat, muscular figure of Odysseus, and knocked the sword from his hand before striking his attacker over the head with the pommel of his own weapon.

Now the others rushed at him as one and Ajax demonstrated to them their folly in not awarding Achilles's armour to him. Limbs and heads were parted from torsos in a blood-drenched rage as Hector's sword carried out the task it had been created for – to slay the enemies of Troy. Last to fall was Menelaus, who had robbed Ajax of Helen twenty years before – another great injustice that he had not been able to avenge because of the oath Odysseus had tricked the other suitors into swearing. He delivered a wound to Menelaus's stomach and as he pleaded for mercy, Ajax smiled and asked him who he thought was the greatest of the Greeks now, before sinking the point of his sword into the Spartan king's throat.

A sound from the shadows at the back of the tent made him turn. In the flickering glow from the hearth, Ajax could see the King of Men standing there with his hands held out like a suppliant pleading for mercy. A soothing smile was on his lips, but his cold blue eyes were full of fear.

'Ajax, I've changed my mind,' he said, his voice shaking. 'Achilles's armour was always meant to be yours, your skill here tonight has proved that beyond doubt.'

'You've had your chance to make the right decision, King of Men,' Ajax sneered. 'But you chose the wrong man and now *I* have come to collect what is rightfully mine. Your pleading and grovelling is meaningless. All your allies are dead. Your great expedition is over. And now *you* will die.'

Agamemnon dropped the shield and made a sudden dart for the entrance. Ajax ran to intercept him but the Mycenaean king was too quick, reaching the gore-spattered canvas flap while Ajax was still on the other side of the hearth. Then, as he tore the flap open, he slipped on the spilled intestines of the dead bard and fell. Squirming on to his back, Agamemnon looked up and saw Ajax towering over him, a vengeful grin on his brutish face as he hacked his sword down through his neck and decapitated him. But Ajax was not satisfied with merely killing the king; reaching down and seizing his jaw he pulled the mouth open and pushed the point of his sword inside. A moment later, the tongue that had awarded the armour of Achilles to Odysseus was in Ajax's fingers. The king of Salamis held it above his head and laughed joyously, before turning and tossing it into the flames of the hearth. The fire fizzled gratefully.

Ajax's eyes now fell on Odysseus, who was groaning as he returned to consciousness. Hanging from one of the posts that held the high roof of the tent up was a halter that Agamemnon used to train his horses. Ajax grabbed this and strode over to the king of Ithaca. Unbuckling the bronze breastplate, he lifted the two halves away from Odysseus's torso then seized the hem of the tunic beneath and tore it open.

'What are you doing?' Odysseus grunted, still groggy from the blow to his head. 'Don't you realize this is madness?'

Ajax raised the halter over his head then brought it down with terrible force across Odysseus's exposed back. He cried out in pain. Another blow followed, then another.

'Stop! This is all madness.'

'This isn't madness, Odysseus. This is *revenge*!'

'No,' Odysseus bit back, staring up at his attacker. 'This *is* madness. The gods have robbed you of your wits, Ajax. Look about yourself.'

Ajax raised his eyes to the carnage he had wreaked in the tent. Bodies and parts of bodies lay everywhere. The walls glowed red in the flames for a moment, and then faded away like a sea mist in a morning breeze. He looked up and saw that the roof of the tent was gone and he was staring instead at the full moon, drifting over a bank of thin cloud and surrounded by dim stars. His mouth opened a little and then, reluctantly at first, he lowered his gaze again and saw that he was back on the slopes overlooking the bay. The fires still burned below and there, dominating the centre of the camp, was Agamemnon's tent. Sounds of feasting and music were carried up to him on the night air and he knew at once that the slaughter he had caused there had been but a figment of his disturbed mind. And yet he could still feel the sticky blood in the palm of his hand as it gripped the sword, and still more blood between his fingers. He held up his hands and saw they were covered in gore to his biceps.

'What have I done?' he whispered to himself, dropping the sword.

But instead of the clang of metal on hard earth, the heavy weapon fell on something soft. Ajax looked down and saw the sword lying across the bodies of two rams. One lay dead without a mark on its body, while the other had been decapitated and its fleece was drenched in its own blood; the head was nearby with its tongue lying beside it. All around were the bodies of sheep, goats and cattle, their moon-silvered cadavers heaped one upon another, score upon score all across the upper slope, drenching the parched grass with their dark blood. Ajax groaned and slumped to his knees, burying his head in his red hands as warm tears flooded his

closed eyelids. A feeling of deep shame settled over him, pressing
him down into the soft fleece of one of the butchered rams.

'Wretched, proud fool. I thought I would teach Agamemnon
and the others a lesson, but instead I have been the pupil of the
gods. They've shown me my true self – an insolent brute and a
man without honour.'

He raised his bloodstained face to the glittering firmament
above and as his cry of despair rolled down the hillside to the
camp below it was answered by the calling of other voices. Looking
up, he saw a line of a dozen or so torches heading up the slope.
Someone must have heard the terrible slaughter or be wondering
why panicked livestock had been driven down among the tents.
Quickly, his eyes wide and his breathing heavy, Ajax snatched up
Hector's sword and ran.

Chapter Forty-Six

FATHER AND SON

Ajax's hut was at the bottom of the slope. The guard stepped aside, shocked by the blood that covered the king's body, and Ajax pushed past him through the canvas flap. The small hearth inside was a mass of smouldering embers that bathed the hut in a warm glow, and the only sounds were the soft breathing of Tecmessa mingled with the baby-snores of little Eurysaces. He crossed the floor and knelt beside them, sword still in hand.

'My love,' he whispered, reaching out and gently touching the locks of thick black hair that hid his wife's face. She did not stir. 'And Eurysaces, my boy.'

He looked down at the child and felt the tears swell up inside him again. He thought of the time he had wasted in battle or in counsel with the other army leaders, rather than spending it with his son. He recalled how he had berated Achilles for threatening to return to Phthia, and how he had declared he would rather give Tecmessa and Eurysaces up before he surrendered his honour. What a fool he had been! He had chased after glory and renown and given barely the scraps of morning and evening to his family. Now that chance was gone and in time he would be little more than a faded memory to Eurysaces; indeed, the boy would know more about him from the stories of his deeds and misdeeds than from his own recollections.

He reached out to touch his son's hair, but stopped himself.

'What if he wakes and sees you, sword in hand and covered

in blood?' Ajax said to himself. 'No, leave him be. Leave them both.'

He stood and took a step back. Then he turned and saw his great, sevenfold shield propped against the back of his chair. He fetched it and laid it down gently next to his son.

'I give this shield to you, Eurysaces,' he said quietly as his tears fell in heavy drops on to the oxhide. 'It was made by Tychus of Hyle, a master of his art. I named you after it, little Broad Shield, and now I hope it will always remind you of your father. Look after your mother for me. I leave her in your care now. Goodbye.'

He left the hut to find the guard had now been joined by two others. There were angry voices coming from the slopes above, where torches were moving this way and that.

'My lord . . .'

'Guard my wife and son. I've done something shameful and men will be angry with me for it, but I don't want my family to suffer for my sake. You – fetch Teucer and Little Ajax. Tell them . . . never mind, just bring them here.'

'But Lord Ajax, where are you going?'

Ajax ignored the soldiers' cries and ran through the tents to the beach, continuing on past the lines of galleys until he saw the dark mound of Patroclus's barrow ahead of him. At its heart was the golden urn Thetis had carried out of the water earlier that day, now filled with the mingled ashes of Achilles and his lover. By now the shouts on the slopes were growing dim and there were no sounds of pursuit, so he slowed to a walk as he approached the barrow. To his right the waves continued to wash up the beach as they had done since the creation of the world, drawn by the silver face of the moon that cast its ghostly light across the ocean. At last Ajax reached the barrow and knelt before it, looking all around to ensure no one else was in sight. Taking Hector's sword, he placed the pommel against the packed earth and pushed it in so that the hilt was buried and the blade stood up towards his chest. Then he sat back on his heels.

'If I'd known what a burden I was carrying when I brought your body back from the Scaean Gate, cousin, I'd have stripped that cursed armour off and thrown it to the Trojans there and then. Now it belongs to a lying scoundrel and my jealousy for it has driven me to terrible desires. I've no honour left, Achilles, and my glory lies slaughtered on the slopes above the camp. Only now do I see the gods were right to deny me your armour, and yet it pains me that they gave it to Odysseus. I only pray that they will destroy him as they've destroyed me. Curse you, Odysseus!'

And with that he fell forward on to the point of the sword.

The full moon had passed its zenith and was beginning to sink behind the topmost branches of the temple of Thymbrean Apollo when Eperitus heard the sound of approaching hooves. All night long he had been walking in circles, stamping his feet against the cold and rubbing his hands up and down his arms while he waited for Astynome to return from Troy, but now he slipped behind a large rock and stared up the slope towards the ridge. Moments later a line of horsemen approached carrying torches. There were a dozen at least, their outlines picked out clearly by the moonlight. One mount carried two figures, a man and a woman, and Eperitus instinctively knew they were his father and Astynome.

The horses stopped a spear's throw from the entrance to the temple and the riders dismounted. Two men scouted forward with their naked swords gleaming, returning shortly afterwards to report the temple empty. Eperitus's eyes could now pick out Apheidas's face in the torchlight as he posted his men in pairs around the circle of trees, before taking Astynome and four men inside.

Eperitus felt his heart thumping hard against his ribcage. His fingers gripped the edge of the boulder as if reluctant to let go and he found himself wondering why he was there at all. It was not too late to return to where he had tethered his horse and ride south to new lands and new adventures. He did not have to become the traitor that Arceisius had accused him of being, or sell his honour for the sake of love as Palamedes had done – to be stoned to death by his comrades in punishment. But Palamedes had also been half Trojan, just as Eperitus was, and perhaps there was no such thing as treachery for men of divided blood. Perhaps they were free to choose their loyalties as they saw fit. But whether he was a traitor or not, he knew in his heart that he could not turn back now. He was an integral part of a larger tale. The gods must always have intended for him to be here, waiting to betray his friends so that he might save them; and though he did not know what lay ahead, he accepted his fate was before him, not behind him.

And still he hesitated, clinging to the boulder like a ship-wrecked sailor to a broken mast. A year ago he would have charged into the temple intending to kill Apheidas or die in the attempt. Now the hatred that had dominated his entire adult life had lost its bite, even died altogether. He thought again of the encounter in the temple of Artemis at Lyrnessus and how his father had confessed himself a reformed man, regretting the mistakes of his youthful ambition. He had begged Eperitus to let the past go and the sadness in his eyes had seemed genuine – the look of a wiser man who had come to realize his family was all he had left in life. Doubtless his offer of peace could just be a trap, but Apheidas had already passed up better chances to take his son's life, and the more Eperitus thought about how he had felt after losing Iphigenia, the more he wanted to believe his father's appeal was genuine. At last, he tore his fingers from the boulder and reached down for the shield and spear that lay beside him. But before he stepped out to approach the nearest pair of Trojan guards – who were still some way off – he turned and gave a low whistle.

'Come on out.'

He sensed the man's breathing stop as he tried not to make any sound.

'Arceisius, I know you've followed me here. Don't force me to come over there and drag you out.'

There was a pause and then a cloaked figure stood up from behind a clump of scrubby bushes and came running over at a stoop.

'Why didn't you tell me you knew I was there?' Arceisius complained. 'At least you've been able to move around and stamp your feet to keep warm; I've been lying there freezing half the night when all you needed to do was come over and put me out of my misery.'

'It'll teach you not to interfere where you're not welcome. But now you're here, what is it you want?'

'To protect you from your own foolishness. If you're going to betray your countrymen then I can't stop you; but if things don't turn out as you're expecting then you could do with an extra sword at your side. And I'm not convinced this isn't a trap.'

'It's not a trap.'

'All the same, I haven't fought alongside you for ten years just to leave you when you need me most. At the very least I'm going to stay by you until they slam the gates of Troy in my face.'

'And much use you'll be with just that sword if it is a trap,' Eperitus sniffed.

'I'd have made too much noise carrying my shield and spear.'

'Not much more than you did without them. But if you insist on coming, then let's go.'

They stood to their full height and walked towards the nearest picket. The two Trojans spotted them quickly and lowered their spears.

'Not a step closer! Who are you and what's your business here?'

'I am Eperitus, son of Apheidas,' Eperitus replied in their own language, naming his sire for the first time in many years. 'And this is Arceisius, son of Arnaeus. I've come to speak with my father.'

'Apheidas is awaiting you,' the guard said, relaxing a little. 'But there was no mention of anyone else. Your friend will have to stay here with us.'

507

'Either Arceisius comes with me or we both leave now.'

After a whispered discussion with his comrade, the soldier nodded and signalled for the two men to follow. He led them up to the top of the ridge from where they could see the dark, moonlit mass of Troy beyond the River Scamander, then turned with his torch held above his head and pointed at their weapons.

'Leave those here with me. That *isn't* negotiable.'

Eperitus hesitated for a moment then lay down his shield and spear, followed shortly after by his sword and dagger. Arceisius gave Eperitus a cynical look then threw his own weapon on the pile. Satisfied, the guard pointed them towards a gap in the circle of laurel trees.

Eperitus led the way into the shadowy interior, where strips of moonlight lay like rib bones across the flagstoned floor. Four soldiers stood at the corners of the temple, their sputtering torches casting a dim glow over the boles of the trees. At the far end was a white altar stone, tinted by the orange torchlight, and behind it an effigy of Apollo carved from the stump of a dead tree. Its legs, as they emerged from the roots, were entwined with thick fronds of ivy up to the knees. Its arms were locked by its sides – a necessity of being shaped from the bole of a tree – but in its left fist it clutched a horn bow and in its right a solid bronze arrow. Apheidas and Astynome stood on either side of the altar. They turned to look as Eperitus and Arceisius entered.

'Eperitus!' Astynome said, crossing the floor and embracing him. 'I thought you might have changed your mind.'

'You were late,' he replied with a smile, kissing her forehead. It was cold from the ride to the temple. 'Dawn isn't very far off.'

'But we're here now and maybe soon we can be married.'

'I hope so.'

'That would be good,' said Apheidas, taking a few paces towards his son. 'Then I will have a daughter, too, and grand-children.'

'You haven't got your son back yet,' Eperitus replied.

'*Yet*, you say. That's more than I had hoped for. I'm glad you came, Son.'

He offered his hand and Astynome stepped away. Eperitus looked down and recalled the last time he had embraced his father in friendship – that same day twenty years ago in Alybas, when Apheidas had later murdered King Pandion and taken the throne for himself. It was still not too late to leave the temple and ride away, he reminded himself, but the moment he took his father's hand he would be declaring himself a traitor to the Greek cause – an act no better than his father's regicide.

'I know what you're thinking, Eperitus, but things have changed since we parted ways in Alybas. You're my only son and I want you back. Nothing is more important to me than that.'

He pushed his hand nearer and smiled. Slowly, Eperitus reached out and took it, feeling his father's rough, hot skin against his own. There was a moment in his heart when Odysseus, Ithaca and all the events of the war seemed to crowd in on him, and then were gone. He had passed through a doorway into a new life, as if the previous twenty years had been by-passed and had transported him and his father from that fateful day in Alybas to this day on the ridge above Troy. He smiled uncertainly at his father then turned to Astynome, whose closeness assured him this was not some strange dream.

Apheidas placed his other hand on Eperitus's shoulder.

'I know you hated me for what I did and that your hatred was real. But something like that doesn't just go away.'

'I'm coming to learn that only weak men allow the past to hold them back.'

'Then was it the knowledge that you're half Trojan that changed your mind? Or was it the love of a Trojan woman?'

'It's of no consequence where the blood in my veins originates from,' Eperitus replied, 'though you're right that Astynome is one reason why I'm here. But it's more than that. I've seen what men's pride does to them, and how this war has turned their noble ideals into monstrous desires. It corrupts men's souls. The war has to end so that good men like Odysseus can return to their families, and if the only thing stopping that is my own selfish pride, then it's time I let the past go. If you can change, Father, then so must I – for Odysseus's sake, and for Astynome's.'

He reached out and took her hand.

'This is the greatness I've always known was in you, Eperitus,' Apheidas said. 'That ability to choose when to do the right thing. And we will all need to make sacrifices if we want peace.'

'But how is peace possible, Father?' Eperitus asked. 'Paris won't surrender Helen and Menelaus won't leave without her. Even if Paris was killed, Agamemnon has no intention of leaving Ilium without first destroying Troy and stealing her wealth. Besides, there's a bitterness between Greeks and Trojans now that there never used to be. How *can* peace be possible?'

Apheidas did not answer immediately. He returned to the altar and ran a fingertip along its rough edges.

'As I said, peace will require sacrifices. Painful sacrifices. Paris and Menelaus, Priam and Agamemnon – will any of them accept peace on anything less than their own terms? Would Hector or Achilles have compromised? Of course not. But I will.'

He looked at his son and there was a new hardness in his features.

'I accepted a long time ago that Troy would never win this war and that peace was our only chance of survival. But that could never happen as long as Hector lived and gave the people hope of victory. That was why I persuaded him to go out and face Achilles.'

'You sent him to his death?' Arceisius asked, incredulously.

'Yes – for the greater good of Troy. To pave the way for peace.'

Eperitus frowned. This was not what he had expected. He looked about at the stony-faced guards, then at Arceisius and Astynome before returning his gaze to his father.

'And what else must happen for the sake of peace?' he asked.

Apheidas gave him a reassuring smile. 'I'm prepared to open the gates and let Agamemnon's army in. An easy conquest, Son, that will see Helen returned to her rightful husband and Troy subjugated to Agamemnon. All I ask in return is that the people are spared and half the remaining wealth is left to them.'

'No!' Astynome protested, glaring at him with disbelieving eyes. 'You never mentioned anything about opening the gates and—'

'What other choice is there?' he snapped back. 'If Troy is to survive then we must make unpalatable decisions. The sacrifice of a few for the good of the many.'

Eperitus looked on in silence. When he had exposed Odysseus's lies he had crossed a threshold. By coming to the temple of Thymbrean Apollo he had ensured he could never reverse that step, and that knowledge had given him the determination to see his betrayal through to the end. He had decided then that he would join his father in Troy and do whatever was required for an end to the war. But now he felt his stomach sink. He had expected Apheidas to propose a resolution acceptable to both sides; a diplomatic coup that would demonstrate his personal desire for peace. Instead, what he was suggesting was not peace at all. It was treachery. It was capitulation.

'What about Priam and Paris?' he demanded. 'What about the Trojan royal line?'

'Agamemnon can't afford to leave Priam or one of his descendants on the throne,' Apheidas answered coldly. 'They'll have to die, of course – right down to Hector's infant son. Then another will be chosen to rule in Priam's place, a Trojan capable of restoring Troy to its former glory and wealth, yet prepared to swear fealty to Agamemnon and his line.'

'Who?' Eperitus asked.

'Don't you understand yet?' Astynome said, turning desperate eyes on her lover. 'After *you* were the one who tried to convince me your father was nothing more than an ambitious, power-hungry murderer? He means himself. *He* wants to be the king of Troy!'

Chapter Forty-Seven

LOVE LOST

The man looked up at the high outer wall of the palace. Its sides were pale in the moonlight and he could see no hand or footholds in the smooth plaster. Looking about, he saw a handcart leaning against a nearby house. A moment later his black-cloaked form was atop the wall and dropping into the courtyard on the other side. He paused briefly, looking and listening for guards, but all he could hear were the voices of two men in the shadows beneath the roofed gateway. Satisfied they were ignorant of his presence, he crossed to the side door that he had been told would give him access to the palace corridors. It was unlocked, and after instinctively reassuring himself of the presence of his sword at his side and the dagger in his belt, he slipped inside.

The corridor within was lit only by a single, sputtering torch that revealed he was alone. Though he was a stranger to Ithaca, the layout of the palace had been explained to him in detail by the men who had hired him and he knew exactly where he would find Telemachus's bedroom. Sliding his dagger from its leather sheath, he stole down the long passageway in silence, pausing briefly as he passed the open doorways of deserted storerooms on each side. Around the corner at the far end was another, shorter passage, again lit by a single torch. In the gloom he could make out the base of a flight of stone steps at the halfway point, leading up to the sleeping quarters above, while, further on, the corridor turned left. Ultimately, it led to the ground-floor bedroom that King

Odysseus had constructed for himself and his wife, but the man had not been hired to kill Penelope, only her son who slept in the room directly above her.

The corridor and steps were unguarded and there was no sound of patrolling footsteps on the floor above. The Ithacans had clearly enjoyed peace for too long on their safe little island, protected from the corruption and violence that had overtaken the mainland since the kings had left for Troy. In northern Greece and the Peloponnese, where the man had learned his trade and been paid well for it, every noble household had armed men guarding its passageways at night. Almost disappointed that his hard-won skills would not be tested, the man slipped down the corridor to the foot of the stairs and looked up. Nothing. He took the steps quietly, but as he reached the top and looked both ways along the narrow corridor, the only sound he could hear was snoring from one of the rooms to his right. And so he gripped his dagger more firmly and moved stealthily towards the door that had been described to him.

He edged it open with his fingertips and looked inside. The room was spacious and by the moonlight that spilled in through the high, narrow window he could see a four-pillared bed with the sleeping boy beneath its piled furs. It did not concern him that his victim was so young – he had even murdered infants before at the behest of those who stood to gain from their deaths – and as he entered and closed the door behind him he whispered a prayer to any god who would accept it that the child would not wake before his blade had finished its work. Then, as he crossed the room, he caught something out of the corner of his eye – a line of twine at ankle height, barely distinguishable from the fleeces that softened the sound of his approach. But it was too late. He caught the line with the toe of his sandal and it tugged at something in the corner of the room. A moment later he saw something fall, followed by the clatter of metallic objects striking the floor in a cacophony of noise that shattered the peace of the night.

Instinctively, the man looked at the window. Realizing it was too high and small for a quick exit, he turned back to the door. But already he could hear the sound of approaching footsteps and the clank of weapons, and the next instant the door was kicked open and four men stood blocking his escape. One of them held a torch that threw a warm, flickering light into the bedroom. In that moment, it occurred to the assassin that he had but one hope of survival: the boy. He leaped across the room in a single bound and threw the furs from the bed, only to find more furs rolled up into the rough shape of a child's body. Somehow he had been expected, and now he was caught.

'Throw down your weapons.'

He turned to see a cloaked woman standing in the doorway, rubbing the sleep from her eyes. The four soldiers had entered the room and were standing two on each side of her, while behind her was a one-handed man leaning on a crutch. The assassin tossed his dagger at the feet of one of the soldiers and followed it with his short sword.

'Who sent you?' Penelope asked in a calm voice that concealed the anger she felt. 'Who sent you to murder my son?'

The man did not answer. He had his instructions if he was caught, and for the sake of his assassin's honour he intended to carry them out, but not yet.

'I've expected an attempt on Telemachus's life for some time now,' the queen explained. 'Hence the twine and the guards in the next room. It's also why my son isn't here. My husband left me to defend his kingdom while he was away, and that includes the heir to his throne. But though you came here to kill my only child, I am prepared to let you live on condition that you tell me who sent you. And when you do, you will be taken in a boat to the Peloponnese and forbidden on your oath to ever set foot on these islands again. Do you understand?'

The assassin nodded.

'I will be only too pleased, my lady,' he said. 'But you won't believe me, for you think of him as a loyal friend.'

'Give me your word of oath and I will believe you.'

'You should also know he is not alone,' the man continued. 'And I am not the only assassin in Greece. They will hire others . . .'

'That's why Telemachus was taken to Sparta several days ago,' said Mentor, hobbling into the room to stand beside Penelope. 'Out of harm's way with Halitherses as a guardian; and there he will stay under the protection of the royal family – *Penelope*'s family – until the war in Troy is over. Then, when Odysseus and the army return, we will deal with your employer's friends. But now, if you want to preserve your villain's life, you'll tell us who paid you to kill Telemachus.'

'You promise I will be freed?' he asked, looking at Penelope. She nodded.

The man smiled. He was an assassin and the only code he followed was not to reveal who had employed him, so to lie on his oath was of no consequence. More importantly, Eupeithes had given him another name if he was captured, an innocent man who was also a member of the Ithacan Kerosia. His implication in the attempt on Telemachus's life would earn him exile at the very least, and without him the Kerosia – and control of Ithaca – would inevitably slip into the hands of Eupeithes.

'As Zeus himself is my witness, the man who hired me was called Nisus of Dulichium.'

'Someone has to rule Troy,' Apheidas said, shooting an angry, silencing glance at Astynome. 'Why not me? I've fought as hard as any man in the army, Trojan or ally, and I'm the only one capable of saving the city from complete destruction. Tell me, Astynome, do you think Priam has been a good king? Do you?'

'Yes!'

Apheidas gave a derisive laugh.

'Commendable loyalty – typically Trojan. But everyone knows he should have sent Helen back the very moment Paris brought her to the palace. Any ruler worth his sceptre would have seen the trouble she would bring, but Priam never could deny a beautiful face. All Helen had to do was flash those eyes at him and expose a little cleavage and he was hers. The old lecher probably fancied he might visit her bed one night.'

'How dare you!' Astynome protested.

'And as for Paris, did he ever show a care for his country after setting eyes upon Helen? No! All he could think about was having her for himself, whatever the consequences for Troy. Priam may have abandoned him as a baby, but he's more like his father than Hector ever was. Neither man deserves to rule this land.'

'And you do?' Eperitus said.

Apheidas turned to his son, taken aback by his sneering tone. Then he brushed away his surprise and forced a smile to his lips.

'Yes, Son, I do. *We* do. Do you think this is all about ambition? That I would open the gates of Troy to its enemies for my own glorification?' He laughed and turned back to the altar, placing his palms on the cold stone and shaking his head. 'Were you never curious as to why your grandfather was forced to flee Ilium?'

'He killed the man who raped and murdered his wife.'

'He killed a member of the *royal family*! Before then, ours had been the wealthiest and most influential of all the noble clans of Troy, second only to the royal family itself. We were forced to leave all that behind when we fled to Greece, and it was only pity and guilt that persuaded Priam to let me come back some years ago – though he didn't return the land and possessions he'd taken from our family. But now I'm going to reclaim all of that and more, and *you*, Eperitus, will become my heir. All I ask is that you take my proposal to Agamemnon – he knows you're a man of honour and will trust you. Persuade him to put our family on the throne of Troy and we will become the easternmost point of his new empire, a safe harbour for Mycenaean merchants to flood Asia with Greek goods – offering him allegiance and paying him tribute for as long as our bloodlines continue. And when I die you will become king, Eperitus, bringing honour and glory back to your grandfather's name, righting the wrong that was done to our family. Astynome will become your queen and your children will establish a new dynasty, restoring Troy to its former glory until, one day, she is strong enough to throw off the shackles of Mycenae and rule herself again.'

His eyes blazed in the torchlight as he imagined a new Troy under his own rule. No longer would he be a mere nobleman; instead, he would avenge the shame of his mother's death and father's exile and claim the throne itself, replacing Priam's unworthy dynasty with his own bloodline. He stared at Eperitus, confident his son would understand. The knowledge his grandfather had been dishonoured by Trojan royalty – and that his own inheritance had been stolen by Priam himself – would clear away his doubts and bring a surge of righteous anger. It was an anger Apheidas had felt all his life, but with Eperitus at his side he would finally see justice and an end to the years of bitterness.

'Dawn is approaching, Son,' he said, calmly now. 'Go. Speak to Agamemnon and let us bring an end to this war.'

'Speak to him yourself,' Eperitus answered, narrowing his eyes at his father. 'You and the King of Men would get on well – two power-hungry murderers who'll stop at nothing to have your way. But I want no part of you or your schemes. I'd hoped you'd changed, Father, but you haven't. You're the same shameful monster that killed King Pandion twenty years ago, and if you think that by putting you on the throne of Troy I'll restore one scrap of glory or honour to my grandfather's name, then you have never been more wrong. You are not my father. As the gods are my witness, I never had a father!'

He turned to Arceisius and Astynome.

'Come on. We're leaving.'

'You don't make a very good traitor,' Arceisius said with a grin.

Astynome laid her hand on Eperitus's arm and together they moved towards the entrance, only to find the way blocked by one of the guardsmen. His spear was aimed at Eperitus's stomach.

'Why are you always so damned stubborn?' Apheidas demanded. 'Isn't this the same selfish pride you said was preventing Odysseus and the others returning to their families? Will you turn your back on them also and have them suffer more interminable, bitter years of war, just because of your ridiculous sense of honour?'

Eperitus's lip curled in contempt.

'Honour has always been a thing of ridicule to you, hasn't it?' he replied, refusing to turn and face his father. 'But it isn't to me. Without honour a man is nothing, no matter how much wealth or power he has. I was a damned fool if I thought I could put my own honour aside to end this war, and you're twice the fool if you think you can turn me to your corrupt ends. I should have killed you in Lyrnessus, Father, but you can be sure I won't miss my chance again.'

He snatched the neck of the guard's spear and pulled the shaft towards himself, throwing his fist into the man's face. The Trojan fell to the floor, his nose pumping blood. Tugging the weapon from his grip, Eperitus turned and hurled it across the temple. Apheidas ducked aside as the bronze point brushed past his ear and embedded itself in the effigy of Apollo.

'Seize him!' he shouted.

The other guards sprang into action at his command. Eperitus, kneeling by the fallen soldier, knocked him unconscious with a second punch and pulled the sword from his belt. He tossed it to Arceisius, who caught it deftly and turned just in time to parry a spear-thrust from the nearest Trojan. Eperitus grabbed the first guard's torch and leapt to his feet, slashing it in an arc before the chests of the other two soldiers and forcing them back.

'Astynome, get behind the altar – *now!*'

One of his assailants jabbed at him with his spear. Twisting aside, Eperitus kicked the shaft from the man's hand and pushed the end of the torch into his face, where it exploded in a shower of flames. The guard screamed in agony and staggered backwards, clutching at his face as he fell to the flagstone. A second scream followed and Eperitus glanced across to see Arceisius plunge his sword into the chest of his opponent.

'Look out!' he warned as two more guards came running in through the entrance with swords drawn and torches held aloft.

'Look out yourself,' Arceisius replied as he ran to meet them.

Eperitus turned just in time to see the other guard rushing at him with his spear held in both hands. Sweeping his torch downward with the speed of his sharp instincts, he knocked the point of the weapon away from his groin and jumped back as the guard swung the butt of his spear up at his face.

'Kill him!' Apheidas ordered from a few paces behind the soldier.

With a determined grimace, yet wary of the flaming brand in Eperitus's hand, the guard edged forward. Eperitus fell back, casting his eyes quickly to either side; Astynome had taken refuge behind the stone altar to his left, but on his right Arceisius's opponents were forcing him back towards the centre of the temple. Inexplicably, Eperitus could also hear the clash of weapons coming from outside of the circle of laurel trees, though he had no time to think what it could mean. He whispered a silent prayer, then stepped backwards on to the shaft of a discarded spear. The gods had heard him.

Throwing his torch at his attacker – who instinctively turned away and shielded his face with his hand, crying out as the flames burnt the soft underside of his forearm – Eperitus dropped to one knee and groped for the abandoned weapon. Seizing the shaft with both hands, he drove it upward at the Trojan's head. In the semi-darkness he had the weapon the wrong way round, but the butt had been fitted with a bronze spike for planting firmly in the ground to resist cavalry attacks. The spike found the flesh beneath the man's chin and carried on through until it punctured his brain and brought him down on to the flagstones. Eperitus tugged the weapon free and looked across, just in time to see Arceisius retreat another two steps to where Apheidas was waiting for him, his long blade glowing orange in the guttering light of the torches.

'No!' Eperitus shouted, leaping forward.

But it was too late. Apheidas placed his left hand firmly on Arceisius's shoulder and plunged the sword into his back, angling it upwards to pierce the heart. Arceisius arched his head back in sudden shock, staring wide-eyed and open-mouthed at the interwoven branches that formed the roof of the temple. Then he gave a choke and blood gushed from his mouth to spill over his chin and neck. His sword fell with a hollow clatter on the flagstones and his body followed a moment later, dropping limp and lifeless to the floor. Astynome gasped and for a few heartbeats the only sound was the clash of bronze from outside the temple.

Then every muscle in Eperitus's body was gripped with rage. Feeling a new surge of strength rushing into his limbs he leapt forward and drove the head of his spear into the nearest Trojan, killing him instantly. As Apheidas fell back, the other soldier turned to meet Eperitus's wrath, a sword in one hand and a torch in the other. With impossible speed, Eperitus's spear found his stomach and brought the man to his knees. The blade fell from his hands as he dropped to one side and curled up about his wound, trying to stem the flow of blood with his fingers. Eperitus dropped his spear and picked up the discarded sword, turning now to face his father.

A watery light was creeping into the sky from the east, settling faintly on the branches and the chiselled contours of the flagstones, bringing with it the faint smell of imminent dawn. There was no colour in the world yet, other than the false orange glow cast by the scattered torches as their flames dwindled, and the hint of scarlet in the dark stain that seeped out from beneath Arceisius's body. Eperitus looked down at the still, blood-smeared features of his friend as he lay on the stone floor, his eyes staring emptily up at the last few stars still glimmering through the branches overhead. Fleeting images of Arceisius whirled past his mind's eye, some of them forced and others unexpected – Arceisius, the young shepherd boy, whom Eperitus had caught following him as he scouted the Taphian positions on Ithaca twenty years ago; Arceisius, his enthusiastic but naïve squire, following him into an ambush by Thessalian bandits on Samos a few days before Agamemnon had arrived with the news of Helen's kidnap; Arceisius, the battle-hardened warrior, looking red-faced and more boyish than ever as he confessed to Odysseus and Eperitus that he had found himself a wife. But Melantho had enjoyed her husband's caresses for the last time. Arceisius had paid the price for Eperitus's treachery, and as he looked down at the soulless pile of flesh that had once been his friend, only one thought possessed him: to kill Apheidas.

His father was half lost in the shadows to one side of the temple, a tall, bulky form shrouded in darkness but betrayed by the gleam of his armour and the naked sword in his hand. His face was dark also, the features only just distinguishable even to Eperitus's eyes. Then, with a cry of fury, Eperitus ran at him. Their swords clashed, scraped across each other and clashed again. Eperitus felt his heart hammering in his chest, both exhilarated and terrified by the closeness of death in a way that rarely touched him on the battlefield. He lunged forward, using his keen senses to guide his sword in the stifled half-light, but his attack was met with an instinctive counter-blow as Apheidas checked him. Again he attacked and again he was repulsed, the thrust of his weapon reciprocated with equal skill and anger by his father. The two men's movements became faster and more forceful as they weaved deadly patterns about each other, trying to find the gap that would lead to victory for one and death for the other. There was no pretence now about either man's intentions: Eperitus had rediscovered his old hatred and was determined to kill his father; Apheidas knew this and would not show his son mercy a second time. To Astynome, watching intently as she gripped the cold stone of the altar, all she could make out in the darkness was two black shapes moving amid flashes of metal, their grunts and curses softening the harsh clatter of their weapons.

'You still haven't the skill or the heart to kill your own father,'

Apheidas said, grinning as he blocked another attack, 'however much I outrage your sense of honour. And it's only a matter of time until I slice that obstinate head from your shoulders.'

He dropped back and scythed at his son's neck, the blade biting into nothing as Eperitus ducked beneath the deadly sweep and lunged with the point of his own sword, narrowly missing as Apheidas twisted aside and chopped down at Eperitus's arm. Eperitus caught the blow against the hilt of his weapon and threw his father's sword-arm into the air. Apheidas jumped back from the follow-up thrust and sensed the altar close behind him.

'Give up all restraint and turn your energy to savage hatred,' Eperitus hissed, advancing on his father with a snarl.

'What's that?' Apheidas said.

'The words of Calchas, priest of Apollo. I wasn't able to beat you in Lyrnessus or by the ships because you planted a seed of doubt in my mind; you made me believe you felt some remorse about the things you'd done. But now I know you for who you *really* are – the same ambitious, lying murderer I'd always thought you were. And don't deceive yourself that I don't hate you enough to kill you, Father. I do and I will.'

He stepped back to pick up a discarded torch and Apheidas lunged. But his attack was weak, half-hearted, and Eperitus beat his sword aside with ease. With his other hand he swung the torch against his father's head, catching him on the ear and provoking a great roar of pain. Apheidas reeled back against the altar, jarring his back and dropping his sword as he pressed his other hand over the charred flesh at the side of his head. Then Astynome screamed a warning, her eyes white in the shadows as she pointed over Eperitus's shoulder. Eperitus turned and saw the guard he had knocked unconscious standing behind him. His nose was a mis-shapen mess of red, but he had a spear poised in his right hand and the point was aimed at Eperitus's heart. The soldier drew back the weapon and, strangely, Eperitus found himself reminded of the temple where he had died saving Odysseus from an assassin's knife. But this time Athena would not restore him to life, and with a sudden pang of regret he wished he had not betrayed his friend. If he was to die, it should have been fighting at Odysseus's side, not as a traitor who had thrown away his honour on a fool's hope.

But as the Trojan pulled the spear back, it fell from his hands and he lurched forward. Blood pumped out from between his lips and, with incredible slowness, he dropped first to his knees and then on to his face, the long shaft of a spear protruding from his back. Behind him, framed in the entrance to the temple by the first light of dawn, was the unmistakeable silhouette of Odysseus. He stepped inside and his eyes fell on the dead face of Arceisius, though he said nothing. Antiphus and Polites followed, the former with his bow across his shoulders and the latter holding a sword in his hand, the blade running with fresh blood.

'Eurylochus said I would find you here,' Odysseus announced.

Eperitus looked at the king, but there was neither anger nor hatred in his eyes. If anything, they were tinged with inexplicable remorse. Then, with sudden shock, he remembered his father. There was a muffled grunt and a short scuffle. Spinning around, he saw Apheidas with his arm about Astynome and his hand over her mouth, pulling her head back. A dagger gleamed against her ribs.

'Harm her and I'll kill you.'

Apheidas gave his son a mocking smile. 'Weren't you going to kill me anyway?'

Eperitus stared at Astynome. Her eyes were wide with fear, silently pleading with him to do something, though he did not know what he *could* do. Then Odysseus crossed the temple floor and stood beside him.

'Let the girl go, Apheidas,' he suggested in a quiet but firm voice. 'Your men are all dead and that leaves just you against the four of us. If you harm her, we will kill you, just as sure as the sun rises in the east and sets in the west.'

'Oh, I'm sure you'll do that anyway – the very moment I let her go.'

Odysseus gave him a reassuring smile and held up his hands submissively.

'We've no desire to kill you. We just want Astynome alive. Let her come to me and I give you my word we'll let you ride back to Troy unharmed.'

'No!' Eperitus protested. 'I've waited twenty years for this moment and he's not leaving this temple alive.'

'There'll be another time for vengeance, Eperitus. Right now we have to get Astynome back.'

'You'll have neither,' Apheidas told them, moving around to the front of the altar. 'Not while I'm holding a knife to the girl's throat. Now, move aside and let us leave unhindered or I'll kill her right now.'

'I can shoot him, Odysseus,' Antiphus said. He had fitted an arrow and pulled the string back so that the flight rested against his cheekbone. The barbed tip was aimed at Apheidas's forehead.

'Lower your bow, Antiphus,' Odysseus answered sharply, knowing that even with Antiphus's aim there was still a risk of harming Astynome. 'We're going to let Apheidas leave. We have no choice.'

'Order him to cut the string,' Apheidas added. 'I don't want an arrow in the back as I ride away.'

Odysseus nodded to Antiphus, who reluctantly pulled out his dagger and did as he was told. The Ithacans all moved back as Apheidas and Astynome edged by them, though Odysseus had to seize Eperitus by the arm and pull him out of their path. Once they were out of the temple, Eperitus shook himself free of the king's grip and ran after them.

Light was spreading across the sky from the east, though the sun had not yet nudged above the mountains and a few stars were still visible overhead. Apheidas and Astynome were standing by the knot of Trojan horses, their breath misting in the cold morning air. Eperitus watched his father help Astynome on to the back of one of the mounts, conscious that Odysseus, Polites and Antiphus had also left the temple and were standing behind him.

'I'll come for you, Astynome,' he called. 'Just tell me where your master's house is in the city and I'll find you.'

'Her master's house?' Apheidas scoffed, mounting behind her and taking the horse's reins in his hands. 'Haven't you realized who Astynome's master is yet?'

Astynome's beautiful features, which until that point had been fearful and despairing, now turned to shock.

'Don't listen to him, Eperitus,' she began, but Apheidas's hand closed over her mouth and stifled her protests.

'*I* am Astynome's master,' Apheidas continued, his features gloating in the half-light. Astynome struggled against his grip then was still. 'Don't you realize it yet, Son? Astynome wasn't in Lyrnessus for any festival of Artemis, she was there because I took her there. I knew that even if I could face you alone, you wouldn't listen to what I had to say. But if I put Astynome into your arms—'

'Enough!' Eperitus shouted.

'If I put Astynome into your arms,' Apheidas insisted, 'if I could get her into your *bed*, she might be able to persuade you to think of me more favourably.'

'That's a lie, damn you. You're not satisfied with killing Arceisius, or deluding me into thinking you felt remorse for your past; now you want to make me believe the woman I love has been deceiving me all along.'

'But she has, and she paid me back handsomely for my faith in her. And even if you've proved to be a disappointment, the other information she brought to me was invaluable. How else do you think we knew about Agamemnon's plan to ambush the Aethiopes?'

'I still don't believe you.'

Apheidas removed his hand from Astynome's mouth.

'Tell him.'

'Yes, tell me,' Eperitus insisted, his tone harsh.

Astynome's face shone with tears, which she refused to wipe away as she stared down at him. The fierce Trojan pride he had seen when he first met her had returned, falling like an impenetrable veil over the warm, intimate smile he had since come to love so deeply.

'It's true, all of it. But what I did I did out of loyalty to Troy and to avenge my dead husband,' she announced. Then the stiffness drained from her and she slumped forward, clutching at the horse's neck and mane. 'But I didn't do any of it to harm *you*, Eperitus. I didn't know you to begin with; I didn't know the sort of man you were. And then, later, Apheidas said that if I could persuade you to meet with him it would bring a peaceful end to the war, that I would help to save Troy from the Greeks. How could I refuse him?'

Eperitus felt cold. He stared at her, feeling the morning air turning the skin on his arms to goosebumps.

'I never knew what he was planning to do,' she continued. 'If I had, I wouldn't have agreed to any of it. But then I wouldn't have met you or fallen in love with you. And that's the only thing that's important now. Let Troy burn and all the armies of Greece perish, but don't stop loving me.'

Apheidas turned the horse about and dug his heels back, sending the animal down the other side of the slope towards the Scamander. Eperitus did not watch them go, though he could see them at the bottom edge of his vision as he stared across at the vast sprawl of Troy on the other side of the valley. Then Odysseus patted him gently on the shoulder.

'Come on,' he said. 'Let's get back to the camp.'

Chapter Forty-Eight

A NEW PROPHECY

Helen woke to the first light of dawn and found herself alone. Without calling her maids, she dressed hurriedly and set off towards the walls of Pergamos. The streets were already alive with a mixture of merchants, tradesmen, slaves and soldiers, all going about their business but none too busy to spare the daughter of Zeus their glances. She ignored them all, well used to the mixture of longing and loathing that followed her every departure from the palace. Soon she was climbing the broad steps that led up to the battlements, where her husband stood with his hands palm-down on the cold stone, staring south-west in the direction of the unseen Greek camp.

Despite the cool morning air and the fresh northerly breeze that whistled over the rooftops and between the crenellated teeth of the parapet, Paris wore nothing more than a thin, knee-length tunic of green wool, belted about the waist. Helen paused, admiring the broad set of his shoulders and the splendid muscles of his arms and legs that held such strength and enduring stamina. For a fleeting moment, as his back was turned to her, she recalled the man she had first fallen in love with: brave, powerful, self-assured – even handsome, in his rugged manner; he was a warrior with a strong sense of duty, but with the courage to sacrifice his honour for love's sake. And as she watched his black hair strain and twist in the wind she knew that she loved him now as much as she had then, when he had stolen her away from Sparta. Only one thing overshadowed their passion for each other – the guilt of what their love had done to Troy.

She climbed to the top step and saw him stiffen slightly, warned of her approach by the tiny particles of stone crunching beneath the leather soles of her sandals. Ignoring the sideward glances of the guards – boys or old men, mostly, since the heavy fighting, interspersed with experienced soldiers too badly wounded to fight in the battle lines again – she placed her hands on his upper back and pressed against the thick layers of muscle with her thumbs, gently kneading the tense knots that lay beneath his skin until she felt his resistance give and his shoulders relax. But moments later he reached back and, without turning to look at her, brushed her hands away.

'What is it, Paris?' she asked, moving beside him and looking up at his face, the familiar scar a bright pink in the clear morning light.

'A horseman,' he said, deliberately misunderstanding her question as he pointed his chin towards the plains. 'Maybe two.'

Helen turned and looked. Her eyes swept over the rooftops of the lower city, skipping over the arc of the impenetrable walls and crossing the pastureland beyond to where the silver line of the Scamander wriggled down towards the bay. As her gaze touched upon the fords she saw a horse picking its way through the swirling waters and the slippery stones beneath, with what were almost certainly two riders on its back. She watched them closely, trying to discern whether they were Trojan or Greek as they reached the near bank of the river and struggled up into the swampy, flower-filled meadows.

'Who are they?' she asked, reaching out and placing her hand on his.

'Apheidas and a girl,' he answered, pulling away. 'One of his household servants, I think.'

Helen felt a sting in her heart as his fingers slipped from hers, sensing that his need of her was slipping away with them. They had not made love since Hector had died, and even killing Achilles had not alleviated the responsibility and guilt he felt for his brother's death or the sense of doom it had brought to Troy. He was punishing himself too much and would not allow her to console him with either her words or her body. But if she lost him, what hope would there be for her in a city full of enemies?

She turned away so that he would not see the tears rimming her eyes.

'Apheidas? What's he doing outside the city walls?'

'Committing treason.'

Helen and Paris turned to see Cassandra at the top of the stairs, a glum expression marring her naturally beautiful features as she stared down at her bare feet. She wore a sable cloak over her pale grey chiton, and with her ashen complexion and her dark hair and eyes she reminded Helen more than ever of Clytaemnestra.

'What do you mean, Sister?' Helen asked, inadvertently adopting the voice she used for children or those who struck her as simple-minded. Paris had already switched his gaze back to the plain before the city walls, where the horse was now approaching the Scaean Gate.

Cassandra shrugged and moved to the battlements, continuing to peer down at her feet as she dropped back against the rough stone.

'I saw it. You know, in here.' She tapped her temple with her finger, sparing Helen a sheepish glance. 'He met with his son in Apollo's temple. Offered to open the city's gates to the Greeks if Agamemnon would give him the throne of Troy. I've always said he can't be trusted, but no one ever believes me anyway.'

Helen narrowed her eyes quizzically. 'So he's going to betray us all?'

'No. He and his son argued, nearly killed each other. There'll be no traitors' deal, and right now all Apheidas is worried about is how to explain what he was doing outside the city walls.'

Paris sighed audibly and leaned his forearms on the parapet.

'Apheidas is a commander in the Trojan army, Sister. He'll have his reasons for going out – a spying mission or a patrol of some kind, most likely.'

'With Astynome, his *maid*?' Cassandra asked, giving him a tired but resentful look.

'Then maybe he's heard the rumour she's sleeping with a Greek in their camp – his own son, by the account I heard – and went to catch her on her return,' Paris replied tersely.

Cassandra returned to the top of the steps, brushing Helen as she passed.

'I shouldn't expect you to believe me, Paris – that's the curse I have to live with – but you don't have to be so wretched about it. At least Hector was polite in his disbelief! But one day the whole city will regret not listening to me, and by then it'll be too late.'

She trudged down the stairs and was gone, but Helen was hardly aware of her passing. As Cassandra had moved by her, their bare arms touching for the briefest of moments, her mind's eye had been filled with a terrible image. The whole of Troy was a mass of fire, from the lowest hovel to the highest palace, the flames towering over the blackened walls to lick at the night sky and fill it with billowing columns of spark-filled smoke. There were screams and the clash of weapons; women were being raped by warriors drunk with victory, while their children were being hurled from the battlements. But at the centre of the inferno, standing tall and black, was a giant horse, a beast so terrible that Helen could sense the evil that had consumed Troy was emanating from it. Then the image was gone as quickly as it had come, so that Helen's mind was left scrambling to pick up the fragments and piece together some memory of what she had imagined. She failed and was left with nothing more than a consuming sense of doom and the image of the horse.

The news of Ajax's suicide reached Odysseus shortly after the skulking Eurylochus had informed him that Eperitus was going to meet with his father in the temple of Thymbrean Apollo. The disbelief he had felt at his captain's treachery quickly turned to remorse over the death of Ajax. Though he had only been a pawn in the vengeance of the gods, Odysseus had acted of his own free will and knew he was as guilty of the great warrior's death as if he had plunged the sword in himself. He also guessed that his actions had been partly responsible for Eperitus's decision to meet with Apheidas, and he was seized by the urgent need to go after him and explain his motives – something he was free to do now that he had carried out the deed. Above all, he had to stop Eperitus from joining his father, if, as Odysseus suspected, that was what he had been driven to.

Later, as they rode slowly back from the temple of Thymbrean Apollo, Eperitus asked the question that had been pricking at him since he had watched his father and Astynome escape.

'What happens now, Odysseus? When I met with Apheidas I betrayed you and the rest of the army, and the punishment for treason is stoning.'

'You said you were trying to end the war so I could go back to Ithaca,' Odysseus said, stroking the oiled mane of his mount. 'So there *was* no betrayal. You knew my heart's desire was always to go home to my family, but you thought I'd forgotten it in some mad desire for the armour of Achilles. I couldn't tell you the real reason why I had to keep the armour from Ajax – though you know now – so you were just trying to save me from its curse. And I forgive you.'

They rode on in silence for a while, then Eperitus turned and looked at the king.

'In that case, am I still captain of the guard?'

'If you want to be. I can't think of anyone better.'

'And I can't think of anyone better to serve. Even if you had wanted Achilles's armour for yourself, Odysseus, you never needed it. You've enough greatness in you to make your own glory, whatever Palamedes might have thought. Besides, even a simple soldier like me can see that Troy isn't going to fall to brute force alone – we've tried that for ten years and failed. It needs brains, the sort of cunning and intelligence the gods blessed you with. And if you can use your wits and determination to bring an end to this war, then your name will be the greatest of all the men who fought at Troy, including Achilles.'

'I'll try,' Odysseus answered. 'With your help. And then, gods willing, perhaps we can go home.'

On their return they found the Greek camp in uproar. Soldiers who had once shouted Great Ajax's name in triumph were now cursing him for the destruction of the army's livestock. Fights had broken out and a few men had been killed, though the violence was rapidly quelled after Agamemnon had sent his Mycenaeans out to keep the peace. He had also summoned the Council of Kings to discuss what to do with Ajax's body, and as Odysseus and Eperitus entered his tent a fierce debate was already taking place. Fighting to master his twitch, Teucer was demanding in an angry stutter that Ajax be given the funeral his heroic deeds had earned. But Menelaus was furious at the slaughter Ajax had caused, as well as the additional shame of his suicide, and was insisting his body should be hurled into the sea or left as carrion for the birds. The majority of the commanders made their agreement known with shouts and energetic gestures at Teucer. To Eperitus's surprise, Little Ajax was among them.

Odysseus strode into the middle of the debate and snatched the staff from Menelaus's grip. He raised his hands for calm and waited for Teucer and Menelaus to move aside before turning to the King of Men, seated in his golden throne.

'What should you care, my lord, if Ajax killed a hundred or even two hundred beasts?' he asked in a soft voice. 'Ten times that number and more have been sacrificed in thanks for the victories Ajax has brought us over the years. And do you think he'd have carried out such an act if the gods hadn't first robbed him of his senses?'

Despite their surprise that Odysseus had spoken in defence of Ajax, there were a few consenting grunts from the circle of on-lookers and a firm nod of agreement from Diomedes. But not all were so quickly persuaded.

'If the gods turned his mind, then he brought it on himself,' Nestor contended. 'He always claimed the glory for his own deeds and never gave the gods their dues. He was asking for trouble.'

'No suicide deserves proper funeral rites!' Little Ajax added, stepping forward. 'Feed his body to the fish!'

His single eyebrow was contorted with anger and his fists were clenched, but beneath his fury Eperitus could see that he was hurt. His namesake's act of self-destruction had been a betrayal that the Locrian was struggling to understand. When Odysseus turned his piercing green eyes on him, though, his head dropped and he retreated back into the crowd.

'A suicide cursed by the gods,' Odysseus said. 'Maybe so, but there was another factor in Ajax's death – the part played by me. If I hadn't been awarded Achilles's armour he would be alive now, and so would your precious livestock.'

'Are you blaming me?' Agamemnon asked, lifting his chin a little from his fist.

'I blame *myself*, Agamemnon, although I was just an instrument in the revenge of the Olympians. My victory – or the dishonour of his own defeat – was too much for Ajax's proud mind to bear. For that reason I beg you, my lord, to employ the greatest power available to any king – the power of mercy. Forget the errors of Ajax's sickness and remember how he always fought in the forefront of every battle, killing many of Troy's greatest men. He was the stalwart of the Greek army, a man that even Hector could not defeat. Indeed, it seems the only man capable of defeating Ajax was Ajax himself! So I ask you to permit Teucer to cremate his half-brother with full funeral rites, which he earned in life by his deeds as a warrior. And if Teucer will forgive *me*, then I would ask him to accept my help in performing the rites.'

There was a murmur of approval and Diomedes demanded that he, also, should be permitted to help. But Agamemnon did not reply at once. He rested his chin back on his fist and stared at Odysseus with a cold, unwavering gaze, taking his time to weigh the arguments as well as to remind the council that he was their leader and all decisions lay ultimately with him. Then he sat up and leaned back with a sigh.

'I will not throw Ajax's body to the fish, as some have demanded,' he began, looking at Menelaus and Little Ajax. A few among the council voiced their relief and pleasure, and even Eperitus felt an unexpected flush of gratitude towards the King of Men, whom he normally loathed. Then Agamemnon held his hand up for silence and they realized their relief had been premature. 'But neither will he receive the full rites due to a great warrior. Ajax took his own life and as such will be allowed a simple burial without honour. Teucer, you have my permission to bury him wherever you choose, as long as it is beyond the walls of this camp.'

And so it was, in spite of all the Trojans he had slain and all the battles he had turned in favour of the Greeks, that Ajax's giant corpse was placed in a lonely suicide's grave on a cliff top overlooking the sea. He was not given a period of mourning or a warrior's cremation, and there were no games in his memory. The only song raised over his body was the wailing of Tecmessa, competing with the howls of the wind and the crashing of the waves below. Eurysaces sat beside her, clutching his mother's black dress as he watched Teucer, Odysseus, Diomedes and Eperitus lower the shrouded body of his father into the pit they had dug. Then each man cut off a lock of his own hair and threw it into the grave, before refilling it with earth. Halfway through, Little Ajax appeared and stood beside them, honouring his friend with his tears as he hung his head and was silent. After a while Teucer put an arm about Tecmessa's shoulder and led her, carrying

Eurysaces, back towards the camp, followed at a distance by Little Ajax.

Once the last of the soil had been replaced, Odysseus and Eperitus returned to the beach where Arceisius's funeral pyre was being prepared. While Odysseus carried out sacrifices and uttered prayers to the callous gods, Eperitus stood back and watched the sun draw gradually closer to the distant horizon. It was a scene he had observed countless times before, but today there was a finality about it, as if some prophetic instinct told him he would not see many more. Then the first pall of smoke twisted up from Arceisius's funeral pyre, spreading a smear of imperfection across the cloudless sky. The smell of burning wood and roasted flesh accompanied it, giving an unpleasant tang to the otherwise clean air that blew in from the Aegean. And all the time the sea breeze filled his ears with the crash and tumble of the white-capped waves, silencing the usual noises of the camp beyond the beach so that the only other sound was the crackle of flames, snapping and popping delightfully as they hastened the destruction of Arceisius's corpse.

A handful of other figures stood watching the pyre: Antiphus, his arms crossed and his eyes red with smoke and tears; Eurybates, busying himself by throwing an armful of faggots on to the fire; Polites, massive and silent, his giant hand resting on the shoulder of the fourth figure, the comparatively diminutive Omeros. In the few months since he had arrived on the shores of Ilium the young bard had shed his gentle layers of fat and had started to grow his hair long, like all the other soldiers in Agamemnon's army. He had lost much of his naïvety, too, surviving the murderous press of the battle line and killing and maiming his share of Trojans in the process. And yet, while the Fates had spared Omeros, Arceisius – the shepherd boy whom Eperitus had transformed into a fearsome warrior – had joined the legions of the dead that the war had created. Such was the will of the gods.

Eperitus turned his eyes from the flames of Arceisius's funeral pyre to where Odysseus was washing the sacrificial blood from his hands. After staring at the burning corpse for a few moments, the king walked to his hut and fetched Achilles's armour, which he planted in the sand before sitting down with his arms folded across his knees. Eperitus joined him and they sat there in silence as the sun crept lower towards the horizon, Odysseus contemplating the patterns on the great, circular shield – as if the answer to all his worries and problems lay in the cyclical movements of the little figures – while Eperitus's mind slipped into a trough of black thoughts about the death of Arceisius, Apheidas's treachery and Astynome's deceit.

After a while his eyes fell on the armour.

'What will you do with it?' he asked, his voice slightly croaky because he had not spoken for so long.

Odysseus shifted, wincing slightly as his muscles complained at the movement.

'Such armour isn't for me, Eperitus, and I've vowed never to wear it. But there's something I didn't tell you. Something that Athena revealed to me in my hut.'

Eperitus turned to him, his curiosity aroused.

'Go on.'

'The gods wanted to destroy Ajax, but they also wanted to prevent him keeping the armour for himself. They say it's meant for another, someone even more worthy than Ajax.'

'Then who? Ajax's son, Eurysaces?'

'No. And I wouldn't curse the poor child with it – you do realize it's cursed, don't you? It's the symbol of everything that's bad about this war.'

'Perhaps we should send it to the Trojans, then. After all, it was Paris who killed Achilles. He's welcome to have the armour, and good riddance to it.'

Odysseus glanced at his friend and smiled, looking a bit more like his old self. He dismissed the suggestion with a shake of his head.

'The Trojans have enough problems of their own. But whoever the rightful owner is, Athena said he is destined to take Achilles's place in the army and that the walls of Troy won't fall without him. I suppose I'll know who to give the armour to when I see him.'

'So is this what you've been thinking about all this time?'

'No, I've been thinking about home. This war isn't infinite, Eperitus. The end must come and I've been wondering how I can hasten it along. I keep thinking of Astynome getting through the gates in the back of that old farmer's cart, and the story Omeros concocted about how I got past those Taphian guards concealed in a pithos of wine. You remember that one? The only problem is I'm not sure how I'm going to smuggle an army inside the Scaean Gate.'

He looked quizzically at Eperitus, who nodded without comprehending a word of what Odysseus was saying.

'But suddenly my mind is full of Ithaca again,' Odysseus continued. 'I've been trying to remember how it looks from the prow of a galley, sailing up from the south – the shape of the hills, the channel between Samos and Ithaca, the harbour below the town, and then the road that leads all the way up to the palace gates. And I can picture what Penelope looks like again, Eperitus. I haven't been able to recall her face for so long, and then I saw her in a dream the night before Ajax killed himself, as clear as if I had only seen her that morning. And I'm going to see her again soon, I'm sure of it.'

'Good,' Eperitus said.

He smiled despite the pain he felt. Odysseus's renewed desire for his home and family reminded him that he had lost his own love, and that all his dreams of marriage and children had been ripped apart by Astynome's betrayal. And yet he could not bring himself to stop loving her, and he knew they would meet again one day – even though the walls of Troy lay between them.

'And there's something else,' Odysseus added, ominously. 'A new prophecy.'

Eperitus shifted round in the sand and looked at his friend.

'Calchas?'

Odysseus nodded. 'Before we left to fetch Ajax's body, Agamemnon took me aside. Calchas came to him early in the morning,
while we were fighting your father in the temple of Thymbrean
Apollo. He says Zeus will not bring an end to the war until a
number of conditions are met, but Apollo has only shown the first
one to him. I suspect one might be the identity of the rightful
owner of Achilles's armour, but, either way, these oracles will only
be revealed by another seer – a Trojan – though Calchas doesn't
know who or when.'

'Then what *does* he know?'

'That for Troy to fall Paris must first be killed by the arrows
of Heracles.'

Eperitus's eyes narrowed in thought.

'But . . . but they belong to Philoctetes,' he said, 'whom *we*
abandoned on Lemnos ten years ago!'

'Yes,' Odysseus said. 'The problem is, we're the only ones who
know where he was marooned, and now Agamemnon wants us to
fetch him back. We leave at dawn tomorrow.'

AUTHOR'S NOTE

The first two books in this series, *King of Ithaca* and *The Gates of Troy*, retold some of the earlier myths associated with Odysseus and the beginnings of the Trojan War. They drew on a handful of lesser-known tales that allowed my imagination plenty of room for manoeuvre. *The Armour of Achilles*, however, is set at the peak of the war, the epic events from which have been told and retold by countless poets, playwrights and other storytellers, both Greek and Roman. Rather than being able to pick over a few myths like a guest at a modest buffet, I now had a feast to choose from and was forced – often reluctantly – to restrict myself to those myths I thought most important and relevant to the tale I wanted to tell.

Chief among the ancient sources for the Trojan War is, of course, Homer. His is the name behind the oldest works of Western literature, *The Iliad* and *The Odyssey*, in which such themes as glory, wrath, fate and homecoming are explored in the brutal and uncertain lives of figures such as Achilles, Hector and Odysseus. Ironically, *The Iliad* covers only a brief, if bloody, period of the war: nearly seven weeks in total. Twenty-one of its twenty-four chapters cover just eight days. It begins with Chryses's appeal to the Greeks for the return of his daughter, Chryseis (also known as Astynome) and ends with the funeral pyre of Hector. Naturally, much of *The Armour of Achilles* follows the action in *The Iliad*, though I have made the gods less prevalent and highlighted Odysseus's part in the story. The events before and after come from a variety of other Greek and

Roman sources, some of which are lost and are known today only from quotes and references by later writers.

The Armour of Achilles begins with the sacking of Lyrnessus, something that happens off-stage as far as the main myths are concerned. As for the stoning of Palamedes, the original version has Odysseus planting gold in his tent to frame him for an act of treason he did not commit, purely out of spite. The ancient writers were often divided in their portrayals of Odysseus: some depicted his keen wits and great oratory as heroic, while others saw his cunning nature as quite the opposite. For obvious reasons, I have tried to make him appear in a more positive light.

The battles with the Amazons and the Aethiopes that follow Hector's funeral are epic stories in their own right and, by necessity, have been curtailed in my own version of them. The death of Achilles happened differently in different sources – some have him stabbed from behind while others say he was shot down with an arrow; in either case, he remained undefeated in individual combat, as befits a hero of his stature. Similarly, the only man who could kill Ajax was himself. He was driven to self-destruction out of pride, unable to bear the humiliation of losing the armour of Achilles to Odysseus. In the original myths, Odysseus wanted the armour for his own personal gain, but again I have tried to save his credibility by giving him a more worthy motive.

There are other threads in *The Armour of Achilles* that are entirely my own invention. The story of Eperitus and his ruth- lessly ambitious father, Apheidas, is one of them. So is the romance between Eperitus and Astynome, though Astynome does appear as a minor figure in the original tales. Equally, the background events on Ithaca can be found nowhere in the myths, even if Penelope's longing for her husband's return is very Homeric. But unfortu- nately for her, she cannot be reunited with Odysseus until the Trojans are defeated and their city razed to the ground. For that to happen, Odysseus must first fulfil the oracles set down by the gods and find a way to breach the impenetrable walls of Troy.

Beware Greeks bearing gifts!

extracts reading groups
competitions books new
discounts extracts extracts events
competitions reading groups
books new discounts
events extracts reading groups
new books
new titles reading groups
interviews events
events extracts extracts
discounts events
new books events interviews
events new interviews
discounts extracts discounts books
www.panmacmillan.com
extracts events reading groups
competitions books extracts new